The Sins Of Silas

KYLIE SNOW

Cover Design: Kylie Snow

Editor: Allison Heddon

ISBN: 979-8-218-51115-9

Contact: kyliesnowauthor@gmail.com

PLAYLIST:

INCANTATIONS:

POTESTAS VERAE MALEFICIS- **THE POWER OF A TRUE WITCH**

REVELARE- **REMOVE GLAMOUR**

VELARE- **ADD GLAMOUR**

AVERTE SONUM INTRA HUNC CIRCULUM-

SOUNDPROOFING SPELL

AVERSA PARS- **SPELL REVERSAL**

LUMEN- **CONJURE MAGE LIGHT**

OCCULTARE NOS AB ASPECTU- **EXPERT CLOAKING SPELL**

CELARE- **NOVICE CLOAKING SPELL**

SANA OMNIA VULNERA EIUS- **EXPERT HEALING SPELL**

ACCIPE CORPUS MEUM ALIBI- **TELEPORTATION SPELL**

OBLIVISCI- **ALTER MEMORIES**

OSTENDE MIHI ALIUD TEMPUS- **MASTER ILLUSION SPELL**

SOMNUM- **SLEEPING SPELL**

CONIUNGERE- **SIPHONING SPELL**

PRONUNCIATION GUIDE

LOCATIONS:

OTACIA- **OH-TAY-SHUH**

FALTRUN- **FALT-RUNE**

FORSMONT- **FOURS-MONT**

WRENDIER- **REN-DYE-ER**

DARANOIS - **DARE-AH-NOY**

AMES- **AIMS**

ROZAVAR- **ROW-ZA-VAR**

OQUERENE- **OH-KUR-EEN**

NEREIDA- **NUR-AY-DUH**

CHARACTERS:

LENA DAELYRA- **LEE-NAH DAY-LIE-RUH**

SILAS- **SIGH-LISS**

TORRIN BRIGHTHELL- **TOUR-IN BRY-THELL**

RYIA- **RYE-UH**

HENDRY BONNEVAU- **HEN-DREE BON-UH-VOW**

ROLAND AUBEZE- **ROW-LIND AWE-BEZ**

EDMUND ESTIELOT- **ED-MUND ES-TA-LOT**

IGON NATARION- **EYE-GONE NAH-TAR-E-ON**

VIOLA SONNET- **VEYE-UH-LA SEWN-IT**

Taira- **Tare-uh**

Saoirse- **Sare-shuh**

Asael Nefeli- **Ah-sigh-all Nuh-fell-ee**

Dagne Nefeli- **Dag-knee Nuh-fell-ee**

Kayin- **Kay-in**

Lucretia- **Lew-cree-shuh**

Gods and Goddesses:

Ravaiana- **Rah-veye-ah-nah**

Azrae- **Az-ray**

Valor- **Val-ler**

Celluna- **Suh-lune-ah**

Tithara- **Tith-are-uh**

To those of you who have ever felt too damaged to be loved or too broken to be fixed.

This is for you.

CONTENT WARNING

Please read with care. This book contains explicit
sexual scenes, explicit language, violence, gore,
torture, burns/burning, miscarriage, child death,
rape, sexual assault, infidelity, panic attacks,
hallucinations, poisoning, enslavement, drug use,
suicidal ideation, homophobia, physical and
mental abuse, grief, loss, and character death.

Your mental health matters.

CHAPTER ONE

SILAS - FIVE YEARS AGO

I awoke to swollen eyes, just as I had the past few nights, and cursed myself when I peered at the clock resting on my night-stand.

6:50 a.m. The council meeting begins in just ten minutes.

Flinging off the comforter cocooning me, I hurried to the bathroom sink, soaking a rag with cold water and wringing it out. I held it to my eyes in an attempt to lessen the puffiness.

It was no surprise I looked this way; I had cried myself to sleep the past couple of nights...ever since my mother was murdered. Last night, I had woken from my sleep in a cold sweat, chest heaving, heart pounding.

Something had felt off. Strange. I didn't know what, but the uneasy sensation made it difficult to fall back asleep.

I pressed the rag to my other swollen eye. The King would not be pleased to witness such weakness. I could only hope he wouldn't be able to tell I had been crying.

I often wondered if the man had a soul. I hadn't seen him shed a single tear since Mother's passing. Though that wasn't entirely alarming...I had never seen my father cry my entire life.

My thoughts drifted to Lena, how it felt holding her last night. Her body against mine, how it felt to kiss her.

I wanted her to be at my side in this castle. I wanted to sleep beside her every night, holding her close. But I hated the thought of her risking her life to see me. It was still unclear if the danger had entirely been eliminated, and I found myself wishing for her to stay away for a while—just until we knew it was secure again. I couldn't stand the thought of anything happening to her.

I scrubbed at my face in frustration. How was I going to ensure our future together? Mother had completely supported our relationship, but now she was gone. The King would never accept Lena as Otacia's princess and future queen.

I placed the cloth down, my eyes looking only slightly less swollen, and was startled by a knock on the door.

"The meeting has begun, Your Highness," Daerin, one of our guards, informed through the door. "The King is not pleased."

"I'll be out momentarily," I called out.

Strange. Usually, it was Torrin who would fetch me.

I chucked off my lounge pants as I heard the steps retreating from my door, then dressed in my fine clothes: a tunic adorned with silver embroidery, trousers that fit tightly against the muscles in my legs, and boots. All were black—the color I wore most days.

Lastly, I placed my silver crown atop my head and studied myself in the mirror beside my bed. The sapphires set in it sparkled from the morning sun filtering into my room.

My hair isn't neat enough, and my damn eyes...

I raked my hands down my face.

I didn't recognize myself most days anymore. Aside from these swollen eyes, wearing these clothes...this crown...it all felt heavy. Too heavy.

I wished I could be an ordinary man...wished I didn't have these responsibilities. All I desired was to be with Lena, to *live*, not just go through the motions as I had every day before meeting the fiery, red-headed beauty.

The corner of my mouth went up at the thought of her. It would be her birthday in just five days. Though I had recently given her my mother's necklace, I still wished to surprise her with something else. I'd pondered various ideas last night, but nothing had stuck out. I'd gifted her several gowns already, and I had just given her jewelry, so earrings seemed uninspired.

Perhaps I could purchase a new weapon for her, or I could write her a poem...though I am not very talented in that regard.

I'd actually written her a handful of poems and letters since I met her, but I still hadn't found the courage to give them to her. I had no problem professing my love in person...but I found myself feeling nervous at the thought of her reading such vulnerable words. I kept them tucked safely under my mattress. I'd give them to her eventually.

So, what else could I gift her?

Lena would always protest whenever I spoiled her, but regardless, her pleas would not sway me. She deserved more than what life had given her thus far.

If only I could turn back the clock and enjoy just one more day outside these castle walls, I would take her to a nice restaurant or even spend another afternoon in the forest lying together, watching the clouds pass through the tree branches. I just wanted one more day of going unnoticed, one more day of experiencing what others perceived as ordinary moments. They were anything but ordinary to me.

I sighed as I exited my quarters, navigating the various white hallways. Had it always been so prosaic and dull in this place? Had it always lacked color and vibrancy?

I was approaching the war room when I saw Finnan with his ear pressed to the black, wooden door.

I suppressed a chuckle, but it came out anyway when I placed a hand on the ten-year-old's shoulder, causing him to jump higher than I knew possible for a human.

He clutched his chest, respiring heavily. "You startled me, Your Highness!"

I raised a brow at him, a smile still on my face. "Are you supposed to be eavesdropping?"

Finnan gave a half-grin, rubbing the back of his neck. "Probably not."

Finnan was the son of Emerson, one of my father's generals. He also happened to be a part of the dreadful meeting being held behind this door.

I ruffled the kid's brown hair, then finally entered the war room, shutting the door behind me and walking toward the group gathered of Otacia's most elite.

Father was sitting at the head of the massive wooden table, stroking his short, black beard as he glowered at the map laid out before him. This room was as gloomy as they come, a stark contrast to the all-white walls just outside. The stone in here was unpainted, and nothing but the large window behind my father provided natural light. The Otacian flag, in our colors navy, black, and silver, was flowing due to the morning breeze blowing in.

"It is a terrible tragedy," Rurik expressed blandly. "But do you think it is connected, Your Majesty?"

Just as Daerin had said, the meeting had already begun. I was to receive a slap for that, I'm sure. I quickly seated myself further down the table. I may be the Prince, but to my father, I had not earned the right to sit beside him.

These meetings had been going on daily since Mother's assassination. Usually for hours at a time. Going over possible threats and connections—brainstorming ways to lure Mages without harming our soldiers.

I hated all of it.

I hated witches, too. Hated that the guilt I felt for setting Amatta on fire was but a speck in the back of my mind.

Did that make me just as much a monster as she? That I could end her life and feel nothing at all?

"How would killing two Outer Ring women be connected?" Emerson asked with lowered brows.

To that, my eyes shot up, my heartbeat quickening. "What did you say?" I asked, sitting straighter in my seat. "What happened?"

The King slowly lifted his glare to me. "You would know if you had been here on time, Silas."

His flat tone sent chills down my spine. Just as I was about to press on the matter, Emerson spoke.

"Arson in the Outer Ring. A cottage was set on fire in the middle of the night while a woman and her daughter were inside."

13

My stomach sank so hard that I felt I'd be sick. I attempted to school my expression, lowering my trembling hands to my lap.

No.

It was just a coincidence. It had to be. The Outer Ring had thousands of residents. It could've been anyone.

"Also, Brighthell is nowhere to be found."

Torrin is missing?

"Has the place been investigated yet?" I pushed. As much as I cared for Torrin, Lena's well-being was my main concern. "Are the citizens alive?"

"We had a handful of soldiers go down to confirm the fire itself, but the investigative crew is about to head out as we speak."

Instantly, I stood, my chair's legs dragging against the floor, making an unpleasant screech.

"Where do you think you're going?" the King demanded through his teeth.

I took in a shaky breath as my father narrowed his eyes at me. "I wish to investigate, Your Majesty," I responded calmly. "If a Mage truly did this..."

If a witch hurt Lena...

"The experience could be good for him, Your Majesty," Emerson interposed. He was perhaps the only person in this room that I liked.

My father studied me for a moment more before ultimately conceding. "Very well. See what you can discover, Silas."

I gave him a grateful nod, then rushed to meet with the soldiers about to head out. After questioning a handful of men if there were any casualties and being provided no answer, I decided to remain silent.

Arming myself with my sword, I mounted Sable, my ebony horse, and made my way toward the Outer Ring.

A pit was in my chest the entire time.

It is some other house. It has to be.

I took slow and steady breaths, preparing myself as we turned the corner before Lena's home.

And I nearly collapsed at the sight of her house.

No.

It was charred...burnt. Although citizens had successfully extinguished the fire, the smoke from the aftermath was still swirling toward the sky.

Instantly, I pulled the reins, squeezing my legs and pushing my hips forward to race my horse toward the house.

"Your Highness!" one of the soldiers called, but I ignored him.

She is alive. She must be alive.

I quickly scrambled off Sable and dashed up to the front door.

"You shouldn't go in, Your Highness," a soldier insisted as he halted me, holding his palms out. "It isn't healthy to breathe in these fumes."

"Out of my way," I seethed, and the soldier's eyes went wide. I was always a kind, respectful prince. I had never ordered anyone around.

He quickly nodded as he stepped out of my path.

I loosened a breath at the state of Lena's living room and kitchen as I entered. The soldier handed me an oil lamp—the soot covering the walls, the windows, everything, made it so there was hardly any natural light.

Hold in the emotion. Don't let them see.

I needed to ask if they survived. The soldiers here knew the answer. But the words wouldn't come out.

15

I slowly crept toward Lena's room, my heartbeat pounding against my chest.

Please...please...

The door was just slightly cracked. I froze for a moment, hand on the knob.

Please be okay...

Finally, I forced myself to step inside...and time stilled. A muffled cry left my lips when I saw what lay in her bed.

No.

"This is a hard sight for anyone to see, Your Highness."

No. No. No.

He cleared his throat. "I insist, these fumes—"

"Leave me," my voice cracked. "Shut the door behind me and leave."

The soldier's brow furrowed. "Your Highness—"

"I wish to say a prayer in private," I whispered. "Please."

His eyes bounced between mine, and he gently nodded, retreating as he closed the door to give me privacy.

As I slowly turned to her, my face crumpled. I was frozen for a long while, unable to believe what was before me. Aside from the orange glow coming from my lamp, the room was nearly pitch black...and eerily silent.

When I finally brought myself to move, my steps felt heavy. I knelt at her side.

"Lena..." I cried softly, unable to restrain my body's trembling. "No...no..."

I placed the oil lamp on the ground beside me. Her hair was gone—those beautiful copper waves disintegrated by the flames. Her face was hardly recognizable.

But it was her.

It was her.

I sobbed quietly as I brushed my fingertips on what was left of her cheek, and at the feeling of her dead body, I wept.

I couldn't get enough air, and it had nothing to do with the smoke. In fact, I wished the fumes would suffocate me, wished they'd take me to wherever she now was.

My best friend.

The love of my life.

Lena.

My eyes trailed over her neck, then darted to her hand.

My mother's necklace, the ring I had given her...someone fucking stole them!

I thought I had felt rage when Mother died, but this? Was this the work of witches? Did they see her climb up to the castle? See her with me?

Was this to punish me? Was it part of their plan? Or was it just some lowlifes looking to steal?

Sweat dripped down my body as I attempted to regulate my breathing.

"You cannot let your will to live be tied to me, Silas. To anyone."

I shook my head as I recalled her final words to me. "You cannot leave me," I wept quietly. "I need you. My life has no meaning without you."

"Because life is unfair, and tragedy can happen at any time."

I cried harder. I placed a kiss on her forehead, my tears dripping onto her burnt corpse. It was morbid...but it was Lena. My Lena.

"You will not give up."

"I can't...Lena," I sobbed.

"You will not break."

I struggled to breathe as I pictured her face. Her beautiful green eyes...her radiant smile.

"Promise me."

My voice was barely a whisper. "I don't accept this. I don't accept it." I kissed her forehead again, holding my lips on her as I attempted to pull myself together.

There was a knock on the door, and a faint voice asked, "Are you finished, Your Highness?"

I withdrew, holding what was left of her face, taking note of every horrific detail, as painful as it was.

"I will always love you." My trembling hand lowered to hold what remained of hers as I whispered, "I will find you in the afterlife, Lena. I promise."

Mother had taught me of the Gods, insisting I know all I could about them. At the feel of my lover's corpse, I didn't know if I believed in such a fantasy anymore. Still, I found myself silently praying to Ravaiana, the Goddess of Life.

Please provide Lena peace. Please tell her how much I love her. Tell her how special she is. How...

I choked on a sob again as there was another knock on the door, more urgent this time.

"Just a second!" I rasped, then resumed my prayer.

Tell her that I will find out who did this to her and that I won't rest until there is justice. I know nothing of the afterlife, nothing about prayers...but please, if you haven't already, provide her safe passage into Elysium. Tell her I will be with her again...and that I'm sorry. I'm so sorry.

I didn't know if I deserved to go to Elysium...to heaven. I had already killed four men, evil as they were. I had killed Amatta, too.

But the entire universe would have to conspire against me if there was a sliver of a chance for my soul to find hers again.

"I will find you," I murmured to her. "I will find you, Flower. I will find you."

One last kiss, and I rose, wiping my eyes and catching my breath.

I just needed to last until I was in my room. Then I could let go.

I retrieved my lamp, then clutched the knob and turned, making sure to avoid eye contact with anyone and everyone. I ignored their expressions of concern, making my way to mount Sable and head home.

I waited for the men to conclude their search, and while I did, I went over the past couple of days, analyzing every little thing.

Lena didn't have many belongings to warrant a theft so extreme. Aside from a few gowns, the necklace and ring were probably all they had of value.

Witches. It had to be witches.

They saw what we did—what I did to Amatta. They must've had a spy watching me, saw how much Lena meant to me, and killed her to make things even.

I grasped the reins in anguish. She should've never come to my room.

This is all my fault.

I could see now that they targeted Lena as an act of revenge, but why Mother? What was their play?

And what were they planning next?

I took in the weather, the bright blue sky, the shining sun. How could the day be so beautiful? How could the world go on like it was nothing when she had suffered so? How was the universe itself not in mourning?

The sky should be grey, rain pouring, thundering cracking as if the Gods themselves were weeping over such a loss.

I barely managed to make it back to the castle in one piece, rushing to my bedroom the second I dismounted Sable. I was silent for a moment when I shut the door behind me. Frozen.

Lena is dead.

Lena is dead.

Lena is dead.

I made it only a few steps before I collapsed to my knees, clutching my chest.

I couldn't breathe.

I couldn't think.

All I could see was her burned, stiff body. All I could smell was the smoke. All I could hear was Amatta's scream, imagining that Lena's cries sounded the same as her life was taken away by flame.

I finally let go completely, wailing into my hands.

"You will not break."

How could she ask that of me? How could she believe it was even possible?

I am broken. I am nothing without her by my side.

I jolted when my door swung open. Turning with fearful eyes, I watched as my father shut my bedroom door behind him.

"You fucking child," he seethed, charging toward me. "Crying over some peasants like a pathetic infant." He gripped the collar of my shirt roughly, pulling me to my feet. "I was told how you acted today. You are an *embarrassment.*"

I glared at him with hatred, tears streaming down my face. "They weren't just some peasants," I spat.

He released my shirt, flinging me back. I stumbled but kept myself from falling.

"Be relieved it was someone from the Outer Ring and not someone of importance," he said simply.

I was full of rage—so much rage.

How dare he.

How fucking dare he.

I didn't think; I just acted. I reeled my arm back and swung my fist across his face.

It made a sickening sound, and pain shot through my knuckles on impact. As scared as I was for what was to come, it felt fucking good inflicting pain on him.

My father slowly curved his head back toward me, touching his now-busted lip, blood coating his fingertips. His malicious gaze met mine, and I watched as he pulled out a dagger.

His voice was dark as he growled, "That will be the last time you disrespect me."

My limbs shook, and my eyes bulged as my father swung at me with his dagger. I dodged quickly, but he persisted. The King was a lot of things—terrible things—but a poor fighter was not one of them.

I managed to dodge his blows until his final swing was successful, and I hissed as the steel blade dragged from just above my lip and up my left cheek.

I grunted as I drew away, my fingertips skimming the blood now coursing down my face.

My father's voice was clipped as he wiped his blade, tucking it back into his side. "See to it that you get stitches." He clicked his tongue. "That's going to leave a nasty scar."

I glared at him, shaking with contempt as my blood dribbled onto the marble floor.

His black eyes scrutinized me with distaste, his lip curling. "Perhaps it shall serve as a reminder. Every time you see your imperfect flesh, I want you to remember just how much of a disappointment you really are."

And with those final words, he left.

I loosened my exhale and gradually stepped to my vanity mirror, blinking at the split open skin, at the trail of red dripping under my chin and down my shirt. My father had slapped me, had punched me...but never had he cut me. The wound burned, I imagined, but no physical pain could outdo the mental.

I want you to remember how much of a disappointment you really are.

I had failed. I had failed my mother. I had failed Minerva. I had failed Lena.

I really was a disappointment, wasn't I?

PART ONE:

MYTHS

CHAPTER TWO
LENA - NOW

"*L*ena," a woman spoke in my head, and I fell to my knees at the sound of Kayin's voice. "*We have work to do.*"

My heart was thumping with intensity. I gripped the blades of grass beneath my fingers as if somehow it would help ground me in this moment.

Kayin? Is that really you?

I hadn't spoken to or heard from the mysterious seer in over half a decade—the evening before Queen Ryia La'Rune's assassination. So many questions drummed around in my head, and all I could do was quickly begin listing them.

Where have you been all this time?

Where are you now?

Were you involved in the Queen's murder?

Just as I was about to ask if she knew where Torrin was, she spoke. Her voice was weaker, more feeble, than I remembered.

"There is much I wish I could tell you, Lena. But I can't." She drew in a long breath. *"It has taken me great effort to contact you. It's..."* She exhaled in relief. *"It's so good to hear your voice."*

She sounded so defeated. Broken. Nothing like the upbeat woman I communicated with for so long.

Are you okay?

Her voice broke as she replied, *"No. I am not."*

The beating in my heart quickened, and I swallowed the unpleasant lump in my throat.

Tell me what I need to do.

She was breathing heavily now. *"You are with the Prince, yes?"*

I am.

"Good." Kayin choked on a cough. *"I can't speak for much longer—our connection isn't strong from this far away."*

Where are you, Kayin?

It was silent for a few moments. *"I am in Otacia."*

My eyes enlarged, and I scrambled up from my place on the ground.

"Otacia?!" I exclaimed out loud. "Are you a prisoner?"

"Do not worry about me," she insisted. *"Our paths shall cross when the time is right."* There was a brief pause. *"What did Igon tell you before he died?"*

I couldn't help but notice the sorrow in her voice as she uttered that out. I still didn't know how the two knew each other.

"He told me he sent Torrin away..." I whispered. "Then told me to find you, to find Oquerene."

I was talking to myself, pacing back and forth like a maniac. If anyone were watching me, they'd surely think I had lost my mind.

"You needn't worry about finding me. Not yet. Did he give you a message of some sort?"

I frowned as I recalled his cryptic words. "Yes...he said, *'Only through fire can the phoenix be reborn from the ashes'*...whatever that means."

She groaned in frustration.

I nervously drummed my fingertips on my legs. "What is it?"

"I don't get visions like I used to...hardly get them at all anymore. The Queen's necklace, do you still have it?"

I blinked and glanced down, beholding the diamond and sapphire necklace lying against my collarbones. I ran my fingers along the delicate gems, the stones glimmering in the moonlight.

"I do...why?" I asked slowly.

"That necklace will give you the answers you need...everything...everything will make sense."

"How would a necklace provide answers?" I questioned skeptically. I felt panic rising within me at her silence. "Kayin, you're scaring me..." I breathed. "Are you in danger?"

"I will talk to you again in time," she claimed. *"Get to Nereida. You will find answers."*

I halted my pacing.

"Wait! Do you know where Torrin is?" I blurted out, hope and dread blooming in my chest at the possibility of answers. "He left last year without a word, though apparently Igon is the one who sent him away."

There was a delay. *"You'll cross paths with Torrin again soon."* She was quiet for a beat longer before she whispered, *"I am so sorry for what happened to you, Lena."*

As quickly as Kayin's voice filled my head, she was gone—nothing audible but the hushed nighttime breeze on this mountaintop.

Kayin...why now after all this time? And how the hell was she speaking to me from all the way in Otacia?

I pinched the bridge of my nose, loosening an aggravated breath.

Igon had refused to offer up much information about her. He had just sworn she was as trustworthy a Mage as they come, and as a seer, keeping her identity unknown was imperative. There was so much I needed to ask her about, and yet, try as I might to communicate, the connection had just...vanished.

And she must've seen what happened to me...with Rurik...

I clutched my chest as I attempted to calm my breathing, the wind doing little to relieve the sweat now dripping from my forehead.

Do not think about it. Do not think about it.

I took a few shaky breaths, willing my tears to stay put. I didn't wish to think of it, certainly not right now when so many were counting on me. I didn't want to be reminded of what those monsters put me through. Reminded of the utter helplessness I felt.

I am alive.

They are gone.

They aren't here.

I am safe.

I couldn't think about it, not now. I needed to focus on saving my people; my trauma could be dealt with later.

They are gone.

They aren't here.

I am safe.

I spent a few minutes collecting myself, rubbing my arms in a comforting motion. I used that time to shove my emotions—my memories—into a bottle.

27

I am safe.

I am safe.

I am safe.

Once I felt composed enough, I slowly started back for camp, feeling even more exhausted after that altercation.

Then, like always, my mind drifted to Silas.

"I cannot bear your kindness. Do not give it to me."

What, did he wish for me to be a raging bitch to him? Did he truly desire hostility? Or perhaps indifference?

How would that help us work toward a better future, considering the animosity he had felt for my people his entire life?

I still felt bitterness, considering all he had done.

Silas, The Witch Slayer.

I had heard stories passed around fires over the years...stories that, once they got gruesome, sent me evacuating to someplace silent.

I never wished to hear those tales. I still didn't. I couldn't picture the man I had loved, the man I knew better than anyone, committing such atrocities. Even after seeing him all these years later, seeing how cold he had become, I still couldn't envision even a fraction of the details I'd heard.

As I made it back, I took in the multiple campsites set up along the top of Mount Rozavar, the mountain weather-controlled by magic.

The fire around our small group was still crackling, and Edmund peered up from examining his new leg, now made of enchanted carbonado, to give me a small smile. Elowen was sitting beside him on a log, marveling at his new arm.

The metal, veiny-like material was...outlandish. Extraordinary.

28

"Thank you again, Lena. Just...thank you," he said with a peaceful grin as I passed by. The flames made his blond waves appear even more golden as they lay against his forehead.

I simply returned his smile, giving him a slight nod, and went to sit beside Merrick on the opposing log across the fire. He was glowering at the two of them, and they were either choosing to ignore him or were so lost in each other that they hadn't noticed him staring.

Roland was sharpening a dagger while talking to Hendry, Viola was off who knows where scouting the skies in bird form to see if any Otacians were near, and I didn't wish to know where the Prince and his wife were.

Those lounging around the flames were spaced far enough away that they couldn't hear Merrick and me speaking. "You could tone down that grimace, you know. You're going to scare off the poor children," I teased lightly.

The handful of Mage children that had traveled on this journey were giggling and dashing around the warm mountaintop, chasing fireflies and capturing them with their magic in little bubbles. If they caught Merrick's twisted face, I had a feeling their stomachs would plunge. He could be unsettling when he wished to be.

Merrick snorted, his expression softening. I set my hand on his shoulder and leaned in close.

"You will never guess who just spoke to me," I whispered in his ear.

I felt him tense, and he turned to look at me, his icy blue eyes turning nearly black—the color they always turned when he read someone's emotions. Sometimes, he used it to detect if someone was lying or to see if someone's emotions matched up with their words. But usually, he just used it to understand others better.

"Torrin?" he breathed.

I shook my head. "Kayin."

His eyes enlarged as he loosened a breath. "Well?" he pressed. "What did she say?"

I let out a humorless laugh through my nose. "Nothing much. She asked if the Prince was here, told me—"

Shit. I can't tell him about the Queen's necklace.

I cleared my throat as my hand slipped from his shoulder and back to my side. "She told me she was in Otacia, and while it wasn't confirmed that she was a prisoner, she told me she was not okay." My eyes fell, and I nervously picked at my nails as I sat down beside him. "She also told me we would meet again in time...Torrin and I."

"That's partly good news, I suppose." Merrick shifted next to me, dragging his teeth along the hooped piercing that wrapped around his bottom lip. "None of this is mere coincidence...does she want us to find her?"

I shook my head again, chewing on the inside of my cheek. "No. She told me to head to Nereida. I didn't even mention the place to her." I gave Merrick a weak smile. "At least that's a sign we're doing one thing right."

Merrick's eyes faded back to icy blue as he studied me. "I trust you, Lena." The corner of his lip crept upward. "It is good she is alive, yes? It's been so long."

"It has..." I angled my head and marveled at the night sky. It really was beautiful up here. I could understand why Immeron chose this place over Ames. The lack of light pollution made the stars all the more visible.

It reminded me of when I was little. I'd struggled with nightmares before we had found our home in Otacia, the fear of my power a constant source of paranoia, even more so in unfamiliar territories. I remember one of our blankets had been eaten up by a pack of moths, causing little holes to form in the fabric. Mother, being the creative woman she was, added more—hundreds of tiny little holes. She scooped me up in her arms, tossing the blanket above us and enclosing us underneath.

The warm light in the room we were staying in at the time had filtered through those tiny tears. *"See, it's like the night sky!"* she had said, and it really was. I felt safe with her beneath the stars.

"Count them, Lena. Count the stars."

I'd fallen asleep in her arms as I counted, finally resting soundly through the night.

Tears began welling in my eyes as they trailed over to Mother's sleeping figure. I would be leaving her for the first time in my life come morning. But she would be safe up here.

She would be safe.

"I never mentioned something to you," I lowered my voice, meeting Merrick's eyes.

He frowned, eyes swirling dark once more. I scooted closer to him and went in to whisper again. I ignored Merrick's scent, or at least tried to. Somehow, he always smelled like fresh snow. Perhaps it was from his continuous use of ice magic.

"Igon gave me a message before he died. 'Only through the fire can the phoenix be reborn from the ashes.'" I searched his eyes. "Does that mean anything to you? I can't comprehend what he meant by it."

Merrick pondered momentarily as Silas and Erabella returned from wherever they had been. My eyes scanned the pair, and I tried my best to ignore their slightly disheveled hair and the subtle flush to their cheeks. Silas wouldn't meet my eyes.

I felt my fire rising, and my eyes averted to the ground.

Calm the flames, Lena.

I felt Merrick tense as well, and when I glanced at him, his darkened eyes were on the two of them. Before he could question me—because I knew like an idiot my emotions soared just now—I pressed, "Well?"

The wind blew his silver-white hair, currently unbound and falling just past his chest. His eyes were narrowed, planted on the ground for only a moment longer before his eyes returned to normal. "No. I...I don't understand it one bit." He crossed his arms as he gazed into the fire.

Silas and Erabella spoke quietly to their men before situating themselves in their shared bedroll. Still, Silas avoided eye contact with me.

"He spoke to me in my mind, Merrick."

Merrick whirled at me, his eyebrows raising.

"Right before he died, Igon spoke to me in my mind. I don't know how."

His jaw clicked, and as my head began to fall, he softly tilted my chin so my eyes could meet his. "I am sure you aren't meant to figure it all out right now." He let go of my chin and patted my shoulder. "Rest. Don't stress all that needs to be figured out—easier said than done, I know." He gave me a lopsided grin. "But get some rest. Tithara only knows when we will be able to get some again."

Wasn't that the truth...

"You should get some then, too," I suggested.

His smile faltered. "I will." His eyes shot to Edmund, who was now holding Elowen's hand as he beamed at her. "Once I know that bastard isn't going to sneak off with my sister."

I laughed through my nose as I stood, about to make my way to my own bedroll. "I've never seen you so overprotective, Merrick."

"I've never seen Elowen..." he began, then sighed, looking at me over his shoulder with a small smile. "Goodnight, Lena."

"Goodnight." I looked back for just another moment, catching the sight of Elowen giggling at something Edmund said, him watching her as if she was the most beautiful thing he had ever seen.

Soul-Ties.

My traitorous eyes shifted to my apparent mate. His eyes were closed, his wife tucked into his side.

I felt that pang of pain in my chest again and didn't feel it ease up, even as I stared off into the stars, even as I drifted to sleep.

CHAPTER THREE

LENA

The mountain was a sea of murmurs the next morning, my people observing warily as our group prepared for the journey south.

Merrick. Elowen. Viola. Silas. Roland. Hendry. Edmund. Erabella. And me, their Supreme.

The handful of days since escaping Fort Laith had drawn us closer together, along with the training we committed to and the small talk that ensued. Still, we weren't entirely comfortable with one another. I imagined it would be a while before we got to that point, understandably so.

The morning began with Ayla bringing us all our new attire, along with Ashton, one of her sons, who brought the armor they had crafted. Immeron's entire family, all five sons, their wives, and Ayla, had spent this week either making our items or traveling to Forsmont for extra supplies.

My entire ensemble was nearly all black, from my tight leather pants to my formfitting top held up with two slim straps. My vambraces, couters, and pauldron all matched, and the leather material was flexible and strong. Lastly, I was given a deep navy cloak. My chest was bare, and there was nothing visible except Ryia's necklace, which rested against my skin.

I couldn't help but notice how my outfit was made with Otacia's colors—black and navy. I wondered if that was done on purpose.

The Mages' attire differed from what was crafted for our human companions. Ours was lighter, as our ability to use protective forcefields and the need to be nimble on our feet was of primary importance.

The humans needed extra cushioning to protect themselves, so their armor was a bit heavier, and the material all matched: all-black, steel plate mail, leather pants, and neutral-colored cloaks. Ayla also packed us some light loungewear, insisting that with the impending heat expected for a summer in Tovagoth, we'd need them.

"I wanted to make the lot of you clothes that wouldn't draw too much attention, as I know you're on the run," Ayla said carefully. "That is why there's a lot of black and silver."

Silas clenched his jaw but attempted to give Ayla a small smile. "Thank you."

The Prince had finally made eye contact with me this morning, but his golden gaze had quickly averted.

"I cannot bear your kindness. Do not give it to me."

I pondered on his words last night and again when I woke up this morning. Did he feel like he deserved my distaste? Or perhaps his feelings for me still lingered a touch...

35

I was pulled out of my thoughts by Ayla strolling over with a pouch in hand. "How does it fit?" she asked with a warm smile, gesturing to my new outfit.

"Like a glove." I grinned back. "Thank you."

Merrick sighed. "It feels so good to be out of those damn prison clothes," he said, brushing his hands along the fabric of his navy robe. He and Elowen both opted for the lightest of options, though both of them wore fighting leathers underneath, with vambraces that matched mine.

Elowen twirled around in her own burgundy and navy robe, the material tight on her slim waist. "It's perfect!"

I chuckled at their excitement, taking note of the belts along their hips and the silver thread woven in their outfits. Elowen's enchanted dagger was secured at her side.

"You look wonderful," Edmund voiced softly, and Elowen flushed, offering him a bashful smile before resuming her spinning.

Ayla clasped her hands together. "Oh, I'm so glad." She turned her attention to the Princess of Otacia, who appeared slightly uncomfortable. "How about you, Era? How does yours fit?"

Era gave her a gracious grin. "It fits perfectly." She wore armor similar to that of the Otacian men, though hers was structured to complement her feminine figure. It was actually quite similar to mine, except instead of leather, it was made of black steel. "I've never worn armor before. I feel...strong with it."

Merrick's eyes flicked to hers, and when she met his gaze, he gave her a slight smile.

Irritation rose within me...simply because Erabella had a personality I was beginning to like.

I didn't want to like her.

36

"We went heavy with yours, just like the other humans. It'll take some getting used to, but it will provide you more protection."

Erabella inclined her head. "I appreciate it. Thank you."

Ayla returned the gesture, then extended her hand toward me, finally handing me the pouch in her hand. I raised a brow.

"Various herbs," she explained. "Some of the ones I find most useful."

Elowen stopped her twirling. "Do you have what's needed for the contraceptive elixir?" she asked.

I nearly choked with laughter when I saw Edmund's and Hendry's eyes blow wide and Merrick's frown deepen. Even Roland seemed surprised the petite healer asked such a thing, but what they didn't realize was whether Elowen planned to sleep with Edmund mattered not.

"It eliminates the monthly bleed," I mumbled to them as I secured the pouch to the belt resting on my hips.

An embarrassed grin formed on Edmund's face as he rubbed the back of his neck, and I noticed a slight flushing of Hendry's cheeks as he began to find the blades of grass at his feet particularly interesting.

Silas's only response was a couple of blinks, but Erabella's mouth popped open. "There is something you can take for that? And it's...safe?"

I narrowed my eyes, feeling a tinge of annoyance. It wasn't uncommon for humans to be wary of anything magic-related.

"It is safe," Viola responded, giving her a wink. "The contraceptive properties are an added bonus."

A dark thought began to cloud my mind, and when I saw how Erabella's face changed, her slight smile as her fingertips brushed Silas's, I quickly diverted my attention to Ayla.

"Anything for invisibility?" I asked a little too loudly as I peeked inside the brown bag. It had been a while since I had the need to make one, but the skill was still fresh in my mind.

"Oh yes, plenty of heliotrope and amaranth," she replied. "I figured it would be better for carrying than a bunch of bottles."

I offered a grateful nod as I tied the pouch shut once more. "This is perfect."

"Now, remember," Immeron started, sauntering over with a folded map. His gaze stopped on the Prince, and then he eyed me, nodding his head backward to suggest we talk in private.

Silas's face remained neutral, but the feathering of his jaw gave away his displeasure.

I trailed Immeron. "Nereida is just past the coast bordering Wrendier," he said quietly, turning back to me when we were far enough away. "Non-Mages have tried to get past the Valley that protects it, but none have ever made it through. To human eyes, it will seem like no land is in sight. You should be able to see it, however." His eyes traveled to the Otacians. "Hopefully, if they're with you, they'll be allowed entry." His finger pointed to an area he marked in between here and Forsmont. "You can go through Half-Life Pass to save you a week of travel to Forsmont. But beware of the dangers."

My eyes nervously went to his. "Exactly what dangers are we talking about?"

He winced. "Bloodsuckers. As I mentioned before, most Vampires are seen up north. But my family tends to steer clear from the pass, based on the whisperings we've heard in Forsmont."

Two of Immeron's other sons had left to gather supplies for my people in the smaller kingdom, and they were still not back.

The journey to Forsmont, taking the route through Halsted, took roughly four weeks total to and from, however, so it wasn't a shock.

"Have you run into any issues in Halsted?"

Halsted was the second largest kingdom in Tovagoth, Faltrun just behind. It was also one of Otacia's most impressive territories...and the most prejudiced.

He shook his head. "Thankfully, we have not. But I'm sure word will have been spread about the Prince's betrayal. I'd say it's the most dangerous place for you all to be, second to Otacia itself."

I pulled my lips to the side as he handed me the worn map. After a moment studying it, my eyes flicked up to his. "How come you didn't travel through Ames?"

Based on the map, Ames and Halsted were equal distance to Mount Rozavar, and Ames was perhaps a day closer to Forsmont. I knew we wouldn't be taking that route, one because the Otacians were probably back in our territory, in case any of us who escaped tried to go home. And two, because I didn't wish to see or smell all the dead bodies that still remained. I wished we could have buried them...but now was not the time.

Immeron's posture stiffened, his deep blue eyes glimmering with an emotion I couldn't place. "Too many memories...I just couldn't be back in that place," he mumbled.

Even though I didn't understand, I nodded. It felt rude to push. "Thank you so much for your hospitality, for taking care of my people."

His smile was genuine as he clasped my shoulder. *"Our* people. We Mages need to look out for one another." His hand fell back to his side. "And thank you for those cuffs. I still have no answers on how they work, but I'm set on figuring it out."

I had given him a spare pair we had kept with us. Whatever powered them was a mystery to us all, even Silas. He said that information was classified; not even the Prince was granted that knowledge. I was determined to get some answers.

I replied with a grin, it slowly falling as I made eye contact with my mother in the distance.

"Excuse me," I said politely. Immeron nodded, and I made my way over to her.

I had talked to her over the past few days, making it clear that she would not be joining me on this journey. She protested every time. But now we were finally here, the day I'd be leaving this mountain. Leaving her.

She brushed her tears away as I approached, doing her best to give me a positive smile. Her face crumpled anyway.

"I should come with you," she begged, her bottom lip protruding.

"No." I grasped her hands in mine, my own voice shaking, knowing this was the last time I'd see her for a while. "I will feel at peace knowing you are safe up here on the mountain."

She shook her head, her copper bangs blowing with the wind. "We haven't been apart your entire twenty-three years of life. I...I don't know what I'll do without you," she cried, cupping my cheek. "You are my life's purpose, Lena."

After a statement like that, I couldn't hold in my emotions. I yanked her into a hug and cried softly. "I will come back," I assured her. "If Nereida is real...if it is a safe place, as Immeron has said, I will return. I will bring all our people there." I pulled back, sniffing as I wiped my tears. I hesitated for a moment. "Kayin spoke to me last night, Mother."

Gulping, her tearful eyes shot wide. "What did she say?"

I gave her the rundown of what Kayin had advised me to do, and once I finished, she took a steady breath, her hand going to her forehead as if she had a headache. "I hate how all of this has been put on your shoulders..."

"This is my fate, and I believe the Gods are watching over me. I think I will be safe...as safe as I can be, anyway," I said with a half-grin. My efforts to make light of the situation fell flat.

"I'm supposed to protect you—" she started.

"And you will be," I promised. "Worrying about your safety would put me in more danger. I need to be focused on the task at hand."

She slowly shook her head, her shoulders drooping in defeat before she pulled me into another hug. "I love you so much, Lena."

My voice shook as I whispered, "I love you, too."

When she released me, I watched her eyes trail behind me, the warmth vanishing from her countenance. When I glanced over my shoulder, I noticed Silas stepping in our direction.

I could tell he didn't wish to make eye contact with either of us, but he finally chose to look at me, my mother's burning gaze too much for him.

"We should go," he proposed as he reached my side. "We're heading to Forsmont, yes? There is a pass that we can take, but we need to get on the road now if there is any hope of making it to its entrance by nightfall."

I blinked. "Do you have excellent hearing, or have you been before?"

A crease formed between his brows. "I've been through it before, three years ago. It's our best bet. I think we should stay as far away from Halsted as we can."

I nodded slowly, and Mother ambled toward him. "Take care of her," she blurted out.

My horrified face darted to her, but her unrelenting regard was for the Prince alone. His honey irises skated to hers in surprise.

Tears slid down her cheeks, but she kept her chin high. "You always protected her before," she said quietly. "I am trusting you with the most important person in my life. Don't let anything happen to her."

Silas blinked a few times before his eyebrows lowered. "You have my word," he promised.

Her lip wobbled, and she gave him a curt nod before stepping away.

"I've never been away from her," I said softly, watching as she made her way over to say goodbye to Merrick, Elowen, and Viola.

I felt Silas's eyes on me. "I know," he replied quietly. "At least you can find solace knowing she is safe up here."

My heart skipped a beat, hearing his gentle tone. I met his eyes, only for a moment, before his jaw clicked, and he strode away.

CHAPTER FOUR

LENA

When we took the portal to the bottom of the mountain, El, Merrick, Viola, and I lifted our hands, turning them ever so slightly to hide the pointed cartilage of our ears.

"It's so weird seeing you with rounded ears, Merrick!" Elowen giggled. It was, but honestly, it was bizarre seeing El and Vi with theirs, too. We never had to hide in Ames.

"I prefer your pointed ones," Edmund murmured to El from his spot behind her on their horse. "But you are beautiful all the same."

I smiled softly when she leaned her head on his shoulder, looking upward into his eyes with a giant smile.

I swear a vein was bulging in Merrick's forehead from how hard he was frowning. Viola drew him out of his anger trance, placing a hand on his shoulder. "Ready to ride?" she joked.

He finally tore his eyes away from his sister. "You sure you're up for it?"

She laughed through her nose, then backed away enough to shift into a stunning, ebony mare. Her violet eyes sparkled, and Merrick patted her back before hopping on.

I flipped my braid off my shoulder, holding the reins to Roland's and my horse, and found Silas staring at me.

I realized this is what I looked like to him before...the ordinary Lena Daelyra of the Outer Ring. I used to hate the magic that ran in my veins and the ears that put a target on my back. But now? Now, I abhorred being forced to hide who I was.

What was going on in his head as his honey eyes studied me? I reminisced about the words he had told me when I discovered his true identity.

"I could tell you wore a mask, hiding your true self because you were scared to be her. It was something I related to. But that's why I enjoyed teasing you...enjoyed pushing your buttons."

I held his unrelenting gaze.

"Because I saw her peering through, begging to come out. And I loved every bit of her."

His eyes flickered, and he was the first to look away. Pain knotted in my stomach as reality sunk in.

You would've never loved a witch, isn't that right, Quill?

...Or is your mask on tight?

We rode mostly in silence for the first few hours to Forsmont, a little small talk amongst the group, but that was it.

It was difficult saying goodbye to my mother for an amount of time I was unsure of. It was difficult watching Silas wrap his arms around his wife, smiling softly while she beamed up at him.

But nothing was more difficult than riding on this damned horse with Roland.

We switched this time, me sitting in front and him behind me, and Gods, did I regret it. It had been a few hours on the road, and we were currently letting our horses drink from a freshwater river. In the distance, the sun was still bright in the sky, warming the air to a comfortable temperature. The terrain before us was mostly bright, green grass—rolling meadows.

We had all hopped off our horses, taken bathroom breaks, and refilled our waterskins. Now, Roland and I were back on our ride, waiting for the mare to finish hydrating.

His strong thighs were pressing against mine, his hands resting comfortably on my hips. I, for one, was not comfortable with the placement. And the bastard could tell—relished in that fact.

"You're awfully stiff, Ginger Snap," he crooned, his hands sliding down my thighs. Chills spread across my entire body as he whispered, "I can help with that later."

Despite what happened to me, I felt safe around Roland. My uncomfortableness didn't stem from disgust or fear of his touch; it was from how much I found myself enjoying it.

Plus, I wasn't in those cuffs. I was far more powerful than him.

"Roland," I said sweetly, leaning back to whisper in his ear. "If you try any more shit, I am literally going to light you on fire."

He snickered. "That wouldn't be kind to ol' Donut here," he replied, patting the horse's white mane. "Wouldn't be fair for her to get caught in the crossfire."

I turned ever so slightly, giving him an artificial smile. "Then don't test me. Or smoked Donut with a side of Roland will be what is served for dinner tonight."

I would never hurt an innocent animal. But I aspired to clarify that I would not tolerate his shameless flirting. Even if I liked it—more than liked it. I refrained from slapping my forehead.

Ugh! What is wrong with me?

He let out a dramatic sigh. "I want to say, *'I'd love for you to eat me for dinner'*, but for Donut's sake, I shall keep my lips sealed."

I narrowed my eyes back at him. "You literally said it anyway."

He gave me a lopsided grin, his hazel eyes sparkling with amusement. "Yeah, but it didn't have the punch it could have had," he retorted.

The sun shining down not only complemented his deep, tanned skin, but the rays also brought out the green hues in his irises. Most of the times I'd seen them, they had appeared on the browner side, but seeing them now as their true color, a combination of olive and ochre, I found them...captivating.

And his eyelashes...I never realized how long they were.

His smile grew, showcasing his bright, white teeth. "Your ogling is making me horny, Ginger Snap," he purred.

My eyes blew wide when I realized I *had* been ogling at him, and I groaned, my grip tightening on the reins as we angled Donut back onto the road. "I can't stand you," I muttered.

He chuckled, and the sound had me clenching my thighs. "Whatever you wanna tell yourself," he replied smoothly.

The others were slowly following us now. "What's your fascination with naming things after desserts?" I prodded, looking down at Donut as she marched.

I felt Roland shrug. "I dunno. Donut just looked like a powdered donut," he explained, patting her mane again. "And you look like a Ginger Snap."

I raised a brow, even though he couldn't see. "I'm crisp and crackly?"

His chuckle so close to my ear sent more chills down my body. "No. I'd instead say you are sweet and spicy." I could hear his smile. "Plus, of course, this hair of yours played a part in my nickname."

"You think I'm *sweet?*" I asked with a disbelieving scoff.

Another sexy laugh. "Okay, well, maybe not sweet to *me*...yet." He squeezed my hip, his lips almost brushing my ear. I sucked in a breath. "But I have a feeling you'll grow fond of me eventually."

How does one breathe again?

"Unlikely," I lied, and Roland laughed through his nose.

"So..." Erabella drawled, pulling me from my fluster. We all halted at the top of a ridge, surveying the terrain before us. Her brown eyes scoped the many hills. "Is it just a straight shot to Forsmont now?"

"The area is mountainous," Silas answered, eyes squinting further down to where the beginnings of a rocky region were evident. "But there is a path throughout we can follow."

"Couldn't we have gone through Halsted?" Edmund asked, his arms tightening around Elowen's waist as he shuddered theatrically. "Avoided the creepy mountains?"

Roland snorted from behind me. "Considering Halsted is Otacia's bitch, that is probably the last place we should be."

The corner of my lip turned up at Roland's comment but quickly fell when Elowen asked, "Does Halsted also have the magic erasing cuffs?"

47

Silas shook his head. "No. Those belong to Otacia and Otacia alone." His eyes flicked to Edmund's. "And Halsted would be less safe than the pass."

"But what if we see vamps?" Edmund pouted, his golden waves blowing with the breeze. "I won't be able to sleep."

Merrick was currently sitting atop Viola, who was still shifted into stallion form. He angled his head toward Silas. "How long is this 'pass' exactly?" he asked, then his icy eyes went to Edmund. "And, what, Vampires are known to reside there?"

"Immeron mentioned the Vampire risk back on the mountain," I said. "But he said they were sighted up north, mostly."

"Half-Life Pass is just under one hundred fifty miles. While it is true most sightings have been in the north," Silas continued grimly, "Halsted has complained of increased Vampire activity. They completely reinforced their borders within the past few months, and they have also been Otacia's major supplier of nightshade longer than that. I wouldn't say we are in the clear down here."

"Nightshade?" Elowen questioned, her big blue eyes round.

"Toxic to Vampires, we've come to find." Hendry tilted his head to look at the healer more fully. "They ingest enough, and it'll kill them. Even touching it burns the shit out of their skin."

Merrick pulled his lips to the side. "Lena, you ever read about that?"

I mulled over all the various texts I'd come across, thinking specifically of the books Igon had encouraged me to read over the years. "No...nothing. Everything I've read says the sun or fire is the only way. Or beheading."

"Did you bring any with you?" Merrick pressed, his eyes darting between the Otacian men. Even Viola's eyes in horse form widened.

"Of course. Nightshade bombs, in fact," Edmund grinned, tapping the bottle secured at his hip. They must've packed some before our escape. His smile morphed into a frown. "But still...it's not simple killing them with it. Their increased speed makes it hard to hit them."

"Well, good thing we have Lena's fire." Elowen grinned, grasping the reins of her and Edmund's horse. "I don't believe they'd stand a chance," she said confidently.

Silas's scowl deepened on the road ahead at the mention of my powers. I had to refrain from rolling my eyes.

"Plus," Merrick added, "it's not like a bite from them will kill or turn you. They won't have the time to drain anyone before Lena lit them on fire."

In order for a Vampire to successfully turn you, you would need to have your blood drained to damn near empty. The point right before death. Then, a Vampire would feed you their blood, blood that contained an ancient virus. Once that occurred, you would start the change. There was no cure once you got to that point—only death could save you from that fate.

"I wouldn't underestimate them," Hendry interjected, his voice calm like always. The man was so composed...I couldn't envision him hysterical or overcome with rage. "We've seen some rip the jugulars out of humans with ease in seconds. It didn't matter how many nightshade bombs we had or how many soldiers went to retaliate. They killed multiple in no time at all." His mismatched eyes slid to mine. "Your fire will help, certainly. But they could still have one of us dead before you get the chance to attack."

That comment made my stomach drop. I gave a grave nod, then focused my attention forward as we all continued to move.

"How did you figure out nightshade was their weakness?" Elowen asked.

Silas's jaw ticked, presumably at the innocent sound of El's voice. "We captured one. Experimented on it for months."

I watched as Erabella lightly caressed his thigh, and he took in a deep breath. I felt my chest ignite, and I quickly averted my vision back to the road ahead.

Calm the flames.

Merrick shot me a perplexed glance. I gave a cheerless smile in response. I really needed to get my emotions in check, for fuck's sake. It was almost as if he was feeling mine without even reading me.

"We've seen animals affected by the Undead's curse," Roland began. "Vampires are already undead in a way, but can they be overtaken by this necromancer, too?"

The group was quiet.

"Let's hope not," I whispered.

It took us a few more hours of riding before we reached the entrance to the enormous mountainscape known as Half-Life Pass. The colossal behemoth of rock and stone loomed above us, a combination of jagged peaks and rust-colored edges. It was remarkable...and completely intimidating as I peered into the slim entrance we'd be trekking through come morning.

Trees encased us, and the sound of crickets threatened to lull me asleep already. The sun was nearly set, and the air was beginning to cool. We'd made it in good time, that was for sure.

"Immeron and his family would travel through here?" Elowen paled as she took in the environment, Edmund lifting her off their ride. The path separating the two towering mountains was slender—just barely wide enough to fit three horses side by side.

"No...I mean, they have. But they normally take the Halsted route," I answered, hesitantly taking Roland's hand as I dismounted our ride.

"It's more of a straight shot this way," Silas commented as he helped Era off their horse. "Less of a risk to your kind, too, all things considered."

When Merrick got off Viola, she instantly shifted back into her regular form, groaning as she stretched.

"Have you taken this path before?" she asked Silas with a wince. Merrick cringed as she rubbed her back, but she gave him a playful wink.

"Not since I was twenty." Silas crossed his arms, his golden eyes squinting as he gazed upward. "Blessedly, there were no dangers when I had gone. Didn't mean it was any less unenjoyable, though."

"Do you feel anything, Lena?" Elowen asked, watching as I took in the environment.

I closed my eyes, inhaling deeply.

To that, Silas asked, "What is she talking about?"

I didn't feel anything amiss. I supposed I had that bit of comfort.

"Sometimes I get a feeling," I answered as my eyes opened. "I can't really explain it. Just sometimes feel when there is a...strange energy."

Roland gave me a playful smile. "That a magical gift, Ginger Snap?"

51

I laughed through my nose. "No, I don't think so. I got a feeling of it before the Undead attacked us during the march, and I had those cuffs on." I stared into his eyes, watching his smile fall as he recalled his treatment of me. As he recalled me saving him. "Those cuffs took my magic, so if it was related to that, I wouldn't have felt a thing. I don't really know how to explain the sensation I get occasionally."

Even when I was in the Western Forest that first day I met Silas, I felt a strange sensation. Silas had, too. Perhaps it was just heightened intuition.

I shrugged, and then, as I went to remove my bedroll from our horse, Roland stepped up, taking over.

"Such a gentleman," I crooned.

He winked. "I have some redeeming qualities."

Silas cleared his throat. "We should begin down the pathway as soon as the sun starts to rise," he said as he laid out his own bedroll. Edmund and Hendry nodded in agreement, then went off to fetch some firewood.

"How come it's called Half-Life Pass, anyway?" Erabella questioned with her head tilted to the side, her blonde bob hovering above her shoulder.

Silas's eyes softened when he looked at his wife. "Legend says Half-Lives used to reside in this pass...that depending on the quality of your soul, they had the ability to snatch you and bring you down to the Underworld." He rolled his eyes. "All fairytales. That would be the last danger we'd run into."

She chewed on her lip, nodding slowly. "How many days will we be in there?"

He kissed her forehead, and my eyes fell to the ground as he replied, "Four."

CHAPTER FIVE
MERRICK

The camp was set up relatively quickly. Edmund and Hendry gathered the wood needed for our fire, and we all ate through the rations of food we had brought along with us. None of us were too eager to walk through the creepy pass, well, at least tonight. We would begin our journey in the morning.

After seeing to our needs, everyone began resting soon after. We were all exhausted, Viola especially. She passed out the second she hit her bedroll.

My eyes trailed over her beautiful face, and guilt overcame me. She was the only one who walked this entire way. You could best believe I would ensure she was one of the people riding a horse through this pass.

"She was pretty tired, huh?" Edmund asked from across the campfire. He and I were taking the first shift, watching over everyone in the event an enemy approached.

My brows scrunched together, and looking at his awkward smile made my fists clench. I was grateful for them taking our side in this war, but that didn't mean I wanted to be friends with any of them. I didn't want to read his emotions—I didn't care about them one bit. So, I chose not to, visualizing a mental wall to cut him off.

I rested my elbow on my knee. "Shifting takes a lot out of her," I grumbled.

His lips pulled to the side as he slowly nodded, eyes skimming those of our group. I followed suit, surveying all of our sleeping companions.

My eyes landed on Erabella, whose blonde hair was tucked behind her rounded ear. Silas was sleeping on his back, his right arm draped around her as she slept with her back against his side.

She stirred, and as her eyes slowly opened, mine darted away, looking up at the massive mountain before me. It was even more menacing to look at in the dark.

Do Vampires truly live inside?

I'd heard tales of them when I was a boy, as my cousin Torrin found them particularly fascinating. Not me. I'd be A-OK without ever seeing one in my life. I couldn't fathom being lost to bloodlust, forced to live in darkness.

I missed him...he was always like the older brother I never had. His thirty-first birthday was last month, and I wondered what he did to celebrate. I couldn't let myself dwell on it...dwell on the fear that something had happened to him.

He was gone for eight years before, after all, following Igon's orders and moving to Otacia. I hoped it wasn't another eight before I saw him again.

"Can't sleep?" Edmund asked Era quietly.

I heard her soft moan as she stretched. "Can't say the ground has grown more comfortable for me," she complained in a sleepy voice.

When I dared another glance, she was staring at me, the flames casting a glow against her tanned skin.

Her lip tilted up. "What, no smart-ass comment about what a princess I am?"

Edmund let out a low whistle, covering his mouth to conceal a smile.

I narrowed my eyes at her and gave her a smirk. "You're in good spirits," I said, tuning into her emotions and watching her smile falter as I did so.

Despite the unpredictable environment we now found ourselves in, she felt safe. She felt comfortable, which was a surprise because the night of our escape, I had felt so much hesitancy from her. I had felt her fear. Her apprehension.

I continued reading her, and I could feel myself flush when I felt her arousal, probably due to the Prince lying beside her. I inhaled sharply, quickly turning my reading off as I held my hands together atop my groin as nonchalantly as I could.

One of the setbacks of being a man.

She gave me a curious expression, but I glanced away again. Perhaps I would tease her about that emotion, but not in front of Edmund. That didn't feel right. Plus, it wasn't the first time I had felt that emotion from someone else. It always felt like an invasion of privacy...though I supposed that's *exactly* what it was.

"How does it work?" she asked gently.

My eyes slid to hers again.

"Reading emotions, how does it work?" she clarified.

Edmund shifted in his place on the ground. "Yeah, that's gotta come in handy. It certainly did at the fort."

I narrowed my eyes at him, then dragged my attention back to Erabella, clicking my tongue. "How does *any* of it work?" Once it was safe for me to do so, I lifted a knee again, resting my elbow atop it. "Before, it was something I couldn't stop. When I first got this power, I felt everything from everyone. It was exhausting...and overwhelming."

"You feel *every* emotion of the people you read?" she questioned with broadened eyes.

I nodded. "Happiness. Sadness. Anger. Jealousy." I paused. "Desire."

I could assume Erabella knew I had felt her arousal when I watched her cheeks turn pink. Edmund examined me with a raised brow.

"I can tell when people lie," I continued grimly. "I feel when they are scared or embarrassed. I feel it all, and I feel it as if it's my own." I stared into the flames of the fire before me. "But emotions aren't always easy to understand. Most people have trouble understanding their *own* emotions."

Just because I could feel what someone felt, like sadness, for example, didn't mean I automatically comprehended it. Someone could be sad about a multitude of things.

I shrugged. "Feeling the emotion is the simple part. Connecting those emotions to understand the *why* is what proves difficult at times."

The firelight danced in Erabella's brown eyes as she scanned me from head to toe. "That sounds awful."

I scoffed. "You've no idea."

"So that's how you knew to trust Silas?" Edmund asked, his face now resting on his carbonado fist, trying to stay awake. "Using that power?"

The feelings I felt from Silas were...strange. I didn't wish to bring that up—especially near his wife.

"I was able to know he was telling the truth about not wishing to harm Lena, yes."

"That power seems like it'll be useful in this war," Edmund replied sleepily.

I nodded, resting back on my palms. I was exhausted, too. But if there really were Vampires, or even just Otacians looking for us, we needed at least one of us alert—ideally a Mage.

I blinked slowly, and my eyes caught Era's again, her own blinks suggesting she'd be back asleep soon. The warm, crackling fire, the pleasant nighttime breeze, and the stars in the sky made it hard for any of us to stay awake after such a long day of travel.

Her mouth parted as if to say something, and I cocked my head to the side, choosing to read her again.

Her words caught in her throat, presumably at the sight of my eye color turning dark, and she laughed softly. "Is it always necessary? To read someone?"

I shrugged nonchalantly. "Amongst those of an enemy king-dom, I'd say so."

Her smile vanished, and after a few moments more of looking at me, she turned to lie on Silas's chest, who, in his sleep, held on to her closer.

I felt a few emotions from her...annoyance and disappoint-ment. But I was not expecting the last one.

Hurt.

I supposed what I said came out pretty bitter...but what did she expect? Her kind had hated mine for decades. A handful of my people were slaughtered by hers just a few weeks ago.

She felt hurt by my words.

I wasn't expecting that fact to bother me, either. But it did.

CHAPTER SIX

LENA

The sun was just rising when Elowen shook me awake, the sky a blend of light blue, pink, and gold behind the myriad of puffy clouds.

"Rise and shine!" she sang in her usual upbeat tone.

I sat up and rubbed my eyes as she retreated, blinking to clear my vision. Elowen had always been a morning person. Even though Mother and I would get up early on Thursday mornings back in Otacia, I always enjoyed it when I could sleep in.

She and Hendry had taken the second watch, so she was already awake and alert. Now, it was time to travel through Half-Life Pass.

I grunted as I brought myself to my feet, rotating my neck and wincing from the unsavory sleeping conditions. I didn't bother changing into the loungewear packed by Ayla; none of us did. It would be safer to utilize those when we found an inn to stay in. Plus, I didn't feel like changing in the forest.

Silas, Hendry, and Edmund were already up, loading the horses again, and I glanced over to see Roland open-mouth snoozing.

"He's a heavy sleeper," Edmund commented with a half-smile, his emerald-green eyes glinting with entertainment.

"And that's saying a lot, coming from Edmund," Hendry added, which earned him a playful nudge from the blond soldier.

I couldn't help the smile curving on my lips.

I think I'm growing to like those two.

Silas refused to look in my direction, and what I now called his signature scowl was plastered on his face.

Did my death really take away that sweet, playful man? Was he always this somber?

I sighed, feeling pain in my chest at the thought. I strode over to Roland, peering down at the slumbering man. His brown hair was tousled, and his face was relaxed. Despite his jaw hanging open, he looked...stupidly cute.

I nudged him with my foot. "Wake up, sleepy head," I crooned.

He winced, swatting me away. "Just...a few minutes," he grumbled.

"I don't think so." I nudged him harder. "Up."

He cracked an eye open, then gave me a devious smirk. "You look especially sexy from this angle, Ginger Snap."

My eyes constricted, and I placed my boot on his chest, causing him to let out an '*oof.*'

"You look especially *unsexy* with drool on your face."

He narrowed his eyes, his smile growing, and replied, "How can I not have drool on my face when I'm picturing you sitting on it?"

My eyes flared, and I withdrew my foot before swiftly kicking him in his side. He let out a grunt, then busted out laughing.

I groaned and turned away, pulling my lips to the side to try and conceal my grin.

What a character.

As I was striding away, Silas hollered to Roland, "Get off your ass and quit behaving like a child!"

Roland rolled his eyes and stood, gathering up his bedroll. "You're no fun, Silas," he muttered.

Once we were all packed, with stacks of fresh-cut wood secured to our horses, we mounted our rides and started the trek through Half-Life Pass. Merrick demanded that Viola ride on Hendry's horse with him and promised he'd be fine walking. They compromised by Viola insisting she'd shift during the latter half of the day so Merrick could rest. The Pass was too bumpy and uneven to ride quickly, so it wasn't like Merrick walking would slow our pace.

The opening between the two large mountains was thin, and I could tell by Elowen's shaking that the healer was nervous. Edmund's vine-like thumb stroked her leg, and she leaned into him.

I found myself marveling at the narrow passageway. The sedimentary was a medley of colors: rust, browns, violets, and silvers, the ripples having their own distinctive hues. It amazed me that the Gods and Goddesses had such an eye for beauty and were so imaginative with their creations.

My thoughts flicked to the Half-Lives, the creatures that supposedly resided here. They were one of the many beings that had gone extinct, spiritual beings that could travel between our world and that of the Gods. Some said they were messengers of Ravaiana, while others believed they were Valor's subjects, slaves of the Underworld.

Who really knew? So much of our history had been wiped out when Solen La'Rune, Silas's great-great-grandfather, had our mystic temples raided and shut down. When the banishments and prejudices really began. Even the books Igon had were but a fraction of our legacy.

I sighed at the state of our world. If Oquerene really was real, I wondered if any Half-Lives happened to survive and resided there.

Four hours later...

"Do we have enough gold for me to get my own horse, Your Highness?" I pinched Roland's thigh, and he hissed.

"C'mon, riding with me isn't so bad," he purred into my ear. He rolled his hips into my backside, subtly enough no one would notice but not so subtly that it had my toes curling.

He had been doing this for nearly the entirety of our trek. It was driving me wild...and not particularly in a bad way. Roland had this way of bringing light to dark situations.

Silas shot Roland a warning glare. "Knock it off," he demanded.

I couldn't see Roland's expression, but I felt him tense behind me. "Prick," he huffed under his breath, certainly quiet enough that the Prince did not hear as he and Erabella's horse rode forward.

I laughed through my nose. "Oh, come on, he isn't that bad."

"You're supposed to be on my side, Ginger Snap," he whispered.

"Is that so?" I rolled my eyes playfully, though Roland couldn't see. "Tell me more of this Weapon, Prince," I asked loudly, changing the subject and nudging our horse forward so I could speak with Silas.

He cocked a brow and looked back at me, the corner of his lip raising as he replied, "I can't trust you fully, not yet."

Roland snickered. "*'He isn't that bad'*. Is that what you just said?"

I pivoted, narrowing my eyes at Roland before diverting back and giving the Prince a glare for reciting my quote. "Oh, it's gonna be like that, is it?"

Silas shrugged, his wife frowning at me from her spot in front of him. "You open up to me; I open up to you." His golden eyes danced in triumph. "Seems only fair, wouldn't you agree?"

I scowled at him. "Fine."

He returned an equally unpleasant sneer. "Fine."

"Get along, you two," Edmund teased.

Hendry's horse halted abruptly. "Whoa...what the fuck is that?" Hendry breathed.

My eyes darted over, and a small gasp escaped my lips as we came to a stop.

Along the rock hung several skeletons, and eerie as they were, the most terrifying exhibition was the bodies that hadn't fully decomposed. A man and a woman. Dry, dead flowers were laced around their limbs and their torsos. Bite wounds were noticeable on what was left of the skin on their necks.

They were shriveled up...but their teeth still remained. These bodies couldn't be older than a few weeks.

Edmund tightened his grip around Elowen's waist, his jaw clicking as he studied the horrific display.

"I'd take that as a warning," Roland said, his tone deep and serious. "I'm surprised there's not more blood."

That was a good point. There was no evidence of blood staining the sedimentary rock or anywhere on the ground.

"Seems these vamps aren't wasteful," Merrick commented, his nose crinkling from the dreadful scent of decay. He angled his head to the side. "But why the display? Why warn off their food supply?"

"It isn't a warning," I whispered.

Silas quickly turned his head, his golden eyes meeting mine. "It's to show us what's to come. A promise."

I nodded gravely, and our eyes lingered for a moment longer before Silas turned his gaze back toward the bodies.

"Let's get away from this place," Viola murmured from her spot behind Hendry.

With that, we moved onward, my gaze lingering for a moment longer on the two individuals who'd died not that long ago.

Why the flowers?

Day one was complete, and we were once again setting up camp. The sky was orange, and as I noticed the temperature cooling, I felt dread at the thought of being in this place in the dark. At the thought of those corpses.

We were all sitting except Erabella, who was taking a bathroom break, and Viola, who was standing nearby. She kept a tasteful distance from where the Princess was but remained close enough in case she heard anything amiss.

I held my index and middle finger out, staring at the flame I conjured. It danced above my fingertips. A decent amount of wood was tied to the horses, but we still needed to be frugal.

My eyes flicked to the sky. I'd light our fire just before dark.

Erabella was ambling back a moment later, and I decided I'd better empty my bladder before bed, too. I stood, and Roland lifted a brow.

"Need some company?"

Silas opened his mouth to scold him, but I responded first. "Yeah, you wanna wipe my ass for me?" I quipped.

He snorted. "Wipe it, smack it, fuck it—"

"Roland," Silas growled.

"What? She's clearly immune to my charms," he stated with a smug grin.

I was already walking away, laughing. "You are an idiot, Roland Aubeze!"

I was shaking my head, and just as I was about to round the corner for some privacy, my eyes caught movement...a moment too late. Instantly, my hands flew upward, grasping the arms of the person now holding a dagger to my neck.

I gasped for breath as I witnessed the soldiers charging in from behind him.

Otacian soldiers had followed us in here.

"THEY FOUND US!" I shouted just before the blade stole my breath.

CHAPTER SEVEN

SILAS

M y heart lurched into my throat at the sound of Lena's warning. Instantly, I was on my feet, quickly opting for my bow for this battle. I pulled the bowstring, readying an arrow as I charged forward.

"How many?!" Hendry yelled, but his words were cut off quickly when Finnan walked forward with Lena, a dagger digging into her neck.

"Let. Her. Go," I gritted out, staring at him through the sight. "NOW, Finnan!"

The fifteen-year-old stared at me with widened eyes. I'd known him since he was a little boy. His father, Emerson, was the best general we had.

"How could you?" he breathed. "How could you betray our kingdom?"

"Let her go!" Roland yelled, attempting to rush toward him. But Finnan dug his weapon deeper, causing Lena to cry out and Roland to freeze.

She could try to burn him, but I feared the second she attempted anything, he would take her life without delay.

"Stay still, Lena," I said carefully, her green eyes welling with tears. I then turned my attention to Finnan. "Release her. We can talk."

"Lower your weapon!" he shouted at me.

I curled my lip. "How dare you speak to your Prince this way."

"Please," Lena whispered. "You can kill me, but there's no chance you'd make it out of here alive."

"SHUT UP!" he yelled at her, his body trembling, his breathing uneven. His blade was digging into her skin now, and I could see the trickle of blood trailing down her neck.

Hendry and Merrick also had their bows readied, and the soldiers behind Finnan had theirs pointed as well.

The sun was almost entirely set, and Lena had not yet started our fire. "This is your final warning, Finnan. Let her go, and you can leave with your life!"

There was petty desperation in my voice, but I couldn't help it. He was just a boy, and I didn't wish to end his life. He was forced into this war and given no choice by his father except to follow the King's command.

"I-I have orders to kill!" he yelled.

But it was becoming clear to me that I was going to have no choice.

"Please don't make him do this," Lena pleaded, and he pushed the dagger closer.

No more.

It happened so quickly, the release of my arrow. I always shot with precision. The arrow just missed Lena's head, striking Finnan's skull right between the eyes. Lena gasped as Finnan's hold on her ceased, and the boy slumped to the ground, his blood pooling beneath him.

I didn't have time to mourn, not as the other Otacian soldiers bellowed, shooting their arrows at once.

Lena, the powerful being I now knew she was, took only a millisecond to catch her breath before swirling, hands going up to create a forcefield so giant that all arrows that hit it ricocheted, falling to the ground.

Merrick lowered his bow, shooting his right hand out to freeze the soldiers' feet to the rocky floor.

"Era!" he shouted, chucking her his bow.

She stumbled and just barely caught the weapon, her eyes blown wide as she looked at him.

"Time for some more practice." He flicked his head toward the men, who were now attempting to free their feet from the ice entrapping them.

"I-I can't!" she exclaimed. "I've never killed before...Gods, I..." She shook her head, her panicked eyes flitting between the Empath and the Otacian soldiers.

"You think they'd hesitate with your life?!" he exclaimed.

I was about to pummel him for raising his voice at her, but I realized he was right.

"Do it, Era," I ordered, and her terrified eyes met mine.

Viola's enchanted sword shifted into a mace, and she ran forward, roaring as she swung at a man's head.

I knew these men. I fought with them...but I also knew how we were trained.

No mercy.

Roland and Edmund rushed in next, and every time one of my father's men released an arrow, Lena shot fire, melting it before it could impale anyone.

Hendry shot from his bow, easily piercing the neck of one of the soldiers. At that moment, I realized that Hendry, Edmund, and Roland knew and had fought with these men, too. Yet here they were, standing by my side without a doubt. I placed my bow down, reaching for the new blade that Immeron crafted for me. Grasping its hilt flecked with purple-red metal, I paced to where the men were trapped.

Hendry, Edmund, and even Roland shouldn't have to live with the guilt of killing our men, haunted by the memory of their desperate faces. So, I started from the back. The soldiers shook in place as their frightened stares met mine.

They knew the type of man I was. They had seen how easily I could kill. They didn't even bother to beg for their lives.

One by one, I began impaling their chests with my weapon. In the front, Era trembled as she held Merrick's bow, the Empath standing beside her, guiding her shot.

She released the arrow just as I completed my second kill, her arrow off the mark. Merrick whispered something to her, and she readied the bow again.

An arrow was traveling toward me as I killed the third, but Lena quickly melted it. She then proceeded to fling her arm out, sending a bolt of electricity straight for the soldier. He shrieked as he convulsed, his eyes rolling back just before he slumped to the ground.

Fourth kill. Viola swung her mace.

Fifth kill. Roland slit the throat of another.

Sixth kill. Lena refroze the feet of those who had managed to break the mold.

Seventh kill. Era's arrow finally struck true, killing the final man with a shot to the heart.

My wife's eyes filled with tears, her knees wobbling as she lowered her weapon.

"You did good, Era," Merrick said gently, placing a hand on her shoulder. Her face scrunched, and she pushed him off, returning his bow as she did so. She crossed her arms and hurried away from the bloodshed.

My eyes trailed over the many bodies before landing on Finnan's, at the young boy's lifeless eyes.

"I...Gods..." Edmund breathed, staring at his corpse. He turned to me. "I am so sorry..."

My lip threatened to tremble, but I knew it wouldn't. Instead, I clenched my jaw so hard it hurt, and as I moved toward the dead body of a boy I knew well, I met eyes with Lena.

Her neck still had blood trailing down it.

"I'm sorry," she whispered. I moved in closer, and Lena stepped aside as I kneeled, roughly retrieving my arrow from Finnan's head.

I wasn't sure what to say, but she shouldn't be sorry. Finnan sealed his fate when he pressed that dagger to her throat...there was nothing any of us could have done.

She stood beside me, watching as I wiped the arrow clean on the boy's shirt. I placed Finnan's dagger back in his hands and crossed his arms over his chest, my eyes locked on his lifeless face.

I could still remember him as a child, running through the castle hallways, listening in on meetings he wasn't old enough for.

He was always so excited to be on the field, to grow up, to make his father proud.

What a fucking waste.

"I'm so sorry," Lena repeated in a whisper as I rose.

My whole body stiffened when she touched me. Her hand was feather light on the back of my arm as if she was scared of me. I angled my head downward, looking into those bright green eyes and hating the pity that shone in them.

"I wish it didn't go down like that," she said quietly.

Everyone around us was staring now. I ground my teeth as I studied at her, then felt the eyes of the Empath. I spared a brief glance in his direction, taking note of his swirling dark eyes. Was it a look of...worry he wore? Of confusion?

I lifted my other arm and couldn't help but notice Lena's body tense, her eyes flaring.

Did she think I would hurt her?

Sighing, I placed my hand over hers, the one still resting on my arm, and gave it a gentle squeeze. Everyone was far enough away not to hear as I leaned down and whispered, "It isn't the first life I've taken for you. I don't expect it to be the last."

A crease formed between her brows, and a lone tear slid down her cheek, her arm slacking to her side.

Elowen ran up to us. "Here," she mumbled as she placed her palm over Lena's neck.

"It wasn't deep. Seriously, you don't even need to heal it," Lena averred.

"Nonsense," Elowen insisted. "If I can heal something, I will."

As I walked away, I noticed Viola staring at me, her arms crossed over her chest.

"You could've let her die...easily," Viola muttered as I was passing her. "But you didn't."

"Is that so surprising?" I questioned, my voice going low.

Merrick's eyes had returned to their icy blue as he observed his sister healing Lena. She pulled her hand away, and the small gash was nowhere to be seen; the only thing left was the blood that dried on Lena's neck.

Lena quickly rushed to our fire but glanced over at me before lighting it. "Should we relocate, Your Highness?"

I blinked, finding myself surprised that Lena had referred to me with that title with warmth in her voice. My eyes trailed back to Finnan, then surveyed all the dead bodies just steps from our campsite. The sun was nearly set, the sky a dark blue.

"Yes," I agreed. "Just until we can't see the bodies anymore."

I sat before the fire, feeling numb. However, that was a normal emotion for me. Standard.

Still, I had learned to find enjoyment in killing. But this...this had brought me no pleasure.

My gaze was emotionless when it drifted up to Lena, who sat across from me. She and I were taking the first shift of the night together, and we had remained silent until now.

The flames danced in her eyes as she stood. "Nereida."

My brows drew together.

She continued, "That is where we are heading. It is past the southern coast. Immeron believes more of my kind live there. Apparently, a ward has been placed on the island so humans cannot see it."

As she began walking away from the fire and our sleeping friends, I stood, striding to her and gripping her elbow.

"Why tell me now?" I asked breathlessly.

She turned, and I held my breath at the sight of her doll-like eyes looking up at me. "Because I trust you." She shrugged. "And you deserve to know."

My eyes bounced between hers. "Thank you," I murmured.

She gave me a small smile, and I gripped her arm tighter as she went to roam away again.

"Where are you going?" I demanded.

She heaved a sigh, then chewed on her lip. "I was just going to pace around," she finally answered. "I...I'm struggling to calm my mind."

I knew that feeling very well. Still, I asked. "Why?"

She blinked over and over, and the shine that began in her eyes let me know she was holding back tears.

"I had never killed anyone before," she whispered. "Today was my first. Well, besides the Undead..." Her shoulders slumped, her eyes falling to the ground before finding mine again. "Was it hard for you? The first time?"

I swallowed, the sound of her sweet voice doing things to me that I'd rather ignore. I thought back to my first kills—the men at Amethyst Pond.

I felt shame...but it mainly stemmed from my fear of what Lena would think about me. I didn't care about their lives, not after they threatened to rape her, a teenage girl at the time, right in front of me.

"Think of those you love, those you wish to protect...and feel no remorse when you kill those who threaten them," I answered. "I never felt bad when that was my reasoning for ending a life."

The way she was looking at me...it was like she could see through all the bullshit. "I know that's not true," she said quietly. "I can see it in your eyes."

I clenched my jaw, and instead of entertaining this conversation, I said, "The Weapon is said to be that of a magic no one has ever seen. Magic to stop all magic...or stop all of humanity. Whoever finds it—hones it—will dictate the fate of the entire world. Ulric wishes to keep it out of the necromancer's hands."

She let out a small gasp and stepped closer to me. My lips parted slightly, my grip on her arm loosening at her proximity.

"Who told you of such a thing?" she asked mutedly.

I did my best to keep my expression neutral, but the quickening of my breathing probably gave away that I didn't want to say it. "We captured a seer years ago. Tortured the information out of him."

Her frown deepened, and I made sure to keep my face void of emotion. "How do you know it wasn't a lie?" she asked.

I licked my lips, then sighed. "We had also captured the seer's daughter. Only upon watching us torture her, us only agreeing to stop once we had answers, did he finally give up everything. He told us the Weapon was in Ames, but if your seer had seen it coming, perhaps he moved it."

There was a moment of silence. "What were their names?"

I gave her a pained expression, slightly ashamed as I admitted, "I don't remember."

She sucked in her lips, shaking her head. "Did you set his daughter free afterward?" she asked, but I could tell she already knew the answer.

I released her arm. "My father had the man's daughter killed in front of him," I responded grimly, then turned to walk away from her. I didn't wish to see the disgust on her face.

But it was she who gripped my arm now, walking around to face me again.

"You are not your father, Silas," she hissed, her voice soft enough that no one could hear if they happened to be awake.

I studied her, my face falling. Only for a minute would I let her see through. "I am hardly better," I replied quietly.

I wanted to hold her...not that I deserved it. I wanted to loosen the tie securing her braid and run my fingers through her hair. I wanted to feel hers running through mine.

Instead, she slid her hand along my arm, currently bare of vambraces. Her expression softened. "You have done all of this to save my people...whether you have your own purpose for doing so or not. I would argue that you are significantly better."

My lips formed a tight line at the sight of her shy smile. Anger rose in me at this interaction, at this entire situation.

"Let us keep our interactions to a minimum," I muttered, then turned to sit back by the fire. "But sit back down. Do not wander," I added over my shoulder gently.

She stood frozen for a moment, then conceded, sitting back across from me.

It was silent in the mountain pass until Lena asked, "Why did you tell me? About the Weapon?"

My eyes slowly lifted from the flames. "Because I trust you, too."

CHAPTER EIGHT

MERRICK

I struggled to rest that night; visions of the many men being slaughtered eliminated any attempt at peaceful thoughts.

My first kills were in Ames the day our village was attacked. As I overheard Lena and Silas's conversation, I realized in some small way that I related to the Prince.

"Think of those you love, those you wish to protect...and feel no remorse when you kill those who threaten them. I never felt bad when that was my reasoning for ending a life."

They weren't aware I was lying awake as I kept my eyes shut. That was exactly how I felt, taking the lives of the soldiers in Ames. I thought of Elowen, of Viola, of Lena. I thought of the many villagers who I'd grown up with, of Igon who had been so kind to all of us.

I felt no remorse...at least not in the moment. Those humans came to kill us, either right then in our village or later in Otacia. I ended them without a second thought.

Still, I found Lena's response...intimate.

"I know that's not true. I can see it in your eyes."

Why were they so gentle with one another? Why did Lena jump in front of one of our kind's biggest enemies to save him? How is it that the Slayer of Witches flipped like a switch, so eager to help?

I could see that perhaps he witnessed our power and realized utilizing it could help him overthrow King Ulric. I could.

But why, when Silas was staring at Lena's injured body back in Fort Laith...why, when I read him, did I feel *love?*

Soul-Ties. It was the only damn explanation.

Still...feeling a love of that magnitude so quickly, regardless of the bond gifted by Celluna, seemed ridiculous. Even the feelings I felt between Edmund and my sister were not nearly as overpowering as what I felt from Silas as he gazed at Lena.

It was now the following morning, and I ran my hands through my hair in frustration as I mulled over everything.

Lena gave up the information on Nereida. My eyes almost fell out of my head when she started telling him everything. And then a gasp threatened to escape from me when he told her what he knew of the Weapon.

I still didn't trust any of these humans...none of this made any sense.

Elowen sauntered over to me, breaking me away from my thoughts and handing me a piece of bread.

"Here you go!" she chirped.

"Thanks," I mumbled, tearing off a piece with my teeth and chewing. I couldn't wait to get some real food again.

I swallowed as she started walking off, but I reached forward and gripped her shoulder to stop her. "Wait."

She turned to me, light pink brow raising.

"How are you holding up?" I asked my sister, tuning into her emotions.

She smiled softly. "I'm alright, Mare." Her eyes flicked to the ground, her smile faltering. "I just can't wait to be out of here...can't wait for the killing to stop."

Elowen hadn't killed anyone yet, but I knew witnessing it affected her.

"I think we have a while before the killing ceases..." Despite myself, I pulled her into a hug. She easily hugged me back, and I felt her delight.

I wasn't the best at showing affection, and once upon a time, I despised my sister. Not because of who she was, but because of what her existence had taken from me. But Elowen had always been loving and sweet. She had always been a good person.

When she pulled away, smiling up at me, my eyes caught Edmund's, who was wearing a nasty glare on his face. I returned the sneer, and his face shifted to adoration as El turned to walk to him.

Jealousy.

I was going to beat the shit out of him if he was the type of boyfriend who was jealous even of family members. Just as I went to confront him, I was stopped by Viola, who was getting ready to shift before we began our second day's trek.

"What are you doing?" I asked.

Her violet eyes slid to mine as she stretched her arms. "Getting ready to turn into the hottest horse you've ever seen." She snorted, and I shook my head.

"You need to rest."

She rolled her eyes. "Merrick, I'll be—"

"You need to rest," I demanded. "If we need you to shift overnight, if we're ambushed again—"

"Fine." She sighed, her hands going up in surrender. "You win. I'll climb atop Hendry's horse again, and you can continue walking."

I smiled, inclining my head ever so slightly. "Thank you. That wasn't so hard, was it?"

My cheeks heated as her violet eyes burned into mine. When she saw my darkened eyes, her full, plump lips curved into a knowing smile.

Desire. Desire for me.

My lips parted, a short exhale escaping from me. "Yeah?" I asked breathlessly, blood rushing to my groin.

"Yes," she answered, her voice downy and sensual. "When we get to Forsmont."

I sucked in my lips to hide my smile. I'd always thought Viola was beautiful; anyone with eyes did. But we'd never crossed a line in our friendship...nor had I ever felt such strong desire from her before, certainly not toward me.

I wonder what changed.

"Okay," I agreed softly.

She bit back her own grin before leaning forward and pressing her soft lips against mine for a fleeting moment. She smiled before walking away.

My whole face had to be red—my pale skin doing no favors to hide my nerves.

Holy shit...Viola just kissed me!

I glanced around to see if anyone had noticed. No one had.

Except for Erabella.

Her brows were raised, and when we met eyes, she quickly glanced away, lips puckered as she studied the rock formations, her hands tucked behind her back.

I didn't need to read her to feel her awkwardness. I chuckled to myself before finishing the rest of my bread.

Then, I tied my hair back into a low pony, pieces falling out in the front, framing my face, and readied myself for another long day of walking.

We were halfway through the second day when we finally took a longer break. My legs were aching from all the steps I completed, and Viola gave me a raised brow as she dismounted Hendry's horse.

"I'm fine," I laughed. "Just building more muscle in my legs is all." My eyes flickered to Lena, who was passed out, resting back on Roland's chest. We determined it would be best for her to be awake at night from here on out—just in case Vampires happened to confront us.

He lightly brushed her arm, and she jolted awake. He murmured something in her ear, and she gave him a hesitant, sleepy smile as he hopped down, giving her a hand off their ride.

Who would've guessed that asshole would've grown so fond of her?

"I'm shifting once we resume," Viola stated.

"I can always walk," Hendry offered, and my surprised eyes met his as he stretched. He shrugged. "I don't mind."

I studied him with my brows drawn tight. "Alright...thanks," I replied skeptically.

"Thank you," Viola added.

He gave a slight smile, then sauntered off toward Silas.

I was frowning as I watched him, sensing no ill feelings.

Vi gave me a soft nudge. "People can just be kind, Merrick."

"Yeah, well, I'm not used to it. Certainly not from humans," I mumbled.

After everyone saw to their needs, I found myself perched against a stone, stuffing my face with more bread, enjoying my mini solitude. I found myself alone in Ames most days, not that I'd complain. Being subjected to everyone else's emotions left me drained more often than not.

I was taking another bite just as Silas ambled up to me. "Would you mind showing Era more with the bow before we continue onward?"

My eyes widened before my surprise turned into a glower.

Really? I'm the only one who walked this whole time, and he wants me to do some more standing?

"Why me and not Hendry?" I muttered with my mouth full.

"You've trained her thus far." He shrugged. "Plus, I asked who she'd prefer, and she said you."

I blinked, then snorted. "Yeah, right."

He crossed his arms, and my smile fell.

"You're being serious?"

Silas's deepening frown sent chills across my body. "Just do it..." He made a pained expression. "...please."

I studied him for a moment longer before sighing. "Fine. Give me a sec."

Era and I walked off for some privacy while I gave her more tips with the bow. No one else planned to train right now, so to avoid embarrassing her, considering her skills were subpar, I suggested I train her further down the pass.

"Here," I adjusted her grip on her bow. "Try like this. Don't keep your arm locked."

"I want to rest," she whined, following my directions and loosening the tightness of the arm holding the weapon.

"You are so damn infuriating," I muttered. I placed my hand on the small of her back, and I felt her stiffen further. "You need to relax your back when you pull the string."

"Right back at you," she mumbled. "And I'm trying. It's hard, and I don't want to be doing this."

"You think I want to be wasting my time this way?" I sneered. I honestly didn't mind teaching her...but her poor attitude was getting on my nerves. "I'm the one who has been walking this whole time, not you, Princess. Shoot the arrow."

She did, missing the target, a bullseye I made on a boulder with my blood. Morbid, I know. But I healed the gash quickly. Erabella had been mortified when she watched me make the cut.

"Yeah, well, that's your choice," she retorted, her chocolate eyes glancing back at me as she retrieved the arrows she fired. "Viola said she was more than happy to let you ride her...or whatever." She cringed.

I snorted, and she turned her head to me as she readied the weapon again.

"So, you two are together?"

"What's it to you?"

She narrowed her eyes. "You make it so hard to be nice to you." She turned her attention back to her target and groaned when her arrow missed again. And again. "I don't see why Silas can't show me how to fight," she muttered to herself.

"Why hasn't he before?" I asked. It did seem odd...but at the same time, princesses usually weren't the ones fighting.

"I tried to get him to. He took no interest in it. I don't get it..."

I felt her hurt and shook it away.

"Yeah, I don't either, but we're both stuck, so quit whining like a baby."

She glared at me. "You're so kind, Merrick."

My lip crept upward. "Again," I ordered, nodding toward the target.

She sighed, shot another, and missed—though this one was closer than the last.

"How does your magic work, anyway?" she inquired, still not too annoyed with me to stop our conversation.

"Pretty sure you asked me that a couple of nights ago, Princess."

She rolled her eyes as she bent over, grasping the arrows. My eyes trailed over her ass like a total creep, and I quickly looked away. "I asked about your gift. Not magic itself," she continued once back at my side.

"We're born with it, yes, but it doesn't surface until we are old enough to manage it, usually." I tilted my head downwards at her and frowned. "Shoot the target."

Era sighed in defeat, shakily aiming the bow at the target. She pulled back the string and, upon release, groaned as her arrow completely missed yet again.

"How old were you when you got it?"

"I was eight."

Why was she asking so many questions? Does she even care about improving her skills?

She released another arrow. Miss.

"That's old enough to handle magic?" she asked in surprise.

I shrugged. "It seems so."

"So, you could just wield ice and fire and all of those things suddenly?"

I shook my head. "No...elemental magic—ice, fire, electricity—those come later in life, if at all." I adjusted her grip on the bow, then continued after she missed another shot. "That type of magic is tied to our emotions. Typically, intense emotions like those aren't experienced until one is older. I can't wield fire or electricity. Just the ice."

She let out a gentle hum as she retrieved the arrows.

"So, what kind of magic did you have then? The non-elemental," she asked once beside me again, drawing the weapon.

"Healing. Forcefields. Enchantment." I bent down beside her, holding her waist with one hand and moving her foot with the other. "You're standing wrong," I murmured. "Your feet should be parallel to your shooting direction."

She sucked in a breath, and her eyes darted down to me, following me as I stood. The corner of my lip raised.

"What?" she asked.

"So many questions."

She lifted her brows. "Is that a bad thing?"

I knew my eyes went dark as I began to read her. Her cheeks flushed, her eyes quickly flickering away.

My smile grew cocky. "You're fascinated by my eyes," I noted.

She scoffed, shooting me a mortified glance. "I am not!"

Lie.

She turned back, shooting another arrow, this one *way* off the mark.

"I think you should focus on improving your skills...or lack thereof," I teased.

She turned to glower at me, and as I continued to absorb her emotions, she diverted, trudging away to reclaim her arrows after missing a few more shots.

"I killed that one man, didn't I?" she shouted over her shoulder.

Those words set my feet in motion, and I seized her arm. She whirled to face me with lowered brows.

"You did," I said gently. "And I was proud. But if the situation would've been less in our favor, you wouldn't have had the time to use those men as living targets. You would've needed to hit true the first time."

Her eyes softened as she gazed up at me, my words causing warm feelings to spread through her body.

She frowned, her little nose crinkling, before resuming her arrow retrieval. "I don't give you permission to read me," she said plainly. "It's an invasion of privacy."

"Be glad I'm not my cousin," I called out.

She shot me a cocked brow over her shoulder.

I shrugged. "He could read thoughts."

Her eyes widened. I was surprised by her expression, by what I felt.

Dread.

"Could?" she asked quietly once she was back by my side, worried my past tense wording was because he was dead.

I hoped and prayed he was not.

"I'm not sure where he is," I admitted solemnly. "He left our village last year without a word."

I felt mild relief from her, and then I ordered her to shoot the bow, this time her arrow at least grazing the bloody bullseye.

"Much better," I praised.

She gave me a satisfied smile, and I found my own lips tilting upward at the sight.

"How are you doing?" I asked a few moments later.

She was squinting through the weapon's sight. "What do you mean?"

I pulled my lips to the side for a moment, feeling awkward even asking about her feelings. I wasn't sure why I even cared. But I remembered the sheer panic on her face when I threw her my bow...the tears that pooled in her eyes once she completed her kill.

I had felt the guilt that overcame her.

"Are you alright? After yesterday."

I could feel that she was not expecting my question. She blinked, lowering the bow to her side. "I..." She shrugged. "I have no choice but to be fine."

I shook my head, my hands going into the pockets of my robe. "It's okay to not be okay, so long as you don't let the negative thoughts rule you." I flicked my now blue eyes to the target. "One more time. You can do it."

Her ochre eyes studied me for a moment longer before she took a deep breath, aimed her bow, and released the string. Just like I knew she could, the arrow struck true, right at the center of the target.

I grinned. "Told you."

She beamed up at me, and the sight...it did something to me.

What the hell?

I blinked, my smile faltering, and cleared my throat. "Let's head back," I murmured. "We can train more tomorrow...if you'd like."

Her eyes dropped, but her smile remained. "I would like that." She looked up at me again. "Thanks, Merrick."

And then she walked away, heading back to our group to finish the second half of the day.

I loosened a breath as her distance from me increased, and I found that my heart was racing.

How odd.

I shook my head, following after her.

I was finally able to sit down, grateful for Hendry allowing me on his horse. The soldier's brown and blue eyes showed no distaste, and perhaps his long legs desired the movement.

After what felt like forever, the group began moving again, and as I tightened my arms around Viola's waist, feeling her desire as she leaned into my hold, I found myself extra excited to get the hell out of this pass.

CHAPTER NINE

LENA

It was the evening of our second night. After our small break, the rest of our travels went by quickly.

We were now halfway through this wretched pass. Blessedly, we encountered no problems in the day. Though with the sun now set and the fire crackling, I knew that if there were any Vampires out here, they were safe to emerge now.

Roland had cooked us dried meat in a small pot of boiling water I had started, seasoning it with spices Ayla had also packed for us. We were all eating now, aside from Viola, who had shifted into a bat—just until I was finished eating.

It was smart, keeping an eye on things with night vision. And because Merrick insisted she save her shifting abilities during our travel, she could do so now with ease.

We decided since my magic was more useful at night, I would take the night shifts. I couldn't believe I had managed to fall asleep against Roland while riding earlier today...but it was nice.

"How's it taste?" Roland asked me from his spot across the fire.

I chewed, enjoying the flavor. "Meh." I gave him a smirk as his eyes narrowed, then chuckled. "Very good. You're a man of many talents, I see."

He laughed. "Good answer." He licked his lips, his smile growing. "Believe me, there are many talents I wish to show you, Lena."

There was something about him using my actual name instead of the nickname he gave that set my cheeks ablaze.

Edmund groaned, slapping Roland's arm from his spot beside him, though he, too, wore a smile. "Too much info, man."

I could safely say I longed to know his other talents...longed to experience them firsthand. I wished I could explore them with him right this moment. But, for Merrick's sake, I tried to reel those feelings back, shaking my head at Roland as I ate.

Finishing my meal, I stood up and stretched just as Viola shifted back, ready to eat her own meal. I walked a small distance from the fire, enjoying the nighttime summer breeze. It was scary in here, honestly, but the moon looming above provided a moderate amount of light. Thankfully, we started our travels at the time the moon would be brightest—it was full this evening.

I heard gravel crunching from behind and tilted my head, watching as Roland strolled up to me.

I swallowed and tilted my head up to meet his eyes. "What's up?"

The moon illuminated his handsome face as his lips turned upward. "Honestly? I want to kiss you."

My eyes shot wide, and I retreated a step. Releasing a scoff, I mumbled, "Quit fucking with me."

His smile fell, and he took a step closer. "I'm not," he whispered. "I want to kiss you." A shy smile emerged, his eyes falling to my lips. "I have since I did in that maid's room, truthfully. Perhaps even before that..."

"Roland," I breathed, pressure forming between my thighs as his lustful eyes found mine.

My gaze drifted over his shoulder, looking at our friends conversing over the fire.

Silas locked eyes with mine, and his brows lowered, his arm wrapping around his wife's waist. My eyes slowly trailed back to Roland's, then fell to his lips.

"Would just a kiss satisfy you?" I murmured, my heart racing so fast it almost hurt.

He stepped closer, his body just inches from mine. He purred into my ear, "Until we are alone...yes."

Fuck.

The need for his body became unbearable as his eyes darkened, as his hands grasped my waist, as—

It happened so fast.

The movement.

The scream.

One second, Roland was before me, about to press his lips to mine.

The next, he was on the ground, wailing in agony as a Vampire began ripping through his throat.

I didn't think, just shrieked—lurching myself forward, engulfing my body in flame as I wrapped my arms around the creature.

It roared, falling back with me holding it still. Silas was running, then managed to plunge his sword through its head just as I released it, backing away. My skin was hot, but I managed to stop before my skin began to burn.

My eyes darted to Roland, who was still lying on the ground, blood gushing from his neck.

I stumbled to him. "ROLAND!" I cried.

He was clutching his throat, choking. His eyes widened as he pointed behind me.

There was no time to react before I was thrown to the ground, almost crashing into our fire. My eyes met the red ones of three other Vampires, and I quickly retrieved my sword, which was sheathed beside me.

My lip curled as I stood. "Elowen, get to Roland!"

The healer was frozen, knees wobbling.

"NOW!" I yelled.

The Vampires just stared, their eyes dilating in hunger. It was two women and a man, the latter staring at me with what almost looked like fright.

Elowen went to move, and one of the females advanced, grasping her.

Edmund chucked one of the nightshade bombs. She was fast, but still, as the contents of the bottle dispersed, the Vampire's skin began sizzling. She released Elowen, falling back.

El screamed, once again freezing from fear, just as I willed my magic into my enchanted blade. I advanced, piercing the creature's torso as flame crept up the metal, and she bellowed, her body turning to dust.

I heard another bottle breaking and more screaming as I withdrew my weapon, and the Vampire below me disintegrated away.

Hendry had chucked another vial of nightshade just as the other female bit Erabella, and I ran, slicing through that one with my burning blade, her body turning to nothing but ash.

My eyes then went to the panicked ones of the male who remained. He went for Silas, moving faster than any creature I'd ever seen.

Silas was ready. He plunged his sword straight into the Vampire's chest. But steel alone couldn't kill a creature like that.

Holding the magical sword that Immeron had gifted me, I twirled it in my hands, readying my stance, and charged toward the Vampire.

I roared as I swung it forward and felt the pulse of energy I had charged it with release in a long burst of flame.

The man screeched as the burning sword slashed his skin. The sword didn't impale deep enough, though—he was still alive.

The bastard pushed Silas off with a quick shove, howling as the steel sword was ripped from his chest. His movements were so quick that by the time I was ready to strike again, he dodged, knocking me to the ground and my sword out of my grasp.

Only a second passed before he gripped my wrist—and bit.

I cried out at the pain, then realized just how hungry this Vampire must have been to quite literally give himself a death sentence.

I gripped his neck with my free hand, ready to burn his flesh and end his life, when his red eyes flicked up to mine as he drank my blood.

His eyes were fearful, filling with tears at his impending doom, but he was so lost to bloodlust that he couldn't stop himself from drinking from me.

I felt it then, the wave of euphoria that came from the pulling of my blood.

My hands trembled on his neck.

Kill him. Kill him.

I stared into his eyes, and I felt pity...why?

"Kill him, Lena!" Silas barked.

The Vampire's eyes fluttered, and tears rushed down his cheeks.

My Gods...

My half-lidded eyes went to Merrick's, who studied the blood drinker with shock and sorrow. His eyes met mine, and I knew based on his expression that he could feel the humanity of the man before me.

"When you're satiated," I breathed. "You run, understand?"

The man's eyes flashed beneath the wavy black hair that lay messily on his forehead.

My eyes rolled back at the pleasure, only for a moment. "Nod, or I kill you now," I mumbled.

He blinked, then nodded, his lips pulling away just to say, "Just a bit more," he rasped.

Hendry readied his bow, arrow aimed at the Vampire's head.

"Don't!" I ordered him.

Hendry was gaping at me as he lowered his weapon.

The Vampire finally tore away, panting and gazing at me with my blood staining his lips.

"What is your name?" he breathed, his red eyes widening.

I felt like I was coming down from a high. "Lena...Lena Daelyra."

His eyes traveled down my body as if trying to log my appearance into his memory. "You shall always be safe here. The Vampires of Half-Life Pass will remember your kindness, Lena Daelyra," he said.

As he went to move, I blurted out, "What is yours?"

He paused, giving me a soft smile. "Daris."

Then he ran, gone in a flash.

My hand trailed to my wound, and a strange feeling of both pleasure and pain came from it.

"What the fuck was that?!" Silas demanded, prowling at me before shaking my shoulders. "Why didn't you kill him?!"

"He...he was just hungry," I muttered.

His gaze burned into mine. "He is a monster!"

"Clearly not," I retorted, shoving his arms away. My eyes quickly found Roland, who was being healed by Elowen.

I rushed over, kneeling beside them. He was out cold. "Is he alright?!"

"Yes," Elowen responded. "He fainted from the blood loss. It'll take a bit to get him fully healed...this wound is more complex. But he'll be good as new by morning."

My lip wobbled as I took in the sight of him. If he wouldn't have made it...

I wasn't even going to go there. He *did* make it.

My thoughts drifted back to Daris. "The look in his eyes..." I peered at the Empath. "You felt it too, didn't you, Merrick?"

He nodded slowly, using his own healing magic on Era's bite mark, her chest rising and falling. "He feared for his life. He was beyond terrified...and," Merrick grasped his collarbones, "he was painfully starving."

"Perhaps the Vampires are like Mages...people believe them to be demons, but really, they wish to survive in this world...to live," Elowen said softly.

When I stared off into the distance, I realized that Daris and I shared a similarity...and that the flowers wrapped around those bodies were not a sick display, but a sign of mourning.

Morning came, and I hadn't gotten a lick of sleep. While Daris had promised our safety for the remainder of our time in this pass, I couldn't be sure.

That, and I found myself nervously watching El as she worked on Roland throughout the night. He slept through it all.

The sun was now rising, and Edmund was up, rubbing El's back as she attempted to keep her eyes open.

Merrick healed Erabella's wound quickly. Thankfully, hers wasn't deep.

"Let me take over," I offered, walking over. Everyone else was still sleeping.

"He doesn't need much more," she murmured, eyelids drooping.

I placed a hand on her shoulder. "I got this."

Edmund gave me a grateful smile, and El nodded. Almost instantly, she fell asleep in Edmund's arms, completely drained from her magic usage. He carried her to her bedroll.

I sat down, bringing Roland's head to my lap, and began healing once I felt that burning in my palms. Elowen was right; it was almost fully healed.

I used my free hand to stroke his cheek and decided I would no longer complain of his incessant flirting or jokes. I would never take any of him for granted again.

Two hours passed, and as the healing was nearing completion, Roland's eyes began to flutter open.

"Hey, you," I said softly.

He blinked, clearing his vision, then smiled. "Hey, you." His brows drew together, his smile dropping as he quickly leaned up, looking around. "Did we—"

"We won. We're all alive."

He angled his head back to me, and I tapped my lap, wishing for him to lie back down. He smiled and obeyed.

I then told him everything that happened after he lost consciousness.

"I can't believe you spared one..."

"I know, but I really believe he will keep his word. Ensure our safety." Despite my nerves, I brought my hand to his cheek again. "I was so scared seeing you like that," I whispered.

His lips parted, color staining his cheeks, and that signature Roland smirk took over. "Aww...you were worried about me, Ginger Snap?"

I smiled softly, my eyes falling to his neck. I traced my fingers over where the wound was. "Very worried..."

He lifted his hand and ran it along the arm that was caressing him. My eyes found his again, his face serious. "Kiss me," he breathed.

No one was awake yet...

My stare slid from his eyes to his lips a few times before that desire ruled me, and I leaned down, pressing my mouth to his.

It was a soft kiss, one that sent warmth throughout my whole body. When I kissed him the second time, his fingers weaved through my hair, holding my face as he kissed me a third.

"Roland," I whispered over his lips.

"Hm?" He kissed me again, sucking my bottom lip into his mouth.

I was about to lose my mind. The need for his entire body, for his touch...

It was almost painful how badly I craved it—craved *him*.

"Fuck," I whispered, pushing away.

Roland chuckled, the sound arousing me further, and I pinched his side, holding back my own laugh.

CHAPTER TEN
LENA

"**T**hank Ravaiana!" Elowen had cried, hopping off the horse and twirling around. "I never wish to travel through there ever again!"

It was another twenty-four hours after Roland awoke that we had made it out of Half-Life Pass, and that final day had dragged the longest. I hadn't gotten Roland's kiss out of my head. To make matters worse, as we were riding on our horse, he'd sneak pecks on my neck when no one was looking. I wasn't even fighting him anymore, nor was he teasing. We simply wanted one another.

It took three more evenings until we could see Forsmont in the distance. We would arrive in the morning. The lights from the kingdom shone like stars from this far away, and I couldn't wait to sleep in an actual bed again...so long as everything went well once we arrived.

And a shower. Gods, I couldn't wait to shower.

"Are you cold?" Edmund asked Elowen as she shivered beside him. The wind tonight was cooler, but still pleasant for a summer evening. We managed to travel with a couple of bottles of mead, waiting to drink until we were near our destination. I was enjoying the slight buzz it gave me.

"A little," she whispered with a smile, and Edmund opened up his arms. She snuggled in closer to him and kissed him on the lips, the action causing Merrick to grunt in distaste.

"Is there a problem?" Edmund asked after pulling his lips away, his tone causing my eyes to widen. Never once had he stood up to all of Merrick's displeased words or actions.

We all looked at Merrick, whose eyes darkened. "My *problem* is you messing with Elowen's feelings."

"Merrick—" Elowen began.

"No, El. I'm sorry, but I still do not love whatever—this—is," he said, twirling his hands toward them.

"Listen, pal, it's clear that you're into Elowen," Edmund said calmly, his back straightening. "I don't think she returns the feeling. So, get over it."

Viola and I choked, and Elowen's hand flew to her mouth, suppressing a chuckle.

Merrick gave him an incredulous look laced with disgust. "I sure as fuck hope she wouldn't return that feeling, considering she is my sister!"

At the sight of Edmund's mouth falling open, the three of us burst out laughing, Edmund's face heating. Even Merrick couldn't hold back his smile as he shook his head and covered his eyes. The others bit down their smiles.

"O-oh." Edmund cringed as he rubbed the back of his neck.

"Looks like you royally misread that, buddy," Roland teased, chuckling as he patted the soldier on the back.

Merrick and Elowen had vastly different features. His skin was fair, hers dark, and his hair was white, hers pink. I could see similarities in their faces. Though, to someone with no knowledge of their relationship, it was understandable not to put two and two together.

Elowen giggled. "You are so cute," she whispered to him and kissed his cheek. "Merrick is overprotective, not for that reason, though." She shivered in repugnance at the thought. "We only share the same father, which is why we don't look entirely alike."

"Well, a brother is a good person to have your back, I suppose," he mumbled, then gave Merrick an embarrassed grin. "Sorry, man."

"I could puke," Merrick muttered, and Edmund chuckled.

"So," Elowen continued, "we all have been traveling for how long now, but we don't really know much about one another." Her eyes went to Silas and Erabella. "How did the two of you meet?"

My smile quickly faded. That was the *last* thing I wanted to hear about. Silas shifted in his seat and quickly glanced away from me.

"Well," Era answered. "We met at Silas's betrothal ball. In fact, I met him in a hallway I wasn't supposed to be in." She laughed softly. "He decided to marry me before even attending the ball, and when we entered together, he introduced me as his fiancée."

"Just like that? You don't get to know each other beforehand?" Viola asked, sipping on the mead.

"That's not how betrothal balls work," Silas replied. "Typically, you meet the proposed woman and her father and see what the joining of their family has to offer the kingdom." He took a sip of his drink. "It is more for politics than anything. So, meeting Era by herself felt more...genuine."

When Era smiled, eyes dropping to the fire, Silas wrapped his arm around her and pulled her into him, kissing the top of her head.

Yep, that hurts.

I took a large gulp of my drink, wishing it would knock me the fuck out.

"What about you guys? Merrick?" Era gave him a smirk. "Since you're not into your sister."

His eyes darkened at her, and he chuckled at her joke. I watched his eyes flick to Viola, then back to the Otacian Princess. "Nothing serious for me just yet, though I did have a crush on Lena when she first came to Ames."

I glanced at him and smiled at the memory.

"You didn't like him back, Lena?"

I tensed, then glimpsed back at her. "I...I just wasn't in a place where I was interested in a relationship."

"How come?"

"Era..." Elowen warned.

She shifted her attention to Elowen, her brows crinkling.

"It's okay." I sighed. My eyes flicked up to Silas, who shared his wife's perplexed expression. I drifted my stare back to Era.

I could feel everyone's eyes on me.

"I lived in Otacia for almost six years. It's the only place other than Ames that felt like home." I inhaled, feeling nervous to continue.

Was it stupid to say I was in love? Was I too young at the time to know what that was?

I continued anyway. "I was in love with a boy I met when I was sixteen. When the King put a kill order out for Mages, my mother and I had to leave, and because I couldn't tell him about what I was...I just left. Leaving him to believe I was dead." I couldn't meet Silas's eyes. "I just...I hadn't been able to move on. Not that soon."

"Well...what about later on? Unless Merrick wasn't interested..."

Elowen sucked in a sharp breath, Merrick shaking his head.

"It's okay, really," I told them, then turned toward Era. "When I left for Ames, I grew sick during my travel. Vomiting, fatigue, I thought I had caught a stomach bug or something." My hands began to shake, and I quickly clasped them together. "It...It wasn't until a few weeks into our journey I realized I had fallen pregnant."

It grew quiet, everyone's eyes widening, and I laughed humorlessly to myself. "My mother left my father with no explanation when she fell pregnant with me. She couldn't bring herself to tell him the truth about who she was. It felt as though history in some way was repeating itself." I smiled sadly to myself, my eyes scanning the ground. "It was a small piece of hope that I had, a small piece of happiness that I couldn't be with the one I loved, but I had a part of him. It wasn't until..." I took in a shaky inhale. "It wasn't until nearly two months after we reached Ames—I was a few months along then—that I...I lost the baby." Tears fell down my face, and I quickly wiped them away with the backs of my hands.

Merrick gently placed a hand on my back, dragging his thumb along my spine. "I couldn't look," I choked. "I didn't even know if they were a boy or girl at the time. But Merrick and Elowen were there to take care of me and helped me bury them."

I didn't mention that Torrin was there. How much he was there for me, too. How much he helped.

Torrin always helped.

I lifted my gaze back up to her, and my eyes finally shifted to Silas. His face was void of all emotion, but his eyes—those golden eyes, gave everything away. There were no tears, but they were devastated all the same.

"Elowen told me months later," I continued quietly. "The baby was a boy."

Silas's lips parted, his shoulders drooping, and I turned my attention back to Erabella as my tears spilled down my face.

"I know that it's silly...after so much time. I have struggled with the idea of moving on. I have tried..."

I shook my head, wiping my tears, feeling utterly stupid even speaking about this.

Era studied me sympathetically. "It's not," she replied softly. "Perhaps he is still in Otacia...what is his name?"

My eyes slowly met Silas's, whose gaze fell to his lap.

"Quill. His name was Quill." My eyes then met Roland's, who, for the first time since knowing him, regarded me with pity.

I fucking hated it.

"It doesn't matter though. There is plenty more I have to worry about right now than a man who has surely moved on from me." I stood up, needing to get the hell out of here. "Excuse me."

I sat by a nearby river, making sure to hold my hands in fists to avoid accidentally freezing the whole damn thing.

Part of me felt embarrassed sharing such a personal story. I wondered if they felt it was foolish that I hadn't been able to move on.

I heard footsteps behind me, twigs and leaves crunching under someone's feet. Part of me hoped it was Silas, but who sat down next to me was Merrick.

I peeked over at him as he rested his elbows on his knees. His eyes were laced with worry as he carefully studied me.

"You alright?" he asked gently.

I sucked in my bottom lip and gazed off into the river. "I will be," I said after a few moments.

We both stared off, the sounds of the running water and crickets filling the air.

Merrick slowly shook his head. "I can't believe it took me so long to figure it out," he whispered.

My head spun to him. "What?"

He met my eyes. "Silas...Silas is Quill, isn't he?"

My eyes widened, and my lips parted briefly before I closed my mouth. Then opened it. Then closed it again.

"Don't bother lying, Lena. I can tell if you lie."

Damn Empath.

I dropped my shoulders in defeat. "I'm sorry I lied," I whispered, my lip beginning to tremble. "Or rather, omitted the truth. Please, Merrick, you can't tell anyone...if they kn—"

"Gods, Lena." He shook his head and then cupped my cheek. "I'm not going to tell. I just can't believe you felt like you couldn't tell me."

I took in a shaky breath. "I didn't want you to think I was making a decision simply based on the fact that I loved him before..."

He frowned, his hand falling back to his lap. "But didn't you? You saved him from Viola. She would have made the kill shot had you not intervened," he reminded me.

I sighed and closed my eyes to prevent tears from falling. "It wasn't just because I loved him. It was because...I knew him better than anyone." My eyes opened. "Quill—Silas was the most loving person you could imagine. He was brave and smart and...I would have never let him die. Never."

"And what if you were wrong? What if he had never come around? What if he still saw our kind as monsters? Would you have killed him if it would have saved our people?"

I stilled, looking down at the ground in consideration before meeting Merrick's now dark eyes once more. "I don't see how killing him would save our people."

"But if—"

"No," I said sternly, and he flinched. "No, I wouldn't have. Just as he would never have killed me."

He studied me for a moment, then sighed. "It makes so much sense why I felt what I did from him," he mumbled.

I blinked. "What?"

His eyes flashed with hurt. "After you were attacked, Elowen insisted I see his intentions before she would heal you. She didn't want to heal you if he intended on breaking you over and over for answers. She wouldn't have put you through it." His jaw ticked. "I felt emotions from him I was not expecting. Sorrow, worry, guilt—" He let out a painful exhale. "So much guilt. But there was one I was surprised to feel. Didn't understand. I thought maybe he was trying to think of something else."

"What was it?" I asked, pulling my knees close.

He smiled softly. "Love."

My eyes enlarged, and I blinked over and over. Merrick just let out a small laugh. "Don't act surprised. You just said he wouldn't have been able to kill you. There's a reason for that."

I chewed on my lip. "It's...complicated."

"So, was Quill a made-up name?"

I smiled at the question, feeling a miniature sense of relief being able to talk about my past freely. "Yes, and no. When I first met him, he told me it was Quill. I had no idea he was the Prince for the first few months of our relationship. Until I was already in love with him."

He paused. "Did Torrin know?"

"Yes...he knows everything."

Merrick dragged his teeth over his lip ring, shaking his head. After a beat, he said, "He got up almost instantly to come to you...Silas."

My heart sped up. "Just now?"

Merrick nodded. "Roland, too, actually. Silas looked like he was gonna rip off his head. But I just...I had to know." He placed his hand on mine. "I promise I won't tell."

"I know. I trust you."

His dark eyes faded back to blue. "I'm going to head back now since I know he wants to speak to you. Unless you don't want that?"

I sighed, my eyes skimming the stars that peeked through the trees. "I'll head back in a few."

He squeezed my hand, then stood, the sound of his steps fading away.

And as I lowered my gaze and observed the river, watching as the moonlight bounced off the ripples, I remembered.

Remembered the night I lost my child.

Remembered the night I got my fire.

CHAPTER ELEVEN

LENA - FIVE YEARS AGO

No...please no...

I sat on the floor in Torrin's room, weeping as I clutched my stomach in agony.

I noticed blood in my underwear when I woke in the middle of the night and immediately went to Torrin, who, in a panic, went to locate Elowen. I didn't wish to involve her...involve *anyone*, but Elowen was the best healer in Ames. I hated putting this pressure on a fourteen-year-old girl.

Another wave of pain washed over me, and I groaned.

I discovered I was pregnant a month before my arrival to Ames. My morning sickness was overwhelming...what little food we found on the road was quickly expelled as my nausea overcame me. Close to the end of our journey, Torrin would carry me as we walked, my body too weak to stand for extended periods of time.

Despite the difficulties, despite the pain, I was overjoyed. I was so happy to have a part of Silas with me...a part of both of us.

I jumped as the door quickly flew open, Torrin rushing in with Elowen and Merrick in tow. If I wasn't so afraid or in so much pain, I may have flushed having them see me like this.

Merrick's eyes swirled dark as Elowen ran to my side, her pink hair tied in a loose braid.

"Please, help me," I cried.

Her aqua eyes filled with tears, and she nodded quickly as she placed her palm over my slightly rounded belly.

Torrin knelt at my other side, holding a cool rag to my forehead. I watched as he attempted to shake his panicked expression.

Elowen's healing magic glowed gold as she held her palm in place, sweat dripping from her forehead.

My voice was quiet as I asked, "Is the baby okay?"

Elowen chewed at her bottom lip, looking with furrowed brows at her palms. Then, her eyes widened, her bottom lip popping free as the glow of her magic faded.

Her chest rose and fell, and tears streamed down her cheeks. "I...I am so sorry, Lena."

No...no...

My face crumpled. "There has to be something you can do...anything," I begged, then wailed as another wave of pain overcame me.

Merrick rushed forward, lowering a large handful of towels to her side, "Do something," he pressed Elowen.

"I can't," she cried softly. "The baby has no heartbeat."

My body shook as her words registered. "No." I shook my head. "I don't accept it."

"Lena," Torrin's voice was a lifeline, a rope that kept me from plummeting to my death. "We will get through this." He flipped over the rag and placed it back on my forehead.

Elowen lifted my dress, and as she lowered my underwear, Merrick cursed.

Blood...so much blood was on the fabric, on the floor, spilling down my legs.

"Your body is expelling the baby," Elowen's voice trembled, and her eyes lifted to mine. "I...I can relieve your pain."

I shook my head rapidly. "No."

"We just need to be here with her, Elowen," Merrick said calmly. I met his nearly black eyes, and as I watched his tears spill, I knew he was feeling exactly what I was. I knew he understood.

I let out a shaky exhale as I nodded to him, then felt my body contract again. Torrin tossed the rag to the ground and wrapped his arm around me, rubbing my lower back. I felt a rush of liquid pour out of me, and Elowen choked on a sob.

My body was overheating, sweat coating my skin.

"It shouldn't be much longer, Lena."

Merrick knelt by my other side and held my hand. "She's burning up," he commented.

"I know," Torrin whispered.

I didn't know how much time had passed, how long I wept for, how long I cramped in horrific pain, gripping Merrick's hand with a force I knew had to hurt before the pain subsided.

I took labored breaths and met Elowen's tearful eyes as she lifted something in one of the cotton towels.

"I can't," I choked on a sob. "Please, please, I can't look!"

My body...my soul...felt like it was tearing in half.

Burning.

"Okay, okay," Elowen responded softly, her eyes going to Torrin's.

"Shit!" Merrick exclaimed, ripping his grip from mine.

My head shot toward him, taking in his blood-red hand.

"Merrick...what did I—"

Torrin instantly scooped me into his arms, not caring that blood was getting all over his clothes. He hurried for the door, and my two other friends followed quickly behind.

It was late. I knew Mother was asleep, Vicsin and Heildee as well. Torrin didn't care if he woke them, it seemed, as he practically flew out of the house. He rushed me outside of Ames, the Mages keeping watch looking at us with concern.

It was the first week of January, and the ground was covered with snow. The winter wind did nothing to cool me. It whipped around us, Torrin's white hair blowing with the movement. When we were further away, just before a river with no trees surrounding us, Torrin placed me directly in the snow.

Merrick and Elowen caught up quickly, the latter taking panicked breaths, the former watching in fear as his tears slipped free.

"Go, you two!" Torrin barked. "It's too dangerous!"

"But Torrin—" Merrick began.

"GO!"

They hesitated before ultimately conceding, sprinting away back toward our village.

My flesh was heating so rapidly my skin started to blister...started to *burn*, despite being enveloped in snow—snow that was melting around me.

I gritted my teeth.

"Try to control your breathing, Lena," Torrin said softly. His fingertips grazed my arm, and he hissed as he withdrew, the heat emulating from me burning him.

"Leave me," I begged, my voice hoarse. "I cannot bear hurting you."

"I will be fine," he assured me. "I have gone through this. I understand."

I knew he didn't mean a miscarriage. Torrin had also acquired fire.

He entrapped his hands in a thin layer of ice, ran them down my arms, then placed them on my chest. They began to melt quickly, so Torrin continued using ice magic, refreezing his hands to keep me cool as best he could.

His scent overwhelmed me—cedar and rain. That scent comforted me during our journey here...comforted me all those days he carried my weakened body.

"When my parents disappeared when I was sixteen, I was so scared...sad..." he began, his voice low and calming. "But, as time went on, those in the village gave up the search and assumed them dead or that they abandoned me. I became so angry."

He leaned in close, using his magic to blow air as frigid as the coldest winter night along the column of my neck. I shivered, but it still wasn't enough to bring my body heat down.

"I was angry our people assumed the worst of them. I was angry they gave up. I was angry that I had no answers."

He blew along the other side of my neck, and I let out a shaky exhale, my eyes fluttering shut.

"When their belongings were discovered abandoned deep in the woods, I knew my parents must've been killed. I knew I'd never see them again."

One last blow of cool air across my lips, and I relaxed ever so slightly at the feeling.

"I am so sorry for this tragedy, Lena," he whispered. "I am so sorry for all you've had to endure." He placed his lips against my forehead, lips covered in frost, the gesture calming me even more so. When his lips thawed, he pulled away. "But you will overcome this."

"How?" My eyes slowly opened, and I saw how cold Torrin looked, frost coating his face, his lips, and his hands to protect himself from me. "Torrin, you're hurting yourself..." My face crumpled. "Please, just g—"

"No," he said sternly. "This could kill you, Lena!"

"And it could kill you just as easily!"

Torrin's brown eyes searched mine, and he let the frost melt from him completely, water droplets trailing down his face. It was a cold winter evening, but the heat emitting from me was enough to keep him warm.

In a blink, Torrin grasped my hand, and he hissed, wincing at the pain.

I went to yank my hand away, but Torrin held firm.

"Torrin! Let go! For fuck's sake...your hand..."

His hand was shaking, burning within my grasp, but he held my gaze with an intensity that made my stomach flip.

"Calm the flames, Lena."

My body shook, and I let out a choked sob as I saw Torrin's flesh melting before me.

"Please, Torrin..."

I could tell he was in so much pain, but he ignored the agony and kept his eyes locked on mine. "I believe in you. Calm the flames."

I bit my lip and closed my eyes.

Calm the flames.

I took in deep breath after deep breath.

Calm the flames.

Calm the flames.

Calm the flames.

"That's it," Torrin comforted.

Calm the flames.

Calm the flames.

Calm the flames.

I felt my temperature dropping and the chilled wind against my skin as I continued to repeat those words.

Calm the flames.

Calm the flames.

Calm the flames.

When I looked down, my skin was red, covered in blisters. But the overwhelming heat...it was gone.

"I knew you could do it," Torrin said with a gleam in his eyes. "That mantra is what has always helped me keep my fire in whenever I feel it wants out." He pressed his lips to my forehead, giving it a gentle kiss. "Now, let's get you to Elowen. She can heal you."

I nodded softly, then glanced down at his hand. His charred hand. "Not until you are healed, first," I insisted.

The corner of his lip turned up. "I can heal myself. I want Elowen working on you."

"She can work on me after."

We both winced in pain as he helped me up. "No. Now, come."

Despite having a burned hand, Torrin lifted me, walking us back to our home. Mother was hysterical when she witnessed him bringing me back inside our house, but thankfully, Merrick was able to calm her down. She wished to be by me while I was being healed, but I insisted on being alone.

I stayed in Torrin's bed while Elowen worked on me. The soothing touch of her healing magic was the best feeling ever. Despite my many protests to have Elowen work on Torrin first, no one listened. Thankfully, Merrick convinced Torrin to allow him to do the healing, though his skills didn't compare to that of his sisters; none of ours did.

It wasn't until morning that I was fully healed. I had fallen asleep at some point. When my eyes finally opened, I turned my head, noticing Torrin was in the room, sleeping soundly on the floor beside me

I studied him...this man who cared for me so deeply.

And once my eyes lowered, my heart sank. Even though Merrick had used healing magic on him, the wounds were so deep that only Elowen's magic could've healed them fully.

I stifled a cry as I beheld Torrin's left hand, which was now permanently covered in burn scars.

CHAPTER TWELVE

LENA - NOW

Silas wasn't coming, and I didn't blame him. The situation was a mess. Plus, he was probably all snuggled up with Era.

The thought made me sick. The truth was, Era was nice. Beautiful. I wanted to hate her...*despise* her...but I couldn't. I was happy he found someone to love, glad he was able to find that happiness, even if it broke me into a million pieces.

I sighed and stood up, my body feeling only slightly warmer, but as I went to turn, I hit something and fell back. Arms reached out and gripped my wrists before I completely fell over. My eyes sprang wide, and I looked up to meet those familiar golden ones.

"Silas!" I exclaimed, my face heating. "I didn't even hear you walk up."

His brows furrowed as he slowly lowered my wrists, still keeping them in his hands.

I gazed up at him, the moonlight bouncing off the river, showing off the sharp lines of his jaw. My eyes trailed from his full lips to the light dusting of facial hair surrounding them, down to the tattoos that covered his neck. I wanted to run my fingers along his skin...wanted to see exactly which places of his body were covered in ink.

I began to vibrate with electricity, and I closed my eyes and swallowed, willing the magic down.

"Lena," he said softly, and my eyes lifted to meet his, which were now laced with concern and...something more. "I...I am so sorry. I had no idea."

I tensed my jaw, and my words were clipped as they came out. "Don't be. It wasn't your fault."

"It doesn't matter whose fault it was." His thumbs brushed the undersides of my wrists, and my lip wobbled. "It was not yours, either. You shouldn't have gone through that alone."

My eyes locked on his. "I wasn't alone," I whispered.

"You shouldn't have gone through it..." his voice cracked, "...without...*me.*"

The tone of his voice ruined me. His hands slid down to hold mine.

I savored the feel of our skin brushing against each other. His hands were rougher than when we were young...but still, they were his.

"I got my fire that night," I said quietly. I bit my bottom lip to prevent the trembling before speaking again. "There's so much I wish happened differently, so much I wish we could have had."

His eyes darkened, and now it was his that lowered to my lips. "You told me you haven't overcome shit, but I think you don't give yourself enough credit, Lena." He lightly squeezed my hands, and my breathing hitched.

Our eyes locked with each other again, and I saw it for a split second.

The longing, the hunger—or perhaps it was all in my head, as it was gone quickly.

He tensed. "Come, I don't wish to have you out here in the dark alone."

My head fell slowly, and I nodded. But as I started to walk away, Silas pulled me into him, wrapping his arms tight around me.

I froze.

He was hugging me.

Silas was hugging me.

I felt pain in the back of my throat as I returned the hug, holding him close. I couldn't help it; tears released from my eyes at the sensation of his body, free of armor, pressed against mine.

Despite our days spent trekking Half-Life Pass, he still smelled like him, that intoxicating aroma of pine and citrus.

Silas.

We stood there for a few moments, our bodies stiff, until we eventually relaxed into the familiar feel of each other's embrace.

Five years...I haven't been in his arms in over five years.

"I've missed you so much," I whispered.

I didn't want to pull away, but I felt Silas's entire body tense at my words. He gently withdrew, his golden eyes pained as he stared.

He shook his head, I don't know if to me or to himself, and squeezed my arm. "Let's get back," he murmured.

So, I followed him.

Roland's eyes were gentle when I glanced at him once I had returned, but as much as I enjoyed the thought of him caring, I also hated the idea of pity. Of appearing broken. I could tell he was unsure how to navigate this awkward situation, so I had just decided to snuggle in my bedroll and be done that evening.

Morning came, and the kingdom of Forsmont was now steps away. Like Ames, the kingdom rested just beside the water. The docks ringing could be heard in the distance, and I felt my nerves rising as we stepped closer to the stone border surrounding their territory.

"I should speak with Leroy myself," Silas said calmly, frowning up at the towers and the men stationed there. "I met with him last year. I know how much he despises the idea of being owned by Otacia."

"You want us to wait out here?" Viola asked him, once again behind Hendry on his horse. Couldn't have her shifting in front of everyone, after all.

"Not out here, but when I meet with him, I should do it alone."

"No," I said immediately, causing everyone's heads to turn to me. I met Silas's lowered brows. "What if they decide to turn on you? We should be there in case they want whatever bounty is on your head. I, at the very least, should be there."

His jaw clicked.

"We appear as humans, do we not?" I continued from my spot in front of Roland. "And as you said, only Otacia wields those wretched cuffs." We slowed our horses just before the kingdom's entrance. "You are *not* going to him alone."

At my last words, Silas began chewing on the inside of his cheek.

"She makes a good point, Silas," Hendry voiced, and I shot him a grateful smile.

"We'll have your back," I insisted. "And Merrick will be able to read them." I ran my eyes along Silas's irritated face. "I want to ensure you are safe."

To that, he scoffed, but as he studied me, he grasped the sincerity of my claim. "I have kept myself alive this far," he muttered.

"I know you have. But they could have you dead in an instant if they wished it."

"Take the lady's gracious help, boss man," Roland added from his spot behind me.

Silas glared at him, then rolled his eyes, letting out a sigh. "Very well...just keep your mouths closed. Let me do the talking."

Everyone agreed, and as we made it to the beginning of the bridge entering the kingdom, we were halted by the soldiers in the towers, who lifted their crossbows at us. Their armor was red and silver—the colors of Forsmont.

"State your business!" one barked out.

"I wish to speak with Leroy Matel," Silas responded, his voice loud and smooth. The voice of a prince. "I am Silas La'Rune, Prince of Otacia."

It was almost comical how the men's eyes bulged, their weapons lowering, their hushed whispers hardly audible.

The same soldier's eyes slid to Silas. "And who do you bring with you, Prince? A small army?"

Silas held his chin up. "Friends."

My heart fluttered, and I couldn't help but notice Viola's surprise at the Prince's words. Merrick's, too.

More hushed mumbling, and the Forsmontian soldier nodded. "Very well. We will grant you access to speak with King Matel."

Silas offered a curt nod, and I held my breath as we crossed the stone bridge. The wooden gate securing the kingdom began to creak open.

Forsmont was half the size of Otacia, and the kingdom wasn't separated by class. In its center, a modest castle stood tall—I could see it from the entrance. White brick, red shingles, and clean glass windows with a large balcony wrapping around the top.

I had heard bits here and there about their leader, Leroy Matel. He was strict but just. His loyalty was to Forsmont. To his people. Otacia endangered the balance of things in this place, and as we trekked through the busy roads of the kingdom, I could understand why Leroy feared change.

The people here wore big smiles, and the buildings all sported fresh coats of paint. The sun even seemed to shine brighter here.

Mother considered us settling down in Forsmont, but the population was deemed too small to risk it—even if a few thousand did live in this place.

I watched those smiles morph into fearful frowns as the citizens beheld Silas. He had a reputation, that was for sure. He was known to be just as vicious as his father.

If only they knew him like I did...or had.

When we finally reached the castle—which honestly, up close, was more like a really nice, brick mansion—we finally dismounted. I held Roland's hand as I stepped off Donut, and he quickly pulled me to his side, the action startling me. The corner of his lip raised as he grazed my ear with his lips.

"I can't wait to get you alone," he murmured.

I shoved him with my hips, a smile creeping over my face. "That is if this goes well. Don't get your hopes up."

He chuckled, then began to stroll away. His brown hair had grown shaggier the past weeks, and despite the fact we all needed showers, I wanted to run my fingers through it.

I hated how attracted I was to the bastard.

Still...the thought of actually being intimate frightened me, especially now that the possibility was becoming more and more real. I wasn't sure I was ready for that. I wasn't sure if I ever would be.

My thoughts sailed, and when my heart began to race, I squeezed my eyes shut.

Fuck...I'm spiraling.

"Lena, are you alright?" Elowen asked. Her voice sounded as if she were underwater.

I am alive.

They are gone.

They aren't here.

I am safe.

I was brought back to reality by a firm hand on my shoulder and worried charcoal eyes on mine.

"You're safe," he said softly. "You're safe."

I nodded over and over again. I knew Merrick felt everything I was feeling. "I'm sorry," I whispered.

"Is everything alright?" a Forsmontian soldier asked skeptically. Silas's eyes were broadened with concern.

"Yes—yes, I'm fine," I muttered. "I think I got off too quickly."

Silas's jaw hardened, and I shot him a tight-lipped smile. He probably thought my nerves had to do with this meeting.

"Don't be sorry, Lena." Merrick squeezed my arm before releasing it. "It's not good to hold everything in...I'm a hypocrite for that, I know." He chuckled as we made our way up the steps. "But please, if you need to talk to someone, I'm here."

I smiled up at him gently. "I know, Mare. Thank you."

His eyes remained dark so as not to alert anyone that it wasn't his normal eye color, and we were all led into the throne room.

I noticed him right away. Their leader stood with crossed arms, his long, golden hair flowing over one of his shoulders. To his right was a male soldier with cobalt blue hair and eyes to match. His arms were also crossed over his broad chest, his narrowed eyes trailing over our group. To Leroy's left was another male, older, wearing a deep frown.

"I'd wish for some privacy, Paul," he said calmly to the man who led us in. "Close the door on your way out."

He must not have known Mages were in his presence, or he wouldn't have been so eager to be alone in a room with us. Well, alone, minus the two men at his side. The door clicked shut behind us.

"Crown Prince of Otacia, to what do we owe the honor?" Leroy gave a crooked smile that didn't meet his eyes. "Or would the term 'Banished Prince' be more fitting?"

I guess word had spread.

Silas tensed at my side, but his face gave away nothing. He tilted his head up slightly. "Is it considered banishment if I chose to leave?"

Leroy's smile remained, his blue eyes trailing over us all before halting on me. His voice was smooth as he said, "Word travels quickly, Prince. It has been said you not only betrayed your kingdom but freed nearly a hundred Mages in captivity."

Shit, shit!

My heartbeat quickened as his gaze slid back to Silas. "I assume there are a few in our company as we speak."

Forsmont had remained separated from Otacia's reign thus far and had never enforced a kill order. That didn't mean that no murders took place. To my left, Merrick's fists clenched, and beside him, Viola eyed the two guards at Leroy's side. The man with blue hair gave Vi a wicked grin, and I could see her refraining from snarling.

"I don't believe I betrayed Otacia at all." Silas's voice was strong and steady. How he was able to keep his nerves at bay, I didn't know. "The King has made his plans for the continent clear. He wishes to be High King."

"So it seems, with how adamant he has been in trying to claim our territory." Leroy plucked a loose string on his red tunic. For a King, he was dressed rather modestly. He didn't even wear a crown. "And, let me guess, you wish to rally our support of your reign, and in exchange, Forsmont keeps our freedom?" He lowered his brows at the Prince of Otacia. There was no kindness in his voice as he said, "Well, keep our freedom until *you* are King. Who knows what you will do with your power?"

"I am a man of my word."

Leroy nodded slowly, his gaze once again going over our group. After a moment, the King exhaled sharply. "Tell you what, Prince." He clapped once, the sound causing me to flinch. He gave an easy smile, crossing his arms. "Slay one of your witches here."

My blood went cold.

"Kill one of them, and Forsmont will join your cause."

Silas blinked, the only sign he was taken aback.

Or...or was he considering?

Elowen's nervous eyes went to Edmund, who pulled her closer to his side. Even Roland tensed beside me.

"I will do no such thing," Silas said cooly. "The Mages are my allies."

Leroy let out a dry laugh, his eyes widening, an incredulous look on his face. "The *Witch Slayer* has made allies with the Mages?" His sky-blue eyes shifted to mine. "What made you agree to such a thing? He promised freedom, and you believed it?"

I was taken by surprise that the leader knew I was one of the Mages. We were all glamoured. Though perhaps word had spread of the red-headed witch leader of Ames.

"Otacia will lift the kill order. Provide us with a home, should we wish it," I answered simply. The blue-haired man scoffed before I continued, "King Matel, there is a dark power spreading across the continent. A necromancer has risen."

To that, Leroy's eyes flared, his arms falling back to his sides.

"We will need to come together if there is any chance of eliminating this threat."

Leroy's frown went to Silas. "How long?"

"Over half a year," Hendry spoke instead. "At least, that's how long we have dealt with their kind."

"Why haven't we been notified of this?" Leroy pushed. Even the two men at his side had paled.

"We were ordered to keep it under wraps," Silas said calmly but not weakly. "It was contained to the north for a while. Though we have had our fair share of run-ins as we have moved south. It seems our efforts to eliminate them have been futile."

Leroy looked at the blue-haired man and then nodded to himself before crossing his arms again.

"Why the change of heart, Prince? You have never shown an ounce of compassion toward the witches. Why now?"

I sucked in my bottom lip and glanced up at Silas to my right. His golden gaze shifted to mine momentarily, and he took a deep breath before facing Leroy.

"I could say it is because they are a powerful ally...but the truth is I was wrong about them."

Leroy blinked, his eyes bouncing between the two of us.

"I was wrong to think they were monsters." Silas glanced at Edmund and nodded toward Leroy. With a gulp, Edmund stepped forward, Elowen still close to his side, as he removed his glove.

The men of Forsmont gasped as they beheld Edmund's artificial limb—as he made a show of rotating his wired carbonado fingers.

"An Undead struck me in the arm. My leg, too." He shot me a grateful glance, and then his green eyes peeked down at Elowen, a devoted smile spreading across his face. "Lena and Elowen saved me. Fought to save me."

The whites of Leroy's eyes became visible as he gaped at the enchanted creation.

"They brought me to an enchanter who made this for me." He began slipping the glove back on. "They didn't have to save me. But they saw me in pain, saw as I was fading, and *begged* to." He lowered his hand to clasp Elowen's, and she smiled brightly at him. "That's the type of people they are."

Leroy only shifted his stare to Silas once the Prince quietly added, "I was saved by them, too."

Silas focused his gaze on me now, and I nearly melted at the sight of his smile. It was small; the corners just barely turned up, but it was *real*.

"I understand your fear," Silas continued, shifting his eyes back to the Forsmontian King. "We've all grown up with tales that have painted Magekind as nothing but aberrations...but I have seen more humanity in them than I have in some of my men."

Leroy's eyes darted between us for a moment before he laughed softly. "You surprise me, Prince." Leroy then raised his hand. ***"Revelare."***

We all watched as Leroy's glamour faded, as the ear his blonde hair was tucked behind turned pointed, and his pupils completely vanished.

As we realized Leroy was a Warlock.

CHAPTER THIRTEEN

LENA

"**H**oly Gods," Viola breathed.

"Dani, come forward." Leroy motioned to the blue-haired man, and he did just that.

He gave Viola another smirk before lifting his hand as Leroy did. *"**Revelare**."*

My mouth hung open as Dani's glamour dropped, though it wasn't the pointed ears or pupilless eyes that shocked me. No, it was Dani shifting into their true form, that of a beautiful female.

Viola's jaw was on the floor. Actually, scratch that, all our jaws were on the ground.

Dani's eyes went to me. "We Warlock's can only glamour ourselves through incantations." She brushed her long, cobalt hair off her shoulder. "Aside from shifting, of course." Her armor was similar to the male version of herself, but now it hugged her feminine curves.

"My sister is a bit more intimidating in male form, well, when we are pretending to be humans, at least," Leroy noted.

She stuck her tongue out at him, and he laughed.

My eyes slid to the Otacians, who all stared as if aliens had invaded Tovagoth, Erabella especially.

"You're...a Warlock? And the King of Forsmont?" I breathed. "How?"

Leroy studied me with those pupilless eyes. "The Warlocks have had influence in Forsmont for decades. As the oppression of our kind progressed, we glamoured ourselves and practiced our traditions in private. Much like you Mages."

"How did you—" Viola began, then swore. "You had shifted...you were watching us."

He nodded. "I was but a bird in the trees this morning, listening to your conversations. You all may have been glamoured, even you, shapeshifter," he commented, pointing at Viola, "but your conversations were noted. You should be careful—you never know who is listening."

Merrick frowned. "Exactly how many of you are here?"

Dani turned her attention to the Empath. "A little over two hundred."

Leroy examined Silas, who had attempted to master his surprise. "I wouldn't have let him kill one of you," he remarked. "I just needed to see if the Slayer of Witches truly had a change of heart."

I wished I could brush a hand along Silas's back. Something to comfort him. Even if he had remained mostly cold toward me, aside from our hug in the forest. Thank the Gods we weren't being watched then.

"The King is a bastard," I stated. "And has brainwashed a good many."

"Is that why you showed kindness? In the hope of changing hearts?" Dani's gaze went to Silas's warily.

"It worked, didn't it?" I half-smiled, and Dani returned the expression. I decided I liked her.

"So, this is all the people willing to join your cause?" The older guard now stepped forward. *"Revelare."* The incantation for undoing glamours, it seemed. Warlocks had to use incantations if they wished to perform any magic that they weren't inherently born with.

The male stayed male, but his age lowered, revealing a boy that had to be around fourteen. His brown hair and hazel eyes reminded me of Roland's, but his fair skin was far different from Roland's golden brown.

"I see why you made yourself old," Roland teased. "No one would take you seriously like that."

In a blink, the boy shifted, claws hitting the ground and a deafening roar sending us stumbling backward as he took on a bear form. Everyone quickly equipped their weapons, ready for whatever shit Roland had just gotten us into.

"Quin!" Leroy reprimanded. "Shift back, now!"

Quin obeyed, easily shifting back into his normal form, a shit-eating grin on his face as he beheld Roland panting.

But the bastard only grinned back. "I like this kid," he wheezed. I couldn't help but look at him in awe, and when Roland caught sight of the presumable hearts in my eyes, he winked at me.

I nervously glanced at the door behind us. "Aren't people going to question hearing that?"

Leroy's smile grew. "Sound-proofing spell. No one heard a thing. But still," he shot a disapproving glare at Quin, "you scared them, Quin!" Leroy rolled his eyes and then gave us an apologetic grin. "The boy takes after his mother, impulsive at times."

Quin's pupilless hazel eyes narrowed, but a smile still remained. "I'm telling her that."

"If you want me sleeping in the street, go right ahead. But who will have your back when you raid the candy cart again?"

"Aunt Dani will."

Ah. So, Quin was Leroy's son. The man appeared to be Torrin's age, probably in his early thirties. He must've been a young father.

Leroy waved a hand. "Let's save the family drama for later." He pinned a stare at Silas. "I have a feeling Forsmont will join your cause, Prince, if it means the safety of our people, both from a dictatorship and us of magical descent from a kill order that has spread across Tovagoth." He moved his hand in that motion again. *"Velare."* He glamoured himself once more. "In two days' time, we will speak with the council. Ultimately, it is their call what we do or do not do."

"But you are their King." Silas frowned. "Is it not your call?"

"Checks and balances are crucial for a successful society. We don't do things like other kingdoms."

Silas merely nodded, and Leroy gestured to the blue-haired Warlock. "Dani will show you to your rooms; we have a handful free in the inn around the block. You guys look like you need a bath...or ten."

Dani led us through a long hallway at the local inn twenty minutes later. I couldn't wait to get into the shower and get this grime off of me...then take the world's best nap.

"You normally wear the skin of a male?" Roland asked Dani.

Dani let out a hum as he walked. "I'd say maybe forty percent of the time. My female form is what I was born with, but I find myself drawn to this form from time to time."

Dani had shifted back into male form, still with those piercing blue eyes, now with pupils, of course. He looked like a normal man.

It was silent for a few more moments as we all walked before Roland spoke again.

"So," he drawled. "How big is your dick?"

I crashed into Merrick, who slammed into Era, and Elowen's petite hand flew over her mouth. The Otacian men gaped at Roland.

"What?" He shrugged, giving us all a crooked grin. "We're all thinking it."

Dani let out a loud laugh. "Wouldn't you like to know?" His chuckling continued as he glanced over his shoulder. "Let's just say the ladies have had no complaints." Dani winked at Roland, shifted his eyes to Viola for a moment, then continued looking forward.

It was easy to say we were all flabbergasted. Roland chortled. "I love this family."

As much as I wished to explore Forsmont, speak more with the Warlocks hosting us, and eat, I quickly jumped into the shower in my own private room, hissing with pleasure as warm water sprinkled over my body. I lathered my hair, the smell of lavender and lemon the most delightful scent, and lastly, covered my legs in soap before sliding the razor Dani gifted me along them. Then my pits. Then, the downstairs region.

I didn't like to be fully bare down there, but it had been too long since I was able to groom myself properly. I was smooth everywhere now.

When I exited the shower, I felt like a new woman. I brushed my teeth, happy to be using a new toothbrush instead of the one I used on our journey. I sighed happily at the taste of mint in my mouth.

When I left the bathroom, I padded across the soft, wooden floors. I slipped on the smooth, cotton loungewear Ayla had made me, and when I snuggled up under the thick comforter, I was easily asleep in seconds.

CHAPTER FOURTEEN

LENA

When my eyes fluttered open, they went directly to the clock at my bedside.

8:10 pm. Damn, I slept for a while.

I sighed, sitting up and rubbing my eyes so hard I saw stars. I wasn't sure what everyone else was up to, but I could assume they all showered and rested just as I had...though my sleeping schedule had been the most screwed up.

My thoughts drifted back to that Vampire. Daris. I glimpsed at my wrist, free of any scarring thanks to Elowen, and wondered how the man had survived in that pass. How long *had* he been surviving? He could be hundreds of years old, for all I knew.

I yawned. I was decently rested, and now all I could think of was Roland and that damned kiss.

Did he even want me anymore? We'd hardly spoken since my confession about my miscarriage, and while he did mention he was eager to get me alone, he could have been teasing.

I decided to hell with it; I was going to go to his room. My hair was all down for once, and my curls were shiny and bouncy from my shower. I crossed my arms, unsure of what I was going to wear. I could head over in this, my shorts and long-sleeved shirt...but perhaps that was too forward.

I glanced around my room until my eyes caught my dresser. On it lay folded-up clothes with a note. I padded over, picking up the small piece of paper.

Some clothes to wear while you visit.

-Dani

I fingered through the garments, entirely grateful. I slipped on a new pair of underwear, then opted for a black dress, its length ending right above my knees. It was held up by two straps, and luckily, I didn't need a bra with it. It was corseted in the back, accentuating my slim waist as I pulled the laces tight. Last was a fresh pair of socks and my boots, which I noticed had been cleaned.

I went back into the bathroom and studied myself in the mirror. I still looked drained...I still felt like a stranger was staring back at me.

My attention went downward as I examined Ryia's necklace, wondering just how this piece of jewelry could provide me with answers of some kind.

Sighing, I peered down at the vanity and noticed a pouch with another note atop it.

In case you like to get dolled up, not that you need any.

-Dani

Yep, I decided I *really* liked Dani. I reached into the pouch and grinned as I layered on black mascara, dusted blush on my cheeks, and put on some lip gloss.

To an unknowing eye, you'd never guess what I had endured the past couple of months. I had leaned out since I was last in Ames...starving will do that. But I still appeared healthy.

My mind was anything but.

Should I even go out? Should I even try with him?

I was startled by a knock at my door. Smoothing the wrinkles out of my dress and brushing my hair behind my ear, I opened the door to find Roland grinning, his smile quickly falling.

He was wearing a maroon tunic, tight black pants, and black boots. His hair had been cut—he must've done that while I slept. The sides were shaved short, the length on top longer, and styled off to the side with some gel.

My lips were parted as I took him in.

"Holy hell, Ginger Snap." His eyes roamed over my body, and then his bright smile shone as we made eye contact. "You look stunning."

I felt my cheeks heating but straightened my back. "I like your haircut," I said softly.

His eyes sparkled. "Yeah?"

"Yeah..." I gave a shy smile, and then I cleared my throat. "I was actually coming to find you. I was wondering if you wanted to...hang out."

He narrowed his eyes, a smile on his face as he replied, "*Hang out?*"

I crossed my arms, mostly to hide the trembling of my hands. "I just wanted to get out of my room," I muttered.

"Well...I'm headed to this spot Dani told me about. Drinks, dancing," he said excitedly. "Want to come with me?"

My grin turned evil. "I'd love to come with you."

Roland blinked, then barked out a laugh. "See! I'm rubbing off on you."

I spared him a glance as I shut and locked my door. "My mind's first response to that is, *'I can rub you off.'* I'd argue that you have corrupted me."

He laughed harder, and my heart skipped a beat as he interlaced our fingers and gazed down at me in what almost appeared like adoration. "I'm so glad I met you," he murmured lovingly. Then, he pulled us toward our destination.

The bar called Lost Anchor was lively, with many people already crowding the tables and couches scattered about. It was a rustic-style cabin that rested along the shore of the sea, with tall wooden beams and twinkle lights dangling from the ceiling.

There was a performer off to the side, playing guitar for tips. The sound was calming as people chatted and drank their cocktails. It was too early for the dancing to begin—Roland informed me that at around ten, the lights get low, and the now empty sunken room and stage in the center of this bar would be crammed with moving, sweaty bodies.

"So..." I drawled as I sat across from him at a high table, Roland handing me the fruity drink he ordered me.

"So..." He sipped from his first glass, grinning like a fool. He had ordered us two drinks each.

I swallowed my beverage, savoring the warmth that spread through me from it, then rested my cheek on my fist. "What'd I miss while I slept the day away?"

My eyes dipped when Roland pulled his glass away from his mouth, his tongue swiping along his bottom lip. His eyes scanned the menu before us. "Nothing much. I woke up around three, nearly cried when I ate something fresh, and got this haircut." He motioned to his cropped hair, then smiled, his eyes lifting. "Then, I waited for you until I couldn't any longer, hence the knocking on your door."

I returned the expression before my stare nervously lowered. "I can't wait to eat," I sighed, peering down to scan the menu. Despite this place being on the water, there were limited seafood options. I decided to order herb-crusted chicken breast and a side of mashed potatoes, and Roland ended up doing the same.

"How original," I teased as we handed our waitress our menus.

Roland's heated smile remained, and as I studied him, sipping from my drink, I couldn't understand how anyone could dislike him.

"Why is your group so annoyed with you at times?" I asked.

He scoffed. "Aren't you always annoyed with me?"

I chuckled and glanced down, sipping my drink again. "Yes. In a good way, though."

The corner of his lip raised. "Oh?"

I met his eyes and beamed when I noticed the amusement shining in them.

"Having been a higher-ranking soldier, I could be a bit of a dick at times," he started. "There were times in training I would be...well, a cocky douchebag." I laughed at his comment. "But honestly, Hendry, Edmund, and I get along perfectly well. They aren't

137

as bold as me, but I have their respect. Otherwise, they wouldn't have been so eager to let me in on your little plan."

That made sense. "And Silas? Where does his animosity come from?"

His brows drew together, his sight falling to his lap. "I'm not sure of that one. He doesn't have much of a sense of humor." He shrugged, and I couldn't help but notice a slight tremor in his hand as he downed his first drink. "Probably jealous," he mumbled.

Silas always had the best sense of humor when I was close to him, but it was obvious he had changed a great deal. Was he actually jealous of Roland?

Both of them were beyond good-looking. I couldn't see it being that. Yes...perhaps if his feelings lingered, he would feel a certain type of way watching him flirt with me. But their conflict appeared to go far back.

"So," I began, changing the subject. "See anyone you want to take to bed tonight?" I questioned boldly.

He smirked at me, then shifted his gaze around the room, puckering his lips and tapping his finger to his mouth. "That girl over there seems like a fun time, or perhaps her friend," he commented, pointing to two elderly women sitting at the rounded bar in front. I giggled, and his hazel irises found mine. "Really, though, there's this beautiful, copper-haired woman I wish to take to my room."

My face heated, and I laughed, eyes falling to the wooden table before looking out at the different people mingling around. My eyes landed on a man whose gaze was locked on Roland.

"It looks like that guy is checking you out." I laughed, and Roland turned his attention to the handsome man.

"Hmm...perhaps if you weren't here, I'd explore that option," he murmured.

I widened my eyes, and when he glanced back at me, he let out a chuckle.

"I actually do like both males and females," he confessed.

"Oh..." I blushed as I sipped on my drink, glancing back at the toned man, who was now focused on someone else after Roland peered in his direction. Was he as attractive as Roland? No. But he was decent.

"Does that surprise you?" he asked while bringing his second drink to his lips.

"A little..." I admitted before I smirked, liquid courage filling my veins. "So, are you a top or bottom?"

He choked on his drink, and when I burst out laughing, a dazzling grin took over his face.

"My, my, Lena. I really have rubbed off on you." He bit his lip. "What do you think?"

I studied him as I leaned back in my chair. Honestly, I couldn't picture him with a male...he was so masculine. Though he, of course, had his pretty face.

My eyes trailed back to the man who had been gawking at him. He had a muscular build similar to Roland's, and his hair was short and dark. I shrugged. "I'd say you like to switch it up."

He chuckled, sipping more of his drink.

"Well?" I pressed, and then my eyes widened at the sight of his reddening cheeks. "Oh. My. Gods! You are blushing!"

"No, I'm not," he mumbled into his glass.

"Yes, you are!" I giggled. "I can't believe I have made *the* Roland actually blush. Am I making you uncomfortable? *Gods*, I hope I am."

He rolled his eyes and nursed his drink. I continued to study him with a shit-eating grin.

"Okay, fine...both have their...pros, I suppose," he conceded, pulling his lips to the side, failing at concealing the enjoyment this conversation provided.

I was the one to blush now, picturing him with another male. "So, which do you prefer, guys or girls?"

He rested his knuckle on his cheek and let his smile loose. He thought for a moment. "Being with men is fun. But I prefer females. Most of the men that I'm attracted to usually don't return the feeling." He shrugged. "Plus, I couldn't see myself coming home and saying, *"Hi honey!"* to a guy."

I tapped on my glass with my long nails. "So...men are more for excitement than love?"

His bottom lip protruded, and he nodded. "That's a good way to put it..." He sipped. "Though I haven't been in love before, with a male or female, so what do I really know?"

I couldn't help my inquisitiveness. "Have you been with any of the soldiers?"

"You're awfully curious, aren't you?" His eyes sparkled. "Just one. Not anyone from our group, obviously."

I was about to open my mouth to ask another question when Roland held a finger to my lips.

"Now, my turn." His lip curved upward, his voice going low. "What do you prefer, Lena?"

My heart began to race. "What do you mean?"

He trailed his index finger over my bottom lip. "Well, I'm assuming you only like men."

"That is correct," I agreed, my eyes getting heavy.

140

"So, what's your type?" he asked, leaning back in his seat and crossing his arms. His self-satisfied smile was infuriating.

Damn him for getting me all hot and bothered.

I thought while staring into my second drink. "Tall. Tan. Tattooed. Dark hair."

Silas. Roland.

I made an internal decision not to think of who else was my type, whose appearance was different from that of the two Otacian men.

"Hmm, it seems I fit the description," he replied smugly, just as our waiter brought over our food. My mouth watered at the smell, and Roland and I were fairly silent the twenty or so minutes it took us to demolish everything.

"That was so good," I huffed, leaning back and patting my belly. "Fuck bread, honestly. I want to eat like that every day."

Roland placed his silverware on his now bare plate. "One day, Ginger Snap, we will be feasting like kings ourselves."

I grinned and surveyed the bar, and my eyes widened to see Hendry chatting with some woman near the bar top. "Whoa," I began, and Roland angled himself in his chair to look behind him.

It was rare to see Hendry with any facial expression, but here he was with a smile. Even from our distance, I could see the dimples in his cheeks. He had had a fresh haircut as well, the sides shaved and the hair on top lying at his brows. His mismatched eyes were focused on the woman in front of him.

A woman around the age of my mother.

Roland let out a soft laugh and turned to face me. "Yeah, Hendry has always been into the older ladies."

My eyes rounded. "No way."

A glint of amusement shone in his eyes. "We've all given him shit here and there. But really, who are we to judge?"

I nodded slowly, my eyes darting back to Hendry. "I suppose you're right." I sat back in my chair, still surveying the two: the woman's hand dragging along Hendry's toned arm, the slight flush in his cheeks. She was pretty but clearly much older than him.

"You seem more surprised by that than by my confession." His lips parted playfully. "Or perhaps you're jealous?"

"Ha-ha." I rolled my eyes. "He's obviously handsome." Very handsome. He had that type of beauty Silas did. Another sip. "But, no, I'm not into him like that."

He looked back again at Hendry, who then noticed our attention. He narrowed his eyes, then rolled them before leading the lady presumably to his room.

"I had a thing for him before," Roland commented, eyes on Hendry as he left the bar.

That caught my attention. I sat up in my chair. "For Hendry? You did?"

Roland set his empty glass down. "I did. A small crush. When I was fifteen...before I'd ever been with anybody before." He laughed, crossing his arms. "Hendry was eighteen at the time. He was strong and clearly the tallest man in any room you walk in."

It was true. He had to be around 6'6".

"He easily could've beaten the shit out of me for coming on to him. But he was kind. He didn't humiliate me or treat me differently. He just apologized and said he didn't return the feeling." Roland gazed at the dance floor again, a band now setting up, and a small smile crept its way on his face. "He still wished to remain friends, though. I appreciated that."

"Do you still have feelings—"

"Gods, no." Roland chuckled and gave a shiver of disgust. "I view him now as a brother. Edmund, too." His smile fell, eyes dropping to the ground. "Same as Silas...even though he hates my guts." Before I could interject, he continued, "But what about you, Ginger Snap?" His hazel eyes became half-lidded as he studied me. "Do you have any feelings for someone?"

My heartbeat quickened, and I smiled bashfully before chugging the remainder of my drink.

As I placed my empty glass down, the lights went off, and loud, sensual music began to play from the band on stage. People began cheering, making their way to the dance floor, moving against each other in dances I had never seen before. The women were slowly rubbing their hips on the men behind them.

The lights started to flash, and the woman singer on stage began to belt. I stared in wonder.

Roland stood, reaching for me. Without exchanging words, I placed my hand in his, and we wandered into the crowd.

Normally, I would be way too shy to attempt anything like this, and if I did, I would be apologetic the entire time. But the drinks made me confident, so I turned my back to Roland. Whether it be liquid courage or Roland's natural confidence, I didn't know, but he placed his hands on my hips, sliding them down my thighs. As I felt the bass vibrating in my chest, I began dancing, grinding up on him and not caring who saw.

I leaned my head back, resting it on his chest as we continued to dance against one another, and I let my eyes shut, savoring the feel. Not two enemies. Not two fugitives on the run. Just two friends living in the moment.

I let out a soft moan as I felt him harden against me. "Roland," I breathed, though I wasn't sure if he heard over the blaring music.

Chills spread across my body as his lips pressed against my neck. A soft kiss followed by a light nip of my skin.

I smelled him now...vanilla and sandalwood. It was intoxicating.

I ground against him harder, and he groaned, turning me to face him. His eyes met mine with profound fixation before focusing on my lips. My heartbeat quickened, and before I knew it, Roland's hand slid behind my neck, angling my face up to him.

He whispered into my ear, "You were headed to me before I knocked on your door, weren't you, Lena?" There he went, using my name as a sexual weapon.

Why did I love it so much?

I nodded.

"Why?" he purred.

"You know why," I murmured, our breaths now mingling.

Those beautiful lips curved into a half-grin. "Not good enough, Ginger Snap. Tell me."

I swallowed. "I want to fuck you," I confessed.

Roland's eyes widened at my bluntness, and I couldn't help the giggle that bubbled in my chest. My laughs quickly evaporated as Roland pressed his mouth to mine, his free hand snaking around my body to grip my ass through the soft fabric.

He grunted into my mouth, then pulled away. "My room. Now."

I left with him. We drunkenly stumbled up the steps in the inn, giggling like children as we made our way to his room when we passed Era in the hallway. Her eyes enlarged just as a knowing smile crossed her face.

I guess what we were about to do was obvious.

CHAPTER FIFTEEN
LENA

We tripped over one another as we rushed into his room and kicked off our shoes. Roland quickly turned on the oil lamp beside his bed, then reached behind and pulled off his shirt. My heart sped up at the sight of his perfect, bronzed body.

With no time to lose, his hungry lips captured mine again, then trailed down, his tongue gliding along my neck.

It felt wonderful, and I desperately wanted to be intimate with him, but despite it, I felt myself start to panic as my eyes found the bed. Images flooded my brain of Rurik violating me—of those soldiers beating me and then watching him force himself inside of me.

I took in a shaky breath. I knew Roland wasn't like those men...not even close. But my body didn't.

I am safe. I am safe. I am safe. I am safe. I am safe.

My whole body stiffened, and Roland was instantly aware of my body language. He pulled back, his hazel eyes examining me with concern.

"Hey," he murmured, grasping my hands. "If you aren't ready, don't worry about it," he said softly.

I drew a few breaths, then sat on his bed in defeat, my cheeks heating in embarrassment. Roland sat beside me a moment later, and his hand gently began rubbing my back. I appreciated how, despite how unserious he was most of the time, it was evident just how much he cared about making me comfortable.

I pulled my lips to the side and looked over at him. Sadness etched his features, and as he held my gaze, a small smile overcame his lips. Another look of pity.

My shoulders sagged, and my eyes traveled to my lap.

This wasn't fucking fair. I wanted this with Roland. I loved how it felt having him kiss me.

I didn't want to be damaged.

Ruined.

"I'm sorry," I whispered.

Roland stopped caressing my back and grasped my chin with his other hand, tilting me to look at him. My throat burned as I glimpsed into his eyes.

"You have nothing to be sorry for, Lena," he assured, his hand sliding up to hold the side of my face. "I understand."

My lip trembled, and I shook my head. "I want to, badly," I said quietly, then bit my lip.

I didn't want those men ruling me. I didn't want them to have a single ounce of power over me. I deserved to be happy, deserved pleasure.

I took in another ragged breath. "I just...I want to be in control...in control of what we do." I angled my body toward him, my hand sliding up his muscular thigh. "Would that be okay with you?"

The corner of his lip went up as he stroked my cheek. "Hell yeah, Ginger Snap." He scooted back on the bed until he was in the center, his arms going behind his head as he leaned against the headboard. "Do whatever you'd like to me."

His smile was infectious. I slowly stood, my eyes never leaving his. The dark, golden lighting in the room accentuated the caramel hues of his irises. The shadows only defined the muscles in his stomach, and I desperately wondered what that trail of hair under his belly button led to.

My heart was pounding so fast.

I am in control.

"Take off your pants."

His eyebrows raised, and he bit back a smile. "As you wish," he purred.

My eyes became heavy as he slowly slid down his trousers, his undergarments coming down along with them. I loosened a breath as his perfect length sprang free.

His smile grew at my expression, and he kicked his pants off and discarded them on the floor.

He tilted his head to the side, an infuriatingly adorable grin on his face as he raised his brow and asked, "Do you like what you see?"

"Very much," I answered quietly.

"I'm glad," he whispered. I loved how comfortable he was around me, how his eyes taunted me.

"Close your eyes."

His eyes twinkled, and he did as I said.

I stood, then slowly began unlacing my dress in the back. "No peeking," I crooned.

His smile grew, showing his bright teeth. "No peeking," he reiterated.

The fabric of my dress fell to the floor, and then I slid down my panties. Once I was completely naked, I kneeled between his legs on the mattress.

I am in control.

"Touch yourself," I ordered quietly.

He kept his eyes shut, then bit his lip and obeyed, his hand lightly sliding up his cock before gripping it and stroking. He let out a breathy moan, his stomach flexing as he drew out his pleasure.

I brought my hand between my legs, not at all surprised by the wetness gathered, and began rubbing circles over my clit. I let out a hum, my eyes rolling back.

Roland was so damn desirable. So confident. His chest rose and fell at an increased pace as he continued pumping himself.

"Now stop," I ordered.

He listened, releasing himself, his hand going back to rest at his side.

I ran my hands along his bare thighs, his cock throbbing at the motion. "I can do *anything* to you?" I asked seductively.

He smirked, his eyes still shut. "*Anything*, Ginger Snap."

I slid my hand up his thigh until my fingers were wrapped around his thick length. He inhaled sharply at my grasp, his head falling back as I began to work him. He released another soft groan, and I halted my movement to allow spit to fall from my mouth and onto his cock.

"Fuck," he moaned as I began to stroke him with my saliva. "Gods, I want to see you."

"Soon," I promised softly, and he hissed as I bent down and wrapped my mouth around his tip, sucking him into my mouth.

"Holy fuck..." he groaned as I bobbed my head up and down. I began swirling my tongue all along his shaft, all along the ridge of his sensitive head. Roland lifted his arm, then froze. "May I touch you?" he asked breathlessly.

I paused my movements. "Yes," I answered, panting.

Roland ran his hand through my hair, his moans growing louder as I quickened my pace, greedily slurping on his length, enjoying the feel of the veins wrapped around it.

"You're a fucking pro at this, Ginger Snap," he respired. "My Gods."

I slid my mouth upward, his cock popping free from my lips.

"You can open your eyes."

Instantly, those hazel eyes met mine, his pupils dilating as he took in my appearance.

"You're so fucking beautiful," he groaned, and I slid my hand over his tip. He shuddered at the movement, and I gripped him, sucking him back into my mouth.

Roland's moaning increased as he gathered all my hair into his hand. I took him deeper, and the sloppy sounds of him fucking my throat had my body begging for friction between my legs.

I licked up and down the sides of him, meeting his lustful eyes, and then lowered myself on the bed and ran my tongue along his balls.

Roland's eyes rolled back as he unleashed a growl deep from his chest, his head falling once again to rest on the headboard. I stroked him as I began to suck on them both.

"You are in control," Roland assured, and his darkened eyes met mine. "But I'd love your pussy in my face, Ginger Snap."

I ran my tongue up his length again, collecting the bead of moisture gathered at his tip on my tongue. I smirked, watching Roland's smile grow as I ran my tongue along his happy trail, and then I climbed up his torso, turning my body around so my pussy was near his face. I leaned down, and Roland gripped my hips, cursing under his breath, before he dragged his wet tongue down my center.

I cried out softly at the pleasure, then grasped his cock and put it back into my mouth. I hadn't done this sex position since I last did it with Silas. Gods, I missed doing it.

Roland eagerly ate my pussy, his fingers digging into my flesh as I sucked his dick. He groaned against me as he slid a finger inside, and my eyes fluttered shut as he began pumping it in and out of me.

I released him from my mouth's grip and quickly stroked his soaked cock. He lashed his tongue against my clit, adding a second finger to fuck me with, and the fingers on his other hand squeezed my ass.

"Fuck, Roland," I cried, my head falling to rest on his body. My inner walls throbbed around his fingers, gripping tight.

"Yes, say my name," he begged against my cunt, then slapped my ass. "You are the sexiest woman alive."

My eyes rolled back as he continued to make out with my pussy, his fingers fucking me faster, the flicks of his tongue becoming more desperate.

I brought him back into my mouth and kept sucking on him until the pleasure became blinding. "Roland," I panted. "I want to come while fucking you."

He removed his fingers, gave me a couple of long, tantalizing licks, and then kissed my sex sweetly before lowering his face. "I want that, too."

I turned my body around, seizing Roland's cock and guiding it to my entrance, his hands roughly gripping my hips.

I slowly began to sit on top of him, and his jaw began to slacken, his eyes going half-lidded as my pussy swallowed all of him.

His moans matched mine as I stretched to accommodate him. I began to move my ass up and down.

His right hand wrapped around my neck, and he pulled my mouth to his, our lips parting so our tongues could slide across each other. And as I found myself lost in his kiss, lost in the feel of our bodies joined, I realized I felt no fear as he took control.

I hummed into his mouth, savoring our mixed taste, just as Roland began to take over, his arms enveloping my torso to hold me tight as he slammed his cock in and out of me.

"Yes," I cried, lost in the feel of that delicious stretch. "Just like that..."

He let out a pleased hum, and I ran my fingers through his hair, lowering my mouth to suck on his earlobe.

"*Fuck*..." he respired, slamming into me harder. "Tell me to come inside you."

"Come in me," I begged. "Please, Roland."

A desperate, needy moan escaped from me at his relentless pace, and the tension that coiled inside me built and built until it blossomed, spilling over. A helpless scream emitted from my chest as I pulsed around his shaft, a feeling of euphoria that I had craved for so long washing over me in waves.

Roland's growl was guttural as his own orgasm took hold, and I felt him pulse inside me as he filled me with his release.

The orgasm was still washing over me as he held me close, our bodies covered in sweat, our hearts pounding against each other.

"Thank you," I breathed, my head buried into the nook of his neck. "Thank you."

He tightened his arms around me. "It was my pleasure...thank you for trusting me." He kissed the top of my head. "And for giving me the best head of my life." He laughed breathlessly. "Best everything, really."

I giggled and raised my head to look into his eyes. I adored the sight of his flushed cheeks.

I kissed his lips softly. "Always full of jokes," I mumbled.

"I'm not kidding." He kissed me. "That was fantastic."

I grinned and kissed him again, lifting myself off of him to stand. "I'll be right back."

I padded to the restroom, saw to my needs, and froze when my hand grasped the doorknob.

I did it. I had sex...and it was *good*. Amazing, even.

I found my eyes watering and took a few breaths to hold the happy tears in before I exited the bathroom.

I may not be fully healed...I wasn't sure it was even possible to go back to how I was before. But I felt like I claimed a part of myself back tonight.

When I stepped out, Roland had the sheets over him. He was lying on his side, and when I began to walk over, he propped himself up on his elbow.

I bent down to put on my underwear when Roland spoke. "Stay," he offered softly, a genuine smile on his face. "I'd like the company of a warm body to sleep beside. Stay."

I hesitated, then bit back my grin. He lifted the sheets, and I slid in beside him, our bodies bare. He pulled my back against his chest, wrapping his arm around me and holding me close.

It felt so lovely. Warm. Safe.

I am safe.

He kissed the top of my head before turning off the oil lamp beside the bed. "Sweet dreams, Ginger Snap," he whispered.

And for the first time in a while, I fell asleep with a smile on my face.

CHAPTER SIXTEEN
LENA

I woke up to the smell of vanilla and sandalwood...and sex. When my hazy gaze opened, I found that I was lying on Roland's chest, our legs tangled together under the sheets.

"Morning, Ginger Snap," he whispered sleepily, a lopsided grin showcasing those gorgeous teeth. His hair was tousled, presumably from my fingers running through it, and he looked...well...sexy as fuck.

"Hi," I whispered back, a smile creeping over me.

"Did you have fun last night?"

I ran a finger down his hard stomach. "Too much fun." Memories flashed in my mind: his thick, wet length in my mouth, his face as I rode him, his lips wet from licking me...

"Flushing at the thought?" he asked in a low purr.

I pinched his side, and he hissed, grinning widely. My eyes couldn't help but notice the hardness of him under the sheet. I bit my lip and met his eyes as he ran a hand along my back.

"Can't get enough, Lena?" He dipped his hand lower and squeezed my ass.

"You're so damn cocky," I laughed, then slid my hand that was resting on his stomach under the sheet, gliding my fingertips over the blunt head of his manhood. He inhaled sharply, his cock throbbing at the touch, and I tightened my hand around him fully and began to stroke.

"Godsdamn," he breathed, his eyes, appearing more sepia-colored this morning, rolling back.

"I might argue that *you* are the one who can't get enough," I purred.

His half-lidded gaze found mine, and he smirked. "Yet *you're* the one grasping my cock."

I loosened my grip and gave him a playful smile. "Do you want me to stop?"

"Please, no."

He moaned as I quickened my pace, then chuckled softly.

"Fine, you're right. I can't get enough." He grasped the hand that was working him, halting me to a stop. He kissed my cheek, then whispered in my ear, "I want to fuck you again, Lena." He pulled back. "May I?"

I bit my lip and nodded, and Roland pulled me onto his lap in a swift movement.

"You are so hot," he whispered, grasping my breast with one hand and angling himself inside me with the other. My breathing hitched as I sat on his thickness, feeling deliciously sore.

Roland ran his hands along my back, then gently pulled me close so I was held in his arms, resting on his chest. His pace quickened, and I unleashed my cries of pleasure as he found both of our releases.

After a few minutes of lying beside each other, sweaty and thoroughly spent yet again, Roland and I had a conversation about our expectations. I told him I wasn't ready for anything serious, certainly not in the middle of a war, so we both agreed we'd have fun with one another—nothing exclusive unless that grew to feel right for us.

"Friends who fuck. That sounds perfect to me," he had purred. I chuckled at that.

I snuck to my room, thankful not to have run into anyone in our group. I quickly saw to my needs, showered, and brushed my teeth, noting the slight difference in my expression in the mirror above the sink.

Satisfied.

I smiled to myself before spitting out the paste Dani was kind enough to offer, and after rinsing my mouth I scrunched my still damp hair with the provided towel and let it dry as I moved on. I fished through the bag of cosmetics Dani gifted me, and once I applied a fresh coat of mascara, blush, and the lip gloss again...it was the first time in a long while I felt like *me*.

After slipping on a black chemise and ochre corset, I made my way down to the dining hall, breakfast being served buffet style. I had a feeling one of the best parts of having Silas's wealth during this journey would be the amazing food we could afford.

A pleasant aroma of coffee, sweets, and bacon filled the room. Silas, Era, Elowen, Edmund, and Viola were already sitting, so I quickly loaded my plate.

Carefully holding my dish, I sauntered over to my group and sat next to Edmund across from Silas and Era. Everyone was busy eating, so I began to do the same, shoving a forkful of syrupy pancakes into my mouth. I had to stifle a moan at how delicious it was.

I tried to keep my eyes off Silas, but his hair, too, had been freshly cut, and the style was remarkably similar to Roland's. In place of armor, he wore a dark shirt, the sleeves rolled up to showcase his golden, tattooed forearms. I wished I could study the designs, but I could only spare quick glances without it seeming odd.

He looked good. Really good.

When he caught my eyes for probably the tenth time, he asked me, "How'd you sleep?"

I tried not to choke on my pancake. "Good. Great." My eyes nervously fell, and I resumed eating.

"You're looking rather well, Lena," Era noted with a smirk. "Very...well rested."

I slowly lifted my glare, wanting to clobber her, but then my eyes sensed Roland. He had just entered and was at the end of the room, picking up a plate and speaking to Hendry. His brown hair was damp, and when his eyes met mine, a sweet smile fell over his face, causing me to suck in my bottom lip and look down at my plate again.

"I suppose I am," I said with a soft laugh, cutting another piece of pancake. Era let out a similar laugh, and when I glanced up, my smile vanished, Silas's expression causing my stomach to drop.

He was *pissed*.

Did Era tell him about last night?!

Oh fuck.

Wait, why was I worried?

If he's upset, he should get the hell over it. He has a wife, after all.

My eyes darted back down to my plate, and I continued to cut my pancakes just as Roland and Hendry reached the table. Roland sat beside me, and Hendry sat next to Silas.

"Got enough pancakes, Ginger Snap?" Roland teased.

I went to stab him with my fork, and he chuckled. "What? I can't be hungry?" I asked as I popped a forkful in my mouth. Three pancakes weren't a lot. Well...jumbo pancakes...and bacon and eggs.

"You must've really exerted yourself, hm?" His eyes went down to my lips.

When I froze, his eyes playfully met mine, and he laughed softly. His eyes danced to his own plate, and he lifted a piece of bacon and took a bite.

I watched the column of his neck work as he chewed and swallowed.

Gods, he is hot. Annoyingly hot.

I refused to look at Silas, but out of the corner of my eye, I noticed his fist clenching where it rested on the table, revealing the whites of his knuckles.

Merrick was the last to arrive. He set his plate down, sitting beside Era.

"This really is an interesting development," Era continued with a grin.

My eyes shot up, but Era was looking at Merrick over her shoulder, the Empath's eyes beginning to swirl dark. He studied her, then raked his gaze across the table.

Enough, for fuck's sake.

Merrick's eyes settled on Silas, then Roland, then me. His dark eyes faded, and his cheeks grew red. "O-oh," he stuttered.

"Uh...what's going on?" Edmund asked slowly, his eyes skating between Erabella and me. Elowen looked over to me with a raised brow.

"Lena, can I talk to you?" Merrick asked quickly.

Tithara, spare me.

I sighed. "Yes," I grumbled, scooting my chair away from the table to meet with him outside in the courtyard.

The breeze was cool this morning as I shoved open the wooden door. The sky was a light grey as if rain might be on the way.

I eyeballed him beside me as we walked, his silver-white hair lying down his back. When we were far enough away, standing near a tall willow tree, he turned to me with a cocked brow, his icy blue eyes going dark once more.

"You need to read me again?" I drawled.

He gave me a deadpan stare. "I'm not my cousin. Although with all the emotions I felt—"

"I slept with Roland."

His eyes broadened, churning back to icy blue.

"I don't see why it's such a big deal!" I exclaimed, throwing my hands up. "Am I not a grown woman capable of making my own decisions?"

"Well, we know it's a big deal to someone." He crossed his arms. "I could feel his rage before even entering the room."

I rolled my eyes. "So he can fuck Era, and that's okay, but I am not allowed to move on? How does that make sense?"

Merrick sighed, pinching the bridge of his nose. "I wasn't agreeing with it, Lena."

"I know...I know." I ran my hand through my hair and let out an aggravated exhale. My eyes flickered to the inn as I saw Silas heading our way. "Fuck me."

Merrick's eyes darted between us. "We'll talk more later. Good luck," he said with a wince as he patted my shoulder. He sauntered away, passing Silas as he trudged over.

I clenched my jaw. "I-I was just going back inside—"

"No," he said sternly, halting me in place.

I didn't bother to hide the annoyance in my voice. "What do you want?"

"Please tell me you did not fuck him," he growled.

I blinked, then let out a humorless laugh. "Who I *fuck* is none of your business," I replied sweetly.

He choked on a laugh, then looked away, waiting a moment before his furious eyes shot back to mine. "Why are you doing this, Lena? To hurt me?"

"Hurt *you*?" I let out a dry laugh. "I have sex with someone, and you make it about you? You're allowed to move on and be happy, and I can't? That's an attack on *you*?"

His eyes darkened with fury, his fists shaking at his sides. "So, you admit it, then," he said in a voice that was all too calm...it unnerved me. "You slept with him."

"Yes. I did." I crossed my arms, giving him my best fake smile.

His eyes flared, just for a moment, his chest rising and falling as he tried and failed to hide the signs of his rage. His body pressed closer, causing us both to fall back under the drooping branches of the willow tree.

"Do you know how easily I could kill him?" he taunted.

I craned my head up to sneer at him once my back hit the tree's trunk. "Do you know how easily I could stop you?" I didn't bother saying kill. We both knew I'd never do that. "Don't you dare fucking threaten me, Silas."

I pushed him back with both palms, but he stayed firmly planted before me.

My gaze scorched into his. "I can watch your wife run her hands along your thighs, see your flushed faces when it's so obvious to *everyone* you two had just screwed," I continued, my lip curled and my eyes now burning from the attempt at holding in my feelings. "But poor Silas can't handle the thought of *me* sleeping with someone." I tilted my head up further and looked at him down my nose. "Fuck off."

I went to trudge past him when he grabbed my arm and pushed me back against the willow tree, holding me in place. Its long and narrow leaves blew around us in the crisp morning wind.

"You have no idea what you're talking about," he said in a low voice. He leaned down, and his breath brushing the shell of my ear ignited something in me I wanted to shove far, far away.

My body stilled, my heart hammering in my chest. Silas's expression changed, too, his eyes dilating, his lips parting. His golden irises studied me, dropping down to my lips, then back to my eyes again as if in a battle.

We were protected beneath this tree—its branches hiding us from any onlookers.

My breathing picked up as he leaned in closer, his lips now grazing my ear. "You can't actually be surprised that I'm angry."

I let out a shaky breath, my eyes falling shut. The dreamy scent of pine and citrus overwhelmed my senses. If I turned my head even slightly, my lips would graze the inked skin of his neck.

"I'm not, Silas...but am I not entitled to feel anger, too?" I whispered.

He stayed close for a beat longer, chills spreading across my body at the feel of his breath against my ear. I flinched as his fingertips trailed up my forearm, my chest rising and falling, my eyes squeezing tightly. I wondered if he would keep touching me under this tree...if his hands would find other places.

But then he drew away, and I thought I would faint at the lazy smile he gave me—Gods, how I have missed that face. Unlike before, though, his smile didn't reach his eyes.

His smiles never reached his eyes anymore.

The expression faded as quickly as it came and went back to that stony look. "You can obviously do as you wish, Lena. But for the love of the Gods, please keep the flirting to a minimum. Unless you want Roland dead."

His audacity was mind-blowing. I let out an incredulous laugh. "Very well," I replied. "So long as you keep your flirting and groping and kissing to a minimum as well." I walked in close, and it was me who whispered in his ear this time, my voice low and sweet. "Or perhaps I'll make a public display and fuck Roland right in front of you."

I pulled my face back, and Silas's pupils were dilated as he stared down at me and wet his lips. There was heat in his gaze...but it wasn't as much anger now as it was hunger.

The corner of his lip tilted up. "Cruel siren," he murmured, and I shuddered as his fingertips grazed my cheek. "You drive me insane."

Holy hell, my entire body was fucking *vibrating*.

"Did he please you as I have?" he purred.

It went against every feeling I had. What I wanted was to say, *'fuck it'* and pull his lips to mine. I wanted to taste him again. Feel his bare body pressed against my naked skin.

But I was upset. So, in typical Lena fashion, I lied.

"He pleased me even better."

The words tasted foul as they came out, and the flickering of Silas's expression nearly had me calling my bluff. But his hurt only shone for a moment before he cocked his head to the side.

"Then I suppose it's better for us both that we have moved on," he said quietly. He turned away, pushing through the hanging willow branches, and Ravaiana, damn me, I wanted to reach for him. But I resisted, even as it ate me alive.

I waited a few moments, collecting myself, steadying my breathing so my heated cheeks would fade before I returned to my friends.

I hated that he affected me this way. Half a decade later and my traitorous body still responded the same to him. Perhaps even more so, knowing just how much I couldn't have him.

I suppose everyone desires what they cannot have, right?

I shook off my nerves, wandering back into the dining hall. I sat down at the table immediately after entering, shoving another forkful of now-cold pancakes in my mouth.

"Everything okay?" Roland asked me with a raised brow, and then he glanced at Silas, who wrapped his arm around Era's waist.

"Yeah," I said after I swallowed a mouthful. "Just peachy."

My eyes darted to the opening double door, and in walked Dani. Her blue hair was up in a high pony, and she wore a tight navy shirt and black leather pants. The straps of her top crossed over her chest and wrapped around her neck, her cleavage visible through the opening.

"Good morning," she greeted, a bright smile on her face as she crossed her arms. "I'm here to take the girls shopping."

I raised a brow, looking over to Erabella, then El, then Viola, all of us equally surprised.

"Shopping?" Viola asked skeptically.

Dani's blue eyes sparkled. "Hell yeah, shopping." She plopped down next to her, resting her elbows on the tabletop. "After you eat, of course."

"What about me?" Roland pouted.

Dani shot him a smirk. "Ladies only, I'm afraid. But don't worry, Leroy will take you guys out to get some clothes, too. 'Cause these—" She motioned to our outfits. "—beautiful as they are, are not fitting for The Freak Show."

"The *Freak Show*?" Edmund asked slowly. Silas narrowed his eyes.

"Yup," Dani said, popping the 'p' as she leaned forward. "It's only the best part of Forsmont." She lowered her voice. "A circus where we Warlocks don't have to hide. Well...not entirely."

"I've always wanted to go to a circus," Elowen said excitedly, and Edmund kissed her temple.

Merrick's jaw ticked, but he didn't acknowledge their affection otherwise. "I didn't see any tents," he commented, eating the last forkful of his waffles. "Where is this Freak Show anyway?

"I guess you'll have to see," she purred.

"We really have more pressing matters to deal with," Silas interjected, but Dani raised a hand.

"An evening of fun won't ruin your plans. In fact, it's probably just what you guys need." She drummed her fingertips along the wooden table. "Now, hurry up and finish eating."

After breakfast, Dani led the girls out of the inn just as Leroy was entering. Roland not so subtly grasped my ass, and I even less subtly swung my fist into his arm. We both were grinning like idiots. I really enjoyed Roland...the lightness to his personality was honestly everything I needed.

I didn't look to see Silas's face, but I hoped it was red with rage. Served him right.

We ambled through the village, and I took note of how tall the buildings were. Tall and crammed. The cobblestone walkways were kept in pristine condition. Even with the drowsy weather, this place was radiating with ebullient energy.

I almost walked right into Vi when she halted to a stop.

"Wait," Viola said. "You brought us to a lingerie store?"

"What?" Dani grinned, grasping the doorknob to an establishment with sexy outfits displayed in the windows. "This place has the best corsets." Dani pushed through the door, the bell chiming above us, and waltzed inside, us following right behind. "We'll find one for each of you and get the rest elsewhere."

"I've never worn a corset before," Elowen commented, eyes wide as she took in all the sexy apparel around us: corsets, bras, garters, and stockings.

"I'm sure Edmund will love it," Erabella teased, and Elowen gave her a bashful smile.

Why is she such a pleasant person?! It's making it hard for me to hate her.

"Oh, absolutely," Dani added. "The Freak Show is a…sexy affair." She ran her fingertips along a sleek black corset. "Well, it can be. The main area is a family event. Animals, clowns, food vendors." Her cobalt gaze slid to Era's. "But there are different tents. One side, my favorite, has exotic dancers on a stage—a variety of different performers. People dress kinky and have a lot of fun."

It was Erabella's turn to flush. "In front of the children?"

"Gods, no." She grimaced. "Those who wish to dress more provocatively must cover themselves in the family areas. Once they enter the adult area, they can remove the outer layers." She waved at the person working, who emerged from the back with a large grin. Dani turned her attention back to us. "I figure we get you guys corsets to wear with a dress, if you want, that is. Anything else you wish to purchase is fine, too."

We girls slowly exchanged glances, then broke off, scanning the various items displayed in this quaint store. Eventually, everyone's apprehension was replaced with smiles and giggles, holding up clothes against our bodies and asking what each other thinks.

Everyone but me.

I was off in a corner, studying a particularly stunning corset, when Dani strode up to me and crossed her arms.

I turned my head toward her, and we had a mini-staring contest before she eventually conceded.

"Alright." She huffed. "What's your deal?"

My brows drew together. "Deal? I don't have a deal." My eyes went back to the corset.

Would this be too much to wear?

"Is it because of what we are?" she asked quietly.

My head spun to hers. "What? No...I'm...I'm just surprised by your kindness," I admitted, looking away. At her silence, my eyes tore away from the rack of clothes, once again finding her bright blue eyes. "Our kinds have been at each other's throats for a long time."

Dani smiled. "While the Warlocks are magical beings as well, yes, there still is some animosity between our kinds. But you somehow convinced the Witch Slayer to be on your side." She shrugged. "If you two can find common ground, if you can look past your differences, why can't we?"

My eyes fell, and as her words registered, a small smile crept on my lips. "I suppose you're right."

Dani clasped my shoulder. "Get the corset. It's hot."

CHAPTER SEVENTEEN

MERRICK

Silas wore a scowl nearly our entire walk after Leroy came to fetch us, taking us on some shopping spree. I found it surprising at times that *this* was the Quill Lena had told me stories about.

The charming, witty, sweet man she fell in love with...what the hell happened to make him change so much?

Then again, I understood. He and I had both lost our mothers. And to make it worse, he lost the love of his life a few days after that tragedy.

I supposed that would make any man turn cold.

"Tell me, Leroy, my man," Roland quipped. "What's this Freak Show all about?"

Leroy gave him a half smile. "No spoilers. It's best to go into it with no expectations."

I watched Silas's frown deepen as his eyes flicked to Roland. Other than the obvious, him bedding his first love, what had made him dislike the soldier so much?

Edmund and Hendry would roll their eyes occasionally at his comments—we all did. But they clearly enjoyed his presence.

The Prince...not so much. Yet he was willing to let him tag along with us for this journey, which meant that in spite of his loathing, he trusted him. So, if he hadn't broken his trust, what exactly did Roland do?

"We first need to get you guys some appropriate attire. Something fancy and not fit for battle. That would surely unnerve the guests."

My eyes darted away when I heard my sister's laugh, and I saw that the girls were striding out of a lingerie store.

My mouth slightly fell open—all of ours did, actually, as Vi shot me a smirk while dangling her bag.

My cheeks heated, and I gave her a shake of my head, grinning like a fool.

Naughty.

"Hell yeah, Ginger Snap!" Roland hollered, and Lena flushed, biting back a smile and giving him her signature middle finger. He chuckled in response.

"She sure is fiery, that one," Hendry noted, crossing his strong arms.

"Feisty as shit. I love it," Roland replied, biting his lip.

Era sheepishly looked to Silas, clutching her own bag, and I watched as he gave her a strained smile.

I felt an unpleasant feeling bubbling in my chest, and I found it was for Era. She really was clueless about the Prince and the

Supreme of Ames's past. She was just innocently going with the flow.

And the Prince...his feelings overwhelmed me.

Silas couldn't fully enjoy these moments with his wife, not with his past staring back at him, *taunting* him.

What he really craved was out of his grasp, the forbidden fruit too high up in that damned tree. His fingertips could only brush the delicate flesh—unable to extend his reach to wrap his fingers around and *pull*.

I felt it then...felt how her presence was nothing more than a constant tease—a reminder that he could not satiate that hunger...could not feast on what it was he truly desired.

And it only enraged him further.

I cleared my throat, blinking rapidly.

Fuck, I wasn't even trying to read him! Why are his emotions bleeding into mine?

Leroy snorted. "C'mon, boys, no getting distracted now." He wiggled his eyebrows. "That's what the evening is for."

We walked along the cobblestone roads, passing many smiling faces, and I found myself liking this place. I'd never traveled outside of Ames...not in my entire life. Despite everything, it was fascinating to see how other groups of people lived.

The people here beamed at Leroy, their expressions displaying no fear. Respect shone in their eyes, and he walked with humility. A far cry from the terror ruling Otacia.

How I wished my people could experience this one day. The freedom to be themselves, travel, and find homes in more than one little place.

"You mentioned you had a wife," Silas said as we walked opposite the girls.

"I do. She doesn't come out for the Show often." He tilted his head back, blue eyes set on the Prince. "We have four children. Quin is the oldest, and our youngest just turned one."

"You both have got your hands full," Edmund commented, a pleasant smile growing on his face. "How'd you two meet?"

Leroy's eyes sparkled as we continued onward. "She's my childhood love. I had a crush on her when we were six years old." He chuckled. "I didn't admit my feelings until we were fifteen. Thank the Gods she felt the same."

We were approaching a tailor's shop, where fine suits were exhibited in the windows. I'd never worn a suit in my life, either.

"Now, fifteen years and four children later, we are happier than ever."

"You're only thirty?" Silas asked, surprised.

"Yeah...why? Do I look older?"

"No," Silas remarked. "You're just very well established for being so young."

Leroy gave him a grin. "I am a King, am I not?"

"A young King," I added. "How did that happen?"

We stopped just outside the door of T & L Tailors. "We don't grant the title of King to just anyone, but we also don't follow the rules of keeping our leader in a royal bloodline...just a certain bloodline."

Warlock bloodline.

"The people here have a voice. Our council picks different candidates, and the people decide who they want to rule. I've been King for five years now, and every three years, we vote." He shrugged. "The same goes for the council. It's the only way we can ensure our safety...staying within the bloodline. I hope one day it won't be so."

He pushed open the windowed door, a bell chiming from above as we strolled in.

"Ah, Leroy! What brings you in?" a male voice called out.

A dark-skinned man with wine-red hair appeared, striding up and giving a brotherly hug to the Warlock. His warm brown eyes skimmed over our group as he pulled away.

It was so bizarre how comfortable everyone was with their King. Even our villagers were a little nervous around our Supreme from time to time.

"I need some suits for my guys here for tonight's show."

A woman with qualities similar to the man before us popped out from the back somewhere. Her big blue eyes skimmed over all of us in surprise. She appeared to be around our age.

"Sure thing. Let me measure you guys, and I'll see what I can find that fits. Taira here—" The man nodded his head toward the woman. "She can make small alterations if needed."

Taira tucked her long, silky hair behind her ear. Not pointed...but perhaps she was another Warlock hiding. "I'd be happy to help."

Leroy grinned at her. "Taira, meet Merrick." He pointed his thumb to me. "He's a Mage like you."

My eyes shot open, flitting between her and Leroy. The whites of her eyes were visible as she gaped at him, then at me.

"Leroy," she hissed, her eyes going to Silas. "What are you—"

"We have a lot to catch up on," he said, chuckling at her panic.

"You have a Mage here?" The red-haired man asked incredulously, his eyes darting around to make sure no one heard.

Taira's gaze hardened. "With the Prince of Otacia."

The man looked like he was about to faint. "Relax, Logan," Leroy muttered, patting his shoulder. "I'll catch you up later." His attention went back to us. "Logan is a human, but his sister got magic from their mother."

"Leroy," she hissed again.

Surprisingly, Silas spoke. "You needn't fear. I'm not going to harm you."

Taira glowered at him, crossing her arms in fear...and in anger. "I will *never* trust you."

Leroy sighed, then gave Silas an apologetic smile. "Don't hold her anger against her."

Silas's eyes widened, and then, for the first time, I witnessed the Prince smile. His golden eyes went back to Taira, whose glare fell away at his expression.

"I don't blame her. I have to prove I am trustworthy first."

Her crossed arms slowly slacked at her sides, her blue eyes shining from unreleased tears.

Leroy clapped. "Alright, back to business. We are here for suits. I'll talk to you two after, I promise."

After over an hour of fishing through various formal attire, we all settled on the outfits we'd be wearing that evening. Leroy insisted we stop for lunch at his home, the modest castle.

Leroy's wife was cleaning dishes as we strolled inside their kitchen. Her hair was a warm brunette, and I noted her eyes were a matching brown when she turned around and smiled at all of us. Quin was at their dining table, working on what appeared to be homework, while the other children were chasing each other, giggling.

"Keep it down, you two," she scolded. "You'll wake your sister." Her loving gaze found her husband. "Oh, hi, honey," she greeted, kissing Leroy on the cheek.

"It smells lovely in here," he complimented, kissing her back.

She gave him a wink. "I made apple pie."

"My favorite," he murmured, then slid his arm around her waist. "This is my wife, Emma. Emma, this is Silas, Roland, Merrick, Hendry, and Edmund."

She beamed at us. "Would you boys like some?"

The most amusing part of eating that apple pie wasn't its delectable flavor, nor was it the goofy children fighting amongst one another. No, it was reading Silas.

He was completely baffled—even if I couldn't read his emotions, his face gave it away. Emma was overly kind, never once showing an ounce of fear toward him.

He even went to take a bite of his pie, then froze, eyes nervously darting to the King's wife.

She chuckled, then leaned down, taking a bite of his pie into her mouth with her own fork. "Baking poisonous pies in a house of children would be quite literally a recipe for disaster."

Silas had inclined his head, the corner of his lip turning up ever so slightly, before conceding and tasting the warm pie. Leroy practically scarfed down his.

"So," Silas began, eyes back on Emma. "Are you Forsmont's Queen then?"

She snorted. "Queen?"

Leroy chuckled. "She even laughs at my title as King." He lifted a glass of milk, gulping down the cold liquid. "Like I said, we do things differently here. Technically, yes, she is Queen. The people call her so."

"And I despise it," she added with an eye-roll, leaning against the counters with crossed arms.

I felt warm emotions spread through Silas as he smiled down at his plate before resuming his eating.

Nostalgia.

"Don't be dramatic," Leroy drawled, and he snickered when she whipped her dish rag at him.

"So that makes little Quin here a prince then, huh?" Roland joked. Quin eyed him from his place on the floor, playing with his baby sister.

"Oh, that's rich," Emma laughed.

"I can be...princely," Quin muttered.

Our empty dishes clanked together as Leroy gathered them in his hands. "Yeah, right," he teased. "Quin could become King if the people vote for him one day, but because the title won't be simply passed to him, no one refers to our children as princes or princesses."

Leroy set the plates into the sink and began scrubbing.

A King...washing his own dishes.

"You clean up nice," Viola purred as we made eye contact through the full-length mirror in my room that evening.

I smiled softly at her before glancing back at my suit. I felt a little ridiculous, but it did suit me well. The deep turquoise piece paired nicely with my porcelain skin, its silver accents matching my piercings.

I turned to face her. Her purple braids were up in two low buns, and she wore a long, white, sleeveless dress paired with a violet corset. It squeezed her waist even tighter than the form-fitting fabric encasing the rest of her.

"You look fantastic," I admired.

She stepped forward, and my heart picked up as she kissed me slowly. I hesitantly gripped her waist, deepening our kiss, before we were interrupted by a knock on my door.

Followed by an immediate entry.

"Hey, we were going to head down—" Edmund began, his eyes bulging when he saw Vi in my arms.

I glared at him, and his whole face turned red. "Sorry, man!" He winced. "I'll wait out here."

The door clicked shut before I could snap at him.

"He's really trying," Viola commented while staring at the door. She turned back to smile at me. "I think it's sweet."

I groaned. "It's not sweet, it's annoying," I muttered.

Viola kissed my cheek, grasping my hand. "C'mon. Let's see what The Freak Show is all about."

CHAPTER EIGHTEEN

LENA

"**L**ook at you, Ginger Snap." Roland's eyes roamed over my body from his seated position on my bed. His gaze lingered on my exposed hips, then on my breasts.

It was now evening, and we were getting ready for the circus Dani and Leroy had raved about. I felt a little scandalous wearing this outfit, but at the same time, I'd never felt more confident. The maroon, off-shoulder dress hugged my body pleasingly, my thighs peeking through the slits on either side, and I'd be lying if I said my ass didn't look nice. But with the black under-bust corset sinching my waist and pushing my breasts up...well, they are what stole the show.

His lips curved into a sinister smile as he stood. "You look..."

I ran my hand over my collarbone suggestively. "Look like what?" I asked sweetly.

He bit back his smile, eyes trailing along me another time. "You look like..." He gave me a mischievous grin. "Like I'm going to have trouble keeping my hands off you."

I grinned back, and his eyes went half-lidded as he drew me close by the small of my back. I gasped softly as he pulled my mouth to his, and after a slow kiss, I smiled against his lips.

"I feel the same way," I purred.

He chuckled lowly. "I'm not even dressed yet," he whispered. He was still wearing his outfit from earlier today.

"Then get dressed." I lightly slapped his ass, and he bit my lip. When he withdrew, I stared up at him, studying this face that I once despised.

"What?" he mumbled, then pecked my lip again.

"I just would've never guessed...any of this." I kissed him slowly. "I wanted you dead last month."

"You never wanted me dead," he murmured over my lips. "You saved me, remember?"

My smile grew against him, and then I pulled away. "We're going to be late. Go get dressed."

He groaned but conceded. I waited on the edge of the bed while Roland changed in the bathroom, him wishing to give me a grand reveal.

I wonder what this Freak Show entails...

I hoped we weren't falling into some trap. Dani and Leroy had been nothing but kind, but Warlocks and Mages had a history of butting heads. I didn't want to think the worst of them...perhaps they were just kind-hearted people. Those still existed, right?

I slipped on my black heeled ankle boots, which I had purchased earlier. Well, technically, Silas purchased them. I wasn't used to wearing heels, but thankfully, they were thick enough that

I felt mostly fine when I walked in them. I still feared tripping and humiliating myself.

I sighed as I stood, practicing my walking skills as I made rounds across the room.

Why am I walking like something's up my ass?!

Okay, fine. I didn't walk great in heels. How princesses did this on the regular was beyond me.

"Well? What do you think?"

I turned at the sound of Roland's voice, and my eyes nearly fell out of my head when I beheld him. His hair was freshly styled, and his suit was a dark grey, hugging his body in all the right places. He looked so...elegant.

He looked exceptional.

He tucked his hands into his pockets, giving me a shit-eating grin. "I look sexy, don't I?"

I bit my lip as my eyes greedily roamed over him. "Gods...*so* sexy."

My smile turned playful at the sight of his reddening cheeks. I'd come to learn that when I was shameless about my attraction to him, it made the overly confident man turn bashful, just for a moment. I relished in it, and found it made me even more attracted to him.

He held out his elbow. "Well, shall we go then, Ginger Snap?"

It was dark when Roland and I stepped outside, the stars illuminating the night sky. I thought of Mother as I observed them, hoping she was doing well up on the mountain. I couldn't let my thoughts linger on her, or I'd cry.

Elowen's mouth fell open, her eyes lighting up as she admired me. "My Gods, Lena!" she exclaimed. "You look incredible!"

Everyone turned to look at me, Elowen's words prompting their curiosity. My cheeks heated as I met all their surprised faces.

But it wasn't until I beheld Silas that my heart stopped. That the world around me stilled.

My lips parted, a soft exhale escaping me at the sight of him. He was wearing a sleek, raven suit. It was gothic—regal. It was low in the front, exposing his muscular, tanned, tattooed chest and the very beginning of his abs.

His jet-black hair was styled back, and his own lips parted, his gold eyes flaring as he took me in. He trailed his stare over every inch of me before settling on my eyes, never leaving once they locked with mine.

Silas had always been beautiful to me, but as he stood right now, he had never appeared more flawless.

I couldn't look away. I needed to look away.

"...Lena?"

I was vaulted back to reality at the sound of Dani's voice. I whirled my head at her. "Sorry, what?"

She laughed. "I said, are you guys ready to go?"

Dani looked incredible. She wore a flowy blue mini dress with a white stay, the sleeves of the dress off-the-shoulder and puffy, just like mine. The hue of the dress's fabric matched her hair, which was currently tied up in a pony.

"Yes," I nodded, smiling shyly. "Yes, we're ready."

She clapped. "Alright, gang! Let's go!" She leaned in close and whispered, "Told ya that corset was hot."

My arm was still linked with Roland's as I walked. Every time I dared a glance in the Prince's direction, his jaw clicked as if he was holding himself back from returning eye contact. His arm was interlocked with Erabella's, and I despised the envy I felt seeing her wear a sapphire blue dress—both of them modeling Otacia's colors.

That could've never been my life...I had to remember that. It was inevitable that falling in love with the Otacian Prince would leave me heartbroken. It was inevitable that he would marry a princess...that he would forget me, that he would move on.

Merrick shot me a worried glance over his shoulder, and I winced when I realized my emotions had risen. I mouthed, "Sorry."

Dani led us down stone steps to a line formed behind a door, one that seemingly led underground.

"Where are we heading?" Edmund asked, eyes narrowed at the security guard granting people access behind the door. He wore a white suit, which paired adorably with Elowen's blush, ruffled dress.

"The Show is through that door. It's held beneath our king-dom," Dani answered, but her eyes were on Viola. "You look great," she complimented.

Viola's purple eyes widened for a moment. "Oh...thank you." She smiled. "You do as well."

Viola really did look stunning, but that wasn't new for her. The shade of her eyes against her deep skin was mesmerizing, even more so with the white dress and violet corset.

181

"I love your buns, Vi," Elowen admired. "Makes me want to grow out my hair."

Edmund ran his fingers through Elowen's pink pixie. "You could put teeny buns in here."

She snorted. "I suppose. I don't think it would look as cute as Vi's."

"It would be adorable," Viola assured, and we all moved forward in the line.

Roland glanced over his shoulder, grinning at Hendry. "I never got to ask, how was that MILF?"

I shot a glare at Roland, then curiously looked back at Hendry, who was shaking his head. "Nunya," he replied.

Hendy's ensemble was light grey, and still, despite a fancy occasion, he kept his hair over his brows. His eye contrast was more apparent in the evening, his blue eye shining bright.

"C'mon," Roland whined. "I gave you all our juicy details."

My head snapped to his, and Roland broke out laughing.

I went to unlink our arms, and he pulled me in close. "I'm teasing, Ginger Snap." He leaned in to whisper in my ear. "I don't kiss and tell—I told you that."

"I can't stand you," I hissed back in his ear, and when he kissed my cheek, I smiled.

Silas kept his back to me.

Twenty minutes passed before we were accepted and led through the door. A scarcely lit, stone hallway was what we trekked through for another ten, and my nerves increased with every step.

Plenty of people had entered before and after us, all giggling in anticipation, murmuring amongst themselves.

Silas was visibly tense, and he kept Era close to his side. I scowled at her from behind, not that she could see me, not that she deserved it.

"Alright," Dani said excitedly, just as we were reaching another entryway, this one enclosed with a thick, red velvet curtain, another soldier keeping guard. "You guys ready?!"

I swallowed, and all of us remained silent. Dani's smile was wide, her eyes trailing over us all, before she sighed, her eyes rolling.

She stepped beside the curtain, her hand grasping the fabric. "Welcome to The Freak Show."

With a dramatic pull, Dani opened the curtain for us, and I froze, my breathing stalling just for a moment before I rushed forward.

"My Gods," I breathed.

My eyes trailed the expansive setting before me—a kingdom beneath a kingdom. Because we were underground, plenty of warm, golden lights scattered about brightened the place—lamp posts, twinkle lights, and more.

Straight ahead was a large stage, and I almost collapsed at the sight of animals I had never seen before.

"You can imagine what those animals really are," Dani murmured into my ear as she stepped beside me.

"Holy shit," Roland whispered.

Tigers. Monkeys. A damn elephant, for fuck's sake. People were filling the hundreds of seats that surrounded the large stage, and my eyes caught the ringleader readying for the show.

"Logan is the ringleader?" Merrick questioned.

"That he is," Dani replied.

The overhead light on the stage was bright. "Mage light?" I whispered.

"Yup," Dani laughed. "Brilliant, right?"

I stumbled forward a step, tilting my head as I studied the surroundings. Food vendors were scattered about, and various games were set up, people already trying to win the small prizes. I heard a loud ding, and when I peered to my right, a man sitting above a tank of water was plunged into the liquid by someone chucking a ball at a bullseye. They roared with laughter as he was submerged.

"This place is remarkable," Elowen said with tearful eyes, covering her smile with her hands.

There were two large tents on either side of the stage. The one to the left had black and grey stripes, and the one to the right was red and gold.

Dani angled her thumb to the black and grey. "That tent is the Adult Only tent. Think exotic dancers, fun cocktails, and...private rooms." Her grin grew as she pointed at the other. "And the red and gold? That is where our 'freaks' work."

Silas raised a brow at her. "Freaks?"

She peeked around, then leaned close to him. "Us Warlocks," she whispered before pulling back. "In one night, many of us make enough silver to last for the month. The workers shift themselves, not enough to give ourselves away, of course." She snorted. "One of the girls gave herself three breasts. You should see how much she makes." Her eyes flicked to the tent. "We've had some wonderful souls wander here, though. Those with real deformities and oddities are the ones who started this show. We've given them a home, a community, and a livelihood after the original one was ransacked by Faltrun." Her eyes sparkled when she faced us again. "Anyway, they are the real stars of the show. We never judged them for how they were born, nor do they judge us." Her eyes trailed our group. "Who wants to check it out with me?"

Roland's hand popped up. "Me!" His eyes shot to mine in question.

"Have fun," I laughed. "I think I'm going to check out the animals first."

Roland gave me a wink, and Hendry and Edmund decided to join along, Edmund's arms going over both men's shoulders before halting.

"Merrick, join us!" Edmund insisted.

My silver-haired friend blinked, and then he let out a breathy laugh, strolling toward the men and Dani.

"I want to check out the animals too!" Elowen said. "I'll meet up with you later?"

Edmund blew her a kiss. "See you soon."

I watched as the guys and Dani wandered over to the red and gold tent, my eyes eventually sliding back to the large center stage. I was mesmerized by the dancers who were now moving their bodies on the steps leading up to the stage, at the animals that, to the human eye, appeared just as that. The humans here had no idea so many Warlocks occupied this space.

I ambled forward, weaving through the numerous bodies that wandered the large open space. I couldn't believe how tall the ceilings were for being underground.

"This is incredible," Erabella murmured beside me, her head craned upward to view the hoops hanging from the ceiling. The crowd roared as acrobats began their aerial performances.

It was captivating to watch their dark and twisty movements, their faces exhibiting no fear as they spun so far from the ground. The crowd 'oohed' and 'aahed' as the performers dared flips.

"I would love to do that," Elowen murmured. "Can you imagine? I bet it feels exhilarating and entirely freeing being up there."

"Or petrifying," I joked. "Then again, for us, we could use a forcefield if we fell."

Elowen shrugged, eyes glued to the acrobats. "Perhaps they have a spell for that...if they are indeed *Warlocks*." She made sure to mouth that last word.

When I realized Silas was nowhere to be found, I quickly scanned the space, sighing in relief when I spotted him. He was still near the entrance, leaning against the stone wall with his arms crossed. Though he wore a scowl on his face, I could read the emotion in his eyes.

He was fascinated. Not only was the show already more impressive than anything we'd ever seen, but it was inspiring how the Warlocks had come up with ingenious ways to support themselves.

"Let's get a closer spot!" Viola pushed.

The girls started moving toward the seating. "I'll meet up with you guys," I laughed, my eyes flitting back to Silas. "I'm going to get grumpy to join us."

Erabella scrunched her eyebrows, then muttered, "Good luck."

I threaded through the bodies again, and he caught my movement toward him almost instantly. "Impressive, huh?" I asked with a smile once I reached him.

He gave a slow nod, his eyes taking in the surroundings once more.

"You're worried," I noted.

He narrowed his eyes at me. "Should I not be?"

I laughed through my nose, crossing my arms. "There are hundreds of humans here. I doubt the W's will try anything."

"How can you be so trusting?" he hissed, anguish in his gaze. "These people view both our kinds as enemies."

I raised a brow at him, then glanced around the space, surveying the humans having the time of their lives and the Warlocks, those in human form, having fun alongside them. When my eyes moved back to Silas, he gave me an eye-roll.

"I like to believe I have good intuition," I said softly, and he stiffened, glancing at me again. "You didn't want to check out the tent with the guys?"

His frown deepened. "No."

I sighed, and my head pivoted when I heard thumping coming from the black and grey striped tent, cheering emulating from within.

I spared another glance at him. "Will you check out the adult tent with me?"

His brows raised, his arms still crossed. "You want me to check out the kinky tent with you?"

My cheeks heated, and I bit back a smile as I slapped his arm. His expression softened, a smile begging to break out on his face.

"You shouldn't be standing here all broody. Let's have...fun."

We stood in silence for a while, and just before I was about to huff in defeat, Silas leaned off the wall, uncrossing his arms. "Fine. Let's check it out."

I sucked in my lips, eating my grin, and dared to lock my elbow with his. His throat bobbed with the action, and I tilted my head up to meet him. "You know I've never worn heeled anything before?"

I glanced down at my shoes as we walked. "I'm struggling to get used to them. My feet already hurt."

The corner of his lip raised ever so slightly. "I think the whole room can tell you're not used to them."

My face fell, and when his eyes playfully met mine, I nudged him with my hip. "Rude."

"You're walking just fine," he assured, then his brows drew together as we approached the tent entrance. "I'm surprised I never bought you any..."

I snorted. "Can you imagine me back then in heels? I would've laughed in your face if you gifted me some."

I felt him staring at the side of my face, and when I glanced upward again, my smile fell at the sight of his lazy grin.

"You would've done no such thing," he murmured. "You would've loved anything I got you."

I clenched my fists, the vibrating throughout my body overwhelming my motor skills.

Hold it in...hold it in...

Tithara, spare me. I'd had trouble from time to time keeping the flames in...even the ice, when my heart ached. But never had the electricity begged to come out like it has the past couple of weeks.

I swallowed, my eyes tearing away from his handsome face.

"You're right...I would have." As we inched closer in line, I thought out loud. "What kind of dances do they do at a circus?"

I felt him shrug beside me. "I'd say the real question is, 'What kind of dances do they do at a 'Freak Show?'"

Only once we made it through the guard blocking the entrance, him marking the tops of our hands with ink, did we weave our way into the tent. We could hear cheering, the music now over, and my eyes widened as we finally made it in.

Another large stage was in the back, currently dark as the previous performers had just ceased their show. The people at the bottom of the pit stood amongst each other, murmuring in anticipation, preparing to dance during the next performance.

As we strode forward, our eyes took in the various people walking about, ordering drinks, or kissing in corners. I sucked in a breath once I noticed that some of the women here were topless.

Silas's eyes remained on me.

I took another step forward, my arms slacking at my sides. "Dance with me?" I asked.

He seemed taken aback for a moment, eyes darting to the large group in front of the stage.

I snorted.

"What's so funny?" he asked with narrowed eyes.

"The face you just gave me...ouch." I winced, my hand going to my chest.

The corner of his mouth went up again.

"Come on," I insisted as I glimpsed up at the stage, the bar, and the many flammable objects that filled the large tent. "If anyone fucks with us, this tent will go burning down, along with everyone inside it." I cocked my head to the side, a smirk on my face. "I'll protect you. Don't worry."

My smirk faltered when he responded with a smile that showcased his perfect teeth. I took in a deep breath and held my elbow out, Silas interlocking his arm with mine once more.

We stood on the outside of the group gathered in front of the stage, and my face warmed at the many suggestive outfits surrounding us. Mine was suggestive, I supposed, but it was still tame enough that I could be around kids. Some of these adults, however, were dressed for the bedroom. Or hardly dressed at all.

The crowd began to cheer as the silhouettes of a handful of people began striding on stage, the lighting still off so we couldn't see exactly who.

Silas leaned down. "Are you nervous?" he whispered in my ear as the music started.

"No..." I lied. People started coming in from behind us, sandwiching us closer.

When the lights above finally snapped on, I gasped. Standing atop the stage were men and women with barely any clothing on—the females wearing covers over their breasts that only hid their nipples, the males wearing the skimpiest undergarments.

The sparkly, pink tassels that hung from the women's covers sparkled as they danced.

My jaw hung open. As the music picked up, fast yet sensual, the people around us began grinding against one another. A woman beside us was leaning against a man's chest, her hands trailing up behind her to run through his hair while his hands trailed her front, gripping her breasts.

It was like the dancing at Lost Anchor, only ten times naughtier. The man beside us began devouring the woman's neck, her eyes rolling back.

"So, this is what you wanted to see?" Silas yelled over the music.

My nervous eyes went to him, and after witnessing my expression, he shot his hand over his mouth to hide his smile.

Mine only grew, and I slapped his arm again. "I guess we figured it out—" I yelled over the music before someone behind me thrust into me, causing me to collide with Silas, who managed to catch me before I fell over.

"S-sorry," I stuttered, looking up at him as he chuckled, holding my arms.

This expression...this smile—was real. It was the first real one I had seen since he came back into my life. The first one that reached his eyes.

I couldn't help but beam up at him. "This is a little more rambunctious than I was expecting!" I laughed, daring to wrap my arms around his neck. I tried to calm my breathing as he placed his hands on my waist.

"Wild indeed," he replied with a half-smile, leaning down to speak in my ear. "A bit more rambunctious than the Summer Solstice festival."

I flushed at the mention of that night. "Well, more than the dancing part of that evening, anyway," I murmured into his ear.

My breathing faltered when I drew away and saw Silas's eyes flare, his lips separating slightly.

Was that too much?

His fingers gripped my waist, just slightly, as his eyes fell to my lips.

I was on high alert, more than aware of his strong thigh pressing between my legs.

My heart rate sped up. Silas's hands slowly slipped from my waist, his fingers brushing the bare skin of my hips, my thighs, through the slits in my dress.

Oh, Gods.

Goosebumps spread from the skin-to-skin contact. My chest was rising and falling, and I didn't even realize that my fingers had slid through the hair at his nape, my other hand now gliding down his bare chest.

His eyes shot to mine, and I couldn't breathe. I couldn't think. But this moment only lasted a beat longer before his hands flew back to his sides, and I instantly withdrew my arms.

"Let's get out of here," he muttered, grasping my hand and pulling me from the crowd.

We pushed through the bodies, and I felt like I could finally take a small breath when we exited that area and made it back to the tent's entrance.

"I'm sorry, Silas...I didn't mean to make it weird," I insisted once we came to a halt.

He let go of my hand and ran his through his hair. "Lena..." He wet his lips, but as he opened his mouth to talk, Erabella, Elowen, and Merrick sauntered up to us.

CHAPTER NINETEEN
MERRICK

"Well...that's not something you see every day," Roland mumbled.

Indeed. Just as Dani had said, a woman with three large breasts and hair as black as night was on stage, waving at the crowd. To her right was a man even taller than Hendry. He had to have been at least eight feet tall. On his shoulder appeared to be a little girl...but also not. She wore a ruffly blue dress and a matching hat.

"The tall guy is Ren, and on his shoulder is Petal. She's actually twenty-seven years old."

Edmund's jaw fell. "So, she shifts to be young?" he whispered.

Dani shook her head. "No. Petal and Ren are not Warlocks. They were just born that way."

My gaze settled on Petal. She was teeny alright, around the size of a three-year-old.

"Ren is actually only twenty years old. He takes care of Petal like a brother," Dani explained as she eyed the tall, strong man. He wore a sheer tank and tight pants, his feet bare as he roamed across the stage floor. People were waiting patiently to compare their heights to the ginger-haired man, girls ogling up at him.

"I've never seen a man taller than myself," Hendry uttered. "He makes *me* feel small."

Roland shot him a devilish grin. "I dare you to go up there and compare."

Hendry chuckled. "Fine. Come with me."

Dani laughed as the two stepped in line, then started speaking to one of the workers. Leaving just Edmund and me.

"Do you see her?" Edmund whispered, pointing at something. I followed his gaze to a woman performing on the other side of the stage. A woman with a beard.

I slapped his hand down.

"Ouch," he pouted.

"It's rude to point," I hissed. "Didn't your mother teach you any manners?"

"Isn't the whole point of this to gawk at the people on stage?" he retorted. "I'm sure I'm not the only one who has pointed."

I rolled my eyes, arms crossing over my chest. Just as Edmund went to continue, a couple of girls wandered up to him.

"Hi," one said sheepishly, her friend next to her giggling as she covered her mouth.

His green eyes widened. "Uh...hi?"

The girl speaking ran her hands through her aqua hair. "My friend over there," she hushed, motioning her head back at a girl standing awkwardly by the stage. "She thinks you're cute. Would you be interested?"

His eyes grew. "Oh, I'm taken. My girlfriend's just outside the tent."

The girls laughed, and the one speaking batted her lashes. "She doesn't have to know. You two could just sneak in one of the private rooms in the other tent."

I was about to tell this bitch to kick rocks, but Edmund beat me to the point.

"My girl is a thousand times sweeter, kinder, and prettier than all of you. Better in every way, actually," he said simply, the girls' faces dropping. "So, no. I'm not interested."

My mouth went slack as he walked away. Dani shot me a perplexed stare, but I gave her a wave of dismissal. I rushed to follow him, leaving the dumbfounded girls behind.

I gaped at the side of his face as I followed him wherever he was going, which appeared to be out of this area.

"What?" he asked, golden brows drawing together.

"What do you mean, 'What?' I've never seen you...behave in such a manner."

He stopped once we exited the tent, running his hand through his blond waves. "Those girls pissed me off, actually thinking I'd do anything like that. It's one thing to admit attraction, but to suggest I betray her in such a way..." He shrugged, looking around the crowds of people playing games. "Elowen is the last person on this planet deserving of any more heartbreak. I just want to be by her now if that's the type of people that are here."

I pulled my lips to the side. "Wow, Edmund. I think you may have actually earned a bit of my respect."

He blinked, then gave a soft smile. "Let's find her."

We strode back to the main stage, where a woman was posing atop an elephant that was prancing its heavy legs about. Acrobats were performing around the border, the ringleader off to the side.

I scanned the space, staring at the various heads until light pink hair and violet caught my eye.

"Over there," I shouted to Edmund, pointing toward Elowen, Viola, and Era.

He gave me a lopsided grin, and when he slapped my arm, I whirled at him.

His smile grew. "It's rude to point!" he mocked. "Didn't your mother teach you any manners?"

I narrowed my eyes at him, and damn me for smiling.

"Ha!" His eyes lit up. "I made you smile!"

I let out a groan just as he called out the girls' names. They turned, and Elowen waved excitedly as they stood from their seats and weaved their way toward us.

Where was Lena...and where was Silas?

"Mare! Edmund! You should've seen the acrobats hanging from the ceiling earlier!" she panted, throwing her arms out. "The rings they held on to were lit on FIRE!"

Edmund chuckled, then pulled her into a hug. She melted in his embrace, and for the first time, I didn't feel disgusted looking at them. Perhaps he really did care for my sister.

Okay, fine. I already had quite literally *felt* that he cared. But I didn't accept it...not until now.

Roland, Hendry, and Dani wandered back to us a moment later.

"Why'd you guys dip?" Dani asked, a crease between her blue brows. "You didn't like it?"

"That wasn't it—" I began.

"I just missed Elowen," Edmund interrupted, and the girls went, *"Aww."*

"I love you," he mumbled to her.

"I love *you*," she whispered back, standing on her tippy toes to kiss him.

Okay. I'm still mildly disgusted.

"We're gonna head to the other tent—see what this adult area is all about," Roland mentioned, his eyes looking over us all. "Whose comin' with?" Then, he frowned. "Where's Lena?"

Erabella glanced around. "She went to get Silas. I'm not sure where they went."

Dani interlocked her arm with Viola, and Vi blinked, her almond-shaped eyes widening at her touch. "Vi and I are going," she announced.

I frowned. Hating to do so but unable to stop, I tuned into their emotions, their feelings seeping into mine.

Viola was mildly uneasy, presumably by Dani's contact, but I could feel the attraction she felt while she looked at her. And Dani certainly felt it back.

Viola's eyes met mine, and her face fell. The unpleasant feeling washed over me—guilt overcoming her because she knew I had sensed her interest.

I mustered up a small smile, knowing it didn't reflect in my eyes. "Go. Have fun."

Her face then changed, her eyes trailing down my body.

Desire.

I cleared my throat, ignoring the feeling in my pants as that emotion bled into mine, and the corner of her lip turned up. "See you later tonight," she purred, and she walked toward the Adult Only tent with Dani. Roland and Hendry followed behind.

I supposed she still felt attraction for me, but it hurt that she felt it for Dani, too.

I hated my gift sometimes.

"I'm gonna go grab a drink," Edmund said, kissing El's temple before trekking to a stand selling alcohol.

"What was that about?" Elowen asked while wiggling her brows.

I knew my cheeks were stained with color. "Nothing."

My eyes went to Era, who gave me a knowing expression. I rolled my eyes, but my lips turned upward by the time my eyes met hers again. Era smiled then, too.

"Are you guys...?" Elowen drawled.

I sucked my lips in and went to turn away when Elowen slapped my arm.

"Ow!" I whined.

"Don't be a baby! Are you guys together?" she pressed, barely hiding her excitement. Era's eyes went down before looking the other way.

"We aren't together, per se."

Images flashed in my mind of what happened between us last night. Everyone was so focused on Lena and Roland this morning that no one realized Viola had snuck into my room.

I'd never had sex with a friend before. Never had sex with *anyone* before. And now I wasn't sure what that meant for our dynamic.

"But you're—"

"Jeez, El, I don't wanna give you any details," I mumbled, wishing I had my own drink in hand.

Era snorted, and Elowen narrowed her eyes at me before a conniving grin took over her face. "Well, I have plenty of details of my own. Just last night, Edmund and I—"

"I will shatter his bones!" I growled.

"Oh, come on, Merrick." Era brushed my arm, and when I shot a glare at her, she laughed. "You and Edmund were getting along a moment ago, and now you want to hurt him again?"

"Getting along is different than liking him," I retorted. My gaze stuck on hers for a moment. She looked fantastic in blue.

"Ugh, forget I mentioned anything," Elowen drawled while waving her hand. When her eyes caught a cotton candy cart rolling around, she bolted.

I chuckled as I watched her approach the worker with a big grin. Edmund waltzed up to stand in line with her, drink in hand.

"You two are entertaining, that's for sure," Era said.

I shot her a half-smile. "Glad I can amuse you."

"It's a surprise—you and Viola..." I raised a brow, and she continued. "After she said what an uneventful evening she had."

My stomach flipped, and I narrowed my eyes, tuning in to read her. But I didn't even have to before she broke out in a giggle, her hand covering her mouth.

"Oh, you think you're funny, huh?"

Her eyes sparkled with merriment. "She was in a rather good mood this morning. Nearly matched Lena's. And El's, for that matter."

She giggled when I fake vomited, and I laughed. "Sounds to me like her evening was rather eventful then...some might say unforgettable."

Era snorted. "Is that so?"

"You don't believe me?" I tuned into her emotions, giving her a smirk. I liked her expression anytime she watched my eyes go dark.

"That's cheating," she drawled.

"Answer." I grinned.

"No, I don't believe you."

My grin only grew.

Liar.

"Ah, you're annoying." Era laughed and shoved my shoulder just as Elowen skipped back over, Edmund right behind her. The spun sugar she held was light pink, just like her hair.

"Some for you, some for you," she said as she handed Era some and then me.

Era took a bite of hers, licking her lips afterward. I realized as I watched her smile softly at me that I'd grown to like her. She came across as cold and uptight when we first met her, but now? Now I could see the real Era. Someone bubbly, kind, and witty, too.

I smiled as I took a bite of my treat. The sweetness was pleasant, and it melted on my tongue.

We made our way over to the Adult Only tent, Edmund and Elowen hand in hand, Era and I following behind. Just as we were getting in line, Era stumbled in her heels. I caught her elbow before she fell.

"Shit," she muttered, then shot me a grateful smile. "Sorry—thanks."

I cocked a brow. "You sure you're a princess?"

She nudged me again. "Your peasantry is rubbing off on me," she teased.

I dragged my teeth over my lip ring, hiding my smile as I shook my head. "You've hurt me."

She laughed. "Yeah, right." We came to a stop as we stood in line. "How was the other tent?"

I tapped my foot as I thought about it. "Unusual...and thoroughly impressive. As is this entire place."

Era smiled, tucking her blonde bob behind her ear. "I love it here."

To that, my brow raised again. "Yeah?"

Her warm brown eyes settled on my blue ones. "Yes. It feels authentic here, don't you think?"

I blinked, tuning in to her.

She felt delighted. Inspired.

And she felt...

She felt...

Her smile slipped, and she cleared her throat, looking away.

Surely...surely those feelings were not for me.

My thoughts were reeling as we stepped through the curtain, and my eyes widened at the lack of clothing displayed before me. Breasts were everywhere. Asses were everywhere. No one was entirely naked, though, from what I saw in front of me, anyway.

"Oh...whoa." It was too dark see, but I imagined my sister's face was beet-red.

When I dared a glance at Era, her hand was covering her mouth. When her broad eyes met mine, I chuckled.

"It doesn't get more authentic than this," I shouted over the music.

She withdrew her hand, sucking in her smile before she inevitably chuckled.

My sister then ran forward, and I followed her steps when I realized she had found Lena and Silas. "Hey, we were looking for you guys!" Elowen chirped as we approached the visibly stressed Prince.

Era's brows drew together, and she wandered to Silas's side, her arm wrapping around his waist.

My eyes slid to Lena's, her chest moving up and down like she'd just run for her life.

Gods, the tension...the lust.

I shook my head, focusing on building up a wall between me and each of them. What were those two doing in here together?

They didn't find a private room together...did they?

"Have you seen Vi? She, Dani, and the guys came in here not too long ago," Elowen asked, eyes darting around the room, a slight cringe on her face as she attempted to avoid looking at any bare body parts.

Lena's eyes flared slightly. "No." She shook her head. "I haven't. It's pretty dark in here..."

Yep. She was anxious as all hell.

Why can't I stop reading her?

"Having fun without me?" Era asked the Prince.

I felt Silas's guilt, just for a moment. He glanced down at Erabella with a hesitant smile. As she angled her head up, puckering her lips, Lena turned, storming off in the opposite direction before she could witness their kiss.

I immediately followed her, Elowen and Edmund on my tail. My sister was munching away at her cotton candy as Edmund was downing his drink.

"I can feel your emotions without even trying," I muttered in annoyance as I reached her side.

She huffed. "Sorry. I wish I didn't feel them. Believe me."

"Did something happen between you two?" I pressed.

Elowen caught up before Lena could reply. "Hey, what was that about?"

"I just want to find Roland," she grumbled, and I decided to stop following her as she continued on her hunt for the soldier.

What happened?

I sighed, shrugging at El and Edmund. My eyes settled on Era kissing Silas, his hands on her hips, her fingers in his hair...and it bothered me.

Why did it bother me?

CHAPTER TWENTY

LENA

There were hundreds of people crammed in the dark tent. How the hell was I going to find Roland?

When I was with him, Silas didn't even cross my mind. I could move on; I just needed to keep my distance. Dancing together in a dim, sex-crazed tent was a poor choice.

Gods...the feeling of his fingertips brushing my thighs still had my electricity buzzing. I knew he didn't have magic, but did my touch affect him similarly? Or was I pathetic for craving him this much?

I was stopped in my tracks by Leroy, whose worried gaze trailed over me. "Everything alright?"

His long, golden hair was loose, and with the low light, I couldn't be certain, but I believed his attire was light blue.

"Yes. Sorry." I flushed, running my hand through my curls. "I just can't find Roland anywhere."

"Ah, I saw him not too long ago with a few of your other friends." His eyes scanned the crowd. "I'm sure they're here somewhere." After looking for a moment more, he turned to me. "How are you enjoying the place?"

My heartbeat calmed, and I was thankful to be directing my thoughts elsewhere. "It's incredible. How did you manage to build this under the ground?"

Leroy smiled, guiding us over to the bar, where he picked up a drink for himself. It seemed the bartender already knew his order. "When Forsmont was built centuries ago, the founders decided to make an underground escape in the event the kingdom got overrun." He sipped what appeared to be whiskey. "We actually have this place stocked, should we ever need to hide down here. No one but the 'royals' know there is an exit passage. They just know of the main area."

I raised a brow. "Yet you told me?"

Leroy gave me a half-smile, rotating the amber liquid in his hand. "Your seer told me of you."

My eyes flared, my head pulling back. "What did you say?"

"Igon Natarion. He stopped in Forsmont a few months ago, telling me about a woman named Lena Daelyra. How she would be replacing him." His eyes fell on his drink. "I didn't realize he'd meant he would be dying."

"Wait." I shook my head, eyebrows scrunching together. "Igon knew of you? Knew Warlocks ruled Forsmont?"

"Apparently so. We'd never heard of Ames before; you guys had done a great job staying secluded to yourselves. His gift must be how he knew of us."

"He didn't mention the Undead, did he? What else did he tell you?"

Leroy finished his glass, setting it on the bar top. "No mention of the Undead, no." His blue eyes settled on mine, arms crossing. "All he mentioned was that the Mages would be seeking unification with the Warlocks...and that the Prince of Otacia would have a change of heart. That his Soul-Tie would be the new leader of Ames."

I swallowed, stiffening in place. My thoughts drifted back to that day...how the order of surrender didn't chime until the moment after I saved Silas.

I danced my fingers on my thigh. "He is my Soul-Tie...yes," I uttered.

"Does he know it?" he asked, disbelief lacing his tone. "Igon didn't go that in-depth. I honestly had trouble even believing him until I saw Silas for myself."

"No, he doesn't. But he and I have a past. A past our friends don't know about."

Leroy stood there, waiting for me to continue.

I sighed. "I used to live in Otacia. It's a long story, but I met Silas when I was sixteen. We were together for a year and a half before my mother and I faked our deaths and fled the kingdom...when the kill order was put in place."

Leroy's jaw fell. "You two have a past?"

My stare drifted over the many bottles of alcohol displayed behind the bar, and I found myself wishing I had my own drink. "He was the love of my life...my best friend. He hid his identity as the Prince for a short while, but I never told him I was a Mage." My eyes burned as I dragged my lip through my teeth. "It killed me to leave him, killed me to see how he had changed. But that man I loved is still there...I've seen him."

Leroy's eyes drifted off in the direction I knew Silas was. "I met Silas last year, and when I tell you his whole demeanor has changed, I mean it." He turned to me. "I could swear the man had no emotions. No feelings. I damn near fell over when he smiled at you during our meeting."

I chuckled at that. "Silas was the warmest, kindest man you could ever imagine." My smile slowly fell. "Loss can change a person...turn them into someone you don't recognize. But he is good. I know he is good."

"I believe you, really I do. Especially considering all your seer told me. Convincing the council, however, will prove difficult." Leroy's gaze saddened. "Many have lost loved ones because of the Prince and his father. But perhaps your stories will convince them."

My face heated. "If we were to speak on that...it would need to be private. Just Silas and me and the council."

He nodded. "I can arrange that."

I loosened a breath, looking back at the dancing bodies, feeling the music vibrating in my bones.

I turned to Leroy. "Can I ask you something?"

Leroy nodded.

"Do phoenixes have any significance to you? Or your people?"

He frowned, his eyes trailing upward as he lost himself in thought. He responded after a few moments. "The phoenix symbolizes a lot of things for various groups of people. In general, it represents immortality. Rebirth. Hope." His blue eyes studied me curiously. "Why do you ask?"

"Igon gave me a message before he died. *Only through fire can the phoenix be reborn from the ashes.*"

"That sure is vague as hell."

I laughed. "That was always the case with him." My smile fell as I recalled his last moments.

"Well...there is the myth of the Immortal Mages."

My head sprang up. "Immortal Mages?"

He nodded. "Back when the Gods originally created Magekind. Mages thousands of years ago were said to be even more powerful...and could live forever. The Warlocks, Angels, Sea Nymphs, Half-Lives, none of them held a fraction of the power your people once held."

"And you're saying Mages of today descended from these Immortal Mages?"

"That's correct. Though through millennia, the bloodline became next to nothing, hence why Mages have the lifetime of a standard human."

How had I never read of this? "Would those Mages still be alive? The original creations?"

Leroy shrugged, motioning to the bartender to get him another drink. "I've thought about it a lot, but legend also says they were wiped out. While time did not affect them, they still could be killed by one thing. Or one being, I should say." He paused, sipping from his new glass just after it was set down. "Azrae."

My stomach flipped at that name. "The God of Vengeance?"

"Yes. Azrae is known as both the God of Vengeance and the God of Justice. He has the power to restore balance at any cost. The original Mages had too much power, power that nearly rivaled that of the Gods." Another sip. "But your riddle sounds like this power, this flame, is bringing something to life...or causing it to go through a rebirth of some sort." He rubbed his jaw. "I'm not sure."

I made a mental note to look more into the history of the original Mages. That is, if I could even find any additional texts on them. "There's only one place I've noticed the phoenix being symbolized," I continued.

Leroy's eyes slid to mine. "The La'Rune family crest."

"Exactly. There are other birds on that crest..." I squinted as I tried to recall them. "A raven, a pelican, and an—"

Leroy's eyes widened. "An owl." He set his glass down. "We have myths among the Warlocks regarding the meaning behind different animals. As you may already know, we came to be by the Gods fusing their power with animals." He winced. "Not breeding—before you get the wrong idea."

I grimaced, and he continued, "As they experimented, they found different properties. Some lines were stronger based on the animal they originated from. We once had a connection to animals millennia ago—used to be able to speak with them. Anyway, the ancients found that each animal symbolizes something." He smiled warmly at me. "Tomorrow, I shall bring that book to you. Perhaps it can help in some way."

I blinked, a smile overcoming my face. "Yes, yes, that would be amazing! Thank you."

Leroy's eyes drifted over my shoulder. "Ah! This one has been looking for you."

I peeked behind me, and there stood Roland, eyes glassy, a giant grin on his face, and cotton candy in his hand.

I snorted. "You're drunk!"

He kissed my cheek. "Am not," he slurred.

Leroy chuckled, clasping my shoulder. "I'll leave you two. Enjoy the rest of the night." He winked, then strolled off with his glass, his other hand in his pants pocket.

I turned back to Roland. "I've been looking everywhere for you."

He took a bite of his treat. "I was admiring the views." He nodded toward the stage with the nearly naked women and men. "None compared to yours, though," he murmured. "You in those tassels? You'd be as rich as a king with those on display." He motioned at my breasts.

I choked on a laugh, rolling my eyes. "Yeah, you've definitely had too much to drink."

His smile grew, and I adored the sight. I stepped forward, kissing him gently on the mouth. I went to pull away, but Roland gripped me with his free hand, deepening our kiss. My mouth watered at the slight sugary flavor of the cotton candy mixed with the lovely taste of his saliva.

Roland drew away, then smiled devilishly as he tore off a piece of spun sugar. "Now be a good girl for me, Ginger Snap," he whispered, "and suck this sweetness off my tongue."

He smirked as he stuck out his tongue, placing the cotton candy on top of it.

It was dark...and there were plenty of others surrounding us that were exploring each other's mouths.

I loosened a breath as I stepped forward, my desire ruling me as I did what he said, wrapping my lips around his tongue and sucking. The sweet flavor melted into my mouth, mixed with the delicious flavor of him.

"Mmm," he moaned as I pulled away. He ripped off another piece. "Again," he whispered, then placed it on his tongue.

I was breathing heavily, my sex throbbing as I sucked his tongue and the sweet treat into my mouth. I gave it a few extra pulls, then sucked his bottom lip into my mouth.

"Fuck," he whispered.

"My turn," I murmured in his ear, reaching over and tearing off a piece of the spun sugar he held. I offered a smug smile as I placed it on my tongue.

I loved Roland's smile. He leaned in, his lips encasing my tongue and sucking gently. I stifled my moan, my hands gripping his strong biceps.

After sucking it off, he slid his hand through my hair, angling my head up to kiss me. Our sweetened saliva mixed, and as he pressed his body into mine, I felt his erection against my stomach.

I wasn't a lover of public displays of affection, at least of this magnitude. But the lights were low, and several couples were doing the same things all throughout this place. And with the way Roland was driving me wild, I couldn't care less who saw. I was so lost in lust that I might be willing to ride him right here, right now.

His voice was low as he whispered in my ear, "You know, there are other places I could lick this off you..." His eyes flicked to the counter in the back.

We stumbled over our steps as we entered the room Roland paid for, our mouths never leaving one another as we kissed with desperation. I only had a moment to study the surroundings while Roland turned to zip shut the fabric, enclosing us in this space. A bed with clean velvet sheets stood in the center of the room, only illuminated by two dim lamps on each nightstand. Mage light, I knew, as actual flames would be a risk. Luxury mirrors were set up on either side of the bed.

Roland pushed me down until my back hit the mattress. His strong arms gripped my thighs, a wicked grin on his face as he parted them. My bare legs slipped through the slits in my dress, completely exposed. He grasped the fabric in the center, pulling it up until just my underwear was visible to him.

He dragged his finger along the dampened fabric, letting out a hum. "So wet for me," he murmured, then hooked his finger around my panties, sliding them down and discarding them on the floor. My breathing became shaky as he knelt before me, prying my legs open further. "Such a perfect pussy," he praised, giving my sex a light slap. I loosened a soft moan, gripping the sheets on the bed beneath me.

He gave me a half-smile, reaching over to tear off a piece of the candy floss. I propped myself up on my elbows, too curious not to watch as he slid the spun sugar over my soaked pussy. The sensation was featherlight yet exhilarating all the same. Roland's eyes were heavy as he witnessed the treat dampen, my arousal absorbing through, the shade of pink darkening.

I bit my lip as he teased my entrance with it, then withdrew it, placing the dampened parts on his tongue and savoring its taste.

"What a combination," he murmured, gliding his tongue along the candy as his heated gaze remained on me.

"Roland," I whispered, raising my hips as I watched him. Moaning could be heard in the rooms beside us; the only thing separating us was the tent material.

He grinned, placing the spun sugar on the bed. He leaned his head down, mouth hovering over my center. "So impatient," he scolded, then flattened his tongue to glide it through my slit. I cried out in pleasure at the feeling, my moans growing as he greedily flicked his tongue over my clit.

"Oh, yes..." I breathed. I should feel shame, knowing others could hear me. But I didn't.

"You taste even better than candy." He pressed his mouth to mine, the taste of sugar and my arousal all over his tongue.

He repeated the process several times, soaking the cotton candy with my wetness, bringing it to his mouth, only to dip his head down and worship my pussy with that tongue of his after eating it. It was the most salacious thing I'd ever done in my entire life, and I didn't want it to stop.

I watched him in the mirror, savoring the view of his perfect profile between my legs.

Once the spun sugar had been completely eaten, Roland's finger slipped inside me, pumping in and out as he licked and sucked relentlessly on my clit. My head eventually fell back, my hands running through his hair as he quickened his pace.

My eyes were squeezed shut, my back arching at the incredible feeling, and as my orgasm built, my mind imagined dark hair and amber eyes. It pictured tattoos on tanned skin.

"Godsdamn it," I cried softly.

I was lost now. I smelled pine and citrus as I recalled him whispering in my ear. I remembered the feeling of his hands on my waist, my fingers in his hair as my body was pressed so close to his.

I pictured him in my room the day he first claimed me. I pictured us in the forest, my mouth sliding up and down his length. I pictured him between my legs, only this time it wasn't the sweet, gentle man from before who I envisioned tasting me, but instead, the dark, tattooed Prince.

Only a few moments passed before I loosened a breathy wail, fisting Roland's hair as I rode out my orgasm on his face.

Roland waited until my throbbing ceased. "Holy hell," he respired as he withdrew his finger from inside me. He prowled over me, capturing my lips with his.

I am a terrible person.

I desired Roland, but my damn treacherous body still wanted Silas, too. I decided I was done thinking about the Prince.

I grasped Roland's erection through his pants, my eyes locked on him, and he groaned.

"I can't wait to stretch you again, Lena," he whispered in my ear.

I moaned softly as he pushed his hardened length against my pussy. I was more than eager to feel him inside me, more than eager to look into his hazel eyes than think about gold ones. But as Roland was fumbling with his belt, a feeling of darkness washed over me.

Wrong.

Wrong. Wrong. Wrong.

I quickly grasped his hand, forcing him to a halt as my eyes darted downward, looking past his shoulder.

He froze. "What's wrong?"

I sat up a second later, pushing Roland off of me. I reached down and quickly slid on my underwear. "I-I don't know."

I stood, closing my eyes.

"Lena, talk to me."

That feeling...It was getting closer.

No...there can't be an Undead here. There would be screaming.

The feeling increased, and I stiffened as the zipper to our room began to pull upward slowly.

"Roland," I hissed softly. "Get behind me."

"What? No, I—"

The material spread, and three figures marched in.

I gasped at what I beheld.

Roland's brows scrunched together. "What the fuck...?"

Three people, two with the bodies of males and one with the body of a female, stood facing us. They wore dark cloaks with the hoods up, and their hands were gloved. But what was most alarming were the porcelain masks concealing their faces. All were white, the lips black, and through the eyeholes, solid black eyes could be seen.

Solid. Black. Eyes.

"Roland!" I cried, shoving him back just as the woman shot an orb of darkness at us—the magic of the Undead. I lifted my hands in an X, grunting as I blocked the move successfully.

There were three of them and one of me.

I can do this.

"Go! Get out of here!" I yelled at Roland over my shoulder, flame creeping up both of my arms.

"I'm not leaving you!" he protested.

Another orb shot forward, and I crossed my arms again, sending the orb back before unleashing my flame toward her. The two others stood with their arms behind their backs.

"Get back up! NOW!"

Roland hesitated, swore, and then bolted out of the room, my flames distracting the creatures enough to allow him out.

My fire began inching up the tent fabric. I cursed, shooting ice over to extinguish the flames.

I need to get us out of this room.

As I went to charge toward them, one of the men raised his arm, and a loud shrieking filled my ears. My brain pounded hard, and I cried out, reaching for my head at the shrill noise and the agonizing pain.

Despite the hurt, I ran forward, flame engulfing my skin. The creatures retreated, scrambling out of the room once they detected my persistence.

That's when I heard the screaming. People were witnessing me enveloped in fire, chasing three bodies that seemed to others like normal people.

People evaded me, and I nearly tripped over my steps in these damn heeled boots, pursuing the figures out of the Adult-Only tent and out into the main area.

I bellowed once we made it out, shooting a bolt of fire out at the female's head. I heard her mask crack once she crashed into the ground. Children around me screamed, their parents holding on to them, gaping at me in terror. The show on stage came to an abrupt halt, the music ceasing.

But their fear shifted the moment the creature stood, her mask now falling free from her face. When she turned to me, my eyes blew wide, a shaky gasp leaving my lungs.

Heildee. Elowen's mother.

She didn't look like a normal Undead...no. Her eyes were solid black. Dark, inky veins covered her face. But she wasn't decaying like those I'd seen before. A symbol was etched into her forehead, presumably by a blade of some sort.

Or by magic.

The symbol was a pentagram with what appeared to be a spider atop it. However, because of the overlap in design, it appeared more like a skull.

A sinister smile took over her face. "Hello, Supreme of Ames," she greeted, her voice hers...and someone else's. A man.

An Undead was *talking*.

"Lena!" I heard Silas yell, but I couldn't turn. I couldn't risk any of them moving a muscle.

Her solid black stare shifted behind me, and the two men behind her followed suit. "The Prince of Otacia...the disgrace of his kingdom." Her smile grew unnaturally wide. "I shall enjoy eradicating you."

"What's going on?!" I heard Leroy yell.

"Mother?" Elowen cried.

Heildee glanced at her daughter, no emotion registering on her face.

She looked back at me. "Or, should I say, *he* will enjoy eradicating you," Heildee said, pointing.

That's when I turned, witnessing a fourth one of them, watching helplessly as the creature raised his hand at Silas.

No.

NO.

I ran. I ran as fast as I could, not worried or caring for one moment if the curse got me as I intercepted their path. As long as it didn't touch Silas.

It couldn't touch Silas.

The other Undead screeched, that same ache spreading in my brain—in everyone's—as the people surrounding me clutched their heads, falling to the ground.

It felt like my brain was bleeding, but I couldn't succumb to the pain. Not yet.

I couldn't let Silas die.

I flung myself at the creature, wrapping my arms around it, and wailed as I unleashed every bit of my fire.

There was no control. My skin burned; my chest hurt. But I released everything I had as the creature beneath me screeched, its skin melting from my touch.

"Lena!" Merrick yelled. I could hear Elowen sobbing from behind me.

I was hurting myself. I was doing too much.

But I couldn't stop. My adrenaline was too high, and all I wanted was for this creature to die.

"LENA!" Silas roared, rushing forward.

"The Lord of the Shadows will rule you one day. All of you," Heildee's distorted voice promised. "You've been warned. He is coming for you all."

I had the sense that the remaining Undead were escaping, but I could only focus on the body beneath me.

The Undead man thrashed, but his movements finally began to slow. I didn't extinguish my flames until his body grew still and quiet. Torrin's words played in my head.

Calm the flames.

Calm the flames.

Calm the flames.

When I finally felt relief from the heat, when I knew I wasn't a danger to others, I grasped my dagger, the one I hid under my corset.

CHAPTER TWENTY-ONE
SILAS

I watched as Lena withdrew a dagger kept tucked into her corset, watched as she straddled the body, wailing as she repeatedly pierced its corpse. Over and over and over again. Black blood splattered on her face and her tattered clothes, pooling on the floor beneath her.

She was sobbing...losing control. I rushed to her not a moment later. I grasped her shoulder, halting her stabbing, and her head spun to face me.

I knew my face didn't hide my emotions. It fucking killed me seeing her like this.

I knelt down beside her, taking her face into my hands. "It's okay, Lena," I whispered, my eyes meeting her frantic ones. "You're alive. You saved all these people. You."

Tears streamed down her cheeks, her fearful gaze softening as I wiped them away. Her lip trembled as I lowered my hands, and she slowly took in the bloodied mess beneath her, then at the crowd, who stared at her, not in fear...but in awe.

"I thought you were done for," she whispered so quietly only I heard it. "I thought it was all over. I...I didn't know if I could stop it."

I wanted to comfort her, but how could I?

"I'm right here, Lena," I said softly. Her skin was bright red—blistered, damaged from the flames she couldn't control.

Burning...so fucking close to burning. I took quick breaths as those memories of her in the cottage haunted me.

She shakily dropped the dagger, then slowly lifted her hands to the porcelain mask. Just as she began pulling it away, she screamed, the mask falling to the ground and shattering as she stumbled off the body.

"No—no, no, no!" she wailed. "Oh, Gods...what did I do!?"

My breathing hitched, my eyes flaring as I took in the body before me.

Igon Natarion.

His solid black eyes were barely open, the same swirling present on his fair skin, the same eerie symbol carved into his forehead. I had thrust my sword into his chest, yet here he was moments ago, walking amongst us.

Lena's face was crumpled as she shook her head back and forth. "I-I killed him! I didn't know...I didn't know..." Her chest was heaving—she was hyperventilating.

"Lena!" I damn near barked, grasping her face with my hands again. Her tearful eyes widened. "You didn't kill him. I did...remember?!"

She choked on a sob, her lip wobbling. "But...but—"

"No. I am the one who ended his life. I am the one responsible, not you."

"Lena, I need to heal you," Elowen said faintly, her tone nasally from crying. Her eyes were bright red, tears still slipping free.

Lena shook her head, and I dragged my thumb gently along her cheek, leaning in close to whisper in her ear, "Let her heal you, Flower."

Lena cried softly, eyes meeting mine for a moment, searching. Then she nodded, wincing as she tried to stand. I was there quickly, lifting her into my arms. She let out a faint whine, her adrenaline fading, the pain becoming more present.

Roland was behind us now, and I felt him stiffen. I didn't care if it made him upset that I was the one holding her. He was the one drunk, not keeping alert in unknown territory. I would reprimand him later.

As we turned, the crowd, humans and Warlocks alike, began to place three fingers on their chests. A symbol known to the people of Forsmont as respect.

"You can bring her to one of the changing rooms in the back. There are a few beds we use after shifting when we need rest," Dani expressed, voice shaking. I nodded, and Elowen followed behind me as we walked, the people splitting apart to let us through with ease.

Lena's eyes were heavy, but still, she gazed up at me as she rested her head on my chest.

"You amazed me out there," I whispered, not caring that Elowen and Dani were listening. "You are incredibly powerful. But more than that, you are brave. So fucking brave. You did what you had to do to save these people."

Her lips formed a small smile, and her eyes slowly fluttered shut, her head falling against my chest.

I halted. "Is she okay?!" I panicked, lightly caressing her cheek.

"Yes," Elowen said gently, touching my arm and motioning forward. "The use of that much magic has left her drained. She just needs rest."

I clenched my jaw and continued striding forward. My eyes continually darted to her chest, making sure I was seeing it rise and fall. When we reached the changing room, I carefully placed Lena on one of the beds. Elowen quickly rushed over to begin her healing.

"She will be asleep for a while," Elowen told me, her hands glowing as they trailed up and down her body.

"I don't mind staying."

She seemed puzzled as she studied me, and I realized this wasn't a normal response for a man who, as far as anyone else knew, hardly knew Lena.

"I...just let me know when she's awake," I mumbled.

Elowen's aqua eyes searched mine, and she nodded, resuming her work.

Dani studied me suspiciously, but I ignored her and exited the room. As I made my way down the corridor, I attempted to steady my breathing...attempted to steady my heart.

She jumped in front of me...willing to take that curse in place of me.

That's twice now. At least the first time, it was her friend. She knew she could stop her with her magic. But these creatures...she was willing to become one of them if it meant saving my life.

I stopped, steadying myself on the tent wall beside me.

I need to calm down.

How could she do such a thing? I wasn't about to yell at her, considering how injured she was. And I was amazed by her bravery...by her strength.

But I would *never* want her to risk herself for me. I had already lost her once, already suffered. I couldn't go through it again.

Elowen's mother...and Igon. It was clear the necromancer made a stop in Ames. Why were they so much different than the Undead we encountered on the road?

I wiped the sweat from my forehead and was just about to continue forward when Merrick emerged. I attempted to straighten myself, to look less unnerved. As if the Empath would fall for it.

We glared at each other in silence for a moment before Merrick's eyes softened.

"If the two of you wish to keep your history under wraps, you'll need to do a better job pretending like she means nothing more than an ally to you."

My eyes widened, my mouth drying. "You...you know?"

He nodded, his eyes going dark. "I put two and two together after Lena spoke of her miscarriage to the group." He slid his hands into his pockets. "I was confused as to why I could sense that you loved her when I read you back at the fort. It made no sense."

I chewed on my lip, and he continued, "But once I sensed your emotions as she told her story...that's when I knew. Knew you were Quill...were the love of her life."

As much as it horrified me to have someone know our secret, part of me also felt like a slight weight was lifted off my chest. I loosened a breath. "You can't tell anyone—"

"Yes, I know. She insisted the same thing."

I crossed my arms and rested my head against the wall.

Deep breaths.

Merrick's eyes remained dark. "Would you have loved her still?"

I tilted my head toward him, brows furrowed.

"Would you have loved her back then if she told you what she was?"

What would I have done if she told me she was a Mage? Would I have been disgusted by her? Would I have had her banished, or after the kill order was placed, have her murdered?

Would I have loved her still, despite it all?

My stare was unwavering as I replied quietly, "Nothing could've made me not love her."

And I knew as his eyes widened slightly, as they returned to an icy blue, he knew I was telling the truth.

I charged up to Leroy after I exited the changing area behind the main stage. "How did those creatures make it past your guards?" I snarled.

Leroy ran a hand through his golden hair, looking at Logan, then back at me. "They killed the guards. All of them."

I shook my head. "They could still be in your kingdom."

His face was weary, his eyes dropping to the ground. "I know...I know."

I chewed on the inside of my cheek, looking around at all the people standing about, debating if it was safer to go up or stay underground. "Well, for starters, we need to assign new guards. We need to reinforce the borders." My eyes trailed back to him. I had felt something off moments before the attack, and apparently,

Lena had too, according to Roland. "Lena gets a sense when those things are nearby. Once she is healed and feeling up to it, she can let us know if she feels anything...hopefully give us some peace of mind."

"You're making orders as if you're our king," Logan said with crossed arms.

My nostrils flared at his tone, but Leroy placed an arm on his shoulder. "Silas has great experience with running a kingdom. I am grateful for any help we can get." Leroy's gaze hardened on mine. "We need to meet with the council the moment she is awake."

It had been ten hours since Lena fell asleep. Her wounds had all been healed by Elowen after about three, and the healer nearly passed out herself, Edmund carrying her to a room they could share.

I was able to catch a few hours of sleep, but not uninterrupted. Every half hour, it seemed my eyes would find themselves open. Era slept beside me in one of those paid adult rooms, which were currently being overlooked by Warlocks.

One thing I hadn't done, that I needed to do, was speak with Roland. So, when I awoke the last time, I made my way to him.

I found him where I expected him to be: at Lena's bedside. She was still sleeping soundly as I entered the room, her copper waves spilling down her chest. Her skin was back to its beautiful porcelain; the only redness was the slight flushing to her cheeks and nose. The blood had been cleaned off her face and hands.

Roland looked over his shoulder, nodded to me, then glanced back at her, his chin resting in his palms.

"Any updates?" I asked as I went to stand beside him.

"None. We're just supposed to let her rest," he replied quietly.

Roland was never quiet, and I knew that meant one thing. "You feel guilty."

He sat upright, and his hazel eyes narrowed on me. "What?"

"You left her. You were drunk, not aware of your surroundings, and you left her. You must feel guilt."

"She needed backup," he gritted out. "And against those things? Humans are basically fucking useless. Even if I hadn't been drinking, I never would've guessed those things would be in here." He ran his hands through his brown hair. "Why do you care so much anyway, huh?"

Play it off.

I shrugged. "She could've died," I said simply. "And she saved my life."

"She has a tendency to do that for you, it seems," he mumbled, and before I could reply, he added, "You're saying you wouldn't have run to get help?"

I was seething with rage when he said he'd left her alone. Even more so when I realized they had been in one of those private rooms together. But I knew he was right. Having other magical beings as backup was what she would have needed.

"You did the best you could," I responded, crossing my arms and looking at Lena again.

Roland was quiet for a handful of moments. "Are you going to hate me for it forever?" he asked quietly.

My heartbeat picked up when he began to speak of our past, and my eyes shot to him. He was staring at his lap.

I don't hate you for it.

I wanted to say that...wanted to *feel* that. I wanted to be able to look at him without being reminded...

Fuck. I can't think about the past right now. Not ever.

Roland's hazel eyes slid to mine, pain laced in his irises, and my eyes darted away.

Leroy stepped inside, his hands nervously going inside his pockets. "We are so grateful for what you did...all of you. We've never had anything like that enter our territory, let alone so many. Our borders are being reinforced as we speak, stronger wards being put in place."

"How did this happen?" Roland questioned, turning in his seat to face him. "What the fuck were those things? Well, obviously, they were dead bodies from Ames."

"These creatures have intelligence," I responded grimly. "Unlike the Undead, who act like wild animals, these versions were smart, killing only enough to get through. As if they knew it would cause attention."

Leroy rested his back against the tent fabric. "They aren't quite like the Undead," he said gravely. "I have my theories." His blue eyes darted nervously between ours. "I think these puppets are Undead. But instead of half-lifted back to life... it's more. Enough to make them smart."

"Puppets?" Roland asked.

Leroy shrugged. "You heard the woman's voice. He was speaking through her, controlling her like a puppet." He loosened a sigh. "It's almost as if they are evolving."

"They're evolving..." I spoke. "Or their master is."

Leroy's gaze fixed on Lena, who still remained asleep. "We haven't had a necromancer around for hundreds of years...we need to locate and finish him before his creations end us all."

CHAPTER TWENTY-TWO

LENA

The last thing I remembered was looking up at Silas, my head lying against his chest, my body burning.

Now, my skin was smooth, and my body felt rested as I opened my eyes. A soft tune was audible—a piano.

I winced as I sat up, rubbing my eyes. I had no idea where I was, but from the looks of it, I was in some sort of dressing room.

The song was slow and ethereal, with a rhythm that ebbed and flowed. I stepped out of the bed, noting my ragged, blood-stained clothes, and pursued the sound of the music.

When I pulled a curtain open, leading me right to the main stage, I stilled once I noticed Roland sitting in front of a piano off to the side, his fingers dancing over the keys. The melody was melancholic...blue.

I stood there for a couple of minutes, studying him closely as he lost himself in the song. He was remarkably adept, no doubt.

When he played the final note, he released a sigh before jumping at the sound of my applause.

"You're awake," he said quietly, almost disbelieving.

"You play piano?!" I exclaimed, my clapping ceasing as I strode up beside him.

He gave a lazy grin, his hands going to his lap. "I am a man of many talents, but really, you're surprised I'm skilled with my fingers?"

I shook my head, biting my lip. "You flirt." I chuckled softly. "How long have I been out? Did anything else happen?" I glanced around. This place appeared completely empty, and the lack of Roland's music left an eerie silence.

"Just under twelve hours. It's almost noon," he answered, his eyes roaming down my body as he stood from the piano bench. "How do you feel? You're looking much better," he murmured, his hand brushing along my cheek.

"Elowen is a miracle worker." I smiled. "I feel fine now."

Physically fine. Mentally, I couldn't get the picture of Igon's corpse out of my head.

His hand continued to graze my cheek. "I'm...I'm sorry for leaving you," he whispered.

My brows went together. "Why are you sorry? I told you to." My hand squeezed his. "I needed help, Roland. And you got it."

His smile didn't reach his eyes, and I leaned in and kissed him softly. "Don't tell me you feel guilty," I murmured.

"What I feel like is useless." He kissed me back. "The help I brought didn't even matter. I should've had a fighting chance to protect you after how many years I have trained. I should've been able to do something."

I wrapped my arms around him, my head resting on his chest. "That is why this necromancer needs to be found. He'll wipe out humanity otherwise."

Roland nodded, his cheek resting on the top of my head as we held each other.

"How are the people?"

"Shaken up. No one has ever seen Undead like that before..." Roland shook his head, a sigh loosening from him as he leaned back. I angled my head up to look at him, and his hazel eyes slowly met mine. "You saved a lot of lives today, Lena."

I nibbled at my bottom lip. "They still got away...it's not like I eliminated them all."

Just as I was finishing my words, Silas strolled up the stage, his eyes widening as he beheld me.

"Hey," he said breathlessly.

I gave him a soft smile. "Hey."

Roland peered at him over his shoulder, both of us stepping out of our embrace. "You're back *again?*"

Silas cleared his throat, glowering at Roland before returning his gaze to me. "Leroy and the council wish to meet with us as soon as possible. Are you feeling up for it? If not, I can meet with them alone."

As if I'd let Silas do it by himself. "No, I'm up for it." My eyes drifted down to my blood-stained clothes. "I just need a change of clothes...and a shower, if that's alright?"

"Of course it's alright," Roland answered. He shot his eyes to Silas. "We'll head back to the inn. Where's this meeting being held?"

Silas crossed his arms. "A room in the castle," he stated blandly. "He only wished for Lena and me to be there."

231

Roland's brows scrunched, but he nodded. As I went to step, he held out his hand.

I gave him a smirk, not taking his hand. "I'm healed now. I'm not helpless."

Roland's grin grew. "Feisty Ginger Snap is back. Good, I missed her."

I showered quickly, and when I reentered my room, I was grateful to see that Roland had left a meal for me on my nightstand. I braided my hair and tossed on a blouse, leather bottoms, and the boots I wore on the road. I didn't know if it was appropriate to bring weapons, but I kept a dagger in my boot.

After inhaling the sandwich Roland left me, I exited my room. Merrick was standing just beside my door, arms crossed and silver hair spilling over his shoulder.

"Whatchya doin'?" I asked, eyes flickering to see if anyone else was standing nearby.

He leaned off the wall. "Just checking on you. That was…" He shook his head. "Seeing Heildee, then Igon like that—"

I sucked in a breath, eyes dropping to the ground.

Merrick cursed. "I'm sorry. I didn't mean to bring it up."

"Don't be sorry." My eyes met his darkened ones. "I…I wish to bury him if they haven't disposed of his body yet. He deserves a resting place."

Merrick smiled gently. "We already did. We can visit him after this meeting, if you'd like."

I bit my quivering lip, nodding as my blurred vision fell to the ground. "How's Elowen?" I asked, changing the subject.

He shook his head slowly, teeth dragging through his lip ring. "After she woke, she couldn't stop crying. Edmund has been with her ever since, locked in their room."

"I suppose I'm just glad no one died." I winced. "Well, I suppose the guards did..." I sighed, brushing my loose hair behind my ear and shaking my head in disgust. "The Lord of the Shadows, this necromancer, really has an ego, doesn't he?"

Merrick scoffed, and we started our walk to Leroy's castle. "Silas mentioned Leroy only wished for you two at the meeting."

I pushed open the door to the inn, and the hot, humid air was an unpleasant wave. The sky was once again grey, and it appeared it had rained during the time I'd slept. "He wishes for me to bring up my past with Silas as a way to sway the council."

Merrick's head swung to me. "Does Silas know?"

I gave him a pained expression. "No."

"I should be there too. Considering I know everything. Perhaps if I can sense their emotions, I can help us say the right things."

I gave him a grateful nod. "I think that's a great idea."

When we rounded a corner, the castle just steps away, I noticed a dark-skinned woman with burgundy hair standing beside the door, Her arms were crossed, a sword on her back. Her blue eyes widened as she saw us.

"Taira." Merrick inclined his head.

"Merrick." She returned the gesture, her gaze flitting to mine. "Silas is already inside." She stepped aside, opening the door for us.

I gave her a small smile before walking in, Merrick in tow, and then we followed the woman as she led us up many stairs. Silas was perched outside of a set of doors, tapping his foot impatiently as he waited to be allowed entry. His eyes slid to mine, then to Merrick's.

"Leroy only wanted us two," Silas stated.

"It'll be fine with Merrick. I'm sure of it," I responded, just as Silas leaned off the wall and Taira opened the large doors. We filtered in.

Silas, Merrick, and I stood in front of the leading council in Forsmont, all sitting before a large, C-shaped table. Light filtered in through the giant glass windows along the perimeter of the room, and I could see the large balcony outside of them, soldiers perched on it, keeping watch.

Leroy was sitting in the far left seat, frowning as his eyes went to Merrick. To his side was a woman with greying brown hair, tied in an updo, and next to her was a man as old as Igon had been. Beside him was a man with copper hair like mine, freckles dusting his nose, ochre eyes studying us with a displeased glare. Then it was two more women, one with long, lilac hair and big blue eyes, and one with hair as dark as Silas's, and slanted, dark eyes to match.

All Warlocks. Their pupilless gazes roved around us.

The Forsmontian King cleared his throat. "Silas La'Rune, Lena Daelyra, and Merrick Astair," he declared, gesturing to his companions. "Meet Aspen, Keir, Evander, Odelia, and Harumi."

Silas inclined his head, and Merrick and I followed his lead. "Thank you for meeting with us," he said.

"Bring in their friends," Keir, the older man with silver hair, said to Leroy. "We wish to hear from them all."

"But Keir, I—"

Evander, the copper-haired male, interrupted. "We wish to hear from all the Mages that traveled with him. Not just the one

234

wrapped around his finger." His following sneer was directed at me.

Leroy shot me a worried glance. I shook my head ever so slightly, and I could only hope he would keep my and Silas's secret in the presence of our friends.

"Very well," the King grumbled. "Taira, will you fetch the rest of their group?"

"Have them wait outside until the rest arrive," Harumi, the dark-haired female, ordered, no compassion on her face.

I stifled a groan of irritation as we were once again led out of the room, forced to stand out in the hallway. Silas's jaw was clenched, his eyes staring off into the distance, Merrick scuffing his boots on the floor.

"Well, what do you think, Silas?" Merrick asked after a beat. "Do you think they'll join our cause?"

His jaw ticked as he shrugged. "No idea. However, after witnessing what happened at The Freak Show, I don't see how they couldn't. We have two enemies against us...it would be foolish to not join forces."

We stood there awkwardly in silence for the fifteen or so minutes it took to get Viola, Elowen, Edmund, Roland, Hendry, and Erabella into this room with us.

Dani was with them this time, in male form. He shot me a weak smile. "Figured it would be good if I was here to vouch for you guys."

I gave him a grateful nod, then reentered the large room with my friends.

The council quieted the moment we entered, eyes scanning us with what appeared like disapproval. Dani went to stand by his brother.

Elowen was nervously chewing on her lip as she surveyed the six Warlocks before us.

"Why is it that after how many centuries of animosity, the Mages wish to ally with the Warlocks?" Odelia, the young woman with lilac hair questioned.

Keir glared at Silas. "The more important question is why are Mages traveling with the Slayer of Witches?"

I shifted my gaze to the Prince. He kept his chin lifted as he returned the glare.

"Silas is on our side," I articulated.

"Interesting," Evander drawled. "You don't call him Your Majesty."

"He isn't our King," Viola retorted, and Silas balled his hands into fists. The brown-eyed Warlock caught his body language.

"Hm..." Evander's smile grew cruel. "Does the disrespect bother you, Witch Slayer?"

I went to speak, but Silas spoke first. "The truth is not disrespectful. I am not their prince or king, nor do I wish to be."

Harumi scoffed. "Well, your father certainly does. He has tried everything besides outright war to get us to kneel before him. Destroying our trade routes was especially a nuisance."

"My father and I have different aspirations."

"And what are yours?" Aspen, the woman beside Leroy, pressed. "I can't imagine someone whose life has been dedicated to genocide has varying goals."

"The Prince has dedicated his life to bettering our kingdom," Era said with a bite to her tone. "He isn't a monster."

To that, every member of the council, aside from Leroy, broke out in laughter. Hendry and Edmund were trying their best to keep their composure, and when Era went to speak again, Silas's fingertips brushed hers, a silent message not to bother. Her gaze went to his, their small moment of intimacy calming her nerves.

I hated it. Or, rather, hated that I hated it.

"Nothing you claim will ever get us to trust a La'Rune. Or to join whatever cause you're against," Evander replied.

"Surely you know there is a necromancer in Tovagoth, considering the tragedy that occurred last night," I redirected.

Keir shot his gaze to me. "We aren't fools." His voice was grave as he tapped his fingers along the tabletop. "We are aware of the threat now."

"It seems the Undead are just now making their way south on the continent. The necromancer must be residing somewhere up north," I insisted. "Defeating Ulric La'Rune is just a small part of this alliance. What we are up against...if we fail...it would cost everything."

Keir's jaw flexed. "According to Leroy, you have not seen Undead quite like the ones from last night, correct?"

"We have not," Silas confirmed grimly. "It has always been the erratic ones, the ones that travel in groups. It appeared like the necromancer was speaking through one of them. He must be evolving, or his power must be growing."

Merrick spoke next. "And now that he can raise animals from the dead and command them the same, who knows how powerful he is?"

Merrick's eyes widened the moment the last of his words came out. I swore.

"Those were not animals you saw," Leroy gritted out. "We have had handfuls of our kind go missing over the past few months. Only magical beings can become Undead. Fuck."

I should've guessed that. Those weren't animals turned Undead that attacked on our way to Mount Rozavar, but Warlocks.

"Mages and Warlocks having to hide who they are makes it nearly impossible to band together to take on this threat. And it's the only thing that will be able to stop whoever this monster is," I expressed.

Evander scoffed, crossing his arms as he leaned back in his chair. His eyes slid to Silas. "Why haven't you gone to your father about this revelation? This grand idea of recruiting the kinds you have slaughtered?"

"Because," I answered for him, "no Mage would ever join forces with Ulric. Not after all the people he has killed."

"And the Prince hasn't killed our people?" Harumi retorted.

I inhaled sharply, and just as I was about to say, *'fuck it,'* Silas spoke.

"I regret what I have done."

My eyes shifted to his golden ones, pain shining in his gaze as he looked at each member of the council.

"But it was never a choice. I *never* had a choice." He glanced at Elowen, then at me, where his eyes stayed. "If it weren't for their kindness, Edmund would be dead. I owe a debt for that alone." His eyes trailed to Harumi, whose scowl lessened. "But it was that kindness, in spite of us killing their people—their families—that made me realize I was wrong.

"I do not wish to be High King. I do not wish to eradicate your people—not anymore. I only wish to rid my kingdom of my father and get rid of the necromancer plaguing our continent."

The council was silent for many moments, absorbing all of what the Prince had said. "What is your plan?" Aspen asked lowly.

"Ally with the southern kingdoms, the ones wishing to remain independent." His gaze shifted to me as if questioning whether or not he should mention my own plan. So, I spoke for him.

"We had a powerful seer in our village. He told me to find Oquerene. I don't know where it is, but his brother told me of Nereida, told me that more Mages should reside there and that if there is any hope of finding Oquerene, it is there we must go."

"Oquerene...a mere whisper among campfires growing up," Aspen muttered. "So, you wish to rally your people to join forces with the Prince?"

"Yes."

"And what of your kill order?" Odelia pressed.

"It will be lifted the moment I am in power," Silas promised. "And Mages will be able to live freely in our lands, should they wish. Your kind, too."

Odelia blinked as if she couldn't believe what she heard.

"And what if you get the throne and change your mind?" Harumi asked. "What keeps you to your word?"

"I have thrown away everything for this. Is that not enough proof?"

"You could always change your mind. Play the part that you did all this to gain information. Play it off."

It was an idea I had thought of many times.

Silas cocked his head toward Merrick. "Have the Empath tell you my intentions."

I looked over at Merrick, his eyes already darkened as he had been reading Silas this entire time. "He tells the truth."

Keir's pupilless gaze hardened on mine. "Is it true? What your seer said of your Soul-Tie?"

My stomach fell to the floor as each of my friends' heads turned to me.

"Is that the reason—"

"It's irrelevant," I interrupted nervously.

Keir contemplated for a moment, and just as he went to speak, horns blared from outside. My head whirled, and I rushed to one of the tall windows in the room to see what was happening. Silas was on my heel, looking over my head.

Silas swore, angling his body toward the council. "You...you didn't summon Otacia, did you?"

Leroy gaped at Keir, who quickly stood from his seat. "Keir...you summoned the Otacians?"

The older Warlock rose from his chair, eyes widening. "I have no idea why they've come," he breathed.

"Are they here to conquer?" Hendry asked Silas, rushing to another window, mismatched eyes broadening at the sight before us. People in the town were scrambling, soldiers rushing toward the front gates.

"The King had plans to take over Forsmont," Silas said quietly, the room going deadly quiet. "But it wasn't supposed to go into effect for another year..."

"Perhaps they seek alliance?" Edmund offered.

Roland shook his head, eyes narrowed as he scanned the outside. "Otacia's number far supersedes that of Forsmont. If anything, they would be heading to Faltrun if they wished for an ally."

I turned my gaze back to the troops rushing toward the entrance.

"How many?" Erabella panicked.

"Too many..." Viola responded, shaking her head slowly. "At least a couple thousand."

Merrick swore, and Elowen squeezed closer to Edmund. "We can't leave them," Elowen said to Silas quietly as she stared out the window.

He frowned. "What—"

"The people here. We cannot let Otacia take over." Her turquoise gaze remained pinned to Silas. "I know those men are your people, Your Majesty," she continued, "but if what you say is true, if we magic folk are to be your allies, then we are your people, too."

Silas blinked, the only sign he was stunned by Elowen referring to him as Your Majesty, not even Your Highness, which was his technical title.

Silas's eyes drifted over the council members, who now all stood, examining the Prince in question.

He bowed slightly. "I will stand by Forsmont."

CHAPTER TWENTY-THREE

MERRICK

A handful of the Forsmontian guard rushed to the castle's balcony, readying their bows, and Hendry joined them. Roland and Edmund had rushed to the front of the castle along with Silas, Lena, and Viola to fight at ground level. Elowen was also stationed down below, ready to heal anyone who needed it.

Era stood, chest rising and falling as she covered her mouth, staring out one of the large glass windows. Silas had ordered her to remain inside.

"Era," I said softly as I tied back my hair. "You ready for some more practice?"

She chewed on her lip, glancing out at the impending army. "Those are my people," she said quietly. "What kind of princess kills her own soldiers?"

I gently grasped her shoulder. "I think instead you should be asking yourself, what kind of soldiers would harm their own princess?"

She studied me with uncertainty, and my hand slid down her arm before holding hers I read her.

"I won't force you to do something you're uncomfortable with. Ever." I squeezed her palm as tears filled her eyes. "If you do not wish to fight, find somewhere safe in the center of the castle and wait."

Leroy rushed forward, ready to descend the steps. "You will not fight, and that's an order!" he shouted at Emma.

She trudged along anyway. "I will defend my kingdom! I will not sit back when my power could be of help."

Leroy halted on the steps, his gaze agonized as he took her in. "The children need you, Emma."

Her lip trembled, but she kept her chin high. "If the kingdom falls, it won't matter, and you know it," she whispered.

"I'm fighting too!" Quin announced as he began following them.

Both parents turned around and said, "No!"

"You need to keep your siblings safe," I interjected, and Quin regarded me with widened eyes. "You're the best person to defend them if it came down to it."

I thought of my own sibling. Elowen would be safe at the bottom of the castle.

She had to be.

Quin blinked, then nodded, following his parents' orders to stay back.

I turned back to Era. "Why don't you stay with them?" I offered, just as a loud boom filled my senses, causing the building to rattle and us all to stumble. I grasped Era's arms before she could fall.

"Fuck! They brought catapults," a guard grumbled. Tears spilled down Era's cheeks.

"Go," I insisted. "Go hide."

Her lip wobbled, and she nodded, escaping somewhere safe.

I rushed out to the balcony, witnessing an influx of Otacians flood in from the damage they caused to the front gate.

Thousands. *Thousands.*

They planned to overthrow this place.

I held my bow, loosening a breath and closing my eyes as I focused my ice magic on the enchanted weapon. I withdrew an arrow from my quiver, aimed my bow, and took a steadying breath as I aimed for one soldier, then another. Blessedly, this castle was stocked with arrows. So long as they were shot through my bow, ice would encapsulate the tips, making the shot more damaging.

I struck through one, then another, then another. But still, it was hardly a dent in the amount that had come rushing forward.

I gasped as I witnessed Warlocks begin to shift, turning into large mountain lions. Hundreds. They rushed for the surplus of soldiers, their large jaws closing around their torsos, their heads. Some had already been impaled with swords, shifting back into their regular forms before falling limp on the ground.

Regardless of who won this battle, it would be a blood bath.

Taira ran up beside me just as I fired my arrow. "What elemental magic have you acquired?" she asked quickly.

"Only ice."

She nodded. "Same." Her blue eyes slid down to the slaughter below. "I'm going down there. You should come with me. There are still plenty of soldiers that have not made it through their forced entry. If we freeze the hole, we may be able to buy ourselves time to regroup."

"Just the two of us?" I asked nervously. Lena had ice, too, but as I glanced down, my friend was wrapped in fire, shooting her flames at the soldiers who advanced.

Taira's chest rose and fell. "It's our only chance."

I slung my bow back over my shoulder and agreed. I nudged Hendry just as he lowered his bow, his mismatched eyes narrowing at me.

"If Era comes out, let her know I'm down there. In case she's looking for me."

Hendry nodded, and I rushed down the steps with Taira. Already injured Forsmontian soldiers were stumbling in, wishing to be treated by my sister. Sweat dripped down Elowen's forehead as she hurried to heal them. As gifted as my sister was, her magic could still be drained as any Mages' could.

I can't worry about that right now.

I bolted to where Edmund and Roland were fighting two Otacian men, and I shot my arm forward, freezing the one in front of Edmund completely, just as Taira shot an ice bolt right into the other's eyeball. He fell back, shrieking in agony as his face dripped red.

"Holy fuck," Roland respired.

Edmund's head shot toward mine. "Thanks, man!"

I offered him a curt nod and resumed my assault, willing the frigid magic to course into my veins. Anytime I used my ice, I thought of my mother. I thought of her final years of life...of how miserable she was. I thought of how skinny she became, having no will to eat.

I thought of the moment I found her body hanging still with a noose tied around her neck.

I allowed that sorrow to run through me, using it as fuel. I bellowed as I struck.

One. Three. Ten. Twenty-four. Thirty-seven.

I killed and killed and killed, and just as Silas had said before, I did it without remorse. I did it to protect. I did it to preserve. Shutting my gift off from feeling the onslaught of horrific emotions around me became easy as I used all my power for my ice.

Taira and I were breathing heavily, weakened from such high magic usage. But we were reaching the opening the Otacians had created, where their soldiers continued to flood in.

"We need to take out the catapult," Taira panted.

My eyes darted to Lena, who was fighting off soldiers with grace...and with rage. She engulfed one after another in flame, their screeches from their burning skin causing half their men to flee and half to charge for her.

Fuck me and my gift that I couldn't seem to get control of. My eyes darted to Silas, whose emotions began to bleed into mine. He was panting heavily...eyes widening at the burning soldiers.

I felt like I was going to vomit. I felt panic and terror flood through me like never before as I clutched my chest.

The Prince was having a panic attack, and his emotions were giving me one as well.

Lena's eyes flashed to his, sensing his unease. She rushed toward him, electrocuting those that separated them.

"Merrick!" Taira wailed just as an Otacian was about to behead me. She was too preoccupied with the one in front of her and couldn't stop the impending blow coming my way.

There was no time. Not even to use a forcefield.

This was it. I was dead.

My eyes squeezed shut, but the sound of an arrow whizzing by, followed by a grunt, had my eyes shooting open. The man before me fell with a thud, and when I whirled at the castle balcony, I saw her.

Erabella. She lowered her bow, panting heavily.

The Otacian Princess came out to fight after all.

And she saved my life.

There was no time for me to shoot her a smile. I whirled my head back and continued killing my way through.

CHAPTER TWENTY-FOUR

SILAS

One by one, I struck my men. Men I had trained alongside, men I had trained myself. The looks of respect and admiration were no longer present on any of their faces as they aimed to strike me down.

It would appear the King did not wish to take me prisoner.

I killed, just like I always had. It was the one thing at which I excelled. However, this slaughter didn't bring me joy. It didn't give me release. No...it just made me realize how my father's beliefs had affected our people. How deeply rooted their fear was.

Warlocks all around me fought against my kingdom alongside the Forsmontian soldiers, who at first were in shock that they had been living amongst them but then quickly focused on the battle at hand.

It was especially endearing seeing Leroy and Emma fight alongside one another. Leroy, a golden mountain lion, and Emma, a brown one. A King and Queen fighting to protect their home, protect their kind, and their human soldiers fighting along with them.

I was grateful my father's ideologies had not affected the people of Forsmont as they had our own.

I was faintly aware of Merrick and Taira to my right, along with Roland and Edmund. While there had already been casualties, Otacian and Forsmontian alike, I was grateful my friends were still alive.

I was fighting with proficiency, just as I always had, until I smelled it.

Burning flesh.

Bright light caught my attention, and when I shifted, I witnessed Lena, once again encased in that glowing flame of hers.

I knew, at least at this point, she was okay. She hadn't overused her magic just yet.

But the sound of the screams and howls of those burning, the scent of scorching skin, and seeing her like this...it was too much.

It was too much.

I couldn't breathe. I couldn't think. Not when it was bringing me back to the worst moment of my life.

It was like I was back in her cottage, back in her room. It was like I was witnessing her wrapped in flame—dying, just as I thought she had five years ago.

I was going to be sick. I was going to faint.

As if sensing my panic, Lena turned, worried green eyes settling on me.

She rushed toward me, grunting as she shot her hand forward, electrocuting the men who separated us—the men who were attempting to harm me.

I couldn't move. Why couldn't I move?

When Lena reached me, she let her flames dissipate before raising her arms, creating an ice wall around the two of us, trapping us inside.

"What's wrong?!" she panicked, eyes darting around my body. "Are you hurt?!"

"I-I just need a minute," I gasped.

"We don't have a minute." Her hand caressed my cheek, her palm hot but not unpleasant. "Silas, we can do this," she insisted, even as her voice shook. "You are the best fighter I've ever seen. I know killing your own must be hard, but—"

"It isn't about the men!" I growled, and Lena flinched. I swallowed, my face falling. "I struggle being around fire...around burned bodies. I struggle with the smell..."

Gods, I am fucking pathetic.

Lena's face instantly changed, understanding etched in her features. "Okay," she said softly. "I won't use the fire then. I promise."

I shook my head. "It's our best shot at winning—"

"I don't care. I have other magic. I'll use it."

Without giving me time to respond, she melted our barrier, firing electricity at the Otacians who had surrounded us with just the slightest movement of her hand.

Blue sparks shot around us in a ring, the soldiers surrounding us dropping to the ground and convulsing as her magic touched them.

Lena smiled at me, and it was the most beautiful sight I'd ever seen.

"We're alive, Silas," she breathed.

And then she ran, gracefully protecting those who fought on our side.

I hated to admit it, but once there was no flame and smoke, I fought better. I was focused.

Lena had encapsulated the three catapults my kingdom had brought in ice, successfully disabling them. Taira and Merrick had frozen the forced entryway, allowing the Forsmontians stationed on the walls to focus their attention on those on the outside while we focused on those on the inside. I wasn't sure of the duration of the battle so far—you tend to lose track of time when you're fighting for your life.

There still had to be a couple hundred Otacians inside Forsmont. While we humans had killed plenty, the few Mages and the hundreds of Warlocks were who made the biggest difference in this battle.

We were winning.

Were.

It happened so quickly. One moment, Emma was a lion, ripping the heads off of the men threatening her home and her family. The next, a soldier withdrew a vial, dotting a substance on his palm before blowing the purple dust at Emma. Whatever it was, it instantly shrank her body back into its normal form.

Leroy roared, but there was nothing he could do—nothing *anyone* could do, as the Otacian soldier lifted his sword and swung, cutting Emma's head clean off of her body.

No.

Leroy released a gut-wrenching bellow just as Emma's head tumbled to the ground, charging for the man who killed his wife. But the soldiers around him were prepared—I could see the handful of them had those vials waiting, secured at their sides.

What the fuck do they have?

Rage overcame me, and I rushed forward, fending off the various Otacians that swung their weapons at me.

This man had five children and was now without his partner. I could not let his kids lose their father, too.

"LEROY!" I shouted. His lion head snapped to me, his turmoil-ridden, pupilless eyes burning into mine. I impaled a man before me. "STOP! THEY CAN TAKE YOUR MAGIC!"

His eyes darted to the soldiers surrounding him, now noticing what was in all of their grasps.

A sword slashed my arm, and I gasped as I fell back.

When I locked eyes with the person who injured me, I recognized him.

Emerson. Finnan's father.

"You are a disgrace to your kingdom!" he spat. "Betraying your own kind to side with the witches!"

I held my gushing wound for a moment before wincing and readying my sword. "I am doing what is right," I growled. "For once in my miserable life."

His eyes welled with tears. "Was it right killing Finnan?!"

My lip trembled, only for a second. We raised our weapons but were both rendered frozen when Lena's wail filled the air. We whirled toward the sound, and I loosened a breath at the sight of her.

Electricity crept up both of her arms and legs, surrounding her hair—it was everywhere. The lighting was an array of blues as it sparked around her.

She looked otherworldly, more powerful than anything I'd ever seen, as she glared at our enemies.

She stared at the men surrounding Leroy, but only for a moment before she unleashed her lightning upon every one of them.

She flung her hands out, and rings of electricity went around each of their throats.

They screamed. They cried. They went to tug at their collars made of lightning, but it was no use. They would be shocked to death if they touched it. They weren't going anywhere.

Lena stared at the men with a curled lip before her eyes darted to Leroy. I then understood what she was doing.

These were his kills.

One by one, Leroy tore their heads off, Lena releasing their electric collars only seconds before Leroy's jaw was around their skulls.

Emerson trembled before me. "This is what you support?!"

"You beheaded his wife!" I hissed. "You came here and attacked!"

Emerson's panicked look went back to the Warlock, who was on the last head. "Retreat," I snarled. "Take what is left of your men and go."

He hesitated, breathing heavily before he gave me a hateful glare. Ultimately, he conceded, yelling, "FALL BACK!"

I glared at Emerson in contempt as he rushed away. I hated that I had killed his son, but he and my father were the ones who allowed his child into battle and who put him up against me. What did they expect to happen?

The remaining soldiers from the outside had managed to break the ice block enough for soldiers to escape. Leroy was still blood-hungry, still full of rage, running after and killing any Otacians he could before they had all fled the kingdom.

CHAPTER TWENTY-FIVE
LENA

The aftermath of a battle was something I never would grow used to. The smell of blood and death surrounded me, and I took a steadying breath as I willed my electricity down.

After Leroy had chased out the last of them, he slowly turned, shifting back into his human form.

As he faced his kingdom, everyone frozen as they stared at him, his lip trembled as he whispered, *"Revelare."*

His glamour faded, his pointed ears and milky-blue eyes on display for the whole kingdom to see. But just like at The Freak Show, the residents showed no disgust, no fear as they held three fingers to their hearts.

Leroy didn't address his people, didn't say anything as he wandered back inside his castle.

My eyes slowly slid to what remained of Emma's head, and I squeezed them shut as I felt the burning pain behind them.

I never got to meet her.

When I opened them, I caught sight of Elowen, Taira, and Viola—now shifted back to Mage form—rushing to the injured soldiers, quickly working on their injuries. The human healers began working on those with lesser wounds.

Merrick was hurrying into the castle.

I needed to be healing people as well. My magic was significantly weakened; I could feel it, but I could still offer my services.

I quickly caught sight of Silas, whose blood was spilling on the ground beneath him as he clutched his arm.

I hurried to him. "You're bleeding." I gripped his arm, examining the wound. I swore colorfully as I took in the nasty gash, then looked him in the eye. "We need to heal this."

Silas frowned as he attempted to tug his arm away. "I'll be fine," he snapped.

Oh, so we're playing this game.

I nodded to a bench a few feet away. "Sit your ass down, Your Highness."

He was hurt, which I had learned meant he would be stubborn. He gave me a cruel smile. "Make me."

"You think I'm not capable of doing so?"

He narrowed his eyes at me, and I squeezed his arm tighter, causing him to hiss.

"Sit."

He hesitated, then huffed as he plopped himself down, removing his vambraces and gloves.

"We need to take off your shirt—"

"No," he said sharply as he removed his pauldron. "My shirt stays on."

I stared at him momentarily, and he refused to meet my eyes.

I was confused, wanting an explanation, but I was too exhausted to argue. "Then we need to cut off the sleeve."

He nodded, looking at the ground as I pulled out my dagger and cut away the material on his shoulder.

I pulled the bloodied rags off, discarding them on the ground for now, and swore when I examined the laceration that trailed from his bicep down half of his forearm. If magic were not here, he would need plenty of stitches. Thank the Gods, no arteries were hit.

I sat beside him on the bench, then closed my palm over his open wound. He sucked in a breath at the pain.

"I'm sorry," I whispered. A healing golden glow began emitting from my palm. First, I needed to repair any muscle that had been severed. Then, I could roam my hand over the rest of the wound to heal it entirely.

Silas just sat in silence, watching the ground. The sounds surrounding us were horrid...sobbing, groaning. Who would've guessed the joyful kingdom we arrived in would be like this just a few days later?

"I know that couldn't have been easy for you," I said softly.

His breathing was uneven. "I knew them all, some closely." He winced as I moved my grip upward. "I led them countless times, fought beside them..."

'None of them joined me' was left unspoken.

"Your father instilled so much fear in them, probably even more so after you left. I'm sure most wished to follow you."

"If that were the case, at least some of them would have joined us," he muttered. "Even one of them."

He was weary, so incredibly fatigued, emotionally and physically. I thought back to the panic in his eyes before I froze a wall around us...before I ceased my fire usage.

That trauma, that stress...it was caused by me. By my death. I knew it.

"Silas?"

He angled his head toward me, his golden eyes glassy and wholly drained. "If you hadn't been there with my people in Ames," I said carefully, "I do not believe any of them would have allowed us to save Edmund. I believe every one of my people would be dead."

His eyes bounced between mine, and I took my free hand and gently slid it against his shoulder. "And I don't think that would be because I wasn't a leader worth following. Sometimes, the situation is...just what it is. And if it wasn't for our history..." I chewed on my lip, then shook my head. "Your people will come around. I'm sure of it."

He sighed softly, then averted his gaze. I healed him in silence for a few more moments.

"You saved Leroy," I said quietly.

He shook his head slowly. "There's no saving him from this loss."

I stiffened, my heart sinking at the depleted look on Silas's face. He'd suffered this loss before and knew all it entailed.

I did this to him.

Just as I went to express regret for all I'd put him through, he turned his head to me. "You hold so much power," he breathed.

I wasn't expecting that response. I blinked. "My magic surfaced when I was incredibly young. I've always felt it, reserved in me like water behind a dam. I think after so many years, I've learned how to hold it in without it harming me." I swallowed. "On the flip side, however, when I do fully let it out, it can be hard to reel it back."

"Is it like that for everyone?"

My eyes went to the ground. "Everything has a cost, and magic always has a price. I do feel mine is...wilder than others. More untamed."

When I met his eyes, my brows raised when I noticed no judgment in his stare.

Slightly, ever so slightly, did the corner of his mouth raise. "That is no surprise. You've always been a spitfire, Flower."

The beating in my chest skipped, my cheeks heating in response to my nickname.

"What was that powder they blew?" I asked.

Silas's jaw clicked, his face heating. "It seems to be a poison of some sort. It must be new, as I have never seen it before."

My eyes nervously went to his wound, now almost healed. "We can't seem to catch a break," I murmured.

Looking down at his arm, Silas pulled away. "That's good enough," he insisted before standing. "Go heal those who need it more."

"I'm almost done—"

He didn't listen; he just began walking toward the castle.

I looked down, studying the blood that covered my hand. His blood.

I knew this external wound did not compare to the one on his inside. I wished I could heal that, too.

After seven hours of constant healing, I was thoroughly spent. I washed all the blood, dirt, and sweat off of my body, crying silently in the shower as I recalled the faces of all the people I had killed.

I knew they were trying to slaughter me, slaughter innocents. But I couldn't help but think of who they may have been outside of the battlefield. They had families. Friends. Perhaps even lovers or children. And I took them from this world.

What gave any of us the right?

I didn't regret it. It had to be done. But I despised that this was my life now. Detested that this was our reality.

As I was squeezing my hair dry, a robe tied around my body, a knock sounded at my door. When I opened it, I was met with tired, hazel eyes.

We didn't speak. Roland just shut the door behind him, eyes lowering as he captured my lips with his. I had spoken with him briefly after the battle, healing a slash in his leg.

We both needed this release...both needed to feel good.

He tore his shirt off, and I grasped his cock as his pants and undergarments fell to the ground. He moaned into my mouth, his fingers untying my robe. When the fabric pooled on the floor, he lifted me by my ass, slamming me against the wall as he devoured my neck.

"Roland," I whispered, and I let out a soft cry as he thrust his thick length inside of me.

"I want to forget today happened," he murmured, the greens in his eyes shining as he stared at me. "Even if it's only for a few moments."

I slid my thumb along his cheek before resting my forehead against his. "Then let's forget," I whispered.

And there was nothing but the sound of skin slapping skin and wild, breathy moans as Roland fucked me against the wall.

CHAPTER TWENTY-SIX
SILAS

L eroy was hunched over, a drink in hand and eyes unfocused as he sat before the fireplace when I entered his study.

I knew how he was feeling. Exactly how. I opened and closed my hands at my sides a few times, unsure if I should even attempt to console him.

Leroy, in the short time I'd known him, had been friendly. Upbeat. Hopeful. I saw no hint of that man now.

And I related.

I slowly made my way to his side, sitting in the armchair beside him. The flames before him reflected in his vacant eyes.

I didn't know if he noticed me sitting next to him until he spoke, his voice a broken whisper as he said, "I'm lost."

My eyebrows raised, shocked that the Warlock was speaking to me about his feelings. Then again, I had purposely come to find him to see how he was doing. I felt a burning sensation behind my eyes and quickly inhaled, caressing my thighs to distract myself. I didn't cry. Not anymore.

But in Leroy, in his pain, I saw myself.

"The love of my life died five years ago," I said solemnly, and Leroy's saddened gaze found mine, his eyebrows drawn together. "I blamed myself for the longest time. Her death appeared to be arson, and it happened just days after my mother's passing."

My eyes slid to the fire before me. "I still remember the feeling. I still remember the smell of her burnt house and the sight of her lifeless body. She was in my arms, in my embrace, only hours prior. I couldn't understand how so much could change so quickly, how my life could fall apart so fast."

I turned to him, tears sliding down his tired face. "We believed Mages to be responsible for both her and my mother's deaths. I let that information destroy me. Let the pain turn me into someone I didn't recognize. Someone I hated."

I took in a shaky breath. I had never spoken about this to anyone.

"I did her a disservice by becoming the man I am today. Don't let it happen to you."

I stood, my heartbeat pounding rapidly from speaking about my emotions. But as I moved to leave, Leroy grasped my wrist.

"Your reputation is less than sparkling," he said. "But the man you showed me today? Fighting against your kingdom, your home, and surely some of your friends to fight alongside innocents? *That* is a man worth following. A man I am sure the love of your life would be proud of."

The burning now spread to my throat. I bit down on my lip, breathing slowly, and gave him a thankful nod.

He released my wrist, eyes going back to the fire. I wished I could be more consoling. Wished I could offer more help.

Instead, I left a large portion of our remaining gold on his kitchen table as I exited his study. I still admired how humble he lived, how the part of the castle that was his home was so modest.

Quin was sitting on the floor, holding a doll for his little sisters, his eyes just as lost as his father's.

He glanced up at me as I was getting ready to walk out. "You lost your mom too, haven't you?" he asked quietly.

He looked so broken...and in him, I saw myself, too. It was like this war was taking my demons and shoving them right in my face.

I nodded. "I did."

His jaw flexed. Leroy's second youngest child, Phoebe, gazed at me with big eyes. She gave me a toothy grin, completely unaware of the loss she had just experienced.

Fuck, it gave me another pang in my chest. "I know how painful it is," I said gently. "How unfair it is."

The door cracked open, and Dani stepped in, carrying Leroy's youngest baby against her chest. Dani's tearful eyes met mine.

"Where's mommy?" their other little girl, Sera, asked. "Why are you crying, Auntie Dani? Does your tummy hurt?"

I turned to Quin, clasping his shoulder. "I can't bring your mother back. I wish I could," I said quietly. "But I promise you, when this war ends, you and your family will never have to hide who you are again. You will know no fear. You will be safe."

Quin's face crumpled, and I couldn't take anymore. I passed Dani, unable to meet her eyes, and left their residence.

Our group was quiet as we readied the horses the following morning. While this battle was technically a win, it was impossible not to feel the weight of all the losses that accompanied it.

We needed to get to Faltrun and gather their support as soon as possible.

Era was especially quiet that evening, and she and I turned in early, holding each other as we fell asleep. With each passing day, it was harder and harder to be intimate with her. Between the stress and Lena's presence, I found myself avoiding my wife's touch and instead finishing myself in the shower.

I felt terrible about it.

My armor was on, and I was standing alone by Sable as he hydrated. I heard the crunching of the twigs and turned to see Dani staring at me with crossed arms and a frown on her face. She was glamoured to appear human.

Her eyes filled with more tears. "Did you mean what you said yesterday? To Quin?"

My brows drew together, and my voice was soft as I replied, "I'd never lie about something like that."

Her lip wobbled, and she exhaled, her hands falling to her sides. "I'm coming with you."

I recoiled. "What?"

"Leroy begged me to, and after seeing how you were with Quin..." She shook her head, then raised her chin. "You *are* a leader worth following."

The same thing Leroy said to me he must've said to Dani.

"What about the children?" I asked.

"Us Warlocks have a great sense of community. They will all pull together to support my brother and his family until my return." Her eyes scanned the group behind me, all of whom were staring at us with raised brows as they mounted their rides. They were too far away to hear our conversation.

"I am powerful, and having a Warlock on your side will help. There is much I can teach the Mages, actually—secrets my kind have kept for millennia." She took a steadying breath. "I...need to help."

I blinked, then gave her a nod. "Then we'd be happy to have you."

She gave a hesitant smile. "Lena is speaking with Leroy. She'll be out in a moment." She adjusted the bag on her back before taking it off and shoving it toward me. "I'll be an extra ride for one of you!" she called out to my group, and I watched in awe as she shifted into a light blue mare, the hair almost iridescent.

I gave her a lopsided grin. "Always a show-off," I teased, and she nudged my shoulder with her nose.

CHAPTER TWENTY-SEVEN

LENA

We were getting ready to leave this morning when Dani insisted I meet her in Leroy's study. When I stepped into the spacious room lined with bookshelves, desks, and a large fireplace with two armchairs in front of it, Dani strolled up to me, a book clutched to her side.

"Do you know why the Warlocks have hated the Mages?"

I crossed my arms, unsure why we were having this conversation. "Not particularly," I answered honestly.

"We envied your power. The Mages were always the superior witches—before that term was stained by bigotry." She held out the thick tome in her hand. My eyes shifted down to the dark and mystifying cover. There was no title.

"I'm not following," I said with furrowed brows, taking the book in my hand. I flipped through the pages. These were all spells.

Warlock spells, many of which were in a language I didn't recognize.

Dani cocked her head to the side. "We hated each other because we both believed our people to be the strongest. We wished to rule over one another." Her smile faltered. "The truth is, despite our shapeshifting capabilities, the Mages are far more powerful. Always have been."

I raised a brow, looking up at her from the archaic pages. "Because of our ability to use magic without the use of incantations?"

Dani gave me a proud grin. "Because of your ability to use *both*."

I blinked over and over before finally releasing a scoff. "What the hell are you talking about?"

Her cobalt eyes sparkled. "It has been a secret long kept. A myth amongst our people. That the Mages were the original beings created by the Gods—created in Oquerene. The Warlocks, the Sea Nymphs, even the Angels are not as strong." She studied her manicured nails, her lips pulling to the side. "Half-lives are below us all, in terms of strength, anyway. But it has always been the Mages who had the most power." Her eyes shifted back to mine. "Us Warlocks have long suspected that the Mages are able to utilize our power, save for the shifting, of course."

I wasn't sure I was breathing. "Why?"

"If the Mages only believed their power to be that of what innately belonged to them, it kept them less powerful. It kept the playing field level."

I was silent for many moments, processing this ridiculous information. "Wait...so if this myth is true, you're saying we can recite spoken spells? Use magic like you?"

"Yes."

"Seems like a simple theory to test out...surely we would've discovered this revelation years ago if that were true."

Dani shook her head. "The Warlocks have done well keeping our spells a secret. Not only that, but training is required to use them properly and get the results you desire. Much like your ability to enchant, you may know the recipe of an elixir or potion you wish to make..." She tapped on the side of her head. "But if you don't know how to make that connection in here, in your body, those words will be nothing but gibberish." She paused. "The pentagram is heavily used in Warlock magic. I believe the necromancer has somehow managed to learn how to wield our power."

My eyes fell to the grimoire, then back to her. "If the Warlocks have kept this secret for centuries, why tell us now?"

She took the spell book back from me, tucking it into the bag resting on her shoulder. "Mages are the most powerful magical beings on the planet. That dark Mage...that necromancer...he has the power to destroy the entire world. I think that is more than enough reason for our people to put our differences aside and work together to stop him."

"Yesterday was proof of that," Leroy added as he ambled into his study, his brows lowered as he spoke to us in a low voice.

I swallowed. I hadn't spoken with Leroy since the battle yesterday...since the death of his wife.

"We have two enemies lusting for power. Two enemies that have no issue ending our people for good. It's time we test this myth." Leroy shifted his eyes to his sister. "Dani will be joining you on your journey."

My eyes widened, then shot to the blue-haired Warlock. "You are?"

"I am." She smiled. "I have much to teach you, and considering we're in a crunch for time, this is the best way." She clasped my shoulder and released a sigh. "I'm going to talk with the Prince." Then, she turned to Leroy, hesitating for a moment before she charged forward, wrapped her arms around him, and squeezed tightly.

"I'll return soon, brother," she whispered.

He sniffed but kept his expression strong, aside from the glimmer in his eyes. He hugged her back. "I know you will. Be safe. I love you."

"I love you too." Dani wiped her eyes as she pulled away, and the two placed their three fingers on their chest before she exited the room.

Leroy's gaze shifted to mine.

"I'm so sorry for your loss," I said quietly.

Leroy nodded, giving me his best attempt at a smile. He then focused his attention on his bookcase, where his fingers trailed various spines. "I need to give you this before you go."

He withdrew an ancient-looking book, fingers skimming through it as he strode over to me. "You asked me about a phoenix on the night of The Freak Show. Last night, I was going through the book I was telling you about."

I stepped forward, Leroy fumbling with the pages until he said, "There." He pointed at the page, and I looked down.

Various animals were listed, with detailed drawings next to each. All had their meanings listed, and I imagined that with how many pages this book possessed, every animal that had ever lived was recorded here.

I read off the ones that had significance. Those of the La'Rune family crest.

Owl: Death

Pelican: Sacrifice

Phoenix: Rebirth

Raven: Prophecy

"Fuck," I muttered. "I remember the La'Rune family crest depicting a pelican guarding a phoenix and a raven from an owl."

"Which would make sense," Leroy continued, "considering the pelican represents sacrifice."

The wheels in my head began spinning. "So, the pelican wished to protect prophecy and rebirth..."

"From death." Leroy flipped through the pages for a moment. "I wonder, though, if the crest is really depicting this." He pointed to a bird just a couple of pages forward. To a white raven. "The crest's raven is an outline. Have you ever noticed that? I wonder if that's because it's a white raven instead of a regular one."

White Raven: Purification

I scratched my head. "I suppose it could be either, but that would make sense." I thought more about the birds. "Igon's compass...a pelican is etched into its backside." My eyes sprang open. "Holy fuck."

"What?"

"Igon knew he was going to die...*sacrifice*..."

Leroy scrubbed at his jaw. "But how does that connect to the Otacian crest?"

I groaned, dragging my hands down my face. "It's like the more I learn, the more confused I am."

Leroy laughed softly through his nose. "Nothing can ever be simple, can it?" Closing the book, he handed it over. "Take it with you. Perhaps you'll learn more, and it can help in some way."

"Thank you," I replied, accepting the Warlock text. "Really...thank you for everything. You and your people were nothing but wonderful and accepting."

"And you and yours were nothing but supportive of ours." He hesitated for a moment. "Dani doesn't know about you and Silas—that you're Soul-Ties. Only the council and I knew that information." He tucked his hands into his pockets. "That man...that man is deeply in love with you."

My eyes flared, and I loosened a breath. "What?"

He gave me a half-smile, as much as he could muster with his broken heart. "He came to speak with me after the battle last night, giving me advice after I'd lost Emma. He spoke of you as if you were dead...told me he did you a disservice by becoming the man that he did."

I bit down on my lip to prevent it from wobbling, my eyes welling with tears.

Leroy's smile fell. "For all the time I knew of Silas La'Rune, I despised him. I saw him as an evil, murderous monster who wanted nothing more than to eliminate our kind. But now that I have experienced what he has, now that I have felt what it's like to have the love of your life ripped away, I understand why he became the man he did. And I forgive him for it."

Leroy's tearful gaze remained on me as I responded quietly, "I also forgive him for it."

He smiled gently. "You'd forgive him regardless...because you are in love with him, too."

A tear slid down my cheek, and as Leroy turned to sit before the fireplace, I departed.

My friends were prepared, and our belongings were packed, new tents gifted by Leroy secured to our rides. But still, there was one thing I had to do before I left.

Say goodbye to Igon.

When I walked back to my group, I asked if Merrick, Viola, and Elowen wanted to come with me. I was surprised that every single one of them, Mage and human alike, wished to pay their respects.

I stood in Forsmont's cemetery, standing before Igon's grave. The site was spacious, but with all the deaths from yesterday, many tearful individuals were surrounding various burial sites.

During the hours I was asleep, recovering from my fire usage after the battle against the Undead puppets, Merrick had a gravestone made for our Supreme.

HERE LIES IGON NATARION.

FRIEND. MENTOR. SUPREME.

It was simple, with no detailed work in the design, as it was made quickly. Just the words.

I covered my mouth, choking on a sob as I took in the freshly piled dirt. My mind flashed with unwanted images: him dying in my arms the first time, and my blade repeatedly puncturing his chest the second.

This man was not related to me by blood, yet he was the closest thing to a father I ever had. He stepped up and took me in as if I was his own.

Five years was not enough time.

Just a few months ago, he was breathing. Smiling. Reading. He was teaching me about magic. He was eating dinner. He was laughing at some joke I had said.

The last moment I had with him before we were attacked was me fucking fighting with him.

It shouldn't have gone this way. He should still be here.

My tearful eyes went to Silas...the one who killed him. Guilt shone in his honey eyes as he took in my brokenness.

My friends said their goodbyes to our leader as I held Silas's gaze. I knew it hurt him to see me like this, which is precisely why he didn't look away.

He believed he deserved every ounce of pain.

Elowen was now weeping profusely just as the Prince said to our group, "May I have a moment with Lena?"

Viola frowned, shaking her head as she and Merrick wandered away, his hand on her back. Elowen couldn't even look at the Prince as she hurried off, Edmund following close behind. Hendry, Roland, and Era looked at him in question, but they left to give us the privacy Silas requested.

After a few moments, it was just us two. I stared at the stone, unwavering, unmoving.

"I'm so sorry, Lena," he whispered, stepping closer. "I wish I could take it back."

I let go then, sobbing into my hands.

Our friends were out of eyesight, though there were still people nearby. But it seemed Silas did not care who saw as he rubbed my back gently.

His voice broke as he uttered, "I'm so fucking sorry."

I dragged my hands away from my face, peeking up at his devastated countenance.

And then I hugged him, enveloping my arms around his waist and burying my face into his chest. He only stiffened for a second before he held me tight, his head tilting down so our cheeks touched. I cried harder.

"I'm sorry, Lena," he whispered.

"I know," I wept. "I forgive you."

He shook his head in protest, the stubble on his cheek brushing against my skin, and I held him tighter.

"You've made it up to me by being here...by helping my people." I sniffed, then gently leaned back, my head craned up to take in his beautiful, forlorn face.

"I am not deserving of forgiveness," he voiced quietly, his arms sliding away from me. "But I will try my best to do the right thing now."

My hands slid from his back to his sides before my right hand went up, stroking his cheek, stroking his scar.

He sucked in a breath, his eyes dilating. "Lena—"

"Deserving or not, you have it from me, Quill."

I let my hand fall, turning back to face Igon's grave once more before our departure. I fished out the bronze compass, running my finger along the pelican etched into its back.

A memento.

Sacrifice.

Only through fire can the phoenix be reborn from the ashes.

What does this all mean, Igon?

CHAPTER TWENTY-EIGHT

MERRICK

I'd be lying if I said I was thrilled to be on the road again. I'd grown accustomed to the warm bed, the hot showers, and being able to piss in private.

We were all back to how we were before, only this time, Viola and I rode on Dani, which I abhorred.

I didn't mind Dani. I just hated that she lusted for my girlfriend...or whatever she was to me. We hadn't put a label on it and had only had sex twice—the first night in Forsmont and the last.

Really, what I actually hated was that Viola returned the attraction. Even though it's normal for people to be attracted to more than one person, I didn't care to know about it.

My eyes slid to Erabella, who gave me a small smile when she saw me looking over at her. I returned the gesture.

Gods. I was such a hypocrite.

After the battle between Otacia and Forsmont, I immediately rushed up the steps inside the castle to find Era.

"You're alright," she had breathed.

I had acted on complete impulse, advancing on her and wrapping her in my embrace.

She had become rigid, but my grip didn't lessen because I felt her warmth at my gesture. She returned the hug a moment later.

I had never been a touchy-feely guy. Ever. But after witnessing her overcome her fear...seeing her have the strength not only to fight but also to take the shot that saved my life...I was left in awe.

I had pulled away, cupping her face in my hands. Her whole face was flushed, those gorgeous brown eyes wide as she stared into mine.

"I am so fucking proud of you," I had praised, my grin wider than it had been since before Ames was overthrown. "I owe you my life, Princess."

She bit her lip, a smile spreading across her face. "I guess my teacher did a good job," she murmured.

My smile began to fall as I studied her. Excitement and wonder bubbled in my chest as I marveled at her sparkling eyes, her cute nose, and her short blonde hair. My pale hands against her tanned face.

I had held her face.

It was an intimate gesture, and when I realized how I'd crossed a boundary, I cleared my throat, hands falling to my sides.

I wanted to read her desperately. But I wouldn't...because I feared what she felt. One way or another.

"I was so scared," she admitted, tears blurring her vision. "I was shaking so badly. I feared I'd miss and strike you instead."

I gave her a lopsided grin. "I'm surprised you didn't," I teased.

She nudged my shoulder, chuckling. "I'm serious, Merrick." Her smile vanished. "If I had killed you..."

I couldn't seem to keep my hands off her. I held her shoulders, angling my head down to look at her. "In that situation, you would not have killed me, Era," I insisted. "Either you would have saved me, or your arrow would've struck me at the same time as that man's sword. Perhaps it would have given me a quicker death."

Her lip wobbled, and she shook her head. "I wouldn't have been able to live with it."

My eyes bounced between hers, and I couldn't stop myself from tuning in to her feelings.

The warmth that flooded into me was like sunlight, revealing just how much she had grown to care for me. Her emotions were heightened...a medley of colors and sounds I couldn't organize. But the warmth was the strongest.

I knew I was pushing...being ballsy. But I had almost just died, so I decided to do what my heart told me.

I leaned down and planted a kiss on her forehead. "Well, good thing your teacher taught you well," I murmured as I pulled away.

Her widened eyes, flushed cheeks, and rapid breathing could've meant multiple things, but I was too scared to find out what.

I knew my eyes had turned blue, not wishing to know how my kiss felt to her. I smiled at her before I strode away.

My eyes now slid back to the road ahead, my arms tightening around Viola. She rested her head on my chest.

Faltrun, thankfully, was only a five-day journey. Once the sun had begun to lower in the sky, Dani came to a halt, and the rest of our friends brought their horses to a stop as well. She neighed, and Viola and I took that as the signal to hop off of her.

In a flash, Dani shifted, wincing as she stretched her arms and let out a loud yawn. "Yep...I'm getting sleepy." Her eyes, now appearing human, slid to me and Vi, then to El and Lena. "Mage practice starts in the morning."

Lena frowned from her position on her and Roland's horse, Donut. I still couldn't believe he named their horse that. "What...out in the open?"

Lena gave us the rundown of Dani's hypothesis during our trek today. I didn't know if I believed her theory, but with all these threats we have faced, I'd be willing to try anything.

Dani's grin grew. "Yup. We have no time to waste." She fished into her back, pulling out a pouch and grasping its contents in her palm. ***"Averte sonum intra hunc circulum"*** she recited as she walked in a circle, sprinkling what appeared like salt on the ground.

"What the hell are you doing?" I questioned.

"Yeah, I'm with Mare Bear—you're creeping me out, Dani," Edmund trembled.

Mare Bear?!

I shot him a scowl over the nickname.

"Averte sonum intra hunc circulum. Averte sonum intra hunc circulum."

Dani then began moving her lips. A smile was on her face, but no sound emitted from her mouth.

"Uh...Dani?" Roland's brows drew together. "Did you star as a mime at The Freak Show and not tell us?"

Her shoulders moved up and down as if laughing, and then she stepped outside of the salt circle. "Soundproofing spell. Good for many reasons." She wiggled her brows at Roland. "Our glamouring spell is simple, only speaking the word once and tilting our hand. The more advanced the spell, the more you have to chant." Her eyes dropped to the salt that was sprinkled on the ground. "The salt acts as a magic binder, absorbing the energy and transmuting it." She casually stepped back into the circle, speaking soundlessly, until she scuffed the salt with her foot, and her voice came through.

"*'Aversa Pars'* is another way to shut off the spell, but sometimes just scuffing the salt works best."

Elowen's round, aqua eyes slid to mine briefly before setting back on the Warlock. "So, you always carry around salt? How do you memorize the spells?"

Dani gave her bag a pat. "Yup, but not just salt. I always keep chalk in my bra. I also carry candles, crystals, and herbs. And, like you Mages sometimes do, a spell book." She fished into her bag, pulling out a nameless tome. "Our ability to enchant isn't innate-like you, nor is it as efficient or as powerful. However, you pair your powers with a spell book like this..." She shook her head, a half-smile on her face. "Well, I'd say we'd be in for some badassery. The salt should bind the spell as it did with mine, but according to myth, with your illusion magic, even disruption to the salt should have no effect."

Lena's arms were crossed, her eyes wide. "I want to try."

Dani's grin widened. "I knew you'd be intrigued, Supreme." She gestured forward.

Lena took a deep breath, tossing her orange braid over her shoulder as she dismounted her horse. She grasped a pouch of salt from Dani.

"Do you remember the words?" Dani asked.

Lena snorted. "No."

"Averte sonum intra hunc circulum."

Lena took in a sharp breath. ***"Averte sonum intra...honk-fer..."***

Dani shook her head. ***"Hunc circulum,"*** she corrected.

"Averte sonum intra hunc circulum. Averte sonum intra hunc circulum." Lena grasped a handful of the salt in her hand, bracing herself to perform the spell.

"Like I said, this is a form of illusion magic," Dani spoke. "Release it. Infuse the salt with it."

Lena kept repeating the spell, over and over, as she dropped the salt. Dancing down her fingertips was a purple, sparkly glow.

"Averte sonum intra hunc circulum. Averte sonum intra hunc circulum. Averte sonum intra hunc circulum."

Lena stopped once the circle was complete. She turned her head toward us and mouthed, *"Can you hear me?"*

We heard nothing.

"By the Gods," Viola breathed. "I cannot believe this."

"Now for the true test," Dani said as she stepped up to Lena, dragging her white boots through the salt. "Speak again, Lena."

Every one of our eyes was wide, waiting in anticipation.

Lena went to speak.

Once again, no sound came out.

"Holy shit..." I mumbled. The Otacian's jaws were on the floor.

Dani threw her arms up. "Hell yeah, bitches!" Her excited eyes danced around us all. "Once Lena—or any one of you, I suppose—grasps higher-level illusion spells, we'll be able to conjure an illusion ring around our camp at night, so no one will be able to hear or see us while we sleep."

Edmund damn near started dancing. "Oh, thank the Gods! Sleeping on the road is especially horrifying...what with all the

Undead." He rubbed the back of his neck. "Wait, you don't know how to?"

Dani shook her head, crossing her arms and pushing out her hip. "It's not that I don't know the spell. I'm just not powerful enough to do it on my own. I'd need at least seven Warlocks performing the incantation with me." She looked at Lena, who was still in the soundproof ring. "I think if you Mages did it together, though, we might stand a chance of it working. But I'm not sure how draining it will be for you. This spell was on the easier side. I wouldn't expect it to go as smoothly when we try something more advanced."

Edmund slowly nodded, and Dani turned to our Supreme. "Alright, Lena. To cancel the spell, you must say ***Aversa Pars.*** Just once, focusing your magic back into the salt."

Lena blinked, then did just that, the violet glow drifting from her fingertips. We couldn't hear her as she spoke the words, but as the magic vanished from her hand, she tilted her head up to us. "Did it work?"

"Wow..." Hendry whispered. "Yeah, it worked."

"So, wait," Era began, shaking her head. "You couldn't do this type of magic before? I'm confused."

I answered for Lena. "We can create illusion elixirs—potions with our magic. We utilize certain properties in various herbs when we make them. I suppose that is our magical binder."

"My mother was able to conjure up false bodies. That was done with no binder." Her guilty eyes slid to Silas, only for a moment. "We can conjure familiars, though that, too, takes a significant amount of magic. This—" She motioned to the salt ring. "This felt like *nothing.*"

"Don't you see?" Dani began. "This has been the missing piece for Mages for centuries. The other half of your power." Her eyes fell to the tome, then back to us all. "This book's title has been glamoured by a powerful being to hide the title. ***Potestas Verae Maleficis.*** The Power of a True Witch."

CHAPTER TWENTY-NINE
LENA

"A true witch?" I asked Dani suspiciously. "You're saying that Mages are the true witches?"

She nodded. "Once you learn how to combine your powers with that in this grimoire, once you learn the Titharan language, you'll be stronger than ever." Her smile turned playful. "You haven't even learned how to teleport yet."

"TELEPORT?!" Elowen screeched, causing us all to jump. She shot her small hand over her mouth. "Sorry," she peeped.

Dani chuckled. "Yes. Gods, you guys are in for some real fun when I teach you what I know."

Hendry's eyes narrowed, his arms crossing as he surveyed the blue-haired Warlock. "If you are able to do all this as well, what makes Mages the 'true witches'?"

"When I tell you our Warlock magic is but a fraction of the Mages, I mean it. We can't just hold out our palms and heal. We can't raise our arms and create a forcefield or have the elements drift from our fingertips at will. We can't conjure familiars. All we can do that is special is shape-shift." Her eyes slid to Viola's. "And the pretty one here can apparently do that, too. So, these spells and incantations are all we have."

"Thank you," I said softly, causing Dani to look at me. "Thank you for your willingness to teach us this."

She smiled. "Don't thank me. Just kick Ulric and this necromancer's asses."

Three days passed. Both evenings, Dani insisted on teaching Viola, Merrick, Elowen, and me everything she could, even though she was the most tired, shifting to carry Viola and Merrick along the journey.

"What is this place?" Edmund asked skeptically as Dani stopped before what appeared to be an abandoned circus.

Shifting back into a human form—this time male—Dani stated, "This was the original Freak Show." He sighed as he surveyed the absolute mess. Large tents were still raised, the fabric lightly tattered. A large wooden carousel was in the center of the scenery, creaking from the evening wind. "Those people you guys met? The ones with oddities who weren't Warlocks? They had their own show here." He stepped up to the carousel. "Remarkable, isn't it? This was crafted by the most talented woodworker I'd ever seen." He pointed to a crank to its left. "He was a strong man—big, beefy guy. You'd never guess that this was his hidden talent. He was the only one strong enough to twist the mechanics for the children to ride."

Elowen's saddened gaze loomed over this desolate place. "What happened?"

"Faltrun," Silas answered for him, his golden gaze flicking to the healer. "Faltrun demanded payments—a commission for the group performing so close to their territory."

Dani nodded. "The people who designed this place and lived here fought back. They were not going to be slaves to a kingdom they were not a part of. Faltrun had this place raided, killing a handful of innocents, including the talented man who created this..." He ran his hands along the wood, now damaged from neglect. "We had only a handful of survivors seeking refuge in Forsmont. Leroy welcomed them with open arms, and through their stories and their ideas, we created something even better. Safer." He shook his head, chewing the inside of his cheek. "Until the damn Undead attacked."

"Faltrun almost sounds as bad as Otacia," Viola mumbled.

Hendry's mismatched eyes slid over, and in his troubled eyes, I could tell he wished to retort but couldn't because she was right.

"When we arrive, I wouldn't expect the treatment you received in Forsmont, that's for sure. While they may not have a kill order for magical beings, we must keep our identity a secret. I don't trust them."

He trailed his sight back to the various tents. "It looks like shit on the outside, but the tents really aren't that bad inside. We took what was salvageable and brought it back to Forsmont already." He clapped his hands together. "After we do some more training, we can set up camp inside."

Roland watched in amusement thirty minutes later as I attempted to create mage light. Dani had pointed to the script in the grimoire. *'Lumen'* could also produce mage light, and the Warlock insisted that if I used the words, I could produce a longer-lasting glow.

Regular mage light was a common innate ability that Mages possessed, but one I hadn't taught myself, as I had my fire to produce light.

My time traveling to Ames five years ago was spent holding my magic in, holding it in like I never had before. The night I got my ice didn't compare to the agony I felt on the road. Once my reality set in...as my days apart from Silas grew.

Those months, the weather had begun to chill, but it was still only autumn. Nevertheless, I would find my fingertips encased in frost, my limbs stiff as I wandered without an ounce of joy.

That time on the road was spent attempting to control that ice. Finding out I was with a child helped a lot, but still, the nights my mind wandered, I found myself growing cold.

I still felt guilt whenever I thought of it...that perhaps my struggle was what harmed my child. That his death was my fault.

"You are not to blame," Torrin had insisted days after my son's passing. "You would've done anything to save him. You are a wonderful mother."

I chewed on my lip as I recalled the memories, trying my hardest not to break down as I conjured up the little glowing orbs.

In the months following that tragedy, my fire and ice fought for dominance. Some days, I was so angry I felt like I could turn

Ames to ash. Others, I would grow so cold that my body couldn't move.

"I am not a mother," I had sobbed. *"I failed."*

He held my face, those warm, brown eyes burning into mine, seeing me for all that I was. Like they always had.

"You are *a mother. And you did not fail." He had pulled me into his arms, rocking me, warming me with his magic. "Your child is with Ravaiana now, roaming the skies in Elysium.* No child shall suffer. Every child is free. *That is engraved in her temple."*

I still struggled with my belief in the Gods and Goddesses sometimes. I especially did after the loss of my baby.

But Torrin believed, and his words comforted me.

"You will be with him again one day...this is not the end," he had *whispered in my mind.*

I sniffed and quickly wiped away my tears as they forced their way down my face at the thought of Torrin.

Roland's smile dissipated just as Merrick leaned over and whispered, "Are you okay?"

I nodded, sniffing once more and taking a shaky breath.

I wasn't. But I needed to shove those emotions down...until I could find a quiet place alone.

Torrin helped me control my ice...had helped me tame my fire. He even taught me how to wield my electricity, to fight with it.

He never told me when he got his.

Anyway, I had much to learn over the past few years. Mage lights were last on my list.

"Lumen," I chanted, my fingers pinching together before flicking them outward. A large orb, the size of cantaloupe, shot out from my hand, floating in the air like a bubble.

I smiled weakly, but the gesture only lasted for a moment before a sinking feeling filled my chest.

"Very good, Lena!" Dani praised, his strong biceps flexing as he clapped.

They can't be here. Not now.

"Now I want to teach you a basic ward. It's—"

Dani was cut off by Elowen's deafening shriek. Our heads whirled toward her as she clasped the sides of her head, falling to her knees.

"Elowen!" Edmund shouted, grasping her arms and searching her face.

A moment later, Silas was wailing, reaching for his head.

I inhaled sharply, flame creeping up my arms and legs. I knew now that Silas had a sensitivity to flame, but it was my strongest form of magic. When it came to the Undead, I would be taking no chances.

My eyes darted around us, in the forest, between the tents.

"They've found us!" Erabella cried, and I whirled to where a singular figure stood.

Vicsin Astair.

"N-no," Elowen sobbed as she fell to her knees, her aqua eyes scrunched in pain. "Father..."

Merrick watched in horror as his father stepped forward, eyes solid black, that same spider and pentagram combo etched into the skin on his forehead. Vicsin's lip raised, his head cocking, and El and Silas cried out harder. Blood began dripping from their noses.

"Stop this!" Roland snarled, withdrawing his sword.

Vicsin's attention skated to him. He laughed. "Silly human." The voice was Vicsin's...and *his*. "You really believe you stand a chance against me?"

"The Lord of the Shadows, is it?" I yelled, and Vicsin's black glaze slid to mine. "What do you want from us?"

His cruel smile grew. "Lena Daelyra...such a powerful Mage." My flames reflected in those cold, soulless eyes. "Isn't it obvious? I want your power for my own."

He tilted his hand, and Elowen shrieked, Silas's screams growing louder.

My heart was beating out of my chest, but I remained strong. "Stop hurting them, and we may come to an agreement."

"What?" Hendry hissed.

"Lena, no—" Dani began.

I ignored them. Vicsin's heartless smile remained, and his hand fell to his side. Elowen gasped, and Silas let out a painful groan. Both of their hands fell to the ground, steadying themselves. I loosened a breath as my friends caught theirs.

"What do you think you have to offer me that I cannot take for myself already?"

I wracked my brain for something, anything I could offer him. "Alliance."

"What?!" Silas choked out, but I didn't look at him. My eyes remained solely on Vicsin—on the necromancer who was looking at me through his eyes.

Vicsin laughed, really laughed. "There is no allying with me. You can either bow or perish."

I was taking a huge risk with my next words...I could only hope my judgment was correct. "I am the only one who knows where the Weapon is."

To that, Vicsin's laughing ceased, his gaze hardening on mine. He stared at me in silence, and the hairs on the back of my neck raised at his chilling appearance...the colorless skin, the dark veins.

"Where?" he gritted out.

I wanted to give him a hateful smile, but I didn't wish to provoke him. "I'll bring it to you...but only if you stay out of my way."

"Lena, no!" Silas begged. "You're making a deal with the devil!"

Vicsin's sadistic grin returned. "Why would you give it to me?"

I prayed he would not call my bluff. "Because I'd rather see it in a Mage's hand than in a La'Rune's."

Silas's fist shook as he gripped the grass beneath him, glaring at me in contempt. "You..."

Something glimmered in Vicsin's eyes...something I couldn't place. He released a breath. "Very well, Miss Daelyra. I won't disturb your travels as you find me my Weapon." His hands flew up, and once again were Elowen and Silas screaming, clutching their heads. My enraged eyes went back to his.

"Don't worry. The hallucinations will only last a few hours. Just know that this is but a sliver of the power I hold." He smiled ruefully. "Consider it a reminder of what is to come should you betray me."

He turned, sprinting away, and I swore as I rushed to my friends' sides.

"Lena," Silas cried in agony, eyes squeezed shut.

"Let's get them in either tent," Dani nervously sputtered, then handed over to me a pouch of salt. "El in one, Silas in the other—we must soundproof, or else we'll alert all of Tovagoth where we are."

Edmund and Merrick lifted a thrashing Elowen while Roland and Hendry lifted Silas. I rushed with Era into the further tent while Dani and Viola went with Elowen.

Silas's scream was so heartbreaking that my eyes flooded with tears. "Dani, what do we do to help them?!" I called out as our distance increased.

His pained eyes shot back to mine. "I have no idea."

They rushed into their tent a moment before we hurried into ours.

The space was nearly empty, with nothing but a few broken chairs,

'Lumen,' I quickly repeated three times, sending the glowing lights into the air to lighten the space. The night was upon us, and this was the quickest option to brighten the space.

Roland and Hendry gently placed Silas on the ground.

When the Prince's eyes shot open, we all fumbled back at the sight of the black gaze that stared back at us. Not all black like the Undead, but Silas's golden irises were gone as if his pupils were completely blown.

I quickly went to work, scattering the salt in a large circle around us. ***"Averte sonum intra hunc circulum. Averte sonum intra hunc circulum."***

His face crumpled. "Lena?" he whispered.

My whole body froze, and my eyes broadened at the tone of his voice. I quickly pivoted my head toward Era and the men. "Leave. It's only going to get worse."

"Averte sonum intra hunc circulum...averte sonum intra hunc circulum."

Erabella's worried eyes darted between the two of us. "I need to be here for him—"

"LENA!" Silas wailed, lunging forward to grasp me, the action causing Era to jolt backward.

I held a forcefield out, shoving Silas down on his ass. He grunted as he hit the ground. "Please," I begged them. "Please leave."

"Are you sure?" Hendry asked desperately. "What if we can help?"

"Yeah—" Roland began, just as Silas turned to his side, lying down.

"I think I'm going to be sick," Silas grumbled, panting as sweat dripped down his forehead.

"Averte sonum intra hunc circulum...averte sonum intra hunc circulum."

The circle was now complete. I glanced at Hendry. "Check if it works."

He did as I asked, stepping out of the circle.

"Can you hear me?"

He shook his head no.

I tilted toward Roland and Era. "Just go. I can handle this," I assured them.

A few more moments of consideration passed, and as Silas began to wail again, Era gave a curt nod, then bolted out of the tent, Hendry and Roland in tow.

"Shh..." I whispered as I hurried to his side, rubbing his back. But Silas's cries wouldn't stop. "I'm here, I'm here."

He flipped over, wide-eyed as he gazed at me. His dark eyes made my stomach turn, knowing that I couldn't just pull him back to reality. Despite all the pain he was in, no tears trailed down his face.

I held my palm to his head. I felt no burning in my palms, no sign of healing being needed.

This magic...it wasn't normal. I couldn't place what was different about it, but I could feel its wrongness.

I willed my healing magic to the front, anyway, hoping that the comforting touch could relieve some of his pain. If Elowen weren't also inebriated with this power, she could make this painless for him, I reckoned.

I bet the Lord of the Shadows knew that.

"I can't." Silas's voice broke as he stared at me. "I have tried, but I can't."

I focused my magic on his temples. I didn't know if it was helping.

"Can't what?" I asked softly.

"I can't!" he wailed, squeezing his eyes shut. I stifled a cry as I watched him begin to hit himself, punching at his head. "I can't stop. I can't turn it off!"

I grasped his hands. His physical strength far superseded my own, but I pulled hard, forcing his assault to a halt. His black eyes shot open, taking me in.

"I know..." I slowly removed one of my hands from his. I gently stroked his cheek, and those haunting eyes fluttered shut. "It will be over before you know it," I promised.

His breaths were shallow. "You left me," he whispered.

My stomach dropped, guilt overtaking me. "I know...I am so sorry..."

"I...if it happens again..." His voice trailed off. "If he finds out...if he sees..." His black eyes shot open, blown wide. "I CAN'T, LENA! I CAN'T!"

His back shot up from the ground, and he crawled back on his palms, stumbling away as if I were something sinister.

"Silas!" I cried, crawling to him and then holding his face in my hands. His frightened eyes locked on mine, his body trembling in trepidation. "What you are seeing is not real. You are safe!" Tears slid down my cheeks. "You are safe with me, Quill."

His lip trembled, his chest rising and falling rapidly. "Safe..." he breathed.

"Yes, safe with me, Quill," I repeated, pressing my lips to his forehead, my eyes squeezing shut as more tears poured out of me. It was wrecking me seeing him like this.

"I don't accept it...I don't." He shook his head back and forth, his eyes shutting.

I knew I couldn't reason with him. He was sputtering nonsense.

The necromancer said hallucinations. What exactly was Silas seeing?

His whole forehead was covered in sweat.

"Silas, let's take your shirt off."

His eyes flared. "No," he growled.

"You are covered in sweat." My fingers only brushed the buttons of his shirt before he roughly gripped my wrist.

"NO!" he shouted.

I flinched. He'd never yelled at me like that before. My voice was small as I asked, "May I unbutton it at least?"

His breathing was staggered, his eyes flashing with so many emotions. "My back." His voice broke. "My back must stay covered."

My eyes softened. "Okay. I promise your back will stay covered."

Slowly, I released each button, revealing skin just as golden beneath it. His body was even more defined than when we were younger, and sweat droplets were trickling down his chest and stomach muscles, the skin covered in ink just like the rest of him.

Part of me missed his bare skin from before, but I found myself loving his flesh for what it was now.

I think I would love any version of him. I don't think I could help it.

When I separated the fabric, my lips parted as I took in the view of the tattoo in the center of his chest.

A dagger. Not just any dagger. It was the exact same hilt as the one I used when we were younger...when he trained me. The first weapon I ever bought myself. The one I held to a girl's neck the first day Silas saw me.

The blade was piercing through a—

"Flower," Silas breathed.

My teary eyes slid up to meet his. "This tattoo..." I traced my fingers along the ink, and Silas shivered at my touch, his body relaxing. "You got it for me?"

"It's...It's your dagger, going through a rose. Your favorite...flower," His breathing quickened. "Over my heart." His face crumpled as he took me in. "I wish I could have saved you," he choked. "I should have kept you safe."

"Silas..." I brought my lips to his forehead again, the taste of his sweat salty against my lips. "I am alive. I am here with you."

"Alive..." he breathed, and as I pulled away, he gripped the back of my neck.

My brows drew together just as Silas yanked me forward, forcing my lips against his.

My eyes shot wide, but they quickly shut at the familiar feel of his mouth against mine. Those perfect, soft lips.

Silas slid his hand in my hair, and our mouths parted at the same time, allowing our tongues to glide along each other's.

His taste...his fucking taste.

He eagerly nipped at my bottom lip, and as I ran my hand along his chest, along those delicious abs, a soft moan escaped me.

"My love," he whispered, and tears began to burn in my eyes.

But as intoxicating as the kiss was, Silas pushed me back, his dark eyes broad as he staggered to his feet. "I...I didn't know," he insisted, his voice shaking. "I..." He shook his head back and forth.

He didn't know what was happening, what was real or not. I wanted to help, but there was nothing I could do as he was further lost in the necromancer's delusion.

CHAPTER THIRTY

SILAS

Her lips were against mine, and everything felt right in the world. My fingers raked through her soft, copper hair. My greedy tongue fervently swirled around hers, my mind calming at the taste of her. I bit her pillow-soft lip, and my heart raced at the sound of her precious moan.

"My love," I breathed against her lips.

I couldn't remember how it got to this point. All I knew was it felt right.

But good things never lasted for me, did they?

It hit me then.

The scent of burning flesh.

I shoved her back on instinct, my eyes quickly darting over her body as I rose to my feet. Her ravishing, perfect body. No burns...no melting flesh. Her skin was its soft, porcelain hue. I swallowed the lump in my throat, shaking my head in an attempt to clear it.

"You left me," she voiced quietly, shifting away.

"I...I didn't know," I insisted. "I..." I continued shaking my head, images of her corpse lying in her bed flashing in my mind. How could I have ever known that wasn't real? That her mother had conjured up false bodies?

Lena's head tilted to the side, studying me over her shoulder with curiosity. The corner of her lip turned upward. "Tell me, Silas, how much do you love your wife?"

I stiffened, and my breathing hitched as her eyes trailed down my body. While her smile was playful, the glare that burned into mine was one that did not belong to her.

I knew it wasn't really Lena, knew what I was seeing wasn't real.

"She may be the one you're fucking," she continued in a low, sultry voice, turning her body to face me, "but you think of me when you're above her...don't you?"

I loosened a breath, stumbling back a step as I whispered, "Stop."

This isn't her. It's just a hallucination.

I blinked repeatedly, wishing to find my way back to reality. But her smile only grew, her arms crossing as she strode toward me. "She has no idea, does she?" she provoked, her eyes lingering on my lips. She lifted her chin, meeting my gaze with a half-lidded stare. "No idea all the ways you fantasize about me."

I bared my teeth, retreating a step, only to have my back against a wall. "Get out of my head," I gritted out.

This isn't her. This isn't her. This isn't her.

She uncrossed her arms once she was standing before me, placing a delicate hand on my chest and trailing it down my tor-so...lower.

"Does the truth frighten you, Silas? Do you hate yourself for it?"

I shuddered, my body's response causing her smile to grow. As much as I desired to shove her away...I couldn't. I couldn't because she looked like her...sounded like her, and I hungered for her touch more than I'd like to admit.

"It's true, is it not?" she asked with a yearning gleam in her sea-green eyes, her brows scrunching together. "Don't you love me?"

My expression turned pained, my voice above a whisper. "Stop...please," I begged.

Lena's eyes softened, and she withdrew her hand. "Is it guilt you feel? Shame for loving me when you're committed to another?" She angled her head downward and stepped back.

My eyes bulged, and I cried out as I witnessed her skin begin to burn and bubble, that sickening stench of burning flesh filling the air. Her whole body was bright red now, her expression a heart-breaking sight. A look of acceptance of her fate, acceptance of a betrayal.

"Lena—" I rushed toward her, but she retreated from me, tears now flowing down her cheeks.

"You gave up on me!" she cried. "You left me!"

I shook my head. "No...*no*, I-I had no idea you were alive!" I went to reach for her again, but she retreated.

"Look." She raised a trembling hand, and I began to hyperventilate at the sight of her skin melting off.

The smell. I knew that smell. The scent permeated the air when I lit Amatta on fire.

I can't. I can't.

Lena.

Lena was on fire.

I was gasping for air in full-fledged panic. "Let me help you!" I begged, but as I ran to her, she lifted her hand, a protective force-field shoving me back. My back slammed against the ground, and I winced at the pain.

"It's too late," she articulated, her voice small. "You've moved on...and I...I am still stuck in that house."

"No." Sweat was beading at my hairline, my brain aching from shaking it back and forth so vigorously. "You didn't die in that house...you—"

"It's all been a dream, Silas," she wept, and I watched in despair as her beautiful hair started to burn off. "You finding me...none of it was real! I'm DEAD!"

My face crumpled. "No...no, no, no..." I was spiraling. "Please—*please*, let me help you!"

"I'm right here, Silas. You're hallucinating. I am right here. I am safe."

I blinked rapidly. "Lena..." I breathed.

That voice...it was her. The real her.

This isn't real. I can't forget.

"What did you have done to my body?" the vision before me asked. "To my mother's?"

I couldn't bear to look at her. Soot covered her red, blistered skin. Her hair was gone. The clothes that remained were tattered. Only those green eyes remained the same.

"I had them buried in the garden," I whispered. "Where your house once stood."

Her bones started to become visible as her skin melted away. The scent...the sight...I couldn't help it; I leaned over and vomited profusely.

"It's okay...let it out...I'm here. You're safe. It's not real."

It felt like a hand was caressing my back. I heaved again and again. When I was through, I hesitantly brought my eyes up to her charred corpse, now standing before me. Her eyes, the only part that had remained intact, now liquified, spilling from their sockets.

My entire body shook. "No...no..." I breathed, my voice hoarse and broken.

"It's not real, Silas."

"You failed me." The corpse's voice—Lena's voice—was all strained and distorted. "You let this happen to me."

"I'm sorry," I cried. "I'm so sorry..."

No.

My eyes widened in panic.

I can't cry. I can't cry. I can't cry.

"H-he is going to hurt me," I trembled. "I can't go through it again. I CAN'T!"

I began to see him. See *them.*

I can't survive this.

I can't go through it again.

Never again.

I covered my eyes, shrinking into myself as I backed away.

"It seems more drastic measures must be taken to break you," the King censured.

All the walls I had built up had threatened to come crumbling down at the sight before me. At the memories I'd tried to forget.

"Help me," I whispered, squeezing my eyes shut. "Please, help me."

"Think about me, Quill. Think of all the good times we've shared."

"Lena," I wept.

"Remember when we went skinny dipping in Amethyst Pond?"

The smell of pine overwhelmed my senses. I carefully opened my eyes and gasped at the sight of Lena swimming in the purple water.

She grinned. "Well, don't keep me waiting!" she giggled, splashing water at me.

My body relaxed at the sight of her, safe and happy. But I stared down at my attire.

"I-I can't take off my shirt," I murmured.

Her head fell to the side, eyes studying me with worry. "Why not?"

My heart began to race again, but Lena was there to pull me back.

"Remember dancing at the festival? How tipsy I was?"

The scene before me shifted, the sun setting to a calming night sky. Tea lights were strung up, and here Lena was amongst dancing bodies in the Outer Ring. She twirled in front of me, wearing the navy gown I had gifted her.

"Dance with me?" she asked shyly.

So, I did. I held my arms out, pulling her into my embrace, and slowly swayed with her.

She rested against me.

"I remember how nervous I was. I knew I wished to make love to you that night."

I held her close. "It was the perfect first time," I said quietly.

"It was. It was entirely perfect."

We were then in her room. My breathing quickened being in here.

She held my hands. She was in a sweater now, in comfortable leggings. "Sleep beside me, Quill. We never could rest with one another."

She crawled into the bed, lifting the blanket for me to join her. I obeyed, feeling the heat of her body already warming mine. We lay facing one another, staring at each other.

"Do you love me?" she asked quietly, her voice a near whisper.

My brows drew together, my eyes bouncing between hers as I lifted my hand, brushing my thumb along the freckles on her cheek. "I will always love you."

Her voice was faint...but I heard her response. Her real response.

"I will always love you, Silas."

Lena smiled, then held me against her chest. It felt so good, so real, that I accepted it. I pretended I wasn't aware of my lucid state, and slowly, I drifted to sleep in her embrace.

CHAPTER THIRTY-ONE

MERRICK

My sister's emotions were bleeding into mine, even without utilizing my gift, as Edmund and I sprinted into one of the weathered tents in this place. I braced myself when she screamed, tears streaming down her face.

"Father!" Elowen whimpered, flailing violently as Edmund and I placed her on the ground. Dani began spreading salt, chanting that spell to keep the sound inside. "STOP!"

"El," Edmund said softly, grasping her hand in an attempt to calm her. "Elowen, baby, I'm right here." When she gradually stopped panicking, when her breathing slowed, he took one hand and held her face. Black irises stared back at him as her eyes shot open.

"Edmund," she whispered, and her face crumpled. "My parents are dead," she cried.

His own face fell, his eyes filling with tears. "I know...I know..."

Viola's palms glowed gold over El's temples, her jaw clenching as she concentrated. "This isn't doing anything," she gritted out.

"It might help speed up the process," Dani said, attempting to be positive as he flipped through his spell book, looking for anything that might help.

"Why are her eyes black?" I shook my head, constructing a mental partition. Her pain...it was too much.

I could now understand why people became unsettled sometimes when my eyes turned dark. It certainly didn't give me fuzzy feelings seeing my sister's.

Elowen sniffled as she struggled to catch her breath. "Why did they have to die?" she wept. "Why did he take them?"

"I'm so sorry, baby," Edmund whispered. "I wish I could've stopped it."

Blood still stained beneath her nose, but blessedly, no more crimson flowed.

Her lip wobbled, her limbs shaking as she turned her attention to me. "M-Merrick..."

I leaned in close, grasping her hands. "Yes? What is it?"

She choked on a sob. "I'm sorry for your mother. I know it's my fault."

My eyes flared, and I dropped her hands, stumbling back.

"I see her, and she blames me," she sobbed. "I know she's right."

"Elowen," Viola shook her head. "Ayana is not here. Your mind is plagued."

"I killed her!" Elowen wailed. "I killed her!"

I clutched my chest, about to break into a million pieces. I wanted to comfort her, but I couldn't. Not when it came to my mother.

I rushed out of the tent, running my hand through my hair. This was fucking torturous, seeing my sister in such agony.

I was grateful Vi took the responsibility of working on her and even more grateful for the soundproofing spell. I could no longer hear her excruciating screams, nor could any potential enemies.

I craved a drink, a smoke—something to take this edge off. I debated rolling up and smoking some of the dagga I had purchased in Forsmont. Elowen hated that I smoked sometimes, so I decided against it. Decided that it wasn't fair for me to feel any amount of bliss when my sister was suffering. I leaned against the fabric of the tent.

Edmund stumbled out a few moments later, aggressively rubbing at his forehead. Being in there was hard for us all. Seeing someone you care for tortured in such a way and being unable to do anything to stop it...it was horrendous.

The sky was darkening, hardly any light from the sun left. Any moment, and the stars would be glittering in the sky.

Edmund stood beside me, resting his head against the thick material. I was too exhausted to bother telling him to bug off.

"I want you to know that I truly care for Elowen," he said quietly. "I know you don't like me very much. I know you despise my presence. But...I love her."

I inhaled the summer air slowly, turning my head to him beside me.

"I love her," he repeated, emerald eyes shining. "I am not some playboy. I have kept to myself my whole life, in the romantic sense." His cheeks flushed. "I mean, she was my first kiss, for fuck's sake."

My jaw fell open at his candor. "Oh..."

I looked away, crossing my arms. I supposed that made me feel better.

"I'm an old-fashioned guy. I was raised to court a woman. Get her family's blessing. Wait until marriage."

My head slowly turned to his again.

"I'm really trying hard on that last one."

"Ugh!" I grimaced. "I don't want any details."

He laughed through his nose, running his carbonado hand through his golden hair. "I'm just saying I care for her. I respect her. And I know that your resentment toward me is because of your love for her. I'm glad for it. I'm glad you care." He paused. "I know we aren't close, but I care and respect for you, too."

My eyes instantly flicked to his, dark as they read him.

Truth.

I clenched my jaw, unsure of how to respond. Edmund continued talking.

"What did she mean by saying she killed your mother?"

I squeezed my hands, the feeling of my ice creeping up my veins.

I didn't want to talk about it, but I chose to give him the short answer. "Elowen is the love child of Vicsin and her mother Heildee. A product of their secret affair."

Edmund's face paled, his artificial arm crossing over his real one. "Your father cheated on your mother."

"That's correct." I rested my head back on the tent where, inside, my sister was undoubtedly wailing in agony. "Only when Heildee gave birth did he leave my mother. Before that, he had lied. He secretly was seeing Heildee for months, pretending to be a good husband to my mother, even though he had grown cold, closed off from her."

I chewed on my lip ring, shaking my head. "My mother was a bright light, and my father's betrayal didn't just dim her. He extinguished her. She killed herself a few years after." I tilted my eyes to Edmund, who wore an expression of tenderness and dismay. "Elowen didn't kill my mother. My father is responsible for that."

I pushed off from my spot, deciding I was my father's son after all. A shit person. I went to smoke the dagga after all.

I plopped myself against the large carousel twenty minutes later, taking a breather and enjoying the herb's ability to spread warmth through my body. I held the joint in my fingers, staring up at the moon looming in the sky.

Elowen used to think it was made of cheese as a child. It was crescent-shaped this evening, but staring at it, I chuckled to myself. It really could pass as cheese.

I took in a third drag, the end glowing orange. I was blowing the smoke out through my lips when my eyes went to Era. She was sitting on the ground with her back against a large tree, her head resting in her hands as she watched me.

I lifted the joint in a silent offer, and she narrowed her eyes, her nose scrunching.

I laughed softly and found myself wandering toward her.

She looked up with tearful eyes as I sat beside her, resting my head against the large trunk.

Her grimace grew. "That smells bad. That stuff isn't good for you, you know."

"Yeah, yeah." It didn't stink *that* bad, at least compared to other herbs that could be smoked for pleasure. Its aroma was like tobacco with a hint of mint. "How are you holding up?" I asked, ignoring her comment and internally cringing.

Isn't it fucking obvious how she's doing?

She sniffed, wiping her nose on the back of her hand. "I hate seeing them suffer."

Them.

I tuned into her emotions, letting her pain wash over me. The buzz from my high helped it hurt less.

I gave her my best attempt at a smile. "It won't be forever. They'll get through this," I assured her gently, pointing my fingertips to the air and conjuring up some mage light as I said, *"Lumen."*

Little orbs that glowed white began floating around us, offering up some light.

Era's eyes sparkled. "Amazing," she breathed, eyes dancing over the little lights. She offered me a shy smile. "I am quite fearful of the dark...I'm grateful for this magic."

Her brown eyes bounced between mine, a glimmer shining in them, reflecting off the mage lights.

"That was your father?" she asked gently.

My eyes flickered, falling to the ground before nodding. "Yeah." I took in another drag.

"I'm so sorry."

I shrugged, blowing the smoke out through my nose, and she placed her hand on mine. The touch made my skin heat.

When I gazed back at her, her eyes trailed back over to the striped tents. "What is happening to the world? How are they growing more powerful?" She squeezed my hand before placing it back in her lap. "A few months ago, life seemed normal. It felt safe."

Her eyes slowly slid to mine, her head now facing me and noting my frown, I'm sure. "Though I suppose it's never felt that way for you," she said quietly.

I flexed my jaw, again trying to muster up a smile. "It wasn't so bad in Ames. Before everything went to shit, anyway."

She gave me a small smile. "We'll get it back. All of it. And it will be better than it was before. I know it."

My eyes flared, and I blinked in surprise.

Her brown eyes twinkled, and she once again looked back at the tents. "We will make this world better. For everyone."

And in reading her emotions, I knew she meant it.

"You will certainly be an exceptional queen one day," I said softly.

Her eyes found mine again, a single tear trailing down her cheek. "Merrick..."

"Try it. You'll feel better," I insisted, offering up the drugs like the bad influence I was.

She scoffed, wiping away her tears. "I'm not a heathen," she said, sticking her nose in the air, her blonde bob flipping with the movement..

I rolled my eyes, and my lip curved into a half-smile. "That mouth of yours says otherwise."

Her head shot back to me, her tears already fading away at my distraction. "I say 'dick' once, and that makes me a heathen?"

I smirked. "No...but twice does. And you just said it for the second time."

She pulled her knees close to her body, sucking in her smile as she shook her head, looking away.

I raised my hands in defeat, the joint still in hand. "You're right. You really are just an uptight princess."

Her almond gaze darted to mine, and her lip curled as she plucked the dagga from my hand, pressed it to her lips, and sucked.

And sucked.

My eyes widened. "Era, that's too much—"

She pulled the joint away from her mouth and began coughing violently, the smoke slipping from her lips.

Quickly, I snatched the dagga, stubbing it out on the tree trunk, and began patting her back as she choked out, "Can't. Breathe!"

I was an asshole for the giggle that escaped me. Her furious gaze shot to mine, and she coughed so hard she gagged.

I grasped her chin, my thumb pulling her bottom lip down, and I leaned in close, my mouth hovering above hers.

The gesture made my heart flutter, especially as her wide-eyed gaze found mine. My lips were just an inch away from kissing her.

I used my magic, sucking the air—the smoke—from her lungs into mine, clearing it back to normal just as my hand trailed down her neck, resting against her chest. My palm didn't burn, but there was a slight tingle. I let the glow out, healing the minor inflammation in her lungs.

Her coughing ceased.

"Better?" I asked.

"You're an asshole," she breathed, but she didn't push me away.

My hand was still on her chest, and our lips were hovering so close. To an onlooker, we'd look like lovers about to devour one another.

I was high and not at all thinking clearly. I was grateful Roland and Hendry were checking in on Edmund, leaving no one to see us.

"I thought I was a dick?" I asked lowly.

She licked her lips. "That too."

My smile grew, and I let myself tune into her.

Yep. She was high now. Usually, the first time didn't work, but the Warlock's version clearly did the trick. I certainly felt fucking amazing right now.

The desire she felt poured into me, washing over me like molten lava. But I enjoyed the burn. Ached for it.

Both of our chests were moving rapidly, our heartbeats in a race with one another.

Why did I feel this way when I was around her?

My thoughts drifted back to a conversation Viola and I had last evening.

"What are we, Vi?" I asked as we lay in our tent.

Her head had tilted to the side, and she shrugged. "Does it matter?" Her hands trailed down my arms. "If it feels good?"

I mentally blocked out her feelings, not wanting to feel desire right at this moment, even though my own was demanding my attention.

"You've been my friend for many years," I said gently. "I just...I never felt this from you before."

"We weren't on the run before...weren't fighting for our lives."

That answered what I assumed. Viola wasn't in love with me. She simply wanted release.

I pulled my lips to the side, looking away and nodding slowly.

Viola cringed. "That came out wrong. Merrick—"

"No, Viola, I get it." I rolled my hoop earring between my fingers. "Friends with benefits. That's fine."

"Once we return to normalcy, whenever that is, maybe we can be something more."

This fixation I felt for Era...this lust...I never felt this magnitude of it before in my life, even when I was thrusting myself into Viola's gorgeous, tight heat. Even as she swirled her tongue on my dick.

What would Era look like with my cock in her mouth? In her pussy?

Wait, what the fuck am I thinking right now?

It was the drugs. That's all this was. Drugs.

She was the first to withdraw, shaking as she did so.

There was no smile on either of our faces as we stared at each other...because there was no denying what just happened. No denying that the desire she felt right now was for me. No denying the desire I felt was for her. Drugs or not.

Guilt flooded her senses, her face crumpling as she eyed Silas's tent.

"Era," I said softly, and her tearful eyes met mine. "It's the dagga making you feel that way. Not me. Don't feel bad."

I was lying, of course. Sure, the herb heightened libido. But it wouldn't make her desire *me*.

Her hands balled into fists, her lip curling. She went to retort, to say what, I didn't know. My eyes picked up movement before she could speak.

I tilted my head, watching as Lena exited Silas's tent. Once again, her emotions overpowered my senses. I swallowed the unpleasantness that washed over me despite the dagga's warmth. Despite Era's.

"How is he?" Era asked a little too loudly, scooting away from me.

"He's back to his old grumpy self," she muttered. "He'd like some water."

My brows creased as Era nodded. She stood, striding away to take care of her husband.

CHAPTER THIRTY-TWO

LENA

Silas had thankfully fallen to sleep. Because of the sound-proofing spell I did on the tent, no one on the outside knew whether I was done or not.

Part of me wanted to keep it this way for a little while. I watched as his breathing calmed and pushed his sweaty hair out of his face.

I loved how sweet he appeared at rest. How beautiful his face was. Even with that scar.

I ran my thumb along the raised, imperfect flesh. It was deep, that was for sure. But its thinness made me believe it was from a blade of some sort.

Silas let out a small sigh in his sleep as I caressed his cheek, his head tilting to rest against my hand.

I will always love you.

Who was he talking to when he said that? Were those words for me?

It was clear toward the end that Silas was hearing my voice, but his responses were still as if someone else was talking to him.

I had told him I'd always love him, too.

And that kiss...how was I supposed to get that kiss out of my head? Will he remember it?

Silas's eyes slowly opened, and I carefully removed my hand from his cheek. A wave of relief washed over me when I saw that his irises were back to their captivating golden hue.

I gave him a small smile. "Hey."

He didn't respond; he just stared at me with a frown that increasingly became more fearful.

My smile faltered. "It's over. You shouldn't have any more hallucinations."

Still no response, those golden eyes just shifting between mine.

"Silas—"

"Leave."

I blinked. "What?"

"I want you to leave," he replied hoarsely, a wince on his face.

"Leave...? Leave this tent, or—"

"The tent. Leave the tent."

I bit down on my lip in an attempt to harbor my emotions. "Very well," I whispered. I stood, and when I tilted my head down to look at him, his eyes were cast downward. "Can I get you anything? Water?"

The muscles in his jaw feathered. "Have someone else bring some."

My heart sank, and I twisted my head away before the burning in my eyes caused tears to pour out.

What did I do?

I halted with the tent fabric in my hand, about to exit. I peeked over my shoulder at him. "Silas, I don't actually know where the Weapon is. I hope you know that. I just said that shit to get him to stop hurting you."

He wouldn't look at me. "Leave."

I dragged my teeth against my lip, biting down hard enough that the slight pain pulled me out of my head.

I exited, striding toward Era. I was sure that was who he wished for. I was sure that's who his words were for.

She was sitting beside Merrick, the two of them in the middle of a conversation—a serious one, it seemed, as they both wore frowns on their faces.

Merrick looked over first, and then Era's brown eyes anxiously went to mine as she scooted away from him.

"How is he?" she asked.

"He's back to his old grumpy self. He'd like some water."

Era nodded, arms wrapping around herself as she ambled toward the tent.

As she left, I replaced her spot, sitting next to Merrick, covering my face.

"That bad, huh?" he asked.

"He couldn't even look at me after," I muttered.

"I'm sure he just needs time to adjust. He's been through a lot of trauma and just had to relive it. Who knows what exactly he saw."

I let my hands fall away from my face, and I studied my friend, his head resting against the tree trunk, his silver hair tied in a low bun. His jaw was set, surely thinking about his sister. "How's El?"

"She's out of it too, I'd imagine, if Silas is. I haven't seen her yet, though."

"How are *you*?"

He snorted, reddened eyes finding mine. His smile fell. "High as a kite. Like a pathetic piece of shit."

I pulled him into a hug, and he returned the gesture, holding me tight. Merrick didn't hug much, but he always hugged me. "Shut up. You aren't a piece of shit."

He was silent for many moments. "I am, Lena. My sister is the one actually suffering, and I can't even handle it filtered through me. I had to numb it. I'm weak."

I leaned back, eyeing the wrapped herb lying on the ground beside him. "If you're weak, then so am I," I responded, picking his joint off the ground and lighting it with my index finger.

I didn't like using substances usually. I craved control—needed it. But honestly, after my interaction with Silas, I could use a bit of numbing, too. So, I inhaled the smoke and let its effects wash over me.

"What?" I hissed quietly two hours later. "I am not getting salt all in our tent."

"Then put it on the outside," Roland offered, leaning back on his elbows, shirtless, with his appealing physique tempting me.

The little mage lights in our tent accentuated every ripple of muscle in Roland's body.

He told me he wanted to fuck me—hard—and urged that I soundproof our tent so he could do so.

"Right. I may as well put up a sign saying, 'Do not disturb. Lena and Roland are screwing in this tent.'"

His sexy grin grew. "I'm sure they already assume that," he purred, leaning up and kissing my neck softly.

My eyes fluttered closed, and I leaned my head back on his shoulder as he sucked on my skin.

"Mmm...that's true..."

Roland's dark chuckle spread goosebumps across my skin. "Come on, Ginger Snap," he pleaded. "I'm desperate."

Nearly an hour later, I was lying on Roland's sweaty chest, catching my breath after he made true to his promise.

"Hope that spell worked," Roland teased. "I think that's the hardest I've made you scream."

I pinched his side, and he slapped my ass.

I grinned, leaning up to look at him. "Tell me more about yourself, Roland."

His eyes danced downward to me. "What do you want to know?"

I quirked my mouth to the side, tapping my lips as I thought about it. "You got any family?"

"I do. Mom and Dad, and four sisters." His fingers drifted up and down my back.

"Four?!"

He laughed. "I know, I know. Our household was always full of drama." He smiled to himself as he reminisced. "I'm the middle child. Two big sisters, two younger ones."

I gently caressed his torso. "Do you miss them?"

His smile slipped, and his eyes returned to mine. "Terribly. It had already been a few months since I saw them by the time we got to Ames." He sighed, sucking in his bottom lip. "I'm sure they've been notified of my betrayal by now. I can only hope they'll understand." He rubbed his eyes with his free hand. "My mother is probably worried sick."

"You seemed to join this cause easily...did you have any doubts?"

"No. I've never liked the King, and I believe in Silas. I believe he'll be a far better leader."

Roland was looking up now, away from me, brows drawn together. The muscle in his jaw was ticking.

"I feel there's something you're not telling me, Roland." I felt him tense slightly, which was proof enough that there was something he was hiding. I leaned up on my elbow. "What happened between you two?"

He gnawed at his lip again, shaking his head as he sat up, running his hands through his short, dark hair. "We just have a past. That's all you need to know." I opened my mouth to press further, but Roland's serious gaze slid to mine. "I won't talk about it."

Thoughts scrambled through my mind, but I couldn't come up with anything that made sense. Roland had to have done something to piss off Silas...but what?

I nodded slowly, my eyes raking down, studying the wings tattooed on his back and down his sides. Angel wings. There was so much about him I knew nothing about.

"What's the inspiration for your tattoo?" I asked, changing the subject.

His shoulders relaxed, clearly happy to be talking about something else. "I've always found the Angels fascinating—even if they don't exist anymore." He shrugged, a smile tugging at his lips. "Plus, I thought it looked badass."

I laughed through my nose, sitting up to run my fingers along his inked skin. "It is badass," I agreed.

"Will you ever get any tattoos?"

I traced the feathers in his wings, goosebumps spreading across his flesh. "I'd like to. I'm just not quite sure what I'd get."

"I'm sure you'd make anything look badass, Ginger Snap." Roland kissed the top of my head, then nudged himself upward, leaving me sitting alone as he slid on his pants.

"Where are you going?" I pouted.

"I just need to clear my head." He leaned down, kissing me gently on the lips. "Sweet dreams, Lena."

My chest hurt as I watched him exit, feeling guilty for asking him about Silas. But still, why would that question cause him distress?

The following morning, we packed up our belongings, and as I mounted Donut, a horse I was growing attached to, Dani held out ***Potestas Verae Maleficis.***

"I'd like you to do some reading," she said as I petted the horse's mane. "I want you to learn how to teleport as soon as possible. Page two-hundred fourteen. You'll notice how that section of spells relies on Titharan symbols. The language." She stretched her arms, preparing to shift. "You'll have the book to look at for reference, but familiarizing yourself with it will help."

"Is this similar to the portal Immeron has on the mountain?" Roland asked as he lifted himself up to sit behind me. I was grateful he'd come back to sleep beside me later in the night.

Dani flipped her ponytail, grinning. "Yes, and no. A stagnant portal is far easier to conjure, especially with your ability to do so innately. Still advanced, but nothing compared to the power of being able to bring yourself directly to the mountaintop from here."

I couldn't even fathom having that much power.

"Have you done it before?" I asked her, leaning back into Roland's body. He slowly caressed my thigh.

Her blue eyes softened. "No. I've never had the strength to. Only a select few Warlocks have succeeded in doing it. We're talking only the best of the best of our kind." She placed the tome in my hand.

I glanced down at the book just as Dani shifted into the stunning stallion, and we all continued our journey further south.

I spent hours flipping through the ancient text. Notes were made in our language, so thankfully, I was able to understand most.

The symbols for the advanced spells all involved a sort of pentagram. Along its lines, various symbols were etched, all with different meanings. At the very beginning of this text, a glossary was present, and every symbol was listed with its purpose, along with the Titharan alphabet.

It was fascinating. Exciting.

As I read, I noticed plenty of mentions of Tithara, the Goddess of Wisdom. Apparently, the Goddess created these symbols as a way for the Gods' magical designs to communicate with their creators—to understand their roots better.

How, I didn't know. That was just what it said.

As I read further, more information about the Gods and Goddesses spread throughout, I found something that caught my eye. I about toppled off of Donut.

First, listed was information I already knew.

Ravaiana – The Goddess of Life

Valor – The God of Death

Tithara – The Goddess of Wisdom

Azrae – The God of Vengeance

Celluna – The Goddess of Love

Then, just below, a prophecy had been made. Centuries ago.

ONLY AFTER THE SIN OF DEATH WILL FOUR GODS RISE TO POWER

The God of Deceit

The Goddess of Sacrifice

The God of Rebirth

The Goddess of Purification

MAY AZRAE SHOW MERCY TO US ALL.

"Whoa...what the fuck," I respired.

Sacrifice. Rebirth. Purification. Those were all the *exact* meanings of three of the four birds on the Otacian crest.

My mind was reeling.

So...The Goddess of Sacrifice protects The God of Rebirth and The Goddess of Purification...from Valor?

"Roland, will you hand me the book in my bag?" I asked nervously.

Silas's eyes finally flitted over to me after ignoring me since he woke up yesterday. "What's wrong?" he pressed, noting the panic in my voice immediately.

Roland plopped the Warlock text in my hand, and I opened it, flipping through the pages with haste.

The only God who was not symbolized in the crest was The God of Deceit. What creature stood for it?

Deceit, Deceit...there.

Spider: Deceit

Spider.

"FUCK!" I blurted, pulling on the reins to force Donut to a halt.

"What?!" Silas demanded.

I rushed off the horse, clutching the books. "Dani!"

Merrick and Vi exchanged a quick, nervous glance before rushing off the Warlock. She shifted back to her human form instantly. "What the bloody hell—"

"This prophecy," I said breathlessly, pointing to the text.

Her eyes skated down to it. "Yeah? What about it?"

"The God of Deceit. The animal that symbolizes deceit is a spider."

She frowned, her eyes widening as she made the connection. "There's no possible way," she breathed, shaking her head.

"Uh, can someone clue us in as to what the fuck you guys are talking about?" Merrick said impatiently.

"If he were a God, what would he need this Weapon for?"

Everyone's face paled from Dani's question.

"It's the only thing that can stop him," I whispered. "Magic to stop all magic."

Silas bared his teeth. "Someone explain. Now."

So, I did. I told him of the animal symbolism in the Otacian crest, of Igon's compass, and of the necromancer's mark.

"If this is real, why would these new Gods be depicted on the Otacian crest? What is the purpose?" Silas prodded. "Why isn't a spider a part of the design?"

"When did the crest get created?" Dani asked.

Silas turned to her. "When the kingdom was founded. Centuries ago."

"Only through fire can the phoenix be reborn from the ashes..." Merrick spoke slowly, reciting Igon's words. "You think...you think Igon wishes you to raise this God of Rebirth?"

I ran my hands through my hair, letting out a dry laugh. "Fuck if I know. Where would I even find him? And what of the other two?"

The pelican symbolizing Igon was an idea out the door now. But still, the pelican being engraved on the compass could not be a coincidence.

"Wouldn't someone know if they're a God already?" Hendry asked, entirely skeptical of this idea. "Wouldn't you be able to tell?"

"No one knows what any of the Gods look like," Elowen responded, her aqua eyes narrowed. "Besides, with the power they possess, I'm sure they could disguise themselves as one of us."

Dani chewed at her nails, pacing in circles before coming to a stop, her hand falling to her side. "Maybe the Warlocks of Daranois have some answers."

I whipped my head to her. "You know where there are more Warlocks?"

"I'm not certain they're there. A coven used to reside there centuries ago. In the caverns." Her eyes slid to the Prince. "Ever since Otacia gained control of Daranois, my people have stayed away. But a powerful Warlock from Daranois wrote **Potestas Verae Maleficis.** If anyone has any further knowledge, it would be them."

Daranois was one of Otacia's first conquered kingdoms. It would be hard to believe any remained, but then again, the fact that Warlocks ruled Forsmont would've seemed improbable a few months ago.

Maybe they still resided there.

"We have to continue to Faltrun," Silas insisted, "and to wherever Lena is being led." He studied me. "Do you think Igon knew of the Gods' identities?"

I shook my head slowly, then shrugged in defeat. "I...I don't know. Seers cannot give up all their information without the potential of altering the future." I flitted my eyes to the sky, picturing our Supreme looking down on us. "If he did, he wouldn't have been able to tell."

Edmund ran a comforting hand down Elowen's trembling arm. "By infiltrating the minds of those he overtakes, does the necromancer have the ability to get into their memories? Would he have been able to see what Igon saw?"

"If he has seen everything Igon has, we'd be fucked already. Igon clearly had an idea where this Weapon was located." I took a steadying breath. "I think the Lord of the Shadows is simply a host—a parasite."

"For all we know," Hendry continued, "this necromancer could be serving this God of Deceit. It doesn't necessarily mean he is him."

"We can only hope." I turned to Dani. "What sin did death—did Valor do that resulted in four new Gods?"

She shrugged. "It has always been a mystery. And the biggest folklore. I mean, this was prophesized hundreds of years ago. I never thought too much about it before."

Merrick placed a hand on my shoulder, sensing my unease. "We can go over ideas as we walk, but Silas is right. We need to keep moving. If the necromancer truly is a God, we need an army now more than ever."

I went over theories in my head for the rest of the day, but I couldn't come up with any ideas on the identity of not only The God of Deceit but the other three Gods that supposedly had been created.

I was fascinated by all I learned. Apparently, the Gods once roamed our planet before Valor's sin caused a punishment, forcing them back into their own realms by Azrae.

Another unclear message was written.

DEATH AND LIFE. EVERYTHING MUST BALANCE.

Ravaiana was forced back to Elysium, and Valor went to the Underworld, otherwise known in this text as Elytial. Celluna, Tithara, and Azrae's realms were not listed.

Azrae, the God of Vengeance, was apparently the only one who was still able to visit here...Sol, our realm was called.

HE WILL RIGHT THE WRONG AT GREAT COST. CELLUNA WILL MAKE SURE OF IT.

I was so sick of these vague answers. There had to be a reason Igon didn't outright tell me everything. He wouldn't make me or my people suffer for no reason.

Or would he?

If Nereida really was a safe haven for our kind, why would he have kept us in Ames? Why would he have us surrender?

It was our final evening before reaching Faltrun. Once more, our tents were set up, and we were ready for, hopefully, our last night of unsavory sleep. This time, Merrick performed the sound-proofing spell around our camp. I had attempted to perform *occultare nos ab aspectu,* a cloaking spell to hide us, but the incantation proved difficult. I was unable to successfully perform it.

"Don't beat yourself up. It takes far more energy to complete. You'll get it eventually," Dani had encouraged.

We were eating dinner: a deer Hendry had managed to shoot down and that Roland had cooked and seasoned. Elowen winced but forced herself to eat it. She never would eat meat in our village; she had always felt too bad for the animals.

I strode up to Silas, who was in the middle of a conversation with Erabella.

"Can I talk to you for a moment?" I asked him, his glare finding mine, threatening me to cower.

Era surprisingly beamed at me. I gave her a tight-lipped smile in return.

He nodded, kissing Era's hand before following me.

Did he do that just to hurt me?

We strolled off further into the forest, and when we had some privacy, I faced him.

"You feel it too, don't you?" I finally asked, looking up at him. "That dark feeling."

Silas shrugged, staring off into the distance. "I don't know," he answered blandly.

"You felt it in the forest that first day I met you," I pressed. "I know you did."

"So what?" His eyes snapped to mine. "I felt it many times after that."

My eyes flickered. "You did?"

He nodded grimly. "I don't remember every moment. I just have felt it from time to time." He exhaled through his nose, looking back into the trees. "I felt it...I felt it the night you supposedly died. So strongly it woke me from my sleep."

I swallowed, eyes looking up at him. "What could that mean? We've only felt it in close proximity to his creations." My eyes flared. "You don't think he was in Otacia, do you? Near the castle?"

He faced me then, glowering at me in contempt. "I. Don't. Know."

He went to storm off as if I'd actually allow that.

"Look at me," I ordered, gripping his arm tightly. He bared his teeth as his eyes flitted down to me. I kept my chin up high. "Don't retreat on me," I demanded. "Don't return to being cold."

He went to tug away, but I held him tighter.

"I would've spewed any bullshit if it meant saving you, saving my friends. I know you're pissed about that—"

"You don't know shit," he retorted.

I balled my fists, then angled my head upward, looking at him through my nose. "He believes I am of use to him. That offers us some protection, at least for now."

"Regardless of if he does or does not call your bluff, he will be following us. Tracking us. I'd hardly call that protection."

330

"He was already following us," I countered. "Only this time, he should hopefully be keeping to himself." Silas didn't respond, so I continued, "I hate your father, Silas. But I wouldn't side with a literal monster just because I fear Ulric...fear whatever his use of the Weapon would be."

Silas's eyes shifted between mine. "They are both monsters," he said quietly.

My gaze softened at the sight of torment behind his eyes. I released his arm from my grasp. He stared for a moment longer as if debating to say more before ultimately treading away.

CHAPTER THIRTY-THREE

LENA

“Like I said before,” Dani said the subsequent daybreak, “I don't trust these bastards. Not one bit.” Her eyes flicked to Vi. “We should spy. Turn into flies and follow in case anything goes awry.”

“Turn into a fly?” Viola asked anxiously, crossing her arms. “I've never turned into something so small before. I don't know if I can muster that much energy.”

She pulled her lips to the side. “Okay, fine. How about a bird?”

Viola nodded slowly. “A bird I can do.”

The Warlock's gaze drifted over us all. “I'll be able to sneak in with you guys. Vi can watch from the outside. If they seem chill, great. Otherwise, I have a way of getting you out if things go bad.”

“What, just tearing off heads?” Roland questioned. “Faltrun's army is triple that of Forsmont, and this time, we don't have your kind here to help us." His worried gaze went to Silas. "What do we do if they wish to turn you in? Keep us prisoners? Kill us?"

Silas sighed, pinching the bridge of his nose.

Dani spoke instead. "I'll be bringing in my magical inventory. If I need to, I can cast an invisibility spell. I could slit necks without being seen." She roughly patted her bag. "I will have a lot in my arsenal."

"How can a fly carry a bag so large?" Hendry asked after chugging from his waterskin. It's clear that even he, the calm and collected one, was anxious about this endeavor.

"The best way I can explain it without confusing you is this: when I shift, it's almost as if my other forms are in a closet. I can dress them up as I wish, and when I switch, they keep the same clothes on."

"Where do you go?" Elowen asked. Her gaze shifted to Viola. "Is it like that for you, Vi?"

Viola smiled at our friend. "That's a good way of putting it. I've never tried the body of another, so I never tried dressing them up."

Dani threw her hair up in her high pony as she spoke. "If you wish to appear as someone else, not just a different version of who you are, you can wear exactly what the person you're trying to imitate is wearing. It's not the same for us Warlocks."

Viola cocked a brow. "Because you can only shift...not innately cast illusions."

"Bingo, babe. Again, this is a perfect example of how Mages are more powerful. You can combine your shifting gift with your illusion magic." Dani grinned, then motioned at herself. "Come on, now. Try to turn into me."

"What?" Vi took a step back, her purple braids bouncing against her back. "I've never—"

"You can do it," Dani said confidently. "And think, if you can shift yourself into one of the guards, that could prove incredibly useful. Plus, it doesn't take as much energy as being a large or teeny creature. C'mon."

Vi took a steadying breath, focusing her vision on the Warlock. Our entire group studied her, Silas especially, as if waiting to see if this power was really true.

After examining Dani for a few moments, Viola exhaled, squeezing her eyes shut before her body morphed into another. In but a blink of an eye, there were two Dani's standing before us.

"I'll be damned," Merrick muttered, his thumb dragging against his lip ring.

"Do me next," Roland pleaded, a wide grin on his handsome face.

Viola turned to him, chuckling. Even her laugh was Dani's. She focused on Roland and then did the same, tuning into the sexy soldier beside me.

"That is crazy," Edmund breathed, eyes darting between her and Roland.

Viola's hazel eyes—Roland's eyes—drifted to Silas, focusing only for a moment before she turned into him next.

His mouth fell open at the sight, staring directly at his doppelganger. "Say something," he instructed in awe.

"Something," Viola spoke, and I got chills at the sound of Silas's voice coming from her lips.

"Bloody amazing," Dani admired. "Don't wear yourself out too much."

"Why didn't you teach her of this before?" Silas questioned further. "This could change everything."

Dani scratched the back of her head. "Honestly? I assumed she'd know she could do that already." She posed with a grace face. "Aren't you guys grateful you got me?"

I smiled. To my surprise, Silas laughed through his nose. "I never thought the day would come that I'd be grateful for a Warlock. Or a Mage, for that matter." He sucked in his lips, then swallowed. "Thank you—all of you. Thank you for joining me in doing this."

Seeing a sliver of vulnerability from the Prince made my face fall. Seeing his humility...his charm. That was Quill who spoke just now.

Despite the tattoos and scars, despite the anger and resentment, that sweet prince who I had seen addressing his kingdom all those years ago was still in there.

My friends also seemed astonished by his comment. Era smiled to herself from her spot in front of him on their horse.

Perhaps he showed her that side of him...perhaps she was the only one who knew Quill now.

My heart lurched in my chest, and I glanced down, rubbing my hands together to attempt to warm them. My ice was pleading to be released.

Viola goggled at him, then shifted back into herself. "Thank you, Prince, for giving our people a chance. We are grateful for you, too." Her smile grew. "I never thought that day would EVER come."

Another laugh, and Silas smiled softly at her. When his gaze drifted to me, his happy expression faded away.

I gave him my best attempt at a smile, but the sadness overwhelmed me...seeing his arms around Era's waist.

"Alright, gang," Edmund chirped, though his hands shook slightly. "Let's do this."

As we strode up to Faltrun, arriving that afternoon, my nerves increased. The odds of having such a pleasant experience as we did in Forsmont were highly unlikely.

"Give us all the info, boss man," Roland had said to Silas a couple of hours prior.

So, he did. The leader of Faltrun was a man named Dimitri Cortev, son of Elvero Cortev, their previous King. While the Cortevs have kept their independence, Silas insisted their leadership was nothing like Forsmont's.

"Even when I met Leroy in the past, I knew he was a just leader. I had respect for him." Silas's face hardened. "But Dimitri...something has always rubbed me the wrong way about him."

"He's a drunk, we know that much," Hendry commented, mismatched eyes constricting in disgust. "Perhaps we can use his inebriation to our advantage."

"Or he'll be less likely to listen to reason," Merrick interjected. "I imagine this could go either way."

"Dimitri craves power. He just doesn't have the means to achieve it like my father does."

"Partnering with a mini-Ulric...seems like a great idea," I mumbled.

Silas slid his gaze to mine. "Better with us than with each other, wouldn't you agree?"

I swallowed, the heat of his gaze too much for me. I nodded and focused back on the road.

Now, we were striding up the gates in Faltrun. Silas greeted them just as he had in Forsmont, the guards here, in their colors of gold and green, studying us warily. We were granted entry, being closely watched and followed as we were led to the castle.

As I focused on the people who roamed the streets of this immense kingdom, I couldn't help but notice how different the energy was here. Like Otacia, this place was split by class. The beggars on the side of the road held up tin cups, pleading for some spare bronze. Drunks were sleeping on the roads, and bards were performing on various corners. I attempted to listen to their poetic words, but my nerves were so high-strung that I could only focus on the clacking of our horse's hoofs as they walked us forward on the broken roads.

Dani was flying around us—I could hear the incessant buzzing. She fit right in here; the filth from the lower class had multiple flies surrounding this area.

How could the King here allow his people to live this way? In Otacia, there was poverty, yes. There were areas worse off in the Outer Ring. But never was it like *this*.

The horrid areas didn't last forever, fortunately. As we found ourselves closer and closer to the enormous brick castle, beggars turned to shoppers. Filth turned to well-kept roads. Weary faces turned to large smiles, though those smiles lacked the genuine spark that those in Forsmont wore.

I didn't like it here.

My eyes found a sign crafted out of driftwood, a business called **The Artist's Guild**.

The words of Ryia La'Rune came to me, visions of the painting in Castle La'Rune seizing my mind.

Death by a lover's fire.

I frowned.

Only through fire can the phoenix be reborn from the ashes.

I thought surely that was a coincidence until I remembered the name of the piece.

Rebirth.

I sucked in a breath, not wanting to appear crazy and have another outburst like before.

Rebirth...could that painting have somehow symbolized the awakening of the God of Rebirth? Ryia had mentioned it was a painting commissioned here. What was the artist's name? Did the artist know something? Or was it simply just a painting inspired by ancient myths?

And why, once again, was there a hint residing in Otacia?

I exhausted an exhale as I dismounted Donut. When I glanced at Merrick, who looked at me in question, I shook my head. Theories could wait until later. Surviving this encounter was all I should focus on.

My eyes flicked up to the blackbird perched atop the stone gargoyle looming above. Viola.

We walked up the steps to the front entrance of the castle, Viola watching us closely just as the fly buzzing around us zoomed inside.

Elowen was stiff as she walked beside me. I brushed her arm in comfort, and she gave me a worried smile. Edmund's gloved hand was around her hip, and his boots were effectively hiding his enchanted limb. Of course, all of us Mages were glamoured.

The inside of the castle matched its outside: bare, grey brick, cream floors, and warm sconces. The walls of the hallway we were led down were lined with Faltrun's flag, art pieces that probably cost thousands of gold pieces, and knight armor that stood menacingly. Less of a modern feel like Otacia's castle.

Wooden doors before us creaked as the guards guiding us flung them open, leading us into a banquet hall.

My jaw dropped at the sight of the long table—big enough to seat maybe thirty people. On it was a spread of enough food to feed an army: soups, breads, and pies. Vegetables, pastries, and every meat imaginable. There was a pig's head, for fuck's sake.

At the back of the room was an elevated throne, a man sitting sloppily in it. We walked past the table as we approached him, and my mouth watered. No one else was in this room except for two guards on either side of the King.

Who is this feast for?

"The Prince of Otacia," Dimitri drawled as we approached, rotating the silver goblet in his hand as he eyed Silas. "What is your excuse for blessing us with your presence?"

His long, frizzy hair was jet-black. His ice-blue eyes popped against his tanned skin, and they were half-lidded, suggesting that the man had consumed a bit too much alcohol or perhaps a substance of some kind.

He didn't appear old, perhaps in his late thirties, but his skin showed signs of aging, the bags under his eyes more prominent than expected for a man his age.

At Silas's pause, Dimitri's eerie grin grew, and he gestured to the banquet table. "Come—sit. You must be famished from your travels. We were just setting up a feast to celebrate our recent triumph."

Silas's brows lowered. "Oh? And what is that?"

Dimitri stood, swaying slightly. "All good things to those who wait," he insisted, raising a finger. He slowly paced to the head of the table, the guards escorting him and watching closely in case they needed to grasp his arms to prevent him from collapsing.

The guard to his right hauled out his chair, but I noticed that his eyes remained on me. He was handsome, so much so that it seemed bizarre seeing him stand behind this King. He was older, probably in his forties, but his skin was smooth, nothing but the crinkles of his eyes giving away his age.

Dimitri Cortev plopped himself down, chugging the remainder of his drink as we all took a seat.

"I come to seek an alliance with Faltrun," Silas said in the drawn-out silence from his spot at the table, eyes hardened on the drunken King. None of us dared to touch any food.

Dimitri's vile smile grew slowly until he was in a full drunken laugh. "You and what army?" His eyes widened, his bright blue eyes piercing as he continued in a mocking tone. "You're a witch sympathizer now, is that it?" His gaze danced over us all. "Do you travel with any now?"

Silas's frown deepened. "No," he lied.

The guard to his right would not stop staring at me, his green eyes almost wide. Almost. He was doing his best to school his expression, but I could see through it.

Dimitri smirked, waving his goblet in the air. "More," he ordered to the brown-haired man intent on gazing at me. "Send Polly in, will you? She's my favorite."

The man listened, finally breaking our stare and hurrying out a door. He was gone only momentarily before a woman with a wine bottle in hand followed him back into the room.

The woman with auburn hair wandered in, her cheeks hollow, her eyes distant. But the frightening thing wasn't just the pointed cartilage of hers that was visible, but the wicked metal binding her wrists.

Cuffs. Otacian cuffs.

Elowen staggered back in her chair, the legs screeching, and it was enough to have Dimitri calling Silas's bluff. "No witches, eh?"

Silas's eyes grew. "You've partnered with Otacia already."

That sinister smirk grew. "Over a year ago, princeling. Your father supplied us with these cuffs just over a year ago. An effort to sway us. It sure as shit worked." As Polly filled his glass, he brushed her arms with his mouth. She bit down hard on her lip, shaking slightly. "With those nasty Undead running around, it only made sense to partner with the King," he murmured, eyes trailing over Polly's body.

I was going to be sick. How was Silas not aware of this?

"You saw an Undead over a year ago?" Silas asked quietly. According to him, it had been just over half a year that they had been dealing with the necromancer's creations.

Dimitri gave a fake look of sympathy. "Aww. Did daddy dearest never tell you that? Good thing, considering what a traitor you've become."

My eyes fluttered around the room, desperately searching for Dani.

"Now, will you surrender? Or shall we have a little blood bath?" His hungry eyes trailed down the Mage prisoner. "Poor Polly here will be forced to clean up all the blood. I do enjoy seeing her bent over, though."

Her eyes filled with tears, but her expression remained blank.

I'm going to kill him. I'm going to fucking kill him.

Soldiers bearing the cuffs advanced, and I had seconds to think. We were fucked if we lost our magic. Then again, Dani and

Vi were in hiding, the Warlock buzzing around this room with the Faltrunians none the wiser.

We could escape and have the upper hand. If Vi shifted into a guard, perhaps their thumbprint could free us.

I could slit Dimitri's throat...burn him alive in his sleep. He'd never see it coming.

Reeling back my homicidal thoughts, I said, "There's no point fighting." I looked at all my friends. "We've been bested."

Silas slowly turned to me, and a silent conversation was passed between us.

"You sure you know what you're doing?"

I have a plan. Trust me.

He swallowed, then nodded slightly.

"Wow, that's it?" Dimitri snorted. "When did the Prince of Otacia become such a pussy?"

Silas's lip curled, but he kept his eyes on mine.

Trust me.

The brown-haired guard just watched me, and his eyes flared as the cuffs secured my wrists and my true appearance was revealed. Merrick and El were next. The only thing I could be grateful for was the fact they remained detached.

Dimitri clicked his tongue. his eyes roaming over us all as our glamours faded. He licked his lips, grasping Polly's ass, her lip trembling. His eyes met mine. "I may have use for you," he said to me, his lip curving.

My heart sped up, sweat beading my hairline.

No. I will not be violated again.

Never again.

"Over my dead fucking body," I spat.

Silas's gaze burned into mine, our eyes never leaving one another. His eyes spoke to me.

"I will not let anything happen to you."

The Otacians were not put in any confines. Their weapons were simply stripped from them, as were ours.

"So, what's your plan?" Silas gritted out, eyes finally darting to Dimitri as he was tugged out of his chair by a guard. "You hand us over to my father?"

Dimitri chuckled, the sound grating against my bones. He laughed so hard he began hacking up a lung.

After he composed himself, his grin grew. "Oh, you have no idea what's to come, princeling."

We were dragged out of our seats, roughly shoved forward. I had no idea where we were being led, but as I heard a buzzing in my ear, my nerves calmed. Just a bit.

The green-eyed guard just watched me. Gods...did he wish to use me as Dimitri suggested? How fucked up were these people?

We walked for a while through various stone hallways. I tried to memorize them all...tried to remember how I could find my way back up here when the time came.

The last door we were brought to was metal, and it was unlocked with a key. We descended the steps, my heart sinking at the sight.

Hundreds of my kind were kept in the enormous cell beneath the fortress, with iron bars and the same familiar cuffs on all their wrists. Gaunt-looking faces studied us with little emotion. Men, women, children—all frail and broken.

All with shaved heads.

And the smell...by the looks of those trapped here, baths were a rare luxury. And they must see to their needs somewhere close by.

Faltrun wasn't turning over Mages to Otacia like they were supposed to.

Faltrun was enslaving them.

We were shoved in, and as my eyes skated over these people—my people—I whirled, grasping the iron bars.

"You fucking bastards!" I shouted as the barred door was locked. "You will pay for this!"

The asshole with the key just disregarded me and began his assent up the stone stairway, the rest of the guards following, leaving only one who just watched at the far end of the room.

My grip on the iron bars tightened, and I fought the urge to shed tears.

We were fucked. So, so fucked.

Then again, if Dani or Vi could manage to free us, all of us, we'd have a fucking army on our hands. A weak, starved army, but an army none the less.

I was pulled out of my thoughts by a voice, a shaky voice.

A voice I hadn't heard in so long.

"Lena?"

As I turned, my knees buckled at the sight of short, white hair and broken, brown eyes.

At the sight of Torrin Brighthell.

Enslaved in this cell.

CHAPTER THIRTY-FOUR

LENA - LAST YEAR

"The news has spread faster than Despia's plague," Viola muttered just as I strolled up to the campfire my friends had set up. Summer was upon us, and being able to enjoy the pleasant nighttime breeze with them, drinking wine and telling stories, was the highlight of my days.

Torrin's nervous eyes met mine from his spot on the ground. I frowned.

What is it?

"Who actually gives a shit?" Merrick responded, inhaling a puff of whatever herb he was smoking. Elowen was scowling at him over the smell. Torrin said nothing. "I feel bad for whatever broad is stuck with that bastard."

"What bastard?" I asked, a soft blanket wrapped around me as I sat next to Torrin. He was stiff, his eyes now glued on the fire.

"Silas La'Rune," Elowen responded.

I froze, my stomach flipping.

"Rumor has it the Prince has a wife," Viola answered, her voice becoming muffled as my head struggled to grasp her words. "The first step to him becoming King one day."

I blinked. Over and over and over.

"Gods, I am not looking forward to that day," Elowen murmured, hugging her knees. "Do you think he'll be worse than his father?"

Silas is married.

Silas has a wife.

"Excuse me," I said quietly, placing my glass on the ground, discarding my blanket, and walking off. My friends thought nothing of it, continuing their conversations as I strode away—faster.

Faster.

"Lena!"

I could just barely hear Torrin call out for me, the heat inside me and around me taking all my attention, all my energy.

Fuck, I was burning. I continually thought of Torrin's words to me, words that have helped me all these years.

Calm the flames.

Calm the flames.

Calm the flames.

I hadn't felt this level of rage, of devastation, of *brokenness* since the first time I got my fire.

I knew it was bound to happen one day, Silas moving on. In fact, I was surprised it hadn't happened sooner. But fuck, it still hurt.

I had already lost our child, and now that he was married to someone else...I had lost him. Forever.

Torrin grabbed my arms and cursed, his hands flying back. "Lena, we need to get you in the lake," he said in a panic.

"No! Just go away, Torrin!"

The lake. That actually sounded good as I stared at the water just steps away, the moonlight reflecting off of the ripples.

I didn't want him near if I was going to combust, and that's surely what it felt like.

I'd already scarred his hand. I didn't want to hurt him ever again.

"We're going!" he growled, not taking no for an answer. He hissed as he grasped my arm, pulling me toward the body of water.

"LET GO! I don't want to hurt you again!" I pulled back, and to my despair, fire shot out of my palms right at Torrin. My eyes widened in horror as I watched the blast of flame head for Torrin's face.

No!

Torrin held out his palms and swirled them before angling my flame to the lake behind us, successfully extinguishing it as the bolt hit the water.

Before I could apologize, Torrin grabbed my waist and hurled me into the water. I landed with a splash; the move catching me by surprise meant water shot up my nose. It burned, but not as bad as my body did.

I emerged, choking for air, brushing the water from my eyes. I blinked a few times, staring at Torrin, who examined me with both fear and worry. The moonlight cast on him made his white-blonde hair appear as if it glowed. His brown eyes were dark and concerned.

"Torrin, I am so—"

He made his way into the lake and, in a few seconds, was standing in front of me. I noticed he didn't even flinch. In fact, the water had warmed from me simply being in here.

I already felt ten times better.

With hesitation, Torrin lifted his hand and softly traced his fingers along my cheek. My eyes fluttered shut, and I let out a soft sigh.

"That's better," he murmured.

He was so close to me. All the horrid emotions I felt were fading, still ever present, but his body...his hand on my face, grounded me.

"Calm the flames, baby," he whispered.

Those words...his voice...this man.

This man who had taken care of me since the moment I met him.

This man whose hand bore scars because he saved me from myself.

It was all I needed.

I leaned forward, pressing my mouth against his, savoring the feeling of his lips on mine.

My body buzzed at the feeling, a whole different type of warmth now spreading through me.

Torrin held the kiss for only a moment before he quickly pulled away, wide-eyed and in shock. My cheeks heated in embarrassment at what I had just done, crossing that line we'd danced around for quite some time now.

Did I just ruin everything?

His eyes bounced between mine, his breathing quick, and an instant later, he pulled me close and kissed me back. My lips parted, as did his, and our tongues began to circle around one another in slow, torturous circles. He tasted so good.

Torrin's strong arms were wrapped around my torso, holding me close, and my hands trailed past his pointed ears and into his platinum hair, my fingers weaving through.

Gods, this feels so good.

I hadn't kissed anyone since the last time I kissed Silas. Even though some men in the village had shown interest, it was never reciprocated. Even Merrick admitted feelings at one point, and as much as I loved him, I couldn't do it.

But Torrin...Gods, I have had feelings for him for a while now. While I always thought he was handsome, I didn't begin desiring him until the last year or so...or at least admitting it to myself. Even still, with my feelings for Silas and our history, the guilt I felt kept me from trying anything with anyone.

But Silas was married now. It was over. It didn't matter that he was my apparent "Soul-Tie".

I had to move on.

I wanted to.

I *needed to*.

I could tell myself I wanted a distraction. But the truth was, I wanted Torrin. I needed *him*.

Torrin kissed me with hunger, with desperation, and I did the same, clinging to his body under the water and wrapping my arms around his waist. He held me up, his hands gliding down to my ass.

I knew Torrin had seen other girls over the last four years, but I didn't know how far he went with any of them...didn't want to know.

Torrin broke the kiss. "Lena, we shouldn't—"

I didn't listen to him. I pressed my mouth back against his, then trailed my hand down between us, grasping his hardened length under the water.

He groaned and drew away, his lips now kissing and sucking on my neck as I rubbed him over his pants.

I moaned softly.

"I need you in my room before all of Ames sees what I do to you," Torrin whispered inside my mind.

I let out a breathy chuckle.

Let them see, I don't care.

He growled, his hands trailing beneath my dress and his fingertips brushing over my center.

I inhaled sharply, his mouth still devouring my neck, those fingers teasing me.

I gripped him harder, and he fully lifted me into his arms. He rushed me out of the water and in between trees, the leaves providing us privacy. His lips never left mine until he placed me on the grass, helping me peel my dress off. I was left in nothing but my bra and underwear.

His shirt came off next, and my mouth parted, viewing his strong physique. I'd seen him shirtless over the years, my eyes always darting away quickly at the feeling the sight of him gave me. But now I could look, could indulge in the view of his attractiveness.

He nervously brought his hands to the buttons of his pants and halted, his cheeks staining with color.

He was nervous, and Gods, if that didn't turn me on. Something about this man...this tall, beautiful man who was over seven years older than me, getting flustered at the idea of being intimate stimulated me further.

You mean so much to me. I want to see you.

He gave me a soft smile. *"You mean everything to me, Lena."*

I bit my lip to prevent it from trembling and brought my hands to my back, unhooking my bra. I watched as Torrin's eyes darkened, a small gasp leaving his lips as my heavy breasts slipped free from their confines, water droplets dripping down the hardened peaks.

"You are ravishing," he said, low voice laced with awe.

I gave him a sheepish smile, and he returned it, unbuttoning his pants and finally sliding the damp material to the ground.

His massive length was rock hard underneath his undergarments, even more pronounced as the wet fabric was tight against his body. He slowly slid them down his muscular thighs, his length springing free.

I was left gazing at his perfect body as he stepped out of them, my eyelids heavy as I did so.

He kneeled down between my legs, his fingers hooking on my underwear and sliding them down my legs, tossing them to the side. His strong hands ran down the insides of my thighs, parting them, and a small moan escaped me as his thumbs slid up my lips.

"Torrin," I breathed, leaning back on my elbows.

"I need your taste on my tongue," he whispered as he lowered himself, his mouth now hovering over my pussy. His hot breath teased me.

All thoughts stopped the moment Torrin's tongue dragged through my slit. My back arched, and I leaned my weight onto one elbow, so I could run my other hand through Torrin's white hair.

His tongue flattened, pulsing on my clit with rapid strokes, and I cried out at the bursts of pleasure it gave me.

He didn't relent, either, as two fingers slipped inside me, pumping in and out. Torrin eagerly began to suck on my clit, and I cried out, finally letting go and resting on my back.

I only lasted a few seconds like that, though, because I wanted to watch that beautiful man's face between my legs.

"You have no idea how long I've dreamt of doing this," he murmured, his brown eyes meeting mine, a grin on his face.

"M-me...too..." I moaned.

"You've dreamt of me eating your pussy?" he asked, sliding his tongue up slowly.

"Mhm..." I lifted my hips, rubbing myself against his face. "Fuck, yes, I have," I breathed.

He let out a hum, licking me fervently again before resuming those torturous slow strokes of his tongue. "How long, Lena?"

I shook my head, not wishing to answer.

He withdrew his fingers, and I nearly whimpered at the loss of the stretch.

My heavy eyes glanced up as he hovered over me, those eyes looking black from his pupils being so wide.

"Answer me," he demanded, rolling his hips forward, his cock gliding through my soaked center.

"Don't...don't make me," I pleaded, eyes rolling back as the head of his cock repeatedly brushed against my clit.

"Answer."

My eyes met his tortured ones. My chest heaved.

"I'm ashamed," I whispered, my eyes filling with tears. "I feel guilty."

The truth was I'd desired him for a long time. I'd found him attractive since the very beginning. It took several months being in

Ames before I allowed my thoughts to drift to him when I pleasured myself.

Years. I had desired him for years.

His lips parted, and I could assume he'd read my thoughts. He leaned forward, pressing a kiss to my forehead just as he thrust himself in.

I whimpered as his thick length slid inside me; the pain of the stretch mixed with the pleasure, drawing out a feeling I had desperately craved. But Torrin's moans, the fucking sounds coming out of him, could make me come by itself.

He slammed into me, over and over, and trailed his hand between my breasts before gripping my neck.

Torrin, this sweet, gentle, quiet man...seeing him unravel, seeing him damn near primal as he drove his cock into me again and again—

"*Fuck!*" I cried out, my voice restricted as his fingers tightened around my throat. "Yes, Torrin..."

His lips captured mine, his hips rolling, and then I pushed him to the side. Torrin breathlessly rolled to his back, and I straddled him, lining his cock with my entrance and sinking back down.

His throat bobbed, and his eyes rolled back as he gripped handfuls of my ass in both palms.

His averted gaze only lasted a few moments, though. As I began to rock my hips back and forth on him, Torrin's eyes opened, heavy as he took in my naked body. His eyes settled on my full breasts, bouncing with each thrust.

He slid a hand up, squeezing one of them before dragging his thumb along my hardened nipple. I shuddered at the feeling, and his eyes darkened further. He wrapped his arms around my back, tugging me to him as he took charge, thrusting himself inside of me while capturing my breast in his mouth.

He held both of them, squeezing them together as his tongue trailed from one nipple to the other.

"These are perfect," he whispered, his eyes finding mine as he sucked. My head fell back, and I moaned as I ground myself against his hips, my pussy tightening around his length. "So beautiful, Lena," he moaned breathlessly.

Taking charge again, Torrin pushed me onto my back and drove himself into me quickly once my legs were wrapped around his back. I ran my hands up his hard abs, mesmerized by the way they flexed and tightened. The friction of our bodies was everything I desired.

My hand trailed up, and I cupped his jaw. "Kiss me," I pleaded.

So, he did. I swirled my tongue around his, and as he groaned into my mouth, my orgasm crashed into me. I dug my nails into his back, my inner walls squeezing him tightly.

He roared, spilling his cum inside of me. His cock and my pussy pulsed, one after another, repeatedly, our orgasms fluttering against each other like butterfly wings. My eyes softly shut, lost in the perfect bliss of our bodies releasing in unison.

We stayed like that for a while, holding each other and breathing heavily, naked on the forest floor. Torrin's half-hard length was still inside of me.

I didn't want him to let me go, but he pulled out, leaning to lay on his back and pulling me to rest against his chest.

As I heard his heartbeat thundering in his chest, I whispered, "I love you, Torrin."

His body went still, and as he went to turn on his side, I leaned off his chest and turned on mine.

His brown eyes traveled between my green ones. "I love *you*, Lena." The corner of his lip turned up ever so slightly as he tucked my hair behind my ear, using the hand I had burned. "I think you have known that, though."

I chewed on my bottom lip, raising my hand to brush it alongside his cheek. "I need to move on. I know that."

Torrin's smile slowly faded. "It'll always be him, Lena."

I froze, then dragged my hand down the side of his neck, his breathing hitching. "It's been four years, Torrin. He's married."

"And if he wasn't?" he questioned. "If he showed up in Ames wishing to be with you again, can you honestly say you'd choose me?"

I hesitated.

Damn me for hesitating.

Torrin's face fell, and as he turned to rest on his back, he dragged his hand along his face.

"I-I just need some time, and—"

"That's bullshit, and we both know it," he snapped.

My lip wobbled, and his brown gaze drifted to me. It killed me to see the hurt behind them.

"I know you can't help how you feel. I'm not angry with you," he said gently. "But it doesn't change how much it hurts."

I sat up on my elbow, feeling entirely comfortable with Torrin seeing my bare chest. "I wasn't lying when I said that I love you, Torrin," I insisted. "I haven't been able to even look at another, except for you. I...I always looked at you."

Once upon a time, I had felt guilty for my attraction to him. But even that first moment when he held my arms, arresting me in Otacia, I believed him to be handsome.

Gods, he was handsome...and so very kind.

His eyes flared, his chest rising and falling. His hand reached up to curl a strand of my hair around his finger, his gaze running along the rest of my copper waves. "I've always looked at you, too."

"If I had the power, I would make you my Soul-Tie. I would," my voice cracked, and Torrin's surprised eyes found mine. "I've always felt so comfortable with you. You have been there through everything. You've saved me from every obstacle, saved me from myself." I held his face again. "I can't imagine my life without you, Torrin."

His lip wobbled, and he pulled me close, kissing me sweetly.

"I can't imagine life without you, either," he whispered over my lips. "I wish I was your Soul-Tie, too."

After an evening of slow kissing, we finally slid on our wet clothes, only to sneak up to his bedroom, remove them, and make love again. And again.

I remembered his heartbeat lulling me to sleep as I lay on his chest. I remembered his scent. Cedar and rain.

And I remembered waking to find myself alone in his bed.

Waking to find he had left Ames without a word.

CHAPTER THIRTY-FIVE
LENA- NOW

I choked on a sob as I ran to him. So quickly were our arms wrapped around each other, our knees sinking to the concrete ground.

We held each other tightly as if one of us would slip away if we so much as loosened our grip.

"Torrin," I cried into his chest, squeezing him close.

"Lena," he breathed, his voice hoarse. His fingers weaved through my hair as he held me. "Lena...how...?" He pulled away gently, his fingertips running up my cheeks, analyzing me as if I were not real, as if it were a dream.

His face, aside from a busted lip, was still as handsome as always, but the circles under his eyes showed how weary he was. My eyes bounced all around him. He was still muscular, but he had leaned out tremendously. And his hair was much shorter now, just like everyone's here, though it looked like it had been a couple of months since it had been shaved.

On both wrists were metal bands with those glowing, red gems. He wore what everyone here seemed to wear, prison clothes that resembled those in Otacia: a brown t-shirt and matching bottoms.

I trembled, afraid of the answer to the question I had to ask. "How long?"

Tears slid down his face. His voice cracked as he answered, "A year."

My face crumpled, and another sob broke free as I pulled him into my embrace again. My fingers drifted through his short platinum hair as I held him, and he ran his hand along my back in a soothing motion, comforting me as we both cried. Just like Torrin to be concerned about me when *he* had been the one enslaved all this time.

Nearly the entire time he'd been gone, he'd been *here*? Did Igon send him to Faltrun? Did he know this was to be his fate?

I could sense Merrick and Elowen walking up behind me, and I sniffed as I pulled away again, holding Torrin's calloused hands in mine.

"Torrin." Elowen's voice was broken as she whispered, "Is that really you?"

He gave her a sad smile, tears still streaming down his face. His eyes slid to Merrick, who was gaping at him.

"You've been here this whole time?" Merrick's voice was rough, and I could tell he was trying to keep from crying.

Torrin's lip trembled as he nodded, and then his eyes went to who was standing behind his cousin.

Silas held Torrin's stare. There was no warmth to his expression, just shock and anger. So much anger. His hands were held in fists at his sides.

Torrin was declared an enemy of Otacia over five years ago when he fled into the night with us. A conspiracy was formed that he was a part of the Queen's murder. A part of mine.

"Holy Gods...I...I don't understand," Edmund whispered, and I knew this was the first time the Otacian men had seen the man who had trained them without his glamour—with his pointed ears.

"You're a Mage?" Hendry's mismatched eyes were blown wide. "You..."

I had never seen such shock on Roland's face either. Before the men could continue, I spoke. "Torrin and I met in Otacia a little over a year before I left." My eyes went to Silas, his golden gaze burning through me. "He is the one who provided my Mother and me safe passage to Ames."

"Torrin is my cousin," Merrick said to them. "Elowen's, too." He gave her a soft smile. "Not by blood, but all the same."

Silas's fists were now trembling, but it was Roland who spoke. "Word has been spread that you were a part of the Queen's assassination."

I had never heard such a stern tone from the normally playful man.

"That is bullshit," Torrin spat. "The Queen was nothing but kind to me. I would never have wished her harm." His eyes skated to Silas. "I know we have much to discuss, Your Highness," he said with gentleness to his tone. "But despite your father and your kingdom's treatment of my people, I grew to love Otacia. It was only when the kill order was put into effect that I left."

359

Silas's voice was low when he said, "The *Mage* that killed my Mother, did you know of her identity?"

Torrin shook his head. "As far as I knew, Amatta was human. I hardly spoke with her." His voice became sharp as he said, "And even when she was publicly burned to death, there was no proof. I saw no pointed ears, no magic on display."

"Are you saying she wasn't a Mage?"

"I'm saying I knew nothing of any of it."

"We don't need to interrogate him right this second," I interjected, squeezing Torrin's palms in silent comfort. His coffee-brown eyes traveled to mine. He gave me a gentle smile.

Before Silas could persist, Merrick's gasp caught our attention.

"Oh, my Gods," Merrick breathed.

A man with a striking resemblance to Torrin walked forward, and a woman with golden hair and brown eyes was at his side. I noticed her hair wasn't shaved, just like how Polly's wasn't.

"Merrick, Elowen, you are so grown," the man whispered, face crumbling.

Merrick ran up to him, finally releasing his cry as he hugged the man tightly. Elowen examined them, unsure fully of who they were.

More tears spilled from Torrin's eyes, and he grinned when he looked at me again. "I found my parents."

My eyes widened, his hands still in mine, and I glanced back at the couple. Tobias and Josie Brighthell went missing when Torrin was sixteen years old, meaning Merrick was nine and Elowen was four the last time they saw them.

"Have you been here this whole time?" Elowen cried softly, walking forward. Merrick hugged Josie next.

Tobias, Merrick's maternal uncle nodded, moving to give Elowen a hug, squeezing her tight. "I'd say I'm so happy to see you, but that would be a lie." He pulled back, grasping El's shoulders, eyes flicking between her and her brother. "What are you doing here?"

Torrin and I stood up just as Merrick replied, "It's a long story. How did *you* two end up here?"

Josie's eyes fell. "We made the mistake of leaving Ames one morning. Not leaving permanently...but Tobias and I wanted a morning to ourselves—wanted to roam the roads and see scenery other than that of our little town." She shook her head. "We planned to be home before dinner, but we were poisoned on the road. Faltrun was looking for slaves even back then."

Tobias gently caressed his wife's back. "The poison they used weakened our magic, causing our glamours to fail." His watery eyes lifted to Merrick's. "When they discovered our magical identity, they didn't kill us. No, they decided to keep us, poisoning us daily—just enough to keep us from fighting back."

"Dear Gods," Elowen murmured.

Josie gave her a sad smile. "Only once the cuffs rolled out did the poisoning cease."

It was evident the two were weak. Dark circles, slim bodies, and skin littered with scars. It was a miracle so many years of abuse hadn't killed them.

"What type of poison?" I asked gently.

Tobias shrugged. "We aren't sure what, exactly. The first time they used it, it was a dust that they blew in our faces. They tainted our meals with it afterward."

My head flew to Silas. "Otacia must've gotten that poison from here...perhaps they are distributing it."

Silas's frown remained, even as Josie said, "You've seen it before?"

I nodded gravely. "Yes. The Otacians used some dust in Forsmont just days ago."

It was quiet as Tobias's eyes narrowed, studying the Prince. "Silas La'Rune travels with you," he noted. "That is most shocking."

There was clear animosity there. It seemed that Silas's reputation had spread even to those down here, enslaved. It was silent for a moment between us all until Elowen spoke again.

She seized Edmund's arm. "As does Edmund." She brought the soldier forward, his cheeks flushing at the action. "My boyfriend."

Torrin's eyes turned to saucers. "*Estielot* is your boyfriend?"

Edmund held Elowen close to his side, and she leaned her head on his chest as she said, "Soul-Tie."

Torrin glanced between the two of them, then grinned. "He is a good man."

To that, Edmund's lip trembled, honored by his once superior's kind remarks.

"Though make sure you lie and tell him the ceremony starts at an earlier time for your wedding day." Torrin smirked. "Estielot could never be on time for anything."

Edmund blinked, and then, despite everything, tipped his head back and laughed. "You got me there, Brighthell."

Hendry and Roland were smiling; even Merrick was, too, but Silas still wore a frown, eyes narrowed.

Torrin's gaze settled on him. "The three of us should speak privately," he said as he glanced between Silas and me. He glimpsed over at his parents, then at his cousins. "You all have plenty to catch up on."

Torrin held my hand again, guiding the three of us over to a corner away from everyone. We weaved through bodies, some looking up at us with tired eyes, some so broken they remained staring at the ground.

When we finally stopped, Silas and Torrin were staring daggers at each other. I nervously stood at Torrin's side.

"How are you here?" Torrin began. "Together, I mean?"

Silas stood glaring, the calm before the storm, as I filled Torrin in on everything. The attack in Ames, Igon's death, him naming me Supreme. I told him of Forth Laith, leaving out my assault, and told him of Immeron and the mountain. He was especially pale-faced when I told him of the necromancer and of the occurrences in Forsmont.

"My Gods." Torrin shook his head. "I...I can't believe Igon is dead. And you being Supreme?"

"Insane, right?" I laughed softly. Gods, it was so nice hearing his voice.

Torrin offered a warm smile, one that caused my heart to skip a few beats. "I was going to say fitting."

My cheeks began to heat just as Silas said, "Explain."

Torrin turned his attention to the Prince. "What do you know?" he asked, his arms crossing over his chest.

"That you left Otacia the same evening Lena supposedly was killed." He shook his head. "I thought this whole time it was you who did it. You who betrayed our kingdom, you who played a part in my mother's death." His eyes went to me, then back to Torrin. "Though Lena is alive, and you two seem rather fond of each other." His fists clenched. "So, explain."

"Torrin had nothing to do with what happened with Ryia, but when we were in Fort Laith, I didn't trust you yet. And I feared if

I mentioned Torrin, knowing the kingdom sought him, it would cause more harm than good."

He darted his gaze between us, his lip curling.

"I remember you two being friendly at my ball. Were you...did you..."

"No," Torrin and I said simultaneously.

"It was Torrin who escorted me home the day I was arrested. He told me that day he was a Mage and, later on, proved it by removing his glamour."

Silas's eyes continued to shift between the two of us, brows remaining lowered as he focused on Torrin. "Were you a spy?"

Torrin swallowed, but his expression remained neutral. "I was to keep an eye on things for the sake of my people, yes."

Torrin told Silas of his ability to read minds, about Igon's orders, and told him how he was meant to be in Otacia all that time.

"So, for the majority of our relationship, you kept this secret?" Silas asked me. "You had this...connection with Torrin?"

"Silas, I never wanted to keep *anything* from you—"

Silas snorted, though he found nothing funny.

I turned to Torrin, needing to tell him an important detail. "Kayin spoke to me, Torrin."

His eyes bulged. "What?" he breathed. "When?"

"When I was on Mount Rozavar. She told me she was in Otacia. She...she didn't seem well." I chewed on my bottom lip, then winced. "I'm assuming you aren't able to hear her, even if she tried to reach out."

His eyes were weary as he shook his head. "No...I've heard nothing. It has been quiet in my head all this time."

My lip wobbled, and Silas asked, "Who is Kayin?"

"A seer," I responded. "Torrin and I haven't ever met her face-to-face, but we have been able to communicate with her telepathically. She..." I dragged my hand down my face. "She is the one who told us awful change was coming, to leave for Ames the night before your mother's death."

Silas's eyes flared, and just as he went to shout, I raised my hand. "But I know she was not responsible. She only saw that it would happen. Believe me, she was working with Igon, and he very much respected Ryia."

"I can't fucking believe any of this." He let out a dry laugh. "Do you even hear yourself?!"

"Silas—"

"I never knew you, did I?" His lip curled as he looked me up and down. "You are a stranger to me."

He went to storm off, but I grasped his arm. He shoved me off and continued to move anyway.

I sped up to him, leaving Torrin. "Silas!" I hissed, looking around at all the weary eyes around us, at my friends' raised brows. "Just let me explain, dammit!"

His face was contorted with rage as he whirled at me. "You've said quite enough!" he hissed back, and he glanced around, lowering his voice before continuing. "You had a secret relationship with another man. You left in the night with him. You chose *him*."

"It wasn't like that at all," I insisted quietly, even though Torrin and I did become intimate with one another years later.

He shook his head, and for a moment—just one moment—sadness shown in his eyes. "There are only so many lies I can look past, Lena. I...I don't know how I can trust you after all this."

I felt my throat closing up. "I swear to the Gods, I will never keep a secret from you again. Ask me anything, and I will tell you."

Silas opened his mouth to respond when a guard opened the door above, dragging us from our conversation.

The descent was quick. The woman from earlier, Polly, was shoved back into our cage. Her cheeks were hollow, her eyes glassy, as she held her crossed arms close to her chest. She wandered forward.

Her face was just...bleak, her eyes distant as if dissociating.

"Josie, Dimitri calls for you," the guard yelled.

Torrin's mother swallowed, her head falling. Tobias grasped her chin, urging her to face him. He whispered something in her ear, then gently kissed her forehead. Tears spilled as she walked away into the guard's grasp.

"What's happening?" I asked quietly as Torrin walked up to Silas and me.

I watched Polly as she shrunk onto the floor, pulling her knees close and lowering her head. I saw myself when I looked at her. I saw my own brokenness...I saw a shell of a person staring back at me.

Torrin's jaw feathered when I gazed up at him. "She is one of Dimitri's *toys*. He rotates through the women here, forcing them to do as he pleases. He doesn't shave the heads of those he takes pleasure in." Torrin's hands were shaking violently at his sides as his eyes followed his mother's disappearing frame. His voice quavered as he said, "He's been using her for years."

My stomach twisted into knots, my mind drifting to Dimitri's words.

"I may have use for you."

My chest began heaving, my eyes watering.

I can't go through it again. I can't.

Torrin's brows drew together as he looked back at me.

I am alive.

They are gone.

They aren't here.

I am...I am not *safe here. I'm not safe at all.*

I blew out a shaky breath, squeezing my eyes shut tightly.

"Lena?" Torrin asked. In my panic, his voice sounded miles away. "Are you okay?"

I was sinking, but Silas's hand on my back brought me back to shore.

While I knew he was still beyond angry, his eyes softened as he studied me, understanding shining in his irises.

"He won't touch you," he promised quietly. "He won't get anywhere near you."

My teary eyes drifted to his, and I was grateful to see the anger behind his eyes gone, at least for now. I nodded my head slowly, hoping he was right.

I wasn't sure how many minutes passed, maybe forty. I had grown accustomed to the horrific smell, and Torrin introduced me to a handful of different people he'd met here. Dani and Viola were nowhere to be found, and while there were plenty of flies buzzing around, I didn't believe Dani to be any of them. I could only hope she and Vi were coming up with a plan.

All the Mages here...they had no willpower to fight, it seemed. Everyone I'd been introduced to could hardly muster even looking at me.

Torrin told me how Mages here have been kept for labor, whether that be serving, cooking, or doing heavy lifting. Or, in the handful of long-haired women's case, giving their bodies over to the King. Rations were slim. If there was no work, they remained here, caged like animals.

It was sick. Vile. I hated Dimitri more than Ulric, and that was saying a lot.

My hands clenched and released at my sides as I stared at Polly. She didn't move, and no one came up to talk to her or check if she was okay. In our shared experience, I found myself wandering toward where she sat, her head buried in her knees.

I sat down beside her, and she didn't so much as budge.

"Hi," I said softly.

She didn't respond.

I wasn't entirely sure what to say, but I knew there was one thing that had always helped me when I was broken...when things seemed hopeless.

"This is not the end, Polly."

That caught her attention. She stiffened, then gradually tilted her head to the side, her grey eyes watery as she inspected me.

"We're breaking free from here," I promised. "And when we do, you'll get your revenge. There will be justice. Your story does not end in this cage."

She stared at me, her expression lacking emotion. Her voice was small as she replied. "You've only been here for an hour. You won't feel that way after being subjected to his wishes for three years. Even three days will change you."

Tithara, guide me...three years she'd been imprisoned here?

I debated placing a hand on her shoulder, but any unwarranted touch could trigger her. I kept my hands firmly planted in my lap. "We will be out of here before you know it," I whispered. "We have a plan."

Her eyes shifted, emotions welling there, but they glazed over the second her head turned, witnessing who was being shoved back into our cage.

Tobias let out a muffled cry at the sight of his wife stumbling back in. Her eye was swollen as if she had been punched, and her long, golden waves were no longer...her head was now shaven bald.

"She's a bit too old for Dimitri's liking now," the man chortled, shoving her until she collapsed onto the floor.

As her knees hit the concrete, Torrin lost all composure. He bared his teeth and roared as he rushed forward, grasping the guard and throwing him on the ground before he could shut the cage door. He quickly straddled him and began pummeling his fist into the man's face. Over and over and over.

"Torrin, stop!" Josie pleaded from her spot on the ground. Her face crumpled as she witnessed her son lose himself to his rage.

Torrin's assault only lasted a few seconds, though, before two more guards rushed in, one flinging Torrin off of his comrade, the other squatting down to assess the wounds.

The one who tossed Torrin off then grasped the collar of Torrin's cotton shirt, and my platinum-haired friend squeezed the man's forearms, attempting to break free from his grasp. Torrin was strong, but nearly a year of mistreatment had weakened him.

"DON'T TOUCH HIM!" I shouted as I stood and rushed for them.

The guard only offered a cruel laugh before sucker-punching Torrin in the face. His head cracked backward, blood splattering over the concrete ground.

Elowen cried out, and as I went to help, Silas roughly seized my arm.

My head whirled back at him. "Let me go, Silas!" I seethed.

He squeezed my arm tighter, and I hissed at the pain. "You can't stop them," he bit out.

I went to argue when he roughly shoved me to the side and charged toward the man himself. He gripped the guard's shoulders, hurling him to the ground.

The soldier's shoulder slammed into the concrete floor, and he gaped at Silas. He only had a moment before the Prince was above him and began beating the absolute shit out of his face.

I'd witnessed Silas fight before, but this rage was unlike anything I'd seen from him before. Raw. Unfiltered.

It was clear he was letting out his frustrations on this man. All anger. All resentment. Not that I'd complain.

I'd never seen a face become so bloodied, never seen Silas's pupils so dark as he repeatedly swung his fist into the man's face.

The enslaved Mages began to cheer, the first sign of life any of them had shown thus far, and as the man beneath Silas went to grasp the dagger secured at his side, Silas snatched his arm, wrenching it back until it made a loud crack.

The guard wailed in agony just as the man tending to the guard injured by Torrin cried for backup. The cheering died down as another soldier hustled in. He sped to the man Silas was still beating, tackling the Prince to the ground.

I ran and grasped the neck of the soldier on top of him. I pulled, not realizing the strength it might take to snap a neck, before he elbowed me in the stomach, causing me to fall back.

"Lena—" Silas began.

The soldier wrapped his hands around Silas's throat before he could finish telling me to get back.

Silas gritted his teeth, grasping the man's hand tightly in an attempt to avoid being strangled. The soldier wouldn't budge.

"LET HIM GO!" I bellowed. It was a petty move, but I didn't give a shit. I gripped the hair on his head and ripped it out from the root.

He shrieked, releasing Silas to reach back for me just as I elbow-locked his neck, pulling him back with me to the ground.

The remaining man cursed before stepping away from the injured soldier. Torrin advanced, and the two began fist-fighting.

The man in my hold easily broke free, as my strength without magic was lacking in comparison to a man of his size. He turned, pressing me into the ground and tightening his hands around my neck. The rest of our friends were about to join in the fight when a loud bang jolted all of us.

"Enough!" A man barked, a handful of soldiers rushing down the steps with him.

My eyes slid to the voice—to the man from before. The one with brown hair and vibrant green eyes.

"Disengage," he chewed out, eyes locking on the man holding my throat as he hurried down the steps. I spiraled into a coughing fit as the guard hesitantly obeyed, releasing me from his tight grip.

"Fen's arm is broken because of him," he spat, pointing at Silas.

"He's lucky it's only his arm," the Prince replied with a smug grin, rising to his feet.

The soldier bared his teeth, but the one originally injured rasped, "The blond started it."

Torrin scoffed, and the green-eyed man clicked his tongue. "Causing issues again, Torrin?"

"He did nothing wrong," I seethed. "Your piece of shit guards antagonized him."

His emerald gaze locked on mine, only for a moment. He cocked his head toward Torrin. "Take him,"

"NO!" I protested just as the guards hustled in, seizing Torrin's arms.

"It's okay, Lena," Torrin said softly before glaring at the soldiers who pulled him forward.

"Don't hurt him," I pleaded, hating how desperate I sounded. But they ignored me, everyone but that damn brown-haired guard, who stared at me with a look I couldn't place.

I stared into his green eyes as every other guard in the room filtered out.

"Where are you taking him?" I gritted out as I stood.

Silas was beside me, his fingers grazing my neck, checking for damage. I couldn't focus on the pleasure his touch provided me. I couldn't focus on anything other than the fire I wished I could unleash upon the bastard before me.

"He's getting punished. Don't worry. He's too valuable an asset to kill."

Silas gave an ingenuine smile from beside me, his hand slipping from my neck. "How comforting."

"Punished how?" I asked in a low voice, heat rising in my body. Fuck this man, and fuck these cuffs.

"A flogging. He's been through it before," he said softly. "He'll be okay."

I felt Silas tense beside me and watched as his eyes slightly flared. Even if he felt betrayed by Torrin, I knew the two had cared for one another. It had to worry him, knowing he was suffering in such a way.

"He didn't do anything to warrant such treatment," I spat. "You're all fucking pathetic."

He ignored my words. "What is your full name?" the man continued, changing the topic.

I blinked and then examined my fingernails, doing my best to seem composed. "What's it to you?"

He grasped the iron bars of the cell, frown deepening. "Your full name," he said sharply.

I scoffed, my eyes sliding up to meet his, and I gave him a cruel smile. "Lena Daelyra, Supreme of Ames." I gave a mocking bow, and my smile vanished as I glared at him, my voice going low. "But there's no need to remember. When I get free of here, which I *will*, I promise I'm scorching every last one of you who have enslaved my people. Nothing will be left of you or this place when I'm finished."

The man's eyebrows rose, and then he mastered his shock as he studied me. A few moments passed.

"No response?" I asked sweetly.

His face became pained. "You...you look so much like her."

I blinked, my brows scrunching together just as Josie wandered to me, placing a comforting hand on my shoulder. I turned to meet her swollen eyes.

"Not that he's entirely innocent, but Waylon has helped us as much as a Faltrunian soldier can. Extra food, warm blankets, things like that. He doesn't agree with the rest of the soldiers or Dimitri's wicked ways...so he helps us where he can."

My eyes sprang wide at the name she used. Quickly, I whirled my head back to the soldier on the other side of the bars.

The handsome man with brown hair and green eyes. Green eyes that were the same color as mine.

The man who Mother named her business after.

Waylon.

Waylon.

My body locked up, and I had trouble finding my voice. "I look like who?" I breathed.

The man's eyes filled with tears, his voice breaking as he said, "Like Minerva."

CHAPTER THIRTY-SIX

LENA

Waylon. My father.

He was just as Mother described: green eyes that matched mine, wavy brown hair cropped close on the sides and longer on top. His skin was a few shades tanner than mine but still lighter than an Otacian-born's skin. And his face...he was clean-shaven, and I could see the very beginning of wrinkles forming—the exhaustion that lay behind an intimidating front.

I was frozen, completely stunned by this revelation, astonished to be standing before a man I had never believed I'd meet.

"Waylon..."

"Waylon Daelyra."

Out of the corner of my eye, I saw Silas's head spin to me. Josie had stepped away, back in Tobias's embrace.

My lip trembled as I looked into my father's eyes. "She loved you very much," I whispered.

His eyes flared. "Is she—"

"She's alive," I said softly. "She's told me a lot about you." I frowned, observing his Faltrunian armor. "Why are you here? Mother said your family has always resided in Renrell."

His jaw clicked. "I couldn't stand being there anymore without her." His eyes dropped to the floor. "It was all a horrible reminder of what could have been. What should have been." He lifted his head. "And you...you're my...we had..."

I nodded slowly, then gestured to my pointed ears. "She didn't know if I would be like you...or like her." I lowered my hand back to my side. "People didn't take kindly to Mages even back then, and she knew how much you loved your home and your family. Out of fear for what it all could entail, what it would put you through...she left."

He shook his head in disbelief. Mother didn't know how Waylon would take to her being a Mage. Most of the humans living in Tovagoth hated us.

I found myself bracing for the worst. For his disgust. His rage.

But tears only slid down his face as Waylon said, "Nothing would have ever kept me away. I would have loved her regardless." His voice shook. "And you, regardless."

My lip wobbled, and my vision became blurred at his words. The closest thing to a father I had was Igon, but I was already an adult when I met him. Having a father was a dream I never thought attainable. It was easier to imagine that he'd hate me than to consider the possibility he might not.

"I would have followed her anywhere," he breathed. "Renrell was never my home. *Minerva* was my home."

I brushed away a stray tear that had fallen down my cheek.

Waylon's fingertips danced nervously at his side. "Did she...did she find love again?"

I shook my head, noting Waylon's sagging shoulders. "Did you?"

His lip quivered. "I tried," he said quietly. "But no one ever could compare. Not to what she and I had. I have been alone ever since."

I felt Silas's eyes on me, but I couldn't meet his stare, not as I said gently, "I have a feeling she has felt the same."

He smiled sadly, and then his gaze flitted around the cell for a few moments. "I will get you out of here," he whispered. "All of you."

I shot my eyes up to my father, loosening a shaky breath. "You wish to free hundreds of slaves?" My voice was barely above a whisper. "Why?"

"You're my daughter," his voice broke. "And these are your people. Your mother's people." He inhaled slowly before nodding to himself, his eyes sweeping across the prison cell yet again. His voice was grave when he said, "I have done my best to help those in here, but my efforts have been pitiful. I've been too fearful of the repercussions. I...I have stood beside injustice for far too long." His eyes slid behind us, to Torrin's mother, and then he settled his sight on Silas. "I suppose you felt the same, Prince? To join their cause."

Silas studied my father. I expected him to reject that idea, to say, as he had told me before, that he had *his own agenda.*

But instead, he said, "I didn't just stand beside injustice." His regretful eyes met mine, but he schooled his expression into neutrality before meeting Waylon's stare again. "I was a major part of it. Hunting, killing...*slaughtering*—" Silas exhaled sharply through his nose. "Many of us must rise up if there is any hope of stopping what my father has put into place. If there is any hope of a better world." Silas stepped closer, his voice just above a whisper. "If you mean what you say, act alone. Do not risk someone turning on you."

Waylon crossed his strong arms. "That's what I planned on. Not many trustworthy people in the royal guard." His eyes shifted to the silver cuffs on my wrists—the bright red gem glowing on each band. "It will take a lot of time to unlink everyone. And I usually am not down here alone—"

As if Valor himself was listening, the door above creaked open. Waylon tilted his head, detecting another soldier initiating his descent into the prison. Considering the other soldiers had been injured, he must be taking over the next shift.

"It has to be tomorrow morning," Waylon spoke calmly. "Before the sun rises."

"What?" I hissed, eyes darting to the soldier who kept walking, still too far away to overhear any conversation.

"My next shift is tomorrow morning. By evening, your heads will be shaved, and the Prince will be tortured for information...potentially even before then." Silas recoiled at the words, clenching his fists as Waylon continued, "You as well, Lena...or worse. I won't allow it." He quickly glanced at the soldier striding down the steps, then settled his eyes on me. "Torrin will be back this evening. When I come in the morning, I'll unlock your group first. He'll need healing."

My stomach sank at the thought of Torrin being harmed at this moment, but I nodded. Waylon's eyes lingered on mine for an extra moment before he strode away, giving a curt nod to the soldier replacing him.

I studied him as his figure disappeared.

My father.

Tears welled in my eyes, taken aback by his kindness. Sure, I may be his blood, but he didn't know me. All he knew was I was a Mage and the political nature of what I was trying to accomplish.

That I was a witch...and at the thought of that term, I found the word not bothering me as much as it once did.

Silas sighed as he retreated, but instead of going by our friends, he left to sit against a wall by himself. Era watched him, crossing her arms in worry. He wouldn't meet her stare, or anyone's, for that matter.

I met Roland's furrowed brows but gave him my index finger, telling him *'one moment'* as I strode toward the Prince. I'm sure Merrick and El were curious about my conversation with a supposed enemy, but I'd fill them in later.

I glimpsed down at Silas's tense expression. "I know we have a lot to discuss," I said in a low voice as I approached him.

Silas scoffed, eyes locked on the ground, elbows resting on his knees. "Indeed."

I slid down beside him on the cold ground, resting my own head against the wall.

He picked at the skin around his nails. "Your father...you said he had died."

"It was easier to explain it that way without outing my secret." I sighed, tilting my head to look at him, noting his bloody knuckles. I wished I could heal them. "I've lied about so much, and for that, I'm sorry. I'm so sorry."

Silas was quiet for a moment. "It appears he cares for you...that's good." He inhaled, then exhaled. "I have always believed Faltrun should remain independent," he continued, changing the subject. "But I had no idea their leader was doing this...enslaving so many." He shook his head and sighed, resting his head against the stone wall as well. "Tovagoth isn't short on shitty men ruling its territories, though I suppose I'm not better," he mumbled, then ran his hand through his hair. "Fuck me."

"You are *much* better. We are all so grateful for your help. I hope you know that." I studied his handsome profile, and a small smile crept on my face. "And there's no privacy here, but since you asked nicely..."

He quickly leaned his head toward me, eyebrows raised, his mouth hanging open. "What did you say?"

I tried and failed at holding in my laughter. I snorted. "Sorry, I was just teasing." Damn, Roland really must be rubbing off on me. Then again, attempting to make light out of hard situations wasn't completely off-brand for me. I feared concentrating on how perilous the morning would be would send me into a full-blown panic attack.

He blinked, over and over, until the corners of his mouth began to rise. "You're awfully bold, Flower."

Flower.

My smile slipped, my eyes dilating. Silas's smirk only grew. "Ah, but I still am able to unnerve you and have the upper hand," he whispered, his eyes falling to my lips.

His golden eyes flicked up to mine. In this lighting, they seemed to glow against his tan skin.

Silas confused me. One minute, he would be looking at me with heat in his honey gaze, offering timid smiles and calming me when I was in my own head. Then, the next, he would be cold. Callous. Distant. His constant shifts in mood gave me whiplash...though I supposed I could be the same way myself. I certainly was in my younger days.

There were times he looked at me, and I could swear I saw hatred. Resentment. And in using my nickname, I truly couldn't decipher the meaning.

"Do you use that name with malice?" I asked quietly.

His smile vanished, his brows furrowing.

My voice shook, just above a whisper, as I pressed, "Do you use it to punish me?"

His frown deepened as he stared at me, chest rising and falling, unsure of what to say.

My eyes flitted away as I stood, ultimately walking away, leaving him to sit alone.

Perhaps he didn't know, either.

CHAPTER THIRTY-SEVEN
SILAS

"*D*o you use it to punish me?"

What the hell did she mean by that?

I was still sitting alone nearly an hour later, lost in my own thoughts and not desiring communication with anyone. Era kept shooting me a look of concern, but I would just shake my head at her. She knew I sometimes needed alone time. I appreciated that about her.

Lena was back by Roland's side, and the sight infuriated me, though I knew I had no right.

I thought she was being flirty with me. I must've misread the scenario, or perhaps my own skills were lacking. I had lost my smoothness after I lost her.

Women had always desired me with little effort. Between my looks and title, I didn't have to flirt or woo any of them. A half-smile and some sex eyes were all it took to get them naked in my bed.

Era was different. Our relationship started out of mutual benefit. At twenty-two, my father demanded I be married. I had put it off as long as I could, fighting tooth and nail against the idea.

The only woman I ever dreamed of marrying was Lena.

Erabella Dreason wasn't supposed to be at the ball last year. Her family detested her and treated her like nothing more than dirt under a rug. She had snuck into her family's carriage, as her younger sister was the one they wished to present to me.

Meeting her in the corridor she was hiding in, speaking of both of our resentments for our parents, I knew that she was the most genuine and unpretentious person in the castle that evening. I'd already had sexual relations with most of the princesses who had been attending at that point, having seen them at the consecutive one that was thrown every six months. None of them stood out to me. They were nothing but a quick and meaningless fuck.

But with Era, it was different.

Even when she became my wife, I never felt like I needed to woo her. We didn't even have sex until a few months after marriage...I didn't wish to force her into something she didn't want.

I would never force something like that.

I had even told her that if she wished to see others, she could just be my wife for the title and that I was okay with it. But for whatever reason, she'd grown fond of me.

I had grown fond of her, too.

Still...it never compared to the love I once had. And how could it? The person I had been back then died along with her. I was a living ghost until those warm, green eyes met mine for the first time in over five years. Until I heard my name whispered from her lips moments before I was about to strike.

I raked my hands down my face.

And now she and Roland were an item. Just fucking perfect.

That bastard was the master at witty banter. I used to think I was good at it.

"He pleased me even better."

I clenched my fists so hard. If I had long nails, my palms would be bleeding. Did she say that to punish *me*? Or was she truly more satisfied with him?

I watched them from across this vile cell, Roland whispering something in her ear, her cheeks flushing as she offered him a bashful smile.

Fuck him. Fuck her. Fuck all of this.

I wanted so desperately to smash my fists into something—anything. My knuckles were already bleeding from beating that guard's face in, but the sting wasn't distracting enough.

My violent thoughts were interrupted by the door opening and Torrin being shoved back inside our cell.

Lena was instantly there, and Torrin winced as she assessed him, his skin raw from being flogged.

Sweat began beading at my hairline, and my breathing became shallow. It was so humid in here...the space felt too small.

I couldn't look at his skin.

I couldn't breathe.

His brown eyes scanned the space until they fell on me. He said something to Lena, her gaze going to me briefly before she nodded and headed back to Roland.

I scowled at Torrin as he hobbled on over to me, but still, he gave me a half smile.

He hissed as he sat beside me on the concrete ground. "That glare is as vicious as ever," he commented.

Torrin had been my inspiration. My mentor. My friend.

But he had deceived me, just as Lena had. They'd deceived me *together*.

As if sensing my thoughts, Torrin said gently, "My friendship with you was always real."

I scoffed. "As was Lena's," I said blandly.

"It was." His eyes lowered to his lap. "It's unfair of you to hold a grudge against her."

My fists shook. He had no idea what he was fucking talking abo—

"She loves you so much," he said quietly.

My muscles loosened, and I relaxed my fists. Otherwise, I said nothing, staring blankly ahead.

She wouldn't have left me if she did.

"You know that, right?" Torrin pressed. "She's always loved you."

I swallowed an unpleasant lump in my throat. "She fancies Roland in her bed these days," I said bitterly.

His eyes enlarged, and his gaze darted over to where they sat beside each other on the opposite side of this disgusting cell.

His cheeks flushed slightly. "Without my ability to read minds, I don't pick up on things as easily," he admitted. He turned his head back to me, clearing his throat. "And you're married."

"No shit."

"So, why does her being with Roland matter?"

I shot him a nasty glare, then scrutinized Roland as he wrapped his arm around her. "If you don't understand the difference, you're dense as hell."

He sighed, running a hand through his short, white hair. "I'm saying just because she's with someone else doesn't mean she doesn't want you."

I tilted my head, narrowing my eyes at him.

I hated that the exhaustion in his expression bothered me. I shouldn't give a single shit about him.

His deep brown gaze held mine. "I see the way you look at her. You still love her too, don't you?"

I curved my head away, inhaling sharply and dramatically resting my head against the wall. My eyes found Lena again, her gaze meeting mine again briefly before she quickly looked away.

I loved her when we were younger. Loved her more than the air that filled my lungs. Loved her more than life itself.

She was my best friend, the only person that ever saw me, truly saw me. She didn't see a prince or a stuck-up Inner Ring boy. Well, not for long, anyway. She saw Quill...and Quill was the real me, even if the name was not.

I had given her all of me...stripped myself bare, and poured my heart, my soul, out to her. I wanted to give her everything this world had to offer. I wanted nothing more than to face every day of the rest of my life with her by my side.

But now? Now, I looked at her and was reminded of five years in hell. Now, I gazed at her ears and was plagued by the thought that while I had given her my entire self, she still didn't trust me enough to give me all of her. Now, I looked at her and saw her soot-filled house and pictured myself weeping on my bedroom floor for six months straight over the memory of her charred corpse.

Now, I stared at her and pictured her eyes rolling back, grinning in pleasure as she was bedded by Roland fucking Aubeze. A smile that, at one point, only belonged to me.

Now, I looked at her, and I was *furious*.

How could I love her when that was my primary emotion? How could I love her when her happiness didn't bring me happiness? That I was only satisfied when she was mine?

"I don't know how I feel for her anymore," I muttered after a beat.

I don't know how I feel about anything.

Torrin also rested his head against the stone wall, eyes narrowing as he stared at the beautiful redhead. "Why did she get so panicked when she saw Polly?" he questioned after a moment. "I've never seen her close in on herself quite like that."

I bit my lip so hard I tasted blood. "She was raped," I answered quietly.

A rough gasp escaped Torrin as he snapped his head toward me. His brows lowered, his lip curling. "Who?" he asked in a tone deeper than I'd ever heard uttered from his lips.

My eyes slid to his. "Rurik. Daerin, Geoff, and Jones almost got to her, too, but I found them before they touched her."

Torrin's hands were shaking against his knees. He lowered them into his lap. "I can assume you took care of them?"

"Of course I did."

"Good." He nodded to himself. "Good."

Torrin sat beside me silently for a few moments. His voice broke as he said quietly, "I'm proud of you."

I felt significant discomfort in my chest. "Don't," I warned in a low voice.

Lena had said the same words to me. Did they have any idea of the things I had done? They couldn't possibly be that daft, could they?

But Torrin continued anyway. "You have always had a good heart, Silas. Even though you have strayed in the past, I always knew you'd do the right thing when the time came."

Before I could protest, Torrin stood, wincing as he did so. His brown eyes slid down to me. "Perhaps the day is not far off. The day we can return to Otacia...the day you finally become the King you are meant to be."

My eyebrows raised at his forgiving words, and my mouth parted to release a sigh. Torrin offered me a small smile before limping away toward his cousins, Elowen and Merrick.

Why did they think so highly of me after all I had done?

What was *wrong* with them?

I had tortured hundreds of their kind, men and women alike.

I had never killed a child, at least. But I'd bring them home, my father imprisoning them until they'd become of age, only to hang them like their family. I only visited those cellars a handful of times, and surprisingly, the children were kept well-fed and clean, given books to read, and presented with hobbies to discover.

There was no point, though. They were to die as adults anyway.

We only had it happen once so far, as the rest of the imprisoned children were still underage. We captured a boy four years ago. He was seventeen at the time. My father said twenty-one was a good age to put them down.

He was hung right before I left for Ames.

I shut off all emotions after what happened to me six months after Lena left...something I couldn't even think about without breaking into a sweat and panicking. I could kill and torture with a straight face as those I was harming begged and pleaded, if not for their own lives, for those they loved that I killed in front of them.

I'd do that, then go home and drink and smoke and fuck, not caring in the slightest that I had committed such atrocities.

But now it was like everything was weighing on me—like my humanity had been lost and was somehow finding its way back.

I hated it. I wanted to go back to not feeling a damn thing.

"Excuse me?" a small voice asked, breaking me from my thoughts.

I shifted my stare over to find a child standing by me. I didn't know if they were a boy or girl, as all the slaves' heads had been shaved. Growing in were tight blonde curls.

My eyebrows raised, and I peered around to see if their parents were nearby. But no one was. No one even had their eyes on the kid.

"Um...how can I help you?"

The child's big blue eyes studied me, clutching a kitten ragdoll. On their little wrists were my father's device. It made my stomach turn.

"I'm Saoirse. I'm four."

My chest felt like it was going to cave in, seeing this child enslaved in such filth.

My son would be this age if he had lived.

My son.

"Hi, Saoirse. I'm Silas. I'm twenty-three," I responded softly.

She smiled and plopped herself down right next to me. My eyes nervously darted around, but still, no one was looking at the little girl. The only eyes that were on us were Lena's, who watched us with a curious gaze.

"Everyone's saying you're a prince," she said matter-of-factly with her little voice.

I pulled my lips to the side, nodding slowly. "That I am."

"Are you here to save us?" she whispered, clutching her doll closer. "I don't like being here. These hurt." She gestured to the cuffs. "And I want to go home."

I examined the device as she held out her wrist. The device had been configured to someone else's fingerprints. I couldn't get it to budge.

I felt like a fool, blindly accepting this device into our army without pestering my father as to where he got them. How they even worked.

I just didn't care at the time.

"I saw you fight the soldier. You're strong."

I wasn't sure what to say to that. "What's your doll's name?" I asked gently, gesturing to the small kitten she held. I'm surprised they let her keep it. Probably Waylon's doing.

"Boots." She picked up one of its plush feet, waving it at me. "See? His paws are white. My mommy said it looked like he was wearing boots."

A small smile crept up my face, but it fell quickly. "Where are your parents?"

"They went to Elysium," she said sadly. "They went to protect me."

I chewed on the inside of my cheek, feeling a weight on me as I stared at this little girl who had no parents.

I didn't know how we would make it out of here. Dimitri could've sent word to my father, though he risked me spilling to Ulric their treachery. No, they wouldn't turn me over to Otacia. They would kill me—that would be their safest bet. But knowing

Dimitri's arrogant tendencies, I could easily see him enjoying my torment for a while before ending my life.

"Will you be my new daddy?" Saoirse asked.

My eyes grew wide. I certainly wasn't envisioning that to be her subsequent comment. "O-oh."

This little girl must not have any idea who I really am. Must not know that because of my father, the world was this way. And because I came from him...honestly, I'd be a shit father.

I cleared my throat. "I think you deserve a better daddy than me." I rubbed the back of my neck. "I am off in battles all the time."

I felt a pang in my chest at the sight of the little girl's face falling. "I don't mind," she insisted. "I'm by myself a lot. I would be a good daughter."

Perhaps I did have a heart because I felt an ache surfacing in my throat, felt my heart shatter at those innocent words. "When did you get here, Saoirse?" I asked, trying to change the subject carefully.

"I dunno." She furrowed her brow in contemplation. "It was...cold when they took me."

Saoirse nestled in close to me, resting her small head on my thigh. I tensed, unsure of what to do.

Big, blue eyes stared up at me. "Princes always come to save the day in my story books. You'll save us, won't you?"

That burning in my throat radiated down into my chest, and I did my best to give her a smile. "I will do everything I can," I promised.

I remained still as Saoirse beamed at me, snuggled closer, and drifted to sleep on my lap.

CHAPTER THIRTY-EIGHT
MERRICK

I stood, leaning against the wall in stupefaction, watching Silas remain seated, allowing the young Mage girl to rest on his leg. The gentleness in his features as he spoke to her was not an expression I thought possible from him.

He himself had drifted to sleep, not wishing to move and wake the young girl.

A new guard was arriving, ready to relieve the current from his watch duty. We were all waiting impatiently for Dani or Vi. It had been several hours in this dirty cage, and we had not seen a sign of either of them. My nerves increased with every second that ticked by.

Waylon said he'd be back before sunrise. That still had to be several hours away.

"You should get some rest," I muttered to Era, who was sitting on the ground beside me. Torrin was catching up with the Otacian men, men he had worked alongside for years, and El and Lena were listening in on their conversations.

Era didn't respond; she just continued to stare at the sleeping Prince.

I let out a sigh at her silence. Her cold demeanor toward me ever since our bizarre moment when we were high was unnerving me. I wasn't entirely sure why it bothered me, but I'd grown to enjoy what I considered the start of a friendship. I enjoyed our banter.

"It's sweet," the new guard standing at our cell door said, eyeing the Prince and the little girl. We all stared daggers at the man before he continued, "Though I'm not surprised...he showed gentleness to Leroy's kids before we left."

Era shuffled up from her spot on the ground. "Dani."

The man grinned. So, Dani had shifted into one of the Faltrunian guards.

"I thought you couldn't shift into other people?" I questioned with a raised brow, trailing my eyes down her new form.

"I can. I'm just without clothing initially." He pointed at his head—the man's head. "This poor bloke is hog-tied in a closet, naked as the day he was born."

Roland snorted.

"So, what's the plan?" Lena pressed, striding toward the cage door. Silas's eyes had just begun blinking open. "Have you spoken to Vi?"

Dani nodded. "She's currently playing the role of Dimitri, sending soldiers out in different directions outside of the castle. When she's done, I'll go on the outside, taking care of as many as I can."

"We need to take him out," Hendry insisted, speaking of the King. "We need him dead."

"I agree." Dani's head turned toward the creaking door, alerting us that someone was walking down. "This castle is massive. Vi is trying to memorize where all the exits are." He paused. "She should be down here soon, though. It won't be much longer."

"Dani," Lena urged. "You can't hurt Waylon."

Dani smiled. "I know. I heard. I've already spoken with him, and he's on board with our plan."

"Hey, what are you doing down here, Eric?" the soldier hollered. "Aren't you supposed to be on watch tower duty?"

Eric—Dani—gave the man a quick once over. "There must have been a miscommunication." He hauled his thumb toward us. "I was told I was taking over watching these ones."

The dark-haired soldier's brows furrowed. "That's not what I was told."

Dani sighed, stepping toward the exit. "Very well. I will go back. It's no worry."

The man shook his head, holding out his hands. "Actually, you can be of help. Cain was just heading down to help me, but he can take watch while you assist me." His glare shifted to Silas. "King Cortev wants the Otacian Prince brought to him."

Dani slowed his steps. "What for?"

The soldier frowned as he began unlocking the cage. "Does it matter? Orders are orders. Help me lug him upstairs."

My eyes nervously shot to Dani's. His jaw clicked, his eyes going to the now-awake Prince.

"Don't hurt him," Era pleaded, as if it would do anything. Silas stood, gently waking the young girl. When she sleepily looked at him, then at Dani and the other guard, she began crying.

"Don't take him!" Her eyes nervously darted up at Silas. "Please, don't leave me!" she cried, grasping onto his leg.

True compassion shone within in the Prince's eyes, and I could swear I felt his torment even with this device numbing me.

"I'll be back," Silas vowed, ruffling the top of her head. "I promise." His eyes went to Lena. "My friend over there will watch over you until I get back, okay?"

Lena's tearful gaze broadened, and she quickly gave Saoirse a smile, gesturing for her to stand beside her.

Tears spilled down the young girl's cheeks just as Silas was roughly pulled out of the cell, Dani wincing at us as he helped guide him away. The other man—Cain—quickly replaced him, and once again, we were separated from our friends.

"He'll be okay. Dani and Vi will make sure of it," Elowen insisted to Saoirse as the men were leaving our range of sight, though her worried gaze gave away her uncertainty.

Era wrapped her arms around herself, wandering away from everyone.

I followed her.

The Otacian Princess glared at me over her shoulder when she sensed me behind her. "Leave me alone."

For once in my life, I wished my gift could work. I wished I knew what she was feeling.

"What's your problem?" I hissed, snatching her arm. Ever since our moment smoking, she'd turned cold.

She slowly turned her head back, eyes going behind me, presumably at our friends, before her gaze found mine. "Don't. Touch. Me."

I blinked, then dropped her arm. "Tell me what your problem is."

"I don't have one."

"That's a fucking lie."

"How would you know?" she challenged. "You don't have your gift."

"Because your nose crinkles when you lie, and your breathing speeds up when you attempt to keep your face void of emotion."

Her eyes slightly expanded, and I stepped in closer. "You aren't that difficult to figure out, Princess," I whispered, not wishing for anyone to hear our conversation. "But what I cannot understand is why you're upset with me."

At her continued silence, I dragged my teeth along my lip ring, dancing my thumb against my leg.

"Is it really because I pressured you with the dagga?" I asked quietly. "Cause you could've slapped me in the face if I was being too forward with it." I continued nibbling on the metal hoop in my lip. "I was just trying to help you feel better."

Her brown eyes shone, her lips turning downward. "No...that's not why I got upset—am upset. I know you were trying to help."

Her chest was rising and falling so quickly, as if she'd just taken a break from running for her life. I trailed my eyes down her fidgeting form, then settled on those seductive eyes of hers, currently appearing more doe-like as she held my eye contact.

I swallowed. "Then why, Era? What did I do?"

She sucked in her lips, shaking her head, then turned away.

If we were alone, I'd grip her arms and pin her to the wall until she gave me answers. Her inability to be real with me drove me crazy, especially when I couldn't feel her emotions, which would probably provide me with some clues.

Instead, I ground my teeth, turning away to give her some space.

Several hours passed, and the plan was officially in motion. We all had attempted to get what sleep we could, all of us but Lena, who had anxiously waited for the Prince to be returned to our cell. He never was.

We expected Waylon or Viola to be down any moment now. I was still left stunned at the fact that Lena's father, of all people, had been working for Dimitri. The longer I thought about it, the more I believed fate really was on our side.

I hoped my thoughts didn't jinx anything for us.

We all had spread across the cage, telling each worn-out Mage our plan of escape, of retaliation. Most appeared unconvinced, with an '*I'll believe it when I see it*' look. But some also felt inspired, especially after witnessing Silas, Lena, and my cousin fighting back hours prior.

Torrin gave me an optimistic grin after we finished telling the seven hundred and forty-six Mages encompassing us the plan.

"I still can't believe you've been trapped here all this time," I uttered to him, the guilt threatening to overtake me. "We should've looked harder for you. We should've done something—"

"Merrick," Torrin interjected, gripping my shoulder. "I chose to leave. It was I that put myself in this situation, and no one else is to blame for my imprisonment but the asshole ruling this kingdom." His smile grew determined. "You're here now. That's all I have dreamed of this entire time. Not you guys being trapped here as well—but reuniting with my family." His face threatened to crumple. "I have missed you and Elowen so much. Lena, Vi...I missed all of you guys."

"We missed you," I said back, pulling my cousin into a quick hug. "We didn't speak of it," I murmured. "But I think we each feared you were dead as the months went on. Lena attempted to gather a search party, but none of the others believed you to be in danger."

I pulled back, and he quickly swiped a tear of his that fell. "I'm sorry I worried you all."

I shook my head. "Why did you leave?"

He offered that broken smile I hated seeing on his face. "I'll tell you everything once we get out of here."

I nodded reluctantly, and at that familiar creaking of a new guard taking the next shift, my stomach fell to see it as someone I didn't recognize.

Where the fuck is Waylon?

"King Cortev told me to take over," the new guard insisted to the old.

He glowered. "I'm on for the next few hours," he responded.

The new guard sighed. "Listen, the King has had more to drink this morning than ever before. He is not in the mood for disobedience, and frankly, neither am I." He crossed his arms. "If I go up and tell him otherwise, you'll be the one to suffer, not me."

The old guard paled, then quickly nodded. "V-very well."

After giving him orders on where to go, the new guard stood at our cell door, watching over us all as the man left.

None of us dare spoke a word.

After the door slammed shut, the soldier smiled. "I can't believe I've never tried this before." He laughed. His eyes widened as he took in my cousin. "Torrin? Is that really you?"

Torrin blinked, and I quickly asked, "Viola?"

The guard's eyes slid to me. "Duh." He winked. "What, you can't recognize me?"

"Where is Dani?" Edmund interjected, rushing up to the iron bars. "What's the plan?"

"She's currently taking out soldiers on the outside. Discreetly as possible. I'm to deal with the inside."

"They took Silas," Lena interrupted, Saoirse holding on to her leg. "You have to help him. Waylon said he would be here before sunrise to start releasing us."

"Does your thumbprint work, Vi?" I pressed.

She glanced down at her hand, the hand of a random soldier, and leaned her arm through, placing it on my cuff link. It didn't budge.

"Dammit," she muttered, then her eyes lit up. "Wait!" She closed her eyes, and we watched as she shifted into Waylon. Placing a hand through the bars, she placed her thumb along the reader on my cuff. It snapped open, the gem losing its light.

"Genius," I praised as she released the other one.

Waylon—Viola—smiled. "Your weapons are stored in the room to the left of the exit. The area is empty; I made sure of it." She turned to my sister. "El," she motioned, "Get over here. You need to heal as many of the injured as possible. Get everyone's strength up as best you can. All of you."

Elowen nodded, reaching her arms through the iron bars and letting Viola free her. She quickly turned, healing Torrin first. He attempted to wave her off, but she insisted anyway.

Viola's gaze slid over us all. "This castle is massive. Where do you think Dimitri is?"

"He has to be with Silas," Lena pressed as she was released next, rubbing her wrists as the device was removed. "Please, Vi, you need to make sure he's okay."

Saoirse glanced up at Lena. "He said he would come back. He promised."

Lena's saddened gaze fell on the child.

"I'll look for him. I didn't see him anywhere the whole time I was looking, but he has to be in here somewhere. Probably wherever Dimitri is."

I didn't need my gift to see the alarm on Lena's face, on Era's.

"Get to healing," Viola insisted. "Waylon will be down in twenty minutes."

My heart was drumming in my chest as Waylon began releasing the Mages one by one.

I was powerful. I knew that much. Lena especially. But the other Mages here were weak—some starved. Even with all of us healing the many injured, I didn't know how much fight those down here had in them. But determination gleamed in their eyes as they beheld my group—beheld Lena.

"Take out Dimitri, then the council, and you rule Faltrun," Waylon mumbled as Mage after Mage stood in line, having the device removed from their wrists.

Polly, along with every woman with long hair, stayed back. Lena shot them each a raised brow.

Polly held her chin up. "The rage will be uncontrollable. I have felt fire in my veins for years. Now is not the time."

Understanding shone in Lena's features as she nodded at the women. I understood, too. Their magic would threaten to destroy them if unleashed after so much time.

"When the battle is over, I will teach you how to control your fire," Lena promised, then bent down to place her hands on Saoirse's arms. The little girl's big blue eyes watered.

"Do you have magic yet, Saoirse?"

She shook her head. "I...I don't think so."

Lena slid her hand up to hold Saoirse's cheek as Waylon removed the small girl's restraints. "This battle is going to be for the grown-ups, okay? You and the other children will need to stay down here until we are all finished."

"You'll come back? My new daddy will come back?"

Era loosened a breath at the little girl's words, and Lena quickly wiped the child's eyes. "Yes, sweetheart. We will be right back. Just wait down here."

Saoirse cried softly, then buried herself in Lena's embrace. "Will you be my new mommy?" she asked, and Lena's face crumpled as she held the little girl close.

Era's eyes widened as we snuck out the cage door, Lena being the last to leave. She held the girl's face as she stood. "Yes, I will. I will take care of you." She glanced back at our group. "We all will. Just stay down here and wait for us."

We quickly rushed up the steps, equipping our weapons that rested in the room upstairs to the left, just as Viola had said. The Mages were waiting nervously in the cell, awaiting Waylon, who would be down there instructing them after our talk.

I shifted to Era, offering her bow over.

She gave a skittish smile, slinging her quiver over her shoulder. Lena kept her sword at her back, and Hendry readied his bow, Edmund and Roland equipping their own swords. Elowen tucked Immeron's dagger at her side, and once we were all ready, we stood around a wooden table.

Waylon cleared his throat, sweat lining his forehead as he laid a map out on the table where our weapons had been resting. "There are three main levels to this castle, and a majority of the soldiers have been strategically placed outside. Archers, the top floor balcony on the east side will provide the best angle, but the southern side will prove useful." He shifted the maps to the second floor. "The council resides on the second floor. Most will be sleeping." He circled in pen different rooms. "This is where you will find them, in their rooms." He scurried over to a cabinet, retrieving two bottles. "Viola made these—said they could turn two of you invisible."

My eyes enlarged, and I glanced down at the corked glass bottles.

"Roland, Edmund, you two should take them," Lena said, eyes drifting from Roland, who stood close to her side, to my sister's boyfriend. "It'll be not only the safest for you, but I assume you have more experience in this."

Roland's lips curved upward. "Yes. Slightly more experienced in assassinations."

She slid her green gaze over. "I don't want them dead. Yet. I want them captured. Tie them up."

Roland's hazel eyes twinkled. "As you wish, Supreme."

She rolled her eyes, the corner of her lip raising.

"The Mages should fight on the ground. I will lead those in the basement out to the main field." He shook his head slowly, his eyes finding his daughter's. "This battle will not be pretty...many lives will be lost. They will need someone leading them."

Lena swallowed, nodding to her father. After a few more comments, he quickly exited the room to fulfill his part in this plan.

"Era and I will take the eastern balcony," I said. Hendry's mismatched eyes met mine. "You good with the southern side?"

He nodded, his gaze flitting to Era. "You sure she's the best for that side?"

Era's face heated at the mention of her lack of skill. But I remembered her clear shot when she saved my life in Forsmont.

"Era is more skilled than you think." I equipped my quiver, slinging my bow against my back as Era and I grasped extra bags of arrows.

Lena observed the elixir bottles. "I'm not sure how long these last," she said, handing one to Roland and one to Edmund. "But make haste to those rooms. Walk with caution in case they wear off."

The men nodded, following her orders by chugging the drinks. Their invisible hands rustled with the parchment, and the second-story map vanished as one of them obtained it.

Lena lastly turned to Torrin. "I need you to lead the people out there," she said calmly, his brows furrowing. "I need to find Silas."

CHAPTER THIRTY-NINE
SILAS

I was shoved to the ground in one of the highest rooms in this castle, judging by the view from the window I found myself gazing out of. I had no idea the time; I just noted it was still dark.

My arms and legs had been secured with chains, my arms elevated, and my feet attached to the ground, leaving me in a kneeling position.

Dani was ordered away the second my chains were attached. He gave me an apologetic frown, and I nodded, understanding there were more pressing matters.

I could at least keep Dimitri distracted.

There was a bed in here. Two nightstands. A desk and chair. Otherwise, this room was rather plain.

Why am I up here?

My question was answered relatively quickly. A few guards took turns pummeling their fists into my stomach, my sides, and my face. After my eyes became swollen and blood started pouring from my broken nose, I was left alone for hours, tugging at my chains, attempting to break free from them to no avail. I squeezed my eyes tight, trying to regulate my breathing at what this position reminded me of.

The door eventually creaked open, Dimitri ambling in. A Mage woman with long, black hair and dark brown eyes was being hauled in behind him. The guards tossed her to the floor, and she stumbled a few steps before hitting the wooden ground.

Dimitri rolled his eyes. "Get up, Deana."

She obeyed, slowly creeping up from the floor, her blank expression nearly as haunting as those overtaken by the necromancer.

"What do you want from me?" I spat the blood that had gathered in my mouth on the floor in front of me, glaring at him from my position on the ground.

I felt my panic rise as Dimitri staggered forward, a sickening grin on his face as he gripped a blade, tearing away at the shirt I wore, and stripped it off me. My armor had already been removed before they secured me in this position.

Sweat mixed with blood as it poured down my face, my breathing labored as his eyes went to my back. No one had seen me shirtless in over five years.

I couldn't move, nor could I meet his eyes as he took in the sight.

"Oh, wow," Dimitri drawled, running his finger along the flesh on my back. I flinched, and he chuckled. "Not what I was expecting back here."

"What do you want?" I seethed, trembling violently.

Dimitri didn't care much for my back. His eyes danced, his sinister smile growing. "Deana, come here, pet."

Deana's hollow gaze met his as she stood, wandering over to him.

"Undress."

My eyes flared, darting away as the woman began to strip.

Dimitri pressed his blade against my neck, and I grunted as my malicious glare found his wretched face.

"Ah, ah, ah," he taunted, wagging his index finger. "Enjoy the free show, princeling."

My nostrils flared, and as he pressed the blade harder against my jugular, I shifted my eyes to the now naked woman, who stood as still as a statue.

The woman had beauty to her, but her body was malnourished. Bruised.

He withdrew his blade and began fumbling with his belt as he turned to her, his back facing me. "On your knees."

"Don't," I barked, sensing where this was going. "Don't touch her!"

He pushed down roughly on her shoulders, her knees hitting the wood with a thud. Her lip trembled, her drained eyes landing on mine.

"DON'T YOU FUCKING TOUCH HER!" I roared, thrashing at my chains. My senses became heightened as I felt the right chain attached to my arm became loosened.

Dimitri only snickered. "She's used to this, princeling." He stroked her jaw as he removed his belt.

Her eyes filled with tears. Still, she kept her gaze on mine.

I pulled and pulled with all my might. As Dimitri released his cock, I tugged my arm so hard that my shoulder dislocated, and the chain finally broke free. Despite the pain, I whipped it at his back, the metal clacking against his skull, knocking him straight to the ground.

Deana shrieked, backing away. I tried so hard to break free of the other restraints, but my arm and both legs were still trapped.

"His thumbprint," I panted to Deana. "Release yourself and get the hell out of here!"

She trembled. "I-I can't...fire will consume me—"

"Then just run," I pleaded.

"What about you?!" she cried.

Dimitri began to stir.

"Go! I'll find a way."

She hesitated, and as Dimitri began to lift himself, she bolted out of the door.

"You," he sputtered, the wound on his skull leaking blood. "You Godsdamn bastard."

He stood, thankfully tucking away his nasty manhood, and turned, slamming a drunken fist into the side of my bruised face.

Stars spread across my vision. "Fuck you." I spat in his face, then broke out in a hysterical laugh at the sight of his angered face. Nothing he could do would be worse than what had already been done to me. He would never have me sniveling or begging for mercy.

His nostrils flared, his lip twitching as he swung into my face again.

And again.

And again.

I choked, blood rushing out of my mouth, my ears ringing from the blunt force.

He grasped my arm, wrenching it at an unnatural angle. "You broke one of my men's arms," he snarled, his foul breath brushing against my face. "I should do the same to you."

I heard it snap, and I cried out as pain shot through my body. One arm was dislocated, one broken.

I was fucked.

"The truth is, princeling, there is no information I need from you." He chuckled, stumbling as he retrieved his blade from the ground. "I just need you dead."

He rushed forward, and I had no time to prepare as he began repeatedly stabbing me in the chest.

Over and over and over.

CHAPTER FORTY

LENA

T orrin had reluctantly agreed to my plan and was now on the outside, leading the prisoners to the fight alongside Elowen. It was better that way, at least to start. Torrin knew everyone inside, and I could tell by the small interactions in the cage that they respected him. Who couldn't, really?

I already could hear the screaming outside as I snuck up an entrance to the second floor. I could only hope Roland and Edmund would be quick with their job capturing the council members.

I had no idea where Silas was, and neither did Waylon. There were hundreds of rooms in the castle. He could be in any of them.

Due to the chaos outside, doors to the rooms began flying open, and royals panicked at the battle beneath them. Some halted in place as I passed them, ducking in fear. Some attempted to grasp me, and I froze their bodies to the walls.

Silas could be dead by now, for all I knew.

"Where is the Prince?!" I yelled at those I passed.

None knew...none gave answers.

"Where is the King?!"

I threatened each with flame, and at their cries, claiming they did not know, I hurried upward.

Cries of torture wouldn't be pleasant for the sleeping. The basement was where we already were, so that left the top floor.

Rushing up the southern staircase, I moved faster than I ever had in my life. The few soldiers that were still remaining attempted to stab me, and I ducked as they swung their weapons, shooting electricity into their bodies, their limbs sizzling before they ultimately collapsed on the ground.

The one I left surviving cowered, and I froze him to the ground, my fingertips dancing with lightning.

"Where. Is. Silas?"

"T-the King took him...I-I don't know which room."

I brought my hands closer to his temples. "I will fry your brain into mush if you do not tell me where he is."

He shook his head, tears spilling. "M-maybe the attic. There's a r-room in the attic he takes his women to."

My stomach dropped, and I raced away, leaving the soldier frozen there.

Dimitri was a sick fuck. I didn't think he would kill him quickly.

There would be time.

There had to be time.

I hated myself for beginning to cry. There were so many steps in this place, so many corridors. I continually darted my eyes down at the map, following the way to the attic.

He had to be there. He had to be okay.

I was rushing around a corner when I slammed into someone. A woman.

I blinked as I took in her naked body. The Mage woman grabbed onto my arms for support, sobbing profusely.

"He saved me," she cried.

"Who saved you?" My eyes darted around her weeping face. "Where is Silas?!" I demanded. "Where is he?!"

"Dimitri stabbed him in the chest so many times...I watched in the doorway—"

I slammed her body against the wall, the wind knocking out of her. Her eyes went wide as I yelled in her face, "WHERE IS HE?!"

The woman shook. "I watched as he finished with him...his head slumping down." Choking on a sob, she replied, "Silas is dead."

CHAPTER FORTY-ONE

MERRICK

Aiming my bow, I released an arrow, the tip incasing in ice, before ripping through a man's chest.

"I wish mine did that!" Erabella yelled, successfully impaling another.

We were perched exactly where Waylon told us to be, and he was right; this spot was excellent.

The battle beneath was in complete disorder, but I was impressed by the Mages' will to fight. All their time without magic had their powers just begging to be released. Still, the army in Faltrun was substantial...triple that of the number of Mages fighting for their freedom.

I tried not to focus on the bodies that dropped.

Era shot her bow with precision, her nerves melting as we fought beside each other.

I was proud of her, but I'd tell her that later.

Things were going well...until they weren't.

My eyes shot to the side at the sound of Era's cry. A soldier within the castle had snuck up on her. I went to shoot a blast of ice through the guy's skull, but Era grasped the dagger resting on her thigh, turning to shove it through the side of his neck.

He gurgled, hands flying to the wound before he ultimately fell to the ground.

That was all the strength she had. She fell to her knees.

"Fuck, Era!" I secured my bow against my back as I quickly rushed to her, her side profusely bleeding. The fucker stabbed her.

"I-I'm fine," she rushed, but I could feel her fear, feel her panic.

"You're not fine," I gritted out, then scooped her into my arms. As Faltrunian soldiers began running toward me, I pushed a force-field out with my mind, using nearly all my power in doing so. It was always easier using my hands—this took all my concentration.

Era wept in my arms, the screams of slaughter and slurs of hate a sick song playing around us.

I didn't know the extent of her wound—how deep it was. I just knew there was a shit ton of blood...and that I was scared.

I was so scared.

If I had acquired fire, perhaps I could cauterize the wound. Though I didn't think I would have it in me to burn her.

Her weeping began to quiet, and when I nervously looked down at her, running as I did so to find us somewhere to hide, her eyes began to flutter shut.

"Era. Era! Don't you dare close your eyes!"

She didn't respond.

Fuck!

I stifled a cry as I made it into an unoccupied room, setting her down on the bed and shoving a dresser in front of the door. The howls of death and the clashing of swords a sound in the distance. Losing my shield, I exhaled sharply as I returned to Era's side.

I needed to use my gift. I needed to be able to sense any emotions of those around me in case I felt someone sneaking up. But I needed to heal Era more. Needed as much power to use toward repairing her.

I placed a panicked hand on her rib cage, and my palms felt like fire. They burned so badly.

"C'mon, Princess...fight," I breathed, a glow emitting from my hand. If Elowen were here, she could have done a much more efficient job. But I had no idea where my sister was. I had no idea if she was even alive.

Era's skin had a bluish hue. Her breathing was shallow, but she was alive...she was still here with me.

I used my free hand to cup her cheek, forcing her head up. "Wake up, Era," I whispered. I shook her chin softly, and her brown eyes began to open slowly. When her eyes focused, meeting mine, tears blurred her vision, her face crumpling.

"It hurts," she cried, her voice hoarse from the wound. I could now tell he had pierced her lung.

"I know." I brushed her falling tears with my thumb, my own lip trembling. "I know."

"Am I going to die?" She coughed and then cried out in agony at the pain.

"No, Princess, you will live." I ground my teeth, willing every ounce of power I had into my palm.

Her voice was quiet and helpless when she said, "Promise?"

I knew I had no right promising such a thing. But I couldn't take the strain in my chest looking at her panicked face, her pained eyes.

I held the side of her face with my free hand. "I promise, Era."

Her eyes bounced between mine, her lips trembling, and she nodded.

I glanced nervously out the window, watching the battle from above. Dani was fighting alongside the Mages down below, shifting into a fly, then her normal form, slicing through soldier after soldier with a sword before shifting back.

It was remarkable, but I didn't know how long she could keep it up.

I still had no idea where Viola was.

The pain in my palm began to subside. Still present, but less severe, that was for sure.

They needed us out there, fighting from above. I knew that.

There was not enough fucking time.

"Merrick."

My stomach plunged at the feel of Era's hand on my cheek, angling me to face her. "You...you have to go."

My eyebrows drew together. "What are you talking about?"

"It's too dangerous, and they need you out there."

"You need me."

It was her thumb that now stroked my face, and I did my best to ignore the chills that spread across my body from it. "Yes. But I am but one person. They need you. Your power."

Spoken like a true princess. Her value had always been to look pretty, please a prince, and birth heirs into the royal family. Her belief was that she wasn't worth anything. I could feel it.

I knew my eyes were swirling dark as I read her, her eyes going half-lidded as I brought my lips to her ear.

"You need me," I repeated in a low voice. "And we are gonna work on how little you value yourself after this."

I drew back and stared at her pained expression, then quickly resumed scanning the battle from the window beside the bed. My palm was growing less and less painful, but I couldn't stitch up this wound as quickly as my sister. At this rate, it would take hours to heal her fully.

"Merrick, go," she demanded with more bite in that sultry voice of hers.

"I will do no such thing," I growled, my eyes breaking away from the window.

A scowl overcame her features. "What if something happens to Elowen? To Viola?" She scoffed. "Are you going to think I'm so valuable if they die because of me? Die because they had less help?"

Panic overtook me momentarily at the thought of losing either of them. My eyes flicked back outside to the increasing number of bodies that lay on the ground.

Era gripped my arm tightly, her gaze burning into mine. "Go. Please."

My chest was rising and falling, my hands trembling with this nauseating fear. I should go; I should make sure both of them are safe. I should fight to protect all those innocent people down there. Era's wound still needed healing, but she wouldn't die from her injuries alone any longer.

But I couldn't move. It was like my body had filled with lead the second I thought of leaving her here alone.

"I can't," I bit out, baring my teeth.

"Merrick—"

"I can't leave you, Erabella. I can't physically leave you...I..." I shook my head, and then my darkened eyes found hers. "You told me before you couldn't live if you'd have killed me in Forsmont."

Her hand still held my face, her thumb running along my cheekbone. "This is different," she whispered.

"You're right," I agreed. "If I had died, it would've been in spite of you trying to save me." I raised my hand to hold her face again, our hands on each other's cheek. "If I leave, you'd die because I tried to save others." My thumb grazed her pouty bottom lip. "I will always save you."

A cry slipped past her lips, and I didn't know what overcame me...perhaps fear of her death, fear of mine. Or maybe it was the feelings I kept trying to push down since the first moment I saw her. I leaned down, capturing her luscious lips with my own.

She stilled, her dainty hand that still held my face shaking.

I read her as I pulled her bottom lip into my mouth, finding confidence in the overwhelming desire that flooded through her body, heightening my own.

She withdrew slightly. "Merrick," she rasped over my lips. "I...we can't—"

I captured her lips again. "Just let me kiss you," I whispered. "Just a few more."

Her heart thundered. I could feel her pulse as my hand slid down to hold the side of her neck. She gave me a rushed nod.

I continued to kiss her slowly, healing her with my other hand. Our tongues never touched—both of us too intimated to deepen our kiss. But when she sucked my lip gently, her tongue gliding against my lip ring, I felt myself losing control. I felt want, need, and desire unlike ever before in my life.

But before we could go any further, Era groaned, her wound spurting out more blood, coating my hand.

"Fuck," I panicked, pulling away from her. I stopped reading her, focusing all my power on healing this wound.

My eyes hesitantly rose to meet her widened ones, noting the significant flush to her cheeks. She blinked rapidly, then averted her gaze, not wishing to look at me.

Clarity washed over me as I accepted that I had just kissed a married woman...and that she had kissed me back.

CHAPTER FORTY-TWO

SILAS

Blood was streaming from the stab wounds in my chest, one still with the knife embedded into it, and I could hardly open my eyes as Dimitri rushed back into the room. He quickly shut the door, eyes widening as he beheld me.

I was surprised I was still breathing, honestly.

"Fucking hell," he muttered, lowering to his knees and taking in my injuries.

"What, need me alive after all?" I choked.

Looking at me, I watched as Dimitri's appearance morphed into my purple-haired companion.

My pathetic lip trembled. "Viola?" I damn near cried.

She immediately placed her palm over the first bleeding wound, beginning to heal it.

"We...we need to get out of here," I panted. "Where is Dimitri?"

"On the run. We'll find him." She assessed my broken arm, noting the out-of-place shoulder on the other side. "I have to stop the bleeding at least," she murmured. "I won't be able to heal your broken arm that fast, but I'll pop the other back in place when I'm done."

I cried out as she quickly withdrew the blade piercing my chest, her glowing palm slapping over the gushing wound.

"Sorry," she winced.

My dizziness had bile gathering in my mouth. "Why are you up here?" I rasped a few moments later. "What's going on?"

"The battle is in full force," she admitted, her palm roaming over the next stab wound. "And I came to find you."

"You came up here looking for *me*?"

"Of course," she answered as if my question was absurd. "That's what friends do."

My breathing began to steady as she weaved my injuries back together. My heavy eyes fell to the bloody floor beneath me. "Friends..."

She offered a sweet smile. "My magic isn't at its best right now. Shifting this much has taken a toll." She took a deep breath. "But I couldn't leave you. Plus, Lena insisted I find you, and she is my Supreme."

I hesitantly glanced up at her. "Where is Lena?"

"In battle, I'd imagine."

Only once my injuries ceased bleeding did she pull her hands away and begin releasing my chains. But it wasn't until Viola finally noticed my back that she gasped, tumbling back, her hand flying over her mouth.

I winced, biting down on my busted lip. "Please," I begged her, disgusted by the desperation in my voice. "Please, no one can know about my back."

"Who..." she began, but in seeing the agony in my eyes, she refrained from asking. Her widened eyes filled with tears, and she nodded. "I won't say a thing. I promise, Silas."

Once the chains clanked against the hardwood floor, she brought her hands to my shoulder. I braced myself, giving her a nod, and I swore colorfully as she set my arm back in place. I bit back a scream as I slid my broken arm through the armhole of a dark shirt—a long-sleeve button-up Viola found tucked in a dresser. Viola helped me cover up the place I kept hidden with no protest.

"I'm sorry," she whispered, quickly buttoning my top.

"Don't be." It was still hard seeing her through my swollen eyes. "I owe you."

She gave me a smile back, and I groaned as she helped me up, assisting me as I limped out of the room.

We only descended the first staircase before I began coughing. Smoke filled the air, the smell of fire invading my nose. When I saw the state of the corridor before me, I loosened a breath.

The hallways had been seared, and every soldier had been turned to ash—I could tell by the charred remains that littered the floors.

My eyes skated down only slightly, and then I saw her.

Encasing her body, her flame glowed brighter than ever before. Hues of blue and violet this time, with sparks of electricity wrapping around her arms and legs, fusing her two elemental powers. When Lena's eyes found mine, she froze, her look of vengeance vanishing.

"Silas," she cried, letting her magic rescind as she ran to me. "Lena..."

When she halted before me, she lifted her fingers, examining my damaged face. Tears were spilling down her cheeks. "T-they said you were dead."

I gave her my best attempt at a smile. "You can't get rid of me that easily." My eyes slid to Viola, who was still helping me walk. "Viola saved my life."

Lena gave her a grateful nod, then wrapped her arm around me. I hissed when she touched my broken arm. "We need to get you healed."

"There's no time—"

"I'm healing you." She shifted her gaze to Vi. "Go. We will join in a moment."

Viola nodded, then rushed off.

Lena guided me into a room, shutting the door behind us, and quickly fished into her bra, withdrawing chalk. The room was off the hall, all empty due to the mayhem Lena had unleashed. She bent down and began drawing on the wooden floor.

It was a pentagram with symbols I couldn't decipher.

"Lena, there's no time," I protested.

She ignored me.

"Stand in it," she ordered after completing the drawing a minute later.

My arm throbbed, so I listened.

"Sana omnia vulnera eius," Lena chanted, a golden glow traveling down to the pentagram. ***"Sana omnia vulnera eius."***

The circle began to glow as she repeated the words, and when Lena's eyes finally shot open, her pupils had vanished.

"Holy fuck," I breathed, and my eyes peeked down. My pain disappeared, and my broken arm was able to move with ease.

Lena blinked, her glow fading, her pupils returning. "It worked. It actually fucking worked," she exhaled, a half grin on her face as she grasped her knees to balance herself.

"You did too much," I murmured, rushing to her and seizing her shoulders. "How did you know that spell?"

"I memorized it on the road. I wasn't sure it would work, but..." Her tired eyes lifted to mine, and then she pulled me into her arms.

I held her back, the feeling of her body pressed against mine providing the most satisfying comfort.

"I love you," she whispered.

My jaw slackened at her soft words, my entire body going rigid as if she had actually frozen me with her ice magic. "Lena..."

"You don't have to say it back. I just had to tell you. I just needed you to know." She withdrew, beaming at me with unreleased tears pooling in her eyes. "Now, put on your armor. Let's take Faltrun as our own."

The battle was pure chaos. The Faltrunian generals were shouting orders—orders that were quickly drowned out by the cacophony of combat. Not only did every soldier in the kingdom come out to fight, but its citizens did as well. By the way that the people here looked at those of magical decent, it was clear their hatred ran just as deep as it did in my own kingdom.

This would not be a simple conquering, but as the Mages here fought with desperation to regain their freedom, their magic overpowered the humans. Sprinting outside, I grasped the first discarded sword I could find. I was stopped in my tracks by a body on the ground.

The body of a child. A young Mage boy.

Lena's eyes widened at the sight of the corpse. "I-I told them to stay inside...the children were supposed to remain inside!"

Bile rose in my throat, and my eyes darted around.

Where is Saoirse?

Panic rose inside me at the thought of that little girl out in this combat, alone, afraid.

"We have to find Saoirse!" I panicked.

Lena agreed, and the two of us charged forward, fighting against any and every soldier who crossed our path.

She was ethereal as she moved, exuding a confident aura I never saw in her before...one I had hoped she'd come into one day. She moved like the wind, searing as she took down those who opposed her, those who threatened her kind.

She was a beautiful whirlwind. A force to be reckoned with.

She was everything I dreamed of and more. A spitfire, a siren.

I hissed as a blade just barely missed decapitating me, distracted by Lena's captivating beauty. Blood coursed down my face, leaking from a cut trailing down my once smooth cheek.

Great. Now both sides were fucked.

I bared my teeth as I engaged in combat, taking down soldier after soldier after soldier.

Hiding behind a house, my eyes caught the sight of several children huddled together, shivering and covering their pointed ears.

I hurried to them, scanning over each face.

She isn't here.

"Where is Saoirse?" I asked them quickly but gently.

A young boy, probably ten, sniffed. "S-she went to fight! She wouldn't listen!"

My heart stopped, and I quickly rotated, skimming the crowd.

When I saw her, everything stilled.

I watched in horror as Saoirse's eyes blew wide, an arrow piercing through her little chest. She held a dagger in her tiny hand, Boots in her other.

She was trying to fight.

The man shook as he held the bow aimed at her, lowering his weapon fearfully as he recognized what he'd just done.

"What did you do?!" I howled, racing up to her and scooping her into my arms. Her dagger slipped from her grasp. I craned my head up at the monster before me, who stood frozen. "WHAT DID YOU DO?!"

I held her, tears spilling down her cheeks. "H-help," she cried.

My eyes darted down to her. "I know it hurts." I quickly assessed the damage.

Fuck...she was gushing blood.

"ELOWEN!" I wailed. But the healer was lost in battle. I doubted she could even hear my cry.

Saoirse clutched onto her bloodied kitten, her lip wobbling, her body trembling with adrenaline. She was losing too much blood.

By some blessing, I caught the pink-haired healer rushing to me.

"Help her," I pleaded as she knelt on the ground beside us.

Elowen's big blue eyes were filled with tears as she waved her hand above the injury.

"L-Lena did a spell. It healed my broken arm—"

"It's pierced her major artery. There's no time to perform such a spell." Her glossy eyes raised, and she mouthed, "*There's nothing I can do.*"

No.

I watched in torment as she withdrew the dagger crafted by Immeron.

The one that could take a life painlessly.

Saoirse was shaking violently in my arms, Elowen behind her, charging the weapon with her magic.

"I'm...scared," she wept, her voice so small.

"Don't be." I tried my hardest to give a smile. "My friend is going to heal you, okay?"

Elowen's face crumpled as she rubbed the top of Saoirse's head, bringing the dagger to her neck.

"You will be just fine," I whispered, stroking her cheek.

I blinked repeatedly as Saoirse lifted her teeny hand, Boots in her other, and placed it on my face. Placed it over my fresh cut.

A golden glow emitted from her little palm as she used her magic to heal the cut on my cheek.

Despite the pain, Saoirse smiled, her eyes threatening to shut. "I...I knew you'd save us."

My face crumpled the moment she uttered those words, the moment right before Elowen dragged her dagger across Saoirse's neck.

Saoirse didn't scream as her throat was cut open. Didn't cry out. I knew that the magical weapon had eliminated all of her pain while it took her life quickly.

The vitality behind her watery eyes withered until her vacant eyes stared back at me, that slight smile of hers fading to a straight line as her hand slipped from my cheek.

Elowen broke into a sob as she withdrew her bloodied blade.

My whole body was shaking.

I saw it then: Roland and Edmund were lugging the council members down, tied up, and at their mercy with the help of a few Mages.

Walking out behind them was Viola, in her true form, Dimitri restrained and in her grasp.

We won.

The Faltrunian soldiers gaped at their captured leaders, dropping their weapons and falling to their knees in surrender.

I felt no satisfaction in our win as my eyes flitted back to the girl in my arms.

This innocent child, bleeding out from a fatal wound, used her final moments to heal a cut on my face.

All she wished for was a mother and father to take care of her...for freedom.

I drifted my hand over her eyelids, closing them forever, tears pouring from my eyes for the first time in years as I held her lifeless body.

PART TWO:

CHRYSALIS

CHAPTER FORTY-THREE

LENA

The Mages had won. Dimitri had been captured, the castle had been secured, and the slaves had all been freed. But at what cost?

Overall, this battle was a success, but as I watched Silas cling to that young girl's dead body, as I witnessed the sobs of both humans and Mages who had lost ones they loved, I realized that there really were no winners in war—just those who suffered a little less.

Roland and Edmund had successfully detained the council, though Edmund had a nasty black eye from being punched. They were lugging them down with the help of a few Mages when my eyes skated to my Soul-Tie.

Silas's eyes were focused on the girl, his entire body stiff yet shaking. He was crying. His face was blank, but the tears were flooding out. When his eyes rose to meet the man who killed Saoirse, I could tell one emotion overpowered them all.

Rage.

I could see it in his eyes as he went to place her on the ground. Saw it when his gaze locked with the kneeling man who took Saoirse's life.

No one interjected when Silas stood, lifted his sword, and stepped toward the man.

"Pl-please—"

The man's words were cut off by Silas's sword plunging into his chest. He choked, panicked eyes shooting toward his fatal wound.

Silas's face held no expression. He withdrew his blade, watching as the man slumped to the ground in a growing puddle of his own blood.

Part of me was surprised he didn't torture the man, but the other part understood. He didn't deserve a moment more of living, even if those moments were unpleasant.

Silas's eyes went to the human council members being led out of the castle in cuffs. His eyes darted to Roland, then Hendry. "You two, with me."

The two men nodded, then moved toward the Prince.

Silas moved forward, but the Mage restraining Dimitri held out his hand. "Their deaths belong to us."

Silas came to a halt. "I don't wish to kill them. I wish to extract information."

"This is kind of our specialty," Roland said with a dark smile aimed toward the King.

The Mage debated, looking at his companions, before agreeing. They all headed inside the castle.

My eyes went to one of the Mage women with long hair—still cuffed. "Why were the children out here?"

She choked on a sob. "Dimitri...he threatened to kill Polly if the rest of us didn't rush out of the castle," she cried. "She begged us to stay, told us she was okay with dying...he slit her throat right in front of us."

"No..." I shook my head, my hand covering my mouth. "I-I promised her she would be free."

"It was clear Dimitri was going to kill us all anyway, so we ran as fast as we could. I...I couldn't keep track of all the children."

My eyes went back to Saoirse, her body, among others, littered on the ground. Many began to lift their dead, bringing them to the graveyard behind the castle.

But Saoirse had no one. How did this little girl have no one?

Then again, if I had lost my mother, what would've become of me?

I was before her in seconds. I knelt down, running my hand against her tight, blonde curls. How could the humans look at her innocent face and shave her head? How could they put cuffs on her tiny wrists?

How could they shoot an arrow in her chest?

My lip wobbled, and I went to lift her but was stopped by a hand on my shoulder.

I looked back, and Torrin's saddened face reflected my own. "Let me help," he offered.

I nodded, removing my arms from Saoirse so Torrin could lift her. She was still clutching that kitten doll.

We walked silently to the graveyard. The residents watched warily from their homes, some fearfully, as they took notice of all the Mages that now ruled this territory.

I paid them no mind. I couldn't focus on anything except lying this sweet girl to rest.

It felt like deja vu. Just like in Forsmont, humans and magical beings alike were mourning their dead after another violent battle.

I wished there were a way to make things right without resorting to violence, but where corruption thrives, lethal force must be used. There was no way around it.

Torrin carefully laid Saoirse on the ground, then lifted a shovel and began to dig where there was an empty spot.

"Let me," I insisted. "You've been put to work long enough."

Torrin kept digging. "Which means I'm efficient." His eyes flitted back to me. "Help El heal those who need it. This will take me about four hours. Come find me after."

"Are you sure?"

He stuck his shovel in the dirt, then ambled toward me, kissing the top of my head. "I'm sure," he murmured. "This will help me clear my head. Plus, our people need your guidance."

"You were the one who led them to victory today," I countered.

He smiled softly, brushing my hair out of my face. "None of this would've been possible without you."

He held my face for a moment, flicked my nose, and returned to the task at hand.

My gaze drifted to the dead child on the ground, the wind drifting over her lifeless form, her short curls blowing with the movement.

None of this would've been possible without you.

It had been a few hours of healing both the Mages and the Faltrun-ian soldiers that had conceded. I reluctantly erased their wounds, many staring at me in disgust.

It was clear it would take a lot to change this place for the better.

Merrick had carried Erabella from somewhere in the castle; apparently, she had been impaled in the lung. Elowen worked on her efficiently as Merrick went to offer help to others.

I had found my way back to Torrin, the kingdom's clocktower chiming twelve in the afternoon. He was panting and sweating, and a sheen of sweat coated his skin as he finished digging her gravesite.

I choked on a sob as I stared at her. Carefully, I removed the doll from her small hands.

"Thank you," I whispered, pulling him into my embrace. "Thank you, Torrin."

His limbs were shaking from exhaustion, but he squeezed me tighter against him.

I wept as Torrin lowered her body into the hole in the ground. I placed a hand on his back. "I'll find you later," I promised him as I pulled away.

Torrin didn't need to ask why I kept the kitten. I walked away before I could see the dirt begin to cover her face.

I scrubbed the doll for what felt like hours, but it was more like thirty minutes, getting as much red out of it as I could. Overall, it appeared clean, but if you looked closely, you could still notice the stains from the little girl's blood.

CHAPTER FORTY-FOUR

SILAS

Roland, Hendry, and Edmund did just as I asked, throwing Dimitri down into the same shit and piss-filled cage we had been kept in.

"Bonnevau, Aubeze, string Dimitri up to the rack."

They did so swiftly, and my chest hummed with excitement.

I glanced over at my blond friend. Edmund was trained to hide any emotion on his face, but I knew he couldn't stomach torture.

"Go. Check on Elowen," I said to him gently. I then whispered something into his ear.

He blinked, bowing. "Thank you, Your Highness. And yes, of course."

My eyes flicked to Roland as Edmund retreated, his hazel eyes looking to me for orders. "Aubeze, cut off a finger. Any finger."

He nodded, then gave Dimitri a smug grin before approaching.

"No! No, no, no—" Dimitri let out a sickening cry as Roland used his dagger to cut off the King's middle finger.

Roland dangled it in front of Dimitri, who was sobbing. "Who would've guessed you'd cry like such a pussy," Roland laughed.

I stepped forward, watching in wonder as the blood poured out of his hand. "You think you could harm me and get away with it?"

My hands twitched. I wanted to torture him myself, but I knew that Hendry desired the same.

My friend was quiet, but within him, just like myself, demons were locked inside.

He had always been the private sort, never wishing to talk about himself. But I could see that glimmer in his eyes. Could see that something haunted him.

When we were teens, I'd try to pry the information out of him, gently, of course, so as not to cause him to withdraw into himself. I never got any answers. Only once I endured what I did, once I changed myself, did I recognize the monsters that lay behind a seemingly composed front. I recognized the shadows in his eyes because I saw them in my own every time I looked in the mirror.

I didn't wish for anyone to pry me, so I stopped doing the same to Hendry.

He enjoyed killing; that much was obvious. I could see his excitement, even if his mouth remained in that straight line.

Sometimes, your demons hold so much power over you that you have to unleash them every now and again. To keep them from taking over completely.

My eyes slid to my friend's mismatched ones, his pupils blown wide in anticipation. I gestured toward Dimitri. "He still has nine more fingers. Do keep one of his thumbs. I want him alive."

A small smile crept along Hendry's slim lips, and he stepped toward Dimitri, whose breathing became increasingly labored as Hendry's long legs stalked toward him.

His eyes studied his shirtless body, analyzing the best place for him to play.

Hendry decided, and Roland and I watched as he sawed Dimitri's nipples off.

Roland winced as Dimitri screeched. "Damn, Hendry, that's cold."

Hendry balanced one on his blade. His eyes flickered up to Dimitri, his voice emotionless as he said, "I'd force-feed you this, but I'd rather not deal with your vomit."

I snorted. "Yeah, I'd rather not as well." My eyes drifted to the various buckets the Mages were forced to defecate in. Hendry's and my eyes met at the same time.

Roland grimaced. "You guys are going to make *me* throw up."

"It's deserved, is it not?" Hendry asked.

Dimitri's panicked gaze was flickering between us three.

Roland shot Hendry a half grin. "Oh, very much deserved, my friend. So, what, shit ball throwing contest?" His eyes fell to the cart of tools. Three pairs of gloves rested on top.

Hendry snickered. "You're sick, Aubeze."

It was sadistic, twisted, and thoroughly disgusting whipping shit at Dimitri, but I have to say, I have never laughed so hard in my life. The King of Faltrun bellowed with rage with each hit to his body. Hendry threw one handful that splattered over Dimitri's face, and Hendry gagged so hard that Roland fell to his knees laughing, me with him. My stomach ached from flexing muscles I hadn't used in that way in years.

"This is fucked," Roland breathed, catching his breath from chuckling so hard.

This was nothing compared to what we had in store for him. But considering he forced hundreds of innocents to live in their own filth, it felt justified throwing shit at him.

I carefully removed the soiled gloves, wincing and trying not to gag myself. I couldn't wait to bathe tonight.

I grasped a blade.

"Time to get some answers." My gaze flicked up. "A year ago, when my father secretly struck a deal with you, you had already seen an Undead?"

Dimitri's nostrils flared. As much as he hated to comply, he knew that doing so would inflict the least amount of pain.

Or so he thought.

"We'd never seen one before," he answered, his voice gravelly, "until Ulric himself brought one to us. It was rabid, feral, and it was only detained because of the cuffs."

To that, my eyes shot wide, meeting Hendry and Roland's equally surprised stare.

We only first learned about the Undead a half-year ago, around the same time the magic-erasing cuffs started rolling out. Yet according to Dimitri, not only did my father have this contraption beforehand, but he was also aware of the Undead. Felt confident enough to have one detained.

He must have had only his close circle aware of this. But why?

"The poison you'd use before the cuffs—what is it?" I continued. "Where are you getting it from?"

He refrained from answering, and when I advanced toward the cart of torture, he shouted, "Okay, okay!"

I slowly turned to him, cocking a brow, awaiting an answer.

His lip curled. "Cortinarius violaceus. Purple shrooms...we grow them here."

"That seems too simple," Roland replied, arms crossed.

"That's because Daranois supplies the substance. We only provide the shrooms."

My eyes narrowed.

"Daranois?" Hendry stepped forward. "Why do they come to you for these mushrooms?"

Dimitri's face was crumpled in pain, his nipples, or lack thereof, surely stinging. "Our soil is good for growing. Daranois...they do something to the shrooms. Turn them into some sort of powder. We call it...siaxcide."

I exchanged glances with my friends. We all knew that Daranois grew plenty on their own...there was a reason their parties lasted for days. They were drug central.

Were they really sourcing this mushroom due to the soil?

"So, Daranois is the one who provides you with siaxcide. Yet somehow, you used this substance almost two decades ago. Otacia would've known if this was going on. A deal between Faltrun and Daranois."

Dimitri choked on a laugh, his head resting back on the rack. "Otacia's witch hunt has blinded them from the dealings in the shadows."

"Their army uses the powder now," I said calmly. "Which means they must know of your involvement."

Dimitri's eyes were slowly shutting.

"Crank it, Hendry."

"NO!" Dimitri screamed. "Wait—wait!" His eyes blinked rapidly as Hendry's hand rested on the handle. "I didn't know the Otacians were aware of the siaxcide. It must be a newer deal."

After seeing what that dust did in Forsmont, I knew we needed to eradicate its production. "Where are you growing them?"

He swallowed. "Free me, and I'll tell you."

I chuckled loudly. "I am my father's son, Dimitri. You know there is no chance of you making it out of here alive." I tilted my head. "The decision of a quick death, or a long, torturous one, is yours."

He glowered viciously. "Bring on the torture," he spat. "Faltrun's economy will tank without the shrooms."

I puckered my lips, nodding slowly as I grasped a pair of shears from the cart. "Very noble, Cortev. It almost sounds like you give a shit about this place." I took delight in seeing the fear in his eyes and thoroughly enjoyed his screams as I snipped the webbing between what remained of his fingers.

"Tell me, Cortev," I continued, pacing around his sobbing body. "Did Ulric know you were keeping a stash of Mages in your castle?"

Snot dripped down his shit-stained face, his lip quivering. Fucking pathetic.

"N-no, the deal was I deliver any witches to him."

I cocked my head to the side and clicked my tongue. "But you decided to keep them for yourself."

His lip curled. "Is that what this is? You're upset I betrayed your kingdom?" He spat at my feet. "You are the biggest betrayer of Otacia."

A grin spread across my face, and Dimitri paled as I stepped closer. He screamed as I thrust my blade into his eye socket.

"Crank it," I ordered Hendry.

He did, turning the handle of the rack, and Dimitri wailed as his limbs began to stretch. "Please! Pleasepleaseplease don't—AHH!"

I ripped the blade free as the machine came to a halt, his eyeball coming out with it, tearing his optic nerve.

Tilting the blade, I surveyed the oozing orb. "Such a shame for these baby blues. I'm sure the ladies loved them." My gaze slid up to his sniveling body, the blood coursing down his face. "I do not care you betrayed the kingdom. I care that you enslaved children. I care that you're a rapist."

Despite his predicament, Dimitri laughed. "You Godsdamn hypocrite. Is that not exactly what Otacia does?! You imprison witch children, and I'm sure plenty of your soldiers have relished in the free pussy."

I stiffened, then flung his eyeball to the ground, thrusting the blade into his thigh. He cried.

"We do not keep them in filth," I spat. "We do not shave their heads, make them piss in buckets, or force them to do labor." I withdrew the blade, red spurting out. "And I do *not* tolerate rape, you fucking pig."

"Oh, aren't you a hero?" He let out a low, breathless laugh. "I think you are struggling to accept what you really are, Silas La'Rune. A monster."

I tilted my head. "That's where you're wrong, Cortev." I gave a sadistic smile. "I know exactly what kind of monster I am."

I wanted to turn the crank. Wanted to watch his limbs rip from his body.

But I had other plans.

As if on cue, in walked twenty-seven women, all with long, flowy hair. All except for Torrin's mother, whose fists shook as she stared up at the strung-up man.

The women he violated.

I had Edmund go to each with an offer of revenge. Every single one came.

They were still weakened, I imagined, but they all stepped forward. My smile slipped when I saw Lena walk in behind them.

Her widened eyes took in the sight before her: Dimitri tied up to the rack, covered in shit and blood. Missing fingers. Missing nipples. A missing eye. And soiled pants.

I supposed it gave a visual of what I had done to Rurik and the others.

I waited for the judgment on her face. Waited for her to look at me in disgust. She did no such thing.

The women all still wore their cuffs.

Deana cried as she beheld me, surprised that I was still alive despite it all.

"The fire will overcome you like nothing you've ever felt before," Lena said calmly, addressing the women. "It can consume you just as easily as your surroundings. Focus it. Hone it. And when you feel it becoming too much, tell yourself to *calm the flames*. Picture your newfound freedom. Picture all the good that is to come for you."

One by one, each woman stepped forward, holding their wrists up to his remaining thumb.

Deana was the first woman to be released from the device. She began shaking as the metal clattered against the ground, her skin turning red.

"You got this, Deana. Calm the flames."

She inhaled and exhaled, squeezing her eyelids tight. She pursed her lips, her breathing wobbly, her skin reddening. When her eyes finally opened, staring at the face of her abuser, she ignited.

The flame crept around her, a beautiful, devastating flame.

Dimitri shuddered, and Deana lifted her chin, tilting her fingers and sending a ring of fire around his throat. He cried out as his skin began to sizzle.

"If there weren't others who also deserved to tear you apart, I would squeeze this ring so tightly your throat would split open." She constricted her fingers, and the King shrieked as it melted his skin.

As I watched in awe, I realized I no longer feared fire. I respected it.

Deana flung her fingers out, and the ring around him vanished, the skin raw and bloody. She stepped aside, allowing the next woman her turn.

Deana's dark gaze found mine, and she walked up to me.

"I owe you, Silas La'Rune," she praised, kneeling before me.

I paused, then gently touched her shoulder. Her brown eyes flicked upward

"Do not kneel before me," I insisted, grasping her hands and helping her to her feet. "Kneel before nobody ever again."

Deana's lips wobbled, and she smiled at me, standing upright.

"I have heard many awful things about you, Prince of Otacia," she whispered. "But it would be an honor to serve you one day." She smiled. "Perhaps someday, your kingdom may be my home."

Her comment warmed me. "If that is your wish, then it shall be granted."

Her cheeks flushed, her smile growing before she turned, watching the next woman come into her power.

I marveled at it—envied their ability to release their rage in such a way. I watched the firelight dance in each of the women's eyes before Torrin's mother gave the final kill shot, Dimitri's head finally slumping down.

Now, it was time to learn what the council knew.

After disposing of another set of gloves a few hours later, I made my way out of the dungeon, ready to take the hottest, longest shower of my life. Roland and Hendry had already left to do so, and the women, along with the rest of the Mages, were choosing their rooms within this castle.

After torturing whatever information the members had, which unfortunately wasn't much, I knew I needed to stop at Saoirse's gravesite before I turned in.

The graveyard was quiet as I stood before the pile of dirt, tears streaming down my face as I pictured her six feet under. A fresh bouquet of roses was placed below a wooden sign that read **SAOIRSE**.

We didn't even know her last name.

I never thought I would let myself cry after what happened to me all those years ago, but nothing was more tragic than this.

My life was filled with so much death and so much loss. Everything I touched found ruin as if I was cursed.

I detected a figure walking up, stopping to stand beside me, copper waves blowing with the evening wind. The sun was just beginning to lower in the sky.

Lena held out her hand to me, and when I turned my head to her, I saw that she was holding Boots.

My face contorted in rage. "Why would you take her doll?!" The thought of Saoirse alone in the dirt without the one thing that brought her comfort had me shaking.

"Because we can never forget," she cried softly, still holding the doll out for me. "Because she should be remembered. Now, and always."

My lip trembled, my eyes slowly blinking as I beheld the doll. I finally lifted my hand, taking the doll from her.

Part of me wanted to do something reckless. Rip it out of anger, toss it as if I didn't care.

But I eventually nodded, eyes welling with tears as I took in the sight of her grave.

If you show any emotion, it will happen again.

As if reading my mind, hearing words that still plagued me, Lena whispered, "It is not a weakness to show emotion, Silas."

My eyes sealed, and I released a frustrated sigh as my head fell forward. It was only a few moments of us standing in silence before I moved my feet, needing to be alone.

She really had no idea what had transpired to make me the way that I was.

Nor would she ever.

445

CHAPTER FORTY-FIVE
MERRICK

The energy in the local tavern was obvious enough, even without using my power to sense the emotions rippling through the people.

The many Faltrunians sat at various tables and along the large square bar, keeping their heads low, nursing their drinks, and mumbling to those around them. Many of them wore frowns, and many of those frowns deepened when they watched me without a glamour weave my way through the space.

From the looks of it, no other Mage was in this place, but I was in desperate need of a drink and truly didn't give a fuck.

Today had been brutal. Mage and Faltrunian alike were slaughtered in a battle that, in idealistic terms anyway, never should have happened.

While we did have access to the royal cellars, meaning unlimited booze, I noticed that Era had wandered to this place. I was intent on finding her.

I weaved my way to the bar, ignoring the glares and the occasional person baring their teeth at me. Sure enough, I noticed her familiar female figure sitting alone at the bar, wearing a long and tight red dress, two skinny straps holding the fabric up.

Era was staring off into space, holding a martini glass in her right hand as I approached her. I placed my hand on the back of her leather stool and gave her a small grin.

"Hey, you."

Era angled her head back toward me. "Hey..." Her voice was soft and quiet, and her brown eyes were dimmed. She anxiously focused back on her drink.

I swallowed, attempting to ignore the attraction I felt toward her.

I still couldn't believe I had kissed her. I had healed her in silence after I pulled away, remaining in that room until the battle had ceased.

I wasn't sure how to even address what happened between us.

"How are you feeling?"

"Good as new."

"I'm glad," I said softly. "Where's Silas?" I looked around the tavern to see if the dark-haired prince was anywhere to be found. I selfishly hoped he wasn't around.

Era sipped her drink. "He turned in early. Today was..." She sighed. "Today was a lot on him."

That it was. Seeing him so torn up about a little Mage girl really showed us all that the Witch Slayer truly did have a heart after all.

I studied her beautiful form.

Something was weighing on her. Though, given all the shit that happened, that was to be expected.

After a few moments, she angled her head to me again, quirking a brow. "It's creepy as hell when you give me those dark eyes, you know."

I blinked, and the corner of my lip turned up.

Liar.

"Creepy?" I questioned.

Her smile took over, and she gestured to the seat beside her. I had to admit, I was surprised she wasn't giving me the cold shoulder again.

I slid in, and the bartender quickly took my order and hurried to fulfill it. The three workers were busting ass, considering all the stressed Faltrunians begging for a buzz. But I also knew the bartender wished to have nothing to do with me. At least she took my order.

I frowned as I surveyed the room. A handful of wary eyes were on the both of us, mostly on me, but still. Era really shouldn't have been alone in here.

"A gimlet?" she asked with a surprised smile, breaking me from my thoughts.

I offered a lazy grin. "What? It's a good drink."

She shrugged, sipping the clear liquid in her glass.

I eyed the olive sitting at the bottom. "A martini. Not surprising," I commented.

Her empty glass clanked on the countertop as she slid it toward the other side of the bar. She rested her cheek on her fist. "How so?"

I nodded my thanks to the bartender as she walked up, setting my drink down in front of me. I placed a few bronze pieces on the wooden bar top and slid my drink to myself, taking a sip of the refreshing cocktail before responding, "I'm just not surprised we both prefer gin."

She blinked, then snorted. "You think us kindred spirits, Merrick?"

I studied the red lipstick she wore and her short blonde hair laying softly along her jawline. Her brown eyes were nearly amber at times, depending on how the light shone in them. The low lighting made it look like flames danced in her irises.

"Merrick?" she asked, her smile falling.

Shit—I was staring.

Creepy indeed. I swallowed, shook my head, again sipping my drink.

"Another, miss?" the plump worker asked Era with a smile—a different treatment than she gave me. I wonder if she knew the Princess of Otacia was who she was serving.

"Please," she slid a handful of bronze, and the woman nodded gratefully before stepping away.

"How are you holding up?" I asked.

She studied me with narrowed eyes. "Why do you feel the need to read me?" she countered coldly. "Do you anticipate me to lie or something?"

I willed my magic down, and my eyes, I knew, shifted to their normal icy blue. "No," I answered honestly. "I just like to know how you're feeling—how others are feeling," I quickly added, looking back to my drink. "Though it is true, most people do not say what they mean. I navigate people better when I feel what they feel."

A moment passed, and I tensed when she placed her hand on mine, her tan starkly contrasting my pale skin. When my gaze shifted to her, she wore a small smile. The bartender slid her drink to Era and hurried away. Era kept her eyes on mine and said, "I don't mind it."

I raised my brow and decided to test her by reading her again. *She means it. And when she looks at me, she feels...*

I felt myself flush slightly. I gave her a tight smile and sipped my drink.

How am I supposed to remain friendly toward her when I can feel how badly she wants me, too?

Her hand gently slid away, and she held her martini glass as she surveyed the room, sucking in that delicious bottom lip.

"Where do you think the others are?" she asked, tucking a strand of golden hair behind her ear.

"The better question is, why did you come here alone?"

She sighed, and instead of dropping her olive in her drink, she decided to slip it off its toothpick and into her mouth. I bit the inside of my cheek as I watched her chew it.

After a moment, she swallowed. "Didn't feel like sleeping just yet."

"How are you holding up...really?" I asked again.

She smiled at me. "You are the first person to ask me that, you know," she admitted softly. She took a sip. "Honestly? Every time I close my eyes, I see that man hovering over me. That sword—" She twisted her lips to the side and stared off into the distance, her left hand's fingertips brushing along her neck. "I have never been so close to death. It..." She took a slow breath through her nose, then faced me again. "You don't know how grateful I am that you were there. That you stayed by me."

I grinned. "Despite your many protests."

She laughed quietly. "Yes..."

It was my turn to place my hand atop hers. "Anytime, Princess," I teased softly.

"I mean it," she insisted, not taking to my dismissive humor. "You saved my life, Merrick."

My smile faded away, and I squeezed her hand gently. "I feel everything you feel, Era. I know you mean it."

Her eyes bounced between mine before they dropped to my lips. Just for a second, they hovered there before she glanced away. She kept her hand under mine.

Comfort.

I smiled softly to myself at the feeling my hand atop hers gave her and dared a drag of my thumb along the tops of her fingers. Her skin was so smooth.

Her eyes slowly shut.

Conflict.

Era gently slid her hand away, finishing her second glass. I quickly worked on my first.

"I'm surprised you want to stick around me," she muttered, eyes looming on her empty glass, her fingertip slowly tracing its edges.

"Why would you say that?"

She gave me a knowing expression, but my brows remained drawn together. She huffed a sigh. "You have disliked me since the moment we met. My people..." she said quietly. "I understand why you don't like us. I just don't understand why you're here."

In this tavern with *her* was left unspoken.

"The only one I truly didn't like was Edmund, and that was 'cause he was trying to bang my sister."

Era giggled.

"I've never disliked you," I said softly.

"Bullshit."

"Truth."

She gave me a blank stare. "I am the princess of a kingdom that is your biggest enemy. And you say you *never* disliked me?"

"Loathed is a better word," I smirked. She grinned and pinched my thigh, and I chuckled. "I had my presumptions of you. As I'm sure you did of me. Mine turned out to be incorrect." I shrugged, and then my smile fell as I asked, "Did yours?"

Her smile faded, too. "Mine were correct," she said quietly.

My heart fell at those words.

As I began to look away, she squeezed my knee. "My assumptions of you were not bad ones, Merrick," she said softly.

I willed myself to ignore what the feeling of her hand on my knee was giving me, and before I imploded, she slipped her hand back to her lap. Her voice went a little high as she asked, "Where's Viola?"

I narrowed my eyes as I read her, sipping on the remainder of my gimlet.

Jealousy.

I choked on my drink and willed my magic down. Era raised a brow, and I nervously drummed my fingers along my knee, which was missing her touch. "Sleeping. All that shifting took a lot out of her. I imagine she'll be sleeping into the late afternoon."

Era wouldn't meet my eyes. "What did you mean when you said, 'I can't'?"

I frowned, my lips pulling to the side as I studied her blank stare at the bar top.

"I don't know."

Her head turned toward me, a little wrinkle now between her brows. "Don't lie."

"What, are you an Empath? Can you tell?"

"Answer me."

"Why did you get jealous mentioning Viola?"

Her eyes widened. She let out an incredulous laugh. "I did no such thing!"

I let my eyes go dark again, a smirk overcoming my face. "You did, Princess. I felt it."

Her eyes narrowed, and she puckered her lips, her eyes now on her empty glass, her index finger tracing the rim.

"Why did you kiss me?" she asked, her voice just above a whisper.

My heart rumbled in my chest, my nerves overtaking me, finally addressing the elephant in the room. "For the same reason you kissed me back."

She swallowed, and her eyes trailed to my mouth, then back up to my eyes. "I'm married."

"I am aware."

"Then why did you kiss me?" she pressed, her brows lowering.

My eyes shifted as they bounced between hers, feeling the anger, the guilt, and the confusion that wrecked her.

I dragged my tongue against my lip ring. "Desire overcame me," I admitted. "I felt like I had no choice."

Excitement brewed in her chest, quickly snuffed out by the overwhelming guilt she felt. "There's always a choice," she whispered, scooting back and standing from her stool. "I should probably head to bed."

I blinked at her sudden withdrawal. "I'll walk you." I quickly offered, my stool squeaking as I stood.

"No, Merrick." She shook her head. "I...I need space."

I went to touch her arm when I was roughly shoved back. "Witch scum! The lady said no!" The drunk human who pushed me yelled. "You'll all be enslaved again one day, filth that you are."

Voices around him mused their agreement. "I bet we can take him," a drunken voice slurred.

The man who pushed me did so again. "I'll hang this ugly bastard by the hooks in his face."

Instantly, Era rushed forward, shoving the man who touched me. "You shut your FUCKING MOUTH!"

Her anger took me aback. Quickly, I squeezed past the angry drunk and placed my hand on the small of her back. "They aren't worth it," I insisted, pushing her toward the exit. "Come, let's go."

"It seems you angered the human whore," another chuckled. "Some are into those pointy-eared pricks. Some fucked up kink or something."

I bared my teeth, ice prickling my insides, begging to be let loose on those fuckers. Era's eyes shone with tears, and she grasped my hand in hers and pushed open the bar's front doors, tugging me along.

We were greeted by the pleasant night air and starry sky. Most places were closed now, and the people were fast asleep. Era continued trudging along, and I tuned into my power, feeling all that she felt.

Rage. Humiliation. Sadness...so much sadness.

"Era," I said softly. She squeezed my hand tighter, her grip near painful, and continued pulling me to the castle. "Era!"

She came to a stop. I quickly walked around to face her. Tears were spilling down her cheeks. "Hey," I said gently, wiping them away and then holding her hands. "Don't let what they said about you hurt. They don't know anything about you."

"I don't give a shit what they said about *me*," she snapped, her brown eyes gazing up at me through wet lashes.

I blinked. "You're upset with what they said about *me*?"

Her lip trembled, and her face crumpled as she said, "I hate how people treat you." Her voice broke as she squeezed my hands. "You are so fucking kind, Merrick, and sweet. And you are *nowhere* near ugly. You are *beautiful*—"

Her eyes widened, and her hand slapped over her mouth.

I gaped at her, and we stood there silently for a few moments. "I-I had a couple of martinis before you showed," she admitted, her cheeks heavily flushed.

Embarrassed. Painfully embarrassed.

I instantly pulled her against me, hugging her tightly. She was stiff for a beat, and then she returned the embrace, burying her face into my chest. She smelled like berries and cream. She smelled heavenly.

"Thank you for caring, Era," I murmured, stroking her golden hair. "Thank you."

I don't know how many moments passed, but I held her until that embarrassment slowly disappeared, until her sob hindered. Then she gently pulled away, wiping her eyes. Our arms were still around each other.

I bit my lip to prevent a grin. "So...you think I'm beautiful?"

She groaned and pushed me away, and I couldn't help but laugh.

We walked up the stairs once inside the castle, and I gave a curt nod to the Mages stationed there before Era and I were in the hallway where our rooms were. Her hand was on her room's doorknob when I said, "Hey, Era?"

She twisted her head toward me, her face showing annoyance by what she presumed I'd say.

"I know things are weird between us. I know It's wrong." I stepped closer, her eyes dilating as I leaned down and whispered, "But I think you're beautiful, too."

At the sight of her fluttering eyelids, I turned on my heel and headed to my room.

CHAPTER FORTY-SIX

LENA

After the chaos of battle, the Mages took over the massive castle. After selecting a room to sleep in, all within close quarters of my friends' rooms, I showered, rinsing off the blood, sweat, and ash from my body.

How many more days will be like this? How many more people will I be forced to kill?

This was the first battle where I truly felt no remorse for what I did. When I believed Silas to be dead, nothing mattered. Nothing mattered but getting justice and seeking revenge on those who had harmed him.

I never understood Silas better than after this battle. I burned a whole wing in this place, rendered unhabitable until further notice. Bodies went up in flames, turning into piles of bones in seconds. I did this all like it was *nothing*. All because I thought I'd lost him.

I didn't wish to think about what any of it meant. I didn't wish to think about my words to him.

I love you.

After drying my hair and slipping on one of the blouses that had been hung in the room, along with a pair of tight pants, I padded my way to the room I knew Torrin was occupying, wishing to see him. Roland was hanging with Hendry and Edmund, but I imagined I'd find him later tonight.

I gave it two knocks, and after a moment, the handsome, platinum-haired man pulled open the door.

He looked so much better now, all clean and in clothes that weren't tattered prison rags.

I smiled up at him softly, and he returned the gesture.

"Hey," he murmured.

"Hey." My grin grew. "You gonna let me in?"

His smile became coy as he laughed through his nose, stepping aside to let me amble into the room. On his nightstand was a bottle of whiskey, and beside it was a glass filled with the amber liquid, nearly empty.

He closed the door behind him, and instantly, the energy in the room shifted.

We stared at each other for a moment, and my lip wobbled before I quickly wrapped my arms around him, holding him close. He smelled just as I remembered...like cedar and a rainy morning.

Home.

"I have missed you so much," I breathed, then pulled back to gaze into his eyes. "Gods, I want to stab you for leaving without a word."

He held me close and let out a soft laugh. "I have missed you. Terribly."

"How could you leave, Torrin? After everything that happened, after what we said…"

Torrin's jaw clicked, and he pulled back, looking back and forth between my eyes.

He didn't want to say.

"Surely our tryst wasn't that bad, was it?" I asked sheepishly.

To that, Torrin's eyes widened, his face flushing. "It wasn't bad *at all*." His hands slid down my arms. "Which is why I had to leave, even if Igon hadn't encouraged me," he admitted quietly.

I frowned. "What do you mean?"

He swallowed, my eyes flitting to his Adam's apple as the lump retracted. "My feelings for you grew too strong, Lena," His arms fell back at his side. "You and Silas are fated for one another. Not you and me. And I couldn't take it. Couldn't take that it would never be me."

"Torrin…" I shook my head, pinching the bridge of my nose.

He glanced away for a moment, then met my eyes with a half-smile. "You and Roland, huh?" he said, changing the subject. "That's quite a surprise."

My eyes widened, my face heating. "How…?"

Torrin tapped at his temple. "I heard his impure thoughts." His hand dropped back to his side. "Silas also told me."

My stomach flipped at the mention of Silas's name. I winced and sucked in my bottom lip. "Are you angry?"

A crease formed between his brows. "No, I want you to be happy. That's all I've ever wanted."

I shook my head. "You need to want *yourself* to be happy. You do everything for everyone else, Torrin." I brought my hand to my chest. "*I* should've been the one to leave Ames. That was your home."

He grasped my hands. "It was *our* home." He leaned forward and kissed my forehead, and butterflies filled my stomach. "Plus," he pulled away with a smile, "Igon would've told you to leave if it was meant to be you."

I took in his face, his beautiful eyes and soft lips, his wispy hair and smooth skin. This man...this man who had always protected me. Always did what was best for the sake of the world and never for himself.

My words were just above a whisper. "Do you think he knew?"

I didn't have to clarify the unspoken words. *Did Igon know you would be enslaved?*

Torrin's eyes dropped to the floor as he thought it over, and then they rose again to meet mine. A crease was between his brows as he said, "It is likely."

"That fucking bastard," I breathed, shaking my head and wrapping my arms around myself.

Torrin placed his hands on my shoulders, his scent reminding me of home as he stepped closer. "He wouldn't do anything like that if it wasn't absolutely necessary."

"I am sick of this fate of the world bullshit," I snapped.

"I found my parents, Lena."

My rage instantly went out at Torrin's broken smile.

"There is that, at least. It was not for nothing."

My lip trembled, and I stepped closer, wrapping my arms around his waist, unable to keep my hands off of him. He held me back tightly.

"You need rest," I whispered.

"*You* need rest," he countered.

I tilted my head back, angling it up to see the corner of his lip raised. And, without thinking, I pressed my lips against his.

He drew away quickly, leaving my embrace. "Lena—no." He shook his head, but his eyes flitted to my mouth.

"I'm sorry." I winced. "I just...I can't stop thinking about the last time I saw you."

He slowly blinked, his hand lifting to brush his thumb along my cheek.

I want to feel you again.

After hearing my thoughts, he cursed softly, pressing his lips to mine. Our mouths opened, and our tongues began to trace. He tasted like mint and whisky. Torrin ran a hand through my hair, his other gripping my ass. I ran my hands up his chest and cupped his face.

He pulled away just enough to get a word in. "Lena," he panted.

Then the door opened. I whirled to see Roland gaping at us. I quickly fixed my hair, and Torrin cleared his throat and moved his hand away from my ass.

A smirk crept over Roland's face. "Getting frisky without me, Ginger Snap?" he leaned against the doorway.

"My apologies—" Torrin began. What he didn't know was that as much as Roland and I cared for one another, what we had between us was simply for fun.

Roland held up a bottle of wine in his hand. "Who wants to get drunk?"

Between the three of us, we were on our fourth bottle of wine. Roland wished to celebrate our win, and considering we had access to the royal cellars, we had a dangerous supply of alcohol. It was something worth celebrating, indeed. Still, my mind couldn't escape the sight of so many lifeless faces.

I just wanted to drink and forget everything tonight.

After the battle, Silas wished to turn in early, understandably. We didn't speak after I gave him Saoirse's doll. The other couples, presumably, turned in as well. Roland wasn't sure where Hendry went after their departure, but knowing him, he was probably off wooing some beautiful female. One of a more mature age.

My face felt flushed, and I didn't know if it was from the alcohol or the unbearable desire I felt watching both Roland and Torrin as the three of us played cards on the rug in front of the bed. I had slept with both of these men. And sitting here, watching both of them lounging, drunk and laughing, I found myself imagining taking them both at the same time.

I shifted in my spot on the floor.

Gods...am I a whore?

Torrin's drunken eyes went to mine, and a smile crept over his face.

"Are you saying you want both of us, Lena?"

My eyes were about to bulge out of my head. I placed my hand of cards on the ground and sipped my drink.

Roland gave me a sideways grin, his elbow resting on his one raised knee, his cheek sitting on his fist. His stare slid to Torrin. "What just happened?"

"Lena wishes to bed us both at the same time."

I choked on my drink and whipped my head up. "Torrin!" I grabbed my stack of cards and tossed them at him, and both men laughed. "I do not wish to. I was just—"

"Fantasizing, Ginger Snap?" His eyes went to Torrin, then back to me. "I'm down if you both are."

My eyes widened and shot to Torrin, whose own face flushed. His eyes trailed down my body before looking at Roland.

All three of us were drunk and definitely not in the right headspace to be making a decision like this.

Torrin tried to hold in a smile as his eyes went back to mine. *Fuck, it's up to me?*

My eyes trailed over Roland's biceps, his golden skin, then went Torrin's muscular thighs, to his darkened eyes.

"What do you want, Lena?" Torrin asked softly.

I blinked, my vision slightly spinning. I was so intoxicated, yet so aroused. I pictured myself sucking on Torrin's cock while Roland took me from behind. Then vice versa, visualizing Torrin sliding into my pussy while I swirled my tongue along Roland's length.

Torrin's eyes widened briefly before he leaned over, brushing his lips against mine. His lips parted, and our tongues began to trace in slow, sexy circles. The flavor of the blackberry wine on his tongue was delightful.

I drew away just enough to glance at Roland, whose teeth were dragging across his bottom lip, his eyes heavy with desire. I gave him a soft smile, and his lip popped free from his teeth, a mischievous grin forming on his face.

Torrin pulled back enough to let Roland in as he crawled toward me. Roland held the back of my neck and dragged my mouth to his. We shared a few slow kisses before he trailed his lips down my neck.

I moaned softly, my eyes fluttering shut only for a moment before opening them to look at Torrin.

For a beat, I expected to see jealousy, but there was nothing but lust in his eyes. His stare flitted down, trailing to where Roland cupped my breast underneath my shirt.

Torrin inched forward as Roland kissed my neck and captured my lips with his. I moaned into his mouth as Roland teased my nipple with his fingers, sucking on the skin of my neck.

I ran my fingers through Torrin's hair as I deepened our kiss, my other arm wrapping around Roland's torso, holding him close.

Fuck...having these two men's lips on me was driving me wild.

Roland's lips pulled away from my neck, a naughty smirk on his face. "Let's take this to the bed, shall we?"

Torrin removed his lips from mine with an equally devilish grin. I squealed as he lifted me, and the three of us rushed to the mattress. Roland threw off his shirt, revealing those delectable, tanned abs, while Torrin stood me in front of the bed, both men now standing before me. He smiled as he took off his shirt, and heat coursed through my body at the sight of him. At the reminder of our night together last year.

My eyes trailed to Roland, to those captivating hazel eyes. That beautiful smile. "You next, Ginger Snap."

I bit back a smile, then began to unbutton my blouse. I pulled off the shirt, revealing a red lace bra.

"Fuck," Torrin breathed, and I watched as Roland's eyes darkened, his lips parting as they took in my heavy breasts.

I smirked as I craned my head upward to look at them both, and then I unbuttoned my pants, sliding them down my thighs and revealing the matching underwear. Roland had never seen this set before, considering I had found it in my room.

Roland wasted no time, unbuttoning his pants and sliding them down his strong legs, his erection springing free.

Torrin's came down a moment later, and soon, both men were standing before me, completely naked. Roland's eyes roamed over Torrin for a moment, and a flush crept up my cheeks at the thought of them being intimate together.

Torrin blushed.

"I don't know if I am drunk enough for that."

I laughed softly, my cheeks heating further, and I watched as Torrin silently relayed my thoughts to Roland. His hazel eyes widened before they slid to mine in amusement.

"Naughty girl." He grinned, licking his lips. "Get on your knees."

I obeyed. I bit my lip as I stared up at both men, their thick cocks looming above me. My eyes met Torrin's, and I decided he deserved something first after all he'd been through...and because I missed him.

Torrin inhaled sharply as I slid my tongue along his shaft, then sucked his length into my mouth. His hand gently glided through my hair as I began to swirl my tongue along him, focusing my attention on the swollen head.

He released a soft moan, and I glanced up at him. His eyes became heavy, his mouth parting as he watched me.

My eyes slid over to Roland, a similar expression on his face as he stroked himself. The corners of his lips rose upward. "She's excellent at that, isn't she?"

Torrin let out a breathy laugh. "That she is."

Their words sent heat between my legs. I continued to suck on Torrin, tasting the saltiness of his precum, before I eventually released him from my mouth and stroked him with my hand. His eyes rolled back, and I turned my attention to Roland, smiling and gesturing him over with my finger.

He rolled his lips inward, stepping forward as Torrin's hand went back to his side. I slid Roland's cock into my mouth next, slurping on him as I worked Torrin with my other hand.

Both of the men's breathing was becoming labored as I drew out their pleasure. Roland gripped my hair forcefully and drove his hips deeper, hitting the back of my throat with every thrust. He groaned as his dick slid free, and I took a moment to catch my breath, saliva dripping down my face.

Torrin held my hand, halting my strokes, then lifted me into his arms. Roland hopped on the bed, remaining in a kneeling position, as Torrin sat me on the mattress.

"I need to see you," he breathed as he reached behind me, unclasping my bra. My breasts spilled free, and Torrin cursed as he lowered me to my back.

Roland angled his cock down, and I resumed sucking on him just as Torrin kissed the sides of my breasts. My back arched when he captured one of my nipples in his mouth, flicking his tongue over the raised peak.

"Torrin," I mumbled over Roland's cock.

Torrin switched sides, giving equal affection to both breasts, before trailing his kisses lower. And lower.

"I can't wait to watch him eat your pussy," Roland murmured.

My half-lidded eyes shot up to see his playful smile. His thumb stroked my cheek as my tongue circled his tip.

It was so much fun having sex with Roland. He held no judgment. He was playful. While I knew he wasn't *in love* with me, I knew he did love me. Just as I loved him.

Just as I loved Torrin.

Torrin yanked down my underwear, and all thoughts vanished the moment he pried open my legs and slid his warm, wet tongue along my center.

I cried out, my hand instinctively gripping his platinum locks, and sucked on Roland quicker as Torrin's tongue teased my clit.

"Fuck...what a sight," Roland moaned, his eyes dilating as he watched Torrin drag his tongue over my pussy, sucking each lip into his mouth.

Torrin continued his skillful strokes, lapping up my arousal. Every time his brown eyes met mine, watching me suck off Roland, my thighs clenched tighter around his head.

When he began thrusting his finger inside of me, I started to come undone.

"I'm going to come," I panted, Roland's cock popping free from my mouth. I stroked Roland with my hand and leaned up to watch. "Yes, just like that," I cried.

Torrin lashed at my bundle of nerves, swirling his tongue rapidly, and I threw my head back, wailing in ecstasy as an orgasm rippled through me, my inner walls clenching around his finger.

As I was catching my breath, I ran my tongue along Roland's length again.

More. I wanted more. I never wanted this moment to end.

"I get her ass, Brighthell," Roland quipped. "But I'm feeling her wet cunt before that."

Gods, the man was so vulgar. I loved it.

Torrin placed a light kiss on my thigh. "Turn around, baby," Torrin demanded, and my sex throbbed.

I love it when you call me that.

Torrin's face was flushed, and I wanted to pull him back between my legs at the sexy smile he gave.

But I got on all fours, facing Torrin, as Roland lined himself up with my entrance. My pussy was already soaked, and Roland slid in with ease, my body stretching to accommodate his size.

I cried out just as Torrin's cock entered my mouth. The sensation of both men claiming me had another orgasm building inside me quickly. Roland was fucking me at the perfect pace; the sound of his skin slapping against mine only heightened my arousal. I gazed up at Torrin, smiling as I worked him.

"Look at how beautiful you are," he whispered, stroking my cheek lovingly. "You take us both so well."

My eyes rolled back as Roland's grip on my hips tightened, groans ripping from his throat as my tight heat sucked him in.

"I need to feel her," Torrin respired.

Roland gave me a couple of harsh, deep thrusts before his dick slid out of me. Torrin's cock sprang free from my mouth, and he laid back on the bed as I straddled him. I lined him up with my entrance and moaned loudly as I sat, his entire length sliding up inside me.

Gods, you feel so damn good.

His strong hands roamed up my thighs before gripping my ass, stretching me for Roland. I was not expecting Roland to lean down and start lapping at my tight exit.

"Roland!" I exclaimed and made to move away, but Torrin held me firm.

"You'll need it," Torrin said softly, then pounded into me harder. The sensation of Torrin filling me and Roland's tongue in forbidden places was driving me into a lust-driven frenzy.

"I can't wait to fill this ass," Roland purred, then slapped my bottom hard before fucking the hole with his tongue.

"Oh, Gods," I moaned, then began licking Torrin's throat. His answering groan rumbled in his chest, and I bounced up and down, savoring the sensation of his thickness impaling me while Roland buried his face between my ass.

As his tongue trailed up and down, I fixated on how close it was to Torrin's cock.

"Would you like to see him lick me, Lena?"

"Fuck," I moaned against his neck. "Yes...yes..."

I knew Torrin had to be communicating with Roland telepathically, as Roland stopped just as Torrin told me to turn.

I lifted off his aching cock, both men's tips red and leaking, and rotated myself so my pussy was now hovering over Torrin's face. My eyes blew wide when Roland smirked, bent down, and took Torrin's cock into his mouth.

Just as Roland began sucking, Torrin groaned, his head falling back momentarily before lapping at my pussy once more.

Holy fuck. Roland was giving Torrin head.

Roland slid his tongue along Torrin's shaft, collecting the precum on the tip, and gave me a mischievous smile. "Share him with me."

Godsdamn.

I bit my lip, stifling a cry as Torrin slid two fingers inside me. I lowered my head, licking up his shaft while Roland did the same.

Our tongues would cross as we pleasured Torrin together, Roland pulling me into long, passionate kisses in between slow, slurpy sucks.

It was such an erotic sight, seeing this beautiful man with a cock in his mouth.

Roland gripped Torrin's dick, angling it toward me. I slid my mouth over, taking all of him in my mouth, and my second orgasm rippled through me at the sight of Roland lowering his mouth, taking Torrin's balls into his mouth.

Torrin moaned loudly, and I came as he fucked me with his fingers, screaming in bliss around his cock.

"*Fuck*," Torrin breathed.

As I popped his dick out of my mouth, Roland dragged his tongue up one more time, Torrin's cock twitching when Roland's tongue teased the tip one last time.

"Turn back around, Lena," Roland ordered.

I did, meeting Torrin's flushed face. I was breathless, high on the most salacious sex of my life.

I could sense his bashfulness, but I ran my fingers through his hair, leaning down to kiss him passionately.

That was so hot.

I tasted myself on his lips, on his tongue, just as I heard Roland spit, feeling his warm saliva spill down my ass. He then positioned himself as Torrin re-entered my pussy, spreading me with his fingers for Roland again.

"Fuck yeah, it was."

Roland started to push inside my ass, and I winced at the pain.

"Have you done this before?" Roland asked gently.

I had a few times with Silas. But it had been over half a decade since. "Not for a very long time," I admitted breathlessly.

"I'll go slow," he promised. "But if it's too much, I'll stop. Just say the word."

I looked back at him, smiling softly, and he leaned down, kissing my back. He pushed in more, and I let out a soft whimper. Torrin began rocking his hips, the pleasure helping to blur the pain.

We kept at that, Torrin pleasing me as Roland got deeper and deeper. I felt so full, both their thick lengths spreading me.

I leaned down again, kissing Torrin slowly. Desperately.

I've missed you.

"I've missed you, too, baby."

My moans grew louder, more needy, as Roland was nearly buried to the hilt. One thing I remembered from before was how intense my orgasms were whenever Silas fucked my ass, swirling his fingers over my clit as he did so. I could only imagine how outstanding the sensation would be with both holes filled.

"Godsdamn," Roland growled. "You are so tight, Lena."

I'd grown to love Roland's nickname for me, but there was something about him calling me Lena, something more intimate about it that further stimulated me.

Both men were moaning, panting, breathing so heavily. I leaned up, my palms on either side of Torrin's face, and he captured my breasts in his hands, guiding them both to his mouth as Roland gripped my hips, driving inside me quicker.

Torrin squeezed my breasts together, dragging his tongue from one nipple to the next, pushing his hips up as Roland held mine down.

I couldn't take anymore. The pleasure rose and rose until I hit that peak. My pussy clenched, and I didn't recognize the sounds that released from my lungs as I screamed, falling forward as Torrin wrapped his arms around me.

The men increased their thrusts until they got choppy, both of them groaning loudly as they spilled themselves inside of me.

I felt them both throbbing within me. Roland's forehead was resting on my back as he caught his breath, Torrin's arms falling slack at his sides.

"Holy fuck..." Roland sighed, pulling out of me slowly. I winced at the uncomfortable feeling, and then Torrin pulled himself out, too.

After a few more moments of regulating his breathing, Roland padded to the bathroom. I heard the sink turn on as he dampened a rag to clean me up.

I leaned up, my gaze flitting down to Torrin. Embarrassment started to rise inside me, as I imagine it did in him, too, but he only smiled, tucking my hair behind my ear.

Roland entered the room again, kissing my back softly before wiping my sex, then my ass. He dried me off after with a soft, dry towel.

I scooted off Torrin just as Roland collapsed on the bed. I, too, felt like I was going to pass out—we were all thoroughly spent.

Torrin chuckled, leaning up on his elbows. "You are not sleeping in here, Aubeze."

Roland turned his head, narrowing his eyes at him. "That's the thanks I get for giving some amazing head?" he teased.

Torrin's cheeks heated, his nervous eyes going to me as I spoke to him gently in his mind.

Have you done that before?

"Never." He grinned. *"I blame the alcohol and your naughty thoughts for corrupting me."*

"We all almost died today. I think it's fine we live a little." Roland yawned, sitting up in the bed before fetching his pants, stumbling a little.

I giggled. "You're shit-faced," I noted.

He threw me a lopsided grin over his shoulder as he slid his pants on. "And you're not? Hm?"

I bit my lip, and he shook his head as he laughed softly.

"Well, I'm off to bed. Does Elowen make any hangover remedies? I think we'll need them come morning."

Torrin ran his hand through his short hair. "I hope so. I have a feeling you're right. My head is spinning."

Roland chuckled. "Goodnight, you two." He gave me a wink, then slipped out of the door, leaving just Torrin and me.

Suddenly, my nerves started to build. Thankfully, when I peered at Torrin, he offered me a kiss on the shoulder. Then, on the cheek.

But then he paused, and I could tell his posture stiffened. He took a shaky breath.

"This can't happen again. Sex between us."

My brows drew together, my arms instinctively covering my chest. "I don't understand...why? Did you not like it?"

"I did like it. But the problem is I like it too much. I like *you* too much. And I know, despite how much wild fun this was, that it is Silas you love."

I went to protest, but he laughed through his nose.

"I know you love me, too. But it'll always be him."

I opened my mouth and shut it a few times, unsure of how to answer. "I just fucked the two of you, and you're bringing up Silas?"

Torrin's saddened eyes crushed me. "I can't be like Roland, hooking up with no strings attached. No feelings. I care too much about you." He stood from the bed, fetching loungewear from the dresser and slipping them up until they rested along his narrow hips.

"You won't leave again, will you?" I asked quietly, dread overcoming me. "I can't lose you again."

He paused before me, running his hand through my messy hair. "No, Lena. I will stay. I promise."

My eyes fell, and I nodded. Then, I stood, slipping back on my underwear, then bra, then outfit. Buttoning my pants proved difficult, and I realized just how tipsy I really was.

I was hurt he didn't wish to sleep beside one another, but I also understood.

Before I exited the room, I hugged him tightly, resting my cheek along his bare chest. "I'm so happy you're okay. I'm so grateful you're here."

"I still can't believe I'm free." He pulled away, eyes shining with unreleased tears. "I will always be in debt to you for that."

My hand slid down to his, holding the one with the burn scars. I ran my thumb along the imperfect skin. "I am the one in debt to you."

I wanted to kiss him, but I refrained, letting my arm fall before slipping out of his room.

As I was walking toward my room, the hallway spinning, my drunken thoughts plagued me.

I had sex with Roland and Torrin. At the same time. Together.

Roland sucked Torrin's dick. I sucked it *with* him.

I rubbed my collarbones. It was fun. Really fun. But I couldn't help but notice the emptiness I felt now.

How could you make love to two people and feel so damn lonely afterward?

Roland only wanted fun, and don't get me wrong, he was fun. And Torrin, despite everything, would never accept being with someone who was Soul-Tied to someone else.

I never could have what I once did...and it killed me.

Just as I was almost to my room, a door to my right opened, and Silas wandered out.

Silas.

Guilt washed over me. Shame.

What would he think if he knew what I just did? Would he be disappointed? Repulsed?

I bit my lip to prevent it from trembling and quickly averted my gaze as I continued forward.

I knew we weren't together anymore, so why was I feeling like I'd betrayed him?

"Lena?"

I froze but didn't turn around. "Yes?" I whispered.

Silas's hand gently grasped my arm, and I turned toward him. He frowned, his golden eyes searching my flushed face.

It was just past 1:00 a.m. Why was he up?

"Are you alright?"

"I'm fine," I croaked. Gods, I couldn't even pretend to be sober. I didn't want to think of my messy hair or my potentially smudged makeup. I hoped to the Gods he couldn't tell what I'd done.

Tears burned in my eyes as I gazed at him. The man I loved more than anything.

Torrin was right.

Damn him for being right.

The sex had been a distraction, a delightful distraction, but like always, the second I saw Silas, my heart sank. Memories of our times together flooded my brain.

Sex with Silas was different. I felt complete when I'd been with him. Cherished. Understood. I felt calm and wild at the same time, worshipped and desired.

I felt loved.

He had always made me feel loved.

My Soul-Tie.

I could never be content without him. I knew this now for certain.

I loved Torrin. I loved Roland. But that love wasn't like my love for Silas. It couldn't compare, no matter how badly I wanted it to.

He continued to study me, worry etching his features. "I can tell when you're lying." His words set a few tears free, and anger filled his eyes. "Did someone hurt you?" he pressed.

"No." I shook free of his grasp. "Leave me alone," I muttered. I didn't wish to be mean to him, but if he continued, I would break down in this hallway.

I clumsily turned and continued to my room. He followed behind.

"Leave me, Silas. Please." My voice broke as I grasped my room's doorknob.

"You're drunk," he commented, placing a hand over mine. My eyes went to his. "Lena, talk to me."

My lip trembled, and I opened my door. "I don't want to. Please, go."

The face he gave me shattered my heart, and then he just nodded. "Goodnight, Lena..."

Then he left. I collapsed on my bed, too wasted to even take my shoes off, and softly cried myself to sleep.

CHAPTER FORTY-SEVEN
LENA

I woke to the most horrific migraine imaginable, not that that should be a shock. My mouth was as dry as a desert, and the need to vomit threatened me enough to have me sprinting to the bathroom.

After hurling my guts up, I brushed my teeth twice as if that would wash away the sins of the evening. I showered, scrubbing my body thoroughly and washing my hair with honey and oat soap before finally exiting the shower and chugging some water from the sink.

After dressing in fresh clothes—a white blouse and black trousers paired with my boots—I made my way to Elowen's room, seeing Torrin already standing at the door, arms resting on the frame.

I walked over just as she handed him a vial, and he downed it instantly.

Her eyes trailed over me. "You too, Lena?" she asked, shaking her head and laughing. "You guys need to not drink so much."

Torrin gave me a half-smile, eyes flitting down my frame, before he turned, exiting the area. I entered Elowen's room, Edmund sharpening a blade in the corner.

"Mornin' Lena," he greeted warmly, his face falling. "Jeez! You look—"

Elowen shot him a death glare, and he rubbed the back of his neck. "L-like you've had a rough night."

You have no idea.

"Yesterday was brutal, Edmund. It's no wonder Lena looks drained." She flitted her eyes to me. "I also whipped up some contraceptive elixirs. It's about time for another."

Elowen went to work at the kitchenette in their room. They were placed in the fancier room on purpose; El was our best healer, and people would need tonics today after the battle.

"How are you holding up?" I asked her gently, sitting on her bed.

She kept her eyes on the task at hand, pouring water into a pot and bringing it to a boil. "I...I don't want to talk about it."

My eyes darted to Edmund, who gave me a sad smile. The strength it must've taken to provide Saoirse with a painless death...I couldn't imagine.

Elowen was a tiny thing, five feet tall, and the youngest one in our group. But inside her was so, so much resilience.

She'd had a whole childhood being hated by her brother. A whole childhood—and adulthood, it felt at times—blaming herself for what happened to Ayana Astair.

She'd helped me through my miscarriage when she was only fourteen years old. She saw both of her parents die, then witnessed them as Undead.

She'd healed my broken frame after I'd been violated. And now, she'd slid a dagger across a helpless child's neck, providing her peace.

Her strength inspired me.

"Has Roland asked for one?"

Edmund snorted. "You already know Roland is probably still sleeping."

I smiled at that. Yeah, he probably was.

"Can you make one for him, too?"

Elowen nodded, crushing herbs from our travels and submerging them into the rolling boil.

As I studied her, I felt something different. I wasn't sure what.

"Hey, Edmund?" I asked, tilting my head to him. "Can El and I have a moment alone?'"

He paused his blade sharpening, just as Elowen said, "I told you I didn't want to talk about it."

I'd never heard such a stern tone from her. Edmund's gaze saddened, and he stood, walking over to her. Her hands were gripping the counters now.

"Ellie...you should talk to her," he murmured, rubbing her back.

Her shoulders shook as she stayed stiffly in place, and she eventually conceded, nodding her head.

I stood from the bed as Edmund kissed the top of her head, then left, giving us some privacy. My head was killing me, but still, my worry for my friend took precedence over it all.

A few moments passed in silence. Elowen finished making the remedies, infusing her magic into the concoctions.

She glanced over her shoulder at me, and my eyes trailed down as she lifted her hand, snuffing out the fire beneath the pot.

I gasped, my eyes shooting back up to hers. "El, you—"

She splayed her fingertips out, and I loosened a breath as fire crept down her hand, down her arm.

Elowen had acquired fire.

"When?" I breathed.

"Last night," she responded quietly, allowing the flame to dissipate. She began filling two bottles of her concoction while I ambled toward her.

"You should have called for me."

"Edmund helped me," she insisted, handing me the remedies, then the contraceptive elixir, her lip trembling. "He is my light. My anchor." She chewed on her bottom lip, brows lowering. "I am so angry, Lena. I have never felt so much bitterness. I've never allowed anything to dull my spirits. But this..." Her aqua eyes drifted toward the window, gazing outside at the kingdom. "There is so much ugliness in this world. I'm finding it difficult to feel hope anymore."

I placed the vials in the cross-body I wore and pulled my friend into a hug.

"Believe me, Elowen, I struggle with that feeling every day." I pulled back, holding her arms. "But you saw beauty in the face of ugliness. What you saw in Edmund changed the course of everything. He is proof that there is hope."

Her light eyes shifted between mine. "As is Silas?"

I swallowed, my arms dropping.

"You saved him first. That is the action that changed the course of everything." She shook her head. "I never saw goodness in him...in any of them. I only saw it in Edmund because he is my Soul-Tie."

I stood still, finding it troublesome to come up with words.

"I've been paying attention to the two of you...two individuals who should hate one another more than anything, fighting vigorously to ensure the other stays alive. He is your Soul-Tie, isn't he?"

My rapid blinking, my mouth opening, then closing, told Elowen all she needed to know.

"You know what really proved it to me?" she asked, her frown disappearing. "When he was being taken away, and Saoirse was crying for him, he told her to go by *you*, not Erabella." She stepped forward, and my heart picked up, nerves running rampant at the idea of her figuring it all out. "It's why he has always shown care toward you."

"Elowen..." I shook my head.

"When did you know?" she pressed.

I wanted to tell her everything, tell her all that her brother and cousin knew. But now was not the time.

"I've felt it for a while," I responded. Not a lie. "But Elowen, a Soul-Tie connection is not enough. The person's character is what dictates how I feel about them." I sighed, running my hand through my curls. I then fished out the vial from my bag and poured its contents down my throat. After swallowing the elixir and curing my hangover, I continued, "Before you recognized what Edmund was to you, you saw in his *actions* he was a good man."

"What action did Silas do that showed you he was a good man, too? Was it his treatment of you after what happened in Forsmont?"

My eyes filled with tears, my voice dropping as I uttered, "It was his treatment of me after I was raped in Fort Laith."

Elowen's eyes flared, her small hand shakily obscuring her mouth. "Lena...I...I had no idea." She shook her head, tears pooling in her eyes. "I knew you had been beaten, but I never would've guessed—"

"It's okay." I sniffed, wiping my eyes and giving her a pitiful smile. "I knew exactly what type of man he was after that. He is broken—tormented by a damaged past. I feel him harboring secrets to keep himself afloat, afraid of drowning in front of everyone...afraid no one would care to bring him to shore." I handed her back the empty vial, feeling as good as new, physically, anyway. "But no matter the cold, emotionless front he presents, his heart is pure. His heart is made of gold, despite his father's attempt to turn it to stone."

Elowen blinked over and over to clear her vision, and she gave me a soft smile. "Edmund loves him. I couldn't understand why for the longest time." She placed a gentle hand on my arm. "You're right. There is beauty camouflaged among the ugly. We just have to look for it." She wrapped her arms around me one more time. "Thank you, Lena."

"If you ever need me, El, please come to me. Fire can be unpredictable at times, especially when those we care for are in danger."

I knocked on Roland's door after leaving Elowen's room, cracking it open to find him in his usual open mouth sleeping position.

I chuckled to myself, quietly walking over to set the vial on the nightstand beside his bed.

He heard my entrance, though, and his mouth shut, his eyes blinking open slowly.

"Morning," I said gently.

"Ugh, my head," he groaned, his hand covering his eyes.

"Here." I picked up the vial. "Open wide."

He peeked at me through his fingers, then smirked before opening his mouth for me. I pulled out the cork, poured the elixir in, and he swallowed.

"Thank the Gods for Elowen," he praised, then sat up in bed, tousling his messy brown hair.

"Honestly," I agreed as I made my way back toward the door.

Roland clutched my arm. "How are you feeling?"

I glanced at him over my shoulder. "Back to normal after that elixir."

He gave me a deadpan look. "That's not what I meant."

I sighed, then sat beside him on the mattress. "I...I don't know."

He studied me with soft eyes.

"Have you ever been in love, Roland?" I asked after a beat, even though I remembered he told me in Forsmont that he had not.

To that, his eyebrows raised, and he rubbed the back of his neck. "I—well...it's not that I don't care for you—"

I snorted, backhanding his chest. "I know you're not in love with me. That's not why I asked." I sighed, my eyes going to the floor. "I asked because I have been...as you know. I have been in love with a man who was in love with me." I turned to face him. "Casual sex is fun, really fun, but it doesn't compare. It's not the same."

My lip wobbled, and Roland held my hand.

"I miss him," I said, my voice a broken whisper.

"Quill?" he asked, remembering my story.

I nodded. "Part of me wishes I never met him...that I didn't know what I was missing. I wish I had nothing to compare it to."

"I thought the saying was *'better to have loved and lost than never to have loved at all'*?"

"The losing hurts so fucking badly...even after all this time." My eyes fell to my lap, Roland's hand still interlaced with mine.

"I do love you, you know," he said quietly.

I swallowed, squeezing his hand. "I love you too," I admitted.

"When this war is over, and we're not almost dying every day...perhaps I could offer you more."

I drew him into a hug. "Your friendship has already offered me so much. I don't ever want that to change." I squeezed him. "And don't think I'm not grateful for yesterday. After how that battle went, I think we all needed release."

He squeezed me back, then pulled away. "So...is this it then? The end of our endeavors?"

I pinched his leg. "I'll keep you posted. But for now, I just need to focus on myself. Focus on winning this damn war."

He gave me an easy smile. "I'm always here if you need me."

I kissed his cheek. "I'm always here for you, too."

Some of the Mages wanted to stay in Faltrun and change it from the inside out. This kingdom lacked morality, and while I knew there had to be some who lived here that had a heart, speciesism wasn't something that could be changed overnight. I admired those who were willing to stay and better this place.

Others, like Torrin's parents, wished to return to the people of Ames. To their home. To safety. I didn't judge anyone who wanted to be as far away from this place as possible.

The sun shone brightly that afternoon, and all of us were standing in the castle's throne room. After a lot of consideration, Deana was named Supreme of Faltrun. I watched a glimmer form in Silas's eyes as he smiled, those of us in the room bowing to her.

My eyes skated to my father, who stood to the side with only a handful of Faltrunian guards behind him. The soldiers who had survived were given three choices: pledge their loyalty to the cause and remain a member of the guard, surrender their titles and stay within the kingdom, or leave entirely. Most surrendered, some left, and very few chose to remain in the army.

After Deana's short coronation, I snatched Dani, pulling her to the side. "I want to teleport to Mount Rozavar."

"Bloody hell," she muttered, pupilless blue eyes focusing on me. "You just wanna jump right to it, huh?"

I crossed my arms, the corners of my lips turning upward. "I performed *Sana omnia vulnera eius* with little difficulty."

At Dani's gaping mouth, I told her how I memorized the spell while traveling and successfully performed it to heal Silas's wounds.

She offered me a lazy grin. "You sure are powerful, Supreme." Her smile faltered. "But this spell isn't for the faint of heart. You will be utterly drained after."

"I thought about it, and I wondered if I could somehow siphon energy from the handful of Mages who wish to come with us.

Despite Elowen's healing, many of them are still weary. I wish to provide them a straight shot to safety, If possible."

Dani pulled her lips to the side. "You can certainly siphon their energy. It's how us Warlocks have performed the spell in the past. The question is if you could manage to teleport us back after leaving all those people behind."

"Can they not send me their energy while standing outside of the circle?"

She thought about it. "I mean, potentially. Without our innate abilities, we've never been able to do it that way. But it sounds...ingenious, really."

I'd read of Mages being able to teleport with their own magic. Like healing or enchantment, it was a type of magic any Mage could learn. The problem was you'd have to be taught it, and I'd never met one who knew how. That, and the power it took, was far beyond the skillset of any Mage I knew.

"It takes significantly more energy to do it the Warlock way," she continued. "But in a dire situation, it is worth it." Her eyes locked with mine. "You've seen a taste of what expending too much of your power looks like. It's not pretty. So, after you complete this, even with your people's help, you'll need to lay off magic—just for a short while."

I nodded my head slowly, my mind thinking back to the detailed pages. "The other types we've learned...I've had to reach into the same place where that specific magic resides inside of me. But if I don't know where this teleporting magic comes from, what do I do?"

Dani hummed. "Teleporting comes from your entire body. It's all of you. Now, while I am not an expert on Mage magic, I know that the hardest part for us in pulling off teleporting is handling the amount of power. I imagine for a Mage, being able to actually reach that level without a magical tether—in our case, the penta-gram—is where the true difficulty resides."

I glanced back to my father, who offered me a warm smile.

Mother would be able to see the love of her life again if I succeeded at this.

I would not fail.

CHAPTER FORTY-EIGHT
LENA

After my talk with Dani, I strode over to my father, who said parting words to his men before approaching me.

"We did it," he said breathlessly. "So many years has this kingdom been corrupt...I can't imagine how it will grow." He paused. "How are you doing?"

I smiled at him. "I'm holding up." I nervously pulled at the hoop earrings in my ears, still awkward in his presence. My hand drifted to my side. "I'm going to attempt a spell...one that will bring some of my people to a place where others reside." I paused. "My mother is there."

His smell fell, his mouth parting as he exhaled.

"Would you...would you like to come with?"

He blinked rapidly, his eyes filling with tears as he smiled, nodding his head. "Yes, I would like that very much."

I beamed back at him. "Well then, fetch your things. We leave tonight."

I wandered through the kingdom by my lonesome, wishing to get some answers to a question that had plagued me ever since I arrived. I angled my head toward the sign looming above an oak door.

The Artist's Guild.

I strolled in and was met with a smile that quickly vanished at the sight of my appearance.

I didn't care. I wasn't going to hide my ears here. I walked forward despite the woman's wide-eyed stare, scanning the various paintings, sculptures, and drawings displayed.

The worker—or owner, I supposed—crossed her arms over her chest as if she was cold. "What can I do for you?" she asked nervously, tucking her green hair behind her rounded ear.

I kept my eyes on the paintings as I wandered around the spacious room. "A friend of mine had a piece commissioned here. It was called 'Rebirth'." I turned to her, noticing her flinch.

I refrained from rolling my eyes.

"D-do you know the artist's name?" she asked.

I shook my head, eyes trailing over the masterpieces once more. "Unfortunately, no. I only remember the description: *Death by a lover's fire.*"

To that, her caramel-colored eyes grew even more expansive. "Oh...oh Gods."

I cocked a brow at her just as she rushed out from behind her desk. "The piece you speak of...my brother painted it."

"Your brother?" I asked, unsure why she was acting panicked.

She nodded toward a room in the back. "Follow me."

I hesitated but decided to obey. There was nothing she could do to harm me. She'd be a fool to try.

I followed, keeping a tasteful distance until the woman stopped. She pointed her delicate hand to a painting before her, one hung higher than the others.

I glanced underneath at the engraving. ***ASAEL NEFELI*** was listed as the artist.

The painting was nearly identical to the one in the castle, although instead of orange and red hues surrounding the dark smoke, the flame was white. Silver sparks appeared to be shooting out from the chaos, sparkling like starlight.

White flame and silver sparks.

My eyes flickered to the name of the painting, and my heart ceased beating when I beheld the description.

Purification: The rise of the phoenix.

"What the fuck," I breathed, then shifted toward the young woman, narrowing my eyes. "Why did your brother name his painting this? What does this all mean?"

"I don't know," she said calmly. "A dark-haired man came into our business fifteen years ago. I was just a little girl at the time—my brother was only fourteen. He was a prodigy, far more skilled than anyone his age." Her weary gaze flitted to the artwork. "It was his first major commission. The man said it was for his daughter: The Queen of Otacia."

My mind reeled, remembering Ryia's words from all those years ago.

"This piece was gifted to me by my father. He had it commissioned by a talented painter in Faltrun. He named the piece Rebirth."

He *named the piece.*

"Who was the one who named the pieces?" I asked.

"Ramiel, the father of the Queen, named them. Asael was just told what to paint."

My brow furrowed, bouncing back to the sister painting. "Why aren't they together?"

She shrugged. "He insisted one stay here—paid quite a bit of gold to do so. Said it was never to be sold."

I studied the painting, searching for a sign, anything.

"Where is your brother now?" I pressed.

"He lives in Halsted...gave up painting to join their forces last year."

That caught my attention. "He gave up all of this to be a soldier for another kingdom?" I asked skeptically.

Her whisky eyes remained on mine. "It makes no sense, does it?" Her eyes flitted back to *Purification.* "My brother loved painting. It was his passion, but when Ramiel returned last year, asking to speak with Asael privately, my brother returned pale-faced and trembling. Something he had said rattled him enough to have him packing for Halsted that evening."

Ramiel...it sounds like this man knows something.

My head spun as I tried to remember the kingdom Ryia hailed from. Was it Halsted? No...perhaps Kalrael?

Silas would know this information. He never spoke to me of his grandfather, but any knowledge would be beneficial at this point.

"What is your name?" I asked her, softening my tone.

She hesitated. "Dagne. Dagne Nefeli."

I nodded, eyes sliding to the painting one last time.

Death by a lover's fire...rise of the phoenix...

"My name is Lena Daelyra," I told Dagne after a moment of pondering.

"I know."

My brows knitted together, and I looked back at her.

"The Queen's father—Ramiel—told Asael of your name."

"How? I've never spoken to the Queen's father before."

But perhaps Ryia had told him about me...

"What did he say about me?" I urged, stepping toward her.

"He said you'd know of the paintings." Her hands clenched the fabric of her dress. "And he told Asael to save you."

I froze, my face dropping. "Save me? From what?"

She swallowed. "I don't know."

"You can do this, Lena," Dani assured.

I took a shaky breath, then began to draw the pentagram that evening. I etched the words ***Accipe corpus meum alibi*** in the Titharan language on the ground with chalk, and our destination, Mount Rozavar, written in the same language at the bottom of the circle.

After the bizarre experience at The Artist's Guild, I began my search for Silas, only to give up shortly after.

I still wasn't ready to face him. I knew he would persist, demanding I tell him what was wrong last night, and I wasn't ready for that conversation just yet. I wanted to be as emotionally stable as I could while attempting a type of magic I'd never used before.

He told him to save you.

It sounded to me like Ramiel was being spoken to by a seer. Perhaps Kayin? Then again, she would have told me if she'd spoken to him or warned me herself of a danger...right?

My stomach sank, thinking about how Igon had led Torrin to danger. Sent him to a place where he was enslaved for a year. Perhaps I'm supposed to suffer...perhaps Kayin knows that.

Godsdamn seers.

"So, she draws some symbols, says a few words, and boom, we're there?" Waylon asked suspiciously, pulling me from my thoughts. Torrin, his parents, and several Mages watched as I drew.

Dani snorted. He was in male form this evening. "If only it were that simple. But, yes, in terms you'll understand...something like that."

"You have to draw from your magic," I described, still working on the design. "Teleporting...it's a type I've never done before."

"And a Warlock taught you this?" His face paled as Dani smirked at him with his pupilless eyes, his arms crossed.

The Mages here stared curiously, having never seen a Warlock and a Mage working together. Certainly, never having seen a Mage utilize what was always believed to be Warlock magic.

I huffed when the design was complete, wiping my forehead with the back of my hand and then placing the chalk back in my bra. "Are you sure you're comfortable trying this?"

He answered immediately. "I need to see her."

I inclined my head, then situated myself inside the circle of symbols I drew, dusting my hands on my pants.

"Whoever wishes to travel with needs to be in physical contact with the spellcaster." Dani grasped my hand, stepped into the circle, and then lifted a brow at my father.

Catching on, Waylon grasped my other hand. It was strange...his touch. Comforting, yet foreign. Familiar, yet not.

Torrin placed a hand on my shoulder, his parents following suit on my other, and a handful of others stepped inside the chalked symbol, putting their hands on my arms and legs wherever they could.

"Focus your magic and your energy toward Lena," Dani instructed.

"H-how do we do that?" someone asked.

But I felt it, felt their energy transfer from their touch, the symbols below us, now glowing purple.

We were ready.

I took a deep breath, squeezing Dani and Waylon's hands, before reaching deep within myself.

I gave it my all as I chanted, *Accipe corpus meum alibi.*

The feeling of teleportation was like no other. I felt my power spike, felt the energy surge through me in an overwhelming rush. But in seconds, the grassy fields on Mount Rozavar were beneath my feet, the warm wind whipping around me and those who traveled with me. The sun was setting, the sky a bright orange.

The wind was knocked from me, and I gasped for air, falling to my knees. Torrin was instantly there, along with my father, making sure I was okay.

"It drains your magic significantly when traveling. She just needs a sec," Dani said simply, stretching his arms.

Torrin rubbed my back and lightly patted it as I choked on the air. "Are you alright?" he asked nervously.

"Super," I rasped, then laughed when I finally got my bearings.

Torrin chuckled, then helped me to my feet. The Mages of Ames examined us with widened eyes, in silence, before one of them cheered, "Our Supreme has returned!"

The crowd on the mountain bellowed with joy, and I grinned as I saw all of them appearing well and content. People I'd grown to care for over the past five years ran forward, hugging me, hugging Torrin, and gasping when seeing Tobias and Josie Brighthell after fifteen years.

Thankfully, because it required a portal to reach this mountain top in general, no one seemed surprised we just appeared, though looks of skepticism began to appear when people realized a Warlock was in their presence.

"Lena? Torrin?!"

I turned to my left to see Mother attempting to push through the crowd, teary-eyed with a grin. Sensing our impending reunion, the crowd parted, and we ran to each other, nearly crashing into one another as we hugged.

"My daughter," she cried. "I have been so worried about you!" She pulled away, holding my face and checking for anything amiss. When satisfied, she looked at Torrin, who was now beside me.

"Hi, Minerva."

She grinned widely. "I have so many questions." She let out a winded laugh.

I bit my lip. "I think you're about to have a lot more."

Her brows furrowed at my comment, and I stepped away so she could see who stood just a few feet behind me.

My mother's jaw fell open, and a moment later, a whimper escaped her, her face crumpling as her hand shot over her mouth.

My father's face mirrored hers. "Minerva."

She choked on a sob. "Waylon."

He rushed to her and pulled her into his embrace. She froze for a moment in utter disbelief before she wrapped her arms around him tightly, weeping into his chest.

"How?" she cried, pulling away after a moment. She turned her face toward me. "How?"

"He saved my life," I said softly. "In Faltrun. It's a long story."

Her teary eyes went back to my father, craning her head to gaze up at him.

"I have spent the past twenty-four years missing you," he whispered, tucking her hair behind her pointed ear. Tears streamed down her face as his finger traced the pointed cartilage. "This would've never scared me away," he whispered.

Her face crumpled again as she brushed her hand against his cheek. "I have missed you, Waylon. I am so sorry..." She began to cry again.

"We'll give you some privacy," I said softly, and Waylon gave us a grateful nod as we walked away, the two of them roaming off in the opposite direction.

Out of the corner of my eye, I saw Immeron striding up to greet us.

"Lena! You're back. Sooner than I imagined. It's perfect, though! I have a little something for Merrick." He paused, his brows going together. "Why are you looking at me like that?"

I beamed. "Gods, do I have much to catch you up on."

It was comical watching Immeron's face shift and contort as I told him all of what had occurred in the past couple of months as we sat at his dining table. I told him of the Vampire encounter in Half-Life Pass and introduced him to Dani, telling him all about the War-locks in Forsmont and how Mages could utilize their magic as our own. I told him about the apparent evolution of the Undead and the encounter with The Lord of the Shadows, including his desire to acquire the Weapon. I finished by telling him of the prophecy in ***Potestas Verae Maleficis***, and how the Otacian crest and Asael's painting all pointed to it. By the time I was finished, the moon was high in the sky.

Immeron just stared at me with his jaw on the floor.

I rolled my ear piercings between my fingers. "Crazy, right?"

"I'm going to have a Godsdamn panic attack," he muttered, and I chuckled. "One thing stuck out to me about this prophecy, though—specifically the painting."

"Oh?"

He stroked his beard, eyes lost in thought. "You said white flame. That is Azrae's power."

My brows drew together. "Azrae? The God of Vengeance?"

"Indeed. All of the Gods and Goddesses had a special type of magic that belonged uniquely to them. Azrae's was white flame. Valor was shadow manipulation. Celluna could bond souls, hence the Soul-Tie bond. Tithara had the power of chronokinesis—the ability to alter time. Ravaiana's was always a secret, however. Or rather, no one had witnessed it to document it." He shuffled in his seat. "Each God has their opposite. It's a balance. Ravaiana is life, and Valor is death. Celluna is Love, and Tithara is Wisdom."

"Mind versus the heart," I mumbled.

Immeron nodded.

"But who is the opposite of Azrae?"

"Azrae is the most fascinating God, in my opinion. Other than Ravaiana's power being unknown, more is unknown of Azrae than any of them. Some call him the God of Vengeance. Some the God of Justice." He inhaled. "Some say the God of Balance. Which would make sense, considering his lack of a counterpart."

"Yes, but the opposite of balance is chaos. There is still an opposite to that."

Immeron shrugged. "We only know a mere fraction of the truth, I imagine."

Withdrawing **Potestas Verae Maleficis** from my crossbody, I flipped to the pages containing the Warlock prophecy. Pointing to it, I handed it over to Immeron for a closer look.

"Purification...Rebirth...I feel as though those must be counterparts, considering how often they've been symbolized among one another," he mumbled, brows drawn tightly as he rubbed the bridge of his nose. "Something about this all seems so familiar, yet I can't place why."

"Igon gave me his compass," I added, fetching it from my bag. "A pelican is engraved on it, and according to this book—" I plopped the other book Leroy gave to me down. "—pelican symbolizes sacrifice. And the spider...the symbol that the necromancer has begun etching on his victim's forehead...it stands for deceit."

My thoughts wandered, going back to those damn paintings.

Death by a lover's fire.

The rise of the phoenix.

Only through fire can the phoenix be reborn from the ashes.

It's clear it is no regular fire, but Azrae's fire. Who is his lover? The Goddess of Purification?

And where is the Weapon?

I scrubbed at my face, and Immeron chuckled. "Imagine what it was like for me all those years with a seer brother. Never fully saying what he meant."

I laughed softly, but the sadness reflected in Immeron's eyes made my smile fall.

Igon was dead, and Silas was the cause. Even if he knew it was coming, it was still a tragedy.

I swallowed, having one last thing to tell him about. "Ramiel—Ryia's father—apparently told Asael to save me. Sounds like a seer's message, no?"

"Indeed," he replied, eyes scanning the Warlock text.

"As far as I'm aware, Igon hasn't been in Otacia...but Kayin has."

"Kayin? Kayin..." His brows drew together tightly.

"Do you know her?"

He blinked, then shook his head. "The name sounds familiar, but I'm afraid not."

"Igon told Torrin and me she was also a seer."

I quickly gave him the rundown of my relationship with Kayin, telling him how I last spoke to her on this very mountaintop.

Immeron rested his elbows on the table. "So, you think Kayin and Ramiel are in cahoots?"

"Unless there's another seer I'm unaware of, which I suppose is possible. But considering Kayin is currently in Otacia, perhaps they are working together."

He rubbed his jaw. "What is their end goal?"

I shrugged, falling back to rest on my chair. "No clue. At this point, I feel as though we are all pawns in a very complicated game."

CHAPTER FORTY-NINE

SILAS

L ena had teleported herself, along with Torrin, her father, and a few other Mages, back to Mount Rozavar last night. Apparently, she thought it wise not to tell me she was doing so.

After successfully ignoring me all day yesterday, she just left. What if she had trouble returning?

According to what I heard through the grapevine, Lena planned on being there for three days. That gave me time to speak with Deana, who insisted I offer tips on how to run a kingdom. I tried to tell her I was just a prince, and while I had my duties, I'd never ruled a kingdom. She didn't mind.

Viola had been helping organize the Mages the entirety of this day, stationing them at different parts of the kingdom, giving them roles, and rationing the castle's coin reserves in an attempt to provide these people with a head start. It was clear now more than ever what Lena meant when she said Viola was a natural-born leader.

I was leaning against the doorframe, waiting for her to finish up her task of passing out silver. When her eyes caught mine, I heard her mumble, "One moment," to the Mage she was working with before striding over to me.

"What's the staring for?" she implored, crossing her arms.

I tilted my head and shrugged. "Just watching."

She narrowed her eyes, and I sighed.

"I wanted to thank you. For saving me." I reached into my back pocket, handing her a black velvet case.

She eyed my gift suspiciously as she accepted it. "What's in…" Her mouth dropped open as she lifted the box's lid.

I didn't know Viola very well, but I figured she might like these. "They're hair rings," I mumbled. "I was having trouble thinking what you might like, and while it doesn't even begin to cover what I owe you, I figured it's a start."

Viola continued staring at the dozens upon dozens of silver hair rings. I thought they'd look pretty in her braids. At the continuous silence, I felt my cheeks heating, wondering if it was a stupid gift.

"Silas…these are great." Her glossy eyes lifted to mine. "I'm shocked. This is really thoughtful."

I snorted. "You say that as if me being a thoughtful man is a ludicrous idea."

She shut the box, then wrapped her arms around me. I stiffened but happily returned the hug.

"Who would've guessed I'd be hugging you…ever."

I chuckled. "I myself am surprised by the gesture."

She pulled back, offering me playful eyes. "You say that as if me being affectionate is a ludicrous idea."

I grinned. "Touché."

She tucked her gift into her bag.

"Hey, do you know where Merrick is?" I asked as nonchalantly as I could.

"Knowing him? Probably smoking on a rooftop somewhere."

After strolling through Faltrun for twenty minutes, I stifled a laugh when I found Merrick exactly where Viola had guessed.

Perched atop a tavern's roof, Merrick held a blunt to his lips, sucking in and blowing out a cloud of smoke. Considering it was still morning, the place was closed, otherwise I had a feeling they'd be pissed for his trespassing.

"How'd you get up there?" I hollered.

Merrick lifted his head, then raised his hand, creating a staircase made of ice for me.

Clever.

I carefully trekked up the steps, and when I joined him atop the room, he let his creation melt.

"Prince Charming," he muttered, resting his head back against the slate shingles. "What's up?"

I cut right to the chase. "Something was wrong with Lena a couple of nights ago," I informed, lying down beside him. "She was walking down the hallway with tears in her eyes. She clearly had consumed a hefty amount of alcohol."

Merrick chuckled. "Didn't we all that night?"

I sighed, lying my head back down. "She almost seemed... guilty of something. I could see it in her eyes."

He raised his joint at me in silent offering. I declined but continued studying his face, noting his hand nervously drumming along the rooftop.

I blinked. "You know something." I sat up. "Tell me."

His icy blue eyes shot to mine as he stubbed the herb out on the roof. "It's not my place to tell you things from her past. That's for her to do."

My brows drew together. "What the hell are you talking about?"

Merrick went to dismiss me again, and I roughly gripped the front of his shirt, pressing him into the roof.

"Let me the fuck go!" he seethed.

My eyes burned into his. "If Lena is hurt, I need to know."

The Empath's eyes swirled dark as he studied me.

"You feel what I feel?" I hissed. "Then you should know how desperately I need to know that she's okay. She completely shut me out, and I need to know why."

Merrick's jaw ticked, and he sighed in defeat. I released his shirt and waited patiently as he found the words.

He sat up, running a hand through his long, silver hair before resting his elbows on his knees. "I...I don't know anything about what happened. Lena just said she didn't want to talk about it. But I imagine it has something to do with Torrin."

"You think Torrin hurt her?"

Merrick shook his head. "Hurt her when he left? Yeah, for sure. But the two of them...they..."

My shoulders slumped, and I felt my blood boiling beneath my skin. "They've slept together?"

Merrick loosened another sigh. "Lena never told me if anything ever happened between them, but I could always feel how much my cousin loved her. And the day we found out he'd left, Lena was devastated, even if she masked it to everyone else."

I was going to kill him. I was going to stab that bastard for taking her away, for touching her.

Sensing my homicidal feelings, Merrick sternly said, "Torrin would never intentionally hurt Lena, Silas."

"He took her from me!" I yelled, then frantically looked around to see if anyone had heard me. Citizens walking down below scowled at me, and I winced.

Calming myself down, I repeated quietly, "He took her from me, and now you're saying he brought her to his bed, too?"

"I don't know if it ever got to that point. But he has always been there for her. He taught her to control her magic. He held her, burning himself as he calmed her fire the night she got it."

I was seeing red. I had noticed the burns on his hand. "He was there comforting her, helping her, as she was losing *our* child..." I curled my lip. "What a great man he is."

"Your father is the one who caused Lena to flee Otacia, not Torrin."

I had heard all I needed to.

"Make me some new steps, please. I need...I need to go think."

Merrick studied me, then raised his hand again, allowing me to leave.

When Lena, Dani, and Torrin returned two evenings later, I did my best to stay composed until I could speak to Torrin in private. Lena had that sparkle back in her eyes, seemingly doing better, as she handed Merrick a crossbow. Apparently, Immeron was working on a new design and decided to gift it to the Empath.

Torrin seemed winded, and it became obvious that he was the one who performed the spell to bring them all back.

I kept a tasteful distance as I followed him to his room that evening. When he entered, I shoved open his door before he had the chance to close it. Torrin backed away, brows lowering as I slammed it shut behind me, the room rattling from the force.

I raised my sword, pointing it at him, his eyes broadening. "So, it wasn't enough to steal the love of my life away from me, but you brought her into your bed as well?"

At the sight of his throat bobbing, I lunged for him. Torrin lifted his palms, holding them out, and the forcefield he projected slammed me back into a dresser.

I bared my teeth, flinging myself forward. "Fight with a weapon, you coward!" I shouted, raising my sword again. "You're the one who trained me. You really don't believe you can take me on?"

I wanted to cut his head clean off of his body. I wanted to pierce him to the wall, gutting him from the inside out.

"I will not fight you!" he barked, holding out his hands. "Nor will I apologize. We almost died in that battle, and the three of us all consented."

My eyes broadened, and I lowered my weapon ever so slightly. "The *three* of you?"

Torrin's eyes slowly widened. "What are you coming here regarding?"

I tightly clenched my sword's handle. "The fact that you slept with her in your village." I angled my blade at him. "But now...now you're going to tell me exactly what the fuck '*the three of us consented*' means."

Torrin was silent, his cheeks turning a bright crimson.

"Did this happen four nights ago? Was that why Lena was in tears at one in the morning, heading to her room?"

A crease formed between his brows. "She was crying?"

"ANSWER ME!" I bellowed, swinging my sword at him. He just barely dodged the move.

Panting, he responded, "Roland and I had sex with Lena. Together."

I felt my entire body reverberating with the fiercest rage. I loosened a shaky exhale, stepping closer, my voice eerily calm. "I will kill you both."

"No, you won't," Torrin responded, lip curled, back to the wall.

I snarled, shoving my sword into the wall just beside his waist. My lips morphed into a sinister grin. "I don't think you fully know what I am capable of, Brighthell."

He looked down his nose at me. "Even if you did want us dead, which you don't, Lena would never forgive you if you did such a thing."

I slid my tongue across my upper teeth, my lips closed. "Doesn't mean I can't rough you up."

His eyes saddened as he let out a sigh. "Do what you must," he whispered. "But I don't regret it."

"You don't regret making her cry? You don't regret taking advantage of her pain?"

"Don't you DARE accuse me of taking advantage of her!" he threatened. "I had no idea she was hurt that badly."

"So, you admit you knew she was hurt?"

His jaw feathered. "Yes," he answered quietly. "Because I told her I couldn't sleep with her again."

I scoffed. "You told her that immediately after fucking her? Do you even give a shit about her at all?!"

"I LOVE HER!" he cried.

I retreated a few steps at his confession.

Emotion welled in his eyes. "I love her," he repeated, and then he sucked in his lips, shaking his head. "But it's you she wants—you that she is destined for. It wounds me too much being intimate with her, knowing it'll never last." His voice broke, a tear slipping free as he whispered, "Knowing I'm her second choice."

My anger bled out, my expression falling as I yanked my sword out of the wall.

Torrin glowered at me. "Does that make you feel better?" he asked bitterly.

My eyes fell to the ground. "No, it does not." After taking a deep, steadying breath, I asked him, "What do you mean she is destined for me?"

He was silent for a moment. "You are her Soul-Tie."

There's that term again, the one Merrick used. I lifted my gaze. "How is there any way to know that for a fact?"

"Igon told me."

I scoffed again. "The seer who misleads you for the sake of destiny?"

Torrin's brows knitted.

"How do you know it's not a lie?" I oppugned. "How do you know you aren't being misguided? Is there really any proof such a bond exists?"

Torrin's eyes flared as if he'd never considered such a thing.

"That's the difference between you and me, Torrin." I sheathed my blade, backing away toward the door. "I wouldn't give a damn if she was my Soul-Tie or not. None of that bullshit would *ever* keep me away."

I turned, grasped the knob, and rotated it.

"Not even your wife?"

I froze, my voice dropping. "What did you say?"

At his silence, I turned back, meeting his sneer.

"The only reason I am married to her is because *you* took Lena away from me. Because you all made me believe she was dead," I spat. All sympathy for Torrin was out the window now. "Don't you *dare* fucking judge me for the mess we've found ourselves in."

And with those final words, I left, slamming the door behind me.

I was bleeding with rage as I made my way over to Lena's room. It was late, but try as I might to get Torrin's words out of my head, they wouldn't cease.

I was pissed. She was crying because Torrin set a boundary with her. She was crying because she wanted *him*.

She had already told me Roland satisfied her better than I had, and if she was this worked up about Torrin...

I released a breath as I stood at her door.

Calm down. Just talk to her.

I knocked, and after a few seconds, I was greeted by a messy bun and bright green eyes.

"Silas—what are you doing here?"

"Let me in," I demanded.

She blinked but stepped aside, allowing me into her room. I slowly closed the door behind us, locking it shut.

Her eyes went to the doorknob. "What's going on? Is everything okay?" she asked, studying me with worry.

I took in a shaky breath, appreciating just how beautiful she looked. I always loved when she'd throw her hair up when we trained together. And with the silk robe she wore, highlighting her sensuous curves...

I cleared my throat, my anger rising. I hated the power she had over me.

"I know about Roland," I said with deathly calm. "About Torrin. Everything."

She stilled, her eyes going wide and eyebrows knitting. We just stood there in silence for a moment.

I was furious. It was still taking every bit of my strength not to go back and bust Torrin's face in. To not kill Roland.

"And?" she prompted, her lip curling with her words. "Are you here to judge me?"

"What should I presume when given that information?"

She scoffed incredulously, then turned away, crossing her arms.

I could feel my face becoming pained. "Both of them, Lena?" I barely got out.

She kept her back to me. "How does that make you feel?" she asked matter-of-factly.

"What do you fucking think?! It makes me angry! Fucking furious!"

"Why?"

I paused. "What do you mean, why?"

"Why does it make you angry?" she demanded.

I was left stunned. She couldn't be seriously asking that.

At my silence, she asked, "Would you have a threesome?"

I took a deep breath. I was a bastard, an asshole, for wanting to hurt her in this moment. "I have before," I said simply. "Multiple times."

That made her spin toward me, and despite my rage, pain lumped in my throat at the sight of her glassy eyes.

"Never with Era. But before I met her, I experimented a lot...I've had a myriad of women in my bed."

It was true. I lost count of how many women I'd slept with. When I thought Lena had died, nothing mattered to me anymore. Sex was the only distraction of mine that didn't involve killing people or destroying my body with substances.

Her hands balled into fists at her sides as she glared at me with contempt.

At one point, we had belonged only to each other. No other person had touched our bodies, and no other lips had brushed against ours.

Didn't she understand I didn't want this? That I didn't ask for any of it?

Her eyes were becoming bloodshot, but she tried her hardest to stand firm. "Would you have shared me with another man, Silas?"

I tensed. I wasn't expecting that to be what came out of her mouth. She wasn't disgusted that I'd slept around, though I'm sure the thought wasn't a pleasant one. No, she was wondering if a man who loved her—*truly* loved her—would be willing to share.

Every relationship was different. People's boundaries varied. It didn't necessarily mean someone didn't love you if they were comfortable sharing.

But I knew the type of man I was. I was possessive. What was mine was mine—no one else's.

"Never," I said softly. "I could never."

Her face fell, and my shoulders sagged, all anger disappearing the second I saw that pain in her face. She pivoted away.

"Lena—"

I went to reach for her, but she shrugged me off, whirling to face me with nothing but wrath etched on her face.

"I HATE YOU!" she screamed, and I recoiled as tears continued to flow down her beautiful face. Her voice shook as she uttered, "I hate you. I hate how badly I crave you. I hate that I will always compare every lover to you and come up short-handed. Every. Single. Time."

I blinked rapidly, surprised by her confession. "I-I thought it was better with Roland—"

"I lied!" she cried, throwing her hands up. "I lied—and how easily did you believe it? How *could* you believe it?" Tears poured down her flushed cheeks. "I want you so badly I can't think straight," she said in a broken whisper. "I know now that I will never be happy...never be satisfied with anyone else. And I know that you are, that you have found your person," she sobbed, her face twisting to rage. "And I *hate* you for it."

An icy coldness took hold of my features as I inched closer to her. "You think I am happy?" I seethed. "You believe I am *satisfied*?!" I gripped her chin tightly and pulled her face up to me, her eyes enlarging at the motion. "I haven't known happiness since you left my life, Lena. I haven't known satisfaction since that last night you were in my bed. How can't you comprehend how desperately I desire you? How, after all these years, am I still in love with you?!"

Her eyes blew wide, and she stiffened as I leaned my face closer, my voice quiet but no less angry. "Do you know how often I dream of you? How often I wish to be holding you in my arms?"

She was staring up at me, her face mere inches from mine. My eyes trailed down to her mouth, and I dragged my thumb along her bottom lip.

"How much strength it takes me to be anywhere near you, to keep what little honor I have...when all I desire is your lips on mine? When all I want is to worship this body of yours?"

Her mouth dropped open, and instantly, my lips were on hers, my hand sliding to grip the back of her neck as our tongues brushed.

As I completely unraveled.

CHAPTER FIFTY

SILAS

I felt like I was dreaming. For so long, this was all I wanted. The dreadful months around her when I couldn't touch her, kiss her, *taste* her.

I didn't know how long we were lost in that kiss. Everything faded away at the feel of her hands running through my hair, her tongue brushing against mine. I gripped her waist and pulled her against me.

I could not get her close enough, not even as my tongue explored her mouth, not even as I broke away and trailed my kisses along her jawline, along her neck.

The taste of her skin was a reminder that I had truly been starving all these years. Her breathy moans had my length straining against my pants.

I sucked on her skin, and her breathing hitched, her grasp on my hair tightening. I found my way to her mouth once more.

When I finally broke away, her pupils were dilated, her cheeks flushed, and her nipples hardened to peaks under her blue silk robe.

I kissed her again, softly this time. "Do you know how badly I have craved you?" I rasped over her lips. "How fucking difficult it has been, enduring your touch, your forgiving words...and now tasting these pillow-soft lips...." I pulled away, and my eyelids became heavy at the sight of those lips wet and swollen from our kiss. My eyes didn't falter from hers as I exhaled, "It has been nothing but torture being in your presence and being unable to have you."

She was breathing fast. "Silas," she began, her thumb sliding along my cheekbone. Along my scar.

I captured her lips once more, and damn me, but my hand cupped her heavy breast. Gods, they were easily three handfuls each.

I had to stop...needed to stop. But I couldn't. Not yet.

My heart was beating so rapidly that I wouldn't be surprised if Lena could hear it. My voice was near guttural when I said, "Remove your robe."

Lena obeyed swiftly, our mouths mere inches from each other as she untied the pale blue material and slid the silk off of her shoulders, it puddling to the floor.

My eyes flared, and my heart surely skipped a few beats as my stare trailed over her smooth, fair skin. Her breasts rose and fell with her rapid breathing, and her skin pebbled as I ran my fingertips along her side, her eyes fluttering closed.

"So damn beautiful," I whispered, and she bit down on her lip, her half-lidded eyes rising to meet mine. My left hand joined my other, sliding down her sides to grip her hips. My gaze flitted between her legs, my mouth watering at the sight.

Fuck. I shouldn't be doing this.

"I want to see you," she whispered.

The sound of her aroused voice eliminated any rational thought. I brought my hands up and began to unbutton my black shirt. The sleeves were cropped midway to my elbow and showcased the tattoos covering my forearms already, but her breathing staggered when I dropped my hands, and my shirt parted to reveal my torso. I knew I was significantly more built than when we were teens—more defined. And just like the rest of me, my chest and stomach were inked.

"I need you to listen to me," I said, my breathing hastening as I roughly gripped her wrists. "You are not to try and remove my shirt. You are not to touch my back skin to skin. Do you understand?"

Her eyebrows furrowed at the request, her lips parting briefly before she closed them and nodded. "Am I allowed to touch your chest?" she asked softly.

I tucked a piece of her copper hair behind her pointed ear. "Yes."

She stepped forward and extended a hand carefully, brushing her fingertips along my pecks, along the tattoo I got for her.

She glanced up to find me studying her, and she trailed her right hand back up to my face, holding me in an embrace as her other hand rested on the dagger piercing the rose.

I missed you so much, Lena.

I wanted to say it, but the words wouldn't come out. I pressed my lips against hers once more, my arms wrapping around her, pulling her until her breasts were squished against my chest. Her neck was angled all the way up as I was nearly a foot taller than her.

I pulled away, and a smug smile took hold of my face as I began to circle around her.

Her breathing quickened.

I stopped behind her, my hands finding her hips once more. I bent down, and my breath against her ear caused her to shudder as I asked, "Does your pussy still weep for me, Lena?"

She gasped softly as my hand trailed down, dipping under the fabric of her panties. My fingers slid through the slickness of her with ease.

I cursed softly, then began skillfully circling my fingers over her clit. Lena's eyes closed, and her head fell back to rest against my chest, another faint moan slipping free of her.

I let out a breathy laugh. "It does." I quickened my tempo, and she bucked against me.

"Fuck," she whispered.

I smiled against her ear, closing my eyes and breathing in her scent. Eucalyptus and spearmint. She always smelled so good.

My lips trailed down to her neck, where I quickly sucked in her skin and bit her.

"Silas!" she squealed, and my tongue moved against the small hurt, the combination of pain and pleasure causing her to shudder.

She moaned, her hand reaching back to feel the hardened length inside my pants. I grunted against the skin on her neck, and she slid her hand up and down.

I cursed again, pulling away and twirling her around to face me. I released her hair from her hair tie, her orange curls falling down her back.

She was stunned as my hand clasped around her neck. My jaw was clenched, my lids heavy as I moved us forward and roughly pushed her against the bed, releasing her neck from my grip. She gasped for air as she hit the soft mattress.

I fell to my knees, prying her thighs apart with no objection, and weaved my arms under her knees. I jerked her toward me and began kissing the sides of her thighs. Slowly. Methodically. When I reached her sex, I gave a light kiss right on top of her undergarments. I knew my breath was hot against her, and I offered her a cruel, teasing smirk before continuing to kiss over the lacy material.

"Silas," she breathed as she propped herself up on her elbows, her shiny copper hair falling well past her breasts. "Are you going to make me beg?"

"I would enjoy it," I admitted, my lips hovering just above her pussy. "But no, my Flower. You never need to beg for this." I slowly slid her underwear off before discarding them on the floor. I loomed over her for a moment, blowing my hot breath over her sensitive privates, and right before she began to protest, my tongue darted out and began lapping at her clit. Her hand shot up over her mouth, muffling her cry.

It had been over half a decade since I tasted her pussy. And while I knew I made her feel good before, I also knew it was evident my sexual skillset had improved. I sure as hell would hope it had, considering how many women I had gone down on since then.

"Scream for me, Lena. I want to hear you come," I mumbled over her clit, and as she lowered her hand, I continued my assault. Her head fell back, and desperate moans escaped her.

My tongue continued to lick up and down, and she met my movements with her own, smothering me with her pussy.

Fuck yes...

She ran her hand through my hair and gripped it, and I grunted against her. I always loved it when she pulled my hair.

"Yes, that's it," I roused. "Grind on my face."

I moved my tongue all around her now, dipping my tongue into her entrance before sliding it back up and then sucking each of her lips into my mouth. Lena rotated her hips, her forbidden sweetness gliding across my lips, across my nose. I inhaled deeply, intoxicated by her heavenly scent.

"Fuck. Silas, please don't stop," she begged, her face flushed as she watched me.

To that, I placed my lips around her clit and sucked, causing her to curse and cry out my name.

My name on her lips...that will be my undoing.

I resisted the urge to grab my aching cock. "You taste even lovelier than I remember, Flower." I groaned, and her left hand joined the other in gripping my raven locks. I could tell she was enjoying the roughness of my facial hair as it slid against her. "So sweet. Your pussy was made for my tongue."

I closed my mouth around her clit again, sucking it in and lashing my tongue rapidly against it before two of my fingers then pushed their way inside. She cursed loudly at the fullness, and I smiled against her.

CHAPTER FIFTY-ONE
LENA

Silas began moving his fingers in and out at an increased pace. The pleasure was blinding, and I couldn't help but squeeze my thighs around his head. He used his free hand to push my legs back so I was opened even wider, unrelenting as he slurped on my pussy. My nails dragged against his scalp, and when he began rapidly pulsing his fingers inside of me, I screamed his name again.

What we were doing was wrong—so wrong. But Gods, it felt so right.

I was reaching the top of the peak, the pleasure exceeding any I had ever felt in my entire life. The forbidden aspect of our affair heightened my arousal, that and the fact it was *him* with his face buried between my legs.

I felt like I was going to lose control of my bladder with the way he had his fingers curved inside me, but the overwhelming need to come was all I could focus on.

"Yes, fuck, yes," I voiced breathlessly.

"Don't hold anything back," he murmured, then closed his mouth over my pussy once more, flicking his fingers and hitting a spot that made me start to see stars as he fucked me with them.

Only a few more seconds passed, and my moans were getting louder, euphoria taking hold. And then, I exploded, screaming his name as my body shuddered against him. I was aware of the liquid pouring out of me as I throbbed—but the sickening pleasure was all I relished in.

"*Fuck*, Lena," he growled as he kept fucking me with his fingers. When my breathing started to level and the stars started to fade, I glimpsed down.

Silas's lips were swollen and wet...no—*dripping* with my release. He smirked at me, golden eyes burning with desire as he withdrew his fingers, slid them into his mouth, and sucked what was left of me off them.

I could only look at him in astonishment. He was the most handsome man I had ever seen, and seeing him like this, lustful and soaked in my release, had me wanting to come again.

He got off his knees and crawled over me on the bed. "Now I want you to come that intensely with my cock inside of you. I want to feel you fluttering around me."

I looked up at him through half-lidded eyes, and as I was still out of breath, I merely gave him a rushed nod. I laced my hand around his neck and pulled him down to kiss me. His tongue danced slowly around mine, the taste of him mixing with the taste of me. We kissed hungrily, starving from all these years apart. Silas pulled away, unzipping his pants. His enormous length sprang free, and I inhaled sharply at the sight. With no time to waste, he angled himself downward, pushing the blunt head against my entrance. It began to slide in effortlessly, considering I was drenched.

He groaned as he pushed in further, and my eyes rolled back at the sensation, at the fullness. He began inching in and out slowly, torturously. When I met his eyes, he was staring down at where we were joined, lips parted and eyes darkened. His breathing staggered as his gaze lifted, and he lowered himself so he was just above me, my arms and legs wrapping around his torso.

I missed him. Gods, I missed him.

He kissed me softly and then plunged himself inside. I cried out, and with no time to waste, Silas began rolling his hips, moving quickly in and out of me.

My head fell back, and I held onto him tightly. "Yes...yes!" I wailed.

"Godsdamn, Lena, I have missed you," he breathed, then quickened his pace. The sound of skin slapping against skin was harmonious with our frantic moans. He pulled back slightly and grasped one of my breasts before sucking my nipple into his mouth.

I felt it then, the electricity. My whole body was buzzing in response to him.

I trailed my right hand to his cheek, my left still around the back of his neck.

I loved seeing him like this, so lost in lust and desire, primal instinct compelling him to slide in me again and again and again.

He slowed down, cupping my face and looking into my eyes. "You are breathtaking," he marveled, his sweetness warming me. "You are exquisite."

He nipped at my ear, kissing my pointed cartilage, and tears began forming in my eyes.

"Flawless," he whispered, leaning back, his fingertips grazing the part of me I had always kept hidden. "Perfect. You are perfect."

My vision grew blurry, and before I could let my tears free, Silas scooped me in his arms, resuming his intense pace.

"Silas!" I dug my nails into his neck, and he groaned, his hand clasping around my neck.

"That's it, sing for me, Lena." His grip on my throat tightened. "There is no sweeter sound than my name cried from your lips."

He trailed kisses along my jawline, his fingers weaving through my copper waves, his pace inside me slowing again.

"You feel so fucking good," he moaned.

"So do you," I panted. "I have missed you so much, Silas."

His breathing quickened, and he withdrew his hand to suck on the skin of my neck. I angled my hips back, taking him even deeper. There was no amount of closeness that would ever feel like enough when it came to him. He growled in response, sliding his soaked shaft in and out of me.

"I haven't known happiness since I left, either," I confessed in a whisper.

I ignored the stinging in my eyes, and Silas lifted his head, studying me. I squeezed my legs around him tighter.

His jaw ticked, and he wrapped his arm behind me, pulling me close. I held on to his back, wishing so badly to be dragging my nails against his skin instead of the fabric of his shirt.

I brought my lips to his neck and kissed his tattooed flesh, screams ripping from my throat as he ruthlessly fucked me.

CHAPTER FIFTY-TWO

SILAS

Her tongue on my neck was enough for me to spill into her easily, but I wanted to enjoy this for as long as I could. I knew that the moment this was over, reality would hit me like never before.

I was cheating on my wife.

I held Lena close as I buried myself inside her, over and over and over again. Her pussy clenched around me, so tight, warm, and wet. I didn't want to stop. I didn't want my reality to be what it was. Her...it was always supposed to be *her*.

I couldn't stop my anger from growing. I knew I had no right. I knew it wasn't her fault. But she left me, lied to me, and I was in this fucked up situation because of it.

I pulled back again, breathing heavily as I stared into those big, green eyes.

I hate you, she had told me.

Did she truly? Did she resent my moving on to the point of hatred?

Did I hate her?

She grabbed the back of my neck and forcefully pulled my lips to hers, and I decided to hell with the difficult thoughts; I was going to enjoy fucking her, consequences be damned.

Lena's desperate moans were always the most beautiful sound. And the way she looked at me...despite our hurt, our resentments, there was longing there. The feel of each other's body was our lifeline. Every touch was an indulgence. The euphoria that even a brush of her fingers provided was far stronger than what any drug or drink could offer me. Except with her, the high of each relapse was just as satisfying as the first.

I couldn't get enough of her. I wasn't ready for the come down...for the withdrawal.

As if sensing my dread, Lena's hand slid to my cheek, her lips parted as she breathed heavily.

I was not a good man. I wasn't deserving of her comfort. My mind kept repeating the same mantra.

Hurt her. Make her hate you.

I was being selfish, enjoying her body like this. Though I supposed I *was* hurting her, giving her a taste of what we both could not have.

I flipped her onto her stomach, then grasped her hips, pulling her ass to my pelvis and thrusting my dick into her tight heat. I gripped her neck and forced her upward, her back pressed against my chest, her head resting on my shoulder.

"I'm happy you hate me, Flower," I murmured in her ear. "And I'm fucking glad I ruined every man for you. Now you have a taste of what I've felt every day for the last five years."

I slid my thumb into my mouth before cupping her breast from behind. I grinned as I watched her shudder, my wet finger circling her pink nipple. A second orgasm rippled through her, a throaty groan tearing from her lungs.

I placed her on her back again, wishing to see her beautiful face as I finished.

I kissed her again, slowly, with intention, knowing once this was finished, nothing would be the same. "I want you to come one more time, Flower."

She nodded breathlessly, kissing me again.

There were no words spoken as we finished, as I gazed into those beautiful meadow eyes, as I angled myself to hit that spot that would make her come harder than she ever had.

Her body was made for mine. Despite our time apart, I knew it better than anyone could. Better than Roland. Better than Torrin.

Lena's eyes rolled back as she screamed, her inner walls contracting around my length, squeezing me tightly. I wanted to come inside her, but I instead pulled out, slapping my cock against her swollen clit as she squirted a second time, wailing in ecstasy. The sight of her, the most beautiful woman in the world, writhing beneath me was all I needed to find my own release. My cock throbbed, and I groaned, borderline fucking whimpered, as I had the most intense orgasm of my life, spilling myself all over her belly and breasts.

I took a few shaky breaths, clarity finally washing over me, and I lifted my stare to Lena's.

Her chest was rising and falling, her panicked eyes searching my own.

My hands shook, and I felt an awful pit in my chest.

How could I do such a thing?

I felt my lip tremble.

"Silas——" Lena started, but I pushed myself off her, retrieving my undergarments and pants. She sat up, watching me with a shameful gaze.

Once my pants were on, I rushed over to the washroom, fetching a cloth to clean her with.

I couldn't look in her eyes. Couldn't accept what I did.

She kept still as I cleaned her flawless body, my body tense as I wiped my arousal off of her chest.

I am a horrible, awful person.

But I knew that already, didn't I? Of all the atrocities I had committed, it was no surprise I'd fuck this up too.

My hands shook as I withdrew my hand and the cloth, placing it back in the bathroom.

I had never been unfaithful...that was one thing I took pride in.

Fucking hell...

When I reemerged, buttoning up my shirt, I finally met eyes with my best friend.

Tears were streaming down her face as she clutched the bedsheet, covering her body.

My hands slowly fell to my sides when I buttoned the final button.

I hated seeing her like this...broken because of me.

But I was broken, too.

I was broken, too.

Hurt her. Make her hate you.

"Do you still hate me?" I asked in a low voice, and I hated myself for the words that came out next. "Because your hatred pales in comparison to the loathing I feel toward you now." Lena's face crumpled, and I stepped closer toward the bed as my frown deepened. "You consume all of me, Lena. You are my waking thought and the final picture I see before I sleep. You are a siren that haunts my dreams. It's been that way since the moment I met you." I sighed in defeat. "There's not a damn second you aren't on my mind."

"Silas," she cried softly.

"You represent all that I could ever desire...and all I can never have." My voice cracked as I whispered, "You have destroyed me...and I resent you for it."

And I fucking hated myself when her response was a choked sob...hated myself for leaving without another word.

I took in a drag of the dagga I purchased at a local tavern, its warmth filling my chest. I noticed the Mages surrounding me, watching me with curious eyes. Apparently, there was an altercation here a few nights ago, and the Mages decided this business was theirs, Deana backing the takeover.

"Long day?"

My eyes shot to the side to see Dani, who sat beside me at the bar, her bright blue eyes looking at me without her pupils. I was happy everyone felt comfortable showing their true selves now, at least here.

I blew out the smoke. "Long life," I muttered.

A crease formed between her brows, but she raised a hand to the worker, who nodded and rolled her a joint. We sat there in silence, Dani eventually taking in her own drag.

"What happened?" she asked.

I chewed on the inside of my cheek, then ran my hand down my face. I opened my mouth to speak, but nothing came out. It wasn't something I could talk about in any capacity, so I took another hit instead.

Dani tilted her head to the side, a smile creeping across her face. "This have anything to do with you being in love with Lena?"

I choked on the smoke, then whirled my head toward her. She let out a chuckle, bringing the rolled herbs to her lips. "Sometimes I'm convinced everyone is fucking blind except me."

I tightened my lips and frowned. "How could you tell?"

She ran her hand through the ends of her long, cobalt hair. "The way you two are constantly fucking each other with your eyes is the biggest giveaway."

I winced, and she continued, "How quickly she was willing to forfeit her life for yours in Forsmont and vice versa in the battle a few days ago."

My heartbeat quickened. "You haven't said...haven't told—"

"No." She placed her joint in the glass bowl set before us. "Human, Mage, Warlock, what have you—our feelings are complex. Difficult. I don't hold judgment toward you for feeling a certain way. Feelings like that...it's not something we can control." She leaned on her knuckles as I took a final hit, mild euphoria coursing through my veins, and watched as I placed my dagga in the glass bowl. "I want to be with Viola, even though she's with Merrick."

I raised my brows. "You don't say," I said sarcastically, and she playfully slapped my arm.

"Yeah, I know I'm even more obvious than you." Her smile faded. "So, what happened?"

Guilt wracked me. My shoulders slumped, and I just shook my head. "I just...I don't know what to do."

"Why did you marry Era?"

I frowned. "I was required to be married. I connected with her that day and just went for it."

"That day?!" Dani asked incredulously. "You met and married her *that day?*"

"Proposed the same day," I corrected. "Married the next."

"Shit," she chuckled, her eyes red and glassy from the drugs. "You humans are odd."

"Royalty is odd. Normal humans don't do it like that...usually, anyway."

"You ever been in any relationships before her?"

My whole body tensed. "Does it matter?"

"Well, if you haven't had any experience, perhaps you are being led by lust."

I gave her a lazy smile. "I'm plenty experienced."

She raised her hands, a grin on her face. "Just checking." She laughed softly, then sipped on the drink that the bartender gave her—free of charge, it seemed—as the man offered her a flirtatious wink. She returned it, and when he stepped away, she rolled her eyes.

"So...Vi, huh?"

"She's the most beautiful woman I've ever seen." She shrugged, sipping the drink and making a pleasantly surprised expression at its apparent palatability. "She's strong. Smart." She sighed. "Merrick is great, but I don't feel they're that into each other."

"Really?" I asked, leaning back in my chair and crossing my arms.

"To be honest, I think he fancies your wife."

My playful grin disappeared. "What?"

"Don't go saying anything. It's just a feeling I get. Then again, your wife has that sort of elegant beauty. He's probably just in awe of it."

I chuckled. "Are you?"

"She's stunning. Not my type." She winked, then purred, "Don't worry, I won't steal her away."

I laughed, but despite the drugs coursing through my system, my emotions came flooding back. Why does the thought of her being with someone else not bother me that much? Yet the thought of Lena with Roland, with Torrin, with both Roland *and* Torrin...

I leaned my head back and loosened a breath. I said such terrible shit to her, things I didn't mean. And the look on her face...

I wanted to fuck her like a wild animal. And I did just that, but the desperation I felt wasn't simple carnal desire. I wanted *all* of her. I wanted to love on her, make her feel good.

And all I did was fuck her and leave. Left her with tears running down her face.

"Can I offer some advice?" Dani asked softly.

I tilted my head to her and nodded.

"Being honest will always be the best, even if it hurts others. Even if it hurts you." Her gaze didn't falter. "And with everything going on, with our lives coming so close to ending countless times now..." She let out a sigh. "I think you would have more regrets not saying how you truly feel. Not doing what your heart tells you."

My eyes fell to my lap. "It isn't so simple," I whispered.

"Love never is. But if you're unhappy, Era deserves to be free." She placed a gentle hand on my arm, and my eyes slid to meet her tender stare. "And you deserve to be as well."

I held her eyes for a few moments before she threw back the rest of her drink and walked off.

I stayed sitting there for a few moments, feeling calmer now, my head somehow clearer, despite the drug warming my body.

I had to go back upstairs.

CHAPTER FIFTY-THREE

LENA

I sobbed into my hands after Silas left the room, never having felt so awful in my life.

I felt disgusting. I felt so, so ashamed.

Era had become my friend. She had been nothing but kind to me, and I slept with her husband.

Slept with her husband only a few days after I had a threesome with two of our other friends.

I cried harder. What the fuck was wrong with me? Both sexual experiences were...blissful. Fantastic, if I was being honest. But both times, I was left feeling empty...and alone.

"Your hatred pales in comparison to the loathing I feel toward you now."

He hates me, and rightfully so. I shouldn't have told him my feelings. I shouldn't have eagerly removed my robe and did everything he asked of me.

I hated that I loved him. Hated him for not being able to have him. And he hated me for the same reason.

How would I face him tomorrow? Face Era? Face Merrick, Torrin, or Roland?

I was a whore.

I wished to cry myself to sleep, but I needed to wash myself, even though I knew I wouldn't feel any less disgusting.

I was standing in the burning hot stream an hour later, silently crying. Try as I might, I was unable to fall asleep, unable to quiet the voices in my head despite my emotional exhaustion. The sting the water gave was a small comfort, distracting me from the war waging in my mind. Once I was ready to pass out, I stepped out. Wringing out my hair and drying my body, I threw on a large cotton T-shirt. I slipped on a pair of underwear and stopped before my bed.

I felt gross even looking at the sheets.

Maybe I should go downstairs and drink away my sorrows.

The thought was intriguing, but I didn't wish to face anyone. Speak to anyone. So, I hesitantly climbed into bed, wrapping myself in the thick comforter.

I stared at the ceiling for a while, eyes leaking.

I was Supreme of Ames. I had a duty to save my people. My heart ached for a man I couldn't have, and the distress was distracting me.

My eyes traveled across the bedroom, and as I was just about to call it quits and go to sleep, my crossbody caught my eye. Specifically, the grimoire tucked inside.

I padded over, lifting the heavy book, and fingered through its pages.

I was about to stop, ready to rest my mind, when the spell on the final page spoke to me.

Oblivisci.

Quickly, I ran to my dresser, slipping a bra on underneath my shirt and pulling on some pants. This spell required help, and I knew exactly who I was going to ask.

I rushed to his room and pounded on the door, and my silver-haired friend came rushing, rubbing his eyes. Viola came scuttling behind him, holding her robe firmly in place.

"Lena?" he whispered.

"I need your help, Merrick."

CHAPTER FIFTY-FOUR
MERRICK

*T*hree hours earlier

I took a steady breath before knocking on Erabella's bedroom door, my now old bow resting on my shoulder. I hoped she and Silas weren't getting it on, but considering I didn't feel any emotions like that coming from behind the door, I figured I was in the clear.

The lock clicked, and Era's eyes widened as she beheld me. My sight trailed down her frame, noting the oversized shirt she wore, no pants.

No bra.

Dear Gods, I was going to faint.

"Hey," she breathed, eyes going down to the bow in my hand. She raised her brow.

I cleared my throat. "Silas in there?"

"No, he went to talk to Torrin earlier. I'm not sure where he is now."

My lips curved into a half-grin. "Can I come in?"

Color stained her cheeks. "I'm not sure that's a good—"

I strode forward anyway, and she stepped aside, rolling her eyes. "What's the point of asking if you're going to do what you want anyway?"

"To be polite," I replied, placing the bow in the corner of the room against the wall.

"Why'd you bring that?" She stepped forward and crossed her arms over her chest.

"I'm giving it to you."

Her mouth dropped open. "What? Why?"

"Lena brought me back a crossbow, remember? I figured you could benefit from my bow since I'll be using the new weapon."

She clicked her tongue. "Figures you'd give me the old model."

"Now, now," I smirked. "Don't be ungrateful."

She laughed softly, focusing her gaze on her new bow. "Does it still shoot ice arrows?"

"Yup. So long as I charge it, anyway."

Her smile slowly faded. "Thank you, Merrick...that is so kind."

The tension in this room, our locked gazes...it set my skin ablaze.

She was so beautiful.

"Anything for you," I murmured.

Her cheeks became redder, her eyes dipping to my lips, trailing along my jaw, along my body.

"If you really meant that," she whispered, her lips curving into a smile, "you'd give me your new bow."

I chuckled, my eyes greedily taking her in, fixated on those long, tanned legs. "So unappreciative."

Her smile turned playful. "I am oh so appreciative of the out-of-date model."

"Smartass," I muttered, my eyes playfully flicking up to meet hers.

She swallowed, skittishly tucking her hair behind her ear. Her eyes darted to the door, her nerves bleeding into mine.

She was anxious about Silas returning with me still in her room.

I crept closer to her, and she released a breath, stumbling back a step.

I halted.

"I-I'm sorry..." she began, then shook her head.

I stepped forward again, and she retreated, eyes pleading.

"I can't, Merrick," she whispered.

Another step forward. "Can't what?" I asked, my voice low.

She backed up again, finding her back against the door. She angled her face upward, panting as she stared at me.

Her desire flooded through me, heightening mine to the point I was breathing heavily, too.

"You...you should go," she whispered.

I tilted my head to the side, leaning in close. My lips brushed the shell of her ear as I murmured, "You're the one blocking the door."

Her eyes fluttered shut, goosebumps spreading across her bronzed skin. Her nipples were begging for my attention, hardened under that dark shirt.

I raised my hand, my movement languid as I caressed her cheek, dragging my thumb along that plump bottom lip of hers.

Her eyes were heavy when she opened them, and desire ruled her. She propelled forward, pressing her lips against mine.

My heart raced, and my hand slipped from her cheek to grasp her waist. Our mouths parted this time, and as my tongue slid against hers, she moaned softly into my mouth.

She tasted like heaven, like strawberries and cream. I knew then I was addicted—no going back. I wanted to taste her daily...taste other places.

I pressed into her, deepening our kiss just as Erabella's hands weaved into my hair. I trailed mine lower, my hand grasping her breast, and she jerked back, her lips vacating mine.

"Merrick—no...I can't," she gasped.

Her hands were still tangled in my hair.

I released her breast, my hand sliding to her waist to join the other. My breathing became labored, our lips still hovering over one another.

"I'm sorry." I winced. "I'm finding it difficult to keep my hands away from you."

Her eyes dropped to my lips, then back. Again and again, her mind battled between right and wrong. Want and need. Loyalty and infidelity.

"I've never felt so strongly for someone, never have felt *want* quite like this before," I admitted breathlessly. I wanted to kiss her again, but I left that decision up to her.

Her right hand slid out of my hair, gently cupping my cheek as she gazed up at me. "What do you feel when you read me?"

I had been reading her this entire time. "Desire. Fear. Guilt."

She wet her lips, her thumb now tracing over my lip ring. "That's all?"

I knew what other emotion she was asking about, but I didn't want to acknowledge it.

Her voice was small as she asked, "Do you feel it for me?"

Yes, of course I do!

I wanted to scream it, shout it to everyone I knew. But that emotion...

"It frightens me," I answered honestly.

Her eyes welled with tears, and she nodded slowly. "Me too," she said quietly. "Mostly because...because..."

Guilt hit her so hard that I wrapped my arms around her, holding her tight. She broke down into my chest, desire fading as the other emotions took precedence.

"Don't cry," I whispered, my own lip wobbling from her emotions overtaking mine. "I'm sorry...I don't wish to hurt you."

She cried harder, fisting my robe's fabric into her hands.

"I'm...I'm so confused," she sobbed loudly.

"Hey." I pulled back, holding her crumpling face in my hands. Tears streamed down my cheeks—tears from her emotions, not my own. "Don't blame yourself. It's my fault. I came here. I initiated."

She went to shake her head, looking away, but I dragged her focus back to me.

"Era—"

"I shouldn't feel this way," she whispered. "I'm married. I-I shouldn't...I can't..."

Anger washed over me, knowing she felt this guilt when her husband desired another, a desire that surpassed what she felt for me.

"Who says you shouldn't?" I challenged. "You married him without even knowing him. Is it such a surprise it isn't working out?"

She swallowed, and her offense took me aback. She hauled her hands away, crossing her arms. "Get out."

I sighed, pulling back and rubbing my forehead. "Era—"

"I said get out!" she yelled, hurrying away from the door. "I-I don't want this. I don't want *you*."

I swallowed, my heart shattering as I turned to her. My eyes skated between hers, waiting for her to change her mind, but she didn't.

I laughed humorlessly through my nose, then stormed out, despite knowing those last words were a lie.

I stomped back into my room just as Viola was exiting the shower, her braids up and in a bun on top of her head, a towel secured around her torso. "Everything okay?" she asked, noticing my irate demeanor.

I sighed, flinging my robe off, my pants and boots the only thing underneath.

Gods, I was frustrated.

Why couldn't Viola feel the way Era did for me? Why didn't she have that overwhelming lust when she stared into my eyes?

Viola was stunning—perfect in every regard. We'd been friends for years. I'd die for her. But emotionally, I wasn't connected to her like I was with Era.

Perhaps I would have been had she not made it clear we were fuck buddies and nothing more.

"I'm fine. Just tired," I fibbed, sitting on the bed and undoing my boots.

"I feel that." She plopped herself down next to me on the mattress. "Better rest up. It's our last evening before being on the road again."

I tossed my boot on the floor, unlacing the other one. "Good idea," I grumbled.

She didn't initiate anything sexual that night, and I was grateful for it.

I felt her before she even reached my door. My heart felt like it was being torn out of my chest, causing me to jolt up in the bed.

"W-what's wrong?" Vi asked groggily, rubbing her eyes as she shot up.

I clutched my chest, squeezing my eyes shut as I attempted to shut out the feelings.

This had been happening more. Other's feelings bleeding into my own without me tuning into my gift...but why?

Viola gripped my shoulder, her violet eyes trailing over me with concern before a knock at our door caused her attention to shift.

I knew who it was. Could feel it. I shuffled out of the bedsheets, grasped the bronze door handle, and opened it to see Lena.

Her big, green eyes were bloodshot, tears trailing down her cheeks. Her lip trembled as she clutched ***Potestas Verae Maleficis***.

"Lena," I whispered, and I felt my own eyes well with tears.

"I need your help, Merrick," she cried softly.

I didn't know what she meant. My brows drew together just as Viola reached my side, her eyes enlarging as she took in our friend's broken form.

"What happened?" Vi pressed. "Are you alright?"

But Lena's eyes remained on mine, and in those moments of silence, I understood. I knew this had something to do with Silas and knew I couldn't say anything.

"Come in," I said gently, stepping aside.

She gave a thankful nod, eyes going to the grimoire in her arms as she entered our room. Fingering through the pages, she opened it up to a spell called *Oblivisci.*

"Here," she sniffled.

My head shot up from the page when I realized what this spell was for. "You want to erase your memories?"

She nodded, and I shook my head in protest.

"That's just ludicrous, Lena. You *need* to remem—"

My eyes darted to Viola and back to Lena. Unspoken words were exchanged within our gazes, words I couldn't say around our friend.

"I won't forget it all," she said quietly. "Just what hurts. I can't be the best leader if I am haunted by..."

Viola's frown deepened, and she looked to me for answers. I couldn't give them.

"Vi, can you give Lena and me some privacy? Just for a few?"

Viola slowly nodded, and I stared at the pages as she quickly got dressed and left, not before Lena blurted out to her, "Actually, can you bring me Dani?"

The bars were still booming, and I could hear the ruckus even from here. If it were Era going out now, all alone, I'd be nervous. But

Viola could rip off someone's head. She could take care of herself amongst predators.

Viola responded, "Of course."

Once the door was closed, Lena knelt on the ground. "We first have to draw this symbol on the floor," her voice wobbled, fetching chalk that was tucked into her bra. She motioned for me to hand over the book, and I obliged.

"I'll stand in it once it's done. We chant **Oblivisci** together and focus our illusion magic on the symbols."

"If you're having Vi get Dani, why do you even need me?"

Lena's slim finger brushed the page and pointed to a specific text. "The spell castor must also know the memory that's to be forgotten. Be thinking of it."

And that's when she told me everything. Told me of memories of her and Silas's romance when they were young. Told me of their encounter in the tent. Told me of their encounter tonight.

"I know what you must be thinking of me...that I am a terrible person."

Knowing my resentment toward my father was left unsaid. Vicsin was unfaithful to my mother, and it destroyed her.

I studied her, still trying to process it all. I felt my own anger, anger toward the situation, anger for Era. Even though I had kissed her, she was truly innocent in all of this.

But damn this gift, because I felt everything Lena did, too. I felt her shame. I felt her heartbreak. I felt her love for Silas, just as I had felt his love for her.

This situation wasn't simple. It wasn't black and white. Still, if I could help her forget, perhaps removing the temptation would help her heal. Help her focus.

Vi returned with Dani a few moments later. The Warlock's blue gaze found Lena's, her brows scrunching together.

"I just want to ensure Merrick does this spell properly." Lena sniffed, handing Dani **Potestas Verae Maleficis**.

Her eyes shot wide, her gaze lifting to Lena. "Can I speak with Lena alone?"

"Pretty sure you can say anything around me," I commented, toying with my piercing.

Lena nodded. "Merrick stays."

Viola groaned, throwing her arms up. "Really? I have to leave *again*?"

"I'll come fetch you right after, babe," Dani replied with a lazy smile.

I narrowed my eyes at her little nickname just as Vi rolled her own, exiting the room once more.

"So..." Dani drawled after the door shut, her eyebrow raised at Lena. "I can say *anything* in front of Merrick?"

"He knows everything about me," Lena insisted. "He's always safe."

I felt warmth bloom in my chest from her comment, and Dani hesitantly lifted her eyes to mine before focusing on Lena again. "Why is it you want to erase your memories? *Which* memories?"

"Memories that are holding me back...distracting me."

Dani's eyes constricted. "Is this about the Prince?"

Mine and Lena's eyes flared, shooting at each other. Lena scoffed, attempting to play it off. "What are you talking about?"

Dani rolled her eyes. "You and Silas are both terrible liars." She plopped the book on the nightstand beside the bed and crossed her arms. "Let's just say I'm an excellent reader of vibes and can tell who it is people are truly desiring." Her eyes slid to mine, and she gave me a knowing, fleeting look.

What the hell does she mean by that?

Before I could think more about it, she diverted her attention to Lena. "Look, clearly whatever happened tonight has both you and the Prince shaken up. I don't think it's healthy to go down this route."

Lena's lip curled. "I am not asking for your advice," she damn near snarled.

The corners of Dani's eyes tightened, and I added gently, "There's a lot you don't know."

Dani propped a hand on her hip. "So, tell me."

"This spell doesn't last forever," Lena groused. "It can be undone. Why are you making this so difficult?"

"How do you think he'll feel if you do this?" Dani challenged.

"He didn't care how he made *me* feel when he fucked me and proceeded to tell me how he loathed me. How I have destroyed him."

Color stained Dani's cheeks, her jaw falling open.

"I shouldn't have done it," Lena whispered with broken rage. "It was a mistake. I know that. I just...I need to focus on saving my people. Not on this. Not on him."

Dani blinked over and over before her mouth snapped shut, and she nodded gravely. Opening up **Potestas Verae Maleficis**, she flipped to the page with the necessary spell.

"This spell needs maintenance, meaning the spellcaster will need to repeat it every so often. That's why the person performing it must also know of the memories wishing to be banished—to keep them away."

"A magical tether is not enough," Lena mumbled.

Dani's eyes remained scanning the page. "That's correct. Merrick will have to repeat this with you every month."

CHAPTER FIFTY-FIVE

LENA

I stood in the pentagram I had sketched, heart racing, a pit in my stomach.

Merrick stood before me, just outside the circle, and Dani was off to the side, still looking at me like this was a mistake.

Merrick's dark eyes focused on me, and I could tell by his lack of persuasion that he felt exactly what I did and understood why I wanted to forget. Even if only for a little while.

Writing in the Titharan language, I spelled out Silas's name—spelled out how I wished to forget every romantic interaction.

My heart pulsed in my chest, anticipating what it would be like. I had fixated on the tan-skinned, golden-eyed man since the very first day I saw him. His witty remarks, his lazy smile, his care. I went from misery, feeling like my existence had no purpose, to actually looking forward to waking in the morning once he entered my life.

I thought of my best friend, of training, and I was grateful at least those memories would stay.

Picturing a version of me that wasn't haunted by our past, of what might have been, felt impossible. Felt dangerous. But I had a purpose outside of him now.

And it needed my focus.

"Say the word and think of the memories. Hold your hands toward the pentagram, Merrick, and release your illusion magic, thinking of the same memories," Dani instructed.

"What if I don't think every single one?" Merrick asked anxiously.

"You're more so here as her tether," Dani explained. "And to be the person who has the knowledge when her memories start to resurface. It'll be necessary when you need to perform it again. Now do it."

We obeyed.

Oblivisci.

Oblivisci.

Oblivisci.

I squeezed my eyes shut, lip trembling, eyes flooding.

I thought of his witty remarks, our banter causing my chest to flutter.

I pictured the moment he dragged his tongue along my lips, licking up the icing from the cinnamon roll he bought me.

I pictured us in Amethyst Pond, the moment his arms went around me, the moment his lips touched mine for the first time.

I pictured our kiss, our hands nervously exploring each other's bodies.

I cried harder.

Oblivisci.

Oblivisci.

Oblivisci.

I pictured us making love the first time, how sweet and gentle he was with me, and pictured all the times after: at my home, in the forest, in the castle. So many times we found ourselves tangled with one another, hearts thundering against our pressed chests.

I pictured him telling me he loved me, kissing my face repeatedly, revealing how much he cherished my existence.

I heard his voice, his flirty words, him calling me Flower. It all felt like a dream, fuzzy and fading.

I felt myself slipping...as If I was about to fall into a deep sleep.

Oblivisci.

Oblivisci.

Oblivisci.

The pentagram began losing its glow, and as the spell reached completion, all those memories, all that pain...

It was all gone.

I woke up feeling slightly refreshed, but when I glanced out the window of my room while packing up my belongings, a heaviness filled my chest.

So many lives lost.

The Mages in captivity had been freed, but still, there was so much uncertainty. Indeed, there would be an uprising at some point. The human citizens of this kingdom couldn't erase their hate or prejudices over the course of a few days.

Fortunately, Torrin had a close relationship with Deana, the Mage taking leadership here. I trusted his judgment—trusted her—seeing how well she handled her fire when she acquired it.

We were preparing to move on to our last territory, Wrendier. I was thankful Dimitri hadn't destroyed our stuff and even more grateful our horses were left unharmed.

My eyes scrunched as I folded up my clothes. Last night was a total blur. I didn't even remember coming to my room and getting in bed. Perhaps all this violence was shrouding my memory.

Slinging my bag over my shoulder after securing my enchanted blade against my back, I left my room, sighing when I accepted it would be another handful of days before I could rest in an actual bed again.

Elowen and Edmund were leaving their room at the same time, and the healer gave me a gentle smile. She sure seemed more upbeat today compared to a few days ago.

I wondered who else was aware of her new ability.

I returned the smile just as Silas and Erabella left their room, all dressed and ready for our next journey. I noticed his eyes widen on me.

I narrowed my stare for a moment before looking away and striding forward.

Do I have something on my face? I didn't notice anything in the mirror earlier...

I heard hurried steps behind me, and as we all made it out the castle's front doors, a hand gripped my shoulder.

I rotated my head, noticing Silas's worried gaze as he held his hand in place.

Era, Elowen, and Edmund continued forward, the rest of our group just steps away, readying their rides. Merrick and Dani were staring at us, the former's eyes dark as night, the latter nervously chewing his lip.

Why is everyone being so weird today?

My frown deepened as I turned my attention back to the Prince. "Um...what's up?"

He leaned down, his lips by my ear and his voice above a whisper. "I returned to your room last night. Where did you go?"

My brows drew together, blinking rapidly. What did he mean he came back to my room?

I couldn't remember much after I returned from Mount Rozavar. The magic usage must've knocked me out.

"Uh, I was probably asleep?"

His golden gaze hardened on mine. "You were not asleep," he growled. "I opened your door. You weren't in your room."

I could see out of the corner of my eye Dani pinching the bridge of his nose, shaking his head.

"Well, I woke up in my bed, so I don't know where else I could've been."

"We goin' or what, boss man?" Roland hollered.

Silas paid him no mind, his hardened gaze softening. "I came to say I was sorry," he whispered.

Okay, now I was really confused. I wracked my brain for something, anything that he would be apologizing for. I was coming up empty-handed.

"Whatever for?"

He drew back. "You know what for, Lena," he snapped.

"Okay," Dani interrupted, wrapping his arm around my shoulders and pulling me away. "Time to hit the road, Prince and Supreme."

My perplexed expression shifted to Dani, and he continued leading me away.

"I forgot to mention you need to replace the old with new. Otherwise, you'll have gaps in your memory." He cringed. "Sorry, we can reconfigure next month."

"What the fuck are you talking about?" I hissed.

"Nothing." Dani withdrew his arms. We had taken a new horse from the kingdom reserve, so now Hendry and Dani shared a horse, Torrin riding on one alone. I debated joining him on his, but he needed space from me.

I flushed thinking about our night, then hopped on Donut, seating myself in front of Roland.

Deana strolled out, a handful of Mage guards protecting her. Her skin was already gaining back color after years of abuse.

"I wish you well on your travels," she said, the guards stepping forward, handing us pouches. "There is silver in there, along with extra herbs and salves. In case you find yourself needing any."

Silas smiled at her. "Thank you, Deana. We wish you well in rebuilding this place. I know you will do a grand job."

She inclined her head, her cheeks staining pink. "If you ever need to come back, you are more than welcome." Her eyes scanned our group. "All of you."

"Do let us know if you locate those mushrooms," Silas added. I had heard through the grape-vine that Silas, Hendry, and Roland had successfully tortured the information out of Dimitri—the source of the poison we saw used in Forsmont. Siaxcide. Well, one of its major ingredients, anyway.

"It's of my main priorites. I won't let you down," she promised.

With our final goodbyes, accepting the gifts from the newly appointed Supreme, we trekked out of Faltrun.

Two kingdoms secured. One to go.

CHAPTER FIFTY-SIX

SILAS

L ena was behaving...oddly. Perhaps it was an attempt to play things off.

Guilt consumed me every time I looked at Era or held her against me. It was wrong to be unfaithful to her. The only thing I kept telling myself was, '*Pretend like it was one more time you made love to Lena in the past,*' though I knew it wasn't the same.

And I couldn't get her out of my damned mind.

I loved Era, and I knew she loved me. But our relationship had started out as a mutual benefit. I was required to get married. It was difficult enough putting it off as long as I did, and Era needed an escape from her shitty family.

I had grown to love her, but it was never like what I had with Lena. Had I known she was alive, I never would have touched another female.

All the Mages, along with Dani, were glamoured again—rounded ears and, in Dani's case, eyes with pupils. Lena's long hair was kept in a braid that was resting on her chest.

I couldn't help but stare at her from the side and note the ease on her face. How was what we had done not eating her alive? Not just the guilt, but the overwhelming desire for more?

I couldn't keep my hand off myself when I showered this morning, biting my lip to contain my moan as I stroked myself to the thought of her naked body and the faces she made while I was driving myself inside of her.

I am a wretched man.

My arms were around my wife's, holding the reins of our horse as we headed for Wrendier. After spending my last moments at Saoirse's grave, we left. Torrin had mentioned how one of the ancient temples was on our way—Temple Celluna—and that it would be a good place to take a break.

Every night that passed until we got there drove me mad. Lena continued to ignore me, hardly even flitting her eyes in my direction. The only bit of peace I had was that she remained in her own tent, not sharing one with either Roland or Torrin.

I didn't initiate with Era, and surprisingly, she didn't initiate anything with me. Just a few soft kisses every night before falling asleep.

Temple Celluna was unlike anything I had ever seen. The white, concrete building was enormous, the very top shaped like a dome. In its intricate design, thousands upon thousands of flowers and leaves were etched into the material. It was miraculous. It had to have taken years to complete.

It had been five days since we left Faltrun, and by some miracle, it had been an easy, danger-free trek.

"Each of the temples has nine points...nine exits," Elowen began.

Lena loosened a breath. "Nine points...for nine Gods."

Elowen's head was craned, studying the architecture just as Dani spoke. "I never knew why each temple was designed in such a way. Now, it makes sense."

"Who runs these temples?" Hendry asked Dani, who sat in front of him.

"Human clerics," she responded. "As I'm sure you all know, humans worship the same Gods we do...same names and all that. They just believe the Gods had no hand in creating us magic folk...that we are abominations. Anomalies."

"Sounds like a great place for us to visit," Merrick drawled with a fake smile. Era turned her head, smiling at his humor.

"Why are they constructed in such a way, then?" Erabella asked. "The nine pillars..."

"These temples were constructed hundreds, if not thousands of years ago," Viola answered, "when our kinds coexisted. It is only in the recent centuries that humans have shifted their beliefs."

"Will we even be welcomed here?" Hendry narrowed his eyes as we were getting closer. "What if they have grown corrupt?"

Dani shrugged. "Then we kick their asses. I dunno."

Roland chuckled. "Can you imagine? Fighting clerics? That just sounds wrong."

As we approached the looming building, the summer sun beaming down on us, no one came out or attempted to stop us from getting closer.

"It's quiet," Lena noted, those stunning eyes searching.

We halted our horses before one of the nine entrances. Pausing for a few moments, and still no sign of life, we hesitantly dismounted our rides.

"Now, be a good little horse for us, Donut, and wait out here," Roland cooed as he stroked his horse's mane.

We all hiked up the many steps leading up to the temple, and as we reached the entrance, Lena began to step in. I instantly tugged at her arm. "Hey, we don't know if there are any traps."

"This place feels...right," she said, slowly staring up at me. "You don't feel anything off, do you?"

I shook my head, releasing her from my grasp and whispering, "No, but that doesn't mean regular enemies don't reside here."

She smiled, and the sight sent my heart racing. "I think we could take any other enemy."

I swallowed, and before she could take the first step inside, I did.

And my shoulders slumped at the sight.

Clerics lay mangled and deceased, their blood splattered against the marble interiors. Black swirled against their flesh, and I knew instantly that the Lord of the Shadows was responsible.

The rest of my friends filtered in, all gasping, covering their noses. This battle had been brutal, and judging by the state of these bodies, it had to have occurred a few weeks ago. The smell was revolting enough to make your eyes water.

"Bloody hell," Dani gasped. "What a mess."

Elowen gagged, and Edmund grasped her shoulders, leading her back outside.

"We should survey the space," Lena said, wincing as she held her hand under her nose. "The necromancer must've been searching for the Weapon here...or looking for answers of some sort."

"Or he is just a sick fuck and enjoys harming others," Merrick replied.

"I agree with Lena," Torrin interjected, eyes trailing upward. "The sanctuary is at the top of this building. I believe the stairs circling upward lead to it." His eyes scanned the surroundings before noticing a set of double doors. "My guess is that leads downward—to the altar room."

"I'll search the sanctuary," Lena offered.

Before Torrin could offer, I said, "I'll go with you."

Lena gave a simple nod, and I noted a feathering in Torrin's jaw. "Fine." His eyes slid to his cousin. "Merrick, you come with me. We'll check out the altar room."

"What about the rest of us?" Dani asked.

Lena turned to the Warlock. "I was thinking that you and Vi scout Wrendier. Considering it is only a day away, I figured you two could fly...see if the kingdom seems anything like Faltrun." She swallowed, her fingers brushing her collarbones. I noticed she did that anytime she was nervous. "For all we know, Ulric could've joined forces with them, as well. I don't want to go through what we did again. We need the upper hand."

Dani nodded. "In an eagle form, we could probably reach the kingdom in five hours and be back another five after that." The Warlock glanced at Viola. "You up for that?"

Viola's full lips pulled into fake consideration. "Let me think, stay in this eerie temple, or soar the skies..." She grinned. "Of course, I'm up for it."

I smiled at her. She was wearing the silver hair rings I purchased for her. They looked badass and beautiful at the same time wrapped around her braids.

"Hendry and Roland, you two keep watch with Elowen and Edmund." I glanced at my wife and at the bow and quiver secured at her back. "You too. Stay close to Hendry."

She nodded, and the men obeyed. As Torrin and Merrick headed for the altar room, Viola and Dani shifting and soaring into the sky, I followed Lena up the marble steps.

She was silent, eyes darting to and from each body that littered the steps. Blessedly, as we ascended, the smell grew less and less pungent.

"I have a question for you," she asked, and my pulse picked up. She angled her head toward me as we continued up the steps. "What do you know of your mother's father, Ramiel?"

My brows lowered. I wasn't expecting that to be the topic of discussion. "Not much. I never met him."

She sighed. "Damn."

"Why do you ask? And how did you know his name?"

"Do you remember your favorite painting? The one in the art gallery in your castle?"

I nodded slowly, unsure where this conversation was going. "How do you know my favorite painting?"

She frowned. "I...your mother told me." Gears appeared to be turning in her mind, but she shook her head. "Anyway, I remembered the painting title." Her green gaze slid to me. "Rebirth."

My brows drew together. "As in the God of Rebirth?"

"I think so." She focused on the steps before us; there was still a ways to go before we reached the top. "Your mother had told me her father had it commissioned in Faltrun. Well, when I was investigating the art shop in town, I saw that it had a sister painting titled Purification."

I swore.

"I know," she agreed. "The crazy part? Your mother's father titled the paintings and came up with the descriptions." She was a few steps ahead of me when she halted, turning to face me. "It makes no sense. Why did Ramiel commission paintings that reference two of the new Gods? Why are those new Gods symbolized in the Otacian crest?"

My eyes flicked between hers. "I wish I knew."

She chewed on her lip, eyes dropping. "Asael Nefeli is the name of the painter. Apparently, Ramiel came back to Faltrun last year and said something that had Asael fleeing to Halsted and becoming a part of their army." Her eyes flicked back to me. "And apparently, he told him to...to save me."

Goosebumps spread across my skin. "Save you? From what?"

"Hell, if I know." She turned, continuing up the steps, boots clicking as they touched each one. "I don't know how Ramiel knew of me...unless your Mother told him of me, told him my name."

"But why would she think you in danger? Other than at the time, the obvious."

Lena stopped again. She looked over her shoulder. "What do you mean, the obvious? She didn't know I was a Mage."

"I know. But she knew of our relationship, one that would not be accepted."

Her brows drew together, eyes going to the floor before she resumed walking.

"No matter, it doesn't make sense for her to tell her father about it, especially if the man wasn't really present in her life. Where does she hail from, by the way?"

"Eretesia. I'd assume my grandfather still resides there."

It was quiet between us for a minute. "Your mother was a good woman. Perhaps her father, too, disagreed with the treatment of my kind. Perhaps he, too, was a witch sympathizer."

"Doubtful he remained one, considering how she was killed," I muttered bitterly, feeling a little winded after walking up so many steps despite how fit I was. When we finally reached the pronaos, thankfully clear of bodies, I grasped her hand.

She stilled, nervous eyes flitting up to mine.

"We need to talk about last night."

Swallowing, she pulled her hand away. "There are more pressing matters, Silas, than where I was. Why do you even care?"

I ran a frustrated hand through my hair, then let out a dry laugh. "Are you really asking me that?" I dropped my hand, stepped closer, and backed her into the hallway's wall. I closed in, placing my palms on the concrete on either side of her head.

"I shouldn't have reacted that way afterward." I acknowledged gently. "I shouldn't have left you in tears. I don't loathe you, not at all, Lena. I loathe the situation we are in. I loathe how I feel because it would be so much easier to feel nothing for you at all."

Her eyes turned to saucers. "S-Silas...what are you—"

"I love you so damn much," I breathed, my face falling. "It *kills* me not being able to have you. It kills me to think that could be the last time I ever make love to you and that I left you in such a way afterward."

I'd never seen such widened eyes on Lena's face. Her head slowly shook back and forth. "I...what...when—"

"You don't have to say anything." I pushed off the wall, stepping back. "I just...I'm sorry, Lena."

I sighed through my nose, head falling, and ambled toward the Sanctuary.

CHAPTER FIFTY-SEVEN

MERRICK

I was a ball of unreleased nerves as Torrin and I began our descent underneath this temple, Torrin's fire hovering over his palm our only source of light. The temperature dropped with every step, and I feared what we'd discover down here.

This was Celluna's temple, the Goddess of Love, but who knew what sacrifices had been made in their altar room?

Admittedly, I didn't know much about the Gods, just the basic stuff most people knew. Elowen was always far more intrigued by it all.

My nerves were also running rampant at the idea of Silas and Lena alone, considering the Prince was bound to discover what we did and probably try to kill me for it.

Torrin came to an abrupt stop, whirling around to me.

Shit!

I slapped my palm on my forehead. I forgot my mind-reading cousin was right beside me.

"What the hell did you do?" he demanded. "What happened?"

I winced, scrubbing at my face. "Lena came to my room the last night in Faltrun...hysterical."

"What happened?"

"I don't think it's my business to say—"

Torrin gripped my robe, slamming me against the concrete wall. "What happened, Merrick?!"

"Fucking hell!" I shouted. "You and Silas are two peas in a pod, throwing people against walls when you're angry!"

His grip lessened, but he still held me. "Tell me, Merrick," he pleaded.

"You know of her past with Silas."

He shook his head, not understanding.

My shoulders slumped. "They...they had sex."

His eyes sprang open just as he loosened a breath. He released the fabric of my robe, stumbling back and clenching his trembling fists.

His rage—his jealousy—overtook me.

"Torrin...I had no idea you felt so strongly for her," I whispered.

"It doesn't matter," he muttered, turning away to tread down the steps.

I staggered forward. "She had me erase her memories."

He halted.

"You did what?" he asked quietly.

"She begged me to. It's not permanent, but she remembers no romantic interactions with him whatsoever."

He whirled at me; his rage had never been more apparent. "How could you do that, Merrick? What the hell were you thinking?!"

I stood my ground. "You may be able to read her mind," I said in a hushed tone, "but I'm the one who felt everything. I felt *all* of her suffering. I knew how unbearable it was for her. I wanted to help."

"Erasing memories is not helpful! She needs to learn to work through it, not run from it."

"I'm surprised this is something you don't want," I commented, and a surge of anger went through him. "Without her tie to him, you and she—"

"This isn't about my wants."

"It never is!" I cried. "I cannot think of a single instance where you have acted selfishly. Why not try?"

"What, should I act on selfish impulse like you?"

I froze, eyes narrowing. "What's that supposed to mean?"

"You think I don't know?" He scoffed. "I've heard your thoughts, Merrick. Hear your inner battle. You desire the Prince's wife."

I clenched my teeth together, shaking my head. "No, I don't," I lied.

Another scoff. "You kissed her, and you say you don't want her?"

"I gave no permission for you to raid my mind!" I yelled. "How dare you!"

Torrin shrugged. "Is it any different than you reading my emotions?"

"It's completely different! Reading thoughts is far more an invasion of privacy."

Torrin's jaw clicked before he said softly, "I'm surprised you did it."

"Did what?"

"Took her memories. If she and Silas got back together, that would leave the Princess for you."

"Believe it or not, Torrin, you're not the only Brighthell to act selflessly," I uttered quietly.

"Then you understand my actions," he said simply as we strode down more steps. "I would want Lena to choose me regardless, not just when she couldn't remember her love for a different man. But she wouldn't...because it's Silas who she wants. Now, and always." He swallowed. "At least Erabella returns the feeling."

I almost tumbled down the stairs. "What did you say?"

"She's attracted to you, that's for sure. She doesn't want to be but can't help herself. She ponders on that kiss more than you do, and that's saying a lot." Torrin turned for the last time. "We have more pressing matters than discussing our messy love lives."

"We've missed a year of cousin bonding."

He cocked a brow at me. "And cousin fighting."

A grin took over my face. "Yeah...and I missed both."

It took ten more minutes until we reached the bottom of the stairs. A single black door stood before us.

"I'll go in first. You cover me," Torrin ordered.

"I hate this creepy shit," I muttered. I withdrew my crossbow, still getting used to the new weapon, and followed Torrin as he slowly pushed the door open. The creaking sound caused the hair on the back of my neck to rise.

Holding his flame, we crept into the eerie space.

The first thing I noticed was the heavy metallic odor. The second was piles of bodies stacked on either side of the room, inky swirls covering their skin.

"Fuck," Torrin grimaced, covering his nose with his elbow.

As we walked a few steps forward, Torrin's fire illuminated someone kneeling before the altar.

Dead bodies were slumped against the walls, lying in the middle of the ground, yet one remained kneeling.

"Miss?" Torrin asked, slowly creeping ahead. "Are you alright?"

Slowly, the woman's head craned back toward us.

Torrin's flame reflected off her solid black eyes, and she smiled.

CHAPTER FIFTY-EIGHT

LENA

My limbs were trembling as I watched Silas wander off into the Sanctuary, a look of utter defeat etched on his face.

I had never been more bewildered in my life.

I love you so damn much.

What the hell was he talking about? Had our minuscule interactions made him desire me?

My heart sped up at the thought of his proximity just moments ago. He was a handsome man; there was no doubt about that. So much so that I was surprised I wasn't attracted to him when we were younger.

"Lena, you need to see this."

His smoky tone unnerved me. Why had I not noticed how pleasant his voice was?

Ambling into the sanctuary, I first let out a breath at its beauty and the pleasant breeze that blew through the opened windows. The mid-day sun filtered through, and rows of benches were placed on either side of a walkway that led up to a pedestal. But when observing the large walls surrounding the massive window behind said pedestal, I realized what it was Silas wanted me to see.

Sprinting forward, running my hands along the concrete, I studied the symbols etched into the wall.

Not just any symbols. It was the Titharan language.

I fetched out **Potestas Verae Maleficis,** hoping to translate. Getting on my knees, I began scribbling my chalk on the ground.

"Rebirth and Purification will fuse, thus creating the first-ever *Realm Travelers,*" Silas read out loud after I completed the first sentence. "You said Oquerene was a different realm, yes?"

"Correct, but..." My eyes frantically darted up and down from **Potestas Verae Maleficis** to the wall, back to my shaking hand. It took a few minutes, but I finished writing out the words.

An Azraeian portal will no longer be the only way. Not two Gods, but two Travelers. They will ensure Deceit's containment.

That dark feeling rushed over me just as a voice boomed, "There's a rift."

I jolted, the chalk flying from my hand. Silas and I whirled around, his sword drawn and my fire flaring as we caught Vicsin sauntering forward, tilting his head as he examined us.

"Learning more about the prophecy, I see," his mixed voice noted.

I lifted my chin. "The Lord of the Shadows, I presume?" I asked sweetly. "You left quite a mess downstairs."

His grin grew, my pulse quickening at his vulgar appearance. I would never grow used to those dark eyes, the inky veins swirling around his lifeless skin, or that symbol etched onto his forehead. "Oh, you have no idea."

I stood, my flame still creeping up my limbs. "What do you mean 'a rift'?"

He tilted his head further, cracking his neck with his hand. "Death's sin did more than just initiate the creation of new Gods," he answered, his voice blending with Vicsin's. "But with the potential fusing of Rebirth and Purification, we risk the creation of the Travelers. There has already been a disruption in our dimension's rift from Azrae, focusing his energy on keeping the Gods away. Less energy being put toward keeping the rift closed has caused our world to be tainted—not just realms within our dimension, but others."

"What the hell are you talking about?" Silas asked lowly. "What makes you believe such things?"

Vicsin released a grating laugh. "Isn't it obvious? There are so many ways our society is advanced, yet there are so many ways we are behind." He strolled forward, hands going behind his back as he stepped around us, moving toward the engravings, chuckling at my translation on the floor. "We have drinks and foods and activities, even clothes and music, that have bled through the rift."

I snorted, replying sarcastically. "What, lacy panties are getting thrown in from the other side?"

The necromancer did not appreciate my humor. "More like the ideas are being planted in our heads—ideas superseding the standard order of evolution. But, occasionally, yes. Something from another dimension finds its way here." He lifted something out of his jacket pocket, raising a brow at me. "Drop this, and I kill one of your friends."

My stomach sank as he chucked something at me. Catching it against my chest, I stared down at the rectangle in my hands.

Lifting it away, I released a gasp when the front of it lit up.

It was a picture of some sort—something captured in time. A woman with golden hair and haunted hazel eyes sat, and in her arms were a young boy and a girl—her children, it seemed. All had rounded ears.

Their clothes were different than what we wore. Blander.

A white bubble appeared just as I was staring at the strange device.

> **Dela: Did u make it home last night? I'm so sorry I dipped…I feel so bad. But OMG mister was packing. 10/10. Pleaseeee forgive me.**

> **Dela: Hopefully you got some too(; You deserve it, Daisy.**

> **Dela: Pick up the phone, bitch!! What on Earth are you doing that's more important than talking to your best friend?**

"What the hell is this?" Silas breathed, viewing the device from over my shoulder.

I touched its glass top, and the words *Enter Passcode* and a number of buttons replaced the messages.

Vicsin stepped closer, holding his hand out for the device. I hesitantly gave it back.

"Something from *Earth*, I'd presume," he answered, solid black eyes focused on the rectangle. His head tilted up. "But don't you see? Their language is the same as ours. They look like us...but don't."

"Why do you care?" Silas bit out. "Isn't your goal world hegemony or some shit like that?"

"I'm a curious man. What can I say?" He tucked the device—the phone, I'm guessing it's called—back into his jacket pocket. "Can you imagine what power and knowledge these other worlds possess? What from our world has bled into theirs?"

My brows lowered. "I find it hard to believe you'd want that power for anything good," I said simply.

The corner of Vicsin's lip turned upward. "Good is complacent. Right and wrong are limiting."

This man was fucking insane. I could take him out right now and provide Vicsin's body peace, but the necromancer wasn't attacking. I didn't wish to provoke him.

"Where did you find that device?"

"Where is the Weapon?" he countered.

I sighed, knowing he didn't plan on giving me any answers. I decided to try a different route. "You mentioned Valor's sin. Do you know what he did to cause all of this?"

Vicsin tilted his head back. "He fell in love with a mortal woman. Bred with her, thus resulting in the God of Deceit." His smile morphed, growing sinister. "Thus, resulting in me."

I swallowed my nerves, not wanting to alert him of my fear. "The God of Deceit created you?"

He scoffed. "Don't you get it, darling?" He placed a palm on his chest. "I *am* the God of Deceit."

Silas breathed in sharply as I whispered, "Valor is your father?"

"By blood, yes. Though he was not the one who raised me." His head tilted to the ancient text etched into the walls, his hand trailing along the engravings. "When Azrae had learned of my father's sin, he banished him from this realm, leaving my mother at the mercy of her husband." He slid his tongue along his teeth. "When I was born with features that did not match my father nor my mother, he killed her."

I felt a pang of pity for him. Just a pang. "My Gods..."

His solid eyes drifted to me. "He was a brutal man. I enjoyed ending his life."

"How did you know you were this God of Deceit?" I breathed. "Who are you?"

I jerked back at the sound of multiple screams from below.

"Oh, you will know all in due time, Supreme." He fixed his attention on Silas. "Unfaithful to your wife, huh?" He clicked his tongue, his grin wide. "I heard your words from earlier. You're just like your mother."

I couldn't even process anything as the wails of our friends grew louder.

"You promised you wouldn't hurt us," I bit out.

"And you promised me the Weapon." He held out his palm toward the floor. "Chop, chop, Supreme. Get me what I need. ***Accipe corpus meum alibi.***"

I only took a moment to process the fact that the necromancer teleported. With an incantation, yes, but without the use of a pentagram.

Silas and I instantly rushed through the pronaos and, as fast as we could, down the many spiral steps, Erabella's scream cutting through.

"Let her go, Godsdamn you!" Merrick bellowed.

When we reached where the sound was coming from, just outside one of the balconies, I was stopped by the sight of Heildee holding Erabella, her arm locked around the Princess's neck.

Era was sobbing, Merrick's arm trembling, his crossbow raised at his stepmother. Hendry's focus was deadly on them.

"Mother, please," Elowen cried, her hands pulling at her pink hair. "You have to be in there. This isn't you!"

Heildee only grinned as she dragged a pointed fingernail along the side of Era's neck, drawing a bit of blood. Biting down, black blood dribbled from Heildee's lip, and she lowered her blood-stained mouth, kissing Era over the tiny cut.

Merrick released a bolt wrapped in ice, shooting right through Heildee's skull.

"Fuck!" Era cried, falling back as Heildee's body crashed to the ground.

"No..." Elowen whispered, wide aqua eyes glued to her mother's dead body.

Silas rushed to Era as Merrick lowered his crossbow. "Are you alright?!" the Prince demanded, helping her off the ground. His eyes trailed over the cut.

"Yeah," she panted. "I-I think so."

"Godsdammit," Hendry growled. "I'm sorry, Silas. It was like she was here in one moment."

"That's because she was," Merrick replied quietly, roughly retrieving his bolt from Heildee's skull. "She did the same spell Lena did for teleporting. She was down in the altar room...waiting."

"I should've felt her," I whispered.

"I don't think so," Merrick said, patting my back gently. "She was kneeling, unmoving. Perhaps the magic was dormant. That could explain why you didn't feel anything."

"The important thing is everyone is alive." Roland turned to me, eyes flitting to Silas. "You guys see anything up there?"

I sighed, then told them everything.

We decided to set up camp in the sanctuary, considering there were no dead bodies up there, and the nighttime breeze offered a small bit of relaxation. We were still waiting for Vi and Dani to return, hopefully with some good news. We sure as shit needed some.

Everyone sat silently for a while after Silas and I told our story, mentioning every odd thing the necromancer told us of other realms, the Travelers, and the worst fact of them all. He was the God of Deceit.

"He offered nothing up as to who the other Gods might be? Where might they reside?" Elowen asked, snuggling into Edmund's hold. He stroked her arms, green eyes worried as he looked to me for answers.

"I can only assume every God is his enemy, except for maybe Valor."

"His father," Torrin whispered. "I didn't know Gods could procreate with mortals."

"Neither did we," Silas admitted. "But it seems Azrae is the key to all of this. He is the only God still here, no? Why isn't he doing anything?"

"And what's all this about an Azraeian portal?" Roland scrubbed at his face, groaning. "Ugh. All of this hurts my head."

Era rubbed at her temples. "You think your head hurts? I have a pounding headache," she complained.

"We still have a destination," I said quietly. "I say we ponder on the road and ask more questions when we get there."

"Do you think he'll follow us there?" Edmund asked quietly.

I didn't wish to think of that possibility. Just as I tried to come up with a response, flapping could be heard in the distance. Two eagles came soaring in, shifting back to our friends as they stood before us, panting and grasping their knees.

"You're not going to like this," Viola gasped.

"What now?" Merrick groaned.

Dani swallowed, pupilless eyes wide with dread. "The Undead have overtaken Wrendier."

CHAPTER FIFTY-NINE
SILAS

"Fucking hell," Merrick muttered, pulling at his hair, releasing a dry laugh. "We really just can't catch a break."

"The good thing is we don't have to travel through their kingdom to reach the shore. We'll avoid them and head to Lena's destination," Hendry responded, squinting at the map he withdrew from his bag. "Though we'll be close to the outer edges. We could be spotted."

"How are we to get over that large ass body of water?" Roland asked, crossing his arms.

"Me," Dani stated, flipping her blue hair over her shoulder as she sat in our circle. "I can shift into a sea dragon—one big enough for you all to join the ride."

"A sea dragon?!" Edmund's green eyes bulged. "Does such a thing exist?"

Dani grinned at him. "In ancient Warlock lore, there are illustrations of sea dragons—history of them existing at one point or another. They may be extinct now, but that passage is enough for me to be able to shift into one."

"Won't that be a lot on you?" Viola asked tenderly, sitting beside her on the ground.

The Warlock's cobalt eyes shifted to hers, and she gave her a small smile. "It will be. I'll need a lot of rest afterward." Her smile turned lazy. "You may need to carry me after we arrive."

Viola laughed through her nose, bashfully glancing away.

"If you all could use your forcefields on Dani's back, so long as we swim away fast enough, we should be able to get away without a scratch," I said, taking the map from Hendry's grasp. "Immeron said he wasn't sure we humans would be accepted." I tilted my head up, an eyebrow raised as I studied Lena through my lashes. "What's our plan if that occurs?"

She held my gaze, looking at me as if I were an outsider or something.

Something was different. Off.

"Two of us can stay behind if you're not allowed in," she proposed. "Viola, you should probably be one of them in case they need to make an escape."

"I can stay back, too," Merrick offered.

"You don't wish to see your people?" Era asked him, tucking her blond hair back. "You don't want to go?"

The corner of his lip turned up. "I do," he said softly. "But you guys will need any protection you can get."

"See, I knew Merrick cared," Edmund crooned, wrapping his arm around the Empath and squeezing tight.

A slight flush crept up his cheeks at my friend's nearness. Merrick shot him a nasty scowl, shrugging him off.

Elowen giggled. "I love seeing you guys get along."

"That's getting along to you?" Merrick mumbled.

Elowen stuck out her tongue at him just as I said, "Merrick, can I talk to you? Privately?"

The Empath frowned but offered me a quick, "Sure."

He stood, and the two of us went to speak in private. Merrick asked no questions, so I could only assume he was aware of what was wrong.

Finding a room on one of the lower levels—a storage room holding various religious artifacts—I attempted to shut the door behind us when a foot prevented me from doing so.

My eyes flitted up to meet Torrin's. "I think you'll want me here," Torrin said, and Merrick sighed.

What does that mean?

I glared at him, allowing him entry, and upon shutting the door, I began to speak. "What is going on with Lena?"

Torrin's eyes slid to Merrick's, his arms crossing. "Tell him, Mare."

I could see the resemblance between the two as they stood beside each other, especially as Merrick's eyes turned charcoal, just a shade darker than Torrin's deep brown.

"Lena and I performed a spell," he began slowly. "Her memories, her feelings for you, became too much to bear." He winced. "She...she wanted to forget."

No.

I blinked.

No fucking way.

"You made her forget me?" I asked in a dangerously low voice.

580

"Not forget you. But all romantic interactions." Merrick puckered his lips, blowing out a shaky breath in an attempt to calm his emotions. "It's not forever. It can be undone. Dani said so."

I crept toward him, Merrick flinching as I yelled, "Dani helped with this?!"

As if knowing what the three of us would be discussing, the blue-haired Warlock pushed open the door.

"Yeah, I did." She waltzed inside, shutting the door closed with her hip.

My furious eyes found hers. "Undo it," I growled.

She crossed her arms, her gaze narrowing. "She told me what you said to her."

"I went right back to her after our talk, and she was gone!" I choked out a bitter laugh. "I guess you lied when you advised, 'be honest.'"

At her silence, I grasped one of the Goddess statues resting on the shelves beside me and whirled it toward the wall behind her, the ceramic shattering upon impact.

Dani bared her teeth as I shouted, "You think this is the solution, Dani?!" My eyes went to Merrick's, then Torrin's. "Does she know everything?"

Merrick shook his head, jaw clicking. "No. Not everything."

"What don't I know?" she asked lowly.

I met her stare with vicious regard, my lip curling. "The only reason I had a change of heart is because I saw Lena in Ames the day my people attacked."

Her frown deepened, not understanding.

I took in an unsteady breath. "I met Lena when I was sixteen...the first day my mother let me out of the castle. Every week, my mother would allow me to sneak out, and every week, I met with her."

Dani's pupilless eyes broadened. "You two knew each other?"

"We didn't just know each other. She was my best friend." My voice broke. "She was the love of my life."

"Lena faked her death when she escaped Otacia. Silas didn't learn of her survival until they crossed paths in Ames," Merrick said quietly.

Dani's hand slowly covered her mouth. "Oh, my Gods...so much makes sense."

"Their history has saved our people up until this point," Torrin said. "Without it, I fear there will be consequences."

"Their history wasn't completely erased," Merrick deflected. "The friendship is still there."

"Our friendship was always laced with flirty banter. We had feelings for each other since the beginning," I responded gravely. "I guarantee she remembers hardly anything."

"I...I didn't know," Dani breathed.

"I don't care. Undo it," I repeated.

"I can't." She pointed to Merrick, cringing as she did so. "The spellcaster must be the one to reverse the spell."

Merrick lifted his shoulders, raising his nose to meet my glare. "I won't do it."

I slowly angled my body toward him. "I will knock your fucking teeth out," I seethed.

Ice surrounded Merrick's fingertips as he replied, "I'm not scared of you."

Torrin gripped his shoulder. "Let's all calm the fuck down." His dark-brown eyes locked on mine. "No one's teeth are getting knocked out."

My fists shook at my sides. "So, what, she'll go the rest of her life not remembering what she and I had?"

Merrick's eyes remained dark as he eyed me. "If it makes her happy, why are you so against it?"

"Because it's not fair! It's not fair that after all I've suffered, all I have endured, she gets to just forget it all!"

The room was silent for a moment. "You could forget, too," Torrin said quietly.

I laughed incredulously. "Oh, I'm sure you'd just love that, wouldn't you, Torrin? Considering you stole her away and proceeded to fuck her."

Merrick's eyes enlarged, darting over to his cousin's. "What?"

Torrin clenched his jaw. "It wasn't like that," he bit out.

"Is he telling the truth, Merrick?" I asked, my eyes not leaving Torrin's.

Merrick's silence was answer enough.

"You can say you wished for her safety. Say it was some unknown seer that forced you to take her away. But you wanted her, didn't you? Even back then." This damn conversation was going so far off-topic, but I couldn't reel in my resentments.

"I've always known she was yours," he said quietly. "Which is why I *agree* that Merrick should give her back her memories. But if he refuses, perhaps that burden could be taken from you as well. Perhaps we should all wipe the slate clean."

"No," Dani shook her head. "This is not why Leroy gave over **Potestas Verae Maleficis**. Hiding from your emotions, from reality, is not a fix."

I shot her a harsh glare. "Where were these beliefs of yours a few nights ago?"

She chewed on the inside of her cheek, then shrugged in defeat. "I fucked up, okay? I just wanted to help."

I scoffed, my focus sliding to the Empath. There was no kindness in my tone as I said, "You will undo the spell one way or another, Merrick."

Ice crawled up his hands. "If you really do love her, Prince, allow her some peace. Even if only for a short while."

I had stormed out right after hearing Merrick's stupid advice.

Allow her some peace.

I laughed to myself as I thought about how ridiculous that request was. Was I allowed peace when I believed she'd burned to death? Was I granted peace when my...when...

I quickly shook my head, covering my eyes.

Don't think about it.

I couldn't sleep, so I snuck away from Era's side later that evening. Now, I found myself perched on one of the many balconies this temple sported, this one a few levels down.

I clutched Saoirse's kitten doll, running my fingertip along one of the loosened beads that made up the cat's eyes. Her death wasn't an act. There was no chance I'd run into her five years from now, discovering she had somehow survived.

I couldn't stop seeing her face...the hope that lay behind those big, blue eyes. She had really believed I was saving her.

I thought of all the Mage children kept in the castle, locked away, being raised for slaughter.

I would free them. I would free them all.

I found it hard to believe I was okay with such sickening behavior...that I had committed such ruthless acts.

I had lost myself to grief. To pain. To *him*. Now, here I was, attempting to reassemble all the broken pieces. No, there was no fixing me, no putting me back together. I could only try to undo as much of the damage I had caused as possible, even if no amount of righteous acts would erase my sins.

I was pulled out of my thoughts when I felt a nudge on my back. When I looked over my shoulder, Lena was staring at me.

My brows lifted, shocked at the idea she was coming anywhere near me. It must have confused her greatly, having me spew out all my feelings earlier.

I took a steadying breath, grasping the railing with one hand and Boots with the other, as Lena stepped beside me. "What's on your mind?" she asked gently.

I ran my hand down the doll's fabric. "How unfair this life is," I whispered. I rotated my head, staring down at her. "What's on *your* mind?"

Her jaw clicked as she stared up into the night sky. The moon loomed over us, stars shimmering above. "I'm afraid," she whispered after a moment. "I'm afraid...not only of crossing those in Wrendier but afraid that Nereida is nothing but a myth. That we've risked so much for nothing."

I carefully placed the doll back in my bag and then put a hand on her shoulder, those stunning eyes hesitantly meeting mine.

"It hasn't been for nothing," I insisted, my eyes softening as they searched her face. "I now have allies in both Forsmont and Faltrun. Those with magic rule in both. I'd say we've made great progress."

I offered her a genuine smile, one that didn't come out much anymore, and I was stunned when she pulled me into an embrace, her head resting against my chest.

"Thank you, Silas," she whispered. "For everything. I couldn't imagine doing this all without your help."

My arms surrounded her a moment later, squeezing her against my body. I breathed in her scent, my nose drifting against her hair. "I couldn't imagine doing this without you, either," I whispered back.

She pulled away gently, smiling up at me as her arms returned to her sides.

My face became pained as I searched hers. "Do you remember a few nights ago?"

I knew she didn't. But still, maybe I could get through to her. Maybe it would trigger something.

"Do you remember our time in Otacia?" I pushed. "When we were younger?"

She frowned, eyes skating the ground. "I remember..." She laughed through her nose, raising her gaze. "I mean, there's not too much to remember. Other than the training. I still appreciate that, you know." She tilted her head to the side. "Why?"

I clenched my fists. "Do you remember Amethyst Pond?"

"You know of that place?"

"You don't remember those lowlifes from Serpent's Cove—how I killed them while you were in the water?"

She thought about it. "No..." she replied slowly. "Silas, are you okay? Maybe you had a bad dream?" Her green eyes studied me with concern.

I let out a shaky exhale. "How could you do that fucking spell?" I gritted out, my face contorting.

She retreated a nervous step. "What spell?"

I ran my hand through my hair and then, after a few seconds, I charged toward her.

Nervously, she backed away. "W-what are you doing?!"

I seized her neck, not roughly, but enough to keep her in place as I pushed her against the building's wall. "How is it fair that your memories get wiped, yet I have to live with mine?" I hissed. "Should I ask Merrick to take mine away, too? Is that what you want?!"

Her eyes bulged. "Merrick...he took my memories?"

I released her neck. "You begged him to!" I cried. When I cupped her face, her green eyes went broad. "You really don't remember anything between us?" My voice broke. "The Summer Solstice festival? Our...our first time?"

She choked on a breath, eyes flitting between mine. "Silas...I...I am so confused." She chewed on her lip. "Have you...did you have something to drink?"

My hands slipped away in defeat, even as I asked one more question. "Do you remember my nickname for you?"

The crease between her brows deepened. "A name? No..."

"Fuck, Lena." I buried my face in my palms. "Fuck."

The silence was deafening, nothing but crickets singing in the trees. That is until Lena replied, "My nickname was *'Fuck'*?"

I glared at her through my fingers. "Not funny," I muttered.

She crossed her arms. "I always wondered what you'd look like drunk."

Incredulously, I slapped my palms on my thighs. "I am not drunk!"

She quirked her lips to the side.

"I'm not!"

She giggled, and Gods, if it wasn't the finest sound. She held her hand above her lips as her chuckling died down, her hand eventually falling to her side. She raised her head to gaze at me.

Something shifted in those beautiful green eyes as she beheld me, something I had seen in them many times before.

Desire.

A smirk spread across my face. "Oh, Flower." I cocked my head to the side, and her breathing fastened. "You may not remember all that I have done to you," I purred, stroking her cheek with my fingertips. "But it seems I still affect you the same."

She blinked rapidly. "Stop fucking with me, Silas," she breathed. "Where is this coming from?"

I debated my next move. I wanted so badly to drag my tongue along her lips. But I remained quiet, studying her perfect mouth,

"You said...you said we made love?" she asked mutedly.

My eyes flicked back to hers. "We did. Just a few nights ago. I..." I sighed, running my hand through the hair at her neck, cradling her head. "I was an ass afterward because I was hurting. Because I was angry with myself. I shouldn't have taken it out on you."

"We..." She licked her lips, then swallowed. "You cheated on Era...with me? Why?"

"Because Lena..." I sighed. "I'm in love with you."

Her widened eyes never faltered, not as she shook her head, her lip curling.

I leaned closer, speaking in her ear. "And you can't comprehend that, can't understand it, because you've forgotten that you're in love with me, too."

I released her, swallowing down my shame at the look of contempt on her face.

My own lip wobbled as I took her in. This woman I loved more than anything. "Lucky you, I suppose. My peace of mind perished the moment I met you. You've branded my soul, marking it as yours, even after all this time." I swallowed, Lena's disdain shifting to sorrow as my words poured out of me. "Or perhaps the Goddess Celluna really did forge that bond between us. I sure as hell feel it now more than ever."

I lifted my fingers, lightly tracing the freckles that danced along her nose, along her cheeks. Her eyes fluttered closed, accepting my gentle touch.

"Nevertheless," I murmured, "even with all the pain that has come with loving you, I would never choose to forget the beauty of the moments we shared. Because for me, those moments with you are the only beautiful memories I have."

I let my fingers fall away, my hand drifting back to my side. She stood before me, lips parted, eyes glossy as they opened.

Without her memory, she had no clue how to respond.

I released a shaky sigh, my gaze dropping. "Let's just get back upstairs," I whispered, nodding toward our destination.

She chewed on her bottom lip, averting her gaze. I kept a tasteful distance as I followed her up the steps, sickened by the distance between us.

It didn't matter what I said. To her, I was a stranger.

CHAPTER SIXTY

LENA

Silas's words tormented me as I attempted to sleep that evening.

Those moments with you are the only beautiful memories I have.

Try as I might to recall something—anything—about our times together, it was just blank.

The pain behind his haunted golden eyes wrecked me. I knew he was my friend and that he had trained me, but it all felt like a fever dream. And hearing how he felt for me, even when I couldn't understand it, made me feel selfish as hell for erasing our history from my mind.

But it wasn't just our history...so much of my life, even the past few years, felt fuzzy. I hardly remembered any of our time on the road and almost nothing about my first few months in Ames.

Panic began to rise in me. What if I didn't get those memories back? Were they really so painful I couldn't handle them?

The following morning, we headed for the eastern side of the southern coast, hoping to bypass Wrendier entirely as we headed for Nereida. When we reached the shoreline a few days later, it dawned on me that we couldn't bring our horses. I felt a wave of sadness parting ways with Donut, though not as much as Roland, who had actual tears in his eyes.

My magic-wielding friends focused their power on the pentagram I drew in the dirt, sending me, Torrin, and our horses to Faltrun. After a quick exchange with leadership, all going seemingly well in the newly taken over town, Torrin teleported us back.

Bending over and grasping his head, Torrin winced as we returned. We had help from a handful more Mages than when I teleported us there, yet Torrin was significantly more drained than I was.

"Are you alright?" I asked nervously as he knelt on the ground.

"Yes...yeah, just need a moment," he breathed.

I frowned, then placed my hands on his shoulders. His brown eyes flicked to mine.

My palms didn't burn, but it felt as though my lungs did. Closing my eyes, I began surging my energy into him, what little I had.

Catching on to what I was doing, Torrin grasped my hands. "No."

"I clearly feel better than you. Just let me—"

Stumbling as he stood, he flung my hands off of him. "I'm fine."

Our friends awkwardly looked away, returning back to the small campfire they'd set as Torrin ambled toward the shoreline.

"I performed **Celare**," Elowen announced gently, a wide smile on her face. "It's a cloaking spell. Our fire is hidden from other's eyes."

"That's amazing, El," I praised, noting the fragrance from the herbs that burned in the fire. Noticing my worried gaze trailing to her cousin, she gave me a sad smile.

I met Silas's eyes for just a moment. The pain that lay behind them almost caused me to rush to my tent, ready for the evening to be over. But I found myself following Torrin off in the distance instead.

He went several feet away from our camp, far away enough that no one could see him. He sat inches away from the tide, the water creeping up the sand. His elbows rested on his knees, and his eyes were glued to the impending waves.

His jaw feathered as I sat beside him, moonlight illuminating his bright hair. He wouldn't look at me.

"It sucks having everyone mad at me," I whispered, eyes turning to watch the ripples in the water. The sounds the ocean made were comforting, threatening to lull me to sleep after such magic usage.

"I'm not mad at you," he mumbled.

I gave him an impassive glance. "Yes, you are."

His chest rose and fell, an exhausted sigh leaving him. "I'm just frustrated," he responded quietly a minute later.

I studied him. "I can't remember why you don't wish to be intimate with me," I whispered. "So, I can only assume..." I trailed off, realizing I had no idea what Torrin did or did not know.

He exhaled through his nose. "Yes, it's because of Silas." He finally tilted his head toward me, making eye contact.

I swallowed. "He said I don't remember that I was in love with him, which is true. I...I only remember loving you."

He sucked in his lips, shaking his head. "You loved him more," he muttered, looking away.

"I said that?"

"You didn't have to."

I sighed through my nose, fisting a handful of sand, the smooth, granular material slipping through the cracks between my fingers. "You really feel we gave it a fair shot?" I asked quietly. "You're satisfied with the attempt?"

He laughed humorlessly through his nose. "Why are you here, Lena?"

"To check on you."

"No." He shook his head. "The real reason."

I swallowed, glancing off to the shore. "I..." I sighed. "I feel guilty."

"You shouldn't be," he replied solemnly. "You can't help that you're in love with him."

"I feel guilty that it is you I want when Silas is hurting so deeply."

His eyes skated to mine. "Lena," Torrin muttered, shaking his head again. "You only want me because you can't remember him."

"I chose to forget him, didn't I? Doesn't that mean the pain of loving him wasn't worth it?"

Torrin's teeth dragged across his bottom lip as he lifted his hand, holding my face. "It wasn't the pain of loving him. It was the pain of being unable to have him."

I went to protest, and Torrin gently placed his lips on mine.

I melted at the feeling, my eyes fluttering shut. When Torrin's lips pulled away, he whispered, "I suppose I understand that pain. I understand why you did it."

"You are able to have me," I whispered over his lips.

He let out a hum, kissing me softly again. "No, I can't." Another kiss. "Because I don't think I could survive the pain that would come with you remembering him again."

I sucked on his bottom lip, and he released a soft sigh. "I could just keep the memories away," I offered quietly.

A light gasp escaped me when Torrin pushed me against the sand, his body looming over mine, holding my arms to the ground.

"Torrin," I breathed.

He leaned down, pressing his lips against mine, his tongue demanding entry. My lips parted, my tongue swirling around his. His mouth trailed down, littering kisses along my jawline.

When a moan slipped free of my lips, Torrin released my arms, falling back beside me with a frustrated groan. His hands raked down his face as he lay against the sand.

Breathing heavily, I said, "I really loved him that much?"

Torrin's silence was answer enough.

Yet again, another evening was spent struggling to rest my mind. I remembered Dani saying there were gaps in my memory due to an error made with the spell. Perhaps that is why all this feels so terrible. Still, when I witnessed the rising sun across the shore, Viola in bird form flying back from an early morning scout, all thoughts about anything else vanished.

My friend shifted back to herself, eyes widening. "I...I saw it."

"Nereida?" I nearly cried. "You've seen it?"

We decided last night it would be wise to have her check and see if the island truly was visible instead of risking our lives passing Wrendier for nothing.

She nodded breathlessly. "Yes, but it seems like an entirely bare island," she stated, and our whole group went quiet. "But, as I got closer, I could feel a barrier of some sort—a ward." She crossed her arms, anxiously rubbing her triceps. "It felt like my magic was being drained almost. I didn't want to get close. Not on my own."

"Drained magic?" Elowen whispered, adjusting the bag on her back. Without our horses, we all had more to carry ourselves. "Are we sure this is a place of good?"

"Kayin told us to go," Torrin interjected. "I trust her."

Silas's narrowed gaze shifted from Torrin to mine. "What do you think, Lena? Would Kayin send you someplace dangerous?"

I thought about the mysterious seer I had yet to meet in person, the seer who apparently was in Otacia, unwell, unless she had managed to leave. I then thought about the other seer who had been in my life, the one who had sent Torrin to a kingdom where he'd been enslaved for an entire year.

My eyes drifted to Torrin, my heart welling with so much love as I took in his eyes and the gentleness behind them. His short hair displayed his handsomeness even better than his longer hair did.

Torrin's cheeks reddened, seemingly reading my mind as I admired him.

What if it's another trap?

"Igon didn't send me into a trap. He sent me somewhere I'd find my parents," he replied softly in my mind. *"Sent me to a place that*

we have now liberated." He offered me a smile that further sent heat throughout me. *"All of this is meant to happen, I believe."*

"It's so awkward watching silent conversations," Roland mumbled to Hendry.

"I'll say."

"Okay." I took a steadying breath. "We're going to go for this and hope for the best." My attention went back to my crossbody. "I want to ensure **Potestas Verae Maleficis** will be kept safe, Gods-forbid we find ourselves in the water."

"Not to worry, Supreme," Dani began. "That grimoire protects itself. The witches who wrote it ensured its preservation." She stretched her limbs. "That doesn't mean it can't get lost at sea, though. Keep your bag secured to yourself." She shifted her body toward the ocean. "Shifting into such a large beast will take a great deal of energy, but based on how long it took Viola to return, this will be the quickest way we can get there."

"We will need to shield," Viola added, tying her braids up in a ponytail. The silver rings in them glinted in the rising sunlight.

I wonder where she got those.

"I could see those special Undead—those puppets—stationed at Wrendier's watchtowers. They paid me no mind as a bird, but a sea dragon will certainly be a different story."

We'd all debated on the idea of taking invisibility elixirs, but the danger of us not being able to see one another while atop such a beast seemed like a bad idea, certainly if one of us fell off.

We stood back as Dani took a bracing breath, striding toward the shore. The tips of her boots submerged in the water. Then, her knees. Then, her waist.

She slowly turned to us. "Alright. Let's do this."

It was an incredible sight, watching Dani morph into a creature so terrifying, so beautiful. Iridescent blue scales covered the length of her new body. Sharp, blue spikes were spread across the length of her spine.

Those same pupilless blue eyes stared at us, sharp, white teeth present as the dragon's mouth parted, releasing a roar.

"Dani says hurry up and get on," Torrin breathlessly said, hurrying to her.

"It will be too bumpy of a ride to get a clear shot should we find ourselves being attacked," Merrick instructed Era as we all hurried forward. "Hide behind my shield, alright?"

There were five of us Mages and five humans, so we each picked one to protect. Our shields could be extended wide, but still. The humans would be sat in front of us, holding on to Dani's spikes, as we wrapped an arm around their torso, balancing ourselves while our other hand created a shield.

Hendry sat in front of Torrin, considering they were both the tallest males here. Roland was in front of Viola, and of course, Elowen was clutching onto Edmund.

My eyes nervously went to the golden-eyed Prince. "You stay in front of me," I said softly.

He nodded, going over to speak with his wife before we mounted. She was wincing, rubbing her head.

My hands grazed Dani's scales. They were smoother than I expected them to feel but still durable. Carefully, we all mounted, situating ourselves on her back.

Sitting toward the rear, Silas and I situated ourselves between one of the spikes in Dani's spine. Silas grasped on while my arms wrapped around his waist, holding him tightly. Our other friends did the same: Torrin's arms around Hendry, Viola's around Roland, Elowen's around Edmund, and Merrick's around Erabella.

It was clear our nerves were shot, considering the silence between us all.

"We ready?" Torrin asked. When we all responded, Dani began moving.

I squeezed my arms around Silas, swallowing as our speed increased. Silas angled his head back. "Don't let go of me."

"I didn't plan on it," I murmured.

Water droplets began sprinkling against my face as Dani went faster, faster, faster. The ripples in the waves had us bouncing slightly, and I found my grip around him tightening.

"We will be passing Wrendier shortly," Torrin spoke, presumably to all of us in our minds.

As the land of Tovagoth began rounding off, I saw it then, the island off in the distance.

"My Gods, do you see it, Silas?" I yelled over the waves.

He shook his head. "No. I see nothing!"

We were zipping forward, water spraying up as Dani led us to the island. I began to sense it then...that darkness I always felt when the necromancer's power was near.

Whipping my head to my right, I flung my right arm out, producing a forcefield. My Mage friends did the same.

Wrendier was far in the distance, but as a dark orb came rushing for us, I knew we'd been spotted.

My shield was hit first. I grunted as it struck, the darkness surging back in the direction it came from.

"Hold on tight!" Silas ordered, grasping the spike close.

The island only had to be a couple of minutes away at the rate Dani was swimming. Still, orb after black orb came hurtling us. My friends and I shot out our forcefields, bouncing their magic back, but they were relentless in their pursuit.

"There's too many of them!" Elowen cried, wincing as another orb hit her forcefield.

"My magic...it's weakening! I can feel it!" Viola yelled, roaring as her shield repeatedly got hit.

"Just a few more seconds. We can make it!" Torrin shouted.

But the second his words were released, I felt myself plunging into the cold sea.

Water rushed up my nose, burning my sinuses. I desperately flung my arms forward, trying to find my way up.

The water was freezing, the waves relentless.

I couldn't find my way back up.

I couldn't breathe.

My head felt like it was imploding with every passing second I went without air, and when I couldn't take it any longer, my body inhaled for me.

Water flooded my lungs, a burning sensation spreading across my chest.

This was it.

This was how I was to die.

My eyes began to shut just as I felt an arm wrap around my waist. I had the sense I was being pulled to shore, the brisk air harsh as my face emerged from the water.

"S-s-stay with me, L-Lena, p-please...please..."

Silas.

The cold was unbearable. My whole body felt like it was shaking violently. But I was still. Motionless. I couldn't move—couldn't open my eyes. My hands and my toes felt numb.

I suddenly felt a pressure on my chest. Over and over and over.

"Fuck!" he roared. "I c-can't lose you, Lena! Please n-not again...please."

I felt the rush of water rising, and I choked. Leaning over, I coughed it all out on the ground beside me.

"Oh...oh, t-thank the Gods," Silas hailed.

I took notice of our surroundings as I sucked in breath after breath, and when I realized what was beneath my fingers, a soft cry escaped me.

Snow. The whole island was covered in snow.

"What..." I breathed, frantically searching all around. "Where is everyone?"

"I don't know," he whispered, his own body trembling from the frigid temperature. Our clothes were suited for a summer in Tovagoth...not this winter. That, plus our soaked bodies, meant we needed to find shelter. Now.

I quickly checked my bag, grateful the grimoire was safe. "W-we need shelter." I could feel the water freezing on me—my hair, my eyelashes, my face. Same with Silas—ice was coating him.

"There's a cabin I s-saw." Without warning, Silas lifted me into his arms.

"Silas, n-no—you're going to hurt yourself!"

I could barely move my hands; it felt as though my body was completely frozen stiff.

He ignored me, trudging through the many inches of snow to a wooden cabin that rested above.

It felt like hours—like slow motion as he plodded forward. Nothing else was present on this bare island.

Where are we?

Kicking open the front door, Silas's eyes desperately darted around the dark home, and he rushed forward until we entered a bedroom.

"Lena, t-there's a f-fireplace here..." He set me down on my feet just steps before it.

"I-I can't." I choked, trembling.

"If you d-don't, w-we will die."

It took everything in me, but I bent down and willed the smallest amount of fire from my fingertips, the thought of Silas dying fueling me with just enough.

"C-come on, come on," I cried.

The fire began small, the crackling sound spreading relief through me.

"We need to take off our c-clothes," he ordered.

I obeyed, peeling off the frozen clothes until I was naked, tossing them to the side, and then I stumbled as close to the fire as I could, my knees dropping to the soft rug in front of it. I was shaking so damn hard.

Silas moved, and a few moments later, after some rustling, he returned to my side with a thick sheet. His body was bare of clothes, but I couldn't focus on anything other than how fucking cold I was.

He laid down next to me, opening up the blanket as I entered, his arms wrapping around me and pulling me close. I nestled into him, my back facing the warm flames.

Our bodies shuddered against one another.

"S-Silas," I breathed.

"I'm here, Flower." His hand rested on the top of my head, holding me against his chest. "I-I'm here."

Flower.

That nickname...the feel of this man's skin against mine.

The scent of pine and citrus.

"Quill?"

His body stiffened, and he pulled away just enough to look at me, his eyes widened. "Lena...do you...are you r-remembering?"

"Yes...in p-pieces but..." I blinked over and over. "The pond, we first kissed in that pond."

He grinned. "Yes. Y-yes, we did."

It seemed this ward, whatever magic-altering barrier had been present, had eliminated the spell put on me. But why did I still have my magic?

"I'm so sorry, Silas," I whispered, tears welling in my eyes as my memories came flooding back to me. "The pain was just so strong." I lifted my shaking hands, my purple fingertips brushing against his cheek. "But it's worse...far worse, not remembering."

His lips trembled, and he pulled me against him, pressing his lips against my forehead.

My breathing calmed in his embrace, at his scent that had always been so soothing. I didn't know how long it was before our shuddering died down, how long it was until we finally began to warm each other and drift off to sleep.

PART THREE:

AWAKEN

CHAPTER SIXTY-ONE
LENA

I awoke facing the firelight, still in Silas's embrace, the room still dark. Everything that had happened began to process slowly. When reality finally hit me, I quickly turned and checked to see if he was alive. Instead, I managed just to wake him.

"Are you alright?" I asked nervously, surveying his handsome face.

"Mhm..." He just smiled sleepily and ran his thumb along my lips. "Do you still remember me?" he asked quietly.

I nodded, heart pounding at how close our naked bodies were. "I do."

His smile began to fall. "I'm so sorry for what I said that night, Lena. I didn't mean it."

I shook my head. "Don't be, Silas. I understand." I remembered his words on the balcony now, and I held no ill feelings toward him at all. Changing the topic, I whispered, "We should switch." I trailed my hand along his chest. "You should be by the fire."

"You've warmed me up just fine," he murmured, his fingers brushing my cheek.

I smiled bashfully, my eyes trailing to his chest. It took me a moment to realize he was completely shirtless in front of me.

"You are not to try and remove my shirt. You are not to touch my back skin to skin."

Sensing my thoughts, Silas carefully sat up. I followed suit, holding both his hands and not caring that the sheet fell to my lap, exposing my bare breasts.

He clenched his jaw, and his breathing began to stagger. He nodded and glanced down, a silent permission to look at his back. At the place he kept hidden.

Slowly, I scooted behind him.

All this time, I wondered what tattoos would be inked, what tattoos held such meaning that he kept them secret.

But when I beheld his back, I choked on a sob.

There were no tattoos. Not a single one.

No...his back was *obliterated.* Several raised gashes were present, leaving minimal skin unblemished. I gently traced my hand on his skin, the action causing him to flinch. The wounds had been so deep, and with how they had healed, it was clear he was continually beaten before the previous injuries had even healed.

He had been tortured. Whipped. Burned. Flayed.

"My Gods, Silas," I breathed, my lip trembling. "Who did this to you?"

He was silent for a few moments before he responded quietly, "My father."

"Ulric?" I asked in disbelief. "I-I don't understand."

Silas turned to face me, his brows drawn together. "When my mother died, my father increased my training. Said I needed to be strong, ruthless, unfeeling. He began to take me on 'hunts', as he called them. Intel would come in about potential threats, and we would ambush and kill everyone...

"I was devastated when I learned you were dead, Lena. My whole world in those couple of weeks had shattered completely." He sighed. "When my father had found me sobbing in my room after seeing your corpse, after I punched him for telling me to be glad it wasn't someone 'of importance' who'd died, he pulled out a dagger. That was the first time my father used something other than his fists to harm me." He pointed to the scar on his left cheek. "This was the first scar he gave me."

I shook my head, fury bubbling inside of me. How could he do that to his own son?

"Ulric wished for me to be like him, cold and merciless. But to go out and end people's lives, seeing the fear in their eyes, hearing their cries as they begged for mercy..." He shuddered. "I hesitated. I wasn't ruthless like my father or the more advanced soldiers. I imagined they had families, people who loved them. It felt wrong just to slaughter them like nothing."

His throat rolled as he swallowed. "That's when the beatings began." His eyes fell to his lap. "My father would do it himself. Any time I showed sympathy, anytime I showed an ounce of compassion, I would be whipped."

My breathing was unsteady as my hand continued to trace his back softly. He slowly eased into my touch.

"That went on for about six months. Eventually, whipping turned to cutting. Cutting to burning. Then back to whipping." He shook his head. "I would go to practice so sore, but I couldn't tell anyone. I was too ashamed. Sometimes, I would fuck up too close together, and I would be whipped over marks that were still healing, opening them up once again. Or burned over fresh burns. My back would constantly ache or itch. I'm shocked I never got an infection."

His tortured eyes found mine again. "I thought it was the worst pain I could experience, next to losing the people I loved more than anything. But..." He released a shaky exhale, his voice a mere whisper. "I was wrong."

He got quiet, and his body began to shake. His eyes shut tight, and his frown and clenched jaw told me that he was trying to stop from crying. I touched his cheek and pulled him to meet my eyes.

A few tears released as he bit down on his lip, and his voice trembled when he spoke again. "I'm going to tell you why I hate Roland, Lena," he whispered, a haunted gleam in his eyes. "But you will not look at me the same again."

My stomach fell at his words.

"It was noticeable to my friends that I had changed after the deaths of my mother and, unbeknownst to them, you. Even more so once my punishments began. Edmund and Hendry would ask me if I was alright, I'd lie, and that would be that.

"But one morning, after a particularly gruesome beating, Roland came up to me. I'd stood up for him before in the past when guys his age tormented him, and while I knew he appreciated that, I was still the Prince. He was never himself around me." He sighed through his nose. "Until that morning."

CHAPTER SIXTY-TWO
SILAS - FIVE YEARS AGO

The beating last night was especially gruesome—the whip splitting open my partially healed wounds.

We had infiltrated a small camp, a camp of witches, and I had frozen with my sword lifted to a woman clinging to a young child. I stood there as one of the older soldiers crept forward, plunging his sword into her chest and ripping the child from her corpse's arms.

"Show no emotion, show no mercy, or you will be beaten again."

I didn't know how to do it. How could I ever be like him? I hated witches, believed them to be evil, but the desperation in that woman's eyes...in her child's...

"They are monsters. It was just an act, and you fell for it like the fool you are."

It was almost impossible to go through the motions during training without crying out in agony. But no one could know of my beatings.

No one can know.

I rotated my hands, staring at how rough they'd become in the last few months. The skin on them was still primarily smooth, but I imagined it wouldn't last.

Maybe once the beatings were done, I could get inked. Perhaps I'd be able to hide all my scars with art one day. The thought of anyone seeing my back humiliated me, though.

I rested outside against the castle wall, Edmund and Hendry throwing me concerned looks. I waved them off, and they shrugged, wandering away.

I hated being distant from them, the only friends I had left. But what was I to talk about? They would notice something was off, and I didn't want to speak about it.

A slight drizzle began, and I sighed, tipping my head up to allow the droplets to pepper my face.

I hated this life. The only thing keeping me going was ridding the world from the evil that took the two most important people away from me. And it turns out I fucking sucked at it.

When I opened my eyes, nearly all our soldiers had dispersed from practice, all except for Roland Aubeze, who was staring at me.

I narrowed my eyes at him, the rain just beginning to dampen his hair. I deepened my glare when he started to walk over, but he seemed determined, as his expression remained strong.

He stopped in front of me, his eyes cast downward to meet my glare. He opened his mouth, but nothing came out.

"What do you want?" I muttered.

His jaw snapped shut, but just for a second. His arms slacked at his sides. "Look, I know you've gone through some awful things," he began, and I tightened my fists. "I know it hurts. But use that pain and turn it into something meaningful." His nose wrinkled as he grimaced at me. "Sulking like this won't do shit."

My mouth fell open. In all the years I'd known Roland, he had hardly uttered a word to me, too intimidated by my title. He was close with Edmund and Hendry but never showed his authentic or playful side to me.

Nor whatever *this* side was.

"I am not sulking," I snapped.

He crossed his arms, a half-smile pulling on his lips. "This is the definition of sulking, Silas."

Sulking...

I wanted to be angry at his disrespect, but he had no idea the torture I was enduring behind the scenes. It had only been three months since Mother and Lena had died...and nearly three months of constant lashings. My back burned so fucking badly right now.

Use that pain and turn it into something meaningful.

Thunder roared in the distance, the rain picking up. It soaked his brown hair, but he remained planted where he was.

"What meaningful thing would you suggest I do?" I asked him, leaning my head against the wall.

His hazel eyes trailed over me, and he shrugged. "I don't know. You got any hobbies?"

I raised a brow. "Hobbies?"

"Yeah, surely the Prince has time to have fun every now and again?"

I thought about it. I couldn't even remember the last time I had fun. I really only did when I was with Lena.

Roland's smile fell when he noticed me struggling to name one single hobby. "You like music?"

I scoffed. "Everyone likes music."

Roland chuckled. "I play piano down at Hidden Rhythm. You should come. Tonight."

I frowned. That lounge was located in the Inner Ring. Now that I had freedom, I could go.

"See you there?" he prodded.

I blinked. "I'll consider it," I mumbled.

His smile grew, and he inclined his drenched face, heading inside the castle.

Roland sat at the piano at Hidden Rhythm later that night. I almost didn't come, but his words compelled me. I dressed in more casual clothes, a hat over my head in the hopes of being unrecognized. Had I left out the castle's front doors, guards would've followed me. But today, I decided to use the pathway I'd taken to see Lena so many times before.

I felt sick the whole walk here thinking of her.

People all around the lounge began to quiet their mumbling as Roland's tanned hands trailed over the keys, his eyes fluttering shut. He was still for only a moment before his fingers began dancing along the white and black.

The song was beautiful, so much so that chills spread across my body once the tune began. Roland wore a faint smile as he played, eyes occasionally glancing up at his sheet music.

He was actually pretty damn good.

It was so complex, the beat picking up, but he didn't miss a single note. It was...melancholic, somehow, the song he played.

The next was upbeat, his hands moving so fast the crowd roared when he completed the melody. Song after song played, and somehow, a half hour had flown by.

A woman stood on stage, getting ready to announce the next performer as Roland stepped off. "Next up, Novalie Briar will be singing 'Loveless'."

The crowd cheered in excitement just as Roland's eyes found me.

"You came!" he exclaimed as he strolled up to me, a giant grin on his face. "Well, what did you think?"

"It was amazing," I admitted. "I had no idea you had such talent."

I didn't miss his cheeks slightly flushing. "Thanks, man." His eyes darted around the room. "I'm surprised no one has recognized you."

I laughed softly. "I'm a master at disguise."

He chuckled, his gaze sliding back to me. "Apparently so."

"Who taught you?"

"My mother," he voiced proudly, adjusting the bag containing his sheet music on his shoulder. "She insisted that my sisters and I have at least one talent. I was always drawn to music."

I nodded, crossing my arms, eyes flitting around the place. "Perhaps you could teach me."

He blinked in surprise, his grin growing. "I'd like that. For tons of gold, of course," he teased.

I snorted. "Sure."

As we headed out, I spoke again. "Hey."

Roland turned to me with a quirked brow.

"Thank you. You've helped me more than you know."

He gave a reserved smile, and when he went to turn away, I grasped his arm.

"Always be real with me, okay?" I insisted. "I...I need some authenticity in my life."

The corners of his lips raised. "Always."

One week later.

"Wow." Roland cringed as he listened to me attempt to play the piano in my room. I had purchased one the following day after seeing him perform. "Turns out the Prince is *not* good at everything."

I scowled at him. "I never said I was good at everything." I tried playing the notes again and groaned when I messed up. "I don't think I'm artistically gifted," I muttered.

"It takes practice. I was this bad once before. When I was four."

I shoved his shoulder playfully, and he snickered.

"Remembering which notes are which takes time," he said from his seat beside me on the bench. "But with daily practice, I'm sure you'll grasp it eventually."

I began the "easy" song, as Roland had called it, and sighed after I completed the first part correctly, only to mess up the second.

He placed a hand on my shoulder, causing me to wince. He quickly removed it.

He didn't know my wince was due to the new wounds I'd gotten the night before.

"Don't give up," he encouraged, rubbing the back of his head. "You'll get the hang of it."

Two and a half months later.

Months went by, and while every beating threatened to turn me into a monster, Roland's goofy personality and our music lessons made me *feel* again, even if only for a little bit. I had grown even closer to him than I had with Edmund and Hendry.

"Wow. I take back what I said about you not being good at everything," he praised after I finished playing a song. "In just a few short months, you've improved dramatically."

"Honestly, it's all I've been doing in my free time." I chewed at my lip. "I loathe being around my father, and other than the training and royal duties, I've been practicing."

"You hate your Dad?"

Yes.

I sighed, standing from the piano bench and walking to my bed. "He's just...nothing like my Mother was." I sat on my mattress, resting my elbows on my knees.

"No kidding," Roland said, standing and striding over to sit beside me. He crossed his arms. "I hardly saw him in training, but now, seeing how he instructs us on the field, I realize just how brutal he is." He paused. "Especially with how he talks to you," he added softly.

"He's always been that way. Well, he was less harsh when I was a boy."

I could sense Roland's eyes drift over to me as I stared ahead. "Does he hurt you?"

My eyes shot wide, and I spun my head toward him.

614

Did he somehow see my back?!

"What makes you ask that?" I asked, attempting to appear unaffected by his question.

His jaw clicked. "He just seems the type."

I laughed through my nose, eyes falling back to the ground. "Don't worry about me."

"Well...I do. I hope you have someone here that sticks up for you," he said quietly.

I gave him a soft smile that I knew didn't reach my eyes. The truth was no one stuck up for me. Not anymore.

I was aware of his thigh pressing against mine as he continued, "You want me to be real with you, yes?"

I nodded, my brows drawing together. "Always."

His fingers nervously drummed along his thighs. I had no time to react as his eyes fell to my lips, and he leaned forward and kissed me.

My instant reaction was to shove him away, so I did.

My eyes were blown wide, as was Roland's, his cheeks tinted pink. I remained gaping at him.

I'd never been attracted to men before. The thought had never crossed my mind.

But human connection...touch. I missed it.

And I was lonely, so fucking lonely that I'd give anything to have a moment where I wasn't dwelling on the past...thinking of *her*.

So, I found myself grasping his jaw and pulling his lips back to mine.

Our kisses were slow for only a moment before I pushed him down against my bed. I hovered over him, kissing him hungrily, my tongue teasing his as his hands ran through my hair.

Who am I? What am I doing?

At that moment, I didn't care. I didn't want to be *me* anymore. I didn't want to be a prince. I didn't want to be a son.

I didn't want to be Silas.

I wanted to be touched in a way that was loving. That was soft. I wanted to feel pleasure again. I wanted to *feel* again.

He tasted like mint and sweet tea—like that drink he'd always order when we went to Hidden Rhythm.

I grunted against his mouth as his hand trailed down to my erection. I broke our kiss, our eyes expansive, chests rising and falling as we took each other in.

He was touching me. No one but Lena had ever touched me.

She died only a few months ago, yet here I was, being intimate with someone else.

But it didn't matter, did it? She was fucking gone.

War was waging in my mind, and I was unsure if I could follow through with this. Roland leaned up, kissing my lips gently just as the door to my room flung open.

I hadn't bothered locking it, never expecting to have been in this situation.

My head whirled in that direction, my stomach sinking as I tumbled off of Roland.

My father's eyes flared, his fists clenching hard. They were trembling as he turned his expression to Roland, who fearfully sat up in bed.

"So, this is why you insisted on defending him last year."

It wasn't like that at all. Yes, he was being attacked for his presumed sexuality. But I did it because his treatment wasn't right, not out of feelings for him.

My father charged toward Roland, but I shot off the bed, blocking his path.

"It's not his fault," I insisted. "I initiated. I-I gave him no choice."

"Silas—" Roland began.

"How long?" the King demanded.

"This was the first time." I trembled. "I swear it on Mother's grave."

Ulric's gaze was the most frightful thing I'd ever seen. He turned his attention back to Roland, who was shaking.

"I never want to see your face again. Get out."

I could feel Roland's gaze on me, but I kept eye contact with my father.

"OUT!" the King shouted, and Roland quickly fled the room.

When he was gone, my father's vicious glare found mine. "You fancy men, huh?"

"No." I shook my head, willing my tears to stay put. "I don't."

"His hand was on your cock," Ulric spat.

I inhaled sharply. I didn't even know what to say.

"I...I'm just confused," I whispered.

"You disgust me. You've been nothing but a failure in everything you do. And now you show me you're a faggot too."

He grasped my arm, pulling me out of the room.

I was just beaten last night. This was going to be so very painful.

I sucked in my lips, my breathing uneven, my throat burning.

Bringing me to one of the extra bedrooms in the castle, my father locked me in there, leaving without a word. I slowly seated myself on the bed, dreading his return.

Don't cry. Don't cry.

Roland should hopefully be off the hook, at least. I could only hope the King believed what I had said.

A few minutes later, my father reentered the room, chains in his hand.

"Take off your shirt and lie on the bed."

I swallowed, then slowly began unbuttoning my top.

I was getting beaten again. I knew this now. Normally, I'd be kneeling on the ground for my punishment, though, not lying on my back.

My stomach fell. Perhaps the beatings will be on my chest now.

I hesitantly did as he said, lying down on the bed, my crusted skin resting against the comforter.

Ulric secured my limbs to the bedposts with the chains. When he was done, he went to leave the room.

"Where are you going?" I asked nervously.

My father's eyes held no emotion. "To get your punishment."

And then he left, leaving me restrained to the bed in the eerie silence. My eyes stung as I stared at the ceiling. Yes, he must be having my front side whipped now, too.

Why did he hate me so much? Why did he wish to harm me?

Several minutes later, and my head turned at the clicking sound of the door lock.

Three men I had never seen before strolled in. One was lanky, with a long mustache and thinning hair. Another big, burly, and bald, his eyes so dark they looked like depthless pits.

The last one appeared more normal, I supposed. Brown hair, brown eyes, and average stature.

But they all shared one thing in common. They studied me like I was their prey.

My eyes darted around, noting no weapons of torture in their hands.

"Are you going to whip me?" I asked quietly.

Father had always been the one giving me my punishments. Who were these men?

The scrawny one tilted his head, letting out a grating laugh as he replied, "Only if you ask."

My heartbeat quickened as they stepped forward, and I nervously tugged at the chains securing me to the bed.

What is happening?

"He's already showing emotion," the big one said, a sinister smile spreading across his face. "Which means we'll have another round with him."

"W-what are you going to do to me?" I whispered.

I shivered in disgust when the average one dragged his fingertips up my bare torso.

No.

He wouldn't.

He wouldn't have this done to me.

The man bent down to whisper in my ear. "Your father says you've been naughty, Your Highness, and so we get to have our way with you."

No.

No, no, no, no!

The scrawny one gripped me through my pants, and I thrashed, desperate to escape.

It was no use. I was fucking trapped.

"Please!" I cried, tears spilling down my face. "Please don't do this! Father!"

The bald one unbuckled his pants, exposing himself as he began to stroke. The average one stood back and watched as the scrawny one pulled down my trousers.

I thrashed again, wailing as I tried with all my might to avoid what they were going to do to me.

"He's soft," the big one complained. "The King said he was into this."

"He'll get there."

"Put him in your mouth."

"GET THE FUCK AWAY FROM ME!" I screamed. "FATHER!"

But the men only laughed at my screams, my pleas. And they went ahead and raped me anyway.

CHAPTER SIXTY-THREE
LENA - NOW

"My father...he had them..." he whispered, his entire body trembling. "He had them..."

My eyes were wide in horror, and I felt fire surge through my veins as tears poured out of my eyes. My voice broke as I uttered, "You were raped?"

His head fell, his tearful eyes dropping to the ground. "By the time I realized what was going to happen, there was nothing I could do. I thrashed and tried to free myself from those fucking chains, but I was trapped," his voice cracked. "I screamed for my father, begging him to help me. He did nothing.

"I had never felt so helpless in my life. The things they did to me, the things they made me do to them..." His face crumpled. "And to top it all off, my body fucking betrayed me." Shame shone in his watery eyes as he gazed up at me. "I-I didn't enjoy it, Lena, I *promise*, not at—"

I grasped his face with both hands, my eyes burning into his. "I know that...Gods," I cried softly. "You don't need to defend yourself, Silas."

The tears he was holding began flooding out. "The sick fucks got off on violating men. They loved seeing me in fear, begging for it to stop." He sniffed. "When it was over, I was shaking so badly. They released me from the chains, and I scrambled away, vomiting on the floor. When my father came back and witnessed me puking, he simply said I was pathetic and whipped me once more."

I wept with him as I lowered my hand, stoking his mangled flesh.

"It wasn't Roland's fault," he cried softly. "He really was helping me. He...I think he actually cared." He shook his head, eyes squeezing shut. "But after that happened to me, I couldn't even look at him without seeing *them*...without being reminded of what happened. So, I pushed him away. I treated him like shit.

"But still, he's always kept that secret of ours. Still, he has stuck by my side." Silas released an exhale, his face crumpling when he had the courage to look at me once again. "You must be disgusted with me."

"Not at all," I insisted, caressing his back. "Not even a little bit, Silas. Nothing like that would change how I look at you. All I can do is admire your strength."

He shook his head. "I wasn't strong. I was a shell of a person then. I thought to myself I would never do anything to get punished again, but it wasn't as if I did something to invoke it, not anymore." His eyes slid to the flames that warmed us. "Every week, I would get put through it all over again. And I was promised it would only stop when I endured it with no emotion, no expression.

"And Gods did I fucking try, but it was impossible. I tried to focus on the only thing that had ever brought me happiness to get me through it." His eyes found mine. "You. But all I could think of when I thought of you was your burnt corpse in your cottage and..." His voice cracked, and he covered his face.

"Silas," I cried, wrapping my arms around him and holding him close.

He wept into the nook of my neck for a few moments before pulling away and wiping his eyes.

"It was almost three months of being raped and beaten every week," he said quietly. "Right before that final week, I told myself if I failed one more time, if I broke just *one* more time, I would end my life. I couldn't go through it any longer.

"As I was lying there the final time, preparing for what they would do, I remembered what you told me when I last saw you. *'You will not give up. You will not break.'* Do you remember telling me that?"

I nodded. "Yes," I breathed. "I do."

"I heard your voice telling me that. Over and over and over again. I willed myself not to react. To go elsewhere. No matter what they were doing to me or having me do to them. I had to have repeated it hundreds of times, thousands.

"When they were done with me, when my father returned, I was lying in the bed, expressionless. All he said was, *'Well done,'* and left." Silas let out a broken laugh, more tears spilling down his face. "I thought I would break down, cry tears of joy that I had finally done it. But I felt *nothing*." His guilt-ridden eyes roamed over me. "I realized that even though I had done what he had asked, and your words guided me through it, I did, in fact, break." His face crumpled. "I lost my fucking soul in the process."

I was sobbing silently, now holding his hands in mine.

"That's why when you were violated under my authority..." A muffled sob broke free of him, and he shook his head. "The thought of *you* going through that...Gods, I had never felt so angry in my entire life."

"You saved me," I reminded him gently.

His face became pained. "It was my fault you were in that position."

I went to protest, but Silas continued his story.

"Once my emotions had successfully been turned off, I found each of those men. I enjoyed killing them. I took my time and strung their lives on for hours before I finally ended them for good." His jaw feathered as he recalled those memories. "After that, I began to kill effortlessly, intent on eradicating the people I thought responsible for killing my mother and you. Killing became...enjoyable to me.

"I didn't have sex for months after that all happened, but once I did..." He exhaled, closing his eyes and pinching the bridge of his nose. "I fucked so many women, Lena. Multiple at one time. So many that I couldn't even give you a number. The sex was a wonderful distraction. But I was always left feeling empty afterward. Same with the killing. But that is all I have known for the last five years, is fucking emptiness."

His eyes lifted to mine. "The only time I felt any desire for a man was with Roland, and really, I think it was because of my loneliness. I have never stared at a man and felt aroused, especially after what happened to me."

He took his free hand and cupped my face. "But that's why I had no fucking right making you feel gross or dirty for what little you've done. Even if it wasn't a little, even if it was as much as I'd done, I would *never* think less of you for that." His pained eyes held mine. "I never meant any of it. I just wanted to hurt you—to push you away."

"I really felt like damaged goods after all that, but not because of what you said. I just felt it in general," I replied softly. "Please don't feel bad for what you said."

"Damaged goods?" He frowned, his hand caressing my cheek. "You aren't an object. You aren't any less of a prize because you've found pleasure in others. Your value doesn't lessen." His golden eyes flitted downward. "If that were the case, then I'd be worthless," he said quietly.

"You are worth everything," I whispered sincerely, bringing the hand of his I held up to my lips and giving it a kiss.

His eyes met mine, and his hand slid back, his fingers lacing through my hair. "*You* are worth everything. Worth more than all the gold in Tovagoth, all the gems and jewels in every royal chamber, worth more than all the paintings and artifacts in the temples." He pressed his lips to my forehead. "Priceless, Lena," he whispered. "You are priceless. That will never change."

He sniffed again, pulling his lips away. "Crying over Saoirse's body...that was the first time I have cried in years. And Gods, there were moments I wanted to. But my body wouldn't let me."

"I'm...I'm so sorry, Silas. I should have been there...I should have been there..."

His broken smile killed me. "When I first saw you were alive, I was so, so angry. I was furious that I had suffered so much and even angrier that it was your choice to leave without telling me. Even though I understood why." He wiped away my tears. "Not only was it never your fault, but in fact, I'm so grateful you left. Because if my father would have found out about you, and he would have, he would have tortured and killed you...and would've made me watch. And I *never* would have recovered from that. Ever."

I leaned forward, kissing the tears off his cheeks. His eyes shut, a soft sigh releasing from his lips.

"I am so sorry I was ever upset with you. I had no right," I apologized.

"Never be sorry to me, ever again," he insisted, then drifted his gaze toward the ground. "I was a much better man with you in my life," he said quietly. "But that's why I hide my back. I've just told Era not to ask about it, and she has listened. I never wanted anyone to ask or show me pity. Be reminded of it. I'm just so ashamed of it all."

"You have nothing to be ashamed of, Silas. You did what you had to in order to *survive*. The person who should be ashamed is your father."

He just shook his head.

"I failed you, Lena. I failed my kingdom. Myself...my mother..." His lip wobbled. "You were right when you said my mother would be horrified to see me like this."

"Silas," I cried as I held his face. "You have *not* failed. Look at where we are and what you have sacrificed to do the right thing."

His face crumpled. "You must be so disappointed in me," he cried softly. "I am so ashamed of who I have become."

"Quill," I whispered as I went to sit on his lap, my legs on either side of him. "I have loved you since the first day I met you," I said with tenderness, his eyes filling with more tears. "And I will love you forever. No matter what, don't you understand that?"

He snaked his arms around my waist. "No, I do not. I don't understand how anyone could love me after all that."

I stroked his cheek and kissed his forehead, pulling back to stare into his eyes again.

"I am not the man you used to love, Lena." The muscle in his jaw feathered before he continued, "I have done unspeakable things. I have tortured and killed hundreds of people. You can't just...you can't just go back to the person you were before all of that. I will forever be haunted by not only everything that has happened to me...but everything I have done."

I held his face as I spoke. "I forgive you," I expressed. "My love for you is limitless, Silas. Unchanging, no matter what you've done. Even if you had never saved my people, and we were all being hung. I would've been heartbroken and angry...but I would've looked into your eyes as I died, and still, I would've loved you."

He shifted his head in refusal, eyes shining from the pooled tears. "I am not deserving of your love, Lena."

"You *are* deserving of it, and so, so much more. It doesn't matter to me that you aren't the man I used to love...because I love you just as you are now." I pulled him into my chest and held him as he finally broke, unleashing a heartbreaking sob.

"I will love every version of you, my Soul-Tie," I whispered.

"I love you so much," he wept. "I am so sorry..."

I hushed him, holding him tightly, my own tears coursing down my face. I stroked his hair and told him I loved him, just like all those years ago.

"He can't hurt you anymore," I whispered. "Never hold back your feelings around me. I will always be a safe person for you, okay?"

He squeezed me tighter, my chest muffling his cries.

CHAPTER SIXTY-FOUR

LENA

Silas had cried into my chest, and as I ran my hand along his back, the motion eventually soothed him to sleep. I drifted off myself soon after.

I didn't know how long I rested for—time felt strange here. But when I awoke, my eyes found him immediately.

Silas sat before the fireplace with his elbows resting on his knees, the delicate sheet tangled between his thighs as he fixated on Saoirse's doll, holding it in his grasp. The flames before him complimented his honey-colored irises, and I stared at him in awe as I observed them dancing in his eyes' reflection.

This man, who I loved with my entire heart, had been through so, so much. His skin, which was once unblemished and smooth, had become scarred, burned, calloused, and covered in tattoos. Ever since we found each other again, I couldn't comprehend why he looked so depleted, how the man who had been all smiles and had teased me non-stop had become cold and closed off.

The rare smiles I had seen had never fully reached his eyes, but as he turned his head to me, catching that I had awoken, his eyes met mine. A soft smile formed on his face, and his eyes sparkled.

I returned the expression, brushing my hand along the side of his leg as I sat up.

His smile then faded as he placed the doll on the floor beside the fireplace, but his eyes remained bright.

"I am desperately in love with you, Lena." He moved his arm and slid his hand along mine—my hand that now rested on his thigh. Our fingers interlocked. "It has only ever been you. No matter what I have done or who I've been with. It was only ever you who held my heart," he assured me.

My heart fluttered, and I scooted closer to him, sitting in between his thighs. I brushed my free hand across his cheek.

"And only you hold mine," I promised, leaning close and kissing his lips softly. I rested my forehead on his. "It has only ever been you, Silas. Even when I have tried to move on, it never compared to what I felt with you."

He released my hand from his grasp and slid his hands to both sides of my face, pulling away just enough so his golden eyes could shift back and forth between mine.

"I don't want to deny myself your lips, your body, your touch, ever again," he murmured, and his gaze dropped to my breasts, then up to my lips, his hands falling to his knees. "Gods, how I wish things were different."

The tension between us quickened my heart rate, and pressure built in between my legs at the memory of the incredible sex we had in Faltrun. My eyes fluttered down to his lips, down to his inked neck, then past his toned stomach to the sheet where the outline of his hardened length was visible. I let out a shaky exhale as I met eyes with him, his pupils dilated so large only a small rim of gold remained.

"Don't deny me. Not anymore," I whispered.

He stared at me for a moment before cursing under his breath and pulling my face to his. His lips collided with mine before both of ours parted, our tongues sliding and dancing against each other in slow, passionate movements. He slid his arms down and wrapped them around me as I sat on his lap, my legs resting on either side of his body. His cock was pushing up against my sensitive flesh—the only thing separating us was the thin fabric of the sheet.

He let out a deep moan as I ground against him, his one hand sliding down to grip my ass, the other one drifting up to release my hair from the tie securing it.

We stayed like that for a moment, lost in lust, kissing sloppily as we rubbed our bodies against each other—desperate, needing, searching. Silas groaned as he gripped the sheet and yanked it away, freeing his stiff cock, the thickness of him bobbing from the movement.

He grabbed me from beneath and lifted me as he stood, tossing me on the bed behind us. He stalked over me, his lustful eyes trailing to my breasts before cupping one with his hand. He bit his bottom lip and dived down, his mouth entrapping the raised peak as he sucked hard. I hissed and arched my back, earning a smirk from the Prince as he slowly swirled his tongue around my nipple.

He sucked once more, then pulled back to stare at me again.

"You are mesmerizing, Lena," he murmured while squeezing my breasts together with both of his strong hands. He allowed saliva to fall from his mouth, spitting gently on my chest. My eyes rolled back as he swirled both peaks with his thumbs, his own eyes darkening as he watched me writhe beneath him.

I let out a breathy moan, raising my hips, desperate for more of him to touch me. But what I truly wanted was to make him feel good.

"I want to suck on you, Silas," I breathed, pushing up and flipping us over so I was straddling him.

He watched me with heavy eyes as I slithered my body down. He sat up against the headboard just as I grasped his cock and slid it into my mouth.

"Lena, *fuck...*"

My entire body hummed with excitement as I took him in my mouth, delighting in the feel of his warm thickness, of his veins, as he slid down my throat. I worked to please him, bouncing my head up and down, thoroughly enjoying the view of his stomach muscles flexing, his eyes half-lidded, and his mouth agape as I sucked on him.

I savored his taste, savored his breathy moans as he fisted the sheet fabric.

"So beautiful," he murmured as he watched me.

I released him from my mouth, giving him a coy smile as I began stroking his cock, twisting my palm along the reddened tip.

His breathing quickened, his moans growing louder.

I felt my magic pooling, that incessant buzzing across my entire body, begging, pleading with me to let it out.

I licked up and down the throbbing length of him before sucking his balls into my mouth and continuing to rub him. "I love you, Silas," I whispered before continuing.

He ran his fingers through my hair. "I love *you,* Lena."

I continued pleasuring him, sucking, slurping, and stroking. Silas's eyes would only close for a second at a time, wishing to watch every second that his cock was in my mouth.

"Sit on my lap, Flower."

Popping his length from my mouth, I obeyed. Silas moved down further on the bed just as I moved up to straddle him. I placed my hands on his shoulders as he lined himself up with my entrance, his other hand holding my waist.

I slowly began sitting, crying out at the feeling of the pleasant stretch.

A throaty groan released from Silas once I was fully seated, and he yanked me toward him, wrapping his arms around me tight as he began ruthlessly fucking me.

I screamed, I moaned, I cried. He grasped me, flipping us over to take me another way. He slid back in slowly, holding my legs up, gazing at where my body was swallowing his. He slid his thumb into his mouth, lowering it to massage my clit.

I gripped one of my breasts, whimpering as he circled his thumb quickly.

I felt my magic rise and rise, and when he lowered himself, his golden eyes meeting mine, a loving smile taking over his face, I finally let it free.

My head fell back as I released my electricity—as my arms and legs wrapped around him, holding him tight. It sparked around his entire body, the blue hues illuminating his golden-brown skin.

His eyes rolled back before closing tightly. "Fuck...fuck," he panted. He squeezed my thighs, driving his hips into me in a wild state of bliss. "You feel so damn heavenly..."

"I love you," I cried in between moans, smiling as tears rolled down my cheeks.

Silas's own slid down his face as he leaned down, kissing my tears away. "I love you, Flower." He grinned, kissing my lips, my jaw, then the tip of my nose. "I will always love you."

The sex became more wild, more frantic as my magic flared. Blissful explosions spread throughout my body with every orgasm he gave me. It had to be over an hour now that his thick length had been sliding in and out of me...that his hands had been greedily exploring every inch of my body, and mine doing the same to his as if attempting to memorize every muscle, every curve.

He was taking me from behind now, and tears were still slipping down my cheeks at how euphoric the sex was. Silas wrapped his hands around my hair, gripping it tight from behind and pulling me upward, my back flush against his chest. Sliding his tongue along the side of my face, he licked my tears away.

"I never want to stop," he murmured into my ear. "I need this forever. I need you forever."

"You have me forever," I breathed, the lightning surrounding us heightening our pleasure. "My heart belongs to you."

He rolled his hips gently, kissing my pointed cartilage as he murmured, "You are even more beautiful with your real ears." More of my tears fell, and he was there to lick them away. "I cherish every part of you. I wouldn't change a damn thing."

He then sucked on my neck, cupping my breast with one hand and squeezing my hip with the other. When he pulled away, sliding his cock out, he laid down on his back. "I want to see your gorgeous face as we finish."

I kissed his cheek before sitting on his cock once more. This time I stayed upright, my hands on his pecs as I lifted myself up and down, smothering his cock with my tight heat.

"You beautiful siren." He grabbed my ass with both hands, his golden eyes illuminated by the lightning that sparked all around us. It was growing wilder. Brighter.

"Come for me, Flower."

His hands slid upward, grasping my hips as he began mercilessly slamming his cock inside of me. I couldn't breathe, couldn't think over the euphoric feeling. Over the perfection of this moment, of the sensation of our bodies joined. My head tipped back, and the guttural moan that ripped free from Silas's throat as he came was the most erotic sight and sound of my life.

My electricity heightened, then finally reached its peak, illuminating the entirety of the room as it flared. I screamed, my nails digging into his chest as my orgasm traveled through my body, stronger and wilder than ever before. My arousal gushed from me, soaking him and the sheets beneath us. I was still shuddering as I collapsed onto him, panting and covered in sweat.

"My Gods..." he rasped. "That...I've never felt a sensation like that."

"Me either. I don't know if I can walk," I joked, heaving a sigh, my limbs trembling

He chuckled, the sound light and sweet. I decided then that it was the most beautiful sound. I wanted nothing more in this life than to see him happy, carefree, and satisfied. I wished to erase every burden on his shoulders and smother every self-deprecating thought he had.

I would show him just how much he was loved, so that he'd never doubt he was deserving of it ever again.

"I love you," he whispered, his arms encasing me. "I love you so damn much." He kissed the top of my head, running his thumb along my cheek. "I have missed making love to you. But I have also missed our friendship. I've missed it all."

My throat burned, but I smiled, kissing his cheek. "I love you more than anything. I've missed it all, too. The only thing that has kept me going these years was the hope I'd find you again...somehow, someway."

He ran his fingers down my spine. "I never want to leave this moment." He sighed, his eyes closing, the corners of his lips raised. "If I died here right now in your arms, it would be the most peaceful death."

My brows drew together. "No one is dying. Don't ever say such a thing."

He let out a hum, continuing to caress my back. "I feel like I'm dreaming. Like I'm high or something."

I did, too, the remnants of our electric lovemaking still buzzing through my body. "I have been wanting to release the electricity during sex...wondering what it felt like." I studied his face as he rotated his head to me, opening those beautiful eyes. "But I only wanted to experience it with you. I acquired this magic because of you, after all. It belongs to you. All of me does."

His smile slowly faded, and he pulled me against him, squeezing tight. "I may not have magic, but all of me belongs to you, too."

CHAPTER SIXTY-FIVE

LENA

We lay there for a while, our limbs tangled together, Silas playing with my hair as we gazed at each other. We didn't have to worry about being caught, rushing, or keeping quiet.

Silas glanced over to the door to the right of the fireplace. "I believe there's a bathroom in there."

He stood, and I eyed his firm backside as he wandered over, peeking into the room. He turned, offering me a smirk.

"What?" I asked with amusement, propping my head up with my fist.

He stepped inside, and after a few seconds, I heard the sound of a faucet going.

A bathtub.

I was shocked there was running water, but then again, something about this place seemed off. Unreal.

"Is it warm?" I called out.

"It is."

I sat up and took in the environment of the room. The flames in the fireplace still crackled, illuminating the room with its warm glow. A painting of the night sky hung above it. I turned my body and stood, walking over to the window to the left of me. Moving the dark blue curtains, I saw how snow completely covered the window, cold air leaking from it. There had to be at least eight feet of it piled up.

I worried for my friends, wondering where they were and if they'd found shelter.

I heard Silas turn off the water, and I continued staring at the window as he walked up beside me.

"How are we going to survive this?" I whispered.

He kissed my shoulder. "One day at a time, Flower."

I turned to him. "And our friends? Do you think they survived?"

His jaw flexed. "I hope so. I still don't understand how the weather changed so drastically."

My thoughts drifted to Immeron's words back on Mount Rozavar before we embarked on this journey.

"...the trial that awaits at The Valley of Awakening. I don't know much of it, but there is a border between regular land and that of Nereida. It is said to show those who cross through it the truths of themselves."

My gaze fell to my hands, still in disbelief that the frostbite had vanished. Silas held my chin and lifted my gaze to his.

"Take a bath with me?" he asked.

I smiled, then squealed when he scooped me into his arms and carried me to the bathroom. Because of the lack of light, I could barely see as he placed me into the hot water. I let out a soft moan as I lowered myself further in. The porcelain tub was deep, and the bubbles, paired with the scent of orange and vanilla, comforted me.

"I have a request," Silas said as he held a candle to me. I let out a soft laugh as I brought my fingertips to the wick, lighting the candle and revealing Silas's beautiful face. He grabbed a few more, and after I lit them all, he placed them in different parts of the bathroom.

He smiled at me as he lowered himself in, and I couldn't keep away from him. I went forward and lifted my soapy hands to his face, pulling his lips to mine. He laughed against my mouth and placed his hands on my hips, pulling me on top of his lap.

I started kissing his neck, and he moaned softly. I could feel him stiffen underneath me, but as much as I wished to make love again, I stopped kissing him and held him tightly, resting my head on his shoulder and letting out a sigh.

He lightly brushed his hands up and down my back, his cheek resting on the top of my head.

"We never had the opportunity to bathe together in my room in the castle," he murmured. "But I had dreamt of it many times."

"What, my cold shower wasn't good enough for you?"

He laughed, leaning down to whisper in my ear. "I did enjoy fucking you in there...even if we were freezing our asses off."

I leaned my head back, raising a brow. "Even when we heard my mother return, and we had to pretend it was just me in the shower?"

"Oh, especially then." His smile grew. "I enjoyed watching you attempt to converse with her through the door while my cock was inside of you. How uneven your words were as I moved in and out."

I shook my head, then kissed his mouth, running my hands through his black hair. "You deviant."

"You loved it."

"I did," I admitted, feeling his length brushing my sex as I straddled him under the water.

"How can I go on after this?" I asked quietly, my hands trailing up his back, caressing the skin that had seen such abuse.

"What do you mean?" he mumbled.

"How can I return to pretending like there's nothing between us?" I pulled away. "How can I be happy when you are with her? When I can't openly show my affection? When I shouldn't be showing affection at all?" I dropped my eyes. "It isn't right to continue doing this when you are with someone else...even though I want to so badly."

"I know...I know," he whispered. "I need to figure out how to end things with Era. I know that."

"You'll actually leave her?" I asked quietly.

He nodded, kissing my temple. "It certainly can't go back to how it was before. I don't know how she will take it. I don't know how anyone will."

"I don't want to pressure you if you aren't ready," I insisted.

"I am more than ready."

"You say that," I said quietly. "But I know you care for Era, Silas. I know that you love her...just as I love Torrin."

His brows lowered, a deep sigh releasing from him.

I shook my head, eyes dropping. "I tried to get him to try again with me...we kissed on the sand last night."

"You wanted to be with him?" Silas asked softly.

I nodded, guilty eyes lifting to meet his. "As far as I could remember, it was he who I lost my virginity to. He and I have this history between us..." I shook my head, tears filling my eyes. "It just kills me to hurt him."

"You are the one who isn't ready," he realized.

I leaned my head against his chest, holding him tight. "I am ready. I never wish to be intimate with anyone else again in my life. I want you and only you. I just...telling the others is what makes me nervous."

Silas held me tighter. "Then we don't have to. We can be committed to one another in private while we navigate the unknown." He paused. "I'll admit...I am nervous about ending things with Erabella. She gave up everything to help me. Committed treason...and to leave her without her title..."

"Then we wait," I whispered, tilting my head up and kissing him slowly.

"I won't sleep with her again. I swear it."

"I know. I won't sleep with anyone else again, either."

My eyes slowly fluttered open, Silas's arms holding me close to his chest. We had made love a handful more times after getting out of the tub, and I don't know when I drifted to sleep nor how long we had been resting. I gazed up at him, sleeping peacefully, his youth more pronounced with his features so soft. His black hair was messy, and his lips were still swollen from our kisses. My heart warmed at the sight of him and the sound of his heart beating against my ear.

I realized this was the first time in our entire relationship that we had been able to sleep next to each other in bed. I had fallen asleep in his arms the first time we made love, but he was gone when I woke.

But here he was. My thoughts wandered to where my friends might be. I hoped they were okay, but I found myself not worrying too much because I was so happy lying here with him. If this really all was a test...surely my friends had succeeded, too.

Silas shifted beneath me, and in his sleep, he nestled in closer to me before his eyes slowly opened.

I stared into the pools of honey that were his eyes, and he gave me a sleepy smile.

"Good morning, Flower," he murmured and planted a kiss on my forehead.

"Did you sleep well?" I asked sleepily.

"Better than I ever have."

I grinned. "Me too." I dragged my finger along the tattoos on his neck, focusing on the artwork. "Are these phoenixes?"

I had never truly studied the design, but now that I did, I noticed the feathers, the beaks, and the flame.

"They are," he murmured. "My mother loved them. Of course, now, with all this prophecy bullshit, I'm wishing I'd picked a different tattoo."

I continued stroking his skin. "I like it...love it, actually."

He let out a hum. "Let's just hope the God of Rebirth isn't a dick."

I giggled, and Silas kissed my lips softly. As he pulled away, my smile faded.

That sound...

"Silas...the birds," I breathed as I shot up, taking note of the room filled with sunlight. Birds sang from outside, and when I pulled back the curtains covering the window beside the bed, I gasped.

Nothing but lush, green fields were in the distance. Not a trace of snow anywhere.

"My Gods," Silas whispered as he stared off from behind me.

We quickly got dressed, grasped our bags, and rushed outside of the cabin. A warm breeze blew through as blades of grass danced, and the sun beamed down, warming my body.

"It's like a summer's day," I whispered. "How—?"

A call in the distance cut off my speech, and when my head turned, I saw our group of friends running to us.

"Lena!" Elowen cried, sprinting for me.

When she reached me and pulled me into a hug, I froze before returning the gesture. Era ran up to Silas, hesitating before hugging him softly.

Silas and I made eye contact, his face lining with guilt, and I quickly glanced away.

I won't sleep with her again. I swear it.

"You're all okay," I whispered. When I met eyes with Merrick, who wore a pained expression, I furrowed my brows in question. He broke our eye contact almost immediately.

"We all got separated when we plunged into the water," Edmund said, running a hand through his light blond hair. "Well, some of us. Merrick and Era disappeared also."

"Something happened to my magic. It forced me back into my standard form, which is why you all plunged into the sea," Dani said. "Thankfully, we've only been separated for an hour."

I frowned. "An hour? That's impossible."

Roland and Hendry exchanged confused expressions while Viola crossed her arms.

"Well, how long would you say you were gone?" Hendry asked warily.

"At least a day and a half, maybe two." I met eyes with Silas, who nodded.

"Yeah, it was certainly far longer than an hour. We almost got killed by this blizzard, and that's when we found—" He turned, and his face went pale.

I glanced behind us and gasped at what I saw. Or rather, what I *didn't* see. "Where...where the fuck did the cabin go?!" I exclaimed.

"Uh...what cabin?" Roland asked.

I narrowed my eyes at him. "The cabin we just emerged from. What do you mean?"

"Lena..." Torrin's eyebrows drew together. "We just saw you and Silas standing out here. Never once did we see a cabin, and we've been walking in nothing but these fields this entire time."

I looked over at Merrick. "How long were you two gone for?"

He clenched his jaw, his eyes swirling dark as he gazed at Era. She quickly averted his gaze and focused on me. "Only an hour or so," she said, crossing her arms.

"Well, we were in the cabin. Otherwise, how would we have gotten these—" I gasped again as I observed my apparel. The new clothes I had adorned had vanished, and I was once again in the clothes Immeron and Ayla had gifted me.

Silas cursed under his breath as he realized his old clothes were on, too.

"What, were you guys wearing other clothes?" Viola asked with a raised brow.

"Yeah, what exactly were you guys up to?" Roland asked with a smirk.

I glared at him, about to throw a fireball at his head. "As Silas said, we were in a blizzard. When we got to the cabin, we changed into dry clothes," I said calmly, definitely leaving out the fact that we warmed each other with our naked bodies. And I would certainly not mention the wild sex that followed.

Torrin's eyes flared. "You got your memories back," he whispered.

I swallowed. "Yes...whatever caused our magic disruption must've canceled the spell."

Torrin nodded gravely, lowering his head.

I focused on putting up a mental wall. I hated hurting him. Roland was never attached to me, so the idea of me hooking up with someone else didn't affect him. Even if he had also had feelings for Silas at one point.

My stomach twisted when I looked back at Silas once more, Era nestled in his chest with arms wrapped around him.

We might not have been able to be with one another right at that moment, but I would always be there for him as a friend. He trusted me with his darkest secrets. And he needed me just as much as I needed him.

Before Roland or anyone else could press on the situation, a sound emitted behind us. A light ringing. We covered our ears, turning to where it came from.

Standing in a line were people dressed in blue and white robes.

"Lena Daelyra," a woman in the center called. "We've been expecting you."

The background behind them warped, the long, plain valley shifting into a massive, marvelous city in the distance. Looming, sandstone buildings and pale blue rooftops called our name—called us home.

The woman's smile grew. "Welcome to Nereida."

CHAPTER SIXTY-SIX

LENA

The smell of salt water and seaweed filled my senses as I gasped at the territory before me.

Nereida. We made it.

As we approached, following the robed Mages, I admired the architecture of the hundreds of sandstone buildings. Most of the women wore shelled tops and flowy skirts, while the men were topless, wearing nothing but a pair of shorts. Their bright smiles went from carefree to wary as they watched our group being led through their home.

I wonder when they last had a visitor.

The tops of many of the buildings were a pearlescent blue color. This place was stunning—more beautiful and brighter than any place on the mainland. It was hard to believe that just yesterday, I had been in the most terrifying snowstorm of my life, and now I was sweating from the heat.

The Mages walking the streets now gawked at the sight of the humans in our group, perhaps as equally as the Warlock, who gladly strutted with us in her usual form, pupilless eyes scanning the scenery.

Roland leaned toward me as we walked. "You think we're the first humans they've seen?"

"It's very likely."

Weaving through the village, I couldn't fathom the number of Mages here. Thousands, maybe more.

They had been here, living—no, thriving—while those of us across the sea had been struggling to survive.

We were led through lush gardens and trickling fountains. A medley of flowers was in bloom, and the aroma mixed with the ocean breeze was an intoxicating scent. Palm trees were looming around us, coconuts hanging, ready to be harvested.

I'd never had coconut before.

We reached the front entry of a massive palace. The elegant sandstone building overlooked the southern sea, the pale blue domes above gleaming in the sunlight. Its size rivaled Castle La-Rune, though its design was far brighter than the gothic architecture in Otacia.

Upon entry, we were met with bright white walls and high ceilings in the grand hall, shimmering crystal chandeliers hanging above.

I studied them in awe as we moved forward. Moving up a set of stairs, I came to an abrupt halt when I caught movement near the sea.

I immediately rushed to the window. "No...there's no possible way," I gasped.

Sitting atop a large boulder perched in the ocean were three Sea Nymphs. Their tails varied in color—one turquoise, one a medley of greens, and one a bright white.

"My Gods!" Elowen exclaimed. Her head whipped to the people leading us. "I thought the Sea Nymphs were extinct!"

The woman who had addressed me smiled. "There's a lot those on the mainland are unaware of."

My eyes slid back to the gorgeous creatures, their upper halves appearing similar to ours. The main difference, other than the whimsical tails, was their ears, which were pointed but also webbed. Along their cheeks and temples, their skin was tinted to match their tails.

I wanted to get closer and see them—meet them. But as we continued onward, I knew meeting the ruler of this land would come first.

Sitting on a throne, a beautiful Mage woman beamed at us. A chunk of white hair framed her face, but otherwise, the rest of her curls were black. But that wasn't her most striking feature—no, that was her skin, which was not brown nor white but a mixture of both, almost marbled. I had never seen someone with such a complexion.

To her right was another woman, one with tanned skin and light sea-green hair whose length rivaled mine. She had it tied in two long fishtail braids, the ends resting at her waist. Her brown eyes studied us with slight surprise.

To the throne's left was a Mage man, his skin a rich brown and eyes a striking green. His dark brown hair was cropped short to his scalp, and his hands were kept politely behind his back. His eyes remained on me.

"Lena Daelyra," The woman on the throne began, her nearly black eyes studying me curiously. "We have been anticipating your arrival. Allow me to introduce myself." A warm smile overcame her face. "I am Lucretia Crane, Supreme of Nereida."

I began to bow, and Lucretia raised her hand. "You and I are equals, Supreme. No need to bow."

I felt my cheeks heat, and I gave an embarrassed smile. "We are pleased to be here."

Lucretia motioned to her right. "This is Kismet, my consort."

The green-haired woman—Kismet—gave a warm smile.

"And this is my son, Valter."

The green-eyed Prince smiled slightly, inclining his head.

I returned the gesture, my eyes sliding back to Lucretia. "How did you know my name?"

Lucretia smiled, lifting a note between her pointed fingernails. "Your seer informed us a few months ago to anticipate your arrival."

"Kayin?" I asked breathlessly.

Lucretia's smile faltered as she lowered the note. "No. A man named Igon."

Gods...Igon really knew a lot. If only he had lived, we would have so many more answers.

I nodded. "He was our Supreme."

"Yes," she responded gravely. "It appears he knew of his impending death."

"I can't believe a place like this actually exists," Viola began. "I can't believe Igon knew yet kept us in Ames."

"We once were a kingdom under the sea," Lucretia explained. "Until The War of Three Pirates, that is." She gestured to a looming statue resting along the northern wall. It was of a male Sea Nymph and what appeared to be a Mage woman in each other's embrace.

The War of Three Pirates...Immeron had mentioned that war.

"I've never read any literature on this place...never heard of it, except from a couple of Mages I know."

"That is for good reason," she explained. "We don't wish for the humans to know of us. While we have a powerful ward protecting our land, it still would prove tiresome if we had a group of people constantly wishing to pass through."

"What of all the rest of your people? We are suffering...our numbers dwindling by the day."

"It seems that is the humans' fault, no?" Her eyes shifted to Dani. "I wasn't expecting a Warlock to be in your company. A long-time enemy of ours."

"Warlocks are not our enemy," I protested as Dani's gaze narrowed.

Lucretia's eyes slid to Silas. "It appears you don't believe humans are, either."

"Bad people exist among every group of people. Our real enemy is the necromancer plaguing our lands."

As my words came out, Valter stiffened. "A necromancer?"

"You don't know?" Dani asked. "Or perhaps you are harboring him, seeing as though there are thousands of Mages here."

I shot Dani a warning glare. Lucretia shook her head, raising her nose. "I'm aware of the threat." To that, Valter shot her a surprised glance. "Those that live here never leave. They have no desire to see the rest of the continent...see all the places where we are discriminated against. As for the necromancer, I became aware of his presence when the Undead recently seized Wrendier. I've had to strengthen our borders due to their continuous desire to get here."

Viola clenched her fists. "You keep to yourselves while the rest of us suffer. With how many of us are here, we could've stood a chance of winning this war before it even began!"

"I have no interest in bringing my people to war. We are happy here. Safe. You're more than welcome to stay."

"You may not be safe here forever," I said calmly. "This necromancer isn't just any Mage...he is a God."

The room became silent.

Lucretia's brows lowered. "What did you say?"

Silas was the one to speak next. "The God of Deceit."

Valter's eyes became saucers. "You know of the prophecy? How are you certain the necromancer is him?"

"I suppose he could be bluffing, but judging the extent of his power, I believe him. He claims Valor fell in love with a human—his mother—resulting in his conception." I swallowed. "He also spoke of a rift. He showed the Prince of Otacia and me a device of some sort. Something from another world."

Valter anxiously peered at his mother, whose own eyebrows were raised. "Do you have this device?" she pressed.

I shook my head. "No. He has it. But he is in desperate search of something called the Weapon. Is it...is it here?"

Kismet frowned. "What kind of weapon do you speak of?"

"All we know of it is that it is a type of magic that no one has ever seen," Silas answered. "A seer told us this...one different from the two mentioned before."

"Magic to stop all magic or all of humanity. It is vital we find it and keep it away from him," I insisted. "Did Igon mention anything about it in his note?"

Lucretia's shoulders slumped, and she shook her head. "No. He mentioned no such thing."

I sighed. "All he said to me was a riddle regarding the God of Rebirth, and he gave me a memento of his before he died."

To that, Valter's head snapped in my direction. "A memento, you say?"

Kismet's eyes slid over to him, and Lucretia clapped happily. "A memento, of course." At my obvious confusion, Lucretia continued. "Have you ever heard of the Chamber of Time? Odds are you haven't since you haven't heard of our lands."

"Tithara's gift was the ability to alter time. Her temple resides on our island," Valter stated. "Now, the Chamber of Time does not alter time, but it allows you to go back for viewing." He smiled. "All you need is a memento of the living or dead, and their memories will play for you." He tilted his head. "Your seer gave you a memento of his. We will use it in the Chamber of Time, and you will see all he did."

Hope blossomed in my chest. "Oh, my Gods! Let's go do it, then. I have the compass in my bag—"

"The Chamber requires charging," Kismet interrupted, and all our eyes went to hers. "It is a powerful, sacred space. We will need a handful of Mages to surge their energy into the altar in order for it to work." Her brown eyes slid over to her lover. "We should get started on it right away. Have it ready the morning after next."

"That would be incredible," I breathed. "Thank you."

Kismet nodded, then stepped away from her spot beside the throne, exiting politely.

Another question popped into my head. "Igon told me to find Oquerene. Do you have any information on the place?"

Valter's eyes flashed. "One does not just find Oquerene."

651

"Ah, the land ruled by the Angels." Lucretia shook her head. "I have not been, nor do I know how one would get there. But what I do know is that the Angels oversee that realm. And Angels have a worse reputation than the Sea Nymphs once did."

"I was told Sea Nymphs had gone extinct," I murmured. "Yet I saw them, basking by the ocean. And now you're telling me Angels exist, too?"

"Why, of course, they do!" Lucretia exclaimed. "Angels, Pixies, Half-lives—there is no shortage of mythical creatures in Oquerene. That is the land of the Gods. Every being they crafted still resides there."

"Like an...afterlife?" Elowen asked.

Valter shook his head. "No, Valor oversees the afterlife. His realm is the Underworld—also known as Elytial. Ravaiana oversees Oquerene, the original place of creation."

"Wait...I thought the Underworld was a hell of sorts," I questioned.

Valter's chuckle was warm as he laughed at my confusion. "There is much knowledge of the Gods that has been lost on the mainland." His green orbs sparkled. "I can show you all I know. Perhaps it would help."

I smiled at his kindness. "Igon told me that...that I would be the savior of our kind," I said with a slight flush to my cheeks. "I'm feeling quite lost, understandably. So, I appreciate any help you're willing to give."

His eyes remained on mine, and after a brief silence, Lucretia said, "You all must be exhausted. I know some of you had a more troublesome time in the Valley of Awakening. It can be hard to readjust after."

My eyes flared, and I felt Silas tense beside me.

Merrick cleared his throat. "You can tell when someone's in there?" he asked cautiously.

"Oh, yes. When someone passes through, they're passing through our defense system." Her eyes raked down him, then slid beside him to Erabella. She said nothing else on the matter.

"Let me guide you all to your rooms," Valter offered, stepping down. When he reached our group, I noted he was around the same height as Silas. "Our beds are incredibly comfortable. You'll all probably sleep like babies."

We were led down the pristine hallways, down an outdoor passage taking us to a separate region of the palace. Once again, I found my eyes drifting off to the sea, gazing upon the Sea Nymphs who swam along the current. There weren't very many, at least from what I could see up here, but still.

I almost felt enraged, knowing we could've been living peacefully here. How long had Igon known about this place?

We continued ambling forward, Valter leading the way.

I supposed this Chamber of Time would give me some answers.

Entering another hallway once back inside, Valter stopped. "All of these rooms are free. Take whichever you like."

As I went to step forward, Valter gently held out his hand. "Supreme, your room will be a floor higher than the others." He offered me a warm smile. "I can show you there." His eyes trailed over our group. "Will anyone be joining you?"

My eyes found Silas's.

I wish.

"Nope. Just me."

"No invitation, Ginger Snap?" Roland pouted.

I chuckled, giving him my middle finger, and followed Valter up a flight of steps.

"Don't like him much?" Valter asked over his shoulder, an easy smile on his face.

I laughed through my nose. "I love him. I love all my friends."

When we stopped in front of an ornate, white door, Valter bowed.

"Now, rest up. Dinner will be brought to you in a couple of hours. You'll get to explore the city tomorrow, and in the evening, a ball will be thrown in your honor."

"A ball? That isn't necessary—"

"Nonsense," he interrupted, his bright green eyes shimmering against his dark skin. 'As you will come to see, we like to be extravagant with our celebrations. And you being here is a celebration indeed."

Heat flooded my cheeks at his compliment. I inclined my head. "Very well."

Valter departed, and gladly so, because the gasp I released upon entry to my room would've been embarrassing for him to hear.

Purple mage light was glowing throughout the room. On the back wall rested a massive bed stacked with multiple pillows and a thick comforter that was calling to me. But the most impressive sight was to my left. Water trickled down the stone wall into a bubbling bath of sorts, large enough to hold multiple people. Blue mage lights were under the water, illuminating the tub.

I set my bag beside my bed, removed my armor, and stepped toward the bubbling water. Kneeling down, I dipped my hand in. It was pleasantly hot.

I grinned, removing the rest of my clothing.

Gods, did I wish Silas were here—

Just as I was about to release my hair from its braid, there was a knock on my door. I quickly grasped one of the white towels beside the bath and wrapped it around my body. I rushed over to open it, expecting Valter to be here telling me something he had forgotten.

But when I opened the door, golden eyes found mine, then trailed down my body.

"Silas...what are you doing here?" I whispered, my head peeking out, my eyes darting down the empty hallway.

He cleared his throat. "I was just making sure you were alright. We don't know these people, and it worried me you were rooming elsewhere." His gaze flitted behind me. "Although now I see why. That bastard wants to woo you."

I slapped his arm, and he smiled playfully down at me. "That 'bastard' is essentially a Prince."

He let out a hum as he raised his arm, leaning against the doorway. "He isn't the first prince enthralled by your charm," he murmured.

I snorted despite my face flushing. "My charm? You think me giving the finger to Roland charmed him?"

"Oh, most definitely," he purred, leaning in closer. "To those who live a life refined and proper, your authenticity is a breath of fresh air. That, and your undeniable beauty."

My eyes became heavy, and I took a steadying breath, grasping one of the stones of my necklace. "I wish you could stay with me in here," I whispered.

His grin slowly fell. "I wish I could, too." His eyes flickered behind me again, just for a moment. "Just don't allow him entry into this room. I doubt there'll be any peace between our kinds if I end up killing him."

I pinched his side, then, without thinking, pulled his face to mine, kissing him.

We held it for a moment. Silas's eyes darkened when I pulled away, and a grin tugged at his lips.

"Oh, my Gods."

Panic surged through me, and when Silas and I whirled our heads to the side, Roland was gaping at us.

CHAPTER SIXTY-SEVEN
LENA

"Oh fuck," I breathed.

Silas went utterly still, and we were all left staring at one another.

"Roland, I can explain—" I began, but he spun away.

Throwing my hand outward, I blocked him from leaving, a protective barrier sealing him in this hallway.

Roland's shoulders rose and fell, and then he rotated his body toward us, brows lowered, eyes narrowed.

"I said I can explain," I bit out. My eyes flicked up to Silas. "I'm sorry. I-I'll talk to him."

Silas's worried gaze went back to his friend, then to mine.

"Go," I ordered him gently.

He sighed, that scowl taking over his face as he turned, walking away.

I released the barrier just as Silas passed Roland, wandering down the steps.

I nodded toward my room. "Come inside."

Roland clenched his jaw, but he followed me.

Closing the door behind him, I sighed through my nose. Roland remained silent as he watched me release my hair from its braid and walk toward the bath.

I allowed my towel to fall, not caring that he saw my naked body, as he'd seen it already many times before.

My eyes fluttered closed as I sunk into the bath. I blew out of my nose, dipping my head under for a moment before emerging. When I wiped the water droplets away from my eyes, the handsome soldier was still staring daggers at me.

I motioned for him to sit beside the bath. He hesitated but removed his boots, rolled up his pant legs, and sat, dipping his calves into the water.

"Well?" he asked.

I took a long breath, smiling to myself. "When I met Quill, back when I was sixteen, I was immediately affected by him. There was this...bond between us. It superseded attraction, though we were surely attracted to one another. I know it now as the Soul-Tie bond." My eyes flitted to Roland, who continued to study me with a hardened jaw.

"Quill lived in the Inner Ring. Well, that is where I met him one morning. Long story short, he'd witnessed a lousy attempt at me defending myself. He agreed to train me once a week after that." I drifted my hands over the bubbles in the water. "It was a few months of that, meeting once a week, falling for one another. But he was so secretive. There was much about him I didn't know."

My eyes roamed up to Roland's, whose stare was growing more confused.

"We had lost our virginities to one another one evening in my home. But after, I was tired of his secrecy. I followed him home the following week, hiding myself with an invisibility elixir. He took a strange path, one that passed beside the castle."

Roland's eyes began to widen.

"I was caught—by Torrin, of all people—for sneaking into the Center. When I was presented to the Queen the following day, beside her was Quill. Beside her...was Silas."

Roland blinked rapidly. "You and him...you knew each other?"

I nodded. "I've been in love with him all these years. I faked my death when the kill order was in place, never having told him what I really was. It changed him."

I could tell Roland's mind was reeling. "That's why he saved you...why he joined your cause. Why, after so many years of hatred of your kind, he seemingly flipped a switch."

"I'm sorry for withholding that information," I spoke honestly. "But we both didn't want our people to think we were joining forces simply because we were in love when we were younger, even though it was a major part."

He took a handful of minutes to process. "Gods, no wonder he's been extra sick of me." He winced. "My flirting with you must've driven him crazy."

"It has been strange between us since reuniting. I have a history with Torrin and obviously have had fun with you. And then there's the fact he is married."

"When did you two...start up again?"

"We had a moment when I returned from the mountain," I admitted, eyes glued to the water. "But it wasn't until we were in the cabin—the Valley of Awakening—that we fully admitted our feelings and worked through everything. Well...worked through most things."

My eyes slowly rose to his at his silence.

"Do you think I'm a bad person?" I asked quietly.

He shook his head. "No, Lena. I think this situation is messy as fuck." He paused. "I think Silas should leave his wife, though I have believed him unhappy with her since the start." He smiled weakly. "I suppose now I know why."

A pang of guilt washed over me. I knew his and Silas's secret, though it was not my place to say what I learned. Maybe all this time, Roland believed Silas to have feelings for him.

Roland's head fell. "I should get back."

"I'm sorry I didn't tell you," I whispered, tears filling my eyes. "I really wanted to move on from him...but I couldn't."

Roland angled his head up, then motioned with his finger for me to come over. I swam forward, stopping once I was between his legs.

He lifted his hand, stroking my cheek with a half-smile. "So much makes sense now," he murmured, then his bottom lip protruded. "Damn...the last time really was our last, wasn't it?"

I bit my lip, then splashed him lightly with water. He chuckled.

I was still attracted to him. But I had no desire for anyone but Silas.

"Afraid so."

"Boo." He sighed, his hand falling back, the corners of his lips rising. "I'm happy for you guys...happy you've found each other again." His smile faltered. "What about Era?"

My shoulders drooped. "There is a lot to be worked out regarding that. We agreed we wouldn't be intimate with anyone else while we figure things out. I...I shouldn't have kissed him." I raked my wet hands down my face.

"You two haven't hooked up since?"

I peeked at him through my fingers, guilt written all over my face.

Roland shook his head. "Naughty, Ginger Snap," he scolded playfully as he stood, removing his legs from the water. "So, Torrin knows about this history?"

I nodded, my fingers falling. "He does. As do Merrick and Dani."

He choked, hand flying to his chest. "Okay, now I'm offended you left me out of the loop."

"To be fair," I began, swimming to the front and resting my arms outside of the bath, "Merrick figured it out because of his gift. Torrin knew because he was there."

He cocked a brow as he dried off his calves. "And Dani?"

"It's another long story. But I guess she noticed the way he and I looked at one another."

He slid back on his socks and boots. "I suppose I need to be more observant." He shot me a wink.

I bit my lip. "I know it's a lot to ask...but please don't tell anyone, Roland."

When he finished lacing his boots, he said, "I won't. The last thing I need is the Prince hating my guts any more than he does."

I offered him a gentle smile. "He doesn't hate your guts. Or you."

"Trust me." He stood up straight. "He does."

He began striding toward the door when I called out, "Roland."

He looked back.

I tried to let him see the truth in my eyes. "Trust me. He doesn't."

Roland sucked in his lips, eyes falling to the ground before he left.

CHAPTER SIXTY-EIGHT

SILAS

"**I**s everything okay with you?" I asked Era from my spot beside her in bed.

She'd hardly uttered any words to me since we'd joined back up. We may have only known each other for a little over a year, but I could tell when something weighed on her mind.

I still couldn't believe Roland had caught Lena and me kissing. I'd have to speak about it with him at some point. Dinner had been delivered to our room, and after eating the delectable, seared fish, we laid in bed, wishing to get some sleep.

Era kept her eyes away, staring up at the ceiling. "Yes. Why wouldn't it be?"

I could also tell when she lied, because it wasn't very often she did so. "Ever since we got split, you've been acting different."

"No, I haven't," she deflected.

She and Merrick had been separated together. Dani had mentioned she believed him to be attracted to her. And as my mind organized my memories, I realized the Empath had always kept close to her.

Did they have a moment together like Lena and I did?

"What happened when you and Merrick were split from us?"

The feathering in her jaw gave away her unease. "Nothing."

I frowned. Clearly, that meant something. But what? Merrick had kept his distance from her since we'd gotten here.

I sighed, not wishing to pester her. She certainly wasn't pestering me...which was curious.

"Very well," I conceded.

After a brief pause in the dark light, she asked quietly, "Do you feel things have changed between us?"

The question spiked my heart rate. "What makes you ask?"

"You've hardly touched me since beginning this journey... have barely even kissed me since before we left Faltrun."

Guilt spread through my chest as I stared at her. I needed to be honest and come clean with the truth of my past and who I was, but the words wouldn't come out.

"I'm just stressed," I deflected.

Her face twisted, and she lifted her hands to rub her temples.

"Is your head alright?" I asked softly.

"I've been getting these headaches...I don't know. Must be from *stress*."

Her sarcasm wasn't lost on me. She didn't believe my excuse.

"Perhaps we can find you a remedy in the morning for it."

She didn't reply.

"Let me rub your back. Perhaps it'll help," I offered.

She looked at me then, eyes wide. Miserable.

I gave her a tight-lipped smile, and I didn't miss the slight tremble of her lips as she turned to her side, allowing me to lift the fabric of her shirt to caress her skin.

My fingers glided over her tanned flesh, and I began to hear her cry.

"Era," I whispered in concern. "What's wrong?"

"Nothing," she cried softly.

I pulled her back against my chest, holding her to me. I was a hypocrite for saying, "Talk to me."

"It's just my head," she mumbled.

I thought over all the possibilities. Did guilt weigh on her, too? Or was my distance causing this much pain?

We'd never been overwhelmingly close, but I would make love to her frequently. I supposed it was clear that something had changed.

"Is Merrick's head hurting, too?"

Her whole body tensed, giving me an answer. "What?" she whispered.

"You two were trapped together. I was just wondering if these headaches were affecting him, too," I murmured, still gliding my hand across her back.

"I...I don't know."

I wanted to ask if she had feelings for him...wanted to tell her it was okay if she did. But on the off chance she didn't, I wasn't ready to speak of my own sentiments.

"Whatever weighs on you, Erabella," I mumbled into her ear, "don't allow it to. I know this journey hasn't been easy, but we've gathered many allies. I think it will be sooner rather than later we can go home."

She let out a faint cry, and I hushed her, relaxing her with my touch.

Even if she wouldn't be my queen, Otacia would always be a home to her. And I'd ensure she was set for the rest of her life, living lavishly and freely, the way she deserved to be.

The morning came, and we were all instructed to dress and head to the dining hall for breakfast. I lifted the white shirt and swim shorts that were left for me, Erabella sliding into her matching shell bra and skirt, showcasing her toned midsection. The skirt was to be pulled away later when we went to the ocean to swim.

She looked beautiful in it, but the weariness in her eyes was unnerving me, as was this headache of hers that was bothering her more and more. I'd sent a request for a healing elixir of sorts, and when she took it, nothing improved.

I held out my elbow, and she lined hers with mine, us heading downstairs. We were the first to arrive in the broad, open space. The windows were all open, the sea breeze pleasant as it blew through, and the sounds of seagulls crying from outside caught my attention.

It was stunning here—the bright blue ocean just steps from our eating area. Otacia wasn't too far from the sea, but it wasn't as tropical of an experience as it was here.

Valter was dressed in a deep green suit, grin broad as he came to greet us. After exchanging pleasantries, he showed us to our seats at the large table. A spread of exotic fruits, breads, and jams was placed elegantly on the table, along with parfaits and coconut meat. The scent of it all had my mouth watering.

Lucretia and her consort, Kismet, had not arrived yet.

Dani sauntered in next, wearing a navy ensemble that complimented his complexion. Roland was at his side, wearing light grey, though all I could focus on was his hazel eyes that stared at me knowingly.

When Merrick entered a moment later, Torrin and Viola were beside him, and his eyes automatically went over to my wife. When I glanced over at her, she was staring down at her lap. The Empath's jaw set, and he sat as far from her as he could.

"Vi, you look amazing," Dani complimented, admiring the sand-colored shell top and skirt. It seemed our outfits were all nearly identical, save for the color differences.

Elowen, Edmund, and Hendry were in next, the healer's aqua-blue outfit matching her eyes.

Two robed figures walked in, and behind them, joining us at last, was Lena.

I did my best to school my expression. Her ensemble was the most elegant of all. Her shell bra was a combination of green hues with glittering gems molded to it. Her skirt was fuller than the others. And across her collarbones, she wore my mother's necklace like always.

It seemed she'd been dolled up. Her orange hair was tied in two fishtail braids, similar to how Kismet's was the day prior. They fell past her full breasts, the tips lying just beside her belly button.

Her cheeks were tinted pink. I knew she wasn't used to presenting in such a way.

"Good morning, Lena," Valter greeted, eyes skating over her. "You look beautiful."

Roland and Torrin's jaws were hanging open while they gazed at her, and even my other male friends were eyeing her a little longer than normal.

She smiled at him. "You don't look so bad yourself," she responded confidently, sitting across from me at the table. When her eyes slid over to mine, they flitted up and down, taking me in as quickly as she could.

Lucretia and Kismet waltzed in a few moments later, arm in arm, Kismet's attire black and Lucretia's white. After a quick greeting, we all began eating.

Breakfast went by relatively quickly. Lena had attempted to talk more about the crisis on the mainland, but Lucretia kept changing the topic of conversation. Whether or not they were willing to help, we at least had this Chamber of Time to give us some answers.

I tried not to overeat, but trying all the different foods was too hard to pass up. From starfruit to durian to kumquats—the latter's name Roland childishly laughed about—I enjoyed it all...except for papaya. I didn't much care for that.

After, everyone excitedly ventured off to the sparkling sea. I told Era I would be a moment, heading back to our room to collect myself.

I wished I could join in, strip off my top, and submerge myself in the water. I wished I was normal.

A soft knock sounded at my door, and when I opened it, Lena walked inside.

"Are you going to swim?" she asked me gently as I shut the door. She now knew exactly why my back was kept covered.

I wanted to swim. I wanted to take my shirt off and feel the warm sun on my body. I didn't want to be held back by my past and ruled by those who abused me.

I began to unbutton my shirt.

"They will ask," I mumbled, my fingers shaking. "I don't want to talk about it."

"Then just say that." Her hand cradled my cheek. "I doubt anyone will pressure you." She gave me a playful smile, grasping her breasts. "I could whip my shell top off. That'll take the attention away."

I snorted. "You do that, and I'll put you over my knee and spank your ass 'til your skin's red."

She bit back a smile. "Don't encourage me," she teased, running her hand down my bare chest.

I dragged my bottom lip through my teeth, eyes falling down to finish unbuttoning the shirt. With a deep breath, I shrugged it off.

Lena's eyes trailed down my body, and her tear-filled eyes met mine. "I am so proud of you."

My lip wobbled, and my own tears threatened to release. "I'll just need a minute," I whispered.

She nodded, stepped forward, and hugged me, her soft hands still foreign against my bare skin. I was still unused to someone's touch there but having her in my arms felt so good.

I held her, stroking her own skin, before giving the top of her head a kiss. "I'll be okay," I said quietly, more to myself than her.

"I know you will be." She pulled back, eyes sparkling, and turned, leaving me alone in the room.

My anxiety was at an all-time high. Here I was about to reveal my greatest weakness, my greatest shame, to everyone I've hidden it from.

I stepped out onto the beach, my feet sinking into the smooth sand, and I felt pain in my throat the second the sun warmed me, the moment the pleasant breeze brushed against my bare skin.

Everyone was already playing in the ocean. Elowen was on Edmund's shoulders, and Roland was attempting to splash her as Edmund splashed him back. Merrick and Era were talking off to the side, floating in the water, and Viola was sauntering along the coast with Dani.

Lena was with Torrin, sitting on the sand, lost in conversation.

Hendry met my eyes first, only steps to my right, a drink in hand. I watched as his widened regard traveled down my back, then back up to my face.

His eyes softened, and he gestured to his cocktail. "Drink?" he asked with a smile.

I gave a small smile back. "Please."

Hendry angled his head at the bartender running the drink stand, ordering another one of the fruity cocktails. As I waited, my eyes caught Era's. The whites of her eyes were completely visible. She'd never seen me topless in our entire marriage. Quickly, she exited the water, making her way to me.

I took a nervous breath, taking the drink Hendry handed me. "I'm always here for you," he said softly. "If you ever need to talk about it."

I swallowed the unpleasant lump rising in my throat. "I know you are."

He departed just as Era ran up to me. "Silas..." she breathed, tears filling her brown eyes.

"I don't want to talk about it," I said quietly. "I just want to pretend it's not there, okay?"

A look of understanding shone in her features. "Of course. Of course." She smiled. "Let's swim?"

I studied my wife's eyes and found myself smiling back as she held my hand.

As we took step after step toward the water, I glanced to my left. Lena's eyes flicked to my and Era's joined hands, and I hated the flash of hurt I saw. But when she lifted her eyes back to mine, the tears that were present were not sadness...but delight. She beamed at me.

Her love was always better than mine, because despite her discomfort seeing me beside another, she was happy for me.

I wanted to scoop her up in my arms and run into the ocean with her. I wanted to kiss her until our lips were swollen and make love to her on the beach, not caring who saw. I think Torrin reiterated the sentiment as his widened eyes returned to her as he spoke, her cheeks heating.

As I focused my attention back on the sea, my eyes met Roland's, whose expression was utterly solemn.

I needed to talk with him...but I wasn't ready yet.

We'd spent hours in the water, and I'd never felt so free in my entire existence. The water and sun against my naked skin was a sensation that healed my inner wounds...if only just a fraction.

As time passed, I forgot that my back was in the state that it was. My confidence slowly returned, showcasing the ways my body was defined. The Sea Nymphs had kept a tasteful distance, but toward the end of our fun, they swam closer. A few of the females smiled at me, blush staining their uniquely colored skin as I overheard them whispering to one another, *"He's so pretty!"*

Most women admired my face, but I was sure that those who would see me topless would find me repulsive.

My eyes trailed back to the love of my life, swimming along-side Elowen and Dani in the waves. It wouldn't matter to me if the world saw me as the ugliest, most pathetic man. Her love and admiration were all I needed, all I wanted.

Era had been beaming the entire time, but I could feel her eyes shifting to the Empath every so often. He kept away, but his eyes would linger on her, too.

When Era's head pain had become too much, she made her exit, heading to our room to rest before the ball. I was going to walk with her, but Hendry offered instead, wishing for me to enjoy as much of this as I could.

He was a great friend.

Viola had also left a while ago. One of Lucretia's hairstylists offered to freshen up her braids, and since it was a time-consuming task, she departed early. I couldn't wait to see her new style at the ball.

I leapt out of the water, heading up to get another drink, when someone stopped me.

"Hey." Roland grasped my arm, eyes bouncing between mine.

I didn't shrug him off; I just stood there, frozen. He had been eyeing me the entire time but hadn't had it in him to come up and talk to me.

"What happened to you?" he asked quietly. "Who did it?"

I swallowed, hesitantly turning to face him. "I don't want to talk about it."

His gentle eyes skated down my face, then back up. "Your father?"

My eyes fell away, and I nodded.

Roland cursed as he released my arm. "I'm so sorry."

"I don't need pity."

"Was it...did he do it because—"

"The beatings started months before that." For the first time in years, my eyes softened at him. My friend, despite my mistreatments. "I'm not ready to talk about it, but I will be eventually. Can you accept that?"

He dragged his teeth over his lip, nodding slowly. "I can...I can accept that."

The corner of my lip raised. "You want a drink?"

CHAPTER SIXTY-NINE

LENA

"Did the ocean please you?" Valter asked me later that afternoon. I could tell he fancied my presence, and I needed more answers. So, when I went to him directly, he decided to bring me to the palace's library.

It was a room in one of those pale blue domes at the top of the palace. White shelves lined the room, filled with books. I strolled across the light wood flooring, sitting in one of the many blue velvet chairs that sat across the multiple desks.

"More than pleased me. Truly, this is the most magical place I've ever seen. Literally and figuratively." My hair was still in those fishtail braids, drying. I had dressed in a casual sweater and leggings that Valter had left in my room. He'd said I would be dressed to the nines tonight, so relaxing attire until then would do. "Immeron—the brother of Igon, our seer—said the Sea Nymphs once ruled this place. I've seen the statues, too."

"Indeed, they did. Until the War of Three Pirates."

"What happened?" I asked curiously, resting my cheek on my fist. "And how are there some still residing here?"

Valter sat across from me, setting down a handful of books. "Three of Tovagoth's most notorious pirates wanted the Sea Nymphs for themselves, not just their own lands but the undersea city itself—Nereida, before it became what it is today. All for different reasons." His green eyes slid to mine. "Do you know the Sea Nymph's greatest power?"

I shook my head.

"Their ability to charm. Seduce. Not to be confused with the Angels's ability to compel, though I suppose they could achieve a similar outcome as charming if they wished. But the Sea Nymphs were a different type of beauty. One look in their eyes and human men and women would fall to their knees. Would give up their gold and their lands.

"One of the pirates, Prince Davian of Balifor, believed this power was too easy to be taken advantage of. He swore to hunt and kill every last one of them. The other pirate, Raden, was his best friend and the Prince of Wrendier. He also believed in doing this to an extent, but he wished to rule the land—to strike a deal so he could use the Sea Nymphs charms to get whatever he wished."

"So, he planned to betray his friend?"

"Indeed. The last pirate was Ketsia. Not only was she the sister of Davian, but she was also betrothed to Raden. She wished to find balance. She didn't believe for one second that her fiancé's plans were just, even as he attempted to convince her that he wished to leave most alive, unlike her brother.

"Ketsia decided to hell with her brother and fiancé's plans. She made the trip to Nereida on foot and passed through the Valley of

Awakening with ease. That ward is cast through the Nymphs, not us Mages. At that point, Nereida was a city underwater. The Sea Nymphs provided her with a magical air bubble so she could travel down below.

"She went to the King and Queen and begged them to spare her people—the Mages. The leaders almost laughed in disbelief. Mages had always been known to be the most powerful. But here was this Mage woman...a woman of importance, right in their clutches.

"They bound her in chains and planned to use her as leverage. She felt like an utter fool for believing the Sea Nymphs could be changed.

"The undersea Prince, Zale, was ordered to get information out of Ketsia by any means necessary. He found Ketsia fascinating and brave, but the two were true enemies. She begged—no, ordered him—to hold his magic, to hold in his charms.

"He agreed but made sure she understood that if she didn't obey, he'd take away her air. But Ketsia was clever. She knew she was more valuable as leverage. Knew he wouldn't harm her.

"The Sea Nymphs and the Mages of both Balifor and Wrendier discussed a deal over forty-three days. During this time, the Prince had been pressured further to torture information out of her. He'd had a Warlock cast a spell on her, shifting her into a dove to be his spy during that time. His parents—his people—most were not kind. But Zale grew fond of Ketsia over time. And when his father swam down to the cell she was kept in, when he watched him repeatedly starve her of air, over and over and over again, despite how he begged and groveled for him to stop, he slit his father's throat."

"My Gods..."

The story made me think of my own love...the man who'd done the same—betrayed his kingdom so I may live.

"Ketsia was shocked, to say the least. Zale released her from her chains and swam her to the shore. He told her to run, run far away, and never come back.

"But she couldn't. Wouldn't. She knew the Prince would be put to death for his crimes. *'Come with me,'* she said. *'Let us change this world for the better. Together.'*

"He hesitated, but knowing there was no home for him, he pushed himself onto the beach, experiencing sunlight for the very first time.

"Ketsia teleported the two of them to her home. She knew from his intel that her brother and fiancé were on the seas.

"This is where their ethics were...questionable. Ketsia and Zale came up with a plan. Sea Nymphs were too feared, and Zale was too far from the ocean. He would need to soak in a tub for a certain number of hours just to keep himself from drying out, from dying. But they decided to play the part that he was human. He would stand beside her on the throne and use his charms to convince everyone that she was Supreme. Not her fiancé, Raden." He smiled. "The very first woman to hold that title."

"Long story short, because it is a very long, in-depth story, the war was not between three pirates, but between her and those of Nereida, her brother and fiancé being another conflict."

"So...she won?"

Valter smiled, and then we were interrupted by a knock on the door.

"Kismet is sort of like that. Though my mother is Supreme, Kismet and she share equal power."

"Kismet is a Sea Nymph?" There were so many questions I needed to ask, including where Valter's father was.

"Enough of story time," Kismet drawled as she entered. "It's time to get ready for the ball!"

Valter rolled his eyes but smiled, standing and making to leave the room.

"Valter."

He turned to me.

"Thank you for the story...it helped more than you know."

He gave a courteous bow. "My pleasure," he purred. "We can discuss more history when the ball is over."

I nodded, and then he was gone. Kismet clapped her hands after he left.

"Chop, chop! I have orders to give you the royal treatment." She wiggled her eyebrows, and a team of ladies scurried in the room carrying cases of cosmetics, baskets of gems and seashells, and what I could see of my gown.

CHAPTER SEVENTY

SILAS

The ballroom was nothing short of amazing, just like the rest of this city. Sparkling chandeliers made of blue crystals hung from the high ceilings, matching the shimmering throne at the front of the room. An enormous table was filled with the most decadent desserts, and on the other side of the room, a large drink fountain trickled with a spiked punch.

Era's head was still bugging her. She looked beautiful, though, with her orange and gold gown.

She was with Elowen, who wore a bright pink ruffled gown that matched the shade of her hair. Edmund was beside her, and that same shade was woven into the design of his grey suit.

I loved seeing such a bright smile on my friend's face with his arm wrapped around her. I loved seeing the admiration in his eyes when he glanced at her.

My gaze trailed down to his carbonado fingers, moving upward to brush against his lover's skin lightly. To think only a few months ago he was about to die...only to be saved by those we were sworn to kill.

I sighed, my stare trailing over to Hendry, who was filling a glass for himself and Roland.

Hendry had been the first of us all to lose his virginity, but he'd never tell us the story of how. Not only that, but he'd also never had an actual girlfriend, just late-night rendezvous with strangers. Strangers who were middle-aged women.

I never quite understood why he preferred them.

I was standing off to the side, waiting for Lena to enter. I could only assume that she was getting dressed in an ensemble to rival Lucretia's, who wore a massive, sparkling blue gown. Kismet sat on her lap, wearing a tight, navy silk dress—certainly less flashy than Lucretia's, but still beautiful.

I waited and waited and waited, and then there she was. It was of great effort to keep my face neutral...impossible.

Lena walked in, accompanied by an ensemble of the Supreme of Nereida's servants. Her gown was made with the most stunning hues of purple and light blue, tight and sleeveless, until right above her knees, where the gown spilled out onto the floor. Its design glittered in the light.

It reminded me of the few Sea Nymphs we'd seen, their captivating tails.

Her copper waves were in a half-up, half-down style, just like how she'd worn it when we met. Only this time, it was far more intricate, with seashells and pearls spread amongst her tight coils.

My knees threatened to buckle at the sight. She was so fucking *ethereal*. Really, the word ethereal didn't do justice to how intoxicating she was. She was otherworldly, her beauty ineffable. No one on this planet could compare.

I watched as Valter's eyes skimmed over her, a smile growing on his face. Jealousy crawled its way through me. I didn't blame other men for looking at her with desire—how could they not? I couldn't, however, eliminate the feeling of wanting to smash in anyone's face who did.

She was *mine*.

Valter seemed like he was about to make his move, but I quickly weaved through the people separating us and swooped in first.

"May I have this dance?" I requested as I reached out my hand to her.

This close, I could see the way they did her makeup. Shades of blue and purple surrounded her eyes, making that warm green appear ever brighter.

Lena's cheeks stained with color at the sight of me, and a small smile tugged at her lips as she replied, "Of course."

I put my hands around her hips and pulled her against me, her hands crossing behind my neck.

"I see Valter is rather fond of you," I noted, my eyes narrowing ever so slightly as I watched him across the room. He wasn't looking this way; he was simply conversing with another guest at this ball.

"Ha, I suppose so." She lifted a brow. "Are you worried he'll woo me?"

I snorted. "I am more worried about how it'll come across if I kick his ass in front of everyone here."

She giggled, and I twirled her in my embrace. "You are such a buffoon."

"You are such a beauty," I whispered, my lips brushing against the shell of her ear.

Her glassy eyes met mine as I drew away. "So are you…"

I blinked, then bit back my grin before the two of us laughed.

"I may have had a little too much wine while they got me ready," she admitted with a chuckle.

"You deserve a good time," I replied softly, so desperately wanting to drag my teeth down the side of her neck.

"We all do." Those damn green eyes greedily took in my face, her fingers running through the hair at my nape.

"Lena," I growly quietly. "You can't do that here."

She tilted her head to the side, giving me innocent eyes. "Can't do what?"

She lightly tugged at my hair, and I felt my cock swelling in my pants.

I leaned my head forward, my lips mere centimeters from her ear. "I have little self-control around you as it is." She let out a breathy exhale, and I grinned. "But you pulling my hair?" I jerked her closer, pressing my erection against her torso. "The threat of me bending you over a table and taking you in front of everyone should frighten you."

I withdrew ever so slightly, pleased to see the goosebumps covering her skin. Pleased to see her half-lidded eyes.

"I wish you could," she uttered, her eyes sinking to my lips. "I wish…"

Dangerous. This was way too dangerous.

My hands tightened on her waist, and Lena's doll-like eyes gazed up at me. "I wish I could stay like this with you. In this moment."

It was hard to ignore the pain behind her expression. The same could probably be said of me. But this was supposed to be a fun night. A happy night. If anyone deserved one, it was her.

"You know I do, too." I twirled her, another sweet giggle slipping free of her lips. I held her close to me again. "Let's try to make it last as long as we can."

I pulled her even closer, and we began to dance to the slow tunes. Her chin rested on my shoulder, my arms holding her against my chest. "I imagined us being like this, you know," I murmured into her ear.

We stayed like that for a few moments, slowly swaying to the music. "I did, too," she replied with a gleam in her eyes. "Even though I knew we couldn't have it. I imagined many evenings like your birthday ball...like the Summer Solstice festival. Dressing up with you and just...having fun." A few more notes played before she said, "I have missed having fun with you, Silas."

I closed my eyes, running my thumb along her back. I knew we were dancing on an exceptionally fine line—knew that anyone looking at us must have had raised eyebrows at the affection we were showing one another. But at that moment, I didn't care.

"I am so grateful you're alive, Flower. It still feels like a dream most days."

She pulled away, her hands still resting on the back of my neck. The energy between us was undeniable.

"You are so damn beautiful," I whispered.

I wanted so badly to kiss her—wanted to meet the strokes of her tongue with my own. Wanted to feel myself buried inside her again. Wanted—

"Silas."

Lena jumped, and we broke our gaze to see Erabella standing beside us, hands on her hips. I then realized the slow music had already stopped and moved on to the next song.

She turned to Lena with narrowed eyes. "I'd like my husband back if you don't mind."

"Oh, right, of course." She bashfully backed up, dusting her dress off.

"Valter wanted to see you, by the way," Era added, her gaze flicking to the handsome Prince at the front of the room.

"Oh! Okay." Lena turned to me and gave me a soft smile. "Thank you for the dance, Your Highness," she said quietly, giving a cute curtsey before walking away.

My eyes were still following her when Era questioned, "What was that?"

"What was what?" I asked dishonestly, putting my hands inside my pockets.

"I'm not stupid. That wasn't just a friendly dance!" she hissed, stepping forward into my view. "You two practically had your tongues down each other's throats!"

I chewed the inside of my cheek, staring off into the distance. "We've been through a lot. We were just...talking."

"Do you have feelings for her?"

My eyes shot back to hers.

Era's lip trembled, her arms crossing as she asked me again, "Do you have feelings for her, Silas?"

I didn't have it in me to lie anymore, nor did I have it in me to tell her the truth.

I hesitated. I fucking hesitated.

I hated myself when I saw my wife's face crumple, and as she went to turn away, I grasped her arm. "I'm sorry, Erabella..."

She refused to meet my stare for a few moments before she shot me a glare over her shoulder, a single tear trailing down her face.

I released her arm and watched as she hurried out of the ballroom.

I should go after her—convince her that it's her that I love. My feelings for Lena aside, she was my wife, and I would choose her.

But I couldn't...because I wouldn't.

I angled my body in the opposite direction, wishing to drown my sorrow in liquor once I saw Lena in Valter's arms, smiling as they danced to the more upbeat tune that was now playing.

This Prince seemed kind—just. He seemed like the type who would never be led astray, whose morals would remain despite anything life threw at him.

Lena fit in with the people here. They treated her with the respect she deserved, unlike Otacia, who viewed her as a mere peasant. As a monster.

She deserved better than me. Better than my kingdom. I knew that. But I didn't know if it was possible for another to love her as much as I did.

I trekked to the punch bowl, filling up another glass.

Viola had her arms crossed beside it, staring off at those on the dance floor. Her purple braids were freshly styled—tight to her scalp. But unlike before, where all her braids reached the ends of her hair, this time, the intricate design remained on her scalp, the rest of her long hair loose and curly. Well, aside from the few braids scattered throughout, adorning the silver rings I had gifted her. A few of her curls were pulled loose, framing her face.

She looked fantastic. In her pointed ears dangled a pair of diamond earrings, and the sparkling grey gown she wore seemed even brighter against her smooth, dark skin.

"Don't dance much?" I asked lightly.

Her purple eyes slid to mine, her lip curving upward. "Not as much fun without a date."

My brows drew together. "I thought you and Merrick—"

"He dumped me just before this."

My eyes widened. "O-oh. My apologies." I turned my head, noticing that the Empath was nowhere to be seen.

She shrugged, sipping her drink. "It's not like we were actually dating. I will always love Merrick. But he was right. He and I aren't a match in that way."

"Still hurts, I imagine," I mumbled, sipping the sweet drink. The alcohol burned in my throat, a warmth blooming in my chest. Just what I needed.

She shrugged again, and I gave her a half-smile. "You're a beautiful woman, Viola. Surely there is someone here who'd wish to have a dance with you."

She quirked a brow at me, and I downed my drink before holding my hand out to her.

She analyzed my offer for a moment, then cursed, throwing her drink back. When she grasped my hand, I led her to the dance floor.

Viola was a confident woman, but as my arm went around her waist, her almond eyes darted up to mine in uncertainty.

"I like the new look," I said, motioning to her new hair.

She grinned as we began to sway. "Thank you. I've been dying to have it done—I'm thankful there are people here who know how to work with my hair type." She hesitated. "And I'm really grateful for the hair rings, Silas."

I laughed through my nose. "I know you are. I'm glad you like them...unless you're wearing them out of pity."

She laughed loudly, her body loosening as we continued to move to the music. "I love them," she assured me.

"Who would've guessed that in the span of a few months, you would go from wishing to decapitate me to being my dancing partner," I teased.

She laughed at that. "I still may wish to decapitate you."

I snorted, then twirled her around. When she was back in my arms, she asked, "What was that with Lena?"

I flexed my jaw. "What do you mean?"

"You two were behaving very...intimately."

I stared into Vi's eyes, then decided to hell with lying. "I am in love with her."

Viola's eyes bulged, a small gasp leaving her lips as we continued our dance. "What did you say?"

"I am in love with Lena." I shrugged in defeat, sighing as I did so.

"Does...does Lena know?" she whispered. "Does she feel the same?"

"It is complicated," I replied quietly.

"No kidding. Have you told Era?"

"She..." I ran my hand along my face, then wrapped it back around Viola's waist. "She asked me just now about my feelings. I froze." When I met Vi's violet gaze and saw that her eyes were filled with compassion and not judgment, I decided to continue. "I don't wish to hurt her. I care for her, too. Be she and I—"

"Aren't a match in that way?"

I supposed Viola did understand. I nodded.

Her lips turned upward. "Who would've guessed the Prince of Otacia would be confiding in me his relationship drama? That we'd be..."

"Friends?"

She failed at holding in a smile. "Yeah. Friends."

I chuckled, twirling her around. "I certainly wouldn't have believed it if you told me so months ago."

She stared off while we swayed. "I can't imagine an arranged marriage to someone you'd never met prior being wildly successful," she continued. "And I suppose you can't help who you catch feelings for." Her eyes widened. "Wait...*wait*—"

"Yes, Lena is my Soul-Tie," I whispered, and Viola blinked rapidly. "Apparently, your seer is the one who told her so, more or less."

"That is why she saved you," she breathed. I resisted the urge to cringe. It wasn't a lie, just not the full story. "Why you helped save her...holy Gods." She glanced over my shoulder, peeking at Edmund and Elowen, who were dancing a few feet away. "What are the odds?"

"Odds that make one believe the universe is on our side."

To that, she beamed. "I am happy I was wrong about you, Silas."

I returned the expression, my eyes trailing along the dance floor. My gaze caught on Dani, who was in their male form, a woman in his arms as they danced.

When I peeked back at Vi, she was staring at him. "What's holding you back?" I asked.

"Hm?" she slowly broke her gaze.

I gave her a knowing look. "Aren't you interested in Dani?"

Her eyes flared, her cheeks heating as she hissed, "No!"

I chuckled, twirling her around. "My apologies."

I didn't suppress my smile, and Viola sighed. "Fine. I have had...thoughts."

I quirked a brow. "Oh?"

She squeezed my side. "Don't say anything."

"I wouldn't dare. I rather like my head just as it is."

She grinned, rolling her eyes. "She...challenges me. She makes me laugh. And, obviously, she's breathtakingly beautiful."

"You aren't into her male form?"

Vi blushed. "I like it, too. Very much."

"Best of both worlds, I suppose," I chuckled.

She laughed, too. "I imagine so." Her eyes fluttered back to Dani, the Mage woman in his arms giggling at a joke he must've said.

"I think you should go for it."

Vi laughed through her nose. "Yeah, right," she replied sarcastically.

"I mean it." I gave Vi a warm smile when she spun her head toward me. "I have a feeling Dani feels the same toward you."

"You've talked?!" she hissed.

I sucked my lips in, pretending to zip them closed.

She bit the corner of her lip, then glanced over to Dani again. He met eyes with her this time, a crooked smile taking over his face.

"Go," I said. "Life's too short for unexplored avenues, no?"

Vi shot me a grateful grin, and I inclined my head just as she made her way to Dani, his eyes flaring ever so slightly, finding their way to mine.

I gave Dani a wink, and as I watched Lena exit somewhere with Valter, I decided to turn in for the evening. There was no point being here without her.

CHAPTER SEVENTY-ONE
LENA

I decided to head over to Valter after that awkward encounter. It was getting increasingly more challenging to act normal around Silas and not like I wanted to rip off his clothes.

Valter looked remarkable, but I was beginning to think that was a normal thing for him. His pale, lavender-colored suit complemented my dress—matching pearls and gems were incorporated into the design.

"Ah, Lena. I was wondering when you would come over," he said warmly.

"Haha, well, having a good amount of punch has helped with the nerves."

I was in Silas's arms almost immediately upon arrival, but I had a decent amount to drink while getting ready.

He laughed, holding out his elbow. He guided me to the center of the dance floor, and we began to sway.

"So, how have you been liking the gala?"

"I've thoroughly enjoyed it." I beamed up at him. "It feels sur-real...being here. Feeling protected." My face fell, my eyes trailing toward the other dancing figures. Did they know how others of their kind suffered? How we have been struggling to survive?

"You aren't happy with my mother's choices," he noted as he twirled me to the beat of the music.

I gave him a pained wince when I got back in his arms, then exhaled. "You should see it out there, Valter. See how our people are barely enduring what the humans have subjected us to. Our numbers are dwindling day by day."

His face offered sympathy, his bright green eyes falling. "I've never left this place. Not once in my twenty-seven years of life." He gave me an apologetic smile. "There is much I do not know. But I want to learn. I'd like to help."

My eyes drifted between his. "I wanted to ask you earlier, since you are so wise in history, if you knew of a tale involving a phoenix—one in reference to the Gods."

Valter's brows drew together. "Hmm...I'd have to check in the library." He gave me a handsome grin. "Want to sneak away for a bit to look?"

I raised a brow at him, continuing to sway in his arms. "That doesn't seem very princely."

He chuckled, twirling me around and capturing me back in his arms. "The truth is my mother wishes for me to find a wife. She's insistent it is you."

My face dropped so fast that Valter chuckled again, pulling me close. "Don't fret," he murmured in my ear. "I know you wish to be with the Otacian Prince."

My eyes hesitantly lifted to his. "It's that obvious?"

His gaze flitted to the side. "It's not so much you as the Prince staring daggers at me since your arrival here." His bright smile went to me. "Igon's note said you'd be with your Soul-Tie. My mother took that as your arrival *uniting* you with your Soul-Tie." He flushed bashfully. "Me...so she thought."

My arms were still around Valter's neck when I glanced over at Lucretia, who sat on her throne, her gaze on us. "Did you believe I was?"

He shrugged, twirling me to the beat again. "I thought you were beautiful. But I don't know what a Soul-Tie bond feels like."

"I'm sorry."

"Don't be," he insisted. "It was more of my mother's dream." He fixed his attention on where Lucretia was sitting. "She'd grown far happier when she found her Soul-Tie. I suppose she just wants that for me." He turned back, smiling as he leaned toward my ear. "Anyway, she'll be supportive of us sneaking off. So, let's go find some information."

"The God of Rebirth," Valter read from one of the many ancient books back in the library. "The heir of both light and dark. Good and evil. Life and death...the phoenix. A seer thousands of years ago prophesized that four gods would rise."

"The same prophecy is found in the Warlock grimoire I...read."

Valter seemed trustworthy, but I didn't want to let him know of it and risk it being taken from me.

"Strange to think," he pondered.

"Not really, considering we Mages have the ability to perform incantations as they do."

"What?"

I wiggled my brows, lifting my hand and drawing my fingers inward before flaring them out. ***"Lumen."***

A small orb of mage light flew from my hand, bouncing around like a bubble in the air.

Valter studied it, brow arching as he returned his stare to me. "Mage light can be conjured by Mages on our own."

I sighed. "True. But it takes less energy for us to use a magical tether—the ones the Warlocks rely on." I walked up to him, trailing my stare to the book in his hands. I took note of the artwork in the ancient passage—two silhouettes of men and two of women.

Valter placed his finger on the woman beside Rebirth. "That is the Goddess of Purification."

"She is supposed to fuse with Rebirth...creating Travelers."

"Wow, you really do know your history," he said surprisingly. "Yes, that is what the prophecy states."

I chewed on my lip. "Fuse how, though?" I pressed.

Valter's expression became grave. "Well, I'd assume in the same way Valor created the God of Deceit."

I frowned, angling my head over. "You think Purification and Rebirth will birth a child? Can Gods even do such a thing with one another?"

Valter shrugged, then ran a hand down his closely cropped hair. "If they can mate with Mages, I don't see why they couldn't with their equals."

"The necromancer—the God of Deceit—he didn't tell me how he'd learned of his identity. I still don't know who he is. He's only spoken to me through his victims."

Valter nodded in contemplation. "Wrendier would've had a higher Mage count than that of other kingdoms, considering centuries ago, Mages ruled that land. My guess is Balifor has been overrun as well."

I swore, eyes pleading as I faced him, grasping his arms. "We need Nereida's help, Valter. There's no way we can stop him on our own."

He swallowed. "I will talk to my mother, but I am not Supreme. I have no real influence."

Panic started to overwhelm me, and Valter placed a hand on my shoulder. "Let's not panic. Tomorrow, the Chamber of Time will be charged. Your seer did not send you here for nothing, I am sure of it."

Valter had managed to calm me down, saying we would figure out more tomorrow after we had a look into Igon's memories.

The ball was nearing its end, so after seeing how much dessert still remained, I scurried over and began helping myself.

My Gods, these treats are divine.

I heard Torrin's voice from behind. "No surprise you're hogging the dessert table."

I turned with my mouth full to see Torrin grinning at me.

I raised a brow, then swallowed. "You aren't doing your job protecting them from my *gaping mouth*."

Torrin chuckled, the sound giving me goosebumps. "I really was smooth back then, wasn't I?"

I giggled, and Torrin held out his hand.

His eyes were gentle as he asked, "Dance with me?"

I smiled, immediately grasping his hand with mine. We strode to the dance floor, only a handful of couples left. Then, we began swaying to the calm music that played.

"Remember how petrified you were when I asked you to dance?" I laughed. "I still remember the bewilderment on your face."

Torrin's cheeks flushed just like they did all those years ago. "I wasn't petrified," he began, then chuckled. "Okay, fine. I was nervous."

"Why? You were clearly the better dancer, just as you are now." I smirked. "You sure loved rubbing it in my face."

His smile slowly began to drop, and that's when I knew.

"Yes," he admitted quietly, having read my mind. "I had feelings for you, even back then."

My throat burned as I rested my head against his chest, feeling his heart pounding.

"You might recall that I developed feelings for you that evening as well," I murmured.

He rested his head against mine as we continued to move slowly. "You thought I was attractive that evening. Your feelings didn't develop until later."

When I tilted my head up at him, he was smiling, though I could see the pain that shone in his eyes.

"I will always love you, you know that, right?" I whispered.

He leaned down, kissing the top of my head. "And I will always love you," he promised.

I spent the rest of the night dancing slowly in his arms, wishing I could offer him more...but accepting that it was the end of our romance.

I tried my best to get a good night's rest, but the anticipation of seeing inside of Igon's head kept me up longer than I'd like.

The walk to the temple was a half-day journey. We'd taken one break in between and eaten a small lunch, and as we began to see the building in the distance, I realized it looked identical to Temple Celluna.

I gazed at the bronze object, rotating it in my hand, staring at the pelican on its back while our group waited for Kismet to lead us inside Temple Tithara, along with Valter, who wished to see the memories as well.

Silas wandered up to my side. "How are you feeling?"

"Nervous. Excited. Scared." I ran my tongue along my teeth. "What if he saw our doom? What if I see one of us die, knowing there is nothing I can do?"

Torrin walked up to me, standing at my other side. "We have all lived thus far."

"And suffered," I whispered.

He smiled sadly just as Kismet approached. "The Chamber is beneath the temple—underwater. There is a passage beneath that will take us there," Kismet informed us as we entered the building.

My heartbeat quickened, remembering the sight of so many deceased clerics. But I sighed in relief as we were met with many living ones this time.

We were led down to the altar room, and Merrick's hand anxiously went to the strap around his chest that held his crossbow.

Thankfully, the people here allowed us to bring our weapons, even though I assumed we wouldn't need them.

Once down in the altar room, we traveled through a hall located at the back of the room.

"Do all the temples have hidden passageways?" Elowen asked, her hand wrapped tightly around Edmund's enchanted one.

"All the temples look alike, but they all have their own unique features," Valter explained from up ahead. "Passageways, perhaps not. But there is something special about them all."

A little further down and the stone walls surrounding us turned to glass. I was in awe of the medley of colorful fish that swam by as we stood beneath the ocean.

"Oh, wow," Dani whispered. "Amazing..."

My friends appreciated the view as we continued onward until we were brought to a large, circular room. Along the entirety of the floor was a pentagram glowing purple.

Dani frowned as she stared up at Kismet. "A pentagram?"

Kismet's brown eyes sharpened, but her smile remained light. "Is it such a surprise one would be here?"

I turned to Valter. "I'm confused. You seemed surprised by my ability to utilize Warlock magic yesterday."

Kismet's brows furrowed, darting between the two of us. "You can utilize Warlock magic?"

I gestured to the pentagram. "Uh, yes? Pentagrams, incantations—all that jazz."

"The pentagram belongs to the Mages," Valter stated. "But the Titharan language...we've never known how to decipher it or speak it."

"So, this Chamber," Dani began, "doesn't utilize a spoken word spell?"

"No," Kismet said, crossing her thin arms. "It requires a charge...and a memento."

"The memento is the tether..." I fished out Igon's compass, my eyes flicking to the statues on either side of the rounded room. "As are the relics. An incantation isn't needed."

Dani walked forward, examining the symbols above the statues. She was able to decipher the language without the grimoire. "Give us an object of value," she read, then walked over to the other relic. "And the truth shall set you free."

"What does the pentagram say, Dani?" Viola asked.

The Warlock knelt down, sliding her hands along the text engraved into the concrete. "*Show me another time.*"

"How does this work, exactly?" Merrick asked Kismet.

She was seemingly shocked by the Warlock being able to decipher the text. "You place a memento in the center of the pentagram, and the clerics will surge in their illusion magic. It will provide you with visions."

Dani swallowed, her brows lowering as she stood. "I think...I think if we speak the incantation, it will be more than just visions." Her pupilless, blue eyes searched the dome-like roof of this underwater room. "This room isn't made of glass, is it?"

"It is," a cleric stated. "Glass infused with clear quartz."

Dani swore, then apologized for using such language in front of a cleric. "Clear quartz is a master crystal, one that amplifies energy." She focused her attention on me. "I believe the incantation won't just provide visions. I believe it will bounce off the quartz and show us the visions as if we were actually there."

"That's ludicrous," Kismet began, but when her gaze flitted down to the Titharan language etched into the pentagram, she sighed. "Very well. We can try it, so long as the clerics are okay with it."

The clerics all stared at Dani with a look of respect. "You speak Tithara's language...words that have been lost to us Mages. If this works, we ask you to teach us."

Dani agreed. "Of course."

I was kneeling now, placing Igon's compass in the center of the pentagram, when a memory hit me—Kayin's words to me back on the mountaintop.

"That necklace will give you the answers you need...everything...everything will make sense."

"Silas," I breathed, glancing over my shoulder at him. My eyes went to the clerics. "Can more than one memento be used?"

One of the clerics nodded. "Certainly. If any of the memories coincide, they will play together. Otherwise, it will play in a timeline."

I gazed at Torrin, silently relaying my message to the Prince.

Ryia's necklace could provide us with answers about her passing.

Torrin glanced at Silas, whose golden eyes widened as they dropped to my collarbones.

Kayin told me it would give me the answers I need. I didn't understand it at the time, but I believe I'm supposed to use it here.

Silas licked his lips, then nodded.

Torrin spoke in my head, *"He said do it."*

"I have something," I said, unclasping the necklace from my neck. "Queen Ryia's necklace." I could sense my friends' confusion, but I ignored it.

"This was the Queen of Otacia's?" Valter asked.

"It was."

"How long has it been in your possession?" another cleric asked.

"Over five years," I answered, holding the jewelry in my palms.

"That likely means you also imprint this memento," she said cautiously. "Which means that some of your memories may play as well, things you may not want the group to see."

I nervously stared at Silas again. We could send others away, but they would still have questions. He nodded once more.

"If it will tell us what happened to the Queen, then it'll be worth it," I whispered, terrified of what may show.

Dani placed a comforting hand on my shoulder. I knew she was aware of my secret, as was Merrick and Roland. Soon, the whole group would know.

"Very well."

I placed the silver and sapphire necklace in the center of the glowing pentagram, then stood. This symbol was easily large enough for us all to stand in, so we did. The clerics surrounded the outside, one by one.

"We will supply the circle with our magic as you speak the incantations, Warlock."

Dani took a deep breath, eyes lowering to the script.

"Ostende mihi aliud tempus. Ostende mihi aliud tempus. Ostende mihi aliud tempus."

The glow around us heightened, morphing our surroundings, and memories began to play.

Giggling could be heard, and a little girl came running from a tower—a familiar tower. I recognized it as Igon's in Ames. Her black hair was pulled back into a braid, and she hurriedly rushed through town, a book clutched to her chest.

"Kayin!" a man's voice called out. Out came a man with familiar topaz eyes, but his hair was darker—black, just like younger Kayin's.

Igon.

What the hell? Igon supposedly moved to Ames much later in life. What is he doing here?

"You know I love you reading, darling," he panted as he caught her. "But those books are valuable."

She pouted, then hesitantly handed back the text.

Seeing Igon in his twenties was...wild. He was handsome—incredibly handsome. His raven hair was kept shorter, and his face was clean-shaven, showing off a sharp jawline. He was fit as an older man, but his body seemed even more toned in his twenties, his skin a sandy tan.

Like always, there was a familiarity to him.

"I was supposed to take it," she explained.

He raised a brow, and his amber eyes glanced down at the book.

"You were supposed to take a book on Otacian history?" Then his eyes widened. "My goodness, Kayin." He squatted down, his hands going to the little girl's arms. "Are you having visions?"

She tilted her head to the side, a puzzled look on her face. She had to be only five years old.

"Otacia will be my home one day," she said.

Igon blinked rapidly before his gaze dropped to the book. "If you have any more, please tell me, okay?" His eyes trailed back to Kayin's, and he offered her a warm smile.

"Yes, papa."

My eyes shot to Torrin's, whose own expression mirrored mine.

Igon...Igon had a child? He was Kayin's father...which meant—

Our surroundings swirled around us, changing before I could finish my thoughts to Torrin. When I beheld the next image, I nearly fell to the ground.

The surprising part of this next vision wasn't that Kayin was a teenager now. No, it was that finally, after all this time, I knew exactly who she was.

"Holy Gods," Torrin breathed, and Silas went wholly still.

Kayin wasn't just Igon's daughter.

She wasn't just your typical Mage with silky black hair and stunning sapphire eyes.

Kayin was Ryia La'Rune.

Kayin was Silas's mother.

CHAPTER SEVENTY-TWO
LENA

My eyes couldn't possibly be wider. They shot over to Silas, who returned the same bewildered expression.

I couldn't believe it. My thoughts jumbled to that night...the night she *died*.

I just spoke to her a few months ago. How is this possible?!

We were in Igon's study in Ames. A golden glow was emitting from Kayin's palms, healing a wound on Igon's arm. Her dark hair was tucked behind her pointed ear.

His hair was still black, free of greys, but a light dusting of facial hair was on his face.

I now realized, looking into his eyes, that they weren't just topaz.

They were golden.

"You need to be more careful," she said quietly to him.

He laughed, his voice unserious as he replied, "I will be just fine, you know this. You've seen it."

Golden...and that's why his smile was always so familiar. He looked like Silas.

"The future can change, *you* know this," she retorted, healing his minor wound.

He sighed. "It was a simple accident, and I would heal fine without magic." His smile faded. "Are you sure you wish to go through with this? Their lineage is..."

Her blue eyes settled on him. "I don't want to marry him. But I have to. It is the only way to save our people and give us a life where we can live freely."

"But how can you be sure?" He sat up now, his eyes surveying the town. I followed his gaze, seeing a man with fair skin and light brown hair walking outside. A human. "I know you love him, Kayin. And he loves you, too."

She squeezed her eyes, and tears came out. "I know. But it must be done, Father. It is the only way."

He brushed his thumb along her cheek lovingly. "The burden of being a seer."

The vision swirled, and we were in a bedroom. Kayin was held in an embrace by the brown-haired man.

"I don't want you to go, Kay," he whispered, his light grey eyes tortured as he pulled away. "Please. I will do anything."

"I don't wish to leave either, Quill," she murmured as she pulled him into a kiss.

My body went into shock. My eyes darted to Silas, whose limbs shook as he gaped at the sight before him.

This was the man who had supposedly killed his sister, Aria. The man whose name he used when he first met me.

Quill Callon.

He was Ryia's—Kayin's lover?

Silas had said his mother had never believed he did it and that she had always spoken of him fondly.

"Why must you follow this vision? You have said yourself that the future can change. What if marrying him does no good?"

She held his face. "It has to. The fate of the world depends on it."

Images flickered, the setting changing. Speaking along the river just outside Ames were Igon and Immeron.

Immeron's hair was just as dark as Igon's, his face just as handsome, though his blue eyes were wary as he looked at his brother.

"She's to become Queen of Otacia? You're sure of it?" Immeron asked wide-eyed.

"Indeed." He turned to him. "They cannot know her real name or where she really came from. Your gift of memory manipulation would come in handy."

Memory manipulation?!

Immeron frowned. "How much manipulation are we talking about?"

"Come with Kayin and me to the castle. Make them believe she is a princess from one of the other kingdoms—Eretesia shall do." He gripped his brother's shoulder. "And another thing, those in Ames cannot know."

Immeron froze. "You can't be asking—"

"I want the people of Ames to forget about Kayin and me. I will come back and reintroduce myself. But they must forget her. She must become Ryia. Embrace this new identity fully."

"What of her friends? Of Quill?" He paused. "Of me? The boys, they—"

Melancholy shone in Igon's eyes.

Immeron scoffed in disbelief. "You want us to forget her, too."

"I would never ask you to forget her. But she could never come up—ever. If somehow she got discovered, her life would be in danger. The boys are too little to keep such a secret..."

"Then we will leave. Live elsewhere. I am not forgetting anyone."

Igon blinked, his brows lowering before the entirety of his eyes glowed white.

I'd never witnessed what it looked like for him to get a vision.

"Igon," Immeron whispered. "What did you see?"

The glow in Igon's eyes faded, and Igon gave Immeron a sad smile.

"*Somnum.*"

Immeron's eyes rolled back, and he sank to the grassy ground at the spell Igon chanted.

Igon grasped a dagger in his hand and slowly dragged it against Immeron's arm, then took out a vial, collecting his blood.

Using his dagger, he carved symbols into his own flesh, wincing at the pain. When complete, he poured his brother's blood over his wounds. Purple glowed from his palm as he held it over the cuts. *"Coniungere."*

His eyes flitted to his sleeping sibling. "Forgive me, my brother. You must forget."

He held his palms over his brother's head, closing his eyes tightly, before rushing away.

Igon knew incantation magic. What exactly did he just do?

Images then flickered, the setting changing more rapidly. Kayin reached Otacia and met Ulric at his betrothal ball. Ulric was already king, considering his father had died when he was eighteen.

He was far less intimidating with a clean-shaven face, but as much as I despised the man, his beauty could not be denied.

These visions were quicker. We witnessed the marriage being secured and the moments of their wedding, along with her crying before and after.

She was in the throne room beside Ulric now, perhaps months later, when a man was brought forward.

Kayin's eyes widened at the sight of him.

The man kneeled before them. "My name is Quill Callon. I am here to offer my services to the royal family."

Ulric scoffed. "Plenty of people wish to aid the La'Rune's." He tilted his head. "What do you have to offer?"

Quill swallowed. "I am an excellent trainer."

Ulric's smile turned sinister.

Swirling again.

Ulric himself was battling with Quill, an initiation of sorts. Kayin nervously observed from the sides, attempting to appear not so.

Quill wasn't lying. He was exceptionally talented, particularly in the use of a sword. But beating Ulric entirely would humiliate the King. He had the upper hand right up until the end when he allowed Ulric to knock him right on his ass, blade just inches from his nose.

Ulric smirked. "Very well, Quill Callon. You may join the Royal Guard."

Memories bled into memories, and now we were in a spare room in the castle.

"Quill—" the Queen began before Quill took her in an embrace and kissed her.

"Nothing can keep me away from you, Kayin," he whispered. "Even if I have to stand by and watch you be with him, start a family—" He choked on a sob. "I will always be here for you. Even if only as a friend."

She kissed him again and again, and the vision changed.

"You're...pregnant," Quill said, almost disbelieving. Kayin sat in a velvet chair and nodded as she stared out of the window, her legs nestled close.

"It feels as though he is strong and healthy," she mumbled.

"You know it's a boy?"

"I have seen him in my visions." She smiled softly.

"Is he...is he mine?"

Her smile faded, her eyes falling to her lap as tears spilled down her cheeks. "No."

It was almost as if this next vision didn't work; it was a jumbled flash, so many I couldn't decipher. Chills raced through my body as our surroundings finally settled. We were in the mountains, somewhere I didn't recognize.

The wind whipped around Ryia as she held the hood pulled over her head. Her rounded belly was prominent.

Stepping outside of the mountains in dark leather were Warlocks—hundreds of them.

"My name is Kayin Natarion," she announced. "And I need a favor."

The Warlocks studied her with distrust. "Why should we help a Mage?"

"Because," Igon advised, walking up beside her, "Ravaiana demands it."

In the blink of an eye, we were back in Castle La'Rune. Once again, the memories flashed quickly, and the picture was unclear.

Why aren't we seeing everything?

"That boy is something else," Quill laughed, he and Kayin watching Silas play with a wooden sword. He was so little...absolutely adorable. But that meant there was a four-year gap in memory.

"I am pregnant again, Quill," she whispered.

His eyes shot to her.

"And I know she has magic. I feel it. I know this time that she is yours." Her eyes met his, and he swallowed. Ryia began to cry, clasping her palm over her mouth to quiet herself. I could tell Quill wanted to comfort her, but there were too many eyes around that would see. It seemed that Quill had become Ryia's aide, no longer just a member of the Royal Guard.

"What does this mean, Ryia?"

"It means...you will have to leave." She ran her hand down her belly. "And you will need to take her with you."

"What?" he hissed.

"Not only is she in danger because she's a Mage, but you...if Ulric finds out—"

"He won't." Quill's grey eyes were pinned on her. "We've kept it a secret this long."

"She will need you." She sniffed. "She will need her father to raise her."

Quill choked on an incredulous scoff. "And what of Silas? Whether he is my blood or not, he is my son."

She clenched her jaw. "I wish you could take him, too," she said quietly. "But he must stay with me."

The vision changed. Ryia was kissing baby Aria on the cheek. The baby's appearance had been glamoured to hide her pointed ears.

She placed her in a basket, then kissed Quill softly. "Get to Daranois. Ask for Enid. She will get you to Oquerene." She pulled him into a tight hug. "I will miss you forever," she breathed.

"You act as if you'll never see me again." His smile fell at her silence. "You...won't?"

She shook her head, tears falling as she cried harder.

"No...no, do not say that." He held her close. "Don't lose hope, Kay," he whispered, stroking her head. "The future can always change."

Memories flickered: Quill escaping with Aria; the panic that ensued when Aria's dead body—which we now knew was a false copy—was found in the Northern Woods. We heard the talking amongst the royals, of how Silas would be held in the castle to ensure his safety.

I was shocked when Amatta appeared, strolling up to Ryia. "I come from Kalrael. Quill wishes for me to keep an eye on you. To ensure your safety."

Ryia raised a brow. "Kalrael?" Then it dawned on her. "Amatta Callon...Quill's sister."

Amatta's smile grew. "I haven't seen him since he left to be with you in Ames. But he sent word."

Ryia pulled her into a hug.

My eyes nervously went to Silas, whose hand was covering his mouth.

We were getting closer now. Was it really Amatta who killed his mother? Was Kayin actually dead?

Regardless, one thing was certain.

Amatta was not a Mage. She was a human.

More memories passed us. Igon ordered a young Torrin Brighthell to go to Otacia—we witnessed the moment he was sworn into the Royal Guard.

"I will need you to give a blood oath," Ryia demanded, only she, Torrin, and Amatta in the throne room.

"Of course," seventeen-year-old Torrin agreed, holding out his palm. Ryia slid a dagger across his flesh and collected his blood in a vial. Torrin asked no questions; Igon must have told him to expect that to happen.

The next second, we were in Ryia's quarters.

"What's the blood oath for?" Amatta asked, tying back her brown hair.

"The boy is a Mage," Ryia answered, and Amatta's eyebrows raised. "A telepath, to be exact."

Ryia took her dagger, etching those same markings into her skin as her father did when he was with Immeron.

"W-what are you doing?" Amatta asked nervously.

Ryia poured Torrin's blood over her wounds, enclosing her glowing purple palm over them.

"Coniungere."

Ryia gave Amatta a smile.

"Utilizing his gift," she responded in Amatta's mind.

Holy fuck.

I turned to Torrin, his brown eyes saucers.

"My Gods...that's how she was able to speak with us."

Our surroundings were shifting again, and now we were in Silas's room.

A lump formed in my throat. He was wearing the outfit he wore the day I met him.

"I'm granting you one day outside the walls," she told him cautiously, his eyes lighting up. "I want you to be a kind leader, a compassionate one, one day. Do not stray from the Inner Ring, though. I don't want to risk you getting caught. I've stationed the guards along this side elsewhere, so be quick. And be back by 10:30."

Silas beamed at her. "Thank you, Mother." I watched as he rushed to his balcony.

Amatta entered a few moments later. "How can you be sure he won't be recognized?"

Ryia shot her a smirk. "I placed a spell on him in his sleep. The second he is outside the castle border, he becomes invisible to the eyes of the guard."

Holy Gods.

It made so much sense now why he wasn't even questioned when he killed that man in Serpent's Cove. It wasn't because he was seemingly from the Inner Ring. It was because they couldn't see him.

My heartbeat quickened the moment I saw him and me.

I saw myself get pushed to the ground by that girl, the others laughing at me. I saw myself rise to my feet and get my bag snatched. I saw myself charge toward her, holding that dagger to the girl's neck after she took a bite of a pastry.

This was it. The moment everyone would know our secret.

Silas charged forward. "Hey!" he growled.

My sixteen-year-old eyes flew to his, and Silas's glare shot to the girl. "See what happens when you take what isn't yours?"

The whole encounter played, Silas getting her to return my bag, only to toss it to the ground, shattering the vial inside.

My friends studied the memories before them with wide eyes, seeing everything.

Past me shook my head. "I'm sorry, I didn't even ask your name. I'm Lena Daelyra," I held out my hand. "And you?"

He examined my hand. "Quill. Quill Callon," he replied, bringing my hand up to his and kissing it.

We watched as my mother panicked when I told her I'd just handed our orders over to him. I cringed as they saw me cry in my room.

They watched as Silas came back, handing over the money, and watched as he went with me to fetch the sage needed for her elixir. They saw us deliver the remaining two orders and saw him grasp my hand, rushing me down the steps of the Outer Ring just in time before the curfew kicked in, giggling at the ridiculousness of it all.

They watched as we made our deal that he'd train me.

They heard the first time he called me Flower.

We were now back in the castle.

"So? How was it?" Ryia asked.

Silas wore a grand smile. "It was amazing. The best day of my life."

I smiled at that.

Ryia's grin faded. "It was only one time, Silas."

His smile disappeared, too. "But I have to go back. I...I have to."

"I'm sorry, Silas. But the answer is no."

I remember this next vision—it was the day after, the day Ryia visited the Outer Ring.

I watched as Ryia's gaze caught mine, as she stilled in place.

"This girl I saw in the Outer Ring," Ryia said to Amatta as our surroundings flashed back to the castle. A smile crept over the Queen's face. "She will be the one my son loves. His Soul-Tie."

"What?" Amatta breathed.

"She is a Mage," Ryia whispered, grasping her silver and sapphire necklace. Visions of Silas and I training in the Western Forest began to play as she spoke. "A powerful one. Or, I should say she will be. Her power...it is unlike anything anyone has ever seen."

Flashes of us kissing in Amethyst Pond played, and I felt my face go hot.

"Silas, have you met anyone?" Ryia asked in the next vision.

"What makes you ask that?" Silas mumbled while fidgeting with his shirt.

The Queen grinned. "Just wondering."

Our entire group witnessed Silas and me at the Summer Solstice festival, dancing in each other's embrace. It cut to us kissing, but thankfully, the rest of the night didn't show.

Everyone saw the moment I followed him, getting captured by Torrin. They witnessed the moment I found out who he really was.

It was heartbreaking seeing Silas in his room after I had left, his mother sitting beside him on the bed.

"What changed?" Silas asked, turning to face her. "That first day out I thought would be my last. Even when I told you about Lena, only speaking about her as a friend, you didn't seem to mind. It just goes against everything I have been told. I am so glad for it, but that doesn't make it any less puzzling."

She gave him a soft smile, placing a hand on his cheek. "It's one of those things I know are meant to be."

Sixteen-year-old Silas returned her expression. "No one can know if *anything* is meant to be."

The year passed. Every one of my friends witnessed how Silas and I became closer. They watched us continue to train. They watched as I attended his birthday ball on the night of his mother's death.

The answers were here now.

We were all in Ryia's room.

"Your Majesty, what's wrong?" Amatta asked, rushing to her side.

Ryia was trembling, tears pouring out of her solid white eyes, a glow emitting from them.

"No...no..." She shook her head, squeezing her eyes shut tight.

First, she sent a message to Torrin.

Find Lena in two days. In the night. Go to Ames.

Then, her message to me.

Lena.

The vision showed us both—our surroundings side by side.

"Talk about a rude awakening."

Change is coming, Lena—horrible, awful change. Find Torrin in two days. In the night. Go to Ames.

"Your Majesty—" Amatta began.

I sat up in my bed.

"What? Leave Otacia? Why?"

Ryia was shaking. *Torrin will help with what needs to be done. When it is time to leave, find him. He will ensure you make it to Ames safely.*

"What needs to be done? What is going to happen?"

Blood began pouring out of her nose.

"Kayin?"

It must happen in order to save Magekind. We will speak again in time.

Ryia's eyes flung open, severing our connection. Her face crumpled as she wiped her nose. "My son...my poor son," she cried. Shaking, she rushed to her drawer to find it empty and let out a curse. "I...I can't let him do this to him...my boy—"

The door slowly crept open. Ryia glanced over her shoulder, and Amatta froze.

Ulric walked in slowly, holding a stack of letters.

His dark eyes were livid, his face contorted. "Oh, Ryia...what have you done?" he growled.

She swallowed, bracing her back against the dresser.

"Amatta, go," Ryia ordered, but as she went to obey, Ulric grasped her, tossing her so hard into the wall her head cracked, and she slumped to the ground, unconscious.

Kayin went to freeze him with her magic, but the King anticipated the move. He plunged a dagger kept at his side into her chest.

She choked, crying out at the pain, eyes wide and tearful as she beheld her husband's blade piercing her.

The vision swirled into nothing.

We were all silent.

"Holy shit," Roland breathed.

When I looked over at Silas, I saw him trembling, tears falling down his face, both hands covering his mouth.

I didn't watch what happened next, but I heard it. Heard Amatta's screams as Silas lit her on fire. I only slid my gaze over to watch his reaction to that final night together.

"You will not give up. You will not break."

Tears spilled down his face as he saw me get my ice, watching as I wailed in agony over the fact that I was leaving him.

I expected it to continue playing my memories now that Kayin was gone.

But I was wrong.

My brows furrowed. We were in a cell of some sort, though I had no idea where.

Kayin lay, groaning at the stab wound in her chest.

This was the night we escaped. She had not died two evenings prior. She was still alive.

"What is this?" Kayin seethed, gesturing to her bound wrists.

The cuffs...those dreaded cuffs. The ones she wore appeared to be an older model, more clunky in design but able to erase magic all the same.

"Something that has been in the works for a while," he commented, grimacing at her from the other side of her cell.

"You really hate Magekind this much, Ulric?" she spat. "Why?"

"What I hate more than anything at this moment is you, dear Ryia." He grasped the bars of the enclosure. "You slept around with human trash and made me believe those children were my own."

Her brows went together. "Silas is yours!" she barked.

Ulric released a guffaw. "You stupid bitch." His dark glare was sickening. Kayin shrunk into the corner of her cell, and the King's cruel smile only grew. "I would've believed it, as I thought he and I shared some physical features. But you miscalculated, Ryia. I figured out Silas wasn't mine the moment I read those letters." He tilted his head to the side. "Do you know why?"

She shook her head, glowering at him with hatred.

Ulric lifted his hand, tilting it ever so slightly.

No.

No.

No.

Kayin's eyes widened in horror as Ulric removed his glamour, showcasing his pointed cartilage.

"You..." she breathed, eyes rounded, head shaking. "How..."

"I guess you and I were both harboring secrets. I knew Silas couldn't be my son the second I read those letters, knowing that if he were mine, he would've been a Mage like us. I was disappointed he didn't receive my magic at first, but now, knowing he isn't my blood..." He cocked his head to the side, a sadistic grin stretching across his face. "I am going to break him, Ryia."

She choked on a sob, "Ulric...*please*, he is yours, I swear—"

"Ask the question, darling."

She shook, swallowing hard. "Why?" she bit out.

Kayin's eyes drifted to the side, and her muffled cry sent chills down my body. Amatta's burnt corpse limped into the cellar, her eyes solid black.

"Do you understand now, Ryia? Do you know what I am?"

"You..." she respired. "You're a necromancer?"

He grinned, his eyes turning that solid black. "I am a God."

CHAPTER SEVENTY-THREE

LENA

Ulric lifted his arm, and dark, shadowy magic emitted from his palm. Kayin attempted to stagger back, but there was nowhere for her to go. As the shadows surrounded her body, entering her mouth, she began to choke. Her hands flew to her throat.

"I loved you," Ulric whispered, his nostrils flaring. "But everything was a lie, wasn't it?"

Her face began to turn blue, her eyes bulging as she tried and failed to take in any air.

"You took all I loved, so I shall do the same to you." His lip curled as he spat, *"Kayin."*

Her eyes rolled back as his shadows suffocated her, and she slumped to the ground.

Everything faded to black.

We were all left in the darkness for a few moments before we were back in Ames. Igon's saddened eyes widened as he beheld my

Mother and Torrin entering our small village, the latter carrying my weak, pregnant body.

"What is it, Igon?" Osrel pressed, gazing as Igon's eyes glowed white.

Images flashed quickly. Fire. Darkness. Bright, white light and silver sparks.

"I've seen this before," Igon breathed. "But now it all makes sense."

I could hardly make out my surroundings, but a woman with bright white hair was surging her power toward something—some darkness. I couldn't make out her face, but it was like the paintings Igon commissioned were coming to life.

This meant the God of Rebirth was being subjected to her power, but I couldn't see him either.

More flickering, and we watched how Igon saw in his mind my reunion with Silas.

We saw as he witnessed his own death.

Igon swallowed. "That girl...my Gods." The white light faded, and his golden gaze didn't waver as he stared at me from his tower, even as it hardened. "A great battle is approaching. Six years from now."

The vision showed Vicsin rushing toward us, a young Merrick and Elowen behind him, crying as they saw their cousin for the first time in years.

"I must teach her everything I know," Igon murmured. "She needs to be able to piece it together when the time comes. She must be kept safe."

My brows lowered, and the final visions passed rapidly.

My friends watched my miscarriage and watched as Torrin helped me once I got my fire.

It was a quick montage of how I trained over the years, getting stronger, and my friends watched as I discovered Silas had a wife.

We could see Torrin and me in the lake, kissing fervently, and the next moment, they could see my panic when he was gone the following day.

Tears filled my eyes as I watched my last moments with Igon...when he told me that he was the one who had sent Torrin away.

Igon winced. "Forced isn't the correct word. Strongly suggested," he said cautiously. "It is known who your Soul-Tie is, Lena. It isn't Torrin."

Past me let out a shaky exhale, my hands clenched to his desk. "Ames was *his* home, not mine. If you cared so much for who I ended up with, then it should've been *me* you suggested to leave." I shook my head in disbelief. "The Prince is married. It doesn't matter who my Soul-Tie is!"

They watched as Merrick and I set our dining table together, only to rush out and witness the chaos as the Otacian army attacked.

They watched as I got thrown to the ground, as I met the eyes of the man about to kill me.

Silas's eyes widened in the vision. "Lena?"

"Silas," I breathed.

Once again, we were back on Mount Rozavar. When the vision became split, when we saw that desolate chamber again, I gasped.

There Kayin sat. Her skin was white, those inky black veins swirling around her flesh. The spider symbol had been etched into her forehead, and her solid dark eyes stared into nothingness.

Silas choked on a sob, seeing his mother in such a way.

But she then began blinking quickly, her fists clenching.

She no longer wore cuffs, because she was controlled by the necromancer. The Lord of the Shadows. The God of Deceit.

Ulric.

She blinked over and over until those sapphire eyes returned.

Panicked, she closed her eyes, searching.

Lena...we have work to do.

We watched my and Kayin's entire conversation, and when our connection was severed, she sighed, coughing up black blood. She squeezed her eyes shut again, only this time, we had no idea who she spoke to.

Save them. Beg and plead with Aleyda if you must. But please, you must save them.

Kayin coughed up more blood, cursing as she did so, and her eyes went back to that solid black. She froze again, remaining seated like a statue.

The final memories that played were rapid, showcasing how the Prince and I had grown closer these past few months.

They saw when Merrick found out, which was the exact moment that Erabella began to cry.

They saw Silas and me argue. They saw us fight.

They saw us kiss. In the tent. In Faltrun. In the Valley of Awakening.

Here, in Nereida.

And then the glow of the pentagram vanished, our surroundings blurring back to the underwater chamber.

Kismet, Valter, and the clerics were frozen in fear.

"Holy shit," Dani respired. "Ulric is the God of Deceit."

"Kayin is alive," Torrin breathed. "She is Undead, but somehow she is still in there."

Era's tearful gaze slid to Silas, then to mine. "You...you two were..." she whispered, backing away. "Oh, my Gods. I'm a fool."

My guilt-ridden eyes filled with their own tears. "Era," I began, walking to her. "I am so sorry—"

She slapped me across the face, and Silas grabbed her wrists. "Be angry with me," he insisted. "Not her."

Her face twisted in contempt before her glare shifted to me. "I considered you my friend," she spat, lip raising. "Both of you can go to hell."

As I lowered my hand from my stinging cheek, she stormed out of the room, leaving down the passage herself. My eyes drifted to Merrick, the Empath shaking his head as he left to follow her.

I swallowed down my shame as I turned to Silas. His eyes were still wide and reddened. "Are you okay?"

"I...I need to go somewhere to think," he whispered, then left out of the passageway. I went to follow him when Viola grabbed my arm.

"That's why you saved him, why you trusted him so easily." She held her forehead. "Gods, Lena. I can't believe you kept that from us this entire time."

I turned to the group, taking in everyone's wide-open eyes.

"I found out a couple of nights ago, but seeing it all is still crazy," Roland added.

"You knew?" Elowen asked him, then tilted her eyes to Torrin. "As did you and Merrick?"

Dani winced, raising her hand. "And me."

Viola whirled to her, and the Warlock gave her an apologetic smile.

"I'm so sorry for lying to you all. It wasn't easy...I just knew how it would sound."

"So, you knew him when we were younger..." Hendry voiced.

"I did." I smiled weakly. "He actually told me about you and Edmund when we were younger. Told me how you were his best friends."

"This is so crazy," Edmund said. "I mean, I always felt this weird chemistry between you two, but—"

"Merrick figured it out and didn't say anything..." Elowen whispered.

I sighed. "I know my and Silas's history is surprising, nor am I proud of how I've handled things. But we should be focusing on the fact that it was King Ulric who killed the Queen...that he is a literal God." I fetched Kayin's necklace from the ground, clasping it back around my neck. "This could be huge in convincing those in Otacia to turn on him."

"That is if they believe us," Roland expressed with crossed arms. "We saw it firsthand here, but if we had just been told it, we would have had trouble believing such a thing."

"If it came from Silas—"

"The kingdom views him as a traitor," Hendry said bluntly. "They may even think you've used magic to warp our minds, that you control Silas and want the crown for yourself."

"That's ridiculous."

"It is, but you know how it is in Otacia. Since the Prince has betrayed his father and sided with the Mages, I can only imagine what story is being spun now."

"Our families," Roland whispered, voice trembling. "Gods, we need to get them out of there."

"Amatta was a human, yet Ulric raised her." Edmund's eyes drifted to his carbonado arm. "I thought that humans touched by the Undead's magic died, and that was that?"

A cleric answered for me. "If touched by the Undead's magic—one of his creations—yes. But a necromancer themselves can raise anyone they'd like."

"There were gaps in the memories." I voiced to the cleric. "We didn't see anything from Igon's early life, and it felt like there was fuzziness in between."

"Yes," one of the clerics responded gravely. "It seems those are memories they wish to remain unseen. They must have taken measures to block it from this spell."

I groaned and pinched the bridge of my nose. "Damn seers."

"And Kayin—Ryia—she is in Otacia, trapped by that necromancer bastard." Torrin clenched his fists. "We have to save her, but how?"

"How was she able to communicate? Even with your blood..." I began. "Dani, do you know anything about what spell he and Kayin performed?"

One of the clerics stepped forward. "I wrote it down—here."

She handed Dani the piece of parchment, and the Warlock studied the symbols. ***"Coniungere,"*** she muttered. "A siphoning spell." Her eyes flicked up. "This one isn't listed in ***Potestas Verae Maleficis.*** I have no idea where they learned such a thing."

"I need to speak with Lucretia immediately," Kismet urged. "You were right, Supreme. We have lived in comfort for far too long. Seeing what we saw..." She shuddered. "His power is a plague. One that needs to be eradicated before he takes over everything."

We all rushed through the passageway and back into the main area of the temple. I had asked if anyone had seen Silas, and I was informed he was in the sanctuary.

I ambled in to see Silas sitting on one of the benches, his head buried in his hands.

I walked over slowly and sat down beside him, my hand on his back.

"This is all such a shock," I whispered. "Worse than I imagined."

"It is." He slowly lowered his hands. "Ulric...he is the necromancer. He is a fucking God." Silas shook his head. "This whole time, I had been slaughtering those I thought hurt my mother—hurt you—and it turns out that those were the good people. It turns out I was being influenced by the evil one all along. The entire time, I was doing his bidding." Tears fell down his face. "I...I fucked up."

"There was no way you could have guessed this, Silas. No possible way."

"I should've seen it...should have known by his cruelty that something was wrong." He buried his face in his palms once more. "My poor mother...she would be so ashamed of me."

"No." I held his face in my hands, turning him to face me. "She would be so *proud* of you. After everything you endured, after everything taught to you, you chose right over wrong. Good over bad. Hard over easy."

"There were many times I did choose wrong, Lena."

"We have all made mistakes."

"None like I have."

"None have endured what you have," I said sternly and kissed him. "If I can forgive what you have done and am proud of you, then I know Ryia—Kayin—would be, too. I know it."

He was silent for a while.

"I killed so many of your kind...I killed my grandfather."

"Igon knew, Silas. He forgave you for a reason."

His eyes looked to mine in desperation. "How can we save her? How can we...*fix* her?"

"I don't know." I ran my hand along his thigh. "But it's a good sign she was able to talk to me, able to break free from whatever trance he's put her in."

"Does that mean all the puppets we've killed...the original soul is still trapped inside them?"

I thought back to Igon in that form, swallowing down the pain. Was he in there? Could we have saved him? "I think it means they must be brought back to life fully."

Silas dragged his hands down his face. "The problem is, Ulric is the only necromancer."

"There must be an answer of some kind...something we can find," I insisted softly. "But that's something to worry about another day."

Silas continued to stare at the ground. "I have always been so unworthy of you."

Just as I went to protest, a voice filled my head.

"Lena."

My whole body jerked at the sound of Kayin's voice in my head. Silas sat up straight, brows drawn tight.

"Kayin," I breathed. "Ryia."

She laughed through her nose. *"So, you finally know the truth,"* she murmured. *"That's good."*

"My mother is speaking to you?" Silas whispered.

I knew we didn't have much time. "Tell me what to do," I pressed. "Tell me how to save you."

"There is so much suffering to come. And there are answers I am not allowed to give you. You have to find them yourself in order to stop him."

My frown deepened, and I stifled a frustrated groan. "I need direction. Just tell me where to go."

"Temple Ravaiana." She choked on a sob. *"I wish things could go differently."*

The tempo of my heart quickened. "What does that mean?"

"Lena, are you talking to my mother?" Silas asked impatiently.

"Tell Silas...tell him I love him so much," she wept. *"Tell him I'm sorry for the hell he has been thrown into. Tell him I am proud, so proud of him."*

"Kayin—"

I felt the connection sever, felt the silence.

"Godsdamn it," I growled.

"Lena."

I turned to Silas, facing his broken expression.

"She told me to tell you that she loves you so much and that she is so sorry for all you've been through." I cupped his cheek, our faces both crumpling. I kissed his lips softly, then smiled. "And she told me to tell you that she is so proud of you."

He began to cry. "No, she doesn't actually feel that way."

I kissed his tears, stroking the scar on his face. "She does. She just told me so, I swear it." My eyes bore into his. "I will never lie to you again."

CHAPTER SEVENTY-FOUR
MERRICK

I stepped out to one of the many balconies in Temple Tithara, where I finally located Era, her hands tightly gripping the white railing. I felt every bit of the betrayal, hurt, and shock that she felt. I wanted to turn it off, the feeling unbearably unpleasant, but I knew if she saw me with my darkened eyes, saw me using my gift, she would know I understood.

"Era," I said softly, touching her arm. She shrugged me off.

"You knew." Her voice was hoarse as she turned to glare at me, unreleased tears just begging to spill out. "You fucking knew all this time. Everything that happened in the Valley...was it because you felt guilty?"

"What?! Of course not." I grasped her hands in mine, and when she tried to pull away, I tightened my grip. "It was with great effort I kept that a secret, especially from you."

I laced my fingers in hers, and she bit her lip, tears finally overflowing as she gazed out at the ocean, the sunlight sparkling across the waves.

"I told you before when we were trapped there that you deserve something *real*, not just some mutual agreement."

She let out a humorless laugh. "And, what?" Those beautiful brown eyes burned into mine. "I deserve *you*?" She pulled her hands away while giving me a skeptical expression. "How are you any better than Silas? Continuing to stay with Viola when you've slept with me?"

I swallowed the lump in my throat. I took a deep breath as I recalled our time together in the Valley of Awakening, as I recalled her writhing beneath me, her moaning my name.

The truth was this. Era and I were not in the Valley of Awakening for a few hours.

We were there for forty-three days.

I wasn't sure we'd ever escape. And as the days passed—as we grew closer, I couldn't deny my feelings for her any longer. Nor could she.

But when we finally were released, after so much time with one another, she grew cold, distant. I knew she felt guilt for it, not knowing the Prince had already betrayed their marriage first.

She crossed her arms and turned to face the sea once more. "You are all the same," she muttered.

I paused, then placed my hand on the small of her back. "You were unfaithful just as I was," I said quietly. "You can't help who you fall in love with, even if it's wrong. Even if you can't have them."

"I am *not* in love with you," she seethed.

In moments like these, I was grateful for my gift.

"I know when you are lying, Erabella," I uttered softly into her ear from behind.

She slowly turned around and hesitated before pushing me hard. I stumbled back, and she cried as she pushed me again. I didn't stop her as she started punching my chest over and over, sobbing as she did so.

After repeatedly hitting me, eventually, she broke down in tears, and I pulled her close. She wept in my arms, and I ran my hand along her back in a soothing motion.

"You aren't in love with *me*," she cried into my chest.

"Yes, yes, I am," I assured her, and I kissed the top of her head. "I ended things with Viola just before the ball."

She sniffed, her head shooting up to me. "You did?"

I nodded. She leaned her head back further, her ochre eyes bouncing between my darkened ones. Her lip trembled. "Why?"

My brows furrowed. "What do you mean, why? It's you I love." I slid my hand into her hair, and her face crumpled. "It's you I want," I whispered. "You must know that."

"If you loved me," her voice broke, "you would have told me. Do you know how humiliating that was for me? Do you have any idea?"

I knew my eyes were still darkened. "I know *exactly* how you feel, Era. That's why it fucking kills me. It kills me that I made this mistake." I kissed the top of her head again, holding my lips there for a moment. "I was worried I'd hurt you more than help. But it's no excuse. I should have told you."

"When you found me when I left the ball, when I had finally noticed something going on between Silas and Lena, you still didn't tell me."

I stroked her back. "I thought that maybe you'd be happy he was fancying her...because it meant you could be with me."

She shook in my grasp. "You lied to me for Lena."

I frowned, pulling away to read Era better. Her tearful brown eyes seared into mine.

Jealousy.

"I love Lena, Era. I do."

A sneer overcame her, and she went to turn away when I grasped her arms fully.

"But my feelings for her, platonic as they are, do not even *compare* to what I feel for you. Not even close."

"You chose her, just as Silas did. You can say the sweetest things, but at the end of the day, your actions showed me exactly how you feel about me." She tugged her arms away, but still, I held her tight. "Now let me go," she snarled.

"Name what I can do to regain your trust, and I will do it. Yell at me, hit me, do what you wish with me. But do *not* shut me out." My hands slid down to hers, gripping her wrists tightly. "Ask me anything, and you will know if it's the truth. I showed you that power in the Valley. I've never shown *anyone* I can do that."

"Let me go!" she cried.

"No! Don't shut me out again!" My voice broke. "Please, Era. We don't have to hide what we have anymore if we don't wish to. Don't go."

I hated the emotion I felt from her. Though I knew she loved me, one other feeling was undeniable...so strong that it overpowered them all.

Resentment.

"You and I have *nothing*," she seethed. "Nothing, Merrick."

And she meant it.

At a loss for words and with a pain in my chest, I finally re-leased her. She jerked away and stood frozen before she trekked back into the temple.

I should have told her. Over a month alone, and still, I had kept it a secret. She had told me so much about herself over those forty-three days, and I had told her things about me that no one knew.

And now I had ruined it all...all for Lena.

Fuck!

I gripped the balcony railing, trembling. How could've I messed this up so badly?

CHAPTER SEVENTY-FIVE

SILAS

Lena studied the engravings on the wall, deciphering yet another strange text as I watched her from my seat on the bench.

My mind was still spiraling. My mother was alive. Well, partially.

And my father...he was who was responsible for the creatures that plagued the continent. It made so much sense. Of course he wished to bring Mages to the kingdom alive, only to execute them in our kingdom.

He was raising an army of the Undead.

How could I have been so blind?

He and my mother both had magic...which meant that if I *were* his son, I, too, would be a Mage. So why was Mother so adamant that I was his?

And how could she be proud of me? I believed Lena, believed Mother had told her those words, but there was no way her visions had shown her the extent of my mistakes....she certainly wouldn't feel that way if she had.

Lena sighed as she placed down the chalk, frowning at the words.

I stood, walking over to her with my hands in my pockets.

PURIFICATION WILL ENSURE BALANCE, JUST AS HER FATHER HAS.

AS HER POWER GROWS, THE RIFT WILL CLOSE.

"Just as her father has," I murmured.

"Balance...Azrae."

I frowned. "So, the Goddess of Purification is the daughter of Azrae?"

"It would seem so," she whispered, just as the Empath came barging in, face contorted in rage.

"What's wrong?!" Lena asked, standing to her feet.

"It wasn't right to put this burden on me...this secret!" he spat.

"Merrick," she said carefully. "I never wanted you to know. Your damn gift is what gave it all away."

"Era is devastated." His eyes were dark, tears beginning to shine. "She is so hurt that I lied to her. For you." He turned his attention to me, his lip curling. "For both of you."

Lena's lip trembled. "I'm so sorry, Merrick."

"Where is she?" I asked. "I need to speak with her."

Merrick scoffed. "Good luck with that. She ran off somewhere in this temple."

I found Era twenty minutes later, her knees to her chest as she sat against the wall in one of the corridors.

"I don't want to talk," she said quietly, brown eyes glued to her lap.

"Era..." I slid down beside her, sighing as I leaned my head back against the wall. "I have messed up so much. I'm sorry you were in the crossfire of all my poor decisions."

She scoffed, and I angled my head toward her. "Why didn't you leave me behind?" she asked, setting her hands on the ground. "Why didn't you dispose of me before we left the fort?"

"Dispose of you?" I shook my head. "Believe me or not, I love you, Era."

She let out a dry laugh, and I reached my hand down to hold hers. "I didn't know how to feel once Lena was back in my life. She was my first love—"

"Yeah, I saw everything, remember?"

"You saw snippets, yes. But none did justice to how close she and I were." I sighed. "I would've never left you behind, one, because I love you, and two, because I didn't know what the King would have done to you. I wanted you safe."

"Yeah, this journey has been real fucking safe. Great job, Your Highness."

My hand still remained on top of hers. "I know I'm not the good guy in this situation, Era. I was unfaithful to you."

Something in her eyes flicked, something I couldn't place.

"Even before you cheated, you weren't a good husband," she whispered.

"I know." I ran my thumb along the backside of her hand. "You deserved better than me this entire time."

"It's not like we were in love when we married," she said, tears spilling down her cheeks. "I knew that. But I had thought, *'If he got to know me, then perhaps he'd love me,'* but your heart...it already had belonged to another."

"You have done nothing wrong. You've been a perfect wife," I insisted.

She shook her head, her frown deepening as she snatched her hand away and rested her head and arms against her raised knees.

"Truly, Era. I just...everything I have gone through has fucked with my head." I tucked my hands in my lap. "I didn't want to feel what I felt with Lena ever again. I didn't desire that level of closeness. Because I remembered what it felt like to lose it."

A few quiet moments passed. "What happened to your back?" she asked quietly. After a moment of silence, she raised her head, brown eyes unrelenting. "Tell me what happened to you, Silas."

My heartbeat quickened, and I raised my legs to rest my elbows on my knees. "The King had me beaten anytime I showed emotion when it came to killing. Any time I showed compassion, or empathy, or fear. He had me tortured for months."

"And...you felt it worked?"

I inhaled, then exhaled. "I didn't lose my humanity until he had me raped as punishment."

Her eyes flared, her legs sinking back down to the floor.

"He had three men he'd kept as prisoners do it. Every week for months straight." Hard as it was, I kept her eye contact. "I lost myself, Era. I...I wasn't always this way. I used to be a decent man."

738

I swallowed at the sight of her glossy eyes. "I think if that had never happened to me...I think I may have been able to love you how you deserved. I think I could've been open, could've told you about my past. Could've moved on.

"But it was like the real me, the Silas who existed before all the death, the torture, the rape..." I chewed on my lip. "I buried him so deep I wasn't sure he existed anymore."

"And then you saw her," Era said quietly.

I nodded, my fingers drumming against the ground. "And it was like these versions of me were battling. The real me wanted back out. But it hurt...being him hurts..."

I couldn't stop the tears from spilling from my eyes, and my stare fell to the ground, feeling pathetic for it.

It was Era who now placed a hand atop mine. "I'm so sorry you went through that."

"I'm sorry I hurt you. I'm sorry I lied. You deserved so much more. You deserved to have had the real me." I gave her a small smile. "I think you would've liked him."

"I liked you just as you were," she said quietly. "I didn't like how closed off you were...didn't like how cold you could be. But I loved you, regardless. You saved me from my family. I'll always be grateful for that." Her hand slipped away. "I ...I just need time—time to adjust to all of this."

"I understand," I whispered.

She winced, rubbing at her temples. "I'd like to be alone now if you don't mind."

I nodded, then stood to give her the space she needed.

My friends—because yes, I considered them all my friends—stared at me, at Lena, with mixed faces when I returned. Era wasn't present; she still wished to remain alone until we were leaving.

I settled my gaze on my men. "I'm sorry I lied to you all."

Edmund shook his head, eyes wide. "Don't be, man. I mean, it makes sense." His eyes went to Lena. "It makes sense why you had a change of heart."

"No wonder you wanted to kick my ass all the time," Roland teased, a half-smile pulling on his face.

For the first time in years, I smiled back at him. His own dropped in shock as he looked at me.

I needed to apologize to him, not just for the treatment recently, but for years of resentment.

I glanced at Hendry, who also wore a happy expression. "I'm happy to see the old you peering through." I could swear I saw a gleam in his eyes. "I missed him."

I sucked in my lips because damn him for making me feel emotional. I glanced back at Roland.

"Can I talk to you?"

He blinked. "Yeah. Of course."

I turned to Lena, brushing my hand down her arm. "Wait to discuss our plans moving forward until I return."

She nodded, her smile encouraging and her eyes gentle.

Roland's hands went inside his pockets, his legs nervously bouncing as he sat beside me on a bench outside of the temple. The warm, summertime air blew past us, ruffling his brown hair.

"I'm sorry," I said quietly.

His brows drew together. "For what? I understand why you've been mad. I was intimate with the love of you—"

"For how I treated you...*after*," I interrupted.

His eyebrows raised, and he offered me a shy smile. "It's okay, Silas."

"No." I shook my head, turning to face him. "It's really not."

I hesitated, but then I told him everything. I told him about my mixed feelings from back then.

I told him of the many beatings.

And then...I told him of the rape.

"My Gods..." Roland breathed after I had finished my story, his eyes overflowing with tears. "I had no idea."

"Regardless of what happened to me, you were my friend. You were there when I needed someone. I never thanked you for it. You didn't deserve my cruelty."

His cheeks flushed, and he rubbed the back of his neck. "You weren't cruel to me." The corner of his lip turned up. "You were an ass."

A small smile formed on my face, but it quickly fell. "Why did you stay by my side?" I asked, my eyes searching his. "After all I did to you?"

He shrugged. "I just figured you were going through an identity crisis of some sort. I wasn't going to hold it against you."

"After *years*?"

He gave me a soft smile. "Even after years...I thought it was 'cause you...maybe you liked men and didn't want to admit it because of your father. But you and Lena? Everything your father put you through? I would've never guessed any of it." He sighed, rubbing the back of his head. "I'm sorry I was intimate with her."

"Don't be. She needed that. Deserved it. And you probably did, too."

His eyes fell to the ground as he dragged his bottom lip through his teeth. "I thought your anger at my flirting with her was because you were jealous I was giving *her* attention." He snorted and gave me an embarrassed smile. "I read that whole thing wrong. Well, right, but in the wrong way."

My shoulders slumped, and my head fell. "I'm really sorry, Roland."

"She's special," he expressed quietly, the corners of his lips raised.

"She is." I glanced up at him again. "I just...I hope we can be friends again," I said sincerely. "I am a broken person. But I'm really trying to be better."

His eyes flickered. "I've always considered you my friend." His smile softened. "Plus, we're all a little broken."

"We need to go to Temple Ravaiana. Kayin spoke to me up in the sanctuary," Lena said softly. Everyone looked at her. "We are going to need a necromancer to bring back Kayin...maybe...I'm not sure." She shook her head. "But perhaps we can find some answers there."

"And if we don't?" Torrin asked. "Where to after that?"

"We need to warn those in Faltrun and Forsmont the truth about Ulric. Everyone needs to know," Dani stated.

"So, we teleport there?" Elowen asked.

Lena pondered on it. "Teleporting takes too much energy. It'd push reaching the temple out a few days, and I want to get there as soon as possible."

"I can go," Dani offered. "Plus, I miss my brother. I can stop in Forsmont, then Faltrun. The mountain, too, if you wish."

"I'll go with," Valter interjected from the hallway.

"What?" Lena breathed, turning to face him.

His shoulders lifted. "You're right. We have stood by the sidelines for far too long." His eyes flashed to Dani. "I already spoke with Kismet. I can come with you and tell your folks about Nereida. Perhaps even bring some to our home for safety—the children."

My stomach sank at his words, thinking of little Saoirse.

Viola said, "Should I come with?"

Dani gave her a lazy smile. "They'll need your shifting abilities, babe. Don't worry." She nudged her hips into Valter, who gave her raised brows. "Valt and I got this."

"Where should we plan on meeting?" Elowen questioned, crossing her golden-brown arms. "Depending on what we do or do not find out at the temple."

Merrick's glare was almost more frightening while his eyes were still icy blue. Almost.

I supposed his bitterness came from feeling Erabella's emotions...or perhaps us hurting her really angered him.

I was still unsure if there was anything between the two of them, but it seemed more and more like there was.

"Let's meet back on the mountain," Lena stated. "I need to talk to Immeron about all we learned. I'll teleport us there after we explore Temple Ravaiana."

Everyone agreed.

"Then we shall leave in the morning."

CHAPTER SEVENTY-SIX

LENA

I hated that we were leaving such a beautiful place so soon. I was going to miss the sea breeze, the carefree attitudes of the residents, and, yes, of course, the outstanding food. We'd hardly spent any time here, but I told myself we would be back one day, hopefully under better circumstances.

Kismet insisted to Lucretia that Nereida should help our cause. I knew from what Valter told me that the two held equal power. Thankfully, they agreed to support our mission, and I said I would return to let them know when the time to fight came.

Lucretia was furious at first when she heard that Valter had already departed with Dani, but her lover was eventually able to calm her down.

The following day came, and I was grateful Kismet had rallied the Sea Nymphs. They worked to balance the tide in our favor.

We rode on a boat sailed by a handful of the Nereidian guard, considering Dani had teleported to Forsmont with Valter already. I missed our Warlock companion, but I knew we'd be reunited with her soon.

We said our thanks to the guard once dropped off on the shoreline and reached Temple Ravaiana by late afternoon. We decided to sleep there after scoping it out. Once again, no clerics lived in the temple, but blessedly, no dead bodies did either.

Silas breathed in as he gazed outside the windows in the sanctuary. Its design was identical to the other two we'd been to so far. "I feel...different here."

Roland raised a brow as he stepped up to him. "You sense something?"

"What do you feel?" I asked carefully. Even I felt nothing.

"Perhaps it's in my head, but I feel almost a...buzz." He glanced around the infrastructure, then focused on the words written in the Titharan language. "Lena, can you read any of this?"

I fished out **Potestas Verae Maleficis** and began my translation just as I had before.

"Do you think it's safe to stay here tonight?" Merrick asked, glancing out a window. "I fear Ulric will find us somehow."

"I'm sure this place is as good as any." Elowen grinned at him. "Plus, this is the home of the Goddess of Life. Surely, she'll be watching over us."

"We should gather some wood for our fire tonight," Hendry stated, peering at the setting sun. "Before it gets dark."

"I'll go with," Edmund offered, kissing Elowen on the temple before walking over to his friend.

Merrick's gaze went to Era, who sat on a bench, rubbing her head and avoiding his stare. "I will, too," Merrick mumbled, following the two men down the temple stairs.

I frowned at the words I had written with chalk on the temple's floor.

RAVAIANA'S DAUGHTER WILL SACRIFICE IT ALL SO HER SON MAY BE REBORN.

HE SHALL DICTATE THE FATE OF THE WORLD.

Viola stepped forward. "Ravaiana's children are the other Gods? A daughter and son..."

"And Azrae's daughter is the other..." I tapped my fingers on the floor, then stood, placing the chalk back in my bra. "But who are they? Where do we find them?"

The golden-eyed Prince spoke. "Ravaiana's realm is Oquerene, yes? Perhaps they reside there."

I rotated my head to him, brows wrinkling. "You think it'll be that easy?" I whispered.

"I don't think getting to Oquerene will be easy, but perhaps once we *do* arrive, things will get easier for us." He tucked my hair behind my ear, then held the side of my face. "Come. We've been traveling a lot. You must be exhausted. You'll need your strength when you bring us back to the mountain in the morning."

I rested my face in his palm, looking up at him lovingly.

"It's still so weird seeing you guys like this," Viola mumbled, and when my eyes slid to her, I chuckled softly. My happy feelings faded the moment I locked eyes with Erabella.

She glared at me with contempt, and I quickly pulled away from Silas, packing my grimoire back into my bag.

CHAPTER SEVENTY-SEVEN
MERRICK

"Y ou've seemed down lately," Edmund commented. "And that's saying a lot, considering you're normally so doom and gloom."

I glared at him, his signature sideways smile slapped on his face. I laughed through my nose, nudging him with my shoulder, and he chuckled.

"Just a lot on my mind."

I couldn't talk about Era. The situation was still so fucked. She and Silas weren't together, yet she joined in on this journey and threw away her title and her comfort, all in support of him. Just for him to leave her for another woman.

I knew what Silas and Lena had was real. I knew the situation had been taxing on them as well. But Era...Era got fucked over, and no one had comforted her. We had all gone on like nothing had changed when everything had.

And she still refused to speak with me. If she would just let me comfort her, if we could just talk, I knew things would be better.

I always wondered if my mother would still be alive today had she found love after my father's affair. If she would've found living to be worthwhile after all. My existence wasn't enough; in fact, it was a constant reminder, I was sure. I was certain every time she looked at me, she'd see my father's face. Be reminded of his betrayal.

That's why I hated seeing Era like this. In her beautiful, broken face, I saw my mother. I saw a woman who would've given her spouse anything but wasn't fully appreciated or worshipped like she deserved.

"A lot of crazy shit in a short amount of time," Edmund mumbled as we cut down some firewood. "I suppose you're feeling...well, all of it."

"As always," I muttered, swinging an ax we found in the temple.

"I can't wait for this war to be over," Edmund sighed. "That little break was good—more than good. But it went by too quickly."

I nodded, lost in thought.

"Was it hard on you? Knowing all that?"

I knew he was referring to the secrets kept for Silas and Lena.

"Painfully. Not only knowing it but feeling everything. I wanted to be angry at them, especially for Era's sake. But I also...couldn't fully. Because I understood."

Our wood pile was looking decent. We only needed enough to cook our dinner, as the temperature tonight shouldn't get too low.

"I hope Era finds a love like that," Edmund said, wiping the sweat off his forehead before bending down to carry some wood. "You too, man. A Soul-Tie bond is the most wonderous thing."

I started gathering wood in my own arms.

"El got her electricity," he mumbled, and I raised a brow at him. His cheeks turned pink, and then his face scrunched in embarrassment.

"I really don't want to hear about you and my sister having sex," I muttered.

I wasn't about to tell him I had also acquired mine.

He laughed, standing straight with his hands full.

I smiled to myself, thinking of Era...thinking of the moment that power spread throughout me...thinking about how she looked when I released it.

I knew Erabella loved me, and when I got back to her, I would show her just how much I loved her. I would beg and grovel if I had to.

I needed to see her smile again. I needed to hold her in my arms. We would work through this and come out even happier. I knew it.

I heard the whizzing passing me only a second before an arrow shot through Hendry's chest.

Hendry's mismatched eyes blew wide, his eyes dropping to his fatal wound before he slumped to the ground, blood pouring out.

"NO!" Edmund bellowed, instantly releasing the wood pile in his arms and withdrawing his sword.

Only a moment went by before the sharp sting of a blade slid across my neck.

Edmund wailed as he whirled in my direction, eyes widened in horror at what he beheld. He thrust his sword into the person behind me.

Liquid poured down my neck as the wood in my arms tumbled to the ground. My eyes enlarged as I contemplated what had just happened.

My neck...my neck had been sliced open.

I brought my hands to the wound, instantly soaking my palms, and blood began to stream out of my mouth.

I stumbled back, falling against one of the tree stumps.

Choking. I was choking. *Dying.* I knew instantly this wound was too harsh for me to survive being separated from Elowen or Lena.

My vision was blurring, but I saw Edmund thrust his sword into another soldier's chest and heard him wail as he took down the last of the men who'd attacked.

Halstedian armor.

Edmund ran to me after successfully killing the men all on his own.

"Fuck!" he roared, falling to his knees in front of me.

"Go—" I managed to choke out, blood splattering out of my mouth.

His eyes darted between Hendry's body and my neck. "No, we need to get you to El. S-she can—"

I grasped his arm, forcing his wide eyes to mine. Tears slid down my face as I shook my head.

Edmund knew I wouldn't make it, and I knew it too. Tears fell down his cheeks, and he clasped my hand in his. I was struggling to keep my eyes open.

"I'm so sorry," he wept. "I love you, brother," he whispered, and the bastard made me cry even harder. I clenched his arm as hard as I could to let him know that despite everything, I loved him, too.

There was so much I wanted to say—so much I still wanted to do in my short life.

A woman I wanted to love fully that I didn't get the chance to.

I spoke to Edmund in my mind, even though I knew he wouldn't hear me.

Take care of my sister...and tell Era that I love her.

As Edmund sobbed, backing away before running toward my friends, a small smile crept over my face as I realized how happy I was to have met them all.

The world began to go black, and I shut my eyes for the final time, thinking of Erabella as I slipped away.

Forever.

CHAPTER SEVENTY-EIGHT
LENA

W e were setting up our bedrolls when Edmund rushed up the steps, panting. Blood stained his clothes.

"What the fuck happened?" Roland exclaimed just as Elowen rushed to him, assessing if there were any wounds.

His chest was rising and falling. "I'm sorry," his voice broke, his face crumpling. "I-I couldn't save them..."

Viola and Roland rushed to the windows, eyes darting outside to check for threats.

I gaped at him, noting that Merrick and Hendry were nowhere to be seen. "Save them?" I asked lowly.

"Where is Merrick?" Elowen's voice trembled as she grasped his shoulders.

Torrin's face crumpled, his hand flying over his mouth as he read Edmund's mind.

No.

Elowen's big blue eyes skated over Edmund's face, searching for an answer. "Where is Merrick, Edmund?!" Elowen shouted, shaking him.

"El...t-they slit his throat—" Edmund choked on a sob, and Elowen's eyes widened.

No. This cannot be.

I clutched my chest. "He's dead?!" I cried.

"No...no..." Elowen collapsed to the ground, a gut-wrenching cry escaping her.

"There was no time," he insisted.

"NO!" she wailed.

"I'm so sorry, El..." Edmund went to touch her arm, and she flinched backward, glaring at him.

"I could have saved him!" she screamed, and I watched as ice began to creep up her arms. "You could have gotten me, and—"

"There is no time," he barked, grasping her freezing arms. "Elowen, we have to go! They are coming!"

"Where is Hendry?" Silas demanded.

Tears coursed down Edmund's cheeks when he met eyes with the Prince. "They killed him."

"No," Roland whispered, tearing his gaze from the window. "No. H-he has to be alright—"

"An arrow went straight through his chest!" Edmund cried. "They are both dead! We have to go!"

I couldn't think. I couldn't process it.

And then there was Era.

Her expression was...blank. Her body was completely still. Utterly emotionless, yet her eyes were filled with tears, and they poured down her face.

"We have to go get him," Elowen wept. "We have to—"

An arrow shot through one of the windows, shattering the glass and grazing Silas's arm as he shoved me out of the way.

"Lena, we need to teleport!" Torrin yelled, ducking down.

"We can't leave him!" Elowen howled, ice creeping up her chest. "I won't go!"

"Elowen—" Torrin began moving toward her with his flame, but multiple objects were tossed into the sanctuary from the pronaos, exploding as they hit the ground. Purple dust filled the room, and my stomach sank when I realized what just happened.

"GRAB YOUR WEAPONS!" I yelled, already feeling the effects of the siaxcide, my magic fading from me.

I rushed to grab my blade—my scabbard beside Era on the bench. She roughly grabbed my wrist as I reached for it.

My eyes shot to hers, burning with rage as I took in her emotionless form. "What are you doing?!" I hissed.

It was all I could get out until I felt something hit the back of my head. Hard.

Suddenly, the world went black.

When I awoke, the first thing I noticed was cuffs around my wrists. My eyes shot wide, and when I forced myself up, wincing from my head pain, a sword was quickly at my throat.

All of us had been knocked out, sitting on the floor of the temple with bound wrists and blades held at our necks.

All of us, except Erabella.

Slowly, we were all gaining consciousness again.

"What's going on?" I hissed.

A soldier, one in Halstedian armor, replied, "The Princess here let us know of your whereabouts." He gestured to her sitting frame. "We've been tracking you ever since."

"What...how..." I shook my head, my watery eyes meeting Era's apathetic ones as I turned to look behind me. "You didn't. You wouldn't."

"She did." The man motioned to one of the soldiers, and the one holding a blade to Silas grasped his arm, pulling him to his feet.

"What are you doing?" I demanded.

They ordered him to sit in front of the altar at the head of the room. His golden eyes flitted to mine, a look I couldn't pinpoint as he stared at me.

"Why have you attacked us?" Silas asked, his voice unusually steady as he walked up the few steps and sat against the wooden altar.

"We have orders from King Ulric."

I bared my teeth, and as I went to stand, the soldier holding me pressed his blade deeper against my throat.

"Do not move, Lena," Silas ordered.

Tears filled my eyes as the man before him withdrew his sword. Dark shadows swirled at its tip.

We all gasped. "What are you doing?!" I repeated.

"Silas La'Rune, you are hereby charged with treason," the man stated as he aimed his blade at him. "Your punishment is execution." He tilted the weapon, the shadows moving as if there were life to them. "The Undead's curse has touched this sword. No witch will be able to save you."

"NO!" I screamed, thrashing against the man who was detaining me. The sword pressed against my throat, drawing blood. "Please, please don't do this—"

Silas went to move, and the man behind me quickly said, "Try anything, and we slit her throat."

Silas's jaw tensed, and his back relaxed against the altar.

"Silas, no!" I cried.

"Don't touch him!" Roland barked.

"Don't!" Viola wept.

The person holding the cursed blade tilted it, examining the dark magic before his eyes flitted to the Prince. "May the Gods have mercy on your soul."

Immediately, I began to panic and tried lashing out of the soldier's grip, even as his blade pressed against me.

"PLEASE!" I begged. "Gods, kill me instead! I will take his place, please..." I cried. "Please, don't hurt him!"

But the soldier didn't listen to my pleas. He only smiled before plunging the cursed sword into Silas's chest.

CHAPTER SEVENTY-NINE
LENA

The world slowed as the cursed weapon went straight through Silas's chest, pinning him to the altar behind him, a trail of crimson pouring out.

"NO!" I screamed as Silas choked, his eyes blowing wide. I flailed out, the sword at my neck digging into my skin.

I didn't care if they slit my throat. I couldn't live without him. I wouldn't want to.

"You fucking bastards!" Roland bellowed, just as Viola broke into a sob, Edmund roaring in despair.

The soldier freed me from his grasp as Silas groaned in agony. I instantly rushed to him.

I sobbed, my cuffed hands holding his face as I stumbled over him. "No...I can't live without you."

"Yes, you can." His hand trembled as he reached for my cheek, brushing away tears. "I love you so much...I only wish we had more time together." He coughed, blood dripping from his mouth.

I cried harder.

"I'm sorry...I'm so sorry," I wept.

"D-don't be, Flower. This was not for nothing." He pulled me into a kiss, my lips on his for a fleeting moment before he cried out at the pain from the curse.

"No...this can't be happening..."

He gave me a broken smile. "I am so grateful I found you again. You have made me truly content, something I never thought possible to feel again."

I choked on a sob at the same time as he did.

"But you know the best part?" he whispered, resting his forehead against mine. "I got to fall in love with you all over again. Not that I had ever stopped." He struggled to breathe, stifling a cough.

"I never stopped either, Silas," I wept, my eyes falling to the blood that poured out of him. "Fuck, let me heal him, please!" I begged.

The soldier laughed. "You could try, but there is no cure for the Undead's curse."

My panicked eyes went to Erabella, who continued to stare at us with no emotion.

"How could you do this?!" I hissed, clinging to Silas's arms.

"Okay, that's enough theatrics," the soldier drawled. As he went to pull me away, Silas held my hand tight.

"Lena," he murmured, tears falling down his cheeks as his golden eyes fixated on me. "Stop him...you're the only one who can." He swallowed. "You will not give up," he choked.

"Silas," I shook my head rapidly. "*Please...*" I cried.

"You will not break."

The guard grabbed me underneath my arms, and I flailed my limbs out as hard as I could.

"NO!" My efforts were futile; I had no magic or way of healing my lover.

When they began tugging me away, a sad smile formed on Silas's face. "I love you, Lena."

"I love you more than anything," I wailed. "Gods, no...please no..."

His eyes were barely open now, his breathing slow and uneven.

I resisted as much as I could, fighting back as they attempted to lug me and my friends out of the temple. That is until a sharp pain blossomed from the back of my head, and my vision turned black.

I woke up in a carriage, the bumps in the road jolting me awake.

My hazy vision darted between my friends, all awake, none of them talking. Elowen was weeping quietly, her head resting on Edmund's chest. Viola sat next to her, her own tears staining her cheeks. I sat up, noting that my head had been resting on Torrin's shoulder. Roland was to my other side, his elbows resting on his knees, his eyes red.

"H-how long have I been out?" I whispered.

"Almost an hour," Torrin said softly, looking sadder than I had ever seen him before.

"Silas?" I cried.

Silence.

"Ravaiana abandoned us," Elowen uttered with a blank stare. "Even in her own temple...she spurned us."

The journey to Halsted took three days, days that passed like years and like seconds at the same time. The townspeople scrutinized us in disgust as they peeked inside our carriage.

I couldn't care less what they thought of us.

Merrick was dead.

Hendry was dead.

Silas...

I shook my head to banish away the tears. I was surprised any remained after how much I had cried.

Silas was dead. There was no possible way he had survived the Undead's curse.

I clenched my fists tightly, unable to wield magic as Otacian cuffs bound my wrists.

I still couldn't accept it. I cried as I pictured how he must've suffered in his final moments.

How did I fuck up this badly? It was seen that Silas would determine the fate of Magekind...how could he do that dead?

Dead...

I thought back to what Kayin had said in Temple Tithara.

"I wish things could go differently."

She cried as she had me tell Silas how much she loved him. She knew of his fate, didn't she?

You will not break.

I would kill King Ulric. I would kill every soldier who chose to obey him. I didn't care if they had families. I didn't care if it would scar my soul. Nothing mattered anymore except seeking revenge and freeing my people and innocent humans from this man's reign—this *monster*.

Once my duty was complete, I would join Silas in the afterlife. Until then, I could not break.

I was shoved into a dank, dark cell only lit by two oil lamps. I was light-headed, and my mouth was dry due to three days without food or water.

I was chained to a chair. About to be interrogated, no doubt.

When a soldier entered the room, I debated finding a way to snap his neck. But when I saw he carried water in his hand, I refrained from any attempt. Not that I really had a chance of successfully doing so.

I didn't recognize him from our travels. His deep green hair flipped out from where it rested along his jawline; his whiskey eyes narrowed as he stepped over with a waterskin.

"Thank you," I rasped before I tilted my head back, guzzling down the water as he poured it into my mouth.

I couldn't wait to kill him and every soldier here.

"The prisoners hardly get fed," he said simply. "When you are given food, I recommend hiding some of it and spreading it out over the course of a few days."

I gave him a fake smile. "Thanks for the advice," I muttered.

"Asael!" Someone pounded on my cell door, and the green-haired man tilted his gaze back. "Cedric will be down any minute. Will you be joining him?"

My Gods.

"I'll be out in a second," Asael responded, and the man outside the door grunted before his steps could be heard fading away.

"Asael..." I breathed. "Asael Nefeli?"

His caramel eyes flared. "How do you know me?"

"You're the painter from Faltrun. Why are you a Halstedian soldier?"

"I am not at liberty to share that information with you," he answered as he turned to leave.

"Wait!" I called out, and Asael slowed his steps. "My name...is Lena Daelyra."

He froze.

"You...you're supposed to save me."

CHAPTER EIGHTY

LENA

A sael slowly turned toward me.

"You..." he whispered. "You're real."

I frowned. "I'm not sure what that means, but you need to get me out of here!"

Asael swallowed. "The directions I was given...they—"

Asael quickly shut his mouth when the iron door creaked open, and a large, muscular form strode in.

Asael had to be around 5'9". This other man, however, was well over six feet. His face was rough, sadistic even. I could sense his wickedness by the way his grin curved when he looked at me.

"Ah, this is the ginger-bitch with the answers we need," Cedric commented, giving me a once over.

I lifted my chin, glaring at him with disdain.

His smile morphed into a nefarious frown. "Where is the Weapon?"

There was that question again. One I myself still did not know.

Ulric wanted the Weapon for himself—feared it.

"Even if I did know," I spat, "what makes you think I'd tell you?"

Cedric crossed his tanned arms. "We have ways of getting answers out of you."

I let out a low laugh. "Do you have any idea what kind of King you serve? Do you know what he really is?"

Cedric's jaw tensed. "Go if you can't handle it, Asael."

Asael just stared at me before saying quietly, "You'd lay a hand on a woman, Cedric?"

Cedric snorted, turning to glower at Asael. "She is a witch, not a woman." To that, he turned, and his fist met my cheek in one hard blow. My face whipped to the side, stars clouding my vision. I clenched my fists, wishing I could break free from these chains.

Cedric was laughing, and as I slowly turned my head back, I met Asael's eyes.

There was so much communication in our unspoken words—in our eye contact.

"I don't believe in the ways of my people," he seemingly said with his expression.

What a hero you are.

"I'd stop it if I could."

Shall I give you a medal?

"Where is the Weapon?" Cedric crooned as he crouched before me, caressing my face. My lip curled, but I held Asael's gaze.

"Just tell him," his eyes pleaded.

Leave if you can't take it.

His caramel eyes narrowed, and Cedric clicked his tongue as he stood, seemingly walking away before turning back and sucker-punching me again.

A small cry escaped my lips at the pain, my head pounding from the blow. I tasted iron and was worried one of my teeth had come loose. Dragging my tongue along each one, all still being in place, I returned my stare to Asael, spitting blood on the floor.

"She's a feisty one," Cedric commented, eyes wild as he studied the damage he had caused.

"What do you know of King Ulric?" Asael asked slowly.

Cedric shot him an annoyed look, but Asael kept his brown eyes on me.

I spat what blood had pooled in my mouth to my left. "I know that he is the necromancer plaguing our lands. The God of Deceit."

Asael's eyes flared, and Cedric barked out a theatrical laugh. "Out of all ridiculous claims you could've made, that one was most unexpected."

I breathed heavily. "It makes perfect sense. He kills Mages in his kingdom, lugs their dead bodies to his dungeons, and has been raising a fucking army this entire time." I let out a humorless laugh. "And all you prejudiced bastards are ensuring your own doom in doing so."

Asael's chest heaved with each breath, his cheeks slightly flushed. Cedric gave him an eyeroll. "Don't believe a word she's saying. She hasn't even had her fingernails ripped off yet." He gave me a sadistic grin. "That's when the real truths come out."

I did my best to school my expression and steady my rapid breathing and my increasing pulse.

I knew by now that they planned on torturing me. I just needed to stay alive long enough to figure out how to get out of here...or stay alive long enough for Asael to free me. Maybe even connect with Kayin if it was possible somehow.

Cedric walked toward me, and I flinched when he grabbed my fingers. "Such pretty little hands," he noted. "Too bad."

I squeezed my eyes shut, tears threatening to overflow, as I heard him step away, fumbling with whatever tool he was going to use to remove my nails. I had noticed the tray of tools earlier, but I purposely chose not to study it.

I will not break.

"Cedric," Asael said quickly. "Let me talk to her."

Cedric scoffed. "Your heart is going to get you killed, Asael. These are not people."

I slowly opened my eyes, tears spilling down my cheeks. Cedric inched closer, thin shards of bamboo in his hands, a hammer in the other. My eyes darted to Asael's, and I knew I no longer hid my look of desperation.

"Let me talk to her," Asael gritted out, grasping Cedric's shoulder.

"Leave, Asael. You're clearly too much of a pansy to be of any use." Cedric let out a whistle, and two men entered.

Asael shot me a panicked gaze, and my face crumpled only for a moment before I glared at Cedric.

"Last chance, Lena Daelyra. Where is the Weapon?" He nodded his head to one of the men, who walked over and held my hand down. Cedric positioned the bamboo at the start of my nail, his other hand readying the hammer.

I will not break.

Asael went to rush forward, but the other soldier gripped him.

"Let me go!" he protested, but the man only held him tighter.

My breathing became labored, my entire body trembling with fear. But I kept Asael's gaze. One person. That was all it would take to set me free. One person witnessing my humanity. One person caring.

Cedric clicked his tongue. "Too bad," he repeated, and he hammered the bamboo shard under my nail.

I shrieked in agony as the bamboo tore through, the pain so horrific I thought I might puke. I couldn't look at my hand, even though I knew the force had ripped my nail completely off.

I will not break.

I hated that I cried. Hated that the men laughed, all but Asael. I lifted my teary eyes to his, his own glassy, a look of horror on his features as he glared at Cedric.

Cedric paid him no mind and went to position the next shard. "Where is the Weapon?" he repeated.

I will not break.

Another wave of dread, and the shard was through, a guttural cry leaving my chest.

"Let me talk to her, dammit!" Asael's voice was hoarse as he begged.

"Vince, take him out of here," Cedric ordered as he began to position another piece of bamboo. I was trembling now, my teeth clenching down hard as I awaited the loss of another nail.

"Hold her still, Lance."

And any shred of hope disappeared the moment Asael was pulled out of the room.

Cedric grinned. "No one here to advocate for you now," he taunted.

I will not break.

"No, you will not, my dear."

I blinked rapidly. Was someone speaking to me in my head?

I was hoping to hear from Kayin, but this voice was masculine. Familiar. Not Torrin. Not Igon.

My vision was blurry from all the tears, from the stars in my vision, but just behind Cedric stood a man.

I couldn't make out his face, only the bright white light swirling around his limbs.

I blinked over and over. His hair was dark brown, and his skin was fair—I could tell that much. His eyes glowed the same color as the magic surrounding his arms...magic as bright as moonlight.

I let out a breathy whisper. "Who are you?"

Lance and Cedric's brows drew together, and they glanced over their shoulders.

Lance snorted. "Looks like the pain is causing her to hallucinate."

I kept my eyes on the mysterious man. His gaze drifted over the two men, his lip curling.

I wailed as the last nail on my right hand was removed.

"Where. Is. The. Weapon?"

"Rot in hell." I spat right in Cedric's face. That made the man with the white glow's lips turn upward.

"I guess you require more drastic measures."

The glowing man began to fade.

"Who are you?" I whispered.

The unknown man's gaze raked over me. *"When you figure that out, you will be freed."*

"Wait! WAIT!" I cried.

"She's lost it entirely," Cedric chortled.

I begged for the stranger to come back, but he didn't. Not as my remaining nails were removed.

Not as a branding iron was brought out. Not as it was pressed flush against my chest.

I screeched as the iron sizzled my skin off.

Silas had gone through this. Silas had survived it.

I will not break.

I would free my people. I would kill Ulric.

Only then would I join Silas in the afterlife. Not before.

So, I repeated that mantra. Repeated it as my skin was repeatedly branded and burned. Repeated it as my skin was whipped. Repeated it as my feet were put in iron boots, and the bones in them were crushed, leaving me unable to stand. Repeated it as I was flayed and cut open and stitched back up for them to do it all over again.

I will not break.

I will not break.

I will not break.

CHAPTER EIGHTY-ONE
LENA - THIRTY DAYS LATER

I'd grown used to being enveloped by darkness, nothing but the occasional sound of dripping water keeping me company as I sat alone in the corner of my cell. Sometimes, like today, I would hear creaking and groaning from up above, which usually meant someone would be coming down to interrogate me.

But this time was different. This time, they hauled me out of my cell for the first time in a month, lugging my broken frame up several concrete steps. I felt like crying when the cool nighttime air kissed my skin.

I was surprised I was still breathing, but as they tied my weak and starved body to a rack in some outdoor courtyard, I knew I would surely die. I knew that as the machine pulled and stretched my limbs to unnatural lengths, my arms and legs would be ripped free of my body.

I was still, my eyes unfocused as they restrained my limp body on the device.

I had held on this long, and I had not broken, despite the sadistic torture they had subjected me to. But still, I had failed. I would not escape here. I couldn't save anyone and would not get justice for those I loved.

I hadn't seen my friends the entire time. I didn't know what horrors they had also endured. I begged to know if they were still alive, but no one listened to my pleas. It was just the same question over and over and over.

"Where is the Weapon?"

I had choked on a sob as they secured the rope around each wrist and ankle. I had tried with all my might the past thirty days, hoping to see the stranger with the white glow. But he never appeared. Neither did Asael.

Once I was secured to the torture device, the soldiers left the courtyard, leaving me to lay in dread until they returned to harm me. To end me.

All I wore was a thin tube top and underwear, and as I peered down at my body, a muffled cry left me.

My hip bones and ribs were entirely visible beneath my skin. My legs were frail, my flesh all shades of purple, yellow, and brown from the beatings. Scars were littered everywhere.

I am so tired...I don't want to fight anymore.

During the first couple of weeks here, I wasn't offered anything but water. I had been given one meal since.

My heavy gaze slowly slid upward, taking in the sight of the thousands of stars twinkling in the sky.

My face began to crumple, and as I accepted that my final moments were upon me, as I stared at the countless pinpricks of light, my mother's words filled my head.

"Count them, Lena. Count the stars."

I bit down my sob, my eyes squeezing tight, a rush of tears spilling down my cheeks.

I opened them.

One.

Two.

Three.

"It's time to sleep, Lena," my mother's voice whispered, and I imagined her holding me close. *"Count the stars."*

Four.

Five.

Six.

"Count the stars."

My eyelids had already begun to flutter shut by the time I was in the double digits. As uncomfortable as this position was, at least I was lying on my back. I could only hope that my death would be swift.

A few more moments of counting passed, and my eyes fell shut. I felt myself drifting off, but the light I saw through my eyelids woke me. I slowly opened them, squinting at the source.

The silhouette of a man.

This time, only the magic surrounding him was glowing. Now, I could see his face fully, see his green eyes and handsome features.

Now, I could see my father's face.

"Waylon?" I breathed.

The corner of his lip pulled up. "Not quite, my dear."

I frowned, studying his face more closely. Without a doubt, he had my father's face, but instead of appearing to be in his forties, he seemed to be in his twenties. His skin showed no signs of aging, and he spoke with an elegant accent I hadn't heard before.

"I...I don't understand." I shook my head. "You look just like my father."

He gave me a lopsided grin. "There is a reason for that, which you shall understand soon." He cocked his head to the side, his touch featherlight against my cheek. "Who am I, Lena? Have you figured it out yet?"

I studied his form, studied the white magic more closely now that I wasn't actively being tortured. It wasn't just white magic...but white *flame*.

And there was only one being said to have such a power.

"Azrae," I breathed.

The God of Vengeance smiled at me. "The Weapon, Lena. Where is it?"

No. Not him, too.

"I won't hurt you," he said gently. "But you need to figure it out if you have any hope of surviving this. Only the Weapon can break you free from here. Only it can stop Ulric."

Silas's words played in my head.

"The Weapon is said to be that of a magic no one has ever seen. Magic to stop all magic...or stop all of humanity. Whoever finds it—hones it—will dictate the fate of the entire world."

"Why can't you just tell me?"

"The Gods cannot interfere. Not with this."

I desperately tried to piece it together.

"You...you are the God of Vengeance. The God of Justice..." I blinked. "Your power, your magic, that is the magic to stop all magic. The white flame in Asael's painting."

Silas's words filtered through.

"He told us the weapon was in Ames, but if your seer had seen it coming, perhaps he moved it."

"In Ames..." I whispered.

Igon's words from the Chamber of Time came to me next.

"I must teach her everything I know. She needs to be able to piece it together when the time comes. She must be kept safe."

I blinked, Kayin's words rushing to me.

"She is a Mage. A powerful one. Or, I should say she will be. Her power...it is unlike anything anyone has ever seen."

"You look...you look like my father." My eyes raised to him. Yes, he looked exactly like Waylon.

Or...Waylon looked exactly like him.

I looked like him.

And the final words that came to me, Igon's words, are what finally made me understand.

"You are more special than you know."

"It's me," I breathed. "*I* am the weapon."

Azrae's eyes sparkled with pride. "And how is that possible, dear?"

It was all starting to make sense now. There was a reason Waylon looked like Azrae. Waylon—who was always described as too handsome to be just a fisherman.

"You changed his appearance to match yours..."

"Why?" Azrae pressed.

Waylon's appearance was altered...because...

"Because I was not sired by Waylon," I breathed. "I was sired by *you.*"

The God of Vengeance's smile grew. "You acquired your power at a young age, far younger than normal. You have grasped magic with ease compared to those around you." He stepped forward, staring down at me as I lay on the rack. "You sense darkness. You feel it even when your friends do not." He leaned down, brushing his hand along my face. "Who are you, Lena?"

The gated door to the courtyard creaked open, but my eyes remained on Azrae despite the bodies that began filtering in.

PURIFICATION WILL ENSURE BALANCE, JUST AS HER FATHER HAS.

"I am a God," I whispered. "I am your daughter. The Goddess of Purification."

"That is right, my dear." The God of Vengeance's smile grew proud. "And you shall bow to *no one.*"

CHAPTER EIGHTY-TWO
SILAS - THIRTY DAYS AGO

My vision was blurring, the pain from my wound radiating from where my chest was impaled down each of my limbs.

I had no concept of time; I believed I was going in and out of consciousness.

Lena...

The pain from this injury was agonizing, and not from the blade that had been thrust into my chest, but from the curse circulating through my body, destroying all my life essence slowly but surely. I supposed the only comfort I had was that I would not turn into one of Ulric's servants. I would be dead any moment.

I wanted to save my kingdom. I wanted to save my mother. I wanted the life with Lena I had always dreamed of.

But this was it—my end.

I supposed I didn't deserve those things, not after the sins I'd committed, not after all the innocent lives I had taken. The irony of dying in this temple was not lost to me.

Lena had forgiven me for all of it. In a way, I couldn't understand how. But no sin she could commit would make me not love her, either.

My Soul-Tie.

I had never believed in such a thing. Even when Merrick first mentioned it, and I learned of the bond gifted by the Goddess Celluna, I had trouble accepting such a thing was real.

But Lena...there was no doubt she and I were fated, no doubt that our paths were meant to cross.

I groaned at the growing pain, my eyes fluttering shut.

There was still so much to be done. So much that had been put on my lover's shoulders. Out of all the reasons I wished I could live, helping and supporting her in all she would endure took precedence.

My heartbeat quickened, more sweat beading at my hairline at the thought of what Ulric would do if he found out what Lena had meant to me, what he would have done to her.

Fuck! If he subjected her to even a fraction of what he did to me...

I attempted to lift my arm to pull the sword out of my chest, but I shrieked at the pain the second I touched the hilt.

Godsdamn it.

Lena was strong. Stronger than me. She could make it, overcome. But I knew my death would be one of no peace, knowing there was nothing I could do to fucking stop what was to happen to her.

I cried. I cried and cried, years of built-up emotion finally releasing as I lived my final moments.

I didn't know how much time passed until my weeping died down...until my eyes became so heavy that I knew my last minutes were approaching.

I was fading when a girl and a man came into my peripheral, and when I glimpsed upward, I blinked rapidly. Part of me debated yelling for help, but the curse had touched me. There was nothing that could be done now.

The girl quickly ran and kneeled at my side, swearing when she took in the sword that had me pinned to the altar. Her jet-black hair spilled past her shoulders.

"We need to get him home—to the healers," she said with urgency to the man behind her, her voice lilting and elegant. I'd never heard such an accent before.

"How will they be able to heal such a thing?" the man panicked, his accent a mix of the unique one and of the people of Tovagoth. "The others are one thing—"

"Look." She pulled my shirt to the side. "It hasn't spread."

I slowly glimpsed into the man's worried grey eyes, and as my blurred vision finally began to focus, I saw a man whom my mother had loved.

A man whose name I used when I first explored my kingdom.

"Quill," I rasped, and Quill's eyes widened.

"Silas, how long ago were you attacked?" the girl beside me pressed, her hand grasping my shoulder.

I blinked over and over, my vision getting hazy again until my gaze finally settled on the girl's eyes.

The same golden ones as mine stared back at me, and I knew then exactly who she was.

"Aria?" I whispered.

Acknowledgements

Wow, did I feel all the emotions writing this book! I laughed, I cried, and I had so much fun. Please forgive me for the crazy cliffhanger! Just know that the next installment will be worth it. (And if you're feeling upset about a certain something...read that last chapter again. Hehe.)

Once again, a giant thank you to my grandma for the many days she has allowed me to work on this manuscript. My goal was to get this out in November, and because of her help, I was able to do so. She is the biggest supporter in my life, and I couldn't have done this without her.

Thank you to my editor, Allison, for taking the time to help polish my manuscript! I loved seeing your reactions to all the twists and turns in this one!

Another massive thank you goes to all the readers who have been so incredibly supportive and excited about this book. Imposter Syndrome is real, especially as an indie author, but the constant hype has gifted me confidence in my work, and I am forever grateful.

In particular, I thank Ashley D. @ravenhoodjunkie1 for all the supportive messages. Your encouragement has meant so much to me, especially those days when I am hard on myself (which is most days). I'm so thankful to have met you!

Shaelin H. @shaelinslibrary, thank you for including The Lies of Lena in so many videos. Marketing has been the most stressful, intimidating part of this journey, and every video that mentioned my book has made me so happy! Thank you so much!

Taylor H. @tays.booktale for the absolute best hype videos. I'm actually typing this page out the day after my release announcement, and your excitement for this book meant everything to me!

Dewi F. @leluviolet, thank you for writing one of my favorite reviews. I cried reading it. You have been so supportive of me and my work, and I appreciate you SO much!

And a giant thank you to all the wonderful people on my Street Team!

Thank you to Isabella, Toni, Jillian, Anna, Alannah, Harli, Regan, Tiffany, Ashley H., Megan, Heather, Amanda B., Princess, Brittany, Alexis, Cara, Peyton, KaLee, Shayna, Jessica, Britney, Kaitlyn, Jade, Stephanie, Kendra, Kaela, Jamie, Danyele, Charlotte, Tabitha, Sky, Danyele, Rita, Josie, Taylor B, Whitney, Amanda L., Carly, Jestine, Samantha, Danielle, Chelsey, Mallory, Destinee, Skylar, Sydney, Raquel, and Bryanna! Every positive comment, post, and review from you guys has meant so much to me. I'm so blessed to have such incredible people in my corner!

And as always, thank you to every person who gives me and my stories a chance! I hope you all enjoyed this book, and I can't wait to finish the third one!

About the Author

Kylie Snow is a wife, mother, and hairstylist residing in Illinois. When she is not writing, she is raising two rambunctious little girls, reading fantasy and dark romance novels, drawing, gaming, or planning her next tattoo.

Socials:
Tiktok: @kyliesnowauthor
IG: @kyliesnowauthor
Website: www.kyliesnow.com

Made in the USA
Coppell, TX
21 June 2025

50780599R00430